EVERYMAN'S LIBRARY

EVERYMAN,
I WILL GO WITH THEE,
AND BE THY GUIDE,
IN THY MOST NEED
TO GO BY THY SIDE

RAYMOND CHANDLER

The Lady in the Lake
The Little Sister
The Long Goodbye
Playback

with an Introduction by
Tom Hiney

EVERYMAN'S LIBRARY

Alfred A. Knopf New York Toronto

256

THIS IS A BORZOI BOOK

PUBLISHED BY ALFRED A. KNOPF

First included in Everyman's Library, 2002
The Lady in the Lake Copyright © 1943 by Raymond Chandler
Copyright renewed 1971 by Mrs. Helga Greene
The Little Sister Copyright © 1949 by Raymond Chandler
Copyright renewed 1976 by Mrs. Helga Greene
The Long Goodbye Copyright © 1953 by Raymond Chandler
Copyright renewed 1981 by Mrs. Helga Greene
Playback Copyright © 1958 by Raymond Chandler
Copyright renewed 1986 by Paul Gitlin and Jonathan S. Gitlin
Introduction Copyright © 2002 by Tom Hiney
Bibliography and Chronology Copyright © 2002 by Everyman
Publishers plc
Typography by Peter B. Willberg

www.randomhouse.com/everymans

ISBN 0-375-41502-5

Book Design by Barbara de Wilde and Carol Devine Carson

Printed and bound in Germany
by GGP Media, Pössneck

RAYMOND CHANDLER

CONTENTS

———

INTRODUCTION

Raymond Chandler once said that writing at its best is magic, casting a spell over readers and drawing them into a high-voltage perspective of the world they can inhabit as their own for a while. The important thing is to break down resistance by offering entertainment, until readers trust the writer well enough to let go and submit to his hard-won honesty and concentrated vision.

This kind of intense relationship with readers was especially important to Chandler, because he had so much to say by the time he came to write books (at the age of forty-nine), so many private and booze-driven insights to relate, so much hypocrisy to expose and, as a lifelong recluse, so few people ever to tell them to. Once he started writing full-time, it poured out of him, in nightly letters and daily scripts, in a torrent of relief and exorcism. He really *needed* to explain and express some of the things he'd been feeling about modern life, and about having watched Los Angeles grow from a small town into a commercial behemoth. He had things to say too, about his childhood in England, his battles in World War One, money, promiscuity, life, God. He also had the hermit's urgency to communicate, and the charm that urgency can generate.

He thought Scott Fitzgerald had such 'charm', and he was pretty sure he had it too. He once told one of the many young writers who wrote to him for advice, 'try to enthrall, not impress', but after helping a few others with their stories he came to the conclusion that writers either had the gift or they didn't, and most didn't. Writing was like red hair, he reckoned: it just happened. And it always came from the belly rather than the head. For at the end of the day, he said, writing was just the expression of a personality.

Through his imagined hero, Philip Marlowe, Chandler's personality was broadcast loud and clear from his house to the world. Like Chandler, Marlowe is a decent, wisecracking semi-alcoholic. He is also a man whose innate nobility transcends the milieu in which it is his fate to operate: a loner, living in '40s Los Angeles, watching society around him and wondering what makes people tick, disgusted at the way they were being fooled by tycoons and politicians, allowing themselves to be fooled, horrified at the tattiness of the mass production stage of civilization he had found himself in. Marlowe is a private eye; so was his childless, shiftless creator. And with the publication of *The Big Sleep* in 1939, an audience began gathering to hear what he had to say.

Two books on, the audience had failed to grow. It was there, enrapt and entertained, but the numbers weren't getting any larger. There had been a lot of anger in *The Big Sleep*, but anger will only drive you so far. In the writing of his second novel, *Farewell, My Lovely*, there was more self-consciousness (he had to completely rewrite it), and by the time he published *The High Window* he was getting tired of his voice. Besides, the all-powerful New York critics weren't taking him seriously. They couldn't see what the French critics were the first to realize: that Chandler had raised the genre of crime fiction into an art form. They just saw him as a crime writer, and he was kept in the 'Also Out This Month' columns, despite the championing of his well-connected New York publisher, Alfred A. Knopf. And no publicity meant few sales.

Although moonlighting for the pulp magazines, Chandler was broke. Most of his delighted readers were crime fans used to getting their books from libraries; without the critics he could not break out of this cycle. He and his wife Cissy were living outside Los Angeles to save on rent while Chandler tried to build his audience. Cissy was ill and needed the desert air, which was frustrating for Chandler because he preferred the mountains north-east of the city around Lake Tahoe, at that stage still hick and low rent country. With the desert finally driving him mad, they moved up there for a year, and it was there that Chandler wrote his fourth novel, *The Lady in the Lake*, in 1943.

A romantic at heart, Chandler had surrounded himself as a boy with Arthurian legend and Victorian Gothic mythology. The poems he wrote throughout his life were often Georgian elegies that hardly seem to come from the same pen as

Marlowe's world. But that part of him was there and was certainly present in his marriage. He believed that for love to be sustained in a marriage a man must always approach his woman as he would an altar, and his own wife, once an opium-smoking, nude-model bohemian, twice divorced and seventeen years his senior, had no objection. Theirs had been a love affair of roses and poems, and now her age was telling and she was dying. When Chandler looked about him at modern California, all 'cheesecake and multiple marriages', advertising and hype and corruption, he could not see where love had gone. He struggled to believe that anything sacred lay still breathing under the rubble of lies and billboards. He was feeling this with particular strength in 1943, and *The Lady in the Lake* of the title is no Avalon priestess, but California's equivalent. A whore by any other name, rotting in Little Fawn Lake after getting herself too close to the underworld for her lascivious kicks. The presentation of the female characters would be misogynist if it wasn't for the fact that the male characters in the story are just as hollow and distasteful, including the lady's husband, who hires Marlowe. Derace Kingsley runs a perfume company whose wealth is based on the elaborate marketing of its indifferent range. '*Gillerlain Regal, The Champagne of Perfumes*. It was definitely the stuff to get. One drop of that in the hollow of your throat and the matched pink pearls started falling on you like summer rain.' Marlowe fails to find much enthusiasm for the job Mr Kingsley gives him. It's just a dirty job. There are no goodies in *The Lady in the Lake*, just degrees of corruption. Even Marlowe feels implicated now and part of the entropy. 'I brushed my hair and looked at the gray in it. There was getting to be plenty of gray in it. The face under the hair had a sick look. I didn't like the face at all.'

Corruption was a reality in '40s California. The prohibition of alcohol in America had, at one estimate, put $2,000,000,000,000 in the way of organized crime syndicates. Italian, Irish and Chinese gangs flourished as everyone, from judges to teachers, continued to buy drink. The unpopularity of the ban, and the vast amount of money needed to enforce it, meant that almost from the start the law backfired and created unintended consequences, among them binge drinking (more alcohol in America was consumed per year during Prohibition than before it), and the underground tycoons who were about the most successful men in the country during the Depression. When the ban was lifted these men had accumulated so much power that they were now entrenched. They moved into land development, funding political campaigns, and narcotics. Such corruption was nowhere more evident than in Chicago and Los Angeles, with their booming populations and proximity to the Canadian and Mexican borders.

A 1937 Grand Jury inquiry had discovered untold levels of graft in Los Angeles: 600 brothels and 18,000 unlicensed bars were operating illegally under the noses of the L.A. police. And that was just on street level. Higher up the crime chain, mobster bosses ruled their bloody kingdoms with impunity. It was discovered in the same year that Bugsy Siegel, supposedly serving a prison sentence, had been sighted on numerous occasions out of prison. The L.A.P.D. apologized to Washington and said Siegel had been let out to go to his dentist. Many policemen and politicians in the city, according to the Grand Jury's report, were directly in the pay of mobsters: 'The District Attorney's Office, Sheriff's office, and the Los Angeles Police Department work in complete harmony and never interfere with important figures in the underworld.' Throughout this time Al Capone roamed free in Chicago, one of the most famous men in the country, and surrounded by some of its best lawyers.

This meant that law and justice were far from being one and the same. The law could be bought for ruthless and greedy ends. Chandler had as much sneaking respect for the sheer gall of mobsters as anyone (he once befriended Lucky Luciano at a hotel in Naples) but he hated their violence, hated the hypocrisy of the culture that bred them, and hated the policemen and politicians who came down hard on the little men while they let mobsters roam free. As someone who'd been thrown in a prison cell for being drunk, he particularly hated the sadism of crooked policemen, who had got as rich as anyone during Prohibition. There are many crooked policemen in *The Lady in the Lake* and official corruption hangs over the story. There are no heroes, and not much sympathy for the victims. Civilization is shown to be a pathetic and cruel sham, very few decent forms of life seem to survive and everyone is tired and nervous.

The Little Sister is not much better in this respect, except that now we have the distraction of watching Marlowe grow increasingly mad, as he confronts his own impotence in the face of the world and loneliness:

I ... leaned back and just sat, not smoking, not even thinking. I was a blank man. I had no face, no meaning, no personality, hardly a name. I didn't want to eat. I didn't even want a drink. I was the page from yesterday's calendar crumpled at the bottom of the wastebasket ... Who would you like to call now? You got a friend somewhere that might like to hear your voice? No. Nobody. Let the telephone ring, please. Let there be somebody to call up and plug me into the human race again. Even a cop. Even a Maglashan. Nobody has to like me. I just want to get off this frozen star.

Meanwhile the other characters in the novel, being Hollywood hangers-on, play out their vicious greed and neuroses around him, with no shred of conviction in Marlowe's mind that the people who hire him are any better than those they hire him to oppose. They are all selfish, short-term and unpleasant. 'There are days like that. Everybody you meet is a dope. You begin to look at yourself in the glass and wonder.' Because, really, what is a smart guy like Marlowe doing risking his life for forty dollars a day in the first place? Is he helping anyone, even himself? But then what else is he meant to do? What livelihood is open to a man with no capital in '40s California, who wants to preserve a little integrity and self-respect? He doesn't want to be an office worker, as he and Chandler had both been in the past, Chandler as an accountant: 'They are what human beings turn into when they trade life for existence and ambition for security.' He knows very clearly what he doesn't like, and doesn't want to be, and in *The Little Sister* he is trying hard to work out what he does still like. And he just can't really think of anything.

Chandler's bitterness towards money slavery was not merely

personal. Having picked up some screenwriting work for Paramount after *The Lady in the Lake* appeared, he was back in Los Angeles where the pay was good and got better. In 1946, Humphrey Bogart took Philip Marlowe and Chandler's name to the masses with Warner Brothers' production of *The Big Sleep*. The film was not expensive to make, but those involved were all Chandler fans (Bogart included) and they caught the tone of his unique voice brilliantly. In my view, it is one of the best films ever made. The buzz about it grew so loud that Warner issued a gloating press release, reporting that even the King and Queen of England had requested a private showing at Balmoral Castle. Cinemas from Buenos Aires through middle America to Beirut were following suit and book sales of Chandler's novels soared, as people discovered him for the first time. He was becoming a rich man, and Hollywood was offering him serious money (more than any screenwriter in history) to stay and write for them. But as soon as he had enough cash in the bank he wanted out. He wanted to get back to his books, alone, no people around. So after five years working for the studio he quit and bought a house in La Jolla, overlooking the ocean near San Diego. Cissy, by now over seventy, was on her last legs.

The draft of *The Little Sister* had been accumulating in his drawer during his time in Hollywood, and he finished it at La Jolla after moving there in the summer of 1946. The book is about a Hollywood which bored him by then, a city he could no longer enjoy, as it moved further from the jacaranda-blossomed adventure town of his youth to the giant 'neon slum' we know and love today. Even the climate had changed. Concerning what were for him old subjects, the story had become something of a bugbear for Chandler, something he wanted to get out of the way. It was the one book he could never bring himself to reread. It was not where his thoughts were. With his wife slowly dying in the house and his own health deteriorating with age and attempted teetotalism, he wondered whether, after all he had fought for, with the biggest audience of his life, he was spent.

But he wasn't. His greatest book and his greatest achievement (in his opinion) lay ahead of him. In the three years that followed, with a fortune in the bank, Chandler nursed Cissy, slept on a couch outside her door in case she needed him in the night, and wrote the book that finally broke the New York critics. It would be, according the *New York Times*, 'a masterpiece'. Harper's kingpin critic Bernard DeVoto called it 'awesome'. With his creative back against the wall, suicide attempts around the corner, *The Long Goodbye* was about love and friendship by a man about to lose the only lasting friendship he had ever had, the friend who had been with him through it all for the last thirty years.

In October 1950, while writing the book, Chandler wrote a letter to a publisher about Hemingway's badly received *Across the River and into the Trees*. 'Apparently Hemingway had been very sick and he was not sure that he was going to get well, and he put down on paper in a rather cursory way how that made him feel to the things he had most valued. I suppose these primping second-guessers who call themselves critics think he shouldn't have written the book at all. Most men wouldn't have. Feeling the way he felt, they wouldn't have had the guts to write anything. I'm damn sure I wouldn't. That's the difference between a champ and knife thrower. The champ may have lost himself temporarily, or permanently, he can't be sure. But when he can no longer throw the high hard one, he throws his heart instead. He throws something. He doesn't just walk off the mound and weep.'

One of the reasons *The Long Goodbye* throws so much at the reader is that here Chandler gives himself not just one but three autobiographical mouthpieces, and moves more of the action out of Los Angeles, to a rich man's suburb called Idle Valley. Marlowe is still Marlowe, heart on sleeve ('An hour crawled by like a sick cockroach. I was a grain of sand on the desert of oblivion'), but joining him now in the sardonic arcade are a cursed and wealthy trash novelist called Roger Wade ('I've written twelve best sellers, and not a damn one of them worth the powder to blow them to hell') and the scarred war hero turned peacetime drifter, Terry Lennox. What the two have in common with Chandler is exposure to hard cash. As the kept husband of a billionaire's daughter (Lennox) and a paperback tycoon (Wade) both have had enough luxury to be sure it is not the promised land. Rich people, Chandler assures his reader, are just as bored and lonely as everyone else in this hollow culture. New demons replace poverty, torments just as fierce. Marlowe, Wade and Lennox are a fraternity of demon seekers, and the momentary gratitude they have for each other's existence has been taken by some critics as homoerotic, but is really a celebration of moments between strangers where small talk is dropped and honesty and hard wit prevail. They are like three members of a doomed cult, as Marlowe tries at one point to explain to Wade's wife:

He wasn't rude to me. He made quite a lot of sense. Your husband is a guy who can take a long hard look at himself and see what is there. It's not a very common gift. Most people go through life using up half their energy trying to protect a dignity they never had.

In 1954 Cissy died, and Chandler went straight off the rails. He would survive five years after her death, and in that time he would blow most of his money on hotels and psychiatry, but would taste the love of women again for the first time since Cissy fell ill. And those short-lived love affairs, all destroyed by Chandler's intensity and return to alcohol, were enough to bring him off his frozen star long enough to know moments of happiness. In *Playback*, his farewell novel, Marlowe finds love, as did Chandler, in his own chaotic way, before dying of pneumonia (he froze in the end) in 1959 at the age of seventy. *Playback*, despite its brevity, has a reckless verve that is all its own. It was the only book Chandler ever wrote while actually drunk at the typewriter, in and out of psychiatric wards, and it is the funniest and most defiant of his stories, because Marlowe just doesn't care anymore. The book's opening catches the new mood:

The voice on the telephone seemed to be sharp and peremptory, but I didn't hear too well what it said – partly because I was only half awake and partly because I was holding the receiver upside down. I fumbled it around and grunted.
  'Did you hear me? I said I was Clyde Umney, the lawyer.'
  'Clyde Umney, the lawyer. I thought we had several of them.'
  'You're Marlowe, aren't you?

'Yeah. I guess so.' I looked at my wrist watch. It was 6:30 A.M., not my best hour.

'Don't get fresh with me, young man.'

'Sorry, Mr. Umney. But I'm not a young man. I'm old, tired, and full of no coffee. What can I do for you, sir?'

'I want you to meet the Super Chief at eight o'clock, identify a girl among the passengers, follow her until she checks in somewhere, and then report to me. Is that clear?'

'No.'

And so on, Chandler getting knocked about and abused by his clients as much as ever, but now there is a sense of acceptance, for he is possessed of a new coping mechanism; the taste of love that can make pain seem irrelevant. Her name is Linda Loring, and his brief time with her is constantly on his mind. It's a sad happiness he feels, for she's gone, but at least he's feeling something again, rather than feeling nothing. He is looking at his earthly problems in a different light. The agony of living is almost funny now. At one point in the story he comes round on the floor of a motel room, having been felled by a hidden thug. His head is pounding but at least someone has put ice cubes over his wound: 'Somebody who loved me very much had put them on the back of my head. Somebody who loved me less had bashed in the back of my skull. It could have been the same person. People have moods.' Chandler certainly had moods, and while his health and sanity were failing he produced a book – writing in four-hour sessions bolstered by high potency vitamin injections and booze – as good as anything he ever wrote. And the message was as much a relief to him as to Marlowe – love is still alive in the twentieth century, twitching but still breathing.

So to what extent does Chandler's magic work? That depends on what you think of Marlowe. Sometimes his honesty is perhaps too clearly born out of loneliness, like an over-assertive drunk, and sometimes he is too concerned with justifying himself rather than expressing himself. He is a proud man (as was his creator) and in presenting him Chandler sometimes failed to heed his own warning to a radio producer: make sure you let Marlowe's opponents sometimes have the final say, the topping wisecrack, otherwise Marlowe becomes too arrogant – however self-critical he can be in private. For although this ploy is used with some success, no one ever really outshines Marlowe face-to-face. He is quicker and wiser and humbler than anyone, contradictory though this may sound, and on all three counts – especially the humility – Marlowe just occasionally becomes annoying.

But then, Hamlet is sometimes annoying too. Chandler's books are not perfect because he was not perfect. 'To know me in the flesh is to move on to better things.' Anxiety and despondency, his constant companions, drove him to create a fictional hero who would preserve his integrity and sense of humor despite every lie and humiliation the world threw at him. Someone who would stay awake while the rest of the world dropped into a coma of consumerism. Not necessarily an enviable vigil, or a pretty one, but one that millions of fans appreciate.

Tom Hiney

SELECT BIBLIOGRAPHY

NOVELS
The Big Sleep. New York: Alfred A. Knopf, 1939; London: Hamish Hamilton, 1939.
Farewell, My Lovely. New York: Alfred A. Knopf, 1940; London: Hamish Hamilton, 1940.
The High Window. New York: Alfred A. Knopf, 1942; London: Hamish Hamilton, 1943.
The Lady in the Lake. New York: Alfred A. Knopf, 1943; London: Hamish Hamilton, 1944.
The Little Sister. London: Hamish Hamilton, 1949; Boston: Houghton Mifflin, 1949.
The Long Goodbye. London: Hamish Hamilton, 1953; Boston: Houghton Mifflin, 1954.
Playback. London: Hamish Hamilton, 1958; Boston: Houghton Mifflin, 1958.

STORIES
'Blackmailers Don't Shoot'. *Black Mask*, December 1933.
'Smart-Aleck Kill'. *Black Mask*, July 1934.
'Finger Man'. *Black Mask*, October 1934.
'Killer in the Rain'. *Black Mask*, January 1935.
'Nevada Gas'. *Black Mask*, June 1935.
'Spanish Blood'. *Black Mask*, November 1935.
'Guns at Cyrano's'. *Black Mask*, January 1936.
'The Man Who Liked Dogs'. *Black Mask*, March 1936.
'Noon Street Nemesis' (republished as 'Pickup on Noon Street'. *Detective Fiction Weekly*, May 30, 1936.
'Goldfish'. *Black Mask*, June 1936.
'The Curtain'. *Black Mask*, September 1936.
'Try the Girl'. *Black Mask*, January 1937.
'Mandarin's Jade'. *Dime Detective Magazine*, November 1937.
'Red Wind'. *Dime Detective Magazine*, January 1938.
'The King in Yellow'. *Dime Detective Magazine*, March 1938.
'Bay City Blues'. *Dime Detective Magazine*, June 1938.
'The Lady in the Lake'. *Dime Detective Magazine*, January 1939.
'Pearls Are a Nuisance'. *Dime Detective Magazine*, April 1939.
'Trouble Is My Business'. *Dime Detective Magazine*, August 1939.
'I'll Be Waiting'. *Saturday Evening Post*, October 14, 1939.

'The Bronze Door'. Unknown Magazine, November 1939.
'No Crime in the Mountains'. *Detective Story*, September 1941.
'Professor Bingo's Snuff'. *Park East*, June–August 1951; *Go*, June–July 1951.
'Marlowe Takes on the Syndicate'. *London Daily Mail*, April 6–10 1959, also published as 'Wrong Pidgeon'. *Manhunt*, February 1961. Reprinted as 'The Pencil'.

BIOGRAPHY
There are several biographies, including *The Life of Raymond Chandler* by Frank MacShane (Cape, 1976), *Raymond Chandler* by William Marling (Twayne, 1986) and Tom Hiney's *Raymond Chandler: An Authorized Biography* (Chatto & Windus, 1997; Grove Atlantic, 2001). *The Raymond Chandler Papers* (ed. Tom Hiney and Frank MacShane, Hamish Hamilton, 2000) includes letters, essays and stories. Miriam Gross's *The World of Raymond Chandler* (Weidenfeld & Nicolson, 1977) offers a pictorial biography and a lavishly illustrated study of the milieu of the Marlowe novels. Jerry Speir's *Raymond Chandler* (Ungar, 1981) contains a useful bibliography.

DATE	AUTHOR'S LIFE	LITERARY CONTEXT
1888	Raymond Thornton Chandler born 23 July in Chicago.	
1892		1892 James M. Cain born.
1894		1894 Dashiell Hammett born.
1895	Parents divorce. Moves to London with his mother.	1895 Twain: *Pudd'nhead Wilson.* Conan Doyle: *The Memoirs of Sherlock Holmes.* Hardy: *Jude the Obscure.*
1896		1896 Chekhov: *The Seagull.* Fitzgerald born.
1899		1899 Chopin: *The Awakening.* James: *The Awkward Age.* Hornung: *Raffles: The Amateur Cracksman.* Hemingway born. Nabokov born.
1900	Attends Dulwich College, as a day student (to 1904).	1900 Dreiser: *Sister Carrie.* Conrad: *Lord Jim.* Freud: *The Interpretation of Dreams.*
1901		1901 Mann: *Buddenbrooks.* Kipling: *Kim.*
1902		1902 Conan Doyle: *The Hound of the Baskervilles.* Steinbeck born.
1904		1904 James: *The Golden Bowl.* Chekhov dies.
1905–6	Attends language schools in France and Germany in preparation for British Civil Service examinations.	1905 Conan Doyle: *The Return of Sherlock Holmes.* 1906 Wharton: *The House of Mirth.* Beckett born.
1907	Returns to London. Works as a civil servant for the Admiralty.	1907 Conrad: *The Secret Agent.* Auden born.
1909–12	Resigns from Admiralty and works as a literary journalist, contributing poems, reviews, sketches and translations to *The Westminster Gazette* and *The Academy.*	1909 Stein: *Three Lives.* 1910 Forster: *Howards End.* Wells: *The History of Mr Polly.*

HISTORICAL EVENTS

1888 The US becomes the leading manufacturing nation in the world.

1892 California earthquake disaster.
1894 Nicholas II becomes Tsar of Russia.
1895 Beginning of Freudian psychoanalysis.

1896 William McKinley elected US president. Klondike Gold Rush.

1899 Outbreak of Boer War. Alfred Hitchcock born.

1900 US population 76 million. US rail network just less than 200,000 miles. First International Socialist Congress in Paris. Planck's quantum theory.

1901 President McKinley assassinated. Succeeded by Theodore Roosevelt, in a progressive era in American politics. Marconi transmits message across the Atlantic. Death of Queen Victoria. Accession of Edward VII.

1904 War breaks out between Japan and Russia.

1905 Einstein's theory of relativity. General strikes, mutiny and incipient revolution in Russia.
1906 San Francisco earthquake.

1907 Cubist exhibition in Paris.

1909 First Ford Model T car.
1910 Death of Edward VII; accession of George V.

DATE	AUTHOR'S LIFE	LITERARY CONTEXT
1912	Returns to America, spends time in St Louis and Omaha, then settles in California. Does odd jobs, including working for a sporting goods firm and on a ranch.	1912 Dreiser: *The Financier.* Mann: *Death in Venice.*
1913–17	Enrols in night-school bookkeeping course and works as an accountant for the Los Angeles Creamery. His mother comes from England to live with him.	1913 Frost: *A Boy's Will.* Cather: *O Pioneers!* Lawrence: *Sons and Lovers.* 1914 Burroughs: *Tarzan of the Apes.* Joyce: *Dubliners.* 1915 Ford: *The Good Soldier.* Lawrence: *The Rainbow.* Kafka: *Metamorphosis.*
1917	Enlists in Canadian army, is assigned to 7th Batallion of Canadian Expeditionary Force, serves in trenches and is made sergeant.	1917 Conan Doyle: *His Last Bow.* Eliot: 'The Love Song of J. Alfred Prufrock'.
1918	In June is transferred to Royal Air Force.	1918 Cather: *My Ántonia.*
1919–22	Discharged and takes a job in a bank in San Francisco before returning to Los Angeles and working for *The Daily Express.* Has an affair with Cissy Pascal, who is seventeen years his senior and now gets a second divorce.	1919 *Black Mask*, pulp magazine, set up. Anderson: *Winesburg, Ohio.* Wodehouse: *My Man Jeeves.* 1920 Fitzgerald: *This Side of Paradise.* Lewis: *Main Street.* Wharton: *The Age of Innocence.* Pound: *Hugh Selwyn Mauberley.* Christie: *The Mysterious Affair at Styles* (first novel). 1921 Dos Passos: *Three Soldiers.* Lawrence: *Women in Love.* Pirandello: *Six Characters in Search of an Author.*
1922	Takes job with Dabney Oil Syndicate as bookkeeper and soon rises to Vice-President.	1922 Carroll John Daly creates the first hard-boiled detective in 'The False Burton Combs'. Eliot: *The Waste Land.* Joyce: *Ulysses.* Mansfield: *The Garden Party.* Hemingway: *In Our Time.*

CHRONOLOGY

1912 Woodrow Wilson elected US president. Sinking of *Titanic*.
Charlie Chaplin's first film.

1913 Completion of new Grand Central Terminal, New York. Post-Impressionist exhibition in New York.

1914 Outbreak of World War I. President Wilson proclaims US neutrality.
Panama Canal opens.

1917 US declares war on Germany. Russian October Revolution.

1918 World War I ends. Civil war in Russia (to 1921).

1919 Versailles Peace Conference, with Wilson's Fourteen Points. Eighteenth
Amendment, prohibiting the manufacture and sale of intoxicating liquors, is
ratified. The 'Red Scare' in the US and a yearlong strike by steelworkers.
Nineteenth Amendment (Female Suffrage) passed.
1920 League of Nations formed. Warren G. Harding elected US president.
The Slump and the 'jazz age' begin.

1921 Washington Conference on disarmament (to 1922).

1922 Establishment of USSR. Mussolini forms a Fascist government in Italy.
Stalin becomes General Secretary of Communist Party. Quota laws restrict
immigration to the US. Revival of Ku Klux Klan. Radio broadcasting
starts. Talking pictures developed.

DATE	AUTHOR'S LIFE	LITERARY CONTEXT
1923		
1924	Mother dies. Marries Cissy.	1924 Forster: *A Passage to India*. Ford: *Parade's End* (to 1928).
1925		1925 Dreiser: *An American Tragedy*. Fitzgerald: *The Great Gatsby*. Loos: *Gentlemen Prefer Blondes*. Stein: *The Making of Americans*. Dos Passos: *Manhattan Transfer*. Woolf: *Mrs Dalloway*. Kafka: *The Trial*.
1926		1926 Fitzgerald: *All the Sad Young Men*. Faulkner: *Soldier's Pay*. Hemingway: *The Sun Also Rises*. Christie: *The Murder of Roger Ackroyd*.
1927		1927 Cather: *Death Comes for the Archbishop*. Wilder: *The Bridge of San Luis Rey*. Woolf: *To the Lighthouse*. Conan Doyle: *The Case Book of Sherlock Holmes*. Proust: *Remembrance of Things Past*.
1928		1928 O'Neill: *Strange Interlude*. Lawrence: *Lady Chatterley's Lover*. Waugh: *Decline and Fall*.
1929		
1930		1930 Faulkner: *As I Lay Dying*. Hammett: *The Maltese Falcon*. Crane: *The Bridge*. Freud *Civilization and its Discontents*. Lawrence dies.
1931		1931 Hammett: *The Glass Key*.
1932	Sacked for drinking and absenteeism, goes to Seattle without Cissy but returns when he becomes ill.	1932 Caldwell: *Tobacco Road*. Erle Stanley Gardner: *The Case of the Velvet Claws* (first Perry Mason novel). Huxley: *Brave New World*. Crane dies.

CHRONOLOGY

1923 Calvin Coolidge elected president after Harding's death.
1924 Death of Lenin. First Labour government in UK.

1925 Al Capone is a powerful force in Chicago.
The 'Monkey Trial' in Dayton, Tennessee, finds for *Genesis*, signalling the withdrawal of Southern culture into otherworldliness.

1926 Television invented by John Logie Baird. First liquid fuel rocket. General strike in the UK.

1927 Lindbergh's solo Atlantic flight. Trotsky expelled from Communist Party in USSR.

1928 First full-length film; first television broadcast; 13 million radios and 26 million cars in use in US. Herbert Hoover elected US president. Amelia Earhart is the first woman to fly the Atlantic solo. Gershwin: *An American in Paris*.
1929 Wall Street Crash on 24 October. Beginning of world depression. US establishes Federal Loans. Museum of Modern Art in New York founded. Land speed record set at 231 mph.
1930 US Unemployment at 13 million. US tariff raised. France begins Maginot Line. Gandhi embarks on civil disobedience campaign in India. Empire State Building opened.

1931 Al Capone found guilty of tax evasion and imprisoned. Britain abandons Gold Standard. Invention of electric razor.
1932 Lindbergh's son kidnapped. Franklin D. Roosevelt elected US president and inaugurates New Deal. Stock prices in US fall to 20% of 1929 value.

DATE	AUTHOR'S LIFE	LITERARY CONTEXT
1933	Studies Erle Stanley Gardner and other representatives of pulp fiction, and spends five months writing his first story, 'Blackmailers Don't Shoot', which is published by pulp detective magazine, *Black Mask*.	1933 Nathaniel West: *Miss Lonelyhearts*. Book burnings in Germany.
1934–39	Lives in and around Los Angeles, writing a total of twenty pulp stories for *Black Mask* and other magazines.	1934 Cain: *The Postman Always Rings Twice* (banned in Boston). Hammett: *The Thin Man*. Fitzgerald: *Tender is the Night*. Miller: *Tropic of Cancer*. Waugh: *A Handful of Dust*. Christie: *Murder on the Orient Express*. 1935 Wolfe: *Of Time and the River*. Lewis: *It Can't Happen Here*. 1936 Cain: *Double Indemnity*. Mitchell: *Gone with the Wind*. Dos Passos: *The Big Money*. Faulkner: *Absalom, Absalom!* Eliot: *Collected Poems*. Wodehouse: *Laughing Gas*. Lorca killed by Fascist militia in Spain. 1937 Hemingway: *To Have and Have Not*. Steinbeck: *Of Mice and Men*. Stevens: *The Man with the Blue Guitar*. Dos Passos: *U.S.A.* Erle Stanley Gardner: *The D.A. Calls it Murder* (first D.A. Douglas Selby novel). Christie: *Death on the Nile* C. S. Forester: *The Happy Return* (first Hornblower novel). 1938 Cummings: *Collected Poems*. Waugh: *Scoop*. Sartre: *Nausea*. Beckett: *Murphy*.
1939	Publishes his first full-length detective story, *The Big Sleep*.	1939 Joyce: *Finnegans Wake*. Steinbeck: *The Grapes of Wrath*.

CHRONOLOGY

1933 The Twenty-First Amendment, repealing Prohibition, ratified. Hitler appointed Chancellor in Germany. USSR recognized by US.

1934 Depth of Great Depression in US; half of the banks have failed. Al Capone sent to Alcatraz.

1935: Nuremberg Laws depriving Jews of rights and citizenship in Germany. Mussolini invades Abyssinia. Transcontinental air service begins in US. Gershwin: *Porgy and Bess*.
1936 Roosevelt re-elected by landslide. Spanish Civil War (to 1939). Abdication of King Edward VIII who wishes to marry the American divorcee Wallis Simpson. Hitler and Mussolini form Rome–Berlin axis. Stalin's Great Purge of Communist Party in Russia (to 1938).

1937 Japanese invasion of China. First jet engine and nylon stockings. In the US around 75 million visit the movies every week. Strikes against Republic Steel in Chicago: four strikers killed and forty-four injured.

1938 Germany annexes Austria; Munich crisis. Hitchcock: *The Lady Vanishes*.

1939 Nazi-Soviet Pact. Hitler invades Poland: World War II begins. First commercial transatlantic flights. Vivien Leigh and Clark Gable star in *Gone with the Wind*.

DATE	AUTHOR'S LIFE	LITERARY CONTEXT
1940–43	Continues with pulp writing and also publishes three full-length works: *Farewell, My Lovely* (1940), *The High Window* (1942) and *The Lady in the Lake* (1943).	1940 Hemingway: *For Whom the Bell Tolls*. Greene: *The Power and the Glory*. Fitzgerald dies. 1941 Fitzgerald: *The Last Tycoon* (posthumous). Cain: *Mildred Pierce*. Nabokov: *The Real Life of Sebastian Knight*. Brecht: *Mother Courage*. Woolf and Joyce die. 1942 Paul: *A Narrow Street*. Camus: *The Stranger*.
1943	Adapts James Cain's crime novel *Double Indemnity* with Billy Wilder for Paramount Studios.	
1944–46	Works for various film studios but is open about his dislike for the industry. Wins Edgar Allen Poe Award in 1946 (and again in 1956).	1944 Williams: *The Glass Menagerie*. Eliot: *Four Quartets*. 1945 Thurber: *The Thurber Carnival*. Orwell: *Animal Farm*. Waugh: *Brideshead Revisited*. Borges: *Fictions*. Dreiser dies.
1946	Moves to La Jolla and begins to detach himself from movie industry.	1946 Cain: *Past All Dishonor*. Goodis: *Dark Passage*.
1947		1947 Williams: *A Streetcar Named Desire*. Cain: *Butterfly*.
1948		1948 Mailer: *The Naked and the Dead*. Cain: *The Moth*. Eliot wins Nobel Prize.
1949	Publishes first post-Hollywood novel, *The Little Sister*. Works on *The Long Goodbye* (to 1952) as Cissy's health deteriorates.	1949 Miller: *Death of a Salesman*. Orwell: *Nineteen Eighty-Four*. Greene: *The Third Man*. Faulkner wins Nobel Prize.
1950	'The Simple Act of Murder' published. Works with Hitchcock on a film version of Patricia Highsmith's *Strangers on a Train*.	1950 Eliot: *The Cocktail Party*.

CHRONOLOGY

1940 France surrenders to Germany. The Battle of Britain. Trotsky assassinated in Mexico. Churchill prime minister in UK. Penicillin developed. Extraction of plutonium from uranium.

1941 Japanese attack Pearl Harbor. US enters war on 11 December. Hitler invades Russia. US introduces 'lease-lend' system of aid to Britain. Orson Welles: *Citizen Kane*. Irving Berlin: 'White Christmas'. Beginnings of 'bebop'.

1942 Rommel defeated at El Alamein. Build-up of American air force in Free China. World's first nuclear reactor constructed at Chicago University.
1943 Russians defeat Germans at Stalingrad. Allied armies victorious in North Africa. Allied invasion of Italy.

1944 Allied landings in Normandy; German retreat; liberation of Paris. Roosevelt elected for fourth term.

1945 Unconditional surrender of Germany and suicide of Hitler. Bombing of Hiroshima and Nagasaki. End of World War II. United Nations founded. Death of Roosevelt. Truman president of US. Attlee prime minister in UK.

1946 Churchill makes 'Iron Curtain' speech. Cold War begins. Film of *The Big Sleep* released with Humphrey Bogart and Lauren Bacall.

1947 India proclaimed independent. Marshall Plan (US aid for European post-war recovery).

1948 Jewish state of Israel comes into existence. Soviet blockade of West Berlin. Gandhi assassinated. Apartheid introduced in South Africa. Month-long strike of coal miners in US. Hitchcock: *Rope*.

1949 Chinese Revolution. North Atlantic Treaty signed in Washington. Orson Welles stars in *The Third Man*.

1950 Senator Joseph McCarthy accuses State Department of being riddled with Communists and begins period of Communist witch-hunts in US (to1954). Korean War begins (to 1953).

DATE	AUTHOR'S LIFE	LITERARY CONTEXT
1951		1951 Jones: *From Here to Eternity*. Salinger: *The Catcher in the Rye*. Frost: *Complete Poems*.
1952		1952 Beckett: *Waiting for Godot*. Ellison: *The Invisible Man*. O'Connor: *Wise Blood*. Steinbeck: *East of Eden*.
1953	*The Long Goodbye* published, cementing Chandler's literary standing among critics on both sides of the Atlantic.	1953 Bellow: *The Adventures of Augie March*. Faulkner: *Requiem for a Nun*. Williams: *Camino Real*. Fleming: *Casino Royale*.
1954	Cissy dies and Chandler attempts suicide shortly afterwards. Briefly admitted to a psychiatric hospital.	1954 Amis: *Lucky Jim*. Fleming: *Live and Let Die*. Hemingway wins Nobel Prize.
1955–57	Lives between La Jolla and Europe, mostly in hotels. Drinks heavily.	1955 Nabokov: *Lolita*. Williams: *Cat on a Hot Tin Roof*. Miller: *A View from the Bridge*. 1956 Highsmith: *The Talented Mr Ripley*. Goodis: *Shoot the Piano Player*. Osborne: *Look Back in Anger*. Fleming: *Diamonds are Forever*. 1957 Kerouac: *On the Road*. Nabokov: *Pnin*.
1958	Publishes *Playback*.	1958 Pasternak: *Doctor Zhivago*. Capote: *Breakfast at Tiffany's*.
1959	Dies in La Jolla on 26 March, aged seventy.	1959 Burroughs: *Naked Lunch*. Bellow: *Henderson the Rain King*. Grass: *The Tin Drum*.

CHRONOLOGY

THE LADY IN THE LAKE

1

THE TRELOAR BUILDING was, and is, on Olive Street, near
Sixth, on the west side. The sidewalk in front of it had been
built of black and white rubber blocks. They were taking
them up now to give to the government, and a hatless pale
man with a face like a building superintendent was watching
the work and looking as if it was breaking his heart.

I went past him through an arcade of specialty shops into
a vast black and gold lobby. The Gillerlain Company was on
the seventh floor, in front, behind swinging double plate glass
doors bound in platinum. Their reception room had Chinese
rugs, dull silver walls, angular but elaborate furniture, sharp
shiny bits of abstract sculpture on pedestals and a tall display
in a triangular showcase in the corner. On tiers and steps and
islands and promontories of shining mirror-glass it seemed to
contain every fancy bottle and box that had ever been
designed. There were creams and powders and soaps and
toilet waters for every season and every occasion. There were
perfumes in tall thin bottles that looked as if a breath would
blow them over and perfumes in little pastel phials tied with
ducky satin bows, like the little girls at a dancing class. The
cream of the crop seemed to be something very small and
simple in a squat amber bottle. It was in the middle at eye
height, had a lot of space to itself, and was labeled *Gillerlain
Regal, The Champagne of Perfumes*. It was definitely the stuff to
get. One drop of that in the hollow of your throat and the
matched pink pearls started falling on you like summer rain.

A neat little blonde sat off in a far corner at a small PBX,
behind a railing and well out of harm's way. At a flat desk in

line with the doors was a tall, lean, dark-haired lovely whose name, according to the tilted embossed plaque on her desk, was Miss Adrienne Fromsett.

She wore a steel gray business suit and under the jacket a dark blue shirt and a man's tie of lighter shade. The edges of the folded handkerchief in the breast pocket looked sharp enough to slice bread. She wore a linked bracelet and no other jewelry. Her dark hair was parted and fell in loose but not unstudied waves. She had a smooth ivory skin and rather severe eyebrows and large dark eyes that looked as if they might warm up at the right time and in the right place.

I put my plain card, the one without the tommy gun in the corner, on her desk and asked to see Mr. Derace Kingsley. She looked at the card and said: "Have you an appointment?"

"No appointment."

"It is very difficult to see Mr. Kingsley without an appointment."

That wasn't anything I could argue about.

"What is the nature of your business, Mr. Marlowe?"

"Personal."

"I see. Does Mr. Kingsley know you, Mr. Marlowe?"

"I don't think so. He may have heard my name. You might say I'm from Lieutenant M'Gee."

"And does Mr. Kingsley know Lieutenant M'Gee?"

She put my card beside a pile of freshly typed letterheads. She leaned back and put one arm on the desk and tapped lightly with a small gold pencil.

I grinned at her. The little blonde at the PBX cocked a shell-like ear and smiled a small fluffy smile. She looked playful and eager, but not quite sure of herself, like a new kitten in a house where they don't care much about kittens.

"I'm hoping he does," I said. "But maybe the best way to find out is to ask him."

She initialed three letters rapidly, to keep from throwing her pen set at me. She spoke again without looking up.

"Mr. Kingsley is in conference. I'll send your card in when I have an opportunity."

I thanked her and went and sat in a chromium and leather chair that was a lot more comfortable than it looked. Time passed and silence descended on the scene. Nobody came in or went out. Miss Fromsett's elegant hand moved over her papers and the muted peep of the kitten at the PBX was audible at moments, and the little click of the plugs going in and out.

I lit a cigarette and dragged a smoking stand beside the chair. The minutes went by on tiptoe, with their fingers to their lips. I looked the place over. You can't tell anything about an outfit like that. They might be making millions, and they might have the sheriff in the back room, with his chair tilted against the safe.

Half an hour and three or four cigarettes later a door opened behind Miss Fromsett's desk and two men came out backwards laughing. A third man held the door for them and helped them laugh. They all shook hands heartily and the two men went across the office and out. The third man dropped the grin off his face and looked as if he had never grinned in his life. He was a tall bird in a gray suit and he didn't want any nonsense.

"Any calls?" he asked in a sharp bossy voice.

Miss Fromsett said softly: "A Mr. Marlowe to see you. From Lieutenant M'Gee. His business is personal."

"Never heard of him," the tall man barked. He took my card, didn't even glance at me, and went back into his office. His door closed on the pneumatic closer and made a sound like "phooey." Miss Fromsett gave me a sweet sad smile and I gave it back to her in the form of an obscene leer. I ate another cigarette and more time staggered by. I was getting to be very fond of the Gillerlain Company.

Ten minutes later the same door opened again and the big shot came out with his hat on and sneered that he was going to get a hair-cut. He started off across the Chinese rug in a swinging athletic stride, made about half the distance to the door and then did a sharp cutback and came over to where I was sitting.

"You want to see me?" he barked.

He was about six feet two and not much of it soft. His eyes were stone gray with flecks of cold light in them. He filled a large size in smooth gray flannel with a narrow chalk stripe, and filled it elegantly. His manner said he was very tough to get along with.

I stood up. "If you're Mr. Derace Kingsley."

"Who the hell did you think I was?"

I let him have that trick and gave him my other card, the one with the business on it. He clamped it in his paw and scowled down at it.

"Who's M'Gee?" he snapped.

"He's just a fellow I know."

"I'm fascinated," he said, glancing back at Miss Fromsett. She liked it. She liked it very much. "Anything else you would care to let drop about him?"

"Well, they call him Violets M'Gee," I said. "On account of he chews little throat pastilles that smell of violets. He's a big man with soft silvery hair and a cute little mouth made to kiss babies with. When last seen he was wearing a neat blue suit, wide-toed brown shoes, gray homburg hat, and he was smoking opium in a short briar pipe."

"I don't like your manner," Kingsley said in a voice you could have cracked a Brazil nut on.

"That's all right," I said. "I'm not selling it."

He reared back as if I had hung a week-old mackerel under his nose. After a moment he turned his back on me and said over his shoulder:

"I'll give you exactly three minutes. God knows why."

He burned the carpet back past Miss Fromsett's desk to his door, yanked it open and let it swing to in my face. Miss

Fromsett liked that too, but I thought there was a little sly laughter behind her eyes now.

2

THE PRIVATE OFFICE was everything a private office should be. It was long and dim and quiet and air-conditioned and its windows were shut and its gray venetian blinds half-closed to keep out the July glare. Gray drapes matched the gray carpeting. There was a large black and silver safe in the corner and a low row of low filing cases that exactly matched it. On the wall there was a huge tinted photograph of an elderly party with a chiseled beak and whiskers and a wing collar. The Adam's apple that edged through his wing collar looked harder than most people's chins. The plate underneath the photograph read: *Mr. Matthew Gillerlain* 1860–1934.

Derace Kingsley marched briskly behind about eight hundred dollars' worth of executive desk and planted his backside in a tall leather chair. He reached himself a panatela out of a copper and mahogany box and trimmed it and lit it with a fat copper desk lighter. He took his time about it. It didn't matter about my time. When he had finished this, he leaned back and blew a little smoke and said:

"I'm a business man. I don't fool around. You're a licensed detective, your card says. Show me something to prove it."

I got my wallet out and handed him things to prove it. He looked at them and threw them back across the desk. The celluloid holder with the photostat license in it fell to the floor. He didn't bother to apologize.

"I don't know M'Gee," he said. "I know Sheriff Petersen. I asked for the name of a reliable man to do a job. I suppose you are the man."

"M'Gee is in the Hollywood sub-station of the sheriff's office," I said. "You can check on that."

"Not necessary. I guess you might do, but don't get flip with me. And remember when I hire a man he's my man. He does exactly what I tell him and he keeps his mouth shut. Or he goes out fast. Is that clear? I hope I'm not too tough for you."

"Why not leave that an open question?" I said.

He frowned. He said sharply: "What do you charge?"

"Twenty-five a day and expenses. Eight cents a mile for my car."

"Absurd," he said. "Far too much. Fifteen a day flat. That's plenty. I'll pay the mileage, within reason, the way things are now. But no joyriding."

I blew a little gray cloud of cigarette smoke and fanned it with my hand. I said nothing. He seemed a little surprised that I said nothing.

He leaned over the desk and pointed with his cigar. "I haven't hired you yet," he said, "but if I do, the job is absolutely confidential. No talking it over with your cop friends. Is that understood?"

"Just what do you want done, Mr. Kingsley?"

"What do you care? You do all kinds of detective work, don't you?"

"Not all kinds. Only the fairly honest kinds."

He stared at me level-eyed, his jaws tight. His gray eyes had an opaque look.

"For one thing I don't do divorce business," I said. "And I get a hundred down as a retainer — from strangers."

"Well, well," he said, in a voice suddenly soft. "Well, well."

"And as for your being too tough for me," I said, "most of the clients start out either by weeping down my shirt or bawling me out to show who's boss. But usually they end up very reasonable — if they're still alive."

"Well, well," he said again, in the same soft voice, and went on staring at me. "Do you lose very many of them?" he asked.

"Not if they treat me right," I said.

8

"Have a cigar," he said.

I took a cigar and put it in my pocket.

"I want you to find my wife," he said. "She's been missing for a month."

"Okay," I said. "I'll find your wife."

He patted his desk with both hands. He stared at me solidly. "I think you will at that," he said. Then he grinned. "I haven't been called down like that in four years," he said.

I didn't say anything.

"Damn it all," he said, "I liked it. I liked it fine." He ran a hand through his thick dark hair. "She's been gone a whole month," he said. "From a cabin we have in the mountains. Near Puma Point. Do you know Puma Point?"

I said I knew Puma Point.

"Our place is three miles from the village," he said, "partly over a private road. It's on a private lake. Little Fawn Lake. There's a dam three of us put up to improve the property. I own the tract with two other men. It's quite large, but undeveloped and won't be developed now for some time, of course. My friends have cabins, I have a cabin and a man named Bill Chess lives with his wife in another cabin rent free and looks after the place. He's a disabled veteran with a pension. That's all there is up there. My wife went up the middle of May, came down twice for weekends, was due down the 12th of June for a party and never showed up. I haven't seen her since."

"What have you done about it?" I asked.

"Nothing. Not a thing. I haven't even been up there." He waited, wanting me to ask why.

I said: "Why?"

He pushed his chair back to get a locked drawer open. He took out a folded paper and passed it over. I unfolded it and saw it was a Postal Telegraph form. The wire had been filed at El Paso on June 14th at 9:19 A.M. It was addressed to Derace Kingsley, 965 Carson Drive, Beverly Hills, and read:

"AM CROSSING TO GET MEXICAN DIVORCE STOP WILL MARRY CHRIS STOP GOOD LUCK AND GOODBYE CRYSTAL."

I put this down on my side of the desk and he was handing me a large and very clear snapshot on glazed paper which showed a man and a woman sitting on the sand under a beach umbrella. The man wore trunks and the woman what looked like a very daring white sharkskin bathing suit. She was a slim blonde, young and shapely and smiling. The man was a hefty dark handsome lad with fine shoulders and legs, sleek dark hair and white teeth. Six feet of a standard type of home-wrecker. Arms to hold you close and all his brains in his face. He was holding a pair of dark glasses in his hand and smiling at the camera with a practiced and easy smile.

"That's Crystal," Kingsley said, "and that's Chris Lavery. She can have him and he can have her and to hell with them both."

I put the photo down on the telegram. "All right, what's the catch?" I asked him.

"There's no telephone up there," he said, "and there was nothing important about the affair she was coming down for. So I got the wire before I gave much thought to it. The wire surprised me only mildly. Crystal and I have been washed up for years. She lives her life and I live mine. She has her own money and plenty of it. About twenty thousand a year from a family holding corporation that owns valuable oil leases in Texas. She plays around and I knew Lavery was one of her playmates. I might have been a little surprised that she would actually marry him, because the man is nothing but a professional chaser. But the picture looked all right so far, you understand?"

"And then?"

"Nothing for two weeks. Then the Prescott Hotel in San Bernardino got in touch with me and said a Packard Clipper registered to Crystal Grace Kingsley at my address was unclaimed in their garage and what about it. I told them to keep it and I sent them a check. There was nothing much in that either. I figured she was still out of the state and that if they had gone in a car at all, they had gone in Lavery's car. The day before yesterday, however, I met Lavery in front of the Athletic Club down on the corner here. He said he didn't know where Crystal was."

Kingsley gave me a quick look and reached a bottle and two tinted glasses up on the desk. He poured a couple of drinks and pushed one over. He held his against the light and said slowly:

"Lavery said he hadn't gone away with her, hadn't seen her in two months, hadn't had any communications with her of any kind."

I said, "You believed him?"

He nodded, frowning, and drank his drink and pushed the glass to one side. I tasted mine. It was Scotch. Not very good Scotch.

"If I believed him," Kingsley said, "— and I was probably wrong to do it — it wasn't because he's a fellow you have to believe. Far from it. It's because he's a no-good son of a bitch who thinks it is smart to lay his friends' wives and brag about it. I feel he would have been tickled pink to stick it into me and break it off that he had got my wife to run away with him and leave me flat. I know these tomcats and I know this one too well. He rode a route for us for a while and he was in trouble all the time. He couldn't keep his hands off the office help. And apart from all that there was this wire from El Paso and I told him about it and why would he think it worth while to lie about it?"

"She might have tossed him out on his can," I said. "That would have hurt him in his deep place — his Casanova complex."

Kingsley brightened up a little, but not very much. He shook his head. "I still more than half way believe him," he said. "You'll have to prove me wrong. That's part of why

I wanted you. But there's another and very worrying angle. I have a good job here, but a job is all it is. I can't stand scandal. I'd be out of here in a hurry if my wife got mixed up with the police."

"Police?"

"Among her other activities," Kingsley said grimly, "my wife occasionally finds time to lift things in department stores. I think it's just a sort of delusion of grandeur she gets when she has been hitting the bottle too hard, but it happens, and we have had some pretty nasty scenes in managers' offices. So far I've been able to keep them from filing charges, but if something like that happened in a strange city where nobody knew her —" He lifted his hands and let them fall with a smack on the desk — "well, it might be a prison matter, mightn't it?"

"Has she ever been fingerprinted?"

"She has never been arrested," he said.

"That's not what I mean. Sometimes in large department stores they make it a condition of dropping shoplifting charges that you give them your prints. It scares the amateurs and builds up a file of kleptomaniacs in their protective association. When the prints come in a certain number of times they call time on you."

"Nothing like that has happened to my knowledge," he said.

"Well, I think we might almost throw the shoplifting angle out of this for the time being," I said. "If she got arrested, she would get searched. Even if the cops let her use a Jane Doe name on the police blotter, they would be likely to get in touch with you. Also she would start yelling for help when she found herself in a jam." I tapped the blue and white telegraph form. "And this is a month old. If what you are thinking about happened around that time, the case would have been settled by now. If it was a first offense, she would get off with a scolding and a suspended sentence."

He poured himself another drink to help him with his worrying. "You're making me feel better," he said.

"There are too many other things that could have happened," I said. "That she did go away with Lavery and they split up. That she went away with some other man and the wire is a gag. That she went away alone or with a woman. That she drank herself over the edge and is holed up in some private sanatorium taking a cure. That she got into some jam we have no idea of. That she met with foul play."

"Good God, don't say that," Kingsley exclaimed.

"Why not? You've got to consider it. I get a very vague idea of Mrs. Kingsley — that she is young, pretty, reckless, and wild. That she drinks and does dangerous things when she drinks. That she is a sucker for the men and might take up with a stranger who might turn out to be a crook. Does that fit?"

He nodded. "Every word of it."

"How much money would she have with her?"

"She liked to carry enough. She has her own bank and her own bank account. She could have any amount of money."

"Any children?"

"No children."

"Do you have the management of her affairs?"

He shook his head. "She hasn't any — excepting depositing checks and drawing out money and spending it. She never invests a nickel. And her money certainly never does me any good, if that's what you are thinking." He paused and then said: "Don't think I haven't tried. I'm human and it's not fun to watch twenty thousand a year go down the drain and nothing to show for it but hangovers and boy friends of the class of Chris Lavery."

"How are you with her bank? Could you get a detail of the checks she has drawn for the past couple of months?"

"They wouldn't tell me. I tried to get some information of the sort once, when I had an idea she was being blackmailed. All I got was ice."

"We can get it," I said, "and we may have to. It will mean going to the Missing Persons Bureau. You wouldn't like that?"

"If I had liked that, I wouldn't have called you," he said.

I nodded, gathered my exhibits together and put them away in my pockets. "There are more angles to this than I can even see now," I said, "but I'll start by talking to Lavery and then taking a run up to Little Fawn Lake and asking questions there. I'll need Lavery's address and a note to your man in charge at the mountain place."

He got a letterhead out of his desk and wrote and passed it over. I read: "Dear Bill: This will introduce Mr. Philip Marlowe who wishes to look over the property. Please show him my cabin and assist him in every way. Yrs. Derace Kingsley."

I folded this up and put it in the envelope he had addressed while I was reading it. "How about the other cabins up there?" I asked.

"Nobody up this year so far. One man's in government service in Washington and the other is at Fort Leavenworth. Their wives are with them."

"Now Lavery's address," I said.

He looked at a point well above the top of my head. "In Bay City. I could find the house but I forget the address. Miss Fromsett can give it to you, I think. She needn't know why you want it. She probably will. And you want a hundred dollars, you said."

"That's all right," I said. "That's just something I said when you were tramping on me."

He grinned. I stood up and hesitated by the desk looking at him. After a moment I said: "You're not holding anything back, are you – anything important?"

He looked at his thumb. "No. I'm not holding anything back. I'm worried and I want to know where she is. I'm damn worried. If you get anything at all, call me any time, day or night."

I said I would do that, and we shook hands and I went back down the long cool office and out to where Miss Fromsett sat elegantly at her desk.

"Mr. Kingsley thinks you can give me Chris Lavery's address," I told her and watched her face.

She reached very slowly for a brown leather address book and turned the leaves. Her voice was tight and cold when she spoke.

"The address we have is 623 Altair Street, in Bay City. Telephone Bay City 12523. Mr. Lavery has not been with us for more than a year. He may have moved."

I thanked her and went on to the door. From there I glanced back at her. She was sitting very still, with her hands clasped on her desk, staring into space. A couple of red spots burned in her cheeks. Her eyes were remote and bitter.

I got the impression that Mr. Chris Lavery was not a pleasant thought to her.

3

ALTAIR STREET LAY on the edge of the V forming the inner end of a deep canyon. To the north was the cool blue sweep of the bay out to the point above Malibu. To the south the beach town of Bay City was spread out on a bluff above the coast highway.

It was a short street, not more than three or four blocks, and ended in a tall iron fence enclosing a large estate. Beyond the gilded spikes of the fence I could see trees and shrubs and a glimpse of lawn and part of a curving driveway, but the house was out of sight. On the inland side of Altair Street the houses were well kept and fairly large, but the few scattered bungalows on the edge of the canyon were nothing much. In the short half block ended by the iron fence were only two houses, on opposite sides of the street and almost directly across from each other. The smaller was number 623.

I drove past it, turned the car in the paved half circle at the end of the street and came back to park in front of the lot next to Lavery's place. His house was built downwards, one of those clinging-vine effects, with the front door a little below street level, the patio on the roof, the bedroom in the basement, and a garage like the corner pocket on a pool table. A crimson bougainvillea was rustling against the front wall and the flat stones of the front walk were edged with Korean moss. The door was narrow, grilled and topped by a lancet arch. Below the grill there was an iron knocker. I hammered on it.

Nothing happened. I pushed the bell at the side of the door and heard it ring inside not very far off and waited and nothing happened. I worked on the knocker again. Still nothing. I went back up the walk and along to the garage and lifted the door far enough to see that a car with white side-walled tires was inside. I went back to the front door.

A neat black Cadillac coupe came out of the garage across the way, backed, turned and came along past Lavery's house, slowed, and a thin man in dark glasses looked at me sharply, as if I hadn't any business to be there. I gave him my steely glare and he went on his way.

I went down Lavery's walk again and did some more hammering on his knocker. This time I got results. The Judas window opened and I was looking at a handsome bright-eyed number through the bars of a grill.

"You make a hell of a lot of noise," a voice said.

"Mr. Lavery?"

He said he was Mr. Lavery and what about it. I poked a card through the grill. A large brown hand took the card. The bright brown eyes came back and the voice said: "So sorry. Not needing any detectives today please."

"I'm working for Derace Kingsley."

"The hell with both of you," he said, and banged the Judas window. I leaned on the bell beside the door and got a cigarette out with my free hand and had just struck the match on the woodwork beside the door when it was yanked open and a big guy in bathing trunks, beach sandals, and a white terry-cloth bathrobe started to come out at me.

I took my thumb off the bell and grinned at him. "What's the matter?" I asked him. "Scared?"

"Ring that bell again," he said, "and I'll throw you clear across the street."

"Don't be childish," I told him. "You know perfectly well I'm going to talk to you and you're going to talk to me."

I got the blue and white telegram out of my pocket and held it in front of his bright brown eyes. He read it morosely, chewed his lip and growled:

"Oh for Chrissake, come on in then."

He held the door wide and I went in past him, into a dim pleasant room with an apricot Chinese rug that looked expensive, deep-sided chairs, a number of white drum lamps, a big Capehart in the corner, a long and very wide davenport in pale tan mohair shot with dark brown, and a fireplace with a copper screen and an over-mantel in white wood. A fire was laid behind the screen and partly masked by a large spray of manzanita bloom. The bloom was turning yellow in places, but was still pretty. There was a bottle of Vat 69 and glasses on a tray and a copper ice bucket on a low round burl walnut table with a glass top. The room went clear to the back of the house and ended in a flat arch through which showed three narrow windows and the top few feet of the white iron railing of the staircase going down.

Lavery swung the door shut and sat on the davenport. He grabbed a cigarette out of a hammered silver box and lit it and looked at me irritably. I sat down opposite him and looked him over. He had everything in the way of good looks the snapshot had indicated. He had a terrific torso and magnificent thighs. His eyes were chestnut brown and the whites of them slightly gray-white. His hair was rather long and curled a little over his temples. His brown skin showed no signs of dissipation. He was a nice piece of beef, but to me that was all he was. I could understand that women would think he was something to yell for.

"Why not tell us where she is?" I said. "We'll find out eventually anyway and if you can tell us now, we won't be bothering you."

"It would take more than a private dick to bother me," he said.

"No, it wouldn't. A private dick can bother anybody. He's persistent and used to snubs. He's paid for his time and he would just as soon use it to bother you as any other way."

"Look," he said, leaning forward and pointing his cigarette at me. "I know what that wire says, but it's the bunk. I didn't go to El Paso with Crystal Kingsley. I haven't seen her in a long time – long before the date of that wire. I haven't had any contact with her. I told Kingsley that."

"He didn't have to believe you."

"Why would I lie to him?" He looked surprised.

"Why wouldn't you?"

"Look," he said earnestly, "it might seem so to you, but you don't know her. Kingsley has no strings on her. If he doesn't like the way she behaves he has a remedy. These proprietary husbands make me sick."

"If you didn't go to El Paso with her," I said, "why did she send this telegram?"

"I haven't the faintest idea."

"You can do better than that," I said. I pointed to the spray of manzanita in the fireplace. "You pick that up at Little Fawn Lake?"

"The hills around here are full of manzanita," he said contemptuously.

"It doesn't bloom like that down here."

He laughed. "I was up there the third week in May. If you have to know. I suppose you can find out. That's the last time I saw her."

"You didn't have any idea of marrying her?"

He blew smoke and said through it: "I've thought of it, yes. She has money. Money is always useful. But it would be too tough a way to make it."

I nodded, but didn't say anything. He looked at the manzanita spray in the fireplace and leaned back to blow smoke in
the air and show me the strong brown line of his throat. After
a moment, when I still didn't say anything, he began to get
restless. He glanced down at the card I had given him and
said:

"So you hire yourself out to dig up dirt? Doing well at it?"

"Nothing to brag about. A dollar here, a dollar there."

"And all of them pretty slimy," he said.

"Look, Mr. Lavery, we don't have to get into a fight.
Kingsley thinks you know where his wife is, but won't tell
him. Either out of meanness or motives of delicacy."

"Which way would he like it?" the handsome brown-faced
man sneered.

"He doesn't care, as long as he gets the information. He
doesn't care a great deal what you and she do together or
where you go or whether she divorces him or not. He just
wants to feel sure that everything is all right and that she isn't
in trouble of any kind."

Lavery looked interested. "Trouble? What kind of trouble?"
He licked the word around on his brown lips, tasting it.

"Maybe you won't know the kind of trouble he is thinking of."

"Tell me," he pleaded sarcastically. "I'd just love to hear
about some kind of trouble I didn't know about."

"You're doing fine," I told him. "No time to talk business,
but always time for a wisecrack. If you think we might try to
get a hook into you because you crossed a state line with her,
forget it."

"Go climb up your thumb, wise guy. You'd have to prove
I paid the freight, or it wouldn't mean anything."

"This wire has to mean something," I said stubbornly. It
seemed to me that I had said it before, several times.

"It's probably just a gag. She's full of little tricks like that.
All of them silly, and some of them vicious."

"I don't see any point in this one."

He flicked cigarette ash carefully at the glass-top table. He gave me a quick up from under look and immediately looked away.

"I stood her up," he said slowly. "It might be her idea of a way to get back at me. I was supposed to run up there one week-end. I didn't go. I was – sick of her."

I said: "Uh-huh," and gave him a long steady stare. "I don't like that so well. I'd like it better if you did go to El Paso with her and had a fight and split up. Could you tell it that way?"

He flushed solidly behind the sunburn.

"God damn it," he said, "I told you I didn't go anywhere with her. Not anywhere. Can't you remember that?"

"I'll remember it when I believe it."

He leaned over to snub out his cigarette. He stood up with an easy movement, not hurried at all, pulled the belt of his robe tight, and moved out to the end of the davenport.

"All right," he said in a clear tight voice. "Out you go. Take the air. I've had enough of your third-degree tripe. You're wasting my time and your own – if it's worth anything."

I stood up and grinned at him. "Not a lot, but for what it's worth I'm being paid for it. It couldn't be, for instance, that you ran into a little unpleasantness in some department store – say at the stocking or jewelry counter."

He looked at me very carefully, drawing his eyebrows down at the corners and making his mouth small.

"I don't get it," he said, but there was thought behind his voice.

"That's all I wanted to know," I said. "And thanks for listening. By the way, what line of business are you in – since you left Kingsley?"

"What the hell business is it of yours?"

"None. But of course I can always find out," I said, and moved a little way towards the door, not very far.

"At the moment I'm not doing anything," he said coldly. "I expect a commission in the navy almost any day."

"You ought to do well at that," I said.

"Yeah. So long, snooper. And don't bother to come back. I won't be at home."

I went over to the door and pulled it open. It stuck on the lower sill, from the beach moisture. When I had it open, I looked back at him. He was standing there narrow-eyed, full of muted thunder.

"I may have to come back," I said. "But it won't be just to swop gags. It will be because I find something out that needs talking over."

"So you still think I'm lying," he said savagely.

"I think you have something on your mind. I've looked at too many faces not to know. It may not be any of my business. If it is, you're likely to have to throw me out again."

"A pleasure," he said. "And next time bring somebody to drive you home. In case you land on your fanny and knock your brains out."

Then without any rhyme or reason that I could see, he spat on the rug in front of his feet.

It jarred me. It was like watching the veneer peel off and leave a tough kid in an alley. Or like hearing an apparently refined woman start expressing herself in four-letter words.

"So long, beautiful hunk," I said, and left him standing there. I closed the door, had to jerk it to get it shut, and went up the path to the street. I stood on the sidewalk looking at the house across the way.

4

IT WAS A wide shallow house with rose stucco walls faded out to a pleasant pastel shade and trimmed with dull green at the window frames. The roof was of green tiles, round rough ones. There was a deeply inset front door framed in a mosaic of multi-colored pieces of tiling and a small flower garden in front, behind a low stucco wall topped by an iron railing which the beach moisture had begun to corrode. Outside the wall to the left was the three-car garage, with a door opening inside the yard and a concrete path going from there to a side door of the house.

Set into the gate post was a bronze tablet which read: "Albert S. Almore, M.D."

While I was standing there staring across the street, the black Cadillac I had already seen came purring around the corner and then down the block. It slowed and started to sweep outwards to get turning space to go into the garage, decided my car was in the way of that, and went on to the end of the road and turned in the widened-out space in front of the ornamental iron railing. It came back slowly and went into the empty third of the garage across the way.

The thin man in sun glasses went along the sidewalk to the house, carrying a double-handled doctor's bag. Halfway along he slowed down to stare across at me. I went along towards my car. At the house he used a key and as he opened the door he looked across at me again.

I got into the Chrysler and sat there smoking and trying to make up my mind whether it was worth while hiring somebody to pull a tail on Lavery. I decided it wasn't, not the way things looked so far.

Curtains moved at a lower window close to the side door Dr. Almore had gone in at. A thin hand held them aside and I caught the glint of light on glasses. They were held aside for quite some time, before they fell together again.

I looked along the street at Lavery's house. From this angle I could see that his service porch gave on a flight of painted wooden steps to a sloping concrete walk and a flight of concrete steps ending in the paved alley below.

I looked across at Dr. Almore's house again, wondering idly if he knew Lavery and how well. He probably knew him,

22

since theirs were the only two houses in the block. But being a doctor, he wouldn't tell me anything about him. As I looked, the curtains which had been lifted apart were now completely drawn aside.

The middle segment of the triple window they had masked had no screen. Behind it, Dr. Almore stood staring across my way, with a sharp frown on his thin face. I shook cigarette ash out of the window and he turned abruptly and sat down at a desk. His double-handled bag was on the desk in front of him. He sat rigidly, drumming on the desk beside the bag. His hand reached for the telephone, touched it and came away again. He lit a cigarette and shook the match violently, then strode to the window and stared out at me some more.

This was interesting, if at all, only because he was a doctor. Doctors, as a rule, are the least curious of men. While they are still internes they hear enough secrets to last them a lifetime. Dr. Almore seemed interested in me. More than interested, bothered.

I reached down to turn the ignition key, then Lavery's front door opened and I took my hand away and leaned back again. Lavery came briskly up the walk of his house, shot a glance down the street and turned to go into his garage. He was dressed as I had seen him. He had a rough towel and a steamer rug over his arm. I heard the garage door lift up, then the car door open and shut, then the grind and cough of the starting car. It backed up the steep incline to the street, white steamy exhaust pouring from its rear end. It was a cute little blue convertible, with the top folded down and Lavery's sleek dark head just rising above it. He was now wearing a natty pair of sun-goggles with very wide white sidebows. The convertible swooped off down the block and danced around the corner.

There was nothing in that for me. Mr. Christopher Lavery was bound for the edge of the broad Pacific, to lie in the sun and let the girls see what they didn't necessarily have to go on missing.

I gave my attention back to Dr. Almore. He was on the telephone now, not talking, holding it to his ear, smoking and waiting. Then he leaned forward as you do when the voice comes back, listened, hung up and wrote something on a pad in front of him. Then a heavy book with yellow sides appeared on his desk and he opened it just about in the middle. While he was doing this he gave one quick look out of the window, straight at the Chrysler.

He found his place in the book, leaned down over it and quick puffs of smoke appeared in the air over the pages. He wrote something else, put the book away, and grabbed the telephone again. He dialed, waited, began to speak quickly, pushing his head down and making gestures in the air with his cigarette.

He finished his call and hung up. He leaned back and sat there brooding, staring down at his desk, but not forgetting to look out of the window every half minute. He was waiting, and I waited with him, for no reason at all. Doctors make many phone calls, talk to many people. Doctors look out of their front windows, doctors frown, doctors show nervousness, doctors have things on their mind and show the strain. Doctors are just people, born to sorrow, fighting the long grim fight like the rest of us.

But there was something about the way this one behaved that intrigued me. I looked at my watch, decided it was time to get something to eat, lit another cigarette and didn't move.

It took about five minutes. Then a green sedan whisked around the corner and bore down the block. It coasted to a stop in front of Dr. Almore's house and its tall buggywhip aerial quivered. A big man with dusty blond hair got out and went up to Dr. Almore's front door. He rang the bell and leaned down to strike a match on the step. His head came around and he stared across the street exactly at where I was sitting.

The door opened and he went into the house. An invisible hand gathered the curtains at Dr. Almore's study window and blanked the room. I sat there and stared at the sun-darkened lining of the curtains. More time trickled by.

The front door opened again and the big man loafed casually down the steps and through the gate. He snapped his cigarette end off into the distance and rumpled his hair. He shrugged once, pinched the end of his chin, and walked diagonally across the street. His steps in the quiet were leisurely and distinct. Dr. Almore's curtains moved apart again behind him. Dr. Almore stood in his window and watched.

A large freckled hand appeared on the sill of the car door at my elbow. A large face, deeply lined, hung above it. The man had eyes of metallic blue. He looked at me solidly and spoke in a deep harsh voice.

"Waiting for somebody?" he asked.

"I don't know," I said. "Am I?"

"I'll ask the questions."

"Well, I'll be damned," I said. "So that's the answer to the pantomime."

"What pantomime?" He gave me a hard level unfriendly stare from his very blue eyes.

I pointed across the street with my cigarette. "Nervous Nellie and the telephone. Calling the cops, after first getting my name from the Auto Club, probably, then looking it up in the city directory. What goes on?"

"Let me see your driver's license."

I gave him back his stare. "You fellows ever flash a buzzer – or is acting tough all the identification you need?"

"If I have to get tough, fellow, you'll know it."

I leaned down and turned my ignition key and pressed the starter. The motor caught and idled down.

"Cut that motor," he said savagely, and put his foot on the running board.

I cut the motor again and leaned back and looked at him.

"God damn it," he said, "do you want me to drag you out of there and bounce you on the pavement?"

I got my wallet out and handed it to him. He drew the celluloid pocket out and looked at my driver's license, then turned the pocket over and looked at the photostat of my other license on the back. He rammed it contemptuously back into the wallet and handed me the wallet. I put it away. His hand dipped and came up with a blue and gold police badge.

"Degarmo, detective-lieutenant," he said in his heavy brutal voice.

"Pleased to meet you, lieutenant."

"Skip it. Now tell why you're down here casing Almore's place."

"I'm not casing Almore's place, as you put it, lieutenant. I never heard of Dr. Almore and I don't know of any reason why I should want to case his house."

He turned his head to spit. I was meeting the spitting boys today.

"What's your grift then? We don't like peepers down here. We don't have one in town."

"Is that so?"

"Yeah, that's so. So come on, talk it up. Unless you want to ride down to the clubhouse and sweat it out under the bright lights."

I didn't answer him.

"Her folks hire you?" he asked suddenly.

I shook my head.

"The last boy that tried it ended up on the road gang, sweetheart."

"I bet it's good," I said, "if only I could guess. Tried what?"

"Tried to put the bite on him," he said thinly.

"Too bad I don't know how," I said. "He looks like an easy man to bite."

"That line of talk don't buy you anything," he said.

26

"All right," I said. "Let's put it this way. I don't know Dr. Almore, never heard of him, and I'm not interested in him. I'm down here visiting a friend and looking at the view. If I'm doing anything else, it doesn't happen to be any of your business. If you don't like that, the best thing to do is to take it down to headquarters and see the day captain."

He moved a foot heavily on the running board and looked doubtful. "Straight goods?" he asked slowly.

"Straight goods."

"Aw hell, the guy's screwy," he said suddenly and looked back over his shoulder at the house. "He ought to see a doctor." He laughed, without any amusement in the laugh. He took his foot off my running board and rumpled his wiry hair.

"Go on – beat it," he said. "Stay off our reservation, and you won't make any enemies."

I pressed the starter again. When the motor was idling gently I said: "How's Al Norgaard these days?"

He stared at me. "You know Al?"

"Yeah. He and I worked on a case down here a couple of years ago – when Wax was chief of police."

"Al's in the military police. I wish I was," he said bitterly. He started to walk away and then swung sharply on his heel. "Go on, beat it before I change my mind," he snapped.

He walked heavily across the street and through Dr. Almore's front gate again.

I let the clutch in and drove away. On the way back to the city, I listened to my thoughts. They moved fitfully in and out, like Dr. Almore's thin nervous hands pulling at the edges of his curtains.

Back in Los Angeles I ate lunch and went up to my office in the Cahuenga Building to see what mail there was. I called Kingsley from there.

"I saw Lavery," I told him. "He told me just enough dirt to sound frank. I tried to needle him a little, but nothing came of it. I still like the idea that they quarreled and split up and that he hopes to fix it up with her yet."

"Then he must know where she is," Kingsley said.

"He might, but it doesn't follow. By the way a rather curious thing happened to me on Lavery's street. There are only two houses. The other belongs to a Dr. Almore." I told him briefly about the rather curious thing.

He was silent for a moment at the end and then he said: "Is this Dr. Albert Almore?"

"Yes."

"He was Crystal's doctor for a time. He came to the house several times when she was — well, when she had been over-drinking. I thought him a little too quick with a hypodermic needle. His wife — let me see, there was something about his wife. Oh yes, she committed suicide."

I said, "When?"

"I don't remember. Quite a long time ago. I never knew them socially. What are you going to do now?"

I told him I was going up to Puma Lake, although it was a little late in the day to start.

He said I would have plenty of time and that they had an hour more daylight in the mountains.

I said that was fine and we hung up.

5

SAN BERNARDINO BAKED and shimmered in the afternoon heat. The air was hot enough to blister my tongue. I drove through it gasping, stopped long enough to buy a pint of liquor in case I fainted before I got to the mountains, and started up the long grade to Crestline. In fifteen miles the road climbed five thousand feet, but even then it was far from cool. Thirty miles of mountain driving brought me to the tall pines and a place called Bubbling Springs. It had a clapboard store and a gas pump, but it felt like paradise. From there on it was cool all the way.

The Puma Lake dam had an armed sentry at each end and one in the middle. The first one I came to had me close all the windows of the car before crossing the dam. About a hundred yards away from the dam a rope with cork floats barred the pleasure boats from coming any closer. Beyond these details the war did not seem to have done anything much to Puma Lake.

Canoes paddled about on the blue water and rowboats with outboard motors put-putted and speedboats showing off like fresh kids made wide swathes of foam and turned on a dime and girls in them shrieked and dragged their hands in the water. Jounced around in the wake of the speedboats people who had paid two dollars for a fishing license were trying to get a dime of it back in tired-tasting fish.

The road skimmed along a high granite outcrop and dropped to meadows of coarse grass in which grew what was left of the wild irises and white and purple lupine and bugle flowers and columbine and penny-royal and desert paint brush. Tall yellow pines probed at the clear blue sky. The road dropped again to lake level and the landscape began to be full of girls in gaudy slacks and snoods and peasant handkerchiefs and rat rolls and fat-soled sandals and fat white thighs. People on bicycles wobbled cautiously over the highway and now and then an anxious-looking bird thumped past on a power-scooter.

A mile from the village the highway was joined by another lesser road which curved back into the mountains. A rough wooden sign under the highway sign said: *Little Fawn Lake 1¾ miles.* I took it. Scattered cabins were perched along the slopes for the first mile and then nothing. Presently another very narrow road debouched from this one and another rough wooden sign said: *Little Fawn Lake. Private Road. No Trespassing.*

I turned the Chrysler into this and crawled carefully around huge bare granite rocks and past a little waterfall and through a maze of black oak trees and ironwood and man-zanita and silence. A bluejay squawked on a branch and a squirrel scolded at me and beat one paw angrily on the pine cone it was holding. A scarlet-topped woodpecker stopped probing in the dark long enough to look at me with one beady eye and then dodge behind the tree trunk to look at me with the other one. I came to a five-barred gate and another sign.

Beyond the gate the road wound for a couple of hundred yards through trees and then suddenly below me was a small oval lake deep in trees and rocks and wild grass, like a drop of dew caught in a curled leaf. At the near end of it was a rough concrete dam with a rope handrail across the top and an old millwheel at the side. Near that stood a small cabin of native pine with the bark on it.

Across the lake the long way by the road and the short way by the top of the dam a large redwood cabin overhung the water and farther along, each well separated from the others, were two other cabins. All three were shut up and quiet, with drawn curtains. The big one had orange-yellow venetian blinds and a twelve-paned window facing on the lake.

At the far end of the lake from the dam was what looked like a small pier and a band pavilion. A warped wooden sign on it was painted in large white letters: *Camp Kilkare*. I couldn't see any sense in that in these surroundings, so I got out of the car and started down towards the nearest cabin. Somewhere behind it an axe thudded.

I pounded on the cabin door. The axe stopped. A man's voice yelled from somewhere. I sat down on a rock and lit a cigarette. Steps came around the corner of the cabin, uneven steps. A man with a harsh face and a swarthy skin came into view carrying a double-bitted axe.

He was heavily built and not very tall and he limped as he walked, giving his right leg a little kick out with each step and swinging the foot in a shallow arc. He had a dark unshaven chin

30

and steady blue eyes and grizzled hair that curled over his ears and needed cutting badly. He wore blue denim pants and a blue shirt open on a brown muscular neck. A cigarette hung from the corner of his mouth. He spoke in a tight tough city voice.

"Yeah?"

"Mr. Bill Chess?"

"That's me."

I stood up and got Kingsley's note of introduction out of my pocket and handed it to him. He squinted at the note, then clumped into the cabin and came back with glasses perched on his nose. He read the note carefully and then again. He put it in his shirt pocket, buttoned the flap of his pocket, and put his hand out.

"Pleased to meet you, Mr. Marlowe."

We shook hands. He had a hand like a wood rasp.

"You want to see Kingsley's cabin, huh? Glad to show you. He ain't selling for Chrissake?" He eyed me steadily and jerked a thumb across the lake.

"He might," I said. "Everything's for sale in California."

"Ain't that the truth? That's his — the redwood job. Lined with knotty pine, composition roof, stone foundations and porches, full bath and shower, venetian blinds all around, big fireplace, oil stove in the big bedroom — and brother, you need it in the spring and fall — Pilgrim combination gas and wood range, everything first class. Cost about eight thousand and that's money for a mountain cabin. And private reservoir in the hills for water."

"How about electric light and telephone?" I asked, just to be friendly.

"Electric light, sure. No phone. You couldn't get one now. If you could, it would cost plenty to string the lines out here."

He looked at me with steady blue eyes and I looked at him. In spite of his weathered appearance he looked like a drinker. He had the thickened and glossy skin, the too notice-able veins, the bright glitter in the eyes.

I said: "Anybody living there now?"

"Nope. Mrs. Kingsley was here a few weeks back. She went down the hill. Back any day, I guess. Didn't he say?"

I looked surprised. "Why? Does she go with the cabin?"

He scowled and then put his head back and burst out laughing. The roar of his laughter was like a tractor backfiring. It blasted the woodland silence to shreds.

"Jesus, if that ain't a kick in the pants!" he gasped. "Does she go with the —" He put out another bellow and then his mouth shut tight as a trap.

"Yeah, it's a swell cabin," he said, eyeing me carefully.

"The beds comfortable?" I asked.

He leaned forward and smiled. "Maybe you'd like a face full of knuckles," he said.

I stared at him with my mouth open. "That one went by me too fast," I said, "I never laid an eye on it."

"How would I know if the beds are comfortable?" he snarled, bending down a little so that he could reach me with a hard right, if it worked out that way.

"I don't know why you wouldn't know," I said. "I won't press the point. I can find out for myself."

"Yah," he said bitterly, "think I can't smell a dick when I meet one? I played hit and run with them in every state in the Union. Nuts to you, pal. And nuts to Kingsley. So he hires himself a dick to come up here and see am I wearing his pajamas, huh? Listen, Jack, I might have a stiff leg and all, but the women I could get —"

I put a hand out, hoping he wouldn't pull it off and throw it in the lake.

"You're slipping your clutch," I told him. "I didn't come up here to enquire into your love life. I never saw Mrs. Kingsley. I never saw Mr. Kingsley until this morning. What the hell's the matter with you?"

He dropped his eyes and rubbed the back of his hand viciously across his mouth, as if he wanted to hurt himself.

Then he held the hand in front of his eyes and squeezed it into a hard fist and opened it again and stared at the fingers. They were shaking a little.

"Sorry, Mr. Marlowe," he said slowly. "I was out on the roof last night and I've got a hangover like seven Swedes. I've been up here alone for a month and it's got me talking to myself. A thing happened to me."

"Anything a drink would help?"

His eyes focused sharply on me and glinted. "You got one?"

I pulled the pint of rye out of my pocket and held it so that he could see the green label over the cap.

"I don't deserve it," he said. "God damn it, I don't. Wait till I get a couple of glasses or would you come into the cabin?"

"I like it out here. I'm enjoying the view."

He swung his stiff leg and went into his cabin and came back carrying a couple of small cheese glasses. He sat down on the rock beside me smelling of dried perspiration.

I tore the metal cap off the bottle and poured him a stiff drink and a light one for myself. We touched glasses and drank. He rolled the liquor on his tongue and a bleak smile put a little sunshine into his face.

"Man that's from the right bottle," he said. "I wonder what made me sound off like that. I guess a guy gets the blues up here all alone. No company, no real friends, no wife." He paused and added with a sidewise look, "Especially no wife."

I kept my eyes on the blue water of the tiny lake. Under an overhanging rock a fish surfaced in a lance of light and a circle of widening ripples. A light breeze moved the tops of the pines with a noise like a gentle surf.

"She left me," he said slowly. "She left me a month ago. Friday, the 12th of June. A day I'll remember."

I stiffened, but not too much to pour more whiskey into his empty glass. Friday the 12th of June was the day Mrs. Crystal Kingsley was supposed to have come into town for a party.

"But you don't want to hear about that," he said. And in his faded blue eyes was the deep yearning to talk about it, as plain as anything could possibly be.

"It's none of my business," I said. "But if it would make you feel any better —"

He nodded sharply. "Two guys will meet on a park bench," he said, "and start talking about God. Did you ever notice that? Guys that wouldn't talk about God to their best friend."

"I know that," I said.

He drank and looked across the lake. "She was one swell kid," he said softly. "A little sharp in the tongue sometimes, but one swell kid. It was love at first sight with me and Muriel. I met her in a joint in Riverside, a year and three months ago. Not the kind of joint where a guy would expect to meet a girl like Muriel, but that's how it happened. We got married. I loved her. I knew I was well off. And I was too much of a skunk to play ball with her."

I moved a little to show him I was still there, but I didn't say anything for fear of breaking the spell. I sat with my drink untouched in my hand. I like to drink, but not when people are using me for a diary.

He went on sadly: "But you know how it is with marriage — any marriage. After a while a guy like me, a common no-good guy like me, he wants to feel a leg. Some other leg. Maybe it's lousy, but that's the way it is."

He looked at me and I said I had heard the idea expressed.

He tossed his second drink off. I passed him the bottle. A bluejay went up a pine tree hopping from branch to branch without moving his wings or even pausing to balance.

"Yeah," Bill Chess said. "All these hillbillies are half crazy and I'm getting that way too. Here I am sitting pretty, no rent to pay, a good pension check every month, half my bonus money in war bonds, I'm married to as neat a little blonde as ever you clapped an eye on and all the time I'm nuts and I don't know it. I go for *that*." He pointed hard at the redwood

34

cabin across the lake. It was turning the color of oxblood in the late afternoon light. "Right in the front yard," he said, "right under the windows, and a showy little tart that means no more to me than a blade of grass. Jesus, what a sap a guy can be."

He drank his third drink and steadied the bottle on a rock. He fished a cigarette out of his shirt, fired a match on his thumbnail and puffed rapidly. I breathed with my mouth open, as silent as a burglar behind a curtain.

"Hell," he said at last, "you'd think if I had to jump off the dock, I'd go a little ways from home and pick me a change in types at least. But little roundheels over there ain't even that. She's a blonde like Muriel, same size and weight, same type, almost the same color eyes. But, brother, how different from then on in. Pretty, sure, but no prettier to anybody and not half so pretty to me. Well, I'm over there burning trash that morning and minding my own business, as much as I ever mind it. And she comes to the back door of the cabin in peekaboo pajamas so thin you can see the pink of her nipples against the cloth. And she says in her lazy, no-good voice: 'Have a drink, Bill. Don't work so hard on such a beautiful morning.' And me, I like a drink too well and I go to the kitchen door and take it. And then I take another and then I take another and then I'm in the house. And the closer I get to her the more bedroom her eyes are."

He paused and swept me with a hard level look.

"You asked me if the beds over there were comfortable and I got sore. You didn't mean a thing. I was just too full of remembering. Yeah – the bed I was in was comfortable."

He stopped talking and I let his words hang in the air. They fell slowly and after them was silence. He leaned to pick the bottle off the rock and stare at it. He seemed to fight with it in his mind. The whiskey won the fight, as it always does. He took a long savage drink out of the bottle and then screwed the cap on tightly, as if that meant something. He picked up a stone and flicked it into the water.

"I came back across the dam," he said slowly, in a voice already thick with alcohol. "I'm as smooth as a new piston head. I'm getting away with something. Us boys can be so wrong about those little things, can't we? I'm not getting away with anything at all. Not anything at all. I listen to Muriel telling me and she don't even raise her voice. But she tells me things about myself I didn't even imagine. Oh, yeah, I'm getting away with it lovely."

"So she left you," I said, when he fell silent.

"That night. I wasn't even here. I felt too mean to stay even half sober. I hopped into my Ford and went over to the north side of the lake and holed up with a couple of no-goods like myself and got good and stinking. Not that it did me any good. Along about 4 A.M. I got back home and Muriel is gone, packed up and gone, nothing left but a note on the bureau and some cold cream on the pillow."

He pulled a dog-eared piece of paper out of a shabby old wallet and passed it over. It was written in pencil on blue-lined paper from a note book. It read:

"I'm sorry, Bill, but I'd rather be dead than live with you any longer. Muriel."

I handed it back. "What about over there?" I asked, pointing across the lake with a glance.

Bill Chess picked up a flat stone and tried to skip it across the water, but it refused to skip.

"Nothing over there," he said. "She packed up and went down the same night. I didn't see her again. I don't want to see her again. I haven't heard a word from Muriel in the whole month, not a single word. I don't have any idea at all where she's at. With some other guy, maybe. I hope he treats her better than I did."

He stood up and took keys out of his pocket and shook them. "So if you want to go across and look at Kingsley's cabin, there isn't a thing to stop you. And thanks for listening to the soap opera. And thanks for the liquor. Here." He picked the bottle up and handed me what was left of the pint.

36

6

WE WENT DOWN the slope to the bank of the lake and the narrow top of the dam. Bill Chess swung his stiff leg in front of me, holding on to the rope handrail set in iron stanchions. At one point water washed over the concrete in a lazy swirl.

"I'll let some out through the wheel in the morning," he said over his shoulder. "That's all the darn thing is good for. Some movie outfit put it up three years ago. They made a picture up here. That little pier down at the other end is some more of their work. Most of what they built is torn down and hauled away, but Kingsley had them leave the pier and the millwheel. Kind of gives the place a touch of color."

I followed him up a flight of heavy wooden steps to the porch of the Kingsley cabin. He unlocked the door and we went into hushed warmth. The closed-up room was almost hot. The light filtering through the slatted blinds made narrow bars across the floor. The living room was long and cheerful and had Indian rugs, padded mountain furniture with metal-strapped joints, chintz curtains, a plain hardwood floor, plenty of lamps and a little built-in bar with round stools in one corner. The room was neat and clean and had no look of having been left at short notice.

We went into the bedrooms. Two of them had twin beds and one a large double bed with a cream-colored spread having a design in plum-colored wool stitched over it. This was the master bedroom, Bill Chess said. On a dresser of varnished wood there were toilet articles and accessories in jade green enamel and stainless steel, and an assortment of cosmetic oddments. A couple of cold cream jars had the wavy gold brand of the Gillerlain Company on them. One whole side of the room consisted of closets with sliding doors. I slid one open and peeked inside. It seemed to be full of women's clothes of the sort they wear at resorts. Bill Chess watched me sourly while I pawed them over. I slid the door shut and pulled open a deep shoe drawer underneath. It contained at least half a dozen pairs of new-looking shoes. I heaved the drawer shut and straightened up.

Bill Chess was planted squarely in front of me, with his chin pushed out and his hard hands in knots on his hips.

"So what did you want to look at the lady's clothes for?" he asked in an angry voice.

"Reasons," I said. "For instance, Mrs. Kingsley didn't go home when she left here. Her husband hasn't seen her since. He doesn't know where she is."

He dropped his fists, and twisted them slowly at his sides. "Dick it is," he snarled. "The first guess is always right. I had myself about talked out of it. Boy, did I open up to you. Nellie with her hair in her lap. Boy, am I a smart little egg!"

"I can respect a confidence as well as the next fellow," I said, and walked around him into the kitchen.

There was a big green and white combination range, a sink of lacquered yellow pine, an automatic water heater in the service porch and opening off the other side of the kitchen a cheerful breakfast room with many windows and an expensive plastic breakfast set. The shelves were gay with colored dishes and glasses and a set of pewter serving dishes.

Everything was in apple-pie order. There were no dirty cups or plates on the drain board, no smeared glasses or empty liquor bottles hanging around. There were no ants and no flies. Whatever loose living Mrs. Derace Kingsley indulged in she managed without leaving the usual Greenwich Village slop behind her.

I went back to the living room and out on the front porch again and waited for Bill Chess to lock up. When he had done that and turned to me with his scowl well in place I said:

"I didn't ask you to take your heart out and squeeze it for me, but I didn't try to stop you either. Kingsley doesn't have to know his wife made a pass at you, unless there's a lot more behind all this than I can see now."

"The hell with you," he said, and the scowl stayed right where it was.

"All right, the hell with me. Would there be any chance your wife and Kingsley's wife went away together?"

"I don't get it," he said.

"After you went to drown your troubles they could have had a fight and made up and cried down each other's necks. Then Mrs. Kingsley might have taken your wife down the hill. She had to have something to ride in, didn't she?"

It sounded silly, but he took it seriously enough.

"Nope. Muriel didn't cry down anybody's neck. They left the weeps out of Muriel. And if she did want to cry on a shoulder, she wouldn't have picked little roundheels. And as for transportation she has a Ford of her own. She couldn't drive mine easily on account of the way the controls are switched over for my stiff leg."

"It was just a passing thought," I said.

"If any more like it pass you, let them go right on," he said.

"For a guy that takes his long wavy hair down in front of complete strangers, you're pretty damn touchy," I said.

He took a step towards me. "Want to make something of it?"

"Look, pal," I said. "I'm working hard to think you are a fundamentally good egg. Help me out a little, can't you?"

He breathed hard for a moment and then dropped his hands and spread them helplessly.

"Boy, can I brighten up anybody's afternoon," he sighed. "Want to walk back around the lake?"

"Sure, if your leg will stand it."

"Stood it plenty of times before."

We started off side by side, as friendly as puppies again. It would probably last all of fifty yards. The roadway, barely wide enough to pass a car, hung above the level of the lake and dodged between high rocks. About half way to the far end another smaller cabin was built on a rock foundation. The third was well beyond the end of the lake, on a patch of almost level ground. Both were closed up and had that long-empty look.

Bill Chess said after a minute or two: "That straight goods little roundheels lammed off?"

"So it seems."

"You a real dick or just a shamus?"

"Just a shamus."

"She go with some other guy?"

"I should think it likely."

"Sure she did. It's a cinch. Kingsley ought to be able to guess that. She had plenty of friends."

"Up here?"

He didn't answer me.

"Was one of them named Lavery?"

"I wouldn't know," he said.

"There's no secret about this one," I said. "She sent a wire from El Paso saying she and Lavery were going to Mexico." I dug the wire out of my pocket and held it out. He fumbled his glasses loose from his shirt and stopped to read it. He handed the paper back and put his glasses away again and stared out over the blue water.

"That's a little confidence for you to hold against some of what you gave me," I said.

"Lavery was up here once," he said slowly.

"He admits he saw her a couple of months ago, probably up here. He claims he hasn't seen her since. We don't know whether to believe him. There's no reason why we should and no reason why we shouldn't."

"She isn't with him now, then?"

"He says not."

"I wouldn't think she would fuss with little details like getting married," he said soberly. "A Florida honeymoon would be more in her line."

"But you can't give me any positive information? You didn't see her go or hear anything that sounded authentic?"

"Nope," he said. "And if I did, I doubt if I would tell. I'm dirty, but not that kind of dirty."

"Well, thanks for trying," I said.

"I don't owe you any favors," he said. "The hell with you and every other God damn snooper."

"Here we go again," I said.

We had come to the end of the lake now. I left him standing there and walked out on a little pier. I leaned on the wooden railing at the end of it and saw that what had looked like a band pavilion was nothing but two pieces of propped-up wall meeting at a flat angle towards the dam. About two feet deep of overhanging roof was stuck on the wall, like a coping. Bill Chess came up behind me and leaned on the railing at my side.

"Not that I don't thank you for the liquor," he said.

"Yeah. Any fish in the lake?"

"Some smart old bastards of trout. No fresh stock. I don't go for fish much myself. I don't bother with them. Sorry I got tough again."

I grinned and leaned on the railing and stared down into the deep still water. It was green when you looked down into it. There was a swirl of movement down there and a swift greenish form moved in the water.

"There's Granpa," Bill Chess said. "Look at the size of that old bastard. He ought to be ashamed of himself getting so fat."

Down below the water there was what looked like an underwater flooring. I couldn't see the sense of that. I asked him.

"Used to be a boat landing before the dam was raised. That lifted the water level so far the old landing was six feet under."

A flat-bottomed boat dangled on a frayed rope tied to a post of the pier. It lay in the water almost without motion, but not quite. The air was peaceful and calm and sunny and held a quiet you don't get in cities. I could have stayed there for hours doing nothing but forgetting all about Derace Kingsley and his wife and her boy friends.

There was a hard movement at my side and Bill Chess said, "Look there!" in a voice that growled like mountain thunder.

His hard fingers dug into the flesh of my arm until I started to get mad. He was bending far out over the railing, staring down like a loon, his face as white as the weather tan would let it get. I looked down with him into the water at the edge of the submerged staging.

Languidly at the edge of this green and sunken shelf of wood something waved out from the darkness, hesitated, waved back again out of sight under the flooring.

The something had looked far too much like a human arm.

Bill Chess straightened his body rigidly. He turned without a sound and clumped back along the pier. He bent to a loose pile of stones and heaved. His panting breath reached me. He got a big one free and lifted it breast high and started back out on the pier with it. It must have weighed a hundred pounds. His neck muscles stood out like ropes under canvas under his taut brown skin. His teeth were clamped tight and his breath hissed between them.

He reached the end of the pier and steadied himself and lifted the rock high. He held it a moment poised, his eyes staring down now, measuring. His mouth made a vague distressful sound and his body lurched forward hard against the quivering rail and the heavy stone smashed down into the water.

The splash it made went over both of us. The rock fell straight and true and struck on the edge of the submerged planking, almost exactly where we had seen the thing wave in and out.

For a moment the water was a confused boiling, then the ripples widened off into the distance, coming smaller and smaller with a trace of froth at the middle, and there was a dim sound as of wood breaking under water, a sound that seemed to come to us a long time after it should have been audible. An ancient rotted plank popped suddenly through the surface, struck out a full foot of its jagged end, and fell back with a flat slap and floated off.

The depths cleared again. Something moved in them that was not a board. It rose slowly, with an infinitely careless languor, a long dark twisted something that rolled lazily in the water as it rose. It broke surface casually, lightly, without haste. I saw wool, sodden and black, a leather jerkin blacker than ink, a pair of slacks. I saw shoes and something that bulged nastily between the shoes and the cuffs of the slacks. I saw a wave of dark blond hair straighten out in the water and hold still for a brief instant as if with a calculated effect, and then swirl into a tangle again.

The thing rolled over once more and an arm flapped up barely above the skin of the water and the arm ended in a bloated hand that was the hand of a freak. Then the face came. A swollen pulpy gray white mass without features, without eyes, without mouth. A blotch of gray dough, a nightmare with human hair on it.

A heavy necklace of green stone showed on what had been a neck, half imbedded, large rough green stones with something that glittered joining them together.

Bill Chess held the handrail and his knuckles were polished bones.

"Muriel!" his voice said croakingly. "Sweet Christ, it's Muriel!"

His voice seemed to come to me from a long way off, over a hill, through a thick silent growth of trees.

7

BEHIND THE WINDOW of the board shack one end of a counter was piled with dusty folders. The glass upper half of the door was lettered in flaked black paint. *Chief of Police. Fire*

Chief. Town Constable. Chamber of Commerce. In the lower corners a USO card and a Red Cross emblem were fastened to the glass.

I went in. There was a pot-bellied stove in the corner and a rolltop desk in the other corner behind the counter. There was a large blue print map of the district on the wall and beside that a board with four hooks on it, one of which supported a frayed and much mended mackinaw. On the counter beside the dusty folders lay the usual sprung pen, exhausted blotter and smeared bottle of gummy ink. The end wall beside the desk was covered with telephone numbers written in hard-bitten figures that would last as long as the wood and looked as if they had been written by a child.

A man sat at the desk in a wooden armchair whose legs were anchored to flat boards, fore and aft, like skis. A spittoon big enough to coil a hose in was leaning against the man's right leg. He had a sweat-stained Stetson on the back of his head and his large hairless hands were clasped comfortably over his stomach, above the waistband of a pair of khaki pants that had been scrubbed thin years ago. His shirt matched the pants except that it was even more faded. It was buttoned tight to the man's thick neck and undecorated by a tie. His hair was mousy brown except at the temples, where it was the color of old snow. He sat more on his left hip than on his right, because there was a hip holster down inside his right hip pocket, and a half foot of .45 gun reared up and bored into his solid back. The star on his left breast had a bent point.

He had large ears and friendly eyes and his jaws munched slowly and he looked as dangerous as a squirrel and much less nervous. I liked everything about him. I leaned on the counter and looked at him and he looked at me and nodded and loosed half a pint of tobacco juice down his right leg into the spittoon. It made a nasty sound of something falling into water.

I lit a cigarette and looked around for an ashtray.

"Try the floor, son," the large friendly man said.

"Are you Sheriff Patton?"

"Constable and deputy sheriff. What law we got to have around here I'm it. Come election anyways. There's a couple of good boys running against me this time and I might get whupped. Job pays eighty a month, cabin, firewood and electricity. That ain't hay in these little old mountains."

"Nobody's going to whip you," I said. "You're going to get a lot of publicity."

"That so?" he asked indifferently and ruined the spittoon again.

"That is, if your jurisdiction extends over to Little Fawn Lake."

"Kingsley's place. Sure. Something bothering you over there, son?"

"There's a dead woman in the lake."

That shook him to the core. He unclasped his hands and scratched one ear. He got to his feet by grasping the arms of his chair and deftly kicking it back from under him. Standing up he was a big man and hard. The fat was just cheerfulness.

"Anybody I know?" he enquired uneasily.

"Muriel Chess. I guess you know her. Bill Chess's wife."

"Yep, I know Bill Chess." His voice hardened a little.

"Looks like suicide. She left a note which sounded as if she was just going away. But it could be a suicide note just as well. She's not nice to look at. Been in the water a long time, about a month, judging by the circumstances."

He scratched his other ear. "What circumstances would that be?" His eyes were searching my face now, slowly and calmly, but searching. He didn't seem in any hurry to blow his whistle.

"They had a fight a month ago. Bill went over to the north shore of the lake and was gone some hours. When he got home she was gone. He never saw her again."

"I see. Who are you, son?"

45

"My name is Marlowe. I'm up from L.A. to look at the property. I had a note from Kingsley to Bill Chess. He took me around the lake and we went out on that little pier the movie people built. We were leaning on the rail and looking down into the water and something that looked like an arm waved out under the submerged flooring, the old boat landing. Bill dropped a heavy rock in and the body popped up."

Patton looked at me without moving a muscle.

"Look, sheriff, hadn't we better run over there? The man's half crazy with shock and he's there all alone."

"How much liquor has he got?"

"Very little when I left. I had a pint but we drank most of it talking."

He moved over to the rolltop desk and unlocked a drawer. He brought up three or four bottles and held them against the light.

"This baby's near full," he said, patting one of them. "Mount Vernon. That ought to hold him. County don't allow me no money for emergency liquor, so I just have to seize a little here and there. Don't use it myself. Never could understand folks letting theirselves get gummed up with it."

He put the bottle on his left hip and locked the desk up and lifted the flap in the counter. He fixed a card against the inside of the glass door panel. I looked at the card as we went out. It read: *Back in Twenty Minutes – Maybe.*

"I'll run down and get Doc Hollis," he said. "Be right back and pick you up. That your car?"

"Yes."

"You can follow along then, as I come back by."

He got into a car which had a siren on it, two red spotlights, two foglights, a red and white fire plate, a new air raid horn on top, three axes, two heavy coils of rope and a fire extinguisher in the back seat, extra gas and oil and water cans in a frame on the running board, an extra spare tire roped to the one on the rack, the stuffing coming out of the upholstery in dingy wads, and half an inch of dust over what was left of the paint.

Behind the right-hand lower corner of the windshield there was a white card printed in block capitals. It read:

"VOTERS, ATTENTION! KEEP JIM PATTON CONSTABLE. HE IS TOO OLD TO GO TO WORK."

He turned the car and went off down the street in a swirl of white dust.

8

HE STOPPED IN front of a white frame building across the road from the stage depot. He went into the white building and presently came out with a man who got into the back seat with the axes and the rope. The official car came back up the street and I fell in behind it. We sifted along the main stem through the slacks and shorts and French sailor jerseys and knotted bandannas and knobby knees and scarlet lips. Beyond the village we went up a dusty hill and stopped at a cabin. Patton touched the siren gently and a man in faded blue overalls opened the cabin door.

"Get in, Andy. Business."

The man in blue overalls nodded morosely and ducked back into the cabin. He came back out wearing an oyster-gray lion hunter's hat and got in under the wheel of Patton's car while Patton slid over. He was about thirty, dark, lithe, and had the slightly dirty and slightly underfed look of the native.

We drove out to Little Fawn Lake with me eating enough dust to make a batch of mud pies. At the five-barred gate Patton got out and let us through and we went on down to the lake. Patton got out again and went to the edge of the water and looked along towards the little pier. Bill Chess was sitting naked on the floor of the pier, with his head in his hands. There was something stretched out on the wet planks beside him.

"We can ride a ways more," Patton said.

47

The two cars went on to the end of the lake and all four of us trooped down to the pier behind Bill Chess's back. The doctor stopped to cough rackingly into a handkerchief and then look thoughtfully at the handkerchief. He was an angular bug-eyed man with a sad sick face.

The thing that had been a woman lay face down on the boards with a rope under the arms. Bill Chess's clothes lay to one side. His stiff leg, flat and scarred at the knee, was stretched out in front of him, the other leg bent up and his forehead resting against it. He didn't move or look up as we came down behind him.

Patton took the pint bottle of Mount Vernon off his hip and unscrewed the top and handed it.

"Drink hearty, Bill."

There was a horrible, sickening smell in the air. Bill Chess didn't seem to notice it, nor Patton nor the doctor. The man called Andy got a dusty brown blanket out of the car and threw it over the body. Then without a word he went and vomited under a pine tree.

Bill Chess drank a long drink and sat holding the bottle against his bare bent knee. He began to talk in a stiff wooden voice, not looking at anybody, not talking to anybody in particular. He told about the quarrel and what happened after it, but not why it had happened. He didn't mention Mrs. Kingsley even in the most casual way. He said that after I left him he had got a rope and stripped and gone down into the water and got the thing out. He had dragged it ashore and then got it up on his back and carried it out on the pier. He didn't know why. He had gone back into the water again then. He didn't have to tell us why.

Patton put a cut of tobacco into his mouth and chewed on it silently, his calm eyes full of nothing. Then he shut his teeth tight and leaned down to pull the blanket off the body. He turned the body over carefully, as if it might come to pieces. The late afternoon sun winked on the necklace of large green stones that were partly imbedded in the swollen neck. They were roughly carved and lusterless, like soapstone or false jade. A gilt chain with an eagle clasp set with small brilliants joined the ends. Patton straightened his broad back and blew his nose on a tan handkerchief.

"What you say, Doc?"

"About what?" the bug-eyed man snarled.

"Cause and time of death."

"Don't be a damn fool, Jim Patton."

"Can't tell nothing, huh?"

"By looking at that? Good God!"

Patton sighed. "Looks drowned all right," he admitted. "But you can't always tell. There's been cases where a victim would be knifed or poisoned or something, and they would soak him in the water to make things look different."

"You get many like that up here?" the doctor enquired nastily.

"Only honest to God murder I ever had up here," Patton said, watching Bill Chess out of the corner of his eye, "was old Dad Meacham over on the north shore. He had a shack in Sheedy Canyon, did a little panning in summer on an old placer claim he had back in the valley near Belltop. Folks didn't see him around for a while in late fall, then come a heavy snow and his roof caved in to one side. So we was over there trying to prop her up a bit, figuring Dad had gone down the hill for the winter without telling anybody, the way them old prospectors do things. Well by gum, old Dad never went down the hill at all. There he was in bed with most of a kindling axe in the back of his head. We never did find out who done it. Somebody figured he had a little bag of gold hid away from the summer's panning."

He looked thoughtfully at Andy. The man in the lion hunter's hat was feeling a tooth in his mouth. He said:

"'Course we know who done it. Guy Pope done it. Only Guy was dead nine days of pneumonia before we found Dad Meacham."

"Eleven days," Patton said.

"Nine," the man in the lion hunter's hat said.

"Was all of six years ago, Andy. Have it your own way, son. How you figure Guy Pope done it?"

"We found about three ounces of small nuggets in Guy's cabin along with some dust. Never was anything bigger'n sand on Guy's claim. Dad had nuggets all of a pennyweight, plenty of times."

"Well, that's the way it goes," Patton said, and smiled at me in a vague manner. "Fellow always forgets something, don't he? No matter how careful he is."

"Cop stuff," Bill Chess said disgustedly and put his pants on and sat down again to put on his shoes and shirt. When he had them on he stood up and reached down for the bottle and took a good drink and laid the bottle carefully on the planks. He thrust his hairy wrists out towards Patton.

"That's the way you guys feel about it, put the cuffs on and get it over," he said in a savage voice.

Patton ignored him and went over to the railing and looked down. "Funny place for a body to be," he said. "No current here to mention, but what there is would be towards the dam."

Bill Chess lowered his wrists and said quietly: "She did it herself, you darn fool. Muriel was a fine swimmer. She dived down in and swum under the boards there and just breathed water in. Had to. No other way."

"I wouldn't quite say that, Bill," Patton answered him mildly. His eyes were as blank as new plates.

Andy shook his head. Patton looked at him with a sly grin. "Crabbin' again, Andy?"

"Was nine days, I tell you. I just counted back," the man in the lion hunter's hat said morosely.

The doctor threw his arms up and walked away, with one hand to his head. He coughed into his handkerchief again and again looked into the handkerchief with passionate attention.

Patton winked at me and spat over the railing. "Let's get on to this one, Andy."

"You ever try to drag a body six feet under water?"

"Nope, can't say I ever did, Andy. Any reason it couldn't be done with a rope?"

Andy shrugged. "If a rope was used, it will show on the corpse. If you got to give yourself away like that, why bother to cover up at all?"

"Question of time," Patton said. "Fellow has his arrangements to make."

Bill Chess snarled at them and reached down for the whiskey. Looking at their solemn mountain faces I couldn't tell what they were really thinking.

Patton said absently: "Something was said about a note."

Bill Chess rummaged in his wallet and drew the folded piece of ruled paper loose. Patton took it and read it slowly.

"Don't seem to have any date," he observed.

Bill Chess shook his head somberly. "No. She left a month ago, June 12th."

"Left you once before, didn't she?"

"Yeah." Bill Chess stared at him fixedly. "I got drunk and stayed with a chippy. Just before the first snow last December. She was gone a week and came back all prettied up. Said she just had to get away for a while and had been staying with a girl she used to work with in L.A."

"What was the name of this party?" Patton asked.

"Never told me and I never asked her. What Muriel did was all silk with me."

"Sure. Note left that time, Bill?" Patton asked smoothly.

"No."

"This note here looks middling old," Patton said, holding it up.

"I carried it a month," Bill Chess growled. "Who told you she left me before?"

"I forget," Patton said. "You know how it is in a place like this. Not much folks don't notice. Except maybe in summertime where there's a lot of strangers about."

Nobody said anything for a while and then Patton said absently: "June 12th you say she left? Or you thought she left? Did you say the folks across the lake were up here then?"

Bill Chess looked at me and his face darkened again. "Ask this snoopy guy – if he didn't already spill his guts to you."

Patton didn't look at me at all. He looked at the line of mountains far beyond the lake. He said gently: "Mr. Marlowe here didn't tell me anything at all, Bill, except how the body come up out of the water and who it was. And that Muriel went away, as you thought, and left a note you showed him. I don't guess there's anything wrong in that, is there?"

There was another silence and Bill Chess stared down at the blanket-covered corpse a few feet away from him. He clenched his hands and a thick tear ran down his cheek.

"Mrs. Kingsley was here," he said. "She went down the hill that same day. Nobody was in the other cabins. Perrys and Farquars ain't been up at all this year."

Patton nodded and was silent. A kind of charged emptiness hung in the air, as if something that had not been said was plain to all of them and didn't need saying.

Then Bill Chess said wildly: "Take me in, you sons of bitches! Sure I did it! I drowned her. She was my girl and I loved her. I'm a heel, always was a heel, always will be a heel, but just the same I loved her. Maybe you guys wouldn't understand that. Just don't bother to try. Take me in, damn you!"

Nobody said anything at all.

Bill Chess looked down at his hard brown fist. He swung it up viciously and hit himself in the face with all his strength.

"You rotten son of a bitch," he breathed in a harsh whisper.

His nose began to bleed slowly. He stood and the blood ran down his lip, down the side of his mouth, to the point of his chin. A drop fell sluggishly to his shirt.

Patton said quietly: "Got to take you down the hill for questioning, Bill. You know that. We ain't accusing you of anything, but the folks down there have got to talk to you."

Bill Chess said heavily: "Can I change my clothes?"

"Sure. You go with him, Andy. And see what you can find to kind of wrap up what we got here."

They went off along the path at the edge of the lake. The doctor cleared his throat and looked out over the water and sighed.

"You'll want to send the corpse down in my ambulance, Jim, won't you?"

Patton shook his head. "Nope. This is a poor county, Doc. I figure the lady can ride cheaper than what you get for that ambulance."

The doctor walked away from him angrily, saying over his shoulder: "Let me know if you want me to pay for the funeral."

"That ain't no way to talk," Patton sighed.

9

THE INDIAN HEAD Hotel was a brown building on a corner across from the new dance hall. I parked in front of it and used its rest room to wash my face and hands and comb the pine needles out of my hair, before I went into the dining-drinking parlor that adjoined the lobby. The whole place was full to overflowing with males in leisure jackets and liquor breaths and females in high-pitched laughs, oxblood fingernails and dirty knuckles. The manager of the joint, a low-budget tough guy in shirt-sleeves and a mangled cigar, was prowling the room with watchful eyes. At the cash desk a pale-haired man was fighting to get the war news on a small radio that was as full of static as the mashed potatoes were full of water. In the deep back corner of the room, a hillbilly orchestra of five pieces, dressed in ill-fitting white jackets and purple shirts, was trying to make itself heard above the brawl at the bar and smiling glassily into the fog of cigarette smoke and the blur of alcoholic voices. At Puma Point, summer, that lovely season, was in full swing.

I gobbled what they called the regular dinner, drank a brandy to sit on its chest and hold it down, and went out on to the main street. It was still broad daylight but some of the neon signs had been turned on, and the evening reeled with the cheerful din of auto horns, children screaming, bowls rattling, skeeballs clunking, .22's snapping merrily in shooting galleries, juke boxes playing like crazy, and behind all this out on the lake the hard barking roar of the speedboats going nowhere at all and acting as though they were racing with death.

In my Chrysler a thin, serious-looking, brown-haired girl in dark slacks was sitting smoking a cigarette and talking to a dude ranch cowboy who sat on my running board. I walked around the car and got into it. The cowboy strolled away hitching his jeans up. The girl didn't move.

"I'm Birdie Keppel," she said cheerfully, "I'm the beautician here daytimes and evenings I work on the Puma Point *Banner*. Excuse me sitting in your car."

"That's all right," I said. "You want to just sit or you want me to drive you somewhere?"

"You can drive down the road a piece where it's quieter, Mr. Marlowe. If you're obliging enough to talk to me."

"Pretty good grapevine you've got up here," I said and started the car.

I drove down past the post office to a corner where a blue and white arrow marked *Telephone* pointed down a narrow road towards the lake. I turned down that, drove past the telephone office, which was a log cabin with a tiny railed lawn in front of it, passed another small cabin and pulled up in front of a huge oak tree that flung its branches all the way across the road and a good fifty feet beyond it.

"This do, Miss Keppel?"

"Mrs. But just call me Birdie. Everybody does. This is fine. Pleased to meet you, Mr. Marlowe. I see you come from Hollywood, that sinful city."

She put a firm brown hand out and I shook it. Clamping bobbie pins into fat blondes had given her a grip like a pair of iceman's tongs.

"I was talking to Doc Hollis," she said, "about poor Muriel Chess. I thought you could give me some details. I understand you found the body."

"Bill Chess found it really. I was just with him. You talk to Jim Patton?"

"Not yet. He went down the hill. Anyway I don't think Jim would tell me much."

"He's up for re-election," I said. "And you're a newspaper woman."

"Jim's no politician, Mr. Marlowe, and I could hardly call myself a newspaper woman. This little paper we get out up here is a pretty amateurish proposition."

"Well, what do you want to know?" I offered her a cigarette and lit it for her.

"You might just tell me the story."

"I came up here with a letter from Derace Kingsley to look at his property. Bill Chess showed me around, got talking to me, told me his wife had moved out on him and showed me the note she left. I had a bottle along and he punished it. He was feeling pretty blue. The liquor loosened him up, but he was lonely and aching to talk anyway. That's how it happened. I didn't know him. Coming back around the end of the lake we went out on the pier and Bill spotted an arm waving out from under the planking down in the water. It turned out to belong to what was left of Muriel Chess. I guess that's all."

"I understand from Doc Hollis she had been in the water a long time. Pretty badly decomposed and all that."

"Yes. Probably the whole month he thought she had been gone. There's no reason to think otherwise. The note's a suicide note."

"Any doubt about that, Mr. Marlowe?"

I looked at her sideways. Thoughtful dark eyes looked out at me under fluffed-out brown hair. The dusk had begun to fall now, very slowly. It was no more than a slight change in the quality of the light.

"I guess the police always have doubts in these cases," I said.

"How about you?"

"My opinion doesn't go for anything."

"But for what it's worth?"

"I only met Bill Chess this afternoon," I said. "He struck me as a quick-tempered lad and from his own account he's no saint. But he seems to have been in love with his wife. And I can't see him hanging around here for a month knowing she was rotting down in the water under that pier. Coming out of his cabin in the sunlight and looking along that soft blue water and seeing in his mind what was under it and what was happening to it. And knowing he put it there."

"No more can I," Birdie Keppel said softly. "No more could anybody. And yet we know in our minds that such things have happened and will happen again. Are you in the real estate business, Mr. Marlowe?"

"No."

"What line of business are you in, if I may ask?"

"I'd rather not say."

"That's almost as good as saying," she said. "Besides Doc Hollis heard you tell Jim Patton your full name. And we have an L.A. city directory in our office. I haven't mentioned it to anyone."

"That's nice of you," I said.

"And what's more, I won't," she said. "If you don't want me to."

"What does it cost me?"

"Nothing," she said. "Nothing at all. I don't claim to be a very good newspaper woman. And we wouldn't print anything that would embarrass Jim Patton. Jim's the salt of the earth. But it does open up, doesn't it?"

"Don't draw any wrong conclusions," I said. "I had no interest in Bill Chess whatever."

"No interest in Muriel Chess?"

"Why would I have any interest in Muriel Chess?"

She snuffed her cigarette out carefully into the ashtray under the dashboard. "Have it your own way," she said. "But here's a little item you might like to think about, if you don't know it already. There was a Los Angeles copper named De Soto up here about six weeks back, a big roughneck with damn poor manners. We didn't like him and we didn't open up to him much. I mean the three of us in the *Banner* office didn't. He had a photograph with him and he was looking for a woman called Mildred Haviland, he said. On police business. It was an ordinary photograph, an enlarged snapshot, not a police photo. He said he had information the woman was staying up here. The photo looked a good deal like Muriel Chess. The hair seemed to be reddish and in a very different style than she has worn it here, and the eyebrows were all plucked to narrow arches, and that changes a woman a good deal. But it did look a good deal like Bill Chess's wife."

I drummed on the door of the car and after a moment I said, "What did you tell him?"

"We didn't tell him anything. First off, we couldn't be sure. Second, we didn't like his manner. Third, even if we had been sure and I had liked his manner, we likely would not have sicked him on to her. Why would we? Everybody's done something to be sorry for. Take me. I was married once – to a professor of classical languages at Redlands University." She laughed lightly.

"You might have got yourself a story," I said.

"Sure. But up here we're just people."

"Did this man De Soto see Jim Patton?"

"Sure, he must have. Jim didn't mention it."

"Did he show you his badge?"

She thought and then shook her head. "I don't recall that he did. We just took him for granted, from what he said. He certainly acted like a tough city cop."

"To me that's a little against his being one. Did anybody tell Muriel about this guy?"

She hesitated, looking quietly out through the windshield for a long moment before she turned her head and nodded.

"I did. Wasn't any of my damn business, was it?"

"What did she say?"

"She didn't say anything. She gave a funny little embarrassed laugh, as if I had been making a bad joke. Then she walked away. But I did get the impression that there was a queer look in her eyes, just for an instant. You still not interested in Muriel Chess, Mr. Marlowe?"

"Why should I be? I never heard of her until I came up here this afternoon. Honest. And I never heard of anybody named Mildred Haviland either. Drive you back to town?"

"Oh no, thanks. I'll walk. It's only a few steps. Much obliged to you. I kind of hope Bill doesn't get into a jam. Especially a nasty jam like this."

She got out of the car and hung on one foot, then tossed her head and laughed. "They say I'm a pretty good beauty operator," she said. "I hope I am. As an interviewer I'm terrible. Goodnight."

I said goodnight and she walked off into the evening. I sat there watching her until she reached the main street and turned out of sight. Then I got out of the Chrysler and went over towards the telephone company's little rustic building.

10

A TAME DOE deer with a leather dog collar on wandered across the road in front of me. I patted her rough hairy neck and went into the telephone office. A small girl in slacks sat at a small desk working on the books. She got me the rate to Beverly Hills and the change for the coin box. The booth was outside, against the front wall of the building.

"I hope you like it up here," she said. "It's very quiet, very restful."

I shut myself into the booth. For ninety cents I could talk to Derace Kingsley for five minutes. He was at home and the call came through quickly but the connection was full of mountain static.

"Find anything up there?" he asked me in a three-highball voice. He sounded tough and confident again.

"I've found too much," I said. "And not at all what we want. Are you alone?"

"What does that matter?"

"It doesn't matter to me. But I know what I'm going to say. You don't."

"Well, get on with it, whatever it is," he said.

"I had a long talk with Bill Chess. He was lonely. His wife had left him – a month ago. They had a fight and he went out and got drunk and when he came back she was gone. She left a note saying she would rather be dead than live with him any more."

"I guess Bill drinks too much," Kingsley's voice said from very far off.

"When he got back, both the women had gone. He has no idea where Mrs. Kingsley went. Lavery was up here in May, but not since. Lavery admitted that much himself. Lavery could, of course, have come up again while Bill was out getting drunk, but there wouldn't be a lot of point to that and there would be two cars to drive down the hill. And I thought that possibly Mrs. K. and Muriel Chess might have gone away together, only Muriel also had a car of her own. But that idea, little as it was worth, has been thrown out by another development. Muriel Chess didn't go away at all. She went down into your private lake. She came back up today. I was there."

"Good God!" Kingsley sounded properly horrified. "You mean she drowned herself?"

"Perhaps. The note she left could be a suicide note. It would read as well that way as the other. The body was stuck down under that old submerged landing below the pier. Bill was the one who spotted an arm moving down there while we were standing on the pier looking down into the water. He got her out. They've arrested him. The poor guy's pretty badly broken up."

"Good God!" Kingsley said again. "I should think he would be. Does it look as if he —" He paused as the operator came in on the line and demanded another forty-five cents. I put in two quarters and the line cleared.

"Look as if he what?"

Suddenly very clear, Kingsley's voice said: "Look as if he murdered her?"

I said: "Very much. Jim Patton, the constable up here, doesn't like the note not being dated. It seems she left him once before over some woman. Patton sort of suspects Bill might have saved up an old note. Anyhow they've taken Bill down to San Bernardino for questioning and they've taken the body down to be post-mortemed."

"And what do you think?" he asked slowly.

"Well, Bill found the body himself. He didn't have to take me around by that pier. She might have stayed down in the water very much longer, or forever. The note could be old because Bill had carried it in his wallet and handled it from time to time, brooding over it. It could just as easily be undated this time as another time. I'd say notes like that are undated more often than not. The people who write them are apt to be in a hurry and not concerned with dates."

"The body must be pretty far gone. What can they find out now?"

"I don't know how well equipped they are. They can find out if she died by drowning, I guess. And whether there are any marks of violence that wouldn't be erased by water and decomposition. They could tell if she had been shot or stabbed. If the hyoid bone in the throat was broken, they could assume she was throttled. The main thing for us is that I'll have to tell why I came up here. I'll have to testify at an inquest."

"That's bad," Kingsley growled. "Very bad. What do you plan to do now?"

"On my way home I'll stop at the Prescott Hotel and see if I can pick up anything there. Were your wife and Muriel Chess friendly?"

"I guess so. Crystal's easy enough to get along with most of the time. I hardly knew Muriel Chess."

"Did you ever know anybody named Mildred Haviland?"

"What?"

I repeated the name.

"No," he said. "Is there any reason why I should?"

"Every question I ask you ask another right back," I said. "No, there isn't any reason why you should know Mildred Haviland. Especially if you hardly knew Muriel Chess. I'll call you in the morning."

"Do that," he said, and hesitated. "I'm sorry you had to walk into such a mess," he added, and then hesitated again and said goodnight and hung up.

The bell rang again immediately and the long-distance operator told me sharply I had put in five cents too much money. I said the sort of thing I would be likely to put into an opening like that. She didn't like it.

I stepped out of the booth and gathered some air into my lungs. The tame doe with the leather collar was standing in the gap in the fence at the end of the walk. I tried to push her out of the way, but she just leaned against me and wouldn't push. So I stepped over the fence and went back to the Chrysler and drove back to the village.

There was a hanging light in Patton's headquarters but the shack was empty and his "*Back in Twenty Minutes*" sign was still against the inside of the glass part of the door. I kept on going down to the boat landing and beyond to the edge of a deserted swimming beach. A few putputs and speedboats were still fooling around on the silky water. Across the lake tiny yellow lights began to show in toy cabins perched on miniature slopes. A single bright star glowed low in the northeast above the ridge of the mountains. A robin sat on the spike top of a hundred-foot pine and waited for it to be dark enough for him to sing his goodnight song.

In a little while it was dark enough and he sang and went away into the invisible depths of sky. I snapped my cigarette into the motionless water a few feet away and climbed back into the car and started back in the direction of Little Fawn Lake.

11

THE GATE ACROSS the private road was padlocked. I put the Chrysler between two pine trees and climbed the gate and pussy-footed along the side of the road until the glimmer of the little lake bloomed suddenly at my feet. Bill Chess's cabin was dark. The three cabins on the other side were abrupt shadows against the pale granite outcrop. Water gleamed white where it trickled across the top of the dam, and fell almost soundlessly along the sloping outer face to the brook below. I listened, and heard no other sound at all.

The front door of the Chess cabin was locked. I padded along to the back and found a brute of a padlock hanging at that. I went along the walls feeling window screens. They were all fastened. One window higher up was screenless, a small double cottage window half way down the north wall. This was locked too. I stood still and did some more listening. There was no breeze and the trees were as quiet as their shadows.

I tried a knife blade between the two halves of the small window. No soap. The catch refused to budge. I leaned against the wall and thought and then suddenly I picked up a large stone and smacked it against the place where the two frames met in the middle. The catch pulled out of dry wood with a tearing noise. The window swung back into darkness. I heaved up on the sill and wangled a cramped leg over and edged through the opening. I rolled and let myself down into the room. I turned, grunting a little from the exertion at that altitude, and listened again.

A blazing flash beam hit me square in the eyes.

A very calm voice said: "I'd rest right there, son. You must be all tuckered out."

The flash pinned me against the wall like a squashed fly. Then a light switch clicked and a table lamp glowed. The flash went out. Jim Patton was sitting in an old brown Morris chair beside the table. A fringed brown scarf hung over the end of the table and touched his thick knee. He wore the same clothes he had worn that afternoon, with the addition of a leather jerkin which must have been new once, say about the time of Grover Cleveland's first term. His hands were empty except for the flash. His eyes were empty. His jaws moved in gentle rhythm.

"What's on your mind, son — besides breaking and entering?"

I poked a chair out and straddled it and leaned my arms on the back and looked around the cabin.

"I had an idea," I said. "It looked pretty good for a while, but I guess I can learn to forget it."

The cabin was larger than it had seemed from outside. The part I was in was the living room. It contained a few articles of modest furniture, a rag rug on the pineboard floor, a round table against the end wall and two chairs set against it. Through an open door the corner of a big black cookstove showed.

Patton nodded and his eyes studied me without rancor. "I heard a car coming," he said. "I knew it had to be coming here. You walk right nice though. I didn't hear you walk worth a darn. I've been a mite curious about you, son."

I said nothing.

"I hope you don't mind me callin' you 'son,'" he said. "I hadn't ought to be so familiar, but I got myself into the habit and I can't seem to shake it. Anybody that don't have a long white beard and arthritis is 'son' to me."

I said he could call me anything that came to mind. I wasn't sensitive.

He grinned. "There's a mess of detectives in the L.A. phone book," he said. "But only one of them is called Marlowe."

"What made you look?"

"I guess you might call it lowdown curiosity. Added to which Bill Chess told me you was some sort of dick. You didn't bother to tell me yourself."

"I'd have got around to it," I said. "I'm sorry it bothered you."

"It didn't bother me none. I don't bother at all easy. You got any identification with you?"

I got my wallet out and showed him this and that.

"Well, you got a good build on you for the work," he said, satisfied. "And your face don't tell a lot of stories. I guess you was aiming to search the cabin."

"Yeah."

"I already pawed around considerable myself. Just got back and come straight here. That is, I stopped by my shack a minute and then come. I don't figure I could let you search the place, though." He scratched his ear. "That is, dum if I know whether I could or not. You telling who hired you?"

"Derace Kingsley. To trace his wife. She skipped out on him a month ago. She started from here. So I started from here. She's supposed to have gone away with a man. The man denies it. I thought maybe something up here might give me a lead."

"And did anything?"

"No. She's traced pretty definitely as far as San Bernardino and then El Paso. There the trail ends. But I've only just started."

Patton stood up and unlocked the cabin door. The spicy smell of the pines surged in. He spat outdoors and sat down again and rumpled the mousy brown hair under his Stetson. His head with the hat off had the indecent look of heads that are seldom without hats.

"You didn't have no interest in Bill Chess at all?"

"None whatever."

"I guess you fellows do a lot of divorce business," he said. "Kind of smelly work, to my notion."

I let that ride.

"Kingsley wouldn't have asked help from the police to find his wife, would he?"

"Hardly," I said. "He knows her too well."

"None of what you've been saying don't hardly explain your wanting to search Bill's cabin," he said judiciously.

"I'm just a great guy to poke around."

"Hell," he said, "you can do better than that."

"Say I am interested in Bill Chess then. But only because he's in trouble and rather a pathetic case – in spite of being a good deal of a heel. If he murdered his wife, there's something here to point that way. If he didn't, there's something to point that way too."

He held his head sideways, like a watchful bird. "As for instance what kind of thing?"

"Clothes, personal jewelry, toilet articles, whatever a woman takes with her when she goes away, not intending to come back."

He leaned back slowly. "But she didn't go away, son."

"Then the stuff should be still here. But if it was still here, Bill would have noticed she hadn't taken it. He would know she hadn't gone away."

"By gum, I don't like it either way," he said.

"But if he murdered her," I said, "then he would have to get rid of the things she ought to have taken with her, if she had gone away."

"And how do you figure he would do that, son?" The yellow lamplight made bronze of one side of his face.

"I understand she had a Ford car of her own. Except for that I'd expect him to burn what he could burn and bury what he could not burn out in the woods. Sinking it in the lake might be dangerous. But he couldn't burn or bury her car. Could he drive it?"

Patton looked surprised. "Sure. He can't bend his right leg at the knee, so he couldn't use the footbrake very handy. But he could get by with the handbrake. All that's different on Bill's own Ford is the brake pedal is set over on the left side of the post, close to the clutch, so he can shove them both down with one foot."

I shook ash from my cigarette into a small blue jar that had once contained a pound of orange honey, according to the small gilt label on it.

"Getting rid of the car would be his big problem," I said. "Wherever he took it he would have to get back, and he would rather not be seen coming back. And if he simply abandoned it on a street, say, down in San Bernardino, it would be found and identified very quickly. He wouldn't want that either. The best stunt would be to unload it on a hot car dealer, but he probably doesn't know one. So the chances are he hid it in the woods within walking distance of here. And walking distance for him would not be very far."

"For a fellow that claims not to be interested, you're doing some pretty close figuring on all this," Patton said dryly. "So now you've got the car hid out in the woods. What then?"

"He has to consider the possibility of its being found. The woods are lonely, but rangers and woodcutters get around in them from time to time. If the car is found, it would be better for Muriel's stuff to be found in it. That would give him a couple of outs – neither one very brilliant but both at least possible. One, that she was murdered by some unknown party who fixed things to implicate Bill when and if the murder was discovered. Two, that Muriel did actually commit suicide, but fixed things so that he would be blamed. A revenge suicide."

Patton thought all this over with calm and care. He went to the door to unload again. He sat down and rumpled his hair again. He looked at me with solid skepticism.

"The first one's possible like you say," he admitted. "But only just, and I don't have anybody in mind for the job. There's that little matter of the note to be got over."

I shook my head. "Say Bill already had the note from another time. Say she went away, as he thought, without leaving a note. After a month had gone by without any word from her he might be just worried and uncertain enough to show the note, feeling it might be some protection to him in case anything had happened to her. He didn't say any of this, but he could have had it in his mind."

Patton shook his head. He didn't like it. Neither did I. He said slowly: "As to your other notion, it's just plain crazy. Killing yourself and fixing things so as somebody else would get accused of murdering you don't fit in with my simple ideas of human nature at all."

"Then your ideas of human nature are too simple," I said. "Because it has been done, and when it has been done, it has nearly always been done by a woman."

"Nope," he said, "I'm a man fifty-seven years old and I've seen a lot of crazy people, but I don't go for that worth a peanut shell. What I like is that she did plan to go away and did write the note, but he caught her before she got clear

67

and saw red and finished her off. Then he would have to do all them things we been talking about."

"I never met her," I said. "So I wouldn't have any idea what she would be likely to do. Bill said he met her in a place in Riverside something over a year ago. She may have had a long and complicated history before that. What kind of girl was she?"

"A mighty cute little blonde when she fixed herself up. She kind of let herself go with Bill. A quiet girl, with a face that kept its secrets. Bill says she had a temper, but I never seen any of it. I seen plenty of nasty temper in him."

"And did you think she looked like the photo of somebody called Mildred Haviland?"

His jaws stopped munching and his mouth became almost primly tight. Very slowly he started chewing again.

"By gum," he said, "I'll be mighty careful to look under the bed before I crawl in tonight. To make sure you ain't there. Where did you get that information?"

"A nice little girl called Birdie Keppel told me. She was interviewing me in the course of her spare-time newspaper job. She happened to mention that an L.A. cop named De Soto was showing the photo around."

Patton smacked his thick knee and hunched his shoulders forward.

"I done wrong there," he said soberly, "I made one of my mistakes. This big bruiser showed his picture to darn near everybody in town before he showed it to me. That made me kind of sore. It looked some like Muriel, but not enough to be sure by any manner of means. I asked him what she was wanted for. He said it was police business. I said I was in that way of business myself, in an ignorant countrified kind of way. He said his instructions were to locate the lady and that was all he knew. Maybe he did wrong to take me up short like that. So I guess I done wrong to tell him I didn't know anybody that looked like his little picture."

The big calm man smiled vaguely at the corner of the ceiling, then brought his eyes down and looked at me steadily.

"I'll thank you to respect this confidence, Mr. Marlowe. You done right nicely in your figuring too. You ever happen to go over to Coon Lake?"

"Never heard of it."

"Back about a mile," he said, pointing over his shoulder with a thumb, "there's a little narrow wood road turns over west. You can just drive it and miss the trees. It climbs about five hundred feet in another mile and comes out by Coon Lake. Pretty little place. Folks go up there to picnic once in a while, but not often. It's hard on tires. There's two, three small shallow lakes full of reeds. There's snow up there even now in the shady places. There's a bunch of old handhewn log cabins that's been falling down ever since I recall, and there's a big broken-down frame building that Montclair University used to use for a summer camp maybe ten years back. They ain't used it in a very long time. This building sits back from the lake in heavy timber. Round at the back of it there's a wash house with an old rusty boiler and along of that there's a big woodshed with a sliding door hung on rollers. It was built for a garage but they kept their wood in it and they locked it up out of season. Wood's one of the few things people will steal up here, but folks who might steal it off a pile wouldn't break a lock to get it. I guess you know what I found in that woodshed."

"I thought you went down to San Bernardino."

"Changed my mind. Didn't seem right to let Bill ride down there with his wife's body in the back of the car. So I sent it down in Doc's ambulance and I sent Andy down with Bill. I figured I kind of ought to look around a little more before I put things up to the sheriff and the coroner."

"Muriel's car was in the woodshed?"

"Yep. And two unlocked suitcases in the car. Packed with clothes and packed kind of hasty, I thought. Women's clothes.

The point is, son, no stranger would have known about that place."

I agreed with him. He put his hand into the slanting side pocket of his jerkin and brought out a small twist of tissue paper. He opened it up on his palm and held the hand out flat.

"Take a look at this."

I went over and looked. What lay on the tissue was a thin gold chain with a tiny lock hardly larger than a link of the chain. The gold had been snipped through, leaving the lock intact. The chain seemed to be about seven inches long. There was white powder sticking to both chain and paper.

"Where would you guess I found that?" Patton asked.

I picked the chain up and tried to fit the cut ends together. They didn't fit. I made no comment on that, but moistened a finger and touched the powder and tasted it.

"In a can or box of confectioner's sugar," I said. "The chain is an anklet. Some women never take them off, like wedding rings. Whoever took this one off didn't have the key."

"What do you make of it?"

"Nothing much," I said. "There wouldn't be any point in Bill cutting it off Muriel's ankle and leaving that green necklace on her neck. There wouldn't be any point in Muriel cutting it off herself – assuming she had lost the key – and hiding it to be found. A search thorough enough to find it wouldn't be made unless her body was found first. If Bill cut it off, he would have thrown it into the lake. But if Muriel wanted to keep it and yet hide it from Bill, there's some sense in the place where it was hidden."

Patton looked puzzled this time. "Why is that?"

"Because it's a woman's hiding place. Confectioner's sugar is used to make cake icing. A man would never look there. Pretty clever of you to find it, sheriff."

He grinned a little sheepishly. "Hell, I knocked the box over and some of the sugar spilled," he said. "Without that

I don't guess I ever would have found it." He rolled the paper up again and slipped it back into his pocket. He stood up with an air of finality.

"You staying up here or going back to town, Mr. Marlowe?"

"Back to town. Until you want me for the inquest. I suppose you will."

"That's up to the coroner, of course. If you'll kind of shut that window you bust in, I'll put this lamp out and lock up."

I did what he said and he snapped his flash on and put out the lamp. We went out and he felt the cabin door to make sure the lock had caught. He closed the screen softly and stood looking across the moonlit lake.

"I don't figure Bill meant to kill her," he said sadly. "He could choke a girl to death without meaning to at all. He has mighty strong hands. Once done he has to use what brains God gave him to cover up what he done. I feel real bad about it, but that don't alter the facts and the probabilities. It's simple and natural and the simple and natural things usually turn out to be right."

I said: "I should think he would have run away. I don't see how he could stand it to stay here."

Patton spat into the black velvet shadow of a manzanita bush. He said slowly: "He had a government pension and he would have to run away from that too. And most men can stand what they've got to stand, when it steps up and looks them straight in the eye. Like they're doing all over the world right now. Well, goodnight to you. I'm going to walk down to that little pier again and stand there awhile in the moonlight and feel bad. A night like this, and we got to think about murders."

He moved quietly off into the shadows and became one of them himself. I stood there until he was out of sight and then went back to the locked gate and climbed over it. I got into the car and drove back down the road looking for a place to hide.

71

12

THREE HUNDRED YARDS from the gate a narrow track, sifted over with brown oak leaves from last fall, curved around a granite boulder and disappeared. I followed it around and bumped along the stones of the outcrop for fifty or sixty feet, then swung the car around a tree and set it pointing back the way it had come. I cut the lights and switched off the motor and sat there waiting.

Half an hour passed. Without tobacco it seemed a long time. Then far off I heard a car motor start up and grow louder and the white beam of headlights passed below me on the road. The sound faded into the distance and a faint dry tang of dust hung in the air for a while after it was gone.

I got out of my car and walked back to the gate and to the Chess cabin. A hard push opened the sprung window this time. I climbed in again and let myself down to the floor and poked the flash I had brought across the room to the table lamp. I switched the lamp on and listened a moment, heard nothing, and went out to the kitchen. I switched on a hanging bulb over the sink.

The woodbox beside the stove was neatly piled with split wood. There were no dirty dishes in the sink, no foul-smelling pots on the stove. Bill Chess, lonely or not, kept his house in good order. A door opened from the kitchen into the bedroom, and from that a very narrow door led into a tiny bathroom which had evidently been built on to the cabin fairly recently. The clean celotex lining showed that. The bathroom told me nothing.

The bedroom contained a double bed, a pinewood dresser with a round mirror on the wall above it, a bureau, two straight chairs, and a tin wastebasket. There were two oval rag rugs on the floor, one on each side of the bed. On the walls Bill Chess had tacked up a set of war maps from the *National*

Geographic. There was a silly-looking red and white flounce on the dressing table.

I poked around in the drawers. An imitation leather trinket box with an assortment of gaudy costume jewelry had not been taken away. There was the usual stuff women use on their faces and fingernails and eyebrows, and it seemed to me that there was too much of it. But that was just guessing. The bureau contained both man's and woman's clothes, not a great deal of either. Bill Chess had a very noisy check shirt with starched matching collar, among other things. Underneath a sheet of blue tissue paper in one corner I found something I didn't like. A seemingly brand-new peach-colored silk slip trimmed with lace. Silk slips were not being left behind that year, not by any woman in her senses.

This looked bad for Bill Chess. I wondered what Patton had thought of it.

I went back to the kitchen and prowled the open shelves above and beside the sink. They were thick with cans and jars of household staples. The confectioner's sugar was in a square brown box with a torn corner. Patton had made an attempt to clean up what was spilled. Near the sugar were salt, borax, baking soda, cornstarch, brown sugar and so on. Something might be hidden in any of them.

Something that had been clipped from a chain anklet whose cut ends did not fit together.

I shut my eyes and poked a finger out at random and it came to rest on the baking soda. I got a newspaper from the back of the woodbox and spread it out and dumped the soda out of the box. I stirred it around with a spoon. There seemed to be an indecent lot of baking soda, but that was all there was. I funneled it back into the box and tried the borax. Nothing but borax. Third time lucky. I tried the cornstarch. It made too much fine dust, and there was nothing but cornstarch.

The sound of distant steps froze me to the ankles. I reached up and yanked the light out and dodged back into the living room and reached for the lamp switch. Much too late to be of any use, of course. The steps sounded again, soft and cautious. The hackles rose on my neck.

I waited in the dark, with the flash in my left hand. A deadly long two minutes crept by. I spent some of the time breathing, but not all.

It wouldn't be Patton. He would walk up to the door and open it and tell me off. The careful quiet steps seemed to move this way and that, a movement, a long pause, another movement, another long pause. I sneaked across to the door and twisted the knob silently. I yanked the door wide and stabbed out with the flash.

It made golden lamps of a pair of eyes. There was a leaping movement and a quick thudding of hoofs back among the trees. It was only an inquisitive deer.

I closed the door again and followed my flashlight beam back into the kitchen. The small round glow rested squarely on the box of confectioner's sugar.

I put the light on again, lifted the box down and emptied it on the newspaper.

Patton hadn't gone deep enough. Having found one thing by accident he had assumed that was all there was. He hadn't seemed to notice that there ought to be something else.

Another twist of white tissue showed in the fine white powdered sugar. I shook it clean and unwound it. It contained a tiny gold heart, no larger than a woman's little fingernail.

I spooned the sugar back into the box and put the box back on the shelf and crumpled the piece of newspaper into the stove. I went back to the living room and turned the table lamp on. Under the brighter light the tiny engraving on the back of the little gold heart could just be read without a magnifying glass.

It was in script. It read: "*Al to Mildred. June 28th 1938. With all my love.*"

74

Al to Mildred. Al somebody to Mildred Haviland. Mildred Haviland was Muriel Chess. Muriel Chess was dead – two weeks after a cop named De Soto had been looking for her.

I stood there, holding it, wondering what it had to do with me. Wondering, and not having the faintest glimmer of an idea.

I wrapped it up again and left the cabin and drove back to the village.

Patton was in his office telephoning when I got around there. The door was locked. I had to wait while he talked. After a while he hung up and came to unlock the door.

I walked in past him and put the twist of tissue paper on his counter and opened it up.

"You didn't go deep enough into the powdered sugar," I said.

He looked at the little gold heart, looked at me, went around behind the counter and got a cheap magnifying glass off his desk. He studied the back of the heart. He put the glass down and frowned at me.

"Might have known if you wanted to search that cabin, you was going to do it," he said gruffly. "I ain't going to have trouble with you, am I, son?"

"You ought to have noticed that the cut ends of the chain didn't fit," I told him.

He looked at me sadly. "Son, I don't have your eyes." He pushed the little heart around with his square blunt finger. He stared at me and said nothing.

I said: "If you were thinking that anklet meant something Bill could have been jealous about, so was I – provided he ever saw it. But strictly on the cuff I'm willing to bet he never did see it and that he never heard of Mildred Haviland."

Patton said slowly: "Looks like maybe I owe this De Soto party an apology, don't it?"

"If you ever see him," I said.

75

He gave me another long empty stare and I gave it right back to him. "Don't tell me, son," he said. "Let me guess all for myself that you got a brand-new idea about it."

"Yeah. Bill didn't murder his wife."

"No?"

"No. She was murdered by somebody out of her past. Somebody who had lost track of her and then found it again and found her married to another man and didn't like it. Somebody who knew the country up here – as hundreds of people do who don't live here – and knew a good place to hide the car and the clothes. Somebody who hated and could dissimulate. Who persuaded her to go away with him and when everything was ready and the note was written, took her around the throat and gave her what he thought was coming to her and put her in the lake and went his way. Like it?"

"Well," he said judiciously, "it does make things kind of complicated, don't you think? But there ain't anything impossible about it. Not one bit impossible."

"When you get tired of it, let me know. I'll have something else," I said.

"I'll just be doggone sure you will," he said, and for the first time since I had met him he laughed.

I said goodnight and went on out, leaving him there moving his mind around with the ponderous energy of a homesteader digging up a stump.

13

AT SOMEWHERE AROUND eleven I got down to the bottom of the grade and parked in one of the diagonal slots at the side of the Prescott Hotel in San Bernardino. I pulled an overnight bag out of the boot and had taken three steps with it when a bellhop in braided pants and a white shirt and black bow tie yanked it out of my hand.

The clerk on duty was an eggheaded man with no interest in me or in anything else. He wore parts of a white linen suit and he yawned as he handed me the desk pen and looked off into the distance as if remembering his childhood.

The hop and I rode a four-by-four elevator to the second floor and walked a couple of blocks around corners. As we walked it got hotter and hotter. The hop unlocked a door into a boy's size room with one window on an airshaft. The air-conditioner inlet up in the corner of the ceiling was about the size of a woman's handkerchief. The bit of ribbon tied to it fluttered weakly, just to show that something was moving.

The hop was tall and thin and yellow and not young and as cool as a slice of chicken in aspic. He moved his gum around in his face, put my bag on a chair, looked up at the grating and then stood looking at me. He had eyes the color of a drink of water.

"Maybe I ought to have asked for one of the dollar rooms," I said. "This one seems a mite close-fitting."

"I reckon you're lucky to get one at all. This town's fair bulgin' at the seams."

"Bring us up some ginger ale and glasses and ice," I said.

"Us?"

"That is, if you happen to be a drinking man."

"I reckon I might take a chance this late."

He went out. I took off my coat, tie, shirt and undershirt and walked around in the warm draft from the open door. The draft smelled of hot iron. I went into the bathroom side-ways – it was that kind of bathroom – and doused myself with tepid cold water. I was breathing a little more freely when the tall languid hop returned with a tray. He shut the door and I brought out a bottle of rye. He mixed a couple of drinks and we made the usual insincere smiles over them and drank. The perspiration started from the back of my neck down my spine and was halfway to my socks before I put the glass down. But I felt better all the same. I sat on the bed and looked at the hop.

"How long can you stay?"

"Doin' what?"

"Remembering."

"I ain't a damn bit of use at it," he said.

"I have money to spend," I said, "in my own peculiar way." I got my wallet unstuck from the lower part of my back and spread tired-looking dollar bills along the bed.

"I beg yore pardon," the hop said. "I reckon you might be a dick."

"Don't be silly," I said. "You never saw a dick playing solitaire with his own money. You might call me an investigator."

"I'm interested," he said. "The likker makes my mind work."

I gave him a dollar bill. "Try that on your mind. And can I call you Big Tex from Houston?"

"Amarillo," he said. "Not that it matters. And how do you like my Texas drawl? It makes me sick, but I find people go for it."

"Stay with it," I said. "It never lost anybody a dollar yet."

He grinned and tucked the folded dollar neatly into the watch pocket of his pants.

"What were you doing on Friday, June 12th?" I asked him. "Late afternoon or evening. It was a Friday."

He sipped his drink and thought, shaking the ice around gently and drinking past his gum. "I was right here, six to twelve shift," he said.

"A woman, slim, pretty blonde, checked in here and stayed until time for the night train to El Paso. I think she must have taken that because she was in El Paso Sunday morning. She came here driving a Packard Clipper registered to Crystal Grace Kingsley, 965 Carson Drive, Beverly Hills. She may have registered as that, or under some other name, and she may not have registered at all. Her car is still in the hotel garage. I'd like to talk to the boys that checked her in and out. That wins another dollar – just thinking about it."

I separated another dollar from my exhibit and it went into his pocket with a sound like caterpillars fighting.

"Can do," he said calmly.

He put his glass down and left the room, closing the door. I finished my drink and made another. I went into the bathroom and used some more warm water on my torso. While I was doing this the telephone on the wall tinkled and I wedged myself into the minute space between the bathroom door and the bed to answer it.

The Texas voice said: "That was Sonny. He was inducted last week. Another boy we call Les checked her out. He's here."

"Okay. Shoot him up, will you?"

I was playing with my second drink and thinking about the third when a knock came and I opened the door to a small, green-eyed rat with a tight, girlish mouth.

He came in almost dancing and stood looking at me with a faint sneer.

"Drink?"

"Sure," he said coldly. He poured himself a large one and added a whisper of ginger ale, put the mixture down in one long swallow, tucked a cigarette between his smooth little lips and snapped a match alight while it was coming up from his pocket. He blew smoke and went on staring at me. The corner of his eye caught the money on the bed, without looking directly at it. Over the pocket of his shirt, instead of a number, the word *Captain* was stitched.

"You Les?" I asked him.

"No." He paused. "We don't like dicks here," he added. "We don't have one of our own and we don't care to bother with dicks that are working for other people."

"Thanks," I said. "That will be all."

"Huh?" The small mouth twisted unpleasantly.

"Beat it," I said.

"I thought you wanted to see me," he sneered.

"You're the bell captain?"

79

"Check."

"I wanted to buy you a drink. I wanted to give you a buck. Here." I held it out to him. "Thanks for coming up."

He took the dollar and pocketed it, without a word of thanks. He hung there, smoke trailing from his nose, his eyes tight and mean.

"What I say here goes," he said.

"It goes as far as you can push it," I said. "And that couldn't be very far. You had your drink and you had your graft. Now you can scram out."

He turned with a swift tight shrug and slipped out of the room noiselessly.

Four minutes passed, then another knock, very light. The tall boy came in grinning. I walked away from him and sat on the bed again.

"You didn't take to Les, I reckon?"

"Not a great deal. Is he satisfied?"

"I reckon so. You know what captains are. They have to have their cut. Maybe you better call me Les, Mr. Marlowe."

"So you checked her out."

"No, that was all a stall. She never checked in at the desk. But I remember the Packard. She gave me a dollar to put it away for her and to look after her stuff until train time. She ate dinner here. A dollar gets you remembered in this town. And there's been talk about the car bein' left so long."

"What was she like to look at?"

"She wore a black and white outfit, mostly white, and a Panama hat with a black and white band. She was a neat blonde lady like you said. Later on she took a hack to the station. I put her bags into it for her. They had initials on them but I'm sorry I can't remember the initials."

"I'm glad you can't." I said. "It would be too good. Have a drink. How old would she be?"

He rinsed the other glass and mixed a civilized drink for himself.

80

"It's mighty hard to tell a woman's age these days," he said. "I reckon she was about thirty, or a little more or a little less."

I dug in my coat for the snapshot of Crystal and Lavery on the beach and handed it to him.

He looked at it steadily and held it away from his eyes, then close.

"You won't have to swear to it in court," I said.

He nodded. "I wouldn't want to. These small blondes are so much of a pattern that a change of clothes or light or make-up makes them all alike or all different." He hesitated, staring at the snapshot.

"What's worrying you?" I asked.

"I'm thinking about the gent in this snap. He enter into it at all?"

"Go on with that," I said.

"I think this fellow spoke to her in the lobby, and had dinner with her. A tall good-lookin' jasper, built like a fast light-heavy. He went in the hack with her too."

"Quite sure about that?"

He looked at the money on the bed.

"Okay, how much does it cost?" I asked wearily.

He stiffened, laid the snapshot down and drew the two folded bills from his pocket and tossed them on the bed.

"I thank you for the drink," he said, "and to hell with you." He started for the door.

"Oh sit down and don't be so touchy," I growled.

He sat down and looked at me stiff-eyed.

"And don't be so damn southern," I said. "I've been knee deep in hotel hops for a lot of years. If I've met one who wouldn't pull a gag, that's fine. But you can't expect me to expect to meet one that wouldn't pull a gag."

He grinned slowly and nodded quickly. He picked the snapshot up again and looked at me over it.

"This gent takes a solid photo," he said. "Much more so than the lady. But there was another little item that made me

81

remember him. I got the impression the lady didn't quite like him walking up to her so openly in the lobby."

I thought that over and decided it didn't mean anything much. He might have been late or have missed some earlier appointment. I said:

"There's a reason for that. Did you notice what jewelry the lady was wearing? Rings, ear-pendants, anything that looked conspicuous or valuable?"

He hadn't noticed, he said.

"Was her hair long or short, straight or waved or curly, natural blond or bleached?"

He laughed. "Hell, you can't tell that last point, Mr. Marlowe. Even when it's natural they want it lighter. As to the rest, my recollection is it was rather long, like they're wearing it now and turned in a little at the bottom and rather straight. But I could be wrong." He looked at the snapshot again. "She has it bound back here. You can't tell a thing."

"That's right," I said. "And the only reason I asked you was to make sure you didn't over-observe. The guy that sees too much detail is just as unreliable a witness as the guy that doesn't see any. He's nearly always making half of it up. You check just about right, considering the circumstances. Thanks very much."

I gave him back his two dollars and a five to keep them company. He thanked me, finished his drink and left softly. I finished mine and washed off again and decided I would rather drive home than sleep in that hole. I put my shirt and coat on again and went downstairs with my bag.

The redheaded rat of a captain was the only hop in the lobby. I carried my bag over to the desk and he didn't move to take it off my hands. The eggheaded clerk separated me from two dollars without even looking at me.

"Two bucks to spend the night in this manhole," I said, "when for free I could have a nice airy ashcan."

The clerk yawned, got a delayed reaction, and said brightly: "It gets quite cool here about three in the morning. From then on until eight, or even nine, it's quite pleasant."

I wiped the back of my neck and staggered out to the car. Even the seat of the car was hot, at midnight.

I got home about two-forty-five and Hollywood was an icebox. Even Pasadena had felt cool.

14

I DREAMED I was far down in the depths of icy green water with a corpse under my arm. The corpse had long blond hair that kept floating around in front of my face. An enormous fish with bulging eyes and a bloated body and scales shining with putrescence swam around leering like an elderly roué. Just as I was about to burst from lack of air, the corpse came alive under my arm and got away from me and then I was fighting with the fish and the corpse was rolling over and over in the water spinning its long hair.

I woke up with a mouth full of sheet and both hands hooked on the head-frame of the bed and pulling hard. The muscles ached when I let go and lowered them. I got up and walked the room and lit a cigarette, feeling the carpet with bare toes. When I had finished the cigarette, I went back to bed.

It was nine o'clock when I woke up again. The sun was on my face. The room was hot. I showered and shaved and partly dressed and made the morning toast and eggs and coffee in the dinette. While I was finishing up there was a knock at the apartment door.

I went to open it with my mouth full of toast. It was a lean, serious-looking man in a severe gray suit.

"Floyd Greer, lieutenant, Central Detective Bureau," he said and walked into the room.

He put out a dry hand and I shook it. He sat down on the edge of a chair, the way they do, and turned his hat in his hands and looked at me with the quiet stare they have.

"We got a call from San Bernardino about that business up at Puma Lake. Drowned woman. Seems you were on hand when the body was discovered."

I nodded and said, "Have some coffee?"

"No thanks. I had breakfast two hours ago."

I got my coffee and sat down across the room from him.

"They asked us to look you up," he said. "Give them a line on you."

"Sure."

"So we did that. Seems like you have a clean bill of health so far as we are concerned. Kind of coincidence a man in your line would be around when the body was found."

"I'm like that," I said. "Lucky."

"So I just thought I'd drop around and say howdy."

"That's fine. Glad to know you, lieutenant."

"Kind of a coincidence," he said again, nodding. "You up there on business, so to speak?"

"If I was," I said, "my business had nothing to do with the girl who was drowned, so far as I know."

"But you couldn't be sure?"

"Until you've finished with a case, you can't ever be quite sure what its ramifications are, can you?"

"That's right." He circled his hat brim through his fingers again, like a bashful cowboy. There was nothing bashful about his eyes. "I'd like to feel sure that if these ramifications you speak of happened to take in this drowned woman's affairs, you would put us wise."

"I hope you can rely on that," I said.

He bulged his lower lip with his tongue. "We'd like a little more than a hope. At the present time you don't care to say?"

"At the present time I don't know anything that Patton doesn't know."

84

"Who's he?"

"The constable up at Puma Point."

The lean serious man smiled tolerantly. He cracked a knuckle and after a pause said: "The San Berdoo D.A. will likely want to talk to you — before the inquest. But that won't be very soon. Right now they're trying to get a set of prints. We lent them a technical man."

"That will be tough. The body's pretty far gone."

"It's done all the time," he said. "They worked out the system back in New York where they're all the time pulling in floaters. They cut patches of skin off the fingers and harden them in a tanning solution and make stamps. It works well enough as a rule."

"You think this woman had a record of some kind?"

"Why, we always take prints of a corpse," he said. "You ought to know that."

I said: "I didn't know the lady. If you thought I did and that was why I was up there, there's nothing to it."

"But you wouldn't care to say just why you were up there," he persisted.

"So you think I'm lying to you," I said.

He spun his hat on a bony forefinger. "You got me wrong, Mr. Marlowe. We don't think anything at all. What we do is investigate and find out. This stuff is just routine. You ought to know that. You been around long enough." He stood up and put his hat on. "You might let me know if you have to leave town. I'd be obliged."

I said I would and went to the door with him. He went out with a duck of his head and a sad half-smile. I watched him drift languidly down the hall and punch the elevator button.

I went back out to the dinette to see if there was any more coffee. There was about two-thirds of a cup. I added cream and sugar and carried my cup over to the telephone. I dialed Police Headquarters downtown and asked for the Detective Bureau and then for Lieutenant Floyd Greer.

The voice said: "Lieutenant Greer is not in the office. Anybody else do?"

"De Soto in?"

"Who?"

I repeated the name.

"What's his rank and department?"

"Plainclothes something or other."

"Hold the line."

I waited. The burring male voice came back after a while and said: "What's the gag? We don't have a De Soto on the roster. Who's this talking?"

I hung up, finished my coffee and dialed the number of Derace Kingsley's office. The smooth and cool Miss Fromsett said he had just come in and put me through without a murmur.

"Well," he said, loud and forceful at the beginning of a fresh day. "What did you find out at the hotel?"

"She was there all right. And Lavery met her there. The hop who gave me the dope brought Lavery into it himself, without any prompting from me. He had dinner with her and went with her in a cab to the railroad station."

"Well, I ought to have known he was lying," Kingsley said slowly. "I got the impression he was surprised when I told him about the telegram from El Paso. I was just letting my impression get too sharp. Anything else?"

"Not there. I had a cop calling on me this morning, giving me the usual looking over and warning not to leave town without letting him know. Trying to find out why I went to Puma Point. I didn't tell him and as he wasn't even aware of Jim Patton's existence, it's evident that Patton didn't tell anybody."

"Jim would do his best to be decent about it," Kingsley said. "Why were you asking me last night about some name – Mildred something or other?"

I told him, making it brief. I told him about Muriel Chess's car and clothes being found and where.

"That looks bad for Bill," he said. "I know Coon Lake myself, but it would never have occurred to me to use that old woodshed – or even that there was an old woodshed. It not only looks bad, it looks premeditated."

"I disagree with that. Assuming he knew the country well enough it wouldn't take him any time to search his mind for a likely hiding place. He was very restricted as to distance."

"Maybe. What do you plan to do now?" he asked.

"Go up against Lavery again, of course."

He agreed that that was the thing to do. He added: "This other, tragic as it is, is really no business of ours, is it?"

"Not unless your wife knew something about it."

His voice sounded sharply, saying: "Look here, Marlowe, I think I can understand your detective instinct to tie everything that happens into one compact knot, but don't let it run away with you. Life isn't like that at all – not life as I have known it. Better leave the affairs of the Chess family to the police and keep your brains working on the Kingsley family."

"Okay," I said.

"I don't mean to be domineering," he said.

I laughed heartily, said goodbye, and hung up. I finished dressing and went down to the basement for the Chrysler. I started for Bay City again.

15

I DROVE PAST the intersection of Altair Street to where the cross street continued to the edge of the canyon and ended in a semi-circular parking place with a sidewalk and a white wooden guard fence around it. I sat there in the car a little while, thinking, looking out to sea and admiring the blue-gray fall of the foothills towards the ocean. I was trying to make up my mind whether to try handling Lavery with a feather or go on using the back of my hand and edge of my tongue. I decided I could lose nothing by the soft approach.

If that didn't produce for me – and I didn't think it would – nature could take its course and we could bust up the furniture.

The paved alley that ran along halfway down the hill below the houses on the outer edge was empty. Below that, on the next hillside street, a couple of kids were throwing a boomerang up the slope and chasing it with the usual amount of elbowing and mutual insult. Farther down still a house was enclosed in trees and a red brick wall. There was a glimpse of washing on the line in the backyard and two pigeons strutted along the slope of the roof bobbing their heads. A blue and tan bus trundled along the street in front of the brick house and stopped and a very old man got off with slow care and settled himself firmly on the ground and tapped with a heavy cane before he started to crawl back up the slope.

The air was clearer than yesterday. The morning was full of peace. I left the car where it was and walked along Altair Street to No. 623.

The venetian blinds were down across the front windows and the place had a sleepy look. I stepped down over the Korean moss and punched the bell and saw that the door was not quite shut. It had dropped in its frame, as most of our doors do, and the spring bolt hung a little on the lower edge of the lock plate. I remembered that it had wanted to stick the day before, when I was leaving.

I gave the door a little push and it moved inward with a light click. The room beyond was dim, but there was some light from west windows. Nobody answered my ring. I didn't ring again. I pushed the door a little wider and stepped inside.

The room had a hushed warm smell, the smell of late morning in a house not yet opened up. The bottle of Vat 69 on the round table by the davenport was almost empty and another full bottle waited beside it. The copper ice bucket had a little water in the bottom. Two glasses had been used, and half a siphon of carbonated water.

I fixed the door about as I had found it and stood there and listened. If Lavery was away I thought I would take a chance and frisk the joint. I didn't have anything much on him, but it was probably enough to keep him from calling the cops.

In the silence time passed. It passed in the dry whirr of the electric clock on the mantel, in the far-off toot of an auto horn on Aster Drive, in the hornet drone of a plane over the foothills across the canyon, in the sudden lurch and growl of the electric refrigerator in the kitchen.

I went farther into the room and stood peering around and listening and hearing nothing except those fixed sounds belonging to the house and having nothing to do with the humans in it. I started along the rug towards the archway at the back.

A hand in a glove appeared on the slope of the white metal railing, at the edge of the archway, where the stairs went down. It appeared and stopped.

It moved and a woman's hat showed, then her head. The woman came quietly up the stairs. She came all the way up, turned through the arch and still didn't seem to see me. She was a slender woman of uncertain age, with untidy brown hair, a scarlet mess of a mouth, too much rouge on her cheekbones, shadowed eyes. She wore a blue tweed suit that looked like the dickens with the purple hat that was doing its best to hang on to the side of her head.

She saw me and didn't stop or change expression in the slightest degree. She came slowly on into the room, holding her right hand away from her body. Her left hand wore the brown glove I had seen on the railing. The right-hand glove that matched it was wrapped around the butt of a small automatic.

She stopped then and her body arched back and a quick distressful sound came out of her mouth. Then she giggled, a high nervous giggle. She pointed the gun at me, and came steadily on.

89

I kept on looking at the gun and not screaming.

The woman came close. When she was close enough to be confidential she pointed the gun at my stomach and said:

"All I wanted was my rent. The place seems well taken care of. Nothing broken. He has always been a good tidy careful tenant. I just didn't want him to get too far behind in the rent."

A fellow with a kind of strained and unhappy voice said politely: "How far behind is he?"

"Three months," she said. "Two hundred and forty dollars. Eighty dollars is very reasonable for a place as well furnished as this. I've had a little trouble collecting before, but it always came out very well. He promised me a check this morning. Over the telephone. I mean he promised to give it to me this morning."

"Over the telephone," I said. "This morning."

I shuffled around a bit in an inconspicuous sort of way. The idea was to get close enough to make a side swipe at the gun, knock it outwards, and then jump in fast before she could bring it back in line. I've never had a lot of luck with the technique, but you have to try it once in a while. This looked like the time to try it.

I made about six inches, but not nearly enough for a first down. I said: "And you're the owner?" I didn't look at the gun directly. I had a faint, a very faint hope that she didn't know she was pointing it at me.

"Why, certainly. I'm Mrs. Fallbrook. Who did you think I was?"

"Well, I thought you might be the owner," I said. "You talking about the rent and all. But I didn't know your name." Another eight inches. Nice smooth work. It would be a shame to have it wasted.

"And who are you, if I may enquire?"

"I just came about the car payment," I said. "The door was open just a teensy weensy bit and I kind of shoved in. I don't know why."

90

I made a face like a man from the finance company coming about the car payment. Kind of tough, but ready to break into a sunny smile.

"You mean Mr. Lavery is behind in his car payments?" she asked, looking worried.

"A little. Not a great deal," I said soothingly.

I was all set now. I had the reach and I ought to have the speed. All it needed was a clean sharp sweep inside the gun and outwards. I started to take my foot out of the rug.

"You know," she said, "it's funny about this gun. I found it on the stairs. Nasty oily things, aren't they? And the stair carpet is a very nice gray chenille. Quite expensive."

And she handed me the gun.

My hand went out for it, as stiff as an eggshell, almost as brittle. I took the gun. She sniffed with distaste at the glove which had been wrapped around the butt. She went on talking in exactly the same tone of cockeyed reasonableness. My knees cracked, relaxing.

"Well, of course it's much easier for you," she said. "About the car, I mean. You can just take it away, if you have to. But taking a house with nice furniture in it isn't so easy. It takes time and money to evict a tenant. There is apt to be bitterness and things get damaged, sometimes on purpose. The rug on this floor cost over two hundred dollars, secondhand. It's only a jute rug, but it has a lovely coloring, don't you think? You'd never know it was only jute, secondhand. But that's silly too because they're always secondhand after you've used them. And I walked over here too, to save my tires for the government. I could have taken a bus part way, but the darn things never come along except going in the wrong direction."

I hardly heard what she said. It was like surf breaking beyond a point, out of sight. The gun had my interest.

I broke the magazine out. It was empty. I turned the gun and looked into the breech. That was empty too. I sniffed the muzzle. It reeked.

I dropped the gun into my pocket. A six-shot .25 caliber automatic. Emptied out. Shot empty, and not too long ago. But not in the last half hour either.

"Has it been fired?" Mrs. Fallbrook enquired pleasantly. "I certainly hope not."

"Any reason why it should have been fired?" I asked her. The voice was steady, but the brain was still bouncing.

"Well, it was lying on the stairs," she said. "After all, people do fire them."

"How true that is," I said. "But Mr. Lavery probably had a hole in his pocket. He isn't home, is he?"

"Oh no." She shook her head and looked disappointed. "And I don't think it's very nice of him. He promised me the check and I walked over −"

"When was it you phoned him?" I asked.

"Why, yesterday evening." She frowned, not liking so many questions.

"He must have been called away," I said.

She stared at a spot between my big brown eyes.

"Look, Mrs. Fallbrook," I said. "Let's not kid around any longer, Mrs. Fallbrook. Not that I don't love it. And not that I like to say this. But you didn't shoot him, did you − on account of he owed you three months' rent?"

She sat down very slowly on the edge of a chair and worked the tip of her tongue along the scarlet slash of her mouth.

"Why, what a perfectly horrid suggestion," she said angrily. "I don't think you are nice at all. Didn't you say the gun had not been fired?"

"All guns have been fired sometime. All guns have been loaded sometime. This one is not loaded now."

"Well, then −" she made an impatient gesture and sniffed at her oily glove.

"Okay, my idea was wrong. Just a gag anyway. Mr. Lavery was out and you went through the house. Being the owner, you have a key. Is that correct?"

THE LADY IN THE LAKE

"I didn't mean to be interfering," she said, biting a finger. "Perhaps I ought not to have done it. But I have a right to see how things are kept."

"Well, you looked. And you're sure he's not here?"

"I didn't look under the beds or in the icebox," she said coldly. "I called out from the top of the stairs when he didn't answer my ring. Then I went down to the lower hall and called out again. I even peeped into the bedroom." She lowered her eyes as if bashfully and twisted a hand on her knee.

"Well, that's that," I said.

She nodded brightly. "Yes, that's that. And what did you say your name was?"

"Vance," I said. "Philo Vance."

"And what company are you employed with, Mr. Vance?"

"I'm out of work right now," I said. "Until the police commissioner gets into a jam again."

She looked startled. "But you said you came about a car payment."

"That's just part-time work," I said. "A fill-in job."

She rose to her feet and looked at me steadily. Her voice was cold saying: "Then in that case I think you had better leave now."

I said: "I thought I might take a look around first, if you don't mind. There might be something you missed."

"I don't think that is necessary," she said. "This is my house. I'll thank you to leave now, Mr. Vance."

I said: "And if I don't leave, you'll get somebody who will. Take a chair again, Mrs. Fallbrook. I'll just glance through. This gun, you know, is kind of queer."

"But I told you I found it lying on the stairs," she said angrily. "I don't know anything else about it. I don't know anything about guns at all. I – I never shot one in my life." She opened a large blue bag and pulled a handkerchief out of it and sniffled.

"That's your story," I said. "I don't have to get stuck with it."

93

She put her left hand out to me with a pathetic gesture, like the erring wife in *East Lynne*.

"Oh, I shouldn't have come in!" she cried. "It was horrid of me. I know it was. Mr. Lavery will be furious."

"What you shouldn't have done," I said, "was let me find out the gun was empty. Up to then you were holding everything in the deck."

She stamped her foot. That was all the scene lacked. That made it perfect.

"Why, you perfectly loathsome man," she squawked. "Don't you dare touch me! Don't you take a single step towards me! I won't stay in this house another minute with you. How *dare* you be so insulting —"

She caught her voice and snapped it in mid-air like a rubber band. Then she put her head down, purple hat and all, and ran for the door. As she passed me she put a hand out as if to stiff-arm me, but she wasn't near enough and I didn't move. She jerked the door wide and charged out through it and up the walk to the street. The door came slowly shut and I heard her rapid steps above the sound of its closing.

I ran a fingernail along my teeth and punched the point of my jaw with a knuckle, listening. I didn't hear anything anywhere to listen to. A six-shot automatic, fired empty.

"Something," I said out loud, "is all wrong with this scene."

The house seemed now to be abnormally still. I went along the apricot rug and through the archway to the head of the stairs. I stood there for another moment and listened again.

I shrugged and went quietly down the stairs.

16

THE LOWER HALL had a door at each end and two in the middle side by side. One of these was a linen closet and the other was locked. I went along to the end and looked in at a spare bedroom with drawn blinds and no sign of being used.

I went back to the other end of the hall and stepped into a second bedroom with a wide bed, a café-au-lait rug, angular furniture in light wood, a box mirror over the dressing table and a long fluorescent lamp over the mirror. In the corner a crystal greyhound stood on a mirror-top table and beside him a crystal box with cigarettes in it.

Face powder was spilled around on the dressing table. There was a smear of dark lipstick on a towel hanging over the wastebasket. On the bed were pillows side by side, with depressions in them that could have been made by heads. A woman's handkerchief peeped from under one pillow. A pair of sheer black pajamas lay across the foot of the bed. A rather too emphatic trace of chypre hung in the air.

I wondered what Mrs. Fallbrook had thought of all this.

I turned around and looked at myself in the long mirror of a closet door. The door was painted white and had a crystal knob. I turned the knob in my handkerchief and looked inside. The cedar-lined closet was fairly full of man's clothes. There was a nice friendly smell of tweed. The closet was not entirely full of man's clothes.

There was also a woman's black and white tailored suit, mostly white, black and white shoes under it, a Panama with a black and white rolled band on a shelf above it. There were other woman's clothes, but I didn't examine them.

I shut the closet door and went out of the bedroom, holding my handkerchief ready for more doorknobs.

The door next to the linen closet, the locked door, had to be the bathroom. I shook it, but it went on being locked. I bent down and saw there was a short, slit-shaped opening in the middle of the knob. I knew then that the door was fastened by pushing a button in the middle of the knob inside, and that the slit-like opening was for a metal key without wards that would spring the lock open in case somebody fainted in the bathroom, or the kids locked themselves in and got sassy.

The key for this ought to be kept on the top shelf of the linen closet, but it wasn't. I tried my knife blade, but that was too thin. I went back to the bedroom and got a flat nail file off the dresser. That worked. I opened the bathroom door.

A man's sand-colored pajamas were tossed over a painted hamper. A pair of heelless green slippers lay on the floor. There was a safety razor on the edge of the washbowl and a tube of cream with the cap off. The bathroom window was shut, and there was a pungent smell in the air that was not quite like any other smell.

Three empty shells lay bright and coppery on the Nile green tiles of the bathroom floor, and there was a nice clean hole in the frosted pane of the window. To the left and a little above the window were two scarred places in the plaster where the white showed behind the paint and where something, such as a bullet, had gone in.

The shower curtain was green and white oiled silk and it hung on shiny chromium rings and it was drawn across the shower opening. I slid it aside, the rings making a thin scraping noise, which for some reason sounded indecently loud.

I felt my neck creak a little as I bent down. He was there all right – there wasn't anywhere else for him to be. He was huddled in the corner under the two shining faucets, and water dripped slowly on his chest, from the chromium showerhead.

His knees were drawn up but slack. The two holes in his naked chest were dark blue and both of them were close enough to his heart to have killed him. The blood seemed to have been washed away.

His eyes had a curiously bright and expectant look, as if he smelled the morning coffee and would be coming right out.

Nice efficient work. You have just finished shaving and stripped for the shower and you are leaning in against the shower curtain and adjusting the temperature of the water. The door opens behind you and somebody comes in. The somebody appears to have been a woman. She has a gun. You look at the gun and she shoots it.

She misses with three shots. It seems impossible, at such short range, but there it is. Maybe it happens all the time. I've been around so little.

You haven't anywhere to go. You could lunge at her and take a chance, if you were that kind of fellow, and if you were braced for it. But leaning in over the shower faucets, holding the curtain closed, you are off balance. Also you are apt to be somewhat petrified with panic, if you are at all like other people. So there isn't anywhere to go, except into the shower.

That is where you go. You go into it as far as you can, but a shower stall is a small place and the tiled wall stops you. You are backed up against the last wall there is now. You are all out of space, and you are all out of living. And then there are two more shots, possibly three, and you slide down the wall, and your eyes are not even frightened any more now. They are just the empty eyes of the dead.

She reaches in and turns the shower off. She sets the lock of the bathroom door. On her way out of the house she throws the empty gun on the stair carpet. She should worry. It is probably your gun.

Is that right? It had better be right.

I bent and pulled at his arm. Ice couldn't have been any colder or any stiffer. I went out of the bathroom, leaving it unlocked. No need to lock it now. It only makes work for the cops.

I went into the bedroom and pulled the handkerchief out from under the pillow. It was a minute piece of linen rag with a scalloped edge embroidered in red. Two small initials were stitched in the corner, in red. *A.F.*

"Adrienne Fromsett," I said. I laughed. It was a rather ghoulish laugh.

I shook the handkerchief to get some of the chypre out of it and folded it up in a tissue and put it in a pocket. I went back upstairs to the living room and poked around in the desk against the wall. The desk contained no interesting letters, phone numbers or provocative match folders. Or if it did, I didn't find them.

I looked at the phone. It was on a small table against the wall beside the fireplace. It had a long cord so that Mr. Lavery could be lying on his back on the davenport, a cigarette between his smooth brown lips, a tall cool one at the table at his side, and plenty of time for a nice long cozy conversation with a lady friend. An easy, languid, flirtatious, kidding, not too subtle and not too blunt conversation, of the sort he would be apt to enjoy.

All that wasted too. I went away from the telephone to the door and set the lock so I could come in again and shut the door tight, pulling it hard over the sill until the lock clicked. I went up the walk and stood in the sunlight looking across the street at Dr. Almore's house.

Nobody yelled or ran out of the door. Nobody blew a police whistle. Everything was quiet and sunny and calm. No cause for excitement whatever. It's only Marlowe, finding another body. He does it rather well by now. Murder-a-day Marlowe, they call him. They have the meat wagon following him around to follow up on the business he finds.

A nice enough fellow, in an ingenuous sort of way.

I walked back to the intersection and got into my car and started it and backed it and drove away from there.

17

THE BELLHOP AT the Athletic Club was back in three minutes with a nod for me to come with him. We rode up to the fourth floor and went around a corner and he showed me a half-open door.

"Around to the left, sir. As quietly as you can. A few of the members are sleeping."

I went into the club library. It contained books behind glass doors and magazines on a long central table and a lighted portrait of the club's founder. But its real business seemed to be sleeping. Outward-jutting bookcases cut the room into a number of small alcoves and in the alcoves were high-backed leather chairs of an incredible size and softness. In a number of the chairs old boys were snoozing peacefully, their faces violet with high blood pressure, thin racking snores coming out of their pinched noses.

I climbed over a few feet and stole around to the left. Derace Kingsley was in the very last alcove in the far end of the room. He had two chairs arranged side by side, facing into the corner. His big dark head just showed over the top of one of them. I slipped into the empty one and gave him a quick nod.

"Keep your voice down," he said. "This room is for afterluncheon naps. Now what is it? When I employed you it was to save me trouble, not to add trouble to what I already had. You made me break an important engagement."

"I know," I said, and put my face close to his. He smelled of highballs, in a nice way. "She shot him."

His eyebrows jumped and his face got that stony look. His teeth clamped tight. He breathed softly and twisted a large hand on his kneecap.

"Go on," he said, in a voice the size of a marble.

I looked back over the top of my chair. The nearest old geezer was sound asleep and blowing the dusty fuzz in his nostrils back and forth as he breathed.

"No answer at Lavery's place," I said. "Door slightly open. But I noticed yesterday it sticks on the sill. Pushed it open. Room dark, two glasses with drinks having been in them. House very still. In a moment a slim dark woman calling herself Mrs. Fallbrook, landlady, came up the stairs with her glove wrapped around a gun. Said she found it on the stairs. Said she came to collect her three months' back rent. Used her key to get in. Inference is she took the chance to snoop around and look the house over. Took the gun from her and found it had been fired recently, but didn't tell her so. She said Lavery was not home. Got rid of her by making her mad and she departed in high dudgeon. She may call the police, but it's much more likely she will just go out and hunt butterflies and forget the whole thing – except the rent."

I paused. Kingsley's head was turned towards me and his jaw muscles bulged with the way his teeth were clamped. His eyes looked sick.

"I went downstairs. Signs of a woman having spent the night. Pajamas, face powder, perfume, and so on. Bathroom locked, but got it open. Three empty shells on the floor, two shots in the wall, one in the window. Lavery in the shower stall, naked and dead."

"My God!" Kingsley whispered. "Do you mean to say he had a woman with him last night and she shot him this morning in the bathroom?"

"Just what did you think I was trying to say?" I asked.

"Keep your voice down," he groaned. "It's a shock, naturally. Why in the bathroom?"

"Keep your own voice down," I said. "Why not in the bathroom? Could you think of a place where a man would be more completely off guard?"

He said: "You don't know that a woman shot him. I mean, you're not sure, are you?"

"No," I said. "That's true. It might have been somebody who used a small gun and emptied it carelessly to look like a woman's work. The bathroom is downhill, facing outwards on space and I don't think shots down there would be easily heard by anyone not in the house. The woman who spent the night might have left – or there need not have been any woman at all. The appearances could have been faked. *You* might have shot him."

"What would I want to shoot him for?" he almost bleated, squeezing both kneecaps hard. "I'm a civilized man."

That didn't seem to be worth an argument either. I said: "Does your wife own a gun?"

He turned a drawn miserable face to me and said hollowly: "Good God, man, you can't really think that!"

"Well does she?"

He got the words out in small pieces. "Yes – she does. A small automatic."

"You buy it locally?"

"I – I didn't buy it at all. I took it away from a drunk at a party in San Francisco a couple of years ago. He was waving it around, with an idea that that was very funny. I never gave it back to him." He pinched his jaw hard until his knuckles whitened. "He probably doesn't even remember how or when he lost it. He was that kind of a drunk."

"This is working out almost too neatly," I said. "Could you recognize this gun?"

He thought hard, pushing his jaw out and half closing his eyes. I looked back over the chairs again. One of the elderly snoozers had waked himself up with a snort that almost blew him out of his chair. He coughed, scratched his nose with a thin dried-up hand, and fumbled a gold watch out of his vest. He peered at it bleakly, put it away, and went to sleep again.

I reached in my pocket and put the gun on Kingsley's hand. He stared down at it miserably.

"I don't know," he said slowly. "It's like it, but I can't tell."

"There's a serial number on the side," I said.

"Nobody remembers the serial numbers of guns."

"I was hoping you wouldn't," I said. "It would have worried me very much."

His hand closed around the gun and he put it down beside him on the chair.

"The dirty rat," he said softly. "I suppose he ditched her."

"I don't get it," I said. "The motive was inadequate for you, on account of you're a civilized man. But it was adequate for her."

"It's not the same motive," he snapped. "And women are more impetuous than men."

"Like cats are more impetuous than dogs."

"How?"

"Some women are more impetuous than some men. That's all that means. We'll have to have a better motive, if you want your wife to have done it."

He turned his head enough to give me a level stare in which there was no amusement. White crescents were bitten into the corners of his mouth.

"This doesn't seem to me a very good spot for the light touch," he said. "We can't let the police have this gun. Crystal had a permit and the gun was registered. So they will know the number, even if I don't. We can't let them have it."

"But Mrs. Fallbrook knows I had the gun."

He shook his head stubbornly. "We'll have to chance that. Yes, I know you're taking a risk. I intend to make it worth your while. If the set-up were possible for suicide, I'd say put the gun back. But the way you tell it, it isn't."

"No. He'd have to have missed himself with the first three shots. But I can't cover up a murder, even for a ten-dollar bonus. The gun will have to go back."

"I was thinking of more money than that," he said quietly. "I was thinking of five hundred dollars."

"Just what did you expect to buy with it?"

He leaned close to me. His eyes were serious and bleak, but not hard. "Is there anything in Lavery's place, apart from the gun, that might indicate Crystal has been there lately?"

"A black and white dress and a hat like the bellhop in Bernardino described on her. There may be a dozen things I don't know about. There almost certainly will be fingerprints. You say she was never printed, but that doesn't mean they won't get her prints to check. Her bedroom at home will be full of them. So will the cabin at Little Fawn Lake. And her car."

"We ought to get the car —" he started to say. I stopped him.

"No use. Too many other places. What kind of perfume does she use?"

He looked blank for an instant. "Oh — Gillerlain Regal, the Champagne of Perfumes," he said woodenly. "A Chanel number once in a while."

"What's this stuff of yours like?"

"A kind of chypre. Sandalwood chypre."

"The bedroom reeks with it," I said. "It smelled like cheap stuff to me. But I'm no judge."

"Cheap?" he said, stung to the quick. "My God, cheap? We get thirty dollars an ounce for it."

"Well, this stuff smelled more like three dollars a gallon."

He put his hands down hard on his knees and shook his head. "I'm talking about money," he said. "Five hundred dollars. A check for it right now."

I let the remark fall to the ground, eddying like a soiled feather. One of the old boys behind us stumbled to his feet and groped his way wearily out of the room.

Kingsley said gravely: "I hired you to protect me from scandal, and of course to protect my wife, if she needed it. Through no fault of yours the chance to avoid scandal is pretty well shot. It's a question of my wife's neck now. I don't believe she shot Lavery. I have no reason for that belief. None at all. I just feel the conviction. She may even have been there last night, this gun may even be her gun. It doesn't prove she killed him. She would be as careless with the gun as with anything else. Anybody could have got hold of it."

"The cops down there won't work very hard to believe that," I said. "If the one I met is a fair specimen, they'll just pick the first head they see and start swinging with their blackjacks. And hers will certainly be the first head they see when they look the situation over."

He ground the heels of his hands together. His misery had a theatrical flavor, as real misery so often has.

"I'll go along with you up to a point," I said. "The set-up down there is almost too good, at first sight. She leaves clothes there she has been seen wearing and which can probably be traced. She leaves the gun on the stairs. It's hard to think she would be as dumb as that."

"You give me a little heart," Kingsley said wearily.

"But none of that means anything," I said. "Because we are looking at it from the angle of calculation, and people who commit crimes of passion or hatred, just commit them and walk out. Everything I have heard indicates that she is a reckless foolish woman. There's no sign of planning in any of the scene down there. There's every sign of a complete lack of planning. But even if there wasn't a thing down there to point to your wife, the cops would tie her up to Lavery. They will investigate his background, his friends, his women. Her name is bound to crop up somewhere along the line, and when it does, the fact that she has been out of sight for a month will make them sit up and rub their horny palms with glee. And of course they'll trace the gun, and if it's her gun —"

His hand dived for the gun in the chair beside him.

"Nope," I said. "They'll have to have the gun. Marlowe may be a very smart guy and very fond of you personally, but he can't risk the suppression of such vital evidence as the gun that killed a man. Whatever I do has to be on the basis that your wife is an obvious suspect, but that the obviousness can be wrong."

He groaned and put his big hand out with the gun on it. I took it and put it away. Then I took it out again and said: "Lend me your handkerchief. I don't want to use mine. I might be searched."

He handed me a stiff white handkerchief and I wiped the gun off carefully all over and dropped it into my pocket. I handed him back the handkerchief.

"My prints are all right," I said. "But I don't want yours on it. Here's the only thing I can do. Go back down there and replace the gun and call the law. Ride it out with them and let the chips fall where they have to. The story will have to come out. What I was doing down there and why. At the worst they'll find her and prove she killed him. At the best they'll find her a lot quicker than I can and let me use my energies proving she didn't kill him, which means, in effect, proving that somebody else did. Are you game for that?"

He nodded slowly. He said: "Yes – and the five hundred stands. For showing Crystal didn't kill him."

"I don't expect to earn it," I said. "You may as well understand that now. How well did Miss Fromsett know Lavery? Out of office hours?"

His face tightened up like a charleyhorse. His fists went into hard lumps on his thighs. He said nothing.

"She looked kind of queer when I asked her for his address yesterday morning," I said.

He let a breath out slowly.

"Like a bad taste in the mouth," I said. "Like a romance that fouled out. Am I too blunt?"

His nostrils quivered a little and his breath made noise in them for a moment. Then he relaxed and said quietly:

"She – she knew him rather well – at one time. She's a girl who would do about what she pleased in that way. Lavery was, I guess, a fascinating bird – to women."

"I'll have to talk to her," I said.

"Why?" he asked shortly. Red patches showed in his cheeks.

"Never mind why. It's my business to ask all sorts of questions of all sorts of people."

"Talk to her then," he said tightly. "As a matter of fact she knew the Almores. She knew Almore's wife, the one who killed herself. Lavery knew her too. Could that have any possible connection with this business?"

"I don't know. You're in love with her, aren't you?"

"I'd marry her tomorrow, if I could," he said stiffly.

I nodded and stood up. I looked back along the room. It was almost empty now. At the far end a couple of elderly relics were still blowing bubbles. The rest of the soft chair boys had staggered back to whatever it was they did when they were conscious.

"There's just one thing," I said, looking down at Kingsley. "Cops get very hostile when there is a delay in calling them after a murder. There's been delay this time and there will be more. I'd like to go down there as if it was the first visit today. I think I can make it that way, if I leave the Fallbrook woman out."

"Fallbrook?" He hardly knew what I was talking about. "Who the hell – oh yes, I remember."

"Well, don't remember. I'm almost certain they'll never hear a peep from her. She's not the kind to have anything to do with the police of her own free will."

"I understand," he said.

"Be sure you handle it right then. Questions will be asked you *before* you are told Lavery is dead, before I'm allowed to get in touch with you – so far as they know. Don't fall into any traps. If you do, I won't be able to find anything out. I'll be in the clink."

"You could call me from the house down there – before you call the police," he said reasonably.

"I know. But the fact that I don't will be in my favor. And they'll check the phone calls one of the first things they do. And if I call you from anywhere else, I might just as well admit that I came up here to see you."

"I understand," he said again. "You can trust me to handle it."

We shook hands and I left him standing there.

18

THE ATHLETIC CLUB was on a corner across the street and half a block down from the Treloar Building. I crossed and walked north to the entrance. They had finished laying rose-colored concrete where the rubber sidewalk had been. It was fenced around, leaving a narrow gangway in and out of the building. The space was clotted with office help going in from lunch.

The Gillerlain Company's reception room looked even emptier than the day before. The same fluffy little blonde was tucked in behind the PBX in the corner. She gave me a quick smile and I gave her the gunman's salute, a stiff forefinger pointing at her, the three lower fingers tucked back under it, and the thumb wiggling up and down like a western gun fighter fanning his hammer. She laughed heartily, without making a sound. This was more fun than she had had in a week.

I pointed to Miss Fromsett's empty desk and the little blonde nodded and pushed a plug in and spoke. A door opened and Miss Fromsett swayed elegantly out to her desk and sat down and gave me her cool expectant eyes.

"Yes, Mr. Marlowe? Mr. Kingsley is not in, I'm afraid."

"I just came from him. Where do we talk?"

"Talk?"

"I have something to show you."

"Oh, yes?" She looked me over thoughtfully. A lot of guys had probably tried to show her things, including etchings. At another time I wouldn't have been above taking a flutter at it myself.

"Business," I said. "Mr. Kingsley's business."

She stood up and opened the gate in the railing. "We may as well go into his office then."

We went in. She held the door for me. As I passed her I sniffed. Sandalwood. I said:

"Gillerlain Regal, the Champagne of Perfumes?"

She smiled faintly, holding the door. "On my salary?"

"I didn't say anything about your salary. You don't look like a girl who has to buy her own perfume."

"Yes, that's what it is," she said. "And if you want to know, I detest wearing perfume in the office. He makes me."

We went down the long dim office and she took a chair at the end of the desk. I sat where I had sat the day before. We looked at each other. She was wearing tan today, with a ruffled jabot at her throat. She looked a little warmer, but still no prairie fire.

I offered her one of Kingsley's cigarettes. She took it, took a light from his lighter, and leaned back.

"We needn't waste time being cagey," I said. "You know by now who I am and what I am doing. If you didn't know yesterday morning, it's only because he loves to play big shot."

She looked down at the hand that lay on her knee, then lifted her eyes and smiled almost shyly.

"He's a great guy," she said. "In spite of the heavy executive act he likes to put on. He's the only guy that gets fooled by it after all. And if you only knew what he has stood from that little tramp" – she waved her cigarette – "well, perhaps I'd better leave that out. What was it you wanted to see me about?"

"Kingsley said you knew the Almores."

"I knew Mrs. Almore. That is, I met her a couple of times."

"Where?"

"At a friend's house. Why?"

"At Lavery's house?"

"You're not going to be insolent, are you, Mr. Marlowe?"

"I don't know what your definition of that would be. I'm going to talk business as if it were business, not international diplomacy."

"Very well." She nodded slightly. "At Chris Lavery's house, yes. I used to go there – once in a while. He had cocktail parties."

"Then Lavery knew the Almores – or Mrs. Almore."

She flushed very slightly. "Yes. Quite well."

"And a lot of other women – quite well, too. I don't doubt that. Did Mrs. Kingsley know her too?"

"Yes, better than I did. They called each other by their first names. Mrs. Almore is dead, you know. She committed suicide, about a year and a half ago."

"Any doubt about that?"

She raised her eyebrows, but the expression looked artificial to me, as if it just went with the question I asked, as a matter of form.

She said: "Have you any particular reason for asking that question in that particular way? I mean, has it anything to do with – with what you are doing?"

"I didn't think so. I still don't know that it has. But yesterday Dr. Almore called a cop just because I looked at his house. After he had found out from my car license who I was. The cop got pretty tough with me, just for being there. He didn't know what I was doing and I didn't tell him I had been calling on Lavery. But Dr. Almore must have known that. He had seen me in front of Lavery's house. Now why would he think it necessary to call a cop? And why would the cop think it smart to say that the last fellow who tried to put the bite on Almore ended up on the road gang? And why would the cop ask me if her folks – meaning Mrs. Almore's folks, I suppose – had hired me? If you can answer any of those questions, I might know whether it's any of my business."

She thought about it for a moment, giving me one quick glance while she was thinking, and then looking away again.

"I only met Mrs. Almore twice," she said slowly. "But I think I can answer your questions – all of them. The last time I met her was at Lavery's place, as I said, and there were quite a lot of people there. There was a lot of drinking and loud talk. The women were not with their husbands and the men were not with their wives, if any. There was a man there named Brownwell who was very tight. He's in the navy now, I heard. He was ribbing Mrs. Almore about her husband's practice. The idea seemed to be that he was one of those doctors who run around all night with a case of loaded hypodermic needles, keeping the local fast set from having pink elephants for breakfast. Florence Almore said she didn't care how her husband got his money so long as he got plenty of it and she had the spending of it. She was tight too and not a very nice person sober, I should imagine. One of these slinky glittering females who laugh too much and sprawl all over their chairs, showing a great deal of leg. A very light blonde with a high color and indecently large baby-blue eyes. Well, Brownwell told her not to worry, it would always be a good racket. In and out of the patient's house in fifteen minutes and anywhere from ten to fifty bucks a trip. But one thing bothered him, he said, how ever a doctor could get hold of so much dope without underworld contacts. He asked Mrs. Almore if they had many nice gangsters to dinner at their house. She threw a glass of liquor in his face."

I grinned, but Miss Fromsett didn't. She crushed her cigarette out in Kingsley's big copper and glass tray and looked at me soberly.

"Fair enough," I said. "Who wouldn't, unless he had a large hard fist to throw?"

"Yes. A few weeks later Florence Almore was found dead in the garage late at night. The door of the garage was shut and the car motor was running." She stopped and moistened her lips slightly. "It was Chris Lavery who found her. Coming home at God knows what o'clock in the morning. She was lying on the concrete floor in pajamas, with her head under a blanket which was also over the exhaust pipe of the car. Dr. Almore was out. There was nothing about the affair in the papers, except that she had died suddenly. It was well hushed up."

She lifted her clasped hands a little and then let them fall slowly into her lap again. I said:

"Was something wrong with it, then?"

"People thought so, but they always do. Some time later I heard what purported to be the lowdown. I met this man Brownwell on Vine Street and he asked me to have a drink with him. I didn't like him, but I had half an hour to kill. We sat at the back of Levy's bar and he asked me if I remembered the babe who threw the drink in his face. I said I did. The conversation then went something very like this. I remember it very well.

"Brownwell said: 'Our pal Chris Lavery is sitting pretty, if he ever runs out of girl friends he can touch for dough.'

"I said: 'I don't think I understand.'

"He said: 'Hell, maybe you don't want to. The night the Almore woman died she was over at Lou Condy's place losing her shirt at roulette. She got into a tantrum and said the wheels were crooked and made a scene. Condy practically had to drag her into his office. He got hold of Dr. Almore through the Physicians' Exchange and after a while the doc came over. He shot her with one of his busy little needles. Then he went away, leaving Condy to get her home. It seems he had a very urgent case. So Condy took her home and the doc's office nurse showed up, having been called by the doc, and Condy carried her upstairs and the nurse put her to bed. Condy went back to his chips. So she had to be carried to bed and yet the same night she got up and walked down to the family garage and finished herself off with monoxide. What do you think of that?' Brownwell was asking me.

"I said: 'I don't know anything about it. How do you?'

"He said: 'I know a reporter on the rag they call a newspaper down there. There was no inquest and no autopsy. If any tests were made, nothing was told about them. They don't have a regular coroner down there. The undertakers take turns at being acting coroner, a week at a time. They're pretty well subservient to the political gang, naturally. It's easy to fix a thing like that in a small town, if anybody with any pull wants it fixed. And Condy had plenty at that time. He didn't want the publicity of an investigation and neither did the doctor.'"

Miss Fromsett stopped talking and waited for me to say something. When I didn't, she went on: "I suppose you know what all this meant to Brownwell."

"Sure. Almore finished her off and then he and Condy between them bought a fix. It has been done in cleaner little cities than Bay City ever tried to be. But that isn't all the story, is it?"

"No. It seems Mrs. Almore's parents hired a private detective. He was a man who ran a night watchman service down there and he was actually the second man on the scene that night, after Chris. Brownwell said he must have had something in the way of information but he never got a chance to use it. They arrested him for drunk driving and he got a jail sentence."

I said: "Is that all?"

She nodded. "And if you think I remember it too well, it's part of my job to remember conversations."

"What I was thinking was that it doesn't have to add up to very much. I don't see where it has to touch Lavery, even if he was the one who found her. Your gossipy friend Brownwell seems to think what happened gave somebody a chance to blackmail the doctor. But there would have to be some evidence, especially when you're trying to put the bite on a man who has already cleared himself with the law."

Miss Fromsett said: "I think so too. And I'd like to think blackmail was one of the nasty little tricks Chris Lavery didn't quite run to. I think that's all I can tell you, Mr. Marlowe. And I ought to be outside."

She started to get up. I said: "It's not quite all. I have something to show you."

I got the little perfumed rag that had been under Lavery's pillow out of my pocket and leaned over to drop it on the desk in front of her.

19

SHE LOOKED AT the handkerchief, looked at me, picked up a pencil and pushed the little piece of linen around with the eraser end.

"What's on it?" she asked. "Fly spray?"

"Some kind of sandalwood, I thought."

"A cheap synthetic. Repulsive is a mild word for it. And why did you want me to look at this handkerchief, Mr. Marlowe?" She leaned back again and stared at me with level cool eyes.

"I found it in Chris Lavery's house, under the pillow on his bed. It has initials on it."

She unfolded the handkerchief without touching it by using the rubber tip of the pencil. Her face got a little grim and taut.

"It has two letters embroidered on it," she said in a cold angry voice. "They happen to be the same letters as my initials. Is that what you mean?"

"Right," I said. "He probably knows half a dozen women with the same initials."

"So you're going to be nasty after all," she said quietly.

"Is it your handkerchief – or isn't it?"

She hesitated. She reached out to the desk and very quietly got herself another cigarette and lit it with a match. She shook the match slowly, watching the small flame creep along the wood.

"Yes, it's mine," she said. "I must have dropped it there. It's a long time ago. And I assure you I didn't put it under a pillow on his bed. Is that what you wanted to know?"

I didn't say anything, and she added: "He must have lent it to some woman who – who would like this kind of perfume."

"I get a mental picture of the woman," I said. "And she doesn't quite go with Lavery."

Her upper lip curled a little. It was a long upper lip. I like long upper lips.

"I think," she said, "you ought to do a little work on your mental picture of Chris Lavery. Any touch of refinement you may have noticed is purely coincidental."

"That's not a nice thing to say about a dead man," I said.

For a moment she just sat there and looked at me as if I hadn't said anything and she was waiting for me to say something. Then a slow shudder started at her throat and passed over her whole body. Her hands clenched and the cigarette bent into a crook. She looked down at it and threw it into the ashtray with a quick jerk of her arm.

"He was shot in his shower," I said. "And it looks as if it was done by some woman who spent the night there. He had just been shaving. The woman left a gun on the stairs and this handkerchief on the bed."

She moved very slightly in her chair. Her eyes were perfectly empty now. Her face was as cold as a carving.

"And did you expect me to be able to give you information about that?" she asked me bitterly.

"Look, Miss Fromsett, I'd like to be smooth and distant and subtle about all this too. I'd like to play this sort of game just once the way somebody like you would like it to be played. But nobody will let me – not the clients, nor the cops, nor the people I play against. However hard I try to be nice I always end up with my nose in the dirt and my thumb feeling for somebody's eye."

She nodded as if she had only just barely heard me. "When was he shot?" she asked, and then shuddered slightly again.

"This morning, I suppose. Not long after he got up. I said he had just shaved and was going to take a shower."

"That," she said, "would probably have been quite late. I've been here since eight-thirty."

"I didn't think you shot him."

"Awfully kind of you," she said. "But it is my handkerchief, isn't it? Although not my perfume. But I don't suppose policemen are very sensitive to quality in perfume – or in anything else."

"No – and that goes for private detectives too," I said. "Are you enjoying this a lot?"

"God," she said, and put the back of her hand hard against her mouth.

"He was shot at five or six times," I said. "And missed all but twice. He was cornered in the shower stall. It was a pretty grim scene, I should think. There was a lot of hate on one side of it. Or a pretty cold-blooded mind."

"He was quite easy to hate," she said emptily. "And poison-ously easy to love. Women – even decent women – make such ghastly mistakes about men."

"All you're telling me is that you once thought you loved him, but not any more, and that you didn't shoot him."

"Yes." Her voice was light and dry now, like the perfume she didn't like to wear at the office. "I'm sure you'll respect the confidence." She laughed shortly and bitterly. "Dead," she said. "The poor, egotistical, cheap, nasty, handsome, treacher-ous guy. Dead and cold and done with. No, Mr. Marlowe, I didn't shoot him."

I waited, letting her work it out of her. After a moment she said quietly: "Does Mr. Kingsley know?"

I nodded.

"And the police, of course."

"Not yet. At least not from me. I found him. The house door wasn't quite shut. I went in. I found him."

She picked the pencil up and poked at the handkerchief again. "Does Mr. Kingsley know about this scented rag?"

"Nobody knows about that, except you and I, and whoever put it there."

"Nice of you," she said dryly. "And nice of you to think what you thought."

"You have a certain quality of aloofness and dignity that I like," I said. "But don't run it into the ground. What would you expect me to think? Do I pull the hankie out from under the pillow and sniff it and hold it out and say, 'Well, well, Miss Adrienne Fromsett's initials and all. Miss Fromsett must have known Lavery, perhaps very intimately. Let's say, just for the book, as intimately as my nasty little mind can conceive. And that would be pretty damn intimately. But this is cheap synthetic sandalwood and Miss Fromsett wouldn't use cheap scent. And this was under Lavery's pillow and Miss Fromsett just never keeps her hankies under a man's pillow. Therefore this has absolutely nothing to do with Miss Fromsett. It's just an optical delusion.'"

"Oh shut up," she said.

I grinned.

"What kind of girl do you think I am?" she snapped.

"I came in too late to tell you."

She flushed, but delicately and all over her face this time. Then, "Have you any idea who did it?"

"Ideas, but that's all they are. I'm afraid the police are going to find it simple. Some of Mrs. Kingsley's clothes are hanging in Lavery's closet. And when they know the whole story — including what happened at Little Fawn Lake yesterday — I'm afraid they'll just reach for the handcuffs. They have to find her first. But that won't be so hard for them."

"Crystal Kingsley," she said emptily. "So he couldn't be spared even that."

I said: "It doesn't have to be. It could be an entirely different motivation, something we know nothing about. It could have been somebody like Dr. Almore."

She looked up quickly, then shook her head. "It could be," I insisted. "We don't know anything against it. He was pretty nervous yesterday, for a man who has nothing to be afraid of. But, of course, it isn't only the guilty who are afraid."

I stood up and tapped on the edge of the desk looking down at her. She had a lovely neck. She pointed to the handkerchief.

"What about that?" she asked dully.

"If it was mine, I'd wash that cheap scent out of it."

"It has to mean something, doesn't it? It might mean a lot."

I laughed. "I don't think it means anything at all. Women are always leaving their handkerchiefs around. A fellow like Lavery would collect them and keep them in a drawer with a sandalwood sachet. Somebody would find the stock and take one out to use. Or he would lend them, enjoying the reactions to the other girls' initials. I'd say he was that kind of a heel. Goodby, Miss Fromsett, and thanks for talking to me."

I started to go, then I stopped and asked her: "Did you hear the name of the reporter down there who gave Brownwell all his information?"

She shook her head.

"Or the name of Mrs. Almore's parents?"

"Not that either. But I could probably find that out for you. I'd be glad to try."

"How?"

"Those things are usually printed in death notices, aren't they? There is pretty sure to have been a death notice in the Los Angeles papers."

"That would be very nice of you," I said. I ran a finger along the edge of the desk and looked at her sideways. Pale ivory skin, dark and lovely eyes, hair as light as hair can be and as dark as night can be.

I walked back down the room and out. The little blonde at the PBX looked at me expectantly, her small red lips parted, waiting for more fun.

I didn't have any more. I went on out.

20

NO POLICE CARS stood in front of Lavery's house, nobody hung around on the sidewalk and when I pushed the front door open there was no smell of cigar or cigarette smoke inside. The sun had gone away from the windows and a fly buzzed softly over one of the liquor glasses. I went down to the end and hung over the railing that led downstairs. Nothing moved in Mr. Lavery's house. Nothing made sound except very faintly down below in the bathroom the quiet trickle of water dripping on a dead man's shoulder.

I went to the telephone and looked up the number of the police department in the directory. I dialed and while I was waiting for an answer, I took the little automatic out of my pocket and laid it on the table beside the telephone.

When the male voice said: "Bay City Police – Smoot talking," I said: "There's been a shooting at 623 Altair Street. Man named Lavery lives there. He's dead."

"Six-two-three Altair. Who are you?"

"The name is Marlowe."

"You right there in the house?"

"Right."

"Don't touch anything at all."

I hung up, sat down on the davenport and waited.

Not very long. A siren whined far off, growing louder with great surges of sound. Tires screamed at a corner, and the siren wail died to a metallic growl, then to silence, and the tires screamed again in front of the house. The Bay City police conserving rubber. Steps hit the sidewalk and I went over to the front door and opened it.

Two uniformed cops barged into the room. They were the usual large size and they had the usual weathered faces and suspicious eyes. One of them had a carnation tucked under his cap, behind his right ear. The other one was older, a little gray and grim. They stood and looked at me warily, then the older one said briefly:

"All right, where is it?"

"Downstairs in the bathroom, behind the shower curtain."

"You stay here with him, Eddie."

He went rapidly along the room and disappeared. The other one looked at me steadily and said out of the corner of his mouth:

"Don't make any false moves, buddy."

I sat down on the davenport again. The cop ranged the room with his eyes. There were sounds below stairs, feet walking. The cop with me suddenly spotted the gun lying on the telephone table. He charged at it violently, like a downfield blocker.

"This the death gun?" he almost shouted.

"I should imagine so. It's been fired."

"Ha!" He leaned over the gun, baring his teeth at me, and put his hand to his holster. His finger tickled the flap off the stud and he grasped the butt of the black revolver.

"You should what?" he barked.

"I should imagine so."

"That's very good," he sneered. "That's very good indeed."

"It's not that good," I said.

He reeled back a little. His eyes were being careful of me. "What you shoot him for?" he growled.

"I've wondered and wondered."

"Oh, a wisenheimer."

"Let's just sit down and wait for the homicide boys," I said. "I'm reserving my defense."

"Don't give me none of that," he said.

"I'm not giving you any of anything. If I had shot him, I wouldn't be here. I wouldn't have called up. You wouldn't have found the gun. Don't work so hard on the case. You won't be on it more than ten minutes."

His eyes looked hurt. He took his cap off and the carnation dropped to the floor. He bent and picked it up and twirled it between his fingers, then dropped it behind the fire screen.

"Better not do that," I told him. "They might think it's a clue and waste a lot of time on it."

"Aw hell." He bent over the screen and retrieved the carnation and put it in his pocket. "You know all the answers, don't you, buddy?"

The other cop came back up the stairs, looking grave. He stood in the middle of the floor and looked at his wrist watch and made a note in a notebook and then looked out of the front windows, holding the venetian blinds to one side to do it.

The one who had stayed with me said: "Can I look now?"

"Let it lie, Eddie. Nothing in it for us. You call the coroner?"

"I thought homicide would do that."

"Yeah, that's right. Captain Webber will be on it and he likes to do everything himself." He looked at me and said: "You're a man named Marlowe?"

I said I was a man named Marlowe.

"He's a wise guy, knows all the answers," Eddie said.

The older one looked at me absently, looked at Eddie absently, spotted the gun lying on the telephone table and looked at that not at all absently.

"Yeah, that's the death gun," Eddie said. "I ain't touched it."

The other nodded. "The boys are not so fast today. What's your line, mister? Friend of his?" He made a thumb towards the floor.

"Saw him yesterday for the first time. I'm a private operative from L.A."

"Oh." He looked at me very sharply. The other cop looked at me with deep suspicion.

"Cripes, that means everything will be all balled up," he said.

That was the first sensible remark he had made. I grinned at him affectionately.

The older cop looked out of the front window again. "That's the Almore place across the street, Eddie," he said.

Eddie went and looked with him. "Sure is," he said. "You can read the plate. Say, this guy downstairs might be the guy —"

"Shut up," the other one said and dropped the venetian blind. They both turned around and stared at me woodenly.

A car came down the block and stopped and a door slammed and more steps came down the walk. The older of the prowl car boys opened the door to two men in plain clothes, one of whom I already knew.

21

THE ONE WHO came first was a small man for a cop, middleaged, thin-faced, with a permanently tired expression. His nose was sharp and bent a little to one side, as if somebody had given it the elbow one time when it was into something. His blue porkpie hat was set very square on his head and chalk-white hair showed under it. He wore a dull brown suit and his hands were in the side pockets of the jacket, with the thumbs outside the seam.

The man behind him was Degarmo, the big cop with the dusty blond hair and the metallic blue eyes and the savage, lined face who had not liked my being in front of Dr. Almore's house.

The two uniformed men looked at the small man and touched their caps.

"The body's in the basement, Captain Webber. Been shot twice after a couple of misses, looks like. Dead quite some time. This party's name is Marlowe. He's a private eye from Los Angeles. I didn't question him beyond that."

"Quite right," Webber said sharply. He had a suspicious voice. He passed a suspicious eye over my face and nodded briefly. "I'm Captain Webber," he said. "This is Lieutenant Degarmo. We'll look at the body first."

He went along the room. Degarmo looked at me as if he had never seen me before and followed him. They went downstairs, the older of the two prowl car men with them. The cop called Eddie and I stared each other down for a while.

I said: "This is right across the street from Dr. Almore's place, isn't it?"

All the expression went out of his face. There hadn't been much to go. "Yeah. So what?"

"So nothing," I said.

He was silent. The voices came up from below, blurred and indistinct. The cop cocked his ear and said in a more friendly tone: "You remember that one?"

"A little."

He laughed. "They killed that one pretty," he said. "They wrapped it up and hid it in back of the shelf. The top shelf in the bathroom closet. The one you can't reach without standing on a chair."

"So they did," I said. "I wonder why."

The cop looked at me sternly. "There was good reasons, pal. Don't think there wasn't. You know this Lavery well?"

"Not well."

"On to him for something?"

"Working on him a little," I said. "You knew him?"

The cop called Eddie shook his head. "Nope. I just remembered it was a guy from this house found Almore's wife in the garage that night."

"Lavery may not have been here then," I said.

"How long's he been here?"

"I don't know," I said.

"Would be about a year and a half," the cop said, musingly. "The L.A. papers give it any play?"

"Paragraph on the Home Counties page," I said, just to be moving my mouth.

He scratched his ear and listened. Steps were coming back up the stairs. The cop's face went blank and he moved away from me and straightened up.

Captain Webber hurried over to the telephone and dialed the number and spoke, then held the phone away from his ear and looked back over his shoulder.

"Who's deputy coroner this week, Al?"

"Ed Garland," the big lieutenant said woodenly.

"Call Ed Garland," Webber said into the phone. "Have him come over right away. And tell the flash squad to step on it."

He put the phone down and barked sharply: "Who handled this gun?"

I said: "I did."

He came over and teetered on his heels in front of me and pushed his small sharp chin up at me. He held the gun delicately on a handkerchief in his hand.

"Don't you know enough not to handle a weapon found at the scene of a crime?"

"Certainly," I said. "But when I handled it I didn't know there had been a crime. I didn't know the gun had been fired. It was lying on the stairs and I thought it had been dropped."

"A likely story," Webber said bitterly. "You get a lot of that sort of thing in your business?"

"A lot of what sort of thing?"

He kept his hard stare on me and didn't answer.

I said: "How would it be for me to tell you my story as it happened?"

He bridled at me like a cockerel. "Suppose you answer my questions exactly as I choose to put them."

I didn't say anything to that. Webber swiveled sharply and said to the two uniformed men: "You boys can get back to your car and check in with the despatcher."

They saluted and went out, closing the door softly until it stuck, then getting as mad at it as anybody else. Webber listened until their car went away. Then he put the bleak and callous eye on me once more.

"Let me see your identification."

I handed him my wallet and he rooted in it. Degarmo sat in a chair and crossed his legs and stared up blankly at the ceiling. He got a match out of his pocket and chewed the end of it. Webber gave me back my wallet. I put it away.

"People in your line make a lot of trouble," he said.

"Not necessarily," I said.

He raised his voice. It had been sharp enough before. "I said they made a lot of trouble, and a lot of trouble is what

I meant. But get this straight. You're not going to make any in Bay City."

I didn't answer him. He jabbed a forefinger at me.

"You're from the big town," he said. "You think you're tough and you think you're wise. Don't worry. We can handle you. We're a small place, but we're very compact. We don't have any political tug-of-war down here. We work on the straight line and we work fast. Don't worry about us, mister."

"I'm not worrying," I said. "I don't have anything to worry about. I'm just trying to make a nice clean dollar."

"And don't give me any of the flip talk," Webber said. "I don't like it."

Degarmo brought his eyes down from the ceiling and curled a forefinger to stare at the nail. He spoke in a heavy bored voice.

"Look, chief, the fellow downstairs is called Lavery. He's dead. I knew him a little. He was a chaser."

"What of it?" Webber snapped, not looking away from me.

"The whole set-up indicates a dame," Degarmo said. "You know what these private eyes work at. Divorce stuff. Suppose we'd let him tie into it, instead of just trying to scare him dumb."

"If I'm scaring him," Webber said, "I'd like to know it. I don't see any signs of it."

He walked over to the front window and yanked the venetian blind up. Light poured into the room almost dazzlingly, after the long dimness. He came back bouncing on his heels and poked a thin hard finger at me and said:

"Talk."

I said, "I'm working for a Los Angeles businessman who can't take a lot of loud publicity. That's why he hired me. A month ago his wife ran off and later a telegram came which indicated she had gone with Lavery. But my client met Lavery in town a couple of days ago and he denied it. The client believed him enough to get worried. It seems the lady is pretty reckless. She might have taken up with some bad company and got into a jam. I came down to see Lavery and he denied to me that he had gone with her. I half believed him but later I got reasonable proof that he had been with her in a San Bernardino hotel the night she was believed to have left the mountain cabin where she had been staying. With that in my pocket I came down to tackle Lavery again. No answer to the bell, the door was slightly open. I came inside, looked around, found the gun and searched the house. I found him. Just the way he is now."

"You had no right to search the house," Webber said coldly.

"Of course not," I agreed. "But I wouldn't be likely to pass up the chance either."

"The name of this man you're working for?"

"Kingsley." I gave him the Beverly Hills address. "He manages a cosmetic company in the Treloar Building on Olive. The Gillerlain Company."

Webber looked at Degarmo. Degarmo wrote lazily on an envelope. Webber looked back at me and said: "What else?"

"I went up to this mountain cabin where the lady had been staying. It's at a place called Little Fawn Lake, near Puma Point, forty-six miles into the mountains from San Bernardino."

I looked at Degarmo. He was writing slowly. His hand stopped a moment and seemed to hang in the air stiffly, then it dropped to the envelope and wrote again. I went on:

"About a month ago the wife of the caretaker at Kingsley's place up there had a fight with him and left, as everybody thought. Yesterday she was found drowned in the lake."

Webber almost closed his eyes and rocked on his heels. Almost softly he asked: "Why are you telling me this? Are you implying a connection?"

"There's a connection in time. Lavery had been up there. I don't know of any other connection, but I thought I'd better mention it."

Degarmo was sitting very still, looking at the floor in front of him. His face was tight and he looked even more savage than usual. Webber said:

"This woman that was drowned? Suicide?"

"Suicide or murder. She left a goodbye note. But her husband has been arrested on suspicion. The name is Chess. Bill and Muriel Chess, his wife."

"I don't want any part of that," Webber said sharply. "Let's confine ourselves to what went on here."

"Nothing went on here," I said, looking at Degarmo. "I've been down here twice. The first time I talked to Lavery and didn't get anywhere. The second time I didn't talk to him and didn't get anywhere."

Webber said slowly: "I'm going to ask you a question and I want an honest answer. You won't want to give it, but now will be as good a time as later. You know I'll get it eventually. The question is this. You have looked through the house and I imagine pretty thoroughly. Have you seen anything that suggests to you that this Kingsley woman has been here?"

"That's not a fair question," I said. "It calls for a conclusion of the witness."

"I want an answer to it," he said grimly. "This isn't a court of law."

"The answer is yes," I said. "There are women's clothes hanging in a closet downstairs that have been described to me as being worn by Mrs. Kingsley at San Bernardino the night she met Lavery there. The description was not exact though. A black and white suit, mostly white, and a Panama hat with a rolled black and white band."

Degarmo snapped a finger against the envelope he was holding. "You must be a great guy for a client to have working for him," he said. "That puts the woman right in this house where a murder has been committed and she is the woman he's supposed to have gone away with. I don't think we'll have to look far for the killer, chief."

Webber was staring at me fixedly, with little or no expression on his face but a kind of tight watchfulness. He nodded absently to what Degarmo had said.

I said: "I'm assuming you fellows are not a pack of damn fools. The clothes are tailored and easy to trace. I've saved you an hour by telling you, perhaps even no more than a phone call."

"Anything else?" Webber asked quietly.

Before I could answer, a car stopped outside the house, and then another. Webber skipped over to open the door. Three men came in, a short curly-haired man and a large ox-like man, both carrying heavy black leather cases. Behind them a tall thin man in a dark gray suit and black tie. He had very bright eyes and a poker face.

Webber pointed a finger at the curly-haired man and said: "Downstairs in the bathroom, Busoni. I want a lot of prints from all over the house, particularly any that seem to be made by a woman. It will be a long job."

"I do all the work," Busoni grunted. He and the ox-like man went along the room and down the stairs.

"We have a corpse for you, Garland," Webber said to the third man. "Let's go down and look at him. You've ordered the wagon?"

The bright-eyed man nodded briefly and he and Webber went downstairs after the other two.

Degarmo put the envelope and pencil away. He stared at me woodenly.

I said: "Am I supposed to talk about our conversation yesterday – or is that a private transaction?"

"Talk about it all you like," he said. "It's our job to protect the citizen."

"You talk about it," I said. "I'd like to know more about the Almore case."

He flushed slowly and his eyes got mean. "You said you didn't know Almore."

"I didn't yesterday, or know anything about him. Since then I've learned that Lavery knew Mrs. Almore, that she committed suicide, that Lavery found her dead, and that Lavery has at least been suspected of blackmailing him – or of being in a position to blackmail him. Also both your prowl car boys seemed interested in the fact that Almore's house was across the street from here. And one of them remarked that the case had been killed pretty, or words to that effect."

Degarmo said in a slow deadly tone: "I'll have the badge off the son of a bitch. All they do is flap their mouths. God damn empty-headed bastards."

"Then there's nothing in it," I said.

He looked at his cigarette. "Nothing in what?"

"Nothing in the idea that Almore murdered his wife, and had enough pull to get it fixed."

Degarmo came to his feet and walked over to lean down at me. "Say that again," he said softly.

I said it again.

He hit me across the face with his open hand. It jerked my head around hard. My face felt hot and large.

"Say it again," he said softly.

I said it again. His hand swept and knocked my head to one side again.

"Say it again."

"Nope. Third time lucky. You might miss." I put a hand up and rubbed my cheek.

He stood leaning down, his lips drawn back over his teeth, a hard animal glare in his very blue eyes.

"Any time you talk like that to a cop," he said, "you know what you got coming. Try it on again and it won't be the flat of a hand I'll use on you."

I bit hard on my lips and rubbed my cheek.

"Poke your big nose into our business and you'll wake up in an alley with the cats looking at you," he said.

I didn't say anything. He went and sat down again, breathing hard. I stopped rubbing my face and held my hand out and worked the fingers slowly, to get the hard clench out of them.

"I'll remember that," I said. "Both ways."

22

IT WAS EARLY evening when I got back to Hollywood and up to the office. The building had emptied out and the corridors were silent. Doors were open and the cleaning women were inside with their vacuum cleaners and their dry mops and dusters.

I unlocked the door to mine and picked up an envelope that lay in front of the mail slot and dropped it on the desk without looking at it. I ran the windows up and leaned out, looking at the early neon lights glowing, smelling the warm, foody air that drifted up from the alley ventilator of the coffee shop next door.

I peeled off my coat and tie and sat down at the desk and got the office bottle out of the deep drawer and bought myself a drink. It didn't do any good. I had another, with the same result.

By now Webber would have seen Kingsley. There would be a general alarm out for his wife, already, or very soon. The thing looked cut and dried to them. A nasty affair between two rather nasty people, too much loving, too much drinking, too much proximity ending in a savage hatred and a murderous impulse and death.

I thought this was all a little too simple.

I reached for the envelope and tore it open. It had no stamp. It read: "Mr. Marlowe: Florence Almore's parents are a Mr. and Mrs. Eustace Grayson, presently residing at the Rossmore Arms, 640 South Oxford Avenue. I checked this by calling the listed phone number. Yrs. Adrienne Fromsett."

An elegant handwriting, like the elegant hand that wrote it. I pushed it to one side and had another drink. I began to feel a little less savage. I pushed things around on the desk. My hands felt thick and hot and awkward. I ran a finger across the corner of the desk and looked at the streak made by the wiping off of the dust. I looked at the dust on my finger and wiped that off. I looked at my watch. I looked at the wall. I looked at nothing.

I put the liquor bottle away and went over to the wash-bowl to rinse the glass out. When I had done that I washed my hands and bathed my face in cold water and looked at it. The flush was gone from the left cheek, but it looked a little swollen. Not very much, but enough to make me tighten up again. I brushed my hair and looked at the gray in it. There was getting to be plenty of gray in it. The face under the hair had a sick look. I didn't like the face at all.

I went back to the desk and read Miss Fromsett's note again. I smoothed it out on the glass and sniffed it and smoothed it out some more and folded it and put it in my coat pocket.

I sat very still and listened to the evening grow quiet outside the open windows. And very slowly I grew quiet with it.

23

THE ROSSMORE ARMS was a gloomy pile of dark red brick built around a huge forecourt. It had a plush-lined lobby containing silence, tubbed plants, a bored canary in a cage as big as a dog-house, a smell of old carpet dust and the cloying fragrance of gardenias long ago.

The Graysons were on the fifth floor in front, in the north wing. They were sitting together in a room which seemed to be deliberately twenty years out of date. It had fat over-stuffed furniture and brass doorknobs, shaped like eggs, a huge wall mirror in a gilt frame, a marble-topped table in the window and dark red plush side drapes by the windows. It smelled of

tobacco smoke and behind that the air was telling me they
had had lamb chops and broccoli for dinner.

Grayson's wife was a plump woman who might once have
had big baby-blue eyes. They were faded out now and
dimmed by glasses and slightly protuberant. She had kinky
white hair. She sat darning socks with her thick ankles
crossed, her feet just reaching the floor, and a big wicker
sewing basket in her lap.

Grayson was a long stooped yellow-faced man with high
shoulders, bristly eyebrows and almost no chin. The upper part
of his face meant business. The lower part was just saying goodbye. He wore bifocals and he had been gnawing fretfully at the
evening paper. I had looked him up in the city directory. He was
a C.P.A. and looked it very inch. He even had ink on his fingers
and there were four pencils in the pocket of his open vest.

He read my card carefully for the seventh time and looked
me up and down and said slowly:

"What is it you want to see us about, Mr. Marlowe?"

"I'm interested in a man named Lavery. He lives across the
street from Dr. Almore. Your daughter was the wife of Dr.
Almore. Lavery is the man who found your daughter the
night she – died."

They both pointed like bird dogs when I deliberately
hesitated on the last word. Grayson looked at his wife and she
shook her head.

"We don't care to talk about that," Grayson said promptly.
"It is much too painful to us."

I waited a moment and looked gloomy with them. Then
I said: "I don't blame you. I don't want to make you. I'd like to
get in touch with the man you hired to look into it, though."

They looked at each other again. Mrs. Grayson didn't shake
her head this time.

Grayson asked: "Why?"

"I'd better tell you a little of my story." I told them what
I had been hired to do, not mentioning Kingsley by name. I

told them the incident with Degarmo outside Almore's house the day before. They pointed again on that.

Grayson said sharply: "Am I to understand that you were unknown to Dr. Almore, had not approached him in any way, and that he nevertheless called a police officer because you were outside his house?"

I said: "That's right. Had been outside for at least an hour though. That is, my car had."

"That's very queer," Grayson said.

"I'd say that was one very nervous man," I said. "And Degarmo asked me if her folks – meaning your daughter's folks – had hired me. Looks as if he didn't feel safe yet, wouldn't you say?"

"Safe about what?" He didn't look at me saying this. He re-lit his pipe, slowly, then tamped the tobacco down with the end of a big metal pencil and lit it again.

I shrugged and didn't answer. He looked at me quickly and looked away. Mrs. Grayson didn't look at me, but her nostrils quivered.

"How did he know who you were?" Grayson asked suddenly.

"Made a note of the car license, called the Auto Club, looked up the name in the directory. At least that's what I'd have done and I saw him through his window making some of the motions."

"So he has the police working for him," Grayson said.

"Not necessarily. If they made a mistake that time, they wouldn't want it found out now."

"Mistake!" He laughed almost shrilly.

"Okay," I said. "The subject is painful but a little fresh air won't hurt it. You've always thought he murdered her, haven't you? That's why you hired this dick – detective."

Mrs. Grayson looked up with quick eyes and ducked her head down and rolled up another pair of mended socks.

Grayson said nothing.

132

I said: "Was there any evidence, or was it just that you didn't like him?"

"There was evidence," Grayson said bitterly, and with a sudden clearness of voice, as if he had decided to talk about it after all. "There must have been. We were told there was. But we never got it. The police took care of that."

"I heard they had this fellow arrested and sent up for drunk driving."

"You heard right."

"But he never told you what he had to go on."

"No."

"I don't like that," I said. "That sounds a little as if this fellow hadn't made up his mind whether to use his information for your benefit or keep it and put a squeeze on the doctor."

Grayson looked at his wife again. She said quietly: "Mr. Talley didn't impress me that way. He was a quiet unassuming little man. But you can't always judge, I know."

I said: "So Talley was his name. That was one of the things I hoped you would tell me."

"And what were the others?" Grayson asked.

"How can I find Talley — and what it was that laid the groundwork of suspicion in your minds. It must have been there, or you wouldn't have hired Talley without a better showing from him that *he* had grounds."

Grayson smiled very thinly and primly. He reached for his little chin and rubbed it with one long yellow finger.

Mrs. Grayson said: "Dope."

"She means that literally," Grayson said at once, as if the single word had been a green light. "Almore was, and no doubt is, a dope doctor. Our daughter made that clear to us. In his hearing too. He didn't like it."

"Just what do you mean by a dope doctor, Mr. Grayson?"

"I mean a doctor whose practice is largely with people who are living on the raw edge of nervous collapse, from drink and dissipation. People who have to be given sedatives and narcotics all the time. The stage comes when an ethical physician refuses to treat them any more, outside a sanatorium. But not the Dr. Almores. *They* will keep on as long as the money comes in, as long as the patient remains alive and reasonably sane, even if he or she becomes a hopeless addict in the process. A lucrative practice," he said primly, "and I imagine a dangerous one to the doctor."

"No doubt of that," I said. "But there's a lot of money in it. Did you know a man named Condy?"

"No. We know who he was. Florence suspected he was a source of Almore's narcotic supply."

I said: "Could be. He probably wouldn't want to write himself too many prescriptions. Did you know Lavery?"

"We never saw him. We knew who he was."

"Ever occur to you that Lavery might have been blackmailing Almore?"

It was a new idea to him. He ran his hand over the top of his head and brought it down over his face and dropped it to his bony knee. He shook his head.

"No. Why should I?"

"He was first to the body," I said. "Whatever looked wrong to Talley must have been equally visible to Lavery."

"Is Lavery that kind of man?"

"I don't know. He has no visible means of support, no job. He gets around a lot, especially with women."

"It's an idea," Grayson said. "And those things can be handled very discreetly." He smiled wryly. "I have come across traces of them in my work. Unsecured loans, long outstanding. Investments on the face of them worthless, made by men who would not be likely to make worthless investments. Bad debts that should obviously be charged off and have not been, for fear of inviting scrutiny from the income tax people. Oh yes, those things can easily be arranged."

I looked at Mrs. Grayson. Her hands had never stopped working. She had a dozen pairs of darned socks finished. Grayson's long bony feet would be hard on socks.

"What's happened to Talley? Was he framed?"

"I don't think there's any doubt about it. His wife was very bitter. She said he had been given a doped drink in a bar and he had been drinking with a policeman. She said a police car was waiting across the street for him to start driving and that he was picked up at once. Also that he was given only the most perfunctory examination at the jail."

"That doesn't mean too much. That's what he told her after he was arrested. He'd tell her something like that automatically."

"Well, I hate to think the police are not honest," Grayson said. "But these things are done, and everybody knows it."

I said: "If they made an honest mistake about your daughter's death, they would hate to have Talley show them up. It might mean several lost jobs. If they thought what he was really after was blackmail, they wouldn't be too fussy about how they took care of him. Where is Talley now? What it all boils down to is that if there was any solid clue, he either had it or was on the track of it and knew what he was looking for."

Grayson said: "We don't know where he is. He got six months, but that expired long ago."

"How about his wife?"

He looked at his own wife. She said briefly: "1618 ½ Westmore Street, Bay City. Eustace and I sent her a little money. She was left bad off."

I made a note of the address and leaned back in my chair and said:

"Somebody shot Lavery this morning in his bathroom."

Mrs. Grayson's pudgy hands became still on the edges of the basket. Grayson sat with his mouth open, holding his pipe in front of it. He made a noise of clearing his throat softly, as if in the presence of the dead. Nothing ever moved slower than his old black pipe going back between his teeth.

"Of course it would be too much to expect," he said and let it hang in the air and blew a little pale smoke at it, and then added, "that Dr. Almore had any connection with that."

"I'd like to think he had," I said. "He certainly lives at a handy distance. The police think my client's wife shot him. They have a good case too, when they find her. But if Almore had anything to do with it, it must surely arise out of your daughter's death. That's why I'm trying to find out something about that."

Grayson said: "A man who has done one murder wouldn't have more than twenty-five per cent of the hesitation in doing another." He spoke as if he had given the matter considerable study.

I said: "Yeah, maybe. What was supposed to be the motive for the first one?"

"Florence was wild," he said sadly. "A wild and difficult girl. She was wasteful and extravagant, always picking up new and rather doubtful friends, talking too much and too loudly, and generally acting the fool. A wife like that can be very dangerous to a man like Albert S. Almore. But I don't believe that was the prime motive, was it, Lettie?"

He looked at his wife, but she didn't look at him. She jabbed a darning needle into a round ball of wool and said nothing.

Grayson sighed and went on: "We had reason to believe he was carrying on with his office nurse and that Florence had threatened him with a public scandal. He couldn't have anything like that, could he? One kind of scandal might too easily lead to another."

I said: "How did he do the murder?"

"With morphine, of course. He always had it, he always used it. He was an expert in the use of it. Then when she was in a deep coma he would have placed her in the garage and started the car motor. There was no autopsy, you know. But if there had been, it was known that she had been given a hypodermic injection that night."

I nodded and he leaned back satisfied and ran his hand over his head and down his face and let it fall slowly to his bony knee. He seemed to have given a lot of study to this angle too.

I looked at them. A couple of elderly people sitting there quietly, poisoning their minds with hate, a year and a half after it had happened. They would like it if Almore had shot Lavery. They would love it. It would warm them clear down to their ankles.

After a pause I said: "You're believing a lot of this because you want to. It's always possible that she committed suicide, and that the cover-up was partly to protect Condy's gambling club and partly to prevent Almore having to be questioned at a public hearing."

"Rubbish," Grayson said sharply. "He murdered her all right. She was in bed, asleep."

"You don't know that. She might have been taking dope herself. She might have established a tolerance for it. The effect wouldn't last long in that case. She might have got up in the middle of the night and looked at herself in the glass and seen devils pointing at her. These things happen."

"I think you have taken up enough of our time," Grayson said.

I stood up. I thanked them both and made a yard towards the door and said: "You didn't do anything more about it after Talley was arrested?"

"Saw an assistant district attorney named Leach," Grayson grunted. "Got exactly nowhere. He saw nothing to justify his office in interfering. Wasn't even interested in the narcotic angle. But Condy's place was closed up about a month later. That might have come out of it somehow."

"That was probably the Bay City cops throwing a little smoke. You'd find Condy somewhere else, if you knew where to look. With all his original equipment intact."

I started for the door again and Grayson hoisted himself out of his chair and dragged across the room after me. There was a flush on his yellow face.

"I didn't mean to be rude," he said. "I guess Lettie and I oughtn't to brood about this business the way we do."

"I think you've both been very patient," I said. "Was there anybody else involved in all this that we haven't mentioned by name?"

He shook his head, then looked back at his wife. Her hands were motionless holding the current sock on the darning egg. Her head was tilted a little to one side. Her attitude was of listening, but not to us.

I said: "The way I got the story, Dr. Almore's office nurse put Mrs. Almore to bed that night. Would that be the one he was supposed to be playing around with?"

Mrs. Grayson said sharply: "Wait a minute. We never saw the girl. But she had a pretty name. Just give me a minute."

We gave her a minute. "Mildred something," she said, and snapped her teeth.

I took a deep breath. "Would it be Mildred Haviland, Mrs. Grayson?"

She smiled brightly and nodded. "Of course, Mildred Haviland. Don't you remember, Eustace?"

He didn't remember. He looked at us like a horse that has got into the wrong stable. He opened the door and said: "What does it matter?"

"And you said Talley was a small man," I bored on. "He wouldn't for instance be a big loud bruiser with an overbearing manner?"

"Oh no," Mrs. Grayson said. "Mr. Talley is a man of not more than medium height, middle-aged, with brownish hair

and a very quiet voice. He had a sort of worried expression.
I mean, he looked as if he always had it."

"Looks as if he needed it," I said.

Grayson put his bony hand out and I shook it. It felt like
shaking hands with a towel rack.

"If you get him," he said and clamped his mouth hard on
his pipe stem, "call back with a bill. If you get Almore, I mean,
of course."

I said I knew he meant Almore, but that there wouldn't be
any bill.

I went back along the silent hallway. The self-operating elevator was carpeted in red plush. It had an elderly perfume in
it, like three widows drinking tea.

24

THE HOUSE ON Westmore Street was a small frame bungalow
behind a larger house. There was no number visible on the
smaller house, but the one in front showed a stenciled 1618
beside the door, with a dim light behind the stencil. A narrow
concrete path led along under windows to the house at the
back. It had a tiny porch with a single chair on it. I stepped
up on the porch and rang the bell.

It buzzed not very far off. The front door was open behind
the screen but there was no light. From the darkness a queru-
lous voice said:

"What is it?"

I spoke into the darkness. "Mr. Talley in?"

The voice became flat and without tone. "Who wants
him?"

"A friend."

The woman sitting inside in the darkness made a vague
sound in her throat which might have been amusement. Or
she might just have been clearing her throat.

"All right," she said. "How much is this one?"

"It's not a bill, Mrs. Talley. I suppose you are Mrs. Talley?"

"Oh, go away and let me alone," the voice said. "Mr. Talley isn't here. He hasn't been here. He won't be here."

I put my nose against the screen and tried to peer into the room. I could see the vague outlines of its furniture. From where the voice came from also showed the shape of a couch. A woman was lying on it. She seemed to be lying on her back and looking up at the ceiling. She was quite motionless.

"I'm sick," the voice said. "I've had enough trouble. Go away and leave me be."

I said: "I've just come from talking to the Graysons."

There was a little silence, but no movement, then a sigh. "I never heard of them."

I leaned against the frame of the screen door and looked back along the narrow walk to the street. There was a car across the way with parking lights burning. There were other cars along the block.

I said: "Yes, you have, Mrs. Talley. I'm working for them. They're still in there pitching. How about you? Don't you want something back?"

The voice said: "I want to be let alone."

"I want information," I said. "I'm going to get it. Quietly if I can. Loud, if it can't be quiet."

The voice said: "Another copper, eh?"

"You know I'm not a copper, Mrs. Talley. The Graysons wouldn't talk to a copper. Call them up and ask them."

"I never heard of them," the voice said. "I don't have a phone, if I knew them. Go away, copper. I'm sick. I've been sick for a month."

"My name is Marlowe," I said. "Philip Marlowe. I'm a private eye in Los Angeles, I've been talking to the Graysons. I've got something, but I want to talk to your husband."

The woman on the couch let out a dim laugh which barely reached across the room. "You've got something," she said.

"That sounds familiar. My God it does! You've got something. George Talley had something too — once."

"He can have it again," I said, "if he plays his cards right."

"If that's what it takes," she said, "you can scratch him off right now."

I leaned against the doorframe and scratched my chin instead. Somebody back on the street had clicked a flashlight on. I didn't know why. It went off again. It seemed to be near my car.

The pale blur of face on the couch moved and disappeared. Hair took its place. The woman had turned her face to the wall.

"I'm tired," she said, her voice now muffled by talking at the wall. "I'm so damn tired. Beat it, mister. Be nice and go away."

"Would a little money help any?"

"Can't you smell the cigar smoke?"

I sniffed. I didn't smell any cigar smoke. I said, "No."

"They've been here. They were here two hours. God, I'm tired of it all. Go away."

"Look, Mrs. Talley —"

She rolled on the couch and the blur of her face showed again. I could almost see her eyes, not quite.

"Look yourself," she said. "I don't know you. I don't want to know you. I have nothing to tell you. I wouldn't tell it, if I had. I live here, mister, if you call it living. Anyway it's the nearest I can get to living. I want a little peace and quiet. Now you get out and leave me alone."

"Let me in the house," I said. "We can talk this over. I think I can show you —"

She rolled suddenly on the couch again and feet struck the floor. A tight anger came into her voice.

"If you don't get out," she said, "I'm going to start yelling my head off. Right now. Now!"

"Okay," I said quickly. "I'll stick my card in the door. So you won't forget my name. You might change your mind."

I got the card out and wedged it into the crack of the screen door. I said: "Well goodnight, Mrs. Talley."

No answer. Her eyes were looking across the room at me, faintly luminous in the dark. I went down off the porch and back along the narrow walk to the street.

Across the way a motor purled gently in the car with the parking lights on it. Motors purl gently in thousands of cars on thousands of streets, everywhere.

I got into the Chrysler and started it up.

25

WESTMORE WAS A north and south street on the wrong side of town. I drove north. At the next corner I bumped over disused interurban tracks and on into a block of junk yards. Behind wooden fences the decomposing carcasses of old automobiles lay in grotesque designs, like a modern battle-field. Piles of rusted parts looked lumpy under the moon. Roof high piles, with alleys between them.

Headlights glowed in my rear view mirror. They got larger. I stepped on the gas and reached keys out of my pocket and unlocked the glove compartment. I took a .38 out and laid it on the car seat close to my leg.

Beyond the junk yards there was a brick field. The tall chimney of the kiln was smokeless, far off over waste land. Piles of dark bricks, a low wooden building with a sign on it, emptiness, no one moving, no light.

The car behind me gained. The low whine of a lightly touched siren growled through the night. The sound loafed over the fringes of a neglected golf course to the east, across the brickyard to the west. I speeded up a bit more, but it wasn't any use. The car behind me came up fast and a huge red spot-light suddenly glared all over the road.

The car came up level and started to cut in. I stood the Chrysler on its nose, swung out behind the police car, and made a U-turn with half an inch to spare. I gunned the motor the other way. Behind me sounded the rough clashing of gears, the howl of an infuriated motor, and the red spotlight swept for what seemed miles over the brickyard.

It wasn't any use. They were behind me and coming fast again. I didn't have any idea of getting away. I wanted to get back where there were houses and people to come out and watch and perhaps to remember.

I didn't make it. The police car heaved up alongside again and a hard voice yelled:

"Pull over, or we'll blast a hole in you!"

I pulled over to the curb and set the brake. I put the gun back in the glove compartment and snapped it shut. The police car jumped on its springs just in front of my left front fender. A fat man slammed out of it roaring.

"Don't you know a police siren when you hear one? Get out of that car!"

I got out of the car and stood beside it in the moonlight. The fat man had a gun in his hand.

"Gimme your license!" he barked in a voice as hard as the blade of a shovel.

I took it out and held it out. The other cop in the car slid out from under the wheel and came around beside me and took what I was holding out. He put a flash on it and read.

"Name of Marlowe," he said. "Hell, the guy's a shamus. Just think of that, Cooney."

Cooney said: "Is that all? Guess I won't need this." He tucked the gun back in his holster and buttoned the leather flap down over it. "Guess I can handle this with my little flippers," he said. "Guess I can at that."

The other one said: "Doing fifty-five. Been drinking, I wouldn't wonder."

"Smell the bastard's breath," Cooney said.

The other one leaned forward with a polite leer. "Could I smell the breath, shamus?"

I let him smell the breath.

"Well," he said judiciously, "he ain't staggering. I got to admit that."

" 'S a cold night for summer. Buy the boy a drink, Officer Dobbs."

"Now that's a sweet idea," Dobbs said. He went to the car and got a half pint bottle out of it. He held it up. It was a third full. "No really solid drinking here," he said. He held the bottle out. "With our compliments, pal."

"Suppose I don't want a drink," I said.

"Don't say that," Cooney whined. "We might get the idea you wanted feetprints on your stomach."

I took the bottle and unscrewed the cap and sniffed. The liquor in the bottle smelled like whiskey. Just whiskey.

"You can't work the same gag all the time," I said.

Cooney said: "Time is eight twenty-seven. Write it down, Officer Dobbs."

Dobbs went to the car and leaned in to make a note on his report. I held the bottle up and said to Cooney: "You insist that I drink this?"

"Naw. You could have me jump on your belly instead."

I tilted the bottle, locked my throat, and filled my mouth with whiskey. Cooney lunged forward and sank a fist in my stomach. I sprayed the whiskey and bent over choking. I dropped the bottle.

I bent to get it and saw Cooney's fat knee rising at my face. I stepped to one side and straightened and slammed him on the nose with everything I had. His left hand went to his face and his voice howled and his right hand jumped to his gun holster. Dobbs ran at me from the side and his arm swung low. The blackjack hit me behind the left knee, the leg went dead and I sat down hard on the ground, gritting my teeth and spitting whiskey.

Cooney took his hand away from his face full of blood.

"Jesus," he cracked in a thick horrible voice. "This is blood. My blood." He let out a wild roar and swung his foot at my face.

I rolled far enough to catch it on my shoulder. It was bad enough taking it there.

Dobbs pushed between us and said: "We got enough, Charlie. Better not get it all gummed up."

Cooney stepped backwards three shuffling steps and sat down on the running board of the police car and held his face. He groped for a handkerchief and used it gently on his nose.

"Just gimme a minute," he said through the handkerchief. "Just a minute, pal. Just one little minute."

Dobbs said, "Pipe down. We got enough. That's the way it's going to be." He swung the blackjack slowly beside his leg. Cooney got up off the running board and staggered forward. Dobbs put a hand against his chest and pushed him gently. Cooney tried to knock the hand out of his way.

"I gotta see blood," he croaked. "I gotta see more blood."

Dobbs said sharply, "Nothing doing. Pipe down. We got all we wanted."

Cooney turned and moved heavily away to the other side of the police car. He leaned against it muttering through his handkerchief. Dobbs said to me:

"Up on the feet, boy friend."

I got up and rubbed behind my knee. The nerve of the leg was jumping like an angry monkey.

"Get in the car," Dobbs said. "Our car."

I went over and climbed into the police car.

Dobbs said: "You drive the other heap, Charlie."

"I'll tear every god damn fender off'n it," Cooney roared.

Dobbs picked the whiskey bottle off the ground, threw it over the fence, and slid into the car beside me. He pressed the starter.

"This is going to cost you," he said. "You hadn't ought to have socked him."

I said: "Just why not?"

"He's a good guy," Dobbs said. "A little loud."

"But not funny," I said. "Not at all funny."

"Don't tell him," Dobbs said. The police car began to move. "You'd hurt his feelings."

Cooney slammed into the Chrysler and started it and clashed the gears as if he was trying to strip them. Dobbs tooled the police car smoothly around and started north again along the brickyard.

"You'll like our new jail," he said.

"What will the charge be?"

He thought a moment, guiding the car with a gentle hand and watching in the mirror to see that Cooney followed along behind.

"Speeding," he said. "Resisting arrest. H.B.D." H.B.D. is police slang for "had been drinking."

"How about being slammed in the belly, kicked in the shoulder, forced to drink liquor under threat of bodily harm, threatened with a gun and struck with a blackjack while unarmed? Couldn't you make a little something more out of that?"

"Aw forget it," he said wearily. "You think this sort of thing is my idea of a good time?"

"I thought they cleaned this town up," I said. "I thought they had it so that a decent man could walk the streets at night without wearing a bulletproof vest."

"They cleaned it up some," he said. "They wouldn't want it too clean. They might scare away a dirty dollar."

"Better not talk like that," I said. "You'll lose your union card."

He laughed. "The hell with them," he said. "I'll be in the army in two weeks."

The incident was over for him. It meant nothing. He took it as a matter of course. He wasn't even bitter about it.

26

THE CELL BLOCK was almost brand-new. The battleship gray paint on the steel walls and door still had the fresh gloss of newness disfigured in two or three places by squirted tobacco juice. The overhead light was sunk in the ceiling behind a heavy frosted panel. There were two bunks on one side of the cell and a man snored in the top bunk, with a dark gray blanket wrapped around him. Since he was asleep that early and didn't smell of whiskey or gin and had chosen the top berth where he would be out of the way, I judged he was an old lodger.

I sat on the lower bunk. They had tapped me for a gun but they hadn't stripped my pockets. I got out a cigarette and rubbed the hot swelling behind my knee. The pain radiated all the way to the ankle. The whiskey I had coughed on my coat front had a rank smell. I held the cloth up and breathed smoke into it. The smoke floated up around the flat square of lighted glass in the ceiling. The jail seemed very quiet. A woman was making a shrill racket somewhere very far off, in another part of the jail. My part was as peaceful as a church.

The woman was screaming, wherever she was. The screaming had a thin sharp unreal sound, something like the screaming of coyotes in the moonlight, but it didn't have the rising keening note of the coyote. After a while the sound stopped.

I smoked two cigarettes through and dropped the butts into the small toilet in the corner. The man in the upper berth still snored. All I could see of him was damp greasy hair sticking out over the edge of the blanket. He slept on his stomach. He slept well. He was one of the best.

I sat down on the bunk again. It was made of flat steel slats with a thin hard mattress over them. Two dark gray blankets were folded on it quite neatly. It was a very nice jail. It was on the twelfth floor of the new city hall. It was a very nice city hall. Bay City was a very nice place. People lived there and thought so. If I lived there, I would probably think so. I would see the nice blue bay and the cliffs and the yacht harbor and the quiet streets of houses, old houses brooding under old trees and new houses with sharp green lawns and wire fences and staked saplings set into the parkway in front of them. I knew a girl who lived on Twenty-fifth Street. It was a nice street. She was a nice girl. She liked Bay City.

She wouldn't think about the Mexican and Negro slums stretched out on the dismal flats south of the old interurban tracks. Nor of the waterfront dives along the flat shore south of the cliffs, the sweaty little dance halls on the pike, the marihuana joints, the narrow fox faces watching over the tops of newspapers in far too quiet hotel lobbies, nor the pickpockets and grifters and con men and drunk rollers and pimps and queens on the board walk.

I went over to stand by the door. There was nobody stirring across the way. The lights in the cell block were bleak and silent. Business in the jail was rotten.

I looked at my watch. Nine fifty-four. Time to go home and get your slippers on and play over a game of chess. Time for a tall cool drink and a long quiet pipe. Time to sit with your feet up and think of nothing. Time to start yawning over your magazine. Time to be a human being, a householder, a man with nothing to do but rest and suck in the night air and rebuild the brain for tomorrow.

A man in the blue-gray jail uniform came along between the cells reading numbers. He stopped in front of mine and unlocked the door and gave me the hard stare they think they have to wear on their pans forever and forever and forever. I'm a cop, brother, I'm tough, watch your step, brother, or we'll fix you up so you'll crawl on your hands and knees, brother, snap out of it, brother, let's get a load of the truth, brother, let's go, and let's not forget we're tough guys, we're cops, and we do what we like with punks like you.

"Out," he said.

I stepped out of the cell and he relocked the door and jerked his thumb and we went along to a wide steel gate and he unlocked that and we went through and he relocked it and the keys tinkled pleasantly on the big steel ring and after a while we went through a steel door that was painted like wood on the outside and battleship gray on the inside.

Degarmo was standing there by the counter talking to the desk sergeant.

He turned his metallic blue eyes on me and said: "How you doing?"

"Fine."

"Like our jail?"

"I like your jail fine."

"Captain Webber wants to talk to you."

"That's fine," I said.

"Don't you know any words but fine?"

"Not right now," I said. "Not in here."

"You're limping a little," he said. "You trip over something?"

"Yeah," I said. "I tripped over a blackjack. It jumped up and bit me behind the left knee."

"That's too bad," Degarmo said, blank-eyed. "Get your stuff from the property clerk."

"I've got it," I said. "It wasn't taken away from me."

"Well, that's fine," he said.

"It sure is," I said. "It's fine."

The desk sergeant lifted his shaggy head and gave us both a long stare. "You ought to see Cooney's little Irish nose," he said. "If you want to see something fine. It's spread over his face like syrup on a waffle."

Degarmo said absently: "What's the matter? He get in a fight?"

"I wouldn't know," the desk sergeant said. "Maybe it was the same blackjack that jumped up and bit him."

"For a desk sergeant you talk too damn much," Degarmo said.

"A desk sergeant always talks too God damn much," the desk sergeant said. "Maybe that's why he isn't a lieutenant on homicide."

"You see how we are here," Degarmo said. "Just one great big happy family."

"With beaming smiles on our faces," the desk sergeant said, "and our arms spread wide in welcome, and a rock in each hand."

Degarmo jerked his head at me and we went out.

27

CAPTAIN WEBBER PUSHED his sharp bent nose across the desk at me and said: "Sit down."

I sat down in a round-backed wooden armchair and eased my left leg away from the sharp edge of the seat. It was a large neat corner office. Degarmo sat at the end of the desk and crossed his legs and rubbed his ankle thoughtfully, looked out of a window.

Webber went on: "You asked for trouble, and you got it. You were doing fifty-five miles an hour in a residential zone and you attempted to get away from a police car that signaled you to stop with its siren and red spotlight. You were abusive when stopped and you struck an officer in the face."

I said nothing. Webber picked a match off his desk and broke it in half and threw the pieces over his shoulder.

"Or are they lying — as usual?" he asked.

"I didn't see their report," I said. "I was probably doing fifty-five in a residential district, or anyhow within city limits. The police car was parked outside a house I visited. It followed me when I drove away and I didn't at that time know it was a police car. It had no good reason to follow me and I didn't like the look of it. I went a little fast, but all I was trying to do was get to a better lighted part of town."

Degarmo moved his eyes to give me a bleak meaningless stare. Webber snapped his teeth impatiently.

He said: "After you knew it was a police car you made a half turn in the middle of the block and still tried to get away. Is that right?"

I said: "Yes. It's going to take a little frank talk to explain that."

"I'm not afraid of a little frank talk," Webber said. "I tend to kind of specialize in frank talk."

I said: "These cops that picked me up were parked in front of the house where George Talley's wife lives. They were there before I got there. George Talley is the man who used to be a private detective down here. I wanted to see him. Degarmo knows why I wanted to see him."

Degarmo picked a match out of his pocket and chewed on the soft end of it quietly. He nodded, without expression. Webber didn't look at him.

I said: "You are a stupid man, Degarmo. Everything you do is stupid, and done in a stupid way. When you went up against me yesterday in front of Almore's house you had to get tough when there was nothing to get tough about. You had to make me curious when I had nothing to be curious about. You even had to drop hints which showed me how I could satisfy that curiosity, if it became important. All you had to do to protect your friends was keep your mouth shut until I made a move. I never would have made one, and you would have saved all this."

Webber said: "What the devil has all this got to do with your being arrested in the twelve hundred block on Westmore Street?"

"It has to do with the Almore case," I said. "George Talley worked on the Almore case – until he was pinched for drunk driving."

"Well, I never worked on the Almore case," Webber snapped. "I don't know who stuck the first knife into Julius Caesar either. Stick to the point, can't you?"

"I am sticking to the point. Degarmo knows about the Almore case and he doesn't like it talked about. Even your prowl car boys know about it. Cooney and Dobbs had no reason to follow me unless it was because I visited the wife of a man who had worked on the Almore case. I wasn't doing fifty-five miles an hour when they started to follow me. I tried to get away from them because I had a good idea I might get beaten up for going there. Degarmo had given me that idea."

Webber looked quickly at Degarmo. Degarmo's hard blue eyes looked across the room at the wall in front of him.

I said: "And I didn't bust Cooney in the nose until after he had forced me to drink whiskey and then hit me in the stomach when I drank it, so that I would spill it down my coat front and smell of it. This can't be the first time you have heard of that trick, captain."

Webber broke another match. He leaned back and looked at his small tight knuckles. He looked again at Degarmo and said: "If you got made chief of police today, you might let me in on it."

Degarmo said: "Hell, the shamus just got a couple of playful taps. Kind of kidding. If a guy can't take a joke —"

Webber said: "You put Cooney and Dobbs over there?"

"Well — yes, I did," Degarmo said. "I don't see where we have to put up with these snoopers coming into our town and stirring up a lot of dead leaves just to promote themselves a job and work a couple of old suckers for a big fee. Guys like that need a good sharp lesson."

"Is that how it looks to you?" Webber asked.

"That's exactly how it looks to me," Degarmo said.

"I wonder what fellows like you need," Webber said. "Right now I think you need a little air. Would you please take it, lieutenant?"

Degarmo opened his mouth slowly. "You mean you want me to breeze on out?"

Webber leaned forward suddenly and his sharp little chin seemed to cut the air like the forefoot of a cruiser. "Would you be so kind?"

Degarmo stood up slowly, a dark flush staining his cheek-bones. He leaned a hard hand flat on the desk and looked at Webber. There was a little charged silence. He said:

"Okay, captain. But you're playing this wrong."

Webber didn't answer him. Degarmo walked to the door and out. Webber waited for the door to close before he spoke.

"Is it your line that you can tie this Almore business a year and a half ago to the shooting in Lavery's place today? Or is it just a smoke screen you're laying down because you know damn well Kingsley's wife shot Lavery?"

I said: "It was tied to Lavery before he was shot. In a rough sort of way, perhaps only with a granny knot. But enough to make a man think."

"I've been into this matter a little more thoroughly than you might think," Webber said coldly. "Although I never had anything personally to do with the death of Almore's wife and I wasn't chief of detectives at that time. If you didn't even know Almore yesterday morning, you must have heard a lot about him since."

I told him exactly what I had heard, both from Miss Fromsett and from the Graysons.

"Then it's your theory that Lavery may have blackmailed Dr. Almore?" he asked at the end. "And that that may have something to do with the murder?"

"It's not a theory. It's no more than a possibility. I wouldn't be doing a job if I ignored it. The relations, if any, between Lavery and Almore might have been deep and dangerous or just the merest acquaintance, or not even that. For all I positively know they may never even have spoken to each other. But if there was nothing funny about the Almore case, why get so tough with anybody who shows an interest in it? It could be coincidence that George Talley was hooked for drunk driving just when he was working on it. It could be coincidence that Almore called a cop because I stared at his house, and that Lavery was shot before I could talk to him a second time. But it's no coincidence that two of your men were watching Talley's home tonight, ready, willing and able to make trouble for me, if I went there."

"I grant you that," Webber said. "And I'm not done with that incident. Do you want to file charges?"

"Life's too short for me to be filing charges of assault against police officers," I said.

He winced a little. "Then we'll wash all that out and charge it to experience," he said. "And as I understand you were not even booked, you're free to go home any time you want to. And if I were you, I'd leave Captain Webber to deal with the Lavery case and with any remote connection it might turn out to have with the Almore case."

I said: "And with any remote connection it might have with a woman named Muriel Chess being found drowned in a mountain lake near Puma Point yesterday?"

He raised his little eyebrows. "You think that?"

"Only you might not know her as Muriel Chess. Supposing that you knew her at all you might have known her as Mildred Haviland, who used to be Dr. Almore's office nurse. Who put Mrs. Almore to bed the night she was found dead in the garage, and who, if there was any hanky-panky about that, might know who it was, and be bribed or scared into leaving town shortly thereafter."

Webber picked up two matches and broke them. His small bleak eyes were fixed on my face. He said nothing.

"And at that point," I said, "you run into a real basic coincidence, the only one I'm willing to admit in the whole picture. For this Mildred Haviland met a man named Bill Chess in a Riverside beer parlor and for reasons of her own married him and went to live with him at Little Fawn Lake. And Little Fawn Lake was the property of a man whose wife was intimate with Lavery, who had found Mrs. Almore's body. That's what I call a real coincidence. It can't be anything else but, but it's basic, fundamental. Everything else flows from it."

Webber got up from his desk and went over to the water cooler and drank two paper cups of water. He crushed the cups slowly in his hand and twisted them into a ball and dropped the ball into a brown metal basket under the cooler. He walked to the windows and stood looking out over the bay. This was before the dimout went into effect, and there were many lights in the yacht harbor.

He came slowly back to the desk and sat down. He reached up and pinched his nose. He was making up his mind about something.

He said slowly: "I can't see what the hell sense there is in trying to mix that up with something that happened a year and a half later."

"Okay," I said, "and thanks for giving me so much of your time." I got up to go.

"Your leg feel pretty bad?" he asked, as I leaned down to rub it.

"Bad enough, but it's getting better."

"Police business," he said almost gently, "is a hell of a problem. It's a good deal like politics. It asks for the highest type of men, and there's nothing in it to attract the highest type of men. So we have to work with what we get — and we get things like this."

"I know," I said. "I've always known that. I'm not bitter about it. Goodnight, Captain Webber."

"Wait a minute," he said. "Sit down a minute. If we've got to have the Almore case in this, let's drag it out into the open and look at it."

"It's about time somebody did that," I said. I sat down again.

28

WEBBER SAID QUIETLY: "I suppose some people think we're just a bunch of crooks down here. I suppose they think a fellow kills his wife and then calls me up on the phone and says: 'Hi, Cap, I got a little murder down here cluttering up the front room. And I've got five hundred iron men that are not working.' And then I say: 'Fine. Hold everything and I'll be right down with a blanket.'"

"Not quite that bad," I said.

"What did you want to see Talley about when you went to his house tonight?"

"He had some line on Florence Almore's death. Her parents hired him to follow it up, but he never told them what it was."

"And you thought he would tell you?" Webber asked sarcastically.

"All I could do was try."

"Or was it just that Degarmo getting tough with you made you feel like getting tough right back at him?"

"There might be a little of that in it too," I said.

"Talley was a petty blackmailer," Webber said contemptuously. "On more than one occasion. Any way to get rid of him was good enough. So I'll tell you what it was he had. He had a slipper he had stolen from Florence Almore's foot."

"A slipper?"

He smiled faintly. "Just a slipper. It was later found hidden in his house. It was a green velvet dancing pump with some little stones set into the heel. It was custom made, by a man in Hollywood who makes theatrical footwear and such. Now ask me what was important about this slipper?"

"What was important about it, captain?"

"She had two pair of them, exactly alike, made on the same order. It seems that is not unusual. In case one of them gets scuffed or some drunken ox tries to walk up a lady's leg." He paused and smiled thinly. "It seems that one pair had never been worn."

"I think I'm beginning to get it," I said.

He leaned back and tapped the arms of his chair. He waited.

"The walk from the side door of the house to the garage is rough concrete," I said. "Fairly rough. Suppose she didn't walk it, but was carried. And suppose whoever carried her put her slippers on – and got one that had not been worn."

"Yes?"

"And suppose Talley noticed this while Lavery was telephoning to the doctor, who was out on his rounds. So he took the unworn slipper, regarding it as evidence that Florence Almore had been murdered."

Webber nodded his head. "It was evidence if he left it where it was, for the police to find it. After he took it, it was just evidence that he was a rat."

"Was a monoxide test made of her blood?"

He put his hands flat on his desk and looked down at them. "Yes," he said. "And there was monoxide all right. Also the investigating officers were satisfied with appearances. There was no sign of violence. They were satisfied that Dr. Almore had not murdered his wife. Perhaps they were wrong. I think the investigation was a little superficial."

"And who was in charge of it?" I asked.

"I think you know the answer to that."

"When the police came, didn't they notice that a slipper was missing?"

"When the police came there was no slipper missing. You must remember that Dr. Almore was back at his home, in reponse to Lavery's call, before the police were called. All we know about the missing shoe is from Talley himself. He might have taken the unworn shoe from the house. The side door was unlocked. The maids were asleep. The objection to that is that he wouldn't have been likely to know there was an unworn slipper to take. I wouldn't put it past him to think of it. He's a sharp sneaky little devil. But I can't fix the necessary knowledge on him."

We sat there and looked at each other, thinking about it.

"Unless," Webber said slowly, "we can suppose that this nurse of Almore's was involved with Talley in a scheme to put the bite on Almore. It's possible. There are things in favor of it. There are more things against it. What reason have you for claiming that the girl drowned up in the mountains was this nurse?"

"Two reasons, neither one conclusive separately, but pretty powerful taken together. A tough guy who looked and acted like Degarmo was up there a few weeks ago showing a photograph of Mildred Haviland that looked something like Muriel Chess. Different hair and eyebrows and so on, but a fair resemblance. Nobody helped him much. He called himself De Soto and said he was a Los Angeles cop. There isn't any Los Angeles cop named De Soto. When Muriel Chess heard about it, she looked scared. If it was Degarmo, that's easily established. The other reason is that a golden anklet with a heart on it was hidden in a box of powdered sugar in the Chess cabin. It was found after her death, after her husband had been arrested. On the back of the heart was engraved: *Al to Mildred. June 28th, 1938. With all my love.*"

"It could have been some other Al and some other Mildred," Webber said.

"You don't really believe that, captain."

He leaned forward and made a hole in the air with his forefinger. "What do you want to make of all this exactly?"

"I want to make it that Kingsley's wife didn't shoot Lavery. That his death had something to do with the Almore business. And with Mildred Haviland. And possibly with Dr. Almore. I want to make it that Kingsley's wife disappeared because something happened that gave her a bad fright, that she may or may not have guilty knowledge, but that she hasn't murdered anybody. There's five hundred dollars in it for me, if I can determine that. It's legitimate to try."

He nodded. "Certainly it is. And I'm the man that would help you, if I could see any grounds for it. We haven't found the woman, but the time has been very short. But I can't help you put something on one of my boys."

I said: "I heard you call Degarmo Al. But I was thinking of Almore. His name's Albert."

Webber looked at his thumb. "But he was never married to the girl," he said quietly. "Degarmo was. I can tell you she led him a pretty dance. A lot of what seems bad in him is the result of it."

I sat very still. After a moment I said: "I'm beginning to see things I didn't know existed. What kind of a girl was she?"

"Smart, smooth and no good. She had a way with men. She could make them crawl over her shoes. The big boob would tear your head off right now, if you said anything against her. She divorced him, but that didn't end it for him."

"Does he know she is dead?"

Webber sat quiet for a long moment before he said: "Not from anything he has said. But how could he help it, if it's the same girl?"

"He never found her in the mountains — so far as we know."

I stood up and leaned down on the desk. "Look, captain, you're not kidding me, are you?"

"No. Not one damn bit. Some men are like that and some women can make them like it. If you think Degarmo went up there looking for her because he wanted to hurt her, you're as wet as a bar towel."

"I never quite thought that," I said. "It would be possible, provided Degarmo knew the country up there pretty well. Whoever murdered the girl did."

"This is all between us," he said. "I'd like you to keep it that way."

I nodded, but I didn't promise him. I said goodnight again and left. He looked after me as I went down the room. He looked hurt and sad.

The Chrysler was in the police lot at the side of the building with the keys in the ignition and none of the fenders smashed. Cooney hadn't made good on his threat. I drove back to Hollywood and went up to my apartment in the Bristol. It was late, almost midnight.

The green and ivory hallway was empty of all sound except that a telephone bell was ringing in one of the apartments. It rang insistently and got louder as I came near to my door. I unlocked the door. It was my telephone.

I walked across the room in darkness to where the phone stood on the ledge of an oak desk against the side wall. It must have rung at least ten times before I got to it.

I lifted it out of the cradle and answered, and it was Derace Kingsley on the line.

His voice sounded tight and brittle and strained. "Good Lord, where in hell have you been?" he snapped. "I've been trying to reach you for hours."

"All right. I'm here now," I said. "What is it?"

"I've heard from her."

I held the telephone very tight and drew my breath in slowly and let it out slowly. "Go ahead," I said.

"I'm not far away. I'll be over there in five or six minutes. Be prepared to move."

He hung up.

I stood there holding the telephone halfway between my ear and the cradle. Then I put it down very slowly and looked at the hand that had held it. It was half open and clenched stiff, as if it was still holding the instrument.

29

THE DISCREET MIDNIGHT tapping sounded on the door and I went over and opened it. Kingsley looked as big as a horse in a creamy Shetland sports coat with a green and yellow scarf around the neck inside the loosely turned-up collar. A dark reddish brown snapbrim hat was pulled low on his forehead and under its brim, his eyes looked like the eyes of a sick animal.

Miss Fromsett was with him. She was wearing slacks and sandals and a dark green coat and no hat and her hair had a wicked luster. In her ears hung ear drops made of a pair of tiny artificial gardenia blooms, hanging one above the other, two on each ear. Gillerlain Regal, the Champagne of Perfumes, came in at the door with her.

I shut the door and indicated the furniture and said: "A drink will probably help."

Miss Fromsett sat in an armchair and crossed her legs and looked around for cigarettes. She found one and lit it with a long casual flourish and smiled bleakly at a corner of the ceiling.

Kingsley stood in the middle of the floor trying to bite his chin. I went out to the dinette and mixed three drinks and brought them in and handed them. I went over to the chair by the chess table with mine.

Kingsley said: "What have you been doing and what's the matter with the leg?"

I said: "A cop kicked me. A present from the Bay City police department. It's a regular service they give down there. As to where I've been – in jail for drunk driving. And from the expression on your face, I think I may be right back there soon."

"I don't know what you're talking about," he said shortly. "I haven't the foggiest idea. This is no time to kid around."

"All right, don't," I said. "What did you hear and where is she?"

He sat down with his drink and flexed the fingers of his right hand, and put it inside his coat. It came out with an envelope, a long one.

"You have to take this to her," he said. "Five hundred dollars. She wanted more, but this is all I could raise. I cashed a check at a night club. It wasn't easy. She has to get out of town."

I said: "Out of what town?"

"Bay City somewhere. I don't know where. She'll meet you at a place called the Peacock Lounge, on Arguello Boulevard, at Eighth Street, or near it."

I looked at Miss Fromsett. She was still looking at the corner of the ceiling as if she had just come along for the ride.

Kingsley tossed the envelope across and it fell on the chess table. I looked inside. It was money all right. That much of his story made sense. I let it lie on the small polished table with its inlaid squares of brown and pale gold.

I said: "What's the matter with her drawing her own money? Any hotel would clear a check for her. Most of them would cash one. Has her bank account got lockjaw or something?"

"That's no way to talk," Kingsley said heavily. "She's in trouble. I don't know how she knows she's in trouble. Unless a pickup order has been broadcast. Has it?"

I said I didn't know. I hadn't had much time to listen to police calls. I had been too busy listening to live policemen.

Kingsley said: "Well, she won't risk cashing a check now. It was all right before. But not now." He lifted his eyes slowly and gave me one of the emptiest stares I had ever seen.

"All right, we can't make sense where there isn't any," I said. "So she's in Bay City. Did you talk to her?"

"No. Miss Fromsett talked to her. She called the office. It was just after hours but that cop from the beach, Captain Webber, was with me. Miss Fromsett naturally didn't want her to talk at all then. She told her to call back. She wouldn't give any number we could call."

I looked at Miss Fromsett. She brought her glance down from the ceiling and pointed it at the top of my head. There was nothing in her eyes at all. They were like drawn curtains.

Kingsley went on: "I didn't want to talk to her. She didn't want to talk to me. I don't want to see her. I guess there's no doubt she shot Lavery. Webber seemed quite sure of it."

"That doesn't mean anything," I said. "What he says and what he thinks don't even have to be on the same map. I don't like her knowing the cops were after her. It's a long time since anybody listened to the police short wave for amusement. So she called back later. And then?"

"It was almost half-past six," Kingsley said. "We had to sit there in the office and wait for her to call. You tell him." He turned his head to the girl.

Miss Fromsett said: "I took the call in Mr. Kingsley's office. He was sitting right beside me, but he didn't speak. She said to send the money down to the Peacock place and asked who would bring it."

"Did she sound scared?"

"Not in the least. Completely calm. I might say, icily calm. She had it all worked out. She realized somebody would have to bring the money she might not know. She seemed to know Derry – Mr. Kingsley wouldn't bring it."

"Call him Derry," I said. "I'll be able to guess who you mean."

She smiled faintly. "She will go into this Peacock Lounge every hour about fifteen minutes past the hour. I – I guess I assumed you would be the one to go. I described you to her. And you're to wear Derry's scarf. I described that. He keeps some clothes at the office and this was among them. It's distinctive enough."

It was all of that. It was an affair of fat green kidneys laid down on an egg yolk background. It would be almost as distinctive as if I went in there wheeling a red, white and blue wheelbarrow.

"For a blimp brain she's doing all right," I said.

"This is no time to fool around," Kingsley put in sharply.

"You said that before," I told him. "You've got a hell of a crust assuming I'll go down there and take a getaway stake to somebody I know the police are looking for."

He twisted a hand on his knee and his face twisted into a crooked grin.

"I admit it's a bit thick," he said. "Well, how about it?"

"It makes accessories after the fact out of all three of us. That might not be too tough for her husband and his confidential secretary to talk out of, but what they would do to me would be nobody's dream of a vacation."

"I'm going to make it worth your while," he said. "And we wouldn't be accessories, if she hasn't done anything."

"I'm willing to suppose it," I said. "Otherwise I wouldn't be talking to you. And in addition to that, if I decide she did do any murder, I'm going to turn her over to the police."

"She won't talk to you," he said.

I reached for the envelope and put it in my pocket. "She will, if she wants this." I looked at my strap watch. "If I start right away, I might make the one-fifteen deadline. They must know her by heart in that bar after all these hours. That makes it nice too."

"She's dyed her hair dark brown," Miss Fromsett said. "That ought to help a little."

I said: "It doesn't help me to think she is just an innocent wayfarer." I finished my drink and stood up. Kingsley swallowed his at a gulp and stood up and got the scarf off his neck and handed it to me.

"What did you do to get the police on your neck down there?" he asked.

"I was using some information Miss Fromsett very kindly got for me. And that led to my looking for a man named Talley who worked on the Almore case. And that led to the clink. They had the house staked. Talley was the dick the Graysons hired," I added, looking at the tall dark girl. "You'll probably be able to explain to him what it's all about. It doesn't matter anyway. I haven't time to go into it now. You two want to wait here?"

Kingsley shook his head. "We'll go to my place and wait for a call from you."

Miss Fromsett stood up and yawned. "No. I'm tired, Derry. I'm going home and going to bed."

"You'll come with me," he said sharply. "You've got to keep me from going nuts."

"Where do you live, Miss Fromsett?" I asked.

"Bryson Tower on Sunset Place. Apartment 716. Why?" She gave me a speculative look.

"I might want to reach you some time."

Kingsley's face looked bleakly irritated, but his eyes still were the eyes of a sick animal. I wound his scarf around my neck and went out to the dinette to switch off the light. When I came back they were both standing by the door. Kingsley had his arm around her shoulders. She looked very tired and rather bored.

"Well, I certainly hope —" he started to say, then took a quick step and put his hand out. "You're a pretty level guy, Marlowe."

"Go on, beat it," I said. "Go away. Go far away."

He gave a queer look and they went out.

I waited until I heard the elevator come up and stop, and the doors open and close again, and the elevator start down. Then I went out myself and took the stairs down to the basement garage and got the Chrysler awake again.

30

THE PEACOCK LOUNGE was a narrow front next to a gift shop in whose window a tray of small crystal animals shimmered in the street light. The Peacock had a glass brick front and soft light glowed out around the stained-glass peacock that was set into the brick. I went in around a Chinese screen and looked along the bar and then sat at the outer edge of a small booth. The light was amber, the leather was Chinese red and the booths had polished plastic tables. In one booth four soldiers were drinking beer moodily, a little glassy in the eyes and obviously bored even with drinking beer. Across from them a party of two girls and two flashy-looking men were making the noise in the place. I saw nobody that looked like my idea of Crystal Kingsley.

A wizened waiter with evil eyes and a face like a gnawed bone put a napkin with a printed peacock on it down on the table in front of me and gave me a Bacardi cocktail. I sipped it and looked at the amber face of the bar clock. It was just past one-fifteen.

One of the men with the two girls got up suddenly and stalked along to the door and went out. The voice of the other man said:

"What did you have to insult the guy for?"

A girl's tinny voice said: "Insult him? I like that. He propositioned me."

The man's voice said complainingly: "Well, you didn't have to insult him, did you?"

One of the soldiers suddenly laughed deep in his chest and then wiped the laugh off his face with a brown hand and drank a little more beer. I rubbed the back of my knee. It was hot and swollen still but the paralyzed feeling had gone away.

A tiny, white-faced Mexican boy with enormous black eyes came in with morning papers and scuttled along the booths trying to make a few sales before the barman threw him out. I bought a paper and looked through it to see if there were any interesting murders. There were not.

I folded it and looked up as a slim, brown-haired girl in coal black slacks and a yellow shirt and a long gray coat came out of somewhere and passed the booth without looking at me. I tried to make up my mind whether her face was familiar or just such a standard type of lean, rather hard, prettiness that I must have seen it ten thousand times. She went out of the street door around the screen. Two minutes later the little Mexican boy came back in, shot a quick look at the barman, and scuttled over to stand in front of me.

"Mister," he said, his great big eyes shining with mischief. Then he made a beckoning sign and scuttled out again.

I finished my drink and went after him. The girl in the gray coat and yellow shirt and black slacks was standing in front of the gift shop, looking in at the window. Her eyes moved as I went out. I went and stood beside her.

She looked at me again. Her face was white and tired. Her hair looked darker than dark brown. She looked away and spoke to the window.

"Give me the money, please." A little mist formed on the plate glass from her breath.

I said: "I'd have to know who you are."

"You know who I am," she said softly. "How much did you bring?"

"Five hundred."

"It's not enough," she said. "Not nearly enough. Give it to me quickly. I've been waiting half of eternity for somebody to get here."

"Where can we talk?"

"We don't have to talk. Just give me the money and go the other way."

"It's not that simple. I'm doing this at quite a risk. I'm at least going to have the satisfaction of knowing what goes on and where I stand."

"Damn you," she said acidly, "why couldn't he come himself? I don't want to talk. I want to get away as soon as I can."

"You didn't want him to come himself. He understood that you didn't even want to talk to him on the phone."

"That's right," she said quickly and tossed her head.

"But you've got to talk to me," I said. "I'm not as easy as he is. Either to me or to the law. There's no way out of it. I'm a private detective and I have to have some protection too."

"Well, isn't he charming," she said. "Private detective and all." Her voice held a low sneer.

"He did the best he knew how. It wasn't easy for him to know what to do."

"What do you want to talk about?"

"You, and what you've been doing and where you've been and what you expect to do. Things like that. Little things, but important."

She breathed on the glass of the shop window and waited while the mist of her breath disappeared.

"I think it would be much better," she said in the same cool empty voice, "for you to give me the money and let me work things out for myself."

"No."

She gave me another sharp sideways glance. She shrugged the shoulders of the gray coat impatiently.

"Very well, if it has to be that way. I'm at the Granada, two blocks north on Eighth. Apartment 618. Give me ten minutes. I'd rather go in alone."

"I have a car."

"I'd rather go alone." She turned quickly and walked away.

She walked back to the corner and crossed the boulevard and disappeared along the block under a line of pepper trees. I went and sat in the Chrysler and gave her her ten minutes before I started it.

The Granada was an ugly gray building on a corner. The plate glass entrance door was level with the street. I drove around the corner and saw a milky globe with *Garage* painted on it. The entrance to the garage was down a ramp into the hard rubber-smelling silence of parked cars in rows. A lanky Negro came out of a glassed-in office and looked the Chrysler over.

"How much to leave this here a short time? I'm going upstairs."

He gave me a shady leer. "Kinda late, boss. She needs a good dustin' too. Be a dollar."

"What goes on here?"

"Be a dollar," he said woodenly.

I got out. He gave me a ticket. I gave him the dollar. Without asking him he said the elevator was in back of the office, by the Men's Room.

I rode up to the sixth floor and looked at numbers on doors and listened to stillness and smelled beach air coming in at the end of corridors. The place seemed decent enough. There would be a few happy ladies in any apartment house. That would explain the lanky Negro's dollar. A great judge of character, that boy.

I came to the door of Apartment 618 and stood outside it a moment and then knocked softly.

31

SHE STILL HAD the gray coat on. She stood back from the door and I went past her into a square room with twin wall beds and a minimum of uninteresting furniture. A small lamp on a window table made a dim yellowish light. The window behind it was open.

The girl said: "Sit down and talk then."

She closed the door and went to sit in a gloomy Boston rocker across the room. I sat down on a thick davenport. There was a dull green curtain hanging across an open door space, at one end of the davenport. That would lead to dressing room and bathroom. There was a closed door at the other end. That would be the kitchenette. That would be all there was.

The girl crossed her ankles and leaned her head back against the chair and looked at me under long beaded lashes. Her eyebrows were thin and arched and as brown as her hair. It was a quiet, secret face. It didn't look like the face of a woman who would waste a lot of motion.

"I got a rather different idea of you," I said, "from Kingsley."

Her lips twisted a little. She said nothing.

"From Lavery too," I said. "It just goes to show that we talk different languages to different people."

"I haven't time for this sort of talk," she said. "What is it you have to know?"

"He hired me to find you. I've been working on it. I supposed you would know that."

"Yes. His office sweetie told me that over the phone. She told me you would be a man named Marlowe. She told me about the scarf."

I took the scarf off my neck and folded it up and slipped it into a pocket. I said:

"So I know a little about your movements. Not very much. I know you left your car at the Prescott Hotel in San Bernardino and that you met Lavery there. I know you sent a wire from El Paso. What did you do then?"

"All I want from you is the money he sent. I don't see that my movements are any of your business."

"I don't have to argue about that," I said. "It's a question of whether you want the money."

"Well, we went to El Paso," she said, in a tired voice. "I thought of marrying him then. So I sent that wire. You saw the wire?"

"Yes."

"Well, I changed my mind. I asked him to go home and leave me. He made a scene."

"Did he go home and leave you?"

"Yes. Why not?"

"What did you do then?"

"I went to Santa Barbara and stayed there a few days. Over a week in fact. Then to Pasadena. Same thing. Then to Hollywood. Then I came down here. That's all."

"You were alone all this time?"

She hesitated a little and then said: "Yes."

"Not with Lavery — any part of it?"

"Not after he went home."

"What was the idea?"

"Idea of what?" Her voice was a little sharp.

"Idea of going to these places and not sending any word. Didn't you know he would be very anxious?"

"Oh, you mean my husband," she said coolly. "I don't think I worried much about him. He'd think I was in Mexico, wouldn't he? As for the idea of it all – well, I just had to think things out. My life had got to be a hopeless tangle. I had to be somewhere quite alone and try to straighten myself out."

"Before that," I said, "you spent a month at Little Fawn Lake trying to straighten it out and not getting anywhere. Is that it?"

She looked down at her shoes and then up at me and nodded earnestly. The wavy brown hair surged forward along her cheeks. She put her left hand up and pushed it back and then rubbed her temple with one finger.

"I seemed to need a new place," she said. "Not necessarily an interesting place. Just a strange place. Without associations. A place where I would be very much alone. Like a hotel."

"How are you getting on with it?"

"Not very well. But I'm not going back to Derace Kingsley. Does he want me to?"

"I don't know. But why did you come down here, to the town where Lavery was?"

She bit a knuckle and looked at me over her hand.

"I wanted to see him again. He's all mixed up in my mind. I'm not in love with him, and yet – well, I suppose in a way I am. But I don't think I want to marry him. Does that make sense?"

"That part of it makes sense. But staying away from home in a lot of crummy hotels doesn't. You've lived your own life for years, as I understand it."

"I had to be alone, to – to think things out," she said a little desperately and bit the knuckle again, hard. "Won't you please give me the money and go away?"

"Sure. Right away. But wasn't there any other reason for your going away from Little Fawn Lake just then? Anything connected with Muriel Chess, for instance?"

171

She looked surprised. But anyone can look surprised. "Good heavens, what would there be? That frozen-faced little drip – what is she to me?"

"I thought you might have had a fight with her – about Bill."

"Bill? Bill Chess?" She seemed even more surprised. Almost too surprised.

"Bill claims you made a pass at him."

She put her head back and let out a tinny and unreal laugh. "Good heavens, that muddy-faced boozer?" Her face sobered suddenly. "What's happened? Why all the mystery?"

"He might be a muddy-faced boozer," I said. "The police think he's a murderer too. Of his wife. She's been found drowned in the lake. After a month."

She moistened her lips and held her head on one side, staring at me fixedly. There was a quiet little silence. The damp breath of the Pacific slid into the room around us.

"I'm not too surprised," she said slowly. "So it came to that in the end. They fought terribly at times. Do you think that had something to do with my leaving?"

I nodded. "There was a chance of it."

"It didn't have anything to do with it at all," she said seriously, and shook her head back and forth. "It was just the way I told you. Nothing else."

"Muriel's dead," I said. "Drowned in the lake. You don't get much of a boot out of that, do you?"

"I hardly knew the girl," she said. "Really. She kept to herself. After all –"

"I don't suppose you knew she had once worked in Dr. Almore's office?"

She looked completely puzzled now. "I was never in Dr. Almore's office," she said slowly. "He made a few house calls a long time ago. I – what are you talking about?"

"Muriel Chess was really a girl called Mildred Haviland, who had been Dr. Almore's office nurse."

172

"That's a queer coincidence," she said wonderingly. "I knew Bill met her in Riverside. I didn't know how or under what circumstances or where she came from. Dr. Almore's office, eh? It doesn't have to mean anything, does it?"

I said: "No. I guess it's a genuine coincidence. They do happen. But you see why I had to talk to you. Muriel being found drowned and you having gone away and Muriel being Mildred Haviland who was connected with Dr. Almore at one time — as Lavery was also, in a different way. And of course Lavery lives across the street from Dr. Almore. Did he, Lavery, seem to know Muriel from somewhere else?"

She thought about it, biting her lower lip gently. "He saw her up there," she said finally. "He didn't act as if he had ever seen her before."

"And he would have," I said. "Being the kind of guy he was."

"I don't think Chris had anything to do with Dr. Almore," she said. "He knew Dr. Almore's wife. I don't think he knew the doctor at all. So he probably wouldn't know Dr. Almore's office nurse."

"Well, I guess there's nothing in all this to help me," I said. "But you can see why I had to talk to you. I guess I can give you the money now."

I got the envelope out and stood up to drop it on her knee. She let it lie there. I sat down again.

"You do this character very well," I said. "This confused innocence with an undertone of hardness and bitterness. People have made a bad mistake about you. They have been thinking of you as a reckless little idiot with no brains and no control. They have been very wrong."

She stared at me, lifting her eyebrows. She said nothing. Then a small smile lifted the corners of her mouth. She reached for the envelope, tapped it on her knee, and laid it aside on the table. She stared at me all the time.

"You did the Fallbrook character very well too," I said. "Looking back on it, I think it was a shade overdone. But at the time it had me going all right. That purple hat that would have been all right on blond hair but looked like hell on straggly brown, that messed-up makeup that looked as if it had been put on in the dark by somebody with a sprained wrist, the jittery screwball manner. All very good. And when you put the gun in my hand like that – I fell like a brick."

She snickered and put her hands in the deep pockets of her coat. Her heels tapped on the floor.

"But why did you go back at all?" I asked. "Why take such a risk in broad daylight, in the middle of the morning?"

"So you think I shot Chris Lavery?" she said quietly.

"I don't think it. I know it."

"Why did I go back? Is that what you want to know?"

"I don't really care," I said.

She laughed. A sharp cold laugh. "He had all my money," she said. "He had stripped my purse. He had it all, even silver. That's why I went back. There wasn't any risk at all. I know how he lived. It was really safer to go back. To take in the milk and newspaper for instance. People lose their heads in these situations. I don't, I didn't see why I should. It's so very much safer not to."

"I see," I said. "Then of course you shot him the night before. I ought to have thought of that, not that it matters. He had been shaving. But guys with dark beards and lady friends sometimes shave the last thing at night, don't they?"

"It has been heard of," she said almost gaily. "And just what are you going to do about it?"

"You're a cold-blooded little bitch if I ever saw one," I said. "Do about it? Turn you over to the police, naturally. It will be a pleasure."

"I don't think so." She threw the words out, almost with a lilt. "You wondered why I gave you the empty gun. Why not? I had another one in my bag. Like this."

Her right hand came up from her coat pocket and she pointed it at me.

I grinned. It may not have been the heartiest grin in the world, but it was a grin.

"I've never liked this scene," I said. "Detective confronts murderer. Murderer produces gun, points same at detective. Murderer tells detective the whole sad story, with the idea of shooting him at the end of it. Thus wasting a lot of valuable time, even if in the end murderer did shoot detective. Only murderer never does. Something always happens to prevent it. The gods don't like this scene either. They always manage to spoil it."

"But this time," she said softly and got up and moved towards me softly across the carpet, "suppose we make it a little different. Suppose I don't tell you anything and nothing happens and I do shoot you?"

"I still wouldn't like the scene," I said.

"You don't seem to be afraid," she said, and slowly licked her lips coming towards me very gently without any sound of footfalls on the carpet.

"I'm not afraid," I lied. "It's too late at night, too still, and the window is open and the gun would make too much noise. It's too long a journey down to the street and you're not good with guns. You would probably miss me. You missed Lavery three times."

"Stand up," she said.

I stood up.

"I'm going to be too close to miss," she said. She pushed the gun against my chest. "Like this. I really can't miss now, can I? Now be very still. Hold your hands up by your shoulders and then don't move at all. If you move at all, the gun will go off."

I put my hands up beside my shoulders, I looked down at the gun. My tongue felt a little thick, but I could still wave it.

Her probing left hand didn't find a gun on me. It dropped and she bit her lip, staring at me. The gun bored into my chest.

"You'll have to turn around now," she said, polite as a tailor at a fitting.

"There's something a little off key about everything you do," I said. "You're definitely not good with guns. You're much too close to me, and I hate to bring this up – but there's that old business of the safety catch not being off. You've overlooked that too."

So she started to do two things at once. To take a long step backwards and to feel with her thumb for the safety catch, without taking her eyes off my face. Two very simple things, needing only a second to do. But she didn't like my telling her. She didn't like my thought riding over hers. The minute confusion of it jarred her.

She let out a small choked sound and I dropped my right hand and yanked her face hard against my chest. My left hand smashed down on her right wrist, the heel of my hand against the base of her thumb. The gun jerked out of her hand to the floor. Her face writhed against my chest and I think she was trying to scream.

Then she tried to kick me and lost what little balance she had left. Her hands came up to claw at me. I caught her wrist and began to twist it behind her back. She was very strong, but I was very much stronger. So she decided to go limp and let her whole weight sag against the hand that was holding her head. I couldn't hold her up with one hand. She started to go down and I had to bend down with her.

There were vague sounds of our scuffling on the floor by the davenport, and hard breathing, and if a floorboard creaked I didn't hear it. I thought a curtain ring checked sharply on a rod. I wasn't sure and I had no time to consider the question. A figure loomed up suddenly on my left, just behind, and out of range of clear vision. I knew there was a man there and that he was a big man.

That was all I knew. The scene exploded into fire and darkness. I didn't even remember being slugged. Fire and darkness and just before the darkness a sharp flash of nausea.

32

I SMELLED OF gin. Not just casually, as if I had taken four or five drinks of a winter morning to get out of bed on, but as if the Pacific Ocean was pure gin and I had nose-dived off the boat deck. The gin was in my hair and eyebrows, on my chin and under my chin. It was on my shirt. I smelled like dead toads.

My coat was off and I was lying flat on my back beside the davenport on somebody's carpet and I was looking at a framed picture. The frame was of cheap soft wood varnished and the picture showed part of an enormously high pale yellow viaduct across which a shiny black locomotive was dragging a Prussian blue train. Through one lofty arch of the viaduct a wide yellow beach showed and was dotted with sprawled bathers and striped beach umbrellas. Three girls walked close up, with paper parasols, one girl in cerise, one in pale blue, one in green. Beyond the beach a curving bay was bluer than any bay has any right to be. It was drenched with sunshine and flecked and dotted with arching white sails. Beyond the inland curve of the bay three ranges of hills rose in three precisely opposed colors, gold and terra cotta and lavender.

Across the bottom of the picture was printed in large capitals SEE THE FRENCH RIVIERA BY THE BLUE TRAIN.

It was a fine time to bring that up.

I reached up wearily and felt the back of my head. It felt pulpy. A shoot of pain from the touch went clear to the soles of my feet. I groaned, and made a grunt out of the groan, from professional pride – what was left of it. I rolled over slowly and carefully and looked at the foot of a pulled-down wall bed; one twin, the other being still up in the wall. The flourish of design on the painted wood was familiar. The picture had hung over the davenport and I hadn't even looked at it.

When I rolled a square gin bottle rolled off my chest and hit the floor. It was water white, and empty. It didn't seem possible there could be so much gin in just one bottle.

I got my knees under me and stayed on all fours for a while, sniffing like a dog who can't finish his dinner, but hates to leave it. I moved my head around on my neck. It hurt. I moved it around some more and it still hurt, so I climbed up on my feet and discovered I didn't have any shoes on.

The shoes were lying against the baseboard, looking as dissipated as shoes ever looked. I put them on wearily. I was an old man now. I was going down the last long hill. I still had a tooth left though. I felt it with my tongue. It didn't seem to taste of gin.

"It will all come back to you," I said. "Some day it will all come back to you. And you won't like it."

There was the lamp on the table by the open window. There was the fat green davenport. There was the doorway with the green curtains across it. Never sit with your back to a green curtain. It always turns out badly. Something always happens. Who had I said that to? A girl with a gun. A girl with a clear empty face and dark brown hair that had been blond.

I looked around for her. She was still there. She was lying on the pulled-down twin bed.

She was wearing a pair of tan stockings and nothing else. Her hair was tumbled. There were dark bruises on her throat. Her mouth was open and a swollen tongue filled it to overflowing. Her eyes bulged and the whites of them were not white.

Across her naked belly four angry scratches leered crimson red against the whiteness of flesh. Deep angry scratches, gouged out by four bitter fingernails.

On the davenport there were tumbled clothes, mostly hers. My coat was there also. I disentangled it and put it on. Something crackled under my hand in the tumbled clothes. I drew out a long envelope with money still in it. I put it in my pocket. Marlowe, five hundred dollars. I hoped it was all there. There didn't seem much else to hope for.

I stepped on the balls of my feet softly, as if walking on very thin ice. I bent down to rub behind my knee and wondered which hurt most, my knee, or my head when I bent down to rub the knee.

Heavy feet came along the hallway and there was a hard mutter of voices. The feet stopped. A hard fist knocked on the door.

I stood there leering at the door, with my lips drawn back tight against my teeth. I waited for somebody to open the door and walk in. The knob was tried, but nobody walked in. The knocking began again, stopped, the voices muttered again. The steps went away. I wondered how long it would take to get the manager with a pass key. Not very long.

Not nearly long enough for Marlowe to get home from the French Riviera.

I went to the green curtain and brushed it aside and looked down a short dark hallway into a bathroom. I went in there and put the light on. Two wash rugs on the floor, a bath mat folded over the edge of the tub, a pebbled glass window at the corner of the tub. I shut the bathroom door and stood on the edge of the tub and eased the window up. This was the sixth floor. There was no screen. I put my head out and looked into darkness and a narrow glimpse of a street with trees. I looked sideways and saw that the bathroom window of the next apartment was not more than three feet away. A well-nourished mountain goat could make it without any trouble at all.

The question was whether a battered private detective could make it, and if so, what the harvest would be.

Behind me a rather remote and muffled voice seemed to be chanting the policeman's litany: "Open it up or we'll kick it in." I sneered back at the voice. They wouldn't kick it in because kicking in a door is hard on the feet. Policemen are kind to their feet. Their feet are about all they are kind to.

I grabbed a towel off the rack and pulled the two halves of the window down and eased out on the sill. I swung half of me over to the next sill, holding on to the frame of the open window. I could just reach to push the next window down, if it was unlocked. It wasn't unlocked. I got my foot over there and kicked the glass over the catch. It made a noise that ought to have been heard in Reno. I wrapped the towel around my left hand and reached in to turn the catch. Down on the street a car went by, but nobody yelled at me.

I pushed the broken window down and climbed across to the other sill. The towel fell out of my hand and fluttered down into the darkness to a strip of grass far below, between the two wings of the building.

I climbed in at the window of the other bathroom.

33

I CLIMBED DOWN into darkness and groped through darkness to a door and opened it and listened. Filtered moonlight coming through north windows showed a bedroom with twin beds, made up and empty. Not wall beds. This was a larger apartment. I moved past the beds to another door and into a living room. Both rooms were closed up and smelled musty. I felt my way to a lamp and switched it on. I ran a finger along the wood of a table edge. There was a light film of dust, such as accumulates in the cleanest room when it is left shut up.

The room contained a library dining table, an armchair radio, a book rack built like a hod, a big bookcase full of novels with their jackets still on them, a dark wood highboy with a siphon and a cut-glass bottle of liquor and four striped glasses upside down on an Indian brass tray. Besides this paired photographs in a double silver frame, a youngish middle-aged man and woman, with round healthy faces and cheerful eyes. They looked out at me as if they didn't mind my being there at all.

I sniffed the liquor, which was Scotch, and used some of it. It made my head feel worse but it made the rest of me feel better. I put the light on in the bedroom and poked into closets. One of them had a man's clothes, tailor-made, plenty of them. The tailor's label inside a coat pocket declared the owner's name to be H. G. Talbot. I went to the bureau and poked around and found a soft blue shirt that looked a little small for me. I carried it into the bathroom and stripped mine off and washed my face and chest and wiped my hair off with a wet towel and put the blue shirt on. I used plenty of Mr. Talbot's rather insistent hair tonic on my hair and used his brush and comb to tidy it up. By that time I smelled of gin only remotely, if at all.

The top button of the shirt wouldn't meet its buttonhole so I poked into the bureau again and found a dark blue crepe tie and strung it around my neck. I got my coat back on and looked at myself in the mirror. I looked slightly too neat for that hour of the night, even for as careful a man as Mr. Talbot's clothes indicated him to be. Too neat and too sober.

I rumpled my hair a little and pulled the tie close, and went back to the whiskey decanter and did what I could about being too sober. I lit one of Mr. Talbot's cigarettes and hoped that Mr. and Mrs. Talbot, wherever they were, were having a much better time than I was. I hoped I would live long enough to come and visit them.

I went to the living room door, the one giving on the hallway, and opened it and leaned in the opening smoking. I didn't think it was going to work. But I didn't think waiting there for them to follow my trail through the window was going to work any better.

A man coughed a little way down the hall and I poked my head out farther and he was looking at me. He came towards me briskly, a small sharp man in a neatly pressed police uniform. He had reddish hair and red-gold eyes.

I yawned and said languidly: "What goes on, officer?"

He stared at me thoughtfully. "Little trouble next door to you. Hear anything?"

"I thought I heard knocking. I just got home a little while ago."

"Little late," he said.

"That's a matter of opinion," I said. "Trouble next door, ah?"

"A dame," he said. "Know her?"

"I think I've seen her."

"Yeah," he said. "You ought to see her now . . ." He put his hands to his throat and bulged his eyes out and gurgled unpleasantly. "Like that," he said. "You didn't hear nothing, huh?"

"Nothing I noticed – except the knocking."

"Yeah. What was the name?"

"Talbot."

"Just a minute, Mr. Talbot. Wait there just a minute."

He went along the hallway and leaned into an open doorway through which light streamed out. "Oh, lieutenant," he said. "The man next door is on deck."

A tall man came out of the doorway and stood looking along the hall straight at me. A tall man with rusty hair and very blue, blue eyes. Degarmo. That made it perfect.

"Here's the guy lives next door," the small neat cop said helpfully. "His name's Talbot."

Degarmo looked straight at me, but nothing in his acid blue eyes showed that he had ever seen me before. He came quietly along the hall and put a hard hand against my chest and pushed me back into the room. When he had me half a dozen feet from the door he said over his shoulder:

"Come in here and shut the door, Shorty."

The small cop came in and shut the door.

"Quite a gag," Degarmo said lazily. "Put a gun on him, Shorty."

Shorty flicked his black belt holster open and had his .38 in his hand like a flash. He licked his lips.

"Oh boy," he said softly, whistling a little. "Oh boy. How'd you know, lieutenant?"

"Know what?" Degarmo asked, keeping his eyes fixed on mine. "What were you thinking of doing, pal — going down to get a paper — to find out if she was dead?"

"Oh boy," Shorty said. "A sex-killer. He pulled the girl's clothes off and choked her with his hands, lieutenant. How'd you know?"

Degarmo didn't answer him. He just stood there, rocking a little on his heels, his face empty and granite-hard.

"Yah, he's the killer, sure," Shorty said suddenly. "Sniff the air in here, lieutenant. The place ain't been aired out for days. And look at the dust on those bookshelves. And the clock on the mantel's stopped, lieutenant. He come in through the — lemme look a minute, can I, lieutenant?"

He ran out of the room into the bedroom. I heard him fumbling around. Degarmo stood woodenly.

Shorty came back. "Come in at the bathroom window. There's broken glass in the tub. And something stinks of gin in there something awful. You remember how that apartment smelled of gin when we went in? Here's a shirt, lieutenant. Smells like it was washed in gin."

He held the shirt up. It perfumed the air rapidly. Degarmo looked at it vaguely and then stepped forward and yanked my coat open and looked at the shirt I was wearing.

"I know what he done," Shorty said. "He stole one of the guy's shirts that lives here. You see what he done, lieutenant?"

"Yeah." Degarmo held his hand against my chest and let it fall slowly. They were talking about me as if I was a piece of wood.

"Frisk him, Shorty."

Shorty ran around me feeling here and there for a gun. "Nothing on him," he said.

"Let's get him out the back way," Degarmo said. "It's our pinch, if we make it before Webber gets here. That lug Reed couldn't find a moth in a shoe box."

"You ain't even detailed on the case," Shorty said doubtfully. "Didn't I hear you was suspended or something?"

"What can I lose?" Degarmo asked, "if I'm suspended?"

"I can lose this here uniform," Shorty said.

Degarmo looked at him wearily. The small cop blushed and his bright red-gold eyes were anxious.

"Okay, Shorty. Go and tell Reed."

The small cop licked his lip. "You say the word, lieutenant, and I'm with you. I don't have to know you got suspended."

"We'll take him down ourselves, just the two of us," Degarmo said.

"Yeah, sure."

Degarmo put his finger against my chin. "A sex-killer," he said quietly. "Well, I'll be damned." He smiled at me thinly, moving only the extreme corners of his wide brutal mouth.

34

WE WENT OUT of the apartment and along the hall the other way from Apartment 618. Light streamed from the still open door. Two men in plain clothes now stood outside it smoking cigarettes inside their cupped hands, as if a wind was blowing. There was a sound of wrangling voices from the apartment.

We went around the bend of the hall and came to the elevator. Degarmo opened the fire door beyond the elevator shaft and we went down echoing concrete steps, floor after floor. At the lobby floor Degarmo stopped and held his hand on the doorknob and listened. He looked back over his shoulder.

"You got a car?" he asked me.

"In the basement garage."

"That's an idea."

We went on down the steps and came out into the shadowy basement. The lanky Negro came out of the little office and I gave him my car check. He looked furtively at the police uniform on Shorty. He said nothing. He pointed to the Chrysler.

Degarmo climbed under the wheel of the Chrysler. I got in beside him and Shorty got into the back seat. We went up the ramp and out into the damp cool night air. A big car with twin red spotlights was charging towards us from a couple of blocks away.

Degarmo spat out of the car window and yanked the Chrysler the other way. "That will be Webber," he said. "Late for the funeral again. We sure skinned his nose on that one, Shorty."

"I don't like it too well, lieutenant. I don't, honest."

"Keep the chin up, kid. You might get back on homicide."

"I'd rather wear buttons and eat," Shorty said. The courage was oozing out of him fast.

Degarmo drove the car hard for ten blocks and then slowed a little. Shorty said uneasily:

"I guess you know what you're doing, lieutenant, but this ain't the way to the Hall."

"That's right," Degarmo said. "It never was, was it?" He let the car slow down to a crawl and then turned into a residential street of small exact houses squatting behind small exact lawns. He braked the car gently and coasted over to the curb and stopped about the middle of the block. He threw an arm over the back of the seat and turned his head to look back at Shorty.

"You think this guy killed her, Shorty?"

"I'm listening," Shorty said in a tight voice.

"Got a flash?"

"No."

I said: "There's one in the car pocket on the left side."

Shorty fumbled around and metal clicked and the white beam of the flashlight came on. Degarmo said:

"Take a look at the back of this guy's head."

The beam moved and settled. I heard the small man's breathing behind me and felt it on my neck. Something felt for and touched the bump on my head. I grunted. The light went off and the darkness of the street rushed in again.

Shorty said: "I guess maybe he was sapped, lieutenant. I don't get it."

"So was the girl," Degarmo said. "It didn't show much but it's there. She was sapped so she could have her clothes pulled off and be clawed up before she was killed. So the scratches would bleed. Then she was throttled. And none of this made any noise. Why would it? And there's no telephone in that apartment. Who reported it, Shorty?"

"How the hell would I know? A guy called up and said a woman had been murdered in 618 Granada Apartments on Eighth. Reed was still looking for a cameraman when you came in. The desk said a guy with a thick voice, likely disguised. Didn't give any name at all."

"All right then," Degarmo said. "If you had murdered the girl, how would you get out of there?"

"I'd walk out," Shorty said. "Why not? Hey," he barked at me suddenly, "why didn't you?"

I didn't answer him. Degarmo said tonelessly: "You wouldn't climb out of a bathroom window six floors up and then burst in another bathroom window into a strange apartment where people would likely be sleeping, would you? You wouldn't pretend to be the guy that lived there and you wouldn't throw away a lot of your time by calling the police, would you? Hell, that girl could have laid there for a week. You wouldn't throw away the chance of a start like that, would you, Shorty?"

"I don't guess I would," Shorty said cautiously. "I don't guess I would call up at all. But you know these sex fiends do funny things, lieutenant. They ain't normal like us. And this guy could have had help and the other guy could have knocked him out to put him in the middle."

"Don't tell me you thought that last bit up all by yourself," Degarmo grunted. "So here we sit, and the fellow that knows

all the answers is sitting here with us and not saying a word."
He turned his big head and stared at me. "What were you
doing there?"

"I can't remember," I said. "The crack on the head seems
to have blanked me out."

"We'll help you to remember," Degarmo said. "We'll take
you up back in the hills a few miles where you can be quiet
and look at the stars and remember. You'll remember all right."

Shorty said: "That ain't no way to talk, lieutenant. Why
don't we just go back to the Hall and play this the way it says
in the rule book?"

"To hell with the rule book," Degarmo said. "I like this
guy. I want to have one long sweet talk with him. He just
needs a little coaxing, Shorty. He's just bashful."

"I don't want any part of it," Shorty said.

"What do you want to do, Shorty?"

"I want to go back to the Hall."

"Nobody's stopping you, kid. You want to walk?"

Shorty was silent for a moment. "That's right," he said at
last, quietly. "I want to walk." He opened the car door and
stepped out on to the curbing. "And I guess you know I have
to report all this, lieutenant."

"Right," Degarmo said. "Tell Webber I was asking for him.
Next time he buys a hamburger, tell him to turn down an
empty plate for me."

"That don't make any sense to me," the small cop said. He
slammed the car door shut. Degarmo let the clutch in and
gunned the motor and hit forty in the first block and a half.
In the third block he hit fifty. He slowed down at the boulevard and turned east and began to cruise along at a legal
speed. A few late cars drifted by both ways, but for the most
part the world lay in the cold silence of early morning.

After a little while we passed the city limits and Degarmo
spoke. "Let's hear you talk," he said quietly. "Maybe we can
work this out."

The car topped a long rise and dipped down to where the boulevard wound through the parklike grounds of the veterans' hospital. The tall triple electroliers had halos from the beach fog that had drifted in during the night. I began to talk.

"Kingsley came over to my apartment tonight and said he had heard from his wife over the phone. She wanted some money quick. The idea was I was to take it to her and get her out of whatever trouble she was in. My idea was a little different. She was told how to identify me and I was to be at the Peacock Lounge at Eighth and Arguello at fifteen minutes past the hour. Any hour."

Degarmo said slowly: "She had to breeze and that meant she had something to breeze from, such as murder." He lifted his hands lightly and let them fall on the wheel again.

"I went down there, hours after she had called. I had been told her hair was dyed brown. She passed me going out of the bar, but I didn't know her. I had never seen her in the flesh. All I had seen was what looked like a pretty good snapshot, but could be that and still not a very good likeness. She sent a Mexican kid in to call me out. She wanted the money and no conversation. I wanted her story. Finally she saw she would have to talk a little and told me she was at the Granada. She made me wait ten minutes before I followed her over."

Degarmo said: "Time to fix up a plant."

"There was a plant all right, but I'm not sure she was in on it. She didn't want me to come up there, didn't want to talk. Yet she ought to have known I would insist on some explanation before I gave up the money, so her reluctance could have been just an act, to make me feel that I was controlling the situation. She could act all right. I found that out. Anyhow I went and we talked. Nothing she said made very much sense until we talked about Lavery getting shot. Then she made too much sense too quick. I told her I was going to turn her over to the police."

Westwood Village, dark except for one all-night service station and a few distant windows in apartment houses, slid away to the north of us.

"So she pulled a gun," I said. "I think she meant to use it, but she got too close to me and I got a headlock on her. While we were wrestling around, somebody came out from behind a green curtain and slugged me. When I came out of that the murder was done."

Degarmo said slowly: "You get any kind of a look at who slugged you?"

"No. I felt or half saw he was a man and a big one. And this lying on the davenport, mixed in with clothes." I reached Kingsley's yellow and green scarf out of my pocket and draped it over his knee. "I saw Kingsley wearing this earlier this evening," I said.

Degarmo looked down at the scarf. He lifted it under the dashlight. "You wouldn't forget that too quick," he said. "It steps right up and smacks you in the eye. Kingsley, huh? Well, I'm damned. What happened then?"

"Knocking on the door. Me still woozy in the head, not too bright and a bit panicked. I had been flooded with gin and my shoes and coat stripped off and maybe I looked and smelled a little like somebody who would yank a woman's clothes off and strangle her. So I got out through the bathroom window, cleaned myself up as well as I could, and the rest you know."

Degarmo said: "Why didn't you lie dormy in the place you climbed into?"

"What was the use? I guess even a Bay City cop would have found the way I had gone in a little while. If I had any chance at all, it was to walk before that was discovered. If nobody was there who knew me, I had a fair chance of getting out of the building."

"I don't think so," Degarmo said. "But I can see where you didn't lose much trying. What's your idea of the motivation here?"

"Why did Kingsley kill her – if he did? That's not hard. She had been cheating on him, making him a lot of trouble, endangering his job and now she had killed a man. Also, she had money and Kingsley wanted to marry another woman. He might have been afraid that with money to spend she would beat the rap and be left laughing at him. If she didn't beat the rap, and got sent up, her money would be just as thoroughly beyond his reach. He'd have to divorce her to get rid of her. There's plenty of motive for murder in all that. Also he saw a chance to make me the goat. It wouldn't stick, but it would make confusion and delay. If murderers didn't think they could get away with their murders, very few would be committed."

Degarmo said: "All the same it could be somebody else, somebody who isn't in the picture at all. Even if he went down there to see her, it could still be somebody else. Somebody else could have killed Lavery too."

"If you like it that way."

He turned his head. "I don't like it any way at all. But if I crack the case, I'll get by with a reprimand from the police board. If I don't crack it, I'll be thumbing a ride out of town. You said I was dumb. Okay, I'm dumb. Where does Kingsley live? One thing I know is how to make people talk."

"965 Carson Drive, Beverly Hills. About five blocks on you turn north to the foothills. It's on the left side, just below Sunset. I've never been there, but I know how the block numbers run."

He handed me the green and yellow scarf. "Tuck that back into your pocket until we want to spring it on him."

35

IT WAS A two-storied white house with a dark roof. Bright moonlight lay against its wall like a fresh coat of paint. There were wrought-iron grills against the lower halves of the front windows. A level lawn swept up to the front door, which was set diagonally into the angle of a jutting wall. All the visible windows were dark.

Degarmo got out of the car and walked along the parkway and looked back along the drive to the garage. He moved down the driveway and the corner of the house hid him. I heard the sound of a garage door going up, then the thud as it was lowered again. He reappeared at the corner of the house, shook his head at me, and walked across the grass to the front door. He leaned his thumb on the bell and juggled a cigarette out of his pocket with one hand and put it between his lips.

He turned away from the door to light it and the flare of the match cut deep lines into his face. After a while there was light on the fan over the door. The peephole in the door swung back. I saw Degarmo holding up his shield. Slowly and as if unwillingly the door was opened. He went in.

He was gone four or five minutes. Light went on behind various windows, then off again. Then he came out of the house and while he was walking back to the car the light went off on the fan and the whole house was again as dark as we had found it.

He stood beside the car smoking and looking off down the curve of the street.

"One small car in the garage," he said. "The cook says it's hers. No sign of Kingsley. They say they haven't seen him since this morning. I looked in all the rooms. I guess they told the truth. Webber and a print man were there late this afternoon and the dusting powder is still all over the main bedroom. Webber would be getting prints to check against what we found in Lavery's house. He didn't tell me what he got. Where would he be – Kingsley?"

"Anywhere," I said. "On the road, in a hotel, in a Turkish bath getting the kinks out of his nerves. But we'll have to try his girl friend first. Her name is Fromsett and she lives at the

Bryson Tower on Sunset Place. That's away downtown, near Bullock's Wilshire."

"She does what?" Degarmo asked, getting in under the wheel.

"She holds the fort in his office and holds his hand out of office hours. She's no office cutie, though. She has brains and style."

"This situation is going to use all she has," Degarmo said. He drove down to Wilshire and we turned east again.

Twenty-five minutes brought us to the Bryson Tower, a white stucco palace with fretted lanterns in the forecourt and tall date palms. The entrance was in an L, up marble steps, through a Moorish archway, and over a lobby that was too big and a carpet that was too blue. Blue Ali Baba oil jars were dotted around, big enough to keep tigers in. There was a desk and a night clerk with one of those mustaches that get stuck under your fingernail.

Degarmo lunged past the desk towards an open elevator beside which a tired old man sat on a stool waiting for a customer. The clerk snapped at Degarmo's back like a terrier.

"One moment, please. Whom did you wish to see?"

Degarmo spun on his heel and looked at me wonderingly. "Did he say 'whom'?"

"Yeah, but don't hit him," I said. "There is such a word."

Degarmo licked his lips. "I knew there was," he said. "I often wondered where they kept it. Look, buddy," he said to the clerk, "we want up to 716. Any objection?"

"Certainly I have," the clerk said coldly. "We don't announce guests at —" he lifted his arm and turned it neatly to look at the narrow oblong watch on the inside of his wrist — "at twenty-three minutes past four in the morning."

"That's what I thought," Degarmo said. "So I wasn't going to bother you. You get the idea?" He took his shield out of his pocket and held it so that the light glinted on the gold and the blue enamel. "I'm a police lieutenant."

The clerk shrugged. "Very well. I hope there isn't going to be any trouble. I'd better announce you then. What names?"

"Lieutenant Degarmo and Mr. Marlowe."

"Apartment 716. That will be Miss Fromsett. One moment."

He went behind a glass screen and we heard him talking on the phone after a longish pause. He came back and nodded.

"Miss Fromsett is in. She will receive you."

"That's certainly a load off my mind," Degarmo said. "And don't bother to call your house peeper and send him up to the scatter. I'm allergic to house peepers."

The clerk gave a small cold smile and we got into the elevator.

The seventh floor was cool and quiet. The corridor seemed a mile long. We came at last to a door with 716 on it in gilt numbers in a circle of gilt leaves. There was an ivory button beside the door. Degarmo pushed it and chimes rang inside the door and it was opened.

Miss Fromsett wore a quilted blue robe over her pajamas. On her feet were small tufted slippers with high heels. Her dark hair was fluffed out engagingly and the cold cream had been wiped from her face and just enough makeup applied.

We went past her into a rather narrow room with several handsome oval mirrors and gray period furniture upholstered in blue damask. It didn't look like apartment house furniture. She sat down on a slender love seat and leaned back and waited calmly for somebody to say something.

I said: "This is Lieutenant Degarmo of the Bay City police. We're looking for Kingsley. He's not at his house. We thought you might be able to give us an idea where to find him."

She spoke to me without looking at me. "Is it that urgent?"

"Yes. Something has happened."

"What has happened?"

Degarmo said bluntly: "We just want to know where Kingsley is, sister. We don't have time to build up a scene."

The girl looked at him with a complete absence of expression. She looked back at me and said:

"I think you had better tell me, Mr. Marlowe."

"I went down there with the money," I said. "I met her as arranged. I went to her apartment to talk to her. While there I was slugged by a man who was hidden behind a curtain. I didn't see the man. When I came out of it she had been murdered."

"Murdered?"

I said: "Murdered."

She closed her fine eyes and the corners of her lovely mouth drew in. Then she stood up with a quick shrug and went over to a small, marble-topped table with spindly legs. She took a cigarette out of a small embossed silver box and lit it, staring emptily down at the table. The match in her hand was waved more and more slowly until it stopped, still burning, and she dropped it into a tray. She turned and put her back to the table.

"I suppose I ought to scream or something," she said. "I don't seem to have any feeling about it at all."

Degarmo said: "We don't feel so interested in your feelings right now. What we want to know is where Kingsley is. You can tell us or not tell us. Either way you can skip the attitudes. Just make your mind up."

She said to me quietly: "The lieutenant here is a Bay City officer?"

I nodded. She turned at him slowly, with a lovely contemptuous dignity. "In that case," she said, "he has no more right in my apartment than any other loud-mouthed bum that might try to toss his weight around."

Degarmo looked at her bleakly. He grinned and walked across the room and stretched his long legs from a deep downy chair. He waved his hand at me.

"Okay, you work on her. I can get all the co-operation I need from the L.A. boys, but by the time I had things explained to them, it would be a week from next Tuesday."

I said: "Miss Fromsett, if you know where he is, or where he started to go, please tell us. You can understand that he has to be found."

She said calmly: "Why?"

Degarmo put his head back and laughed. "This babe is good," he said. "Maybe she thinks we should keep it a secret from him that his wife has been knocked off."

"She's better than you think," I told him. His face sobered and he bit his thumb. He looked her up and down insolently.

She said: "Is it just because he has to be told?"

I took the yellow and green scarf out of my pocket and shook it out loose and held it in front of her.

"This was found in the apartment where she was murdered. I think you have seen it."

She looked at the scarf and she looked at me, and in neither of the glances was there any meaning. She said: "You ask for a great deal of confidence, Mr. Marlowe. Considering that you haven't been such a very smart detective after all."

"I ask for it," I said, "and I expect to get it. And how smart I've been is something you don't really know anything about."

"This is cute," Degarmo put in. "You two make a nice team. All you need is acrobats to follow you. But right now —"

She cut through his voice as if he didn't exist. "How was she murdered?"

"She was strangled and stripped naked and scratched up."

"Derry wouldn't have done anything like that," she said quietly.

Degarmo made a noise with his lips. "Nobody ever knows what anybody else will do, sister. A cop knows that much."

She still didn't look at him. In the same level tone she asked: "Do you want to know where we went after we left your apartment and whether he brought me home — things like that?"

"Yes."

"Because if he did, he wouldn't have had time to go down to the beach and kill her? Is that it?"

I said, "That's a good part of it."

"He didn't bring me home," she said slowly. "I took a taxi on Hollywood Boulevard, not more than five minutes after we left your place. I didn't see him again. I supposed he went home."

Degarmo said: "Usually the bim tries to give her boy friend a bit more alibi than that. But it takes all kinds, don't it?"

Miss Fromsett said to me: "He wanted to bring me home, but it was a long way out of his way and we were both tired. The reason I was telling you this is because I know it doesn't matter in the least. If I thought it did, I wouldn't tell you."

"So he did have time," I said.

She shook her head. "I don't know. I don't know how much time was needed. I don't know how he could have known where to go. Not from me, not from her through me. She didn't tell me." Her dark eyes were on mine, searching, probing. "Is this the kind of confidence you ask for?"

I folded the scarf up and put it back in my pocket. "We want to know where he is now."

"I can't tell you because I have no idea." Her eyes had followed the scarf down to my pocket. They stayed there. "You say you were slugged. You mean knocked unconscious?"

"Yes. By somebody who was hidden out behind a curtain. We still fall for it. She pulled a gun on me and I was busy trying to take it away from her. There's no doubt she shot Lavery."

Degarmo stood up suddenly: "You're making yourself a nice smooth scene, fellow," he growled. "But you're not getting anywhere. Let's blow."

I said: "Wait a minute. I'm not finished. Suppose he had something on his mind, Miss Fromsett, something that was eating pretty deep into him. That was how he looked tonight.

196

Suppose he knew more about all this than we realized – or than I realized – and knew things were coming to a head. He would want to go somewhere quietly and try to figure out what to do. Don't you think he might?"

I stopped and waited, looking sideways at Degarmo's impatience. After a moment the girl said tonelessly: "He wouldn't run away or hide, because it wasn't anything he could run away or hide from. But he might want a time to himself to think."

"In a strange place, in a hotel," I said, thinking of the story that had been told me in the Granada. "Or in a much quieter place than that."

I looked around for the telephone.

"It's in my bedroom," Miss Fromsett said, knowing at once what I was looking for.

I went down the room and through the door at the end. Degarmo was right behind me. The bedroom was ivory and ashes of roses. There was a big bed with no footboard and a pillow with the rounded hollow of a head. Toilet articles glistened on a built-in dresser with paneled mirrors on the wall above it. An open door showed mulberry bathroom tiles. The phone was on a night table by the bed.

I sat down on the edge of the bed and patted the place where Miss Fromsett's head had been and lifted the phone and dialed long distance. When the operator answered I asked for Constable Jim Patton at Puma Point, person to person, very urgent. I put the phone back in the cradle and lit a cigarette. Degarmo glowered down at me, standing with his legs apart, tough and tireless and ready to be nasty. "What now?" he grunted.

"Wait and see."

"Who's running this show?"

"Your asking me shows that I am – unless you want the Los Angeles police to run it."

He scratched a match on his thumbnail and watched it burn and tried to blow it out with a long steady breath that just bent the flame over. He got rid of that match and put another between his teeth and chewed on it. The phone rang in a moment.

"Ready with your Puma Point call."

Patton's sleepy voice came on the line. "Yes? This is Patton at Puma Point."

"This is Marlowe in Los Angeles," I said. "Remember me?"

"Sure I remember you, son. I ain't only half awake though."

"Do me a favor," I said. "Although I don't know why you should. Go or send over to Little Fawn Lake and see if Kingsley is there. Don't let him see you. You can spot his car outside the cabin or maybe see lights. And see that he stays put. Call me back as soon as you know. I'm coming up. Can you do that?"

Patton said: "I got no reason to stop him if he wants to leave."

"I'll have a Bay City police officer with me who wants to question him about a murder. Not your murder, another one."

There was a drumming silence along the wire. Patton said: "You ain't just bein' tricky, are you, son?"

"No. Call me back at Tunbridge 2722."

"Should likely take me half an hour," he said.

I hung up. Degarmo was grinning now. "This babe flash you a signal I couldn't read?"

I stood up off the bed. "No. I'm just trying to read his mind. He's no cold killer. Whatever fire there was is all burned out of him by now. I thought he might go to the quietest and most remote place he knows – just to get a grip of himself. In a few hours he'll probably turn himself in. It would look better for you if you got to him before he did that."

"Unless he puts a slug in his head," Degarmo said coldly. "Guys like him are very apt to do that."

"You can't stop him until you find him."

"That's right."

We went back into the living room. Miss Fromsett poked her head out of her kitchenette and said she was making coffee, and did we want any. We had some coffee and sat around looking like people seeing friends off at the railroad station.

The call from Patton came through in about twenty-five minutes. There was light in the Kingsley cabin and a car was parked beside it.

36

WE ATE SOME breakfast at Alhambra and I had the tank filled. We drove out Highway 70 and started moving past the trucks into the rolling ranch country. I was driving. Degarmo sat moodily in the corner, his hands deep in his pockets.

I watched the fat straight rows of orange trees spin by like the spokes of a wheel. I listened to the whine of the tires on the pavement and I felt tired and stale from lack of sleep and too much emotion.

We reached the long slope south of San Dimas that goes up to a ridge and drops down into Pomona. This is the ultimate end of the fog belt, and the beginning of that semi-desert region where the sun is as light and dry as old sherry in the morning, as hot as a blast furnace at noon, and drops like an angry brick at nightfall.

Degarmo stuck a match in the corner of his mouth and said almost sneeringly:

"Webber gave me hell last night. He said he was talking to you and what about."

I said nothing. He looked at me and looked away again. He waved a hand outwards. "I wouldn't live in this damn country if they gave it to me. The air's stale before it gets up in the morning."

"We'll be coming to Ontario in a minute. We'll switch over to Foothill Boulevard and you'll see five miles of the finest grevillea trees in the world."

"I wouldn't know one from a fire plug," Degarmo said.

We came to the center of town and turned north on Euclid, along the splendid parkway. Degarmo sneered at the grevillea trees.

After a while he said: "That was my girl that drowned in the lake up there. I haven't been right in the head since I heard about it. All I can see is red. If I could get my hands on that guy Chess –"

"You made enough trouble," I said, "letting her get away with murdering Almore's wife."

I stared straight ahead through the windshield. I knew his head moved and his eyes froze on me. I didn't know what his hands were doing. I didn't know what expression was on his face. After a long time his words came. They came through tight teeth and edgeways, and they scraped a little as they came out.

"You a little crazy or something?"

"No," I said. "Neither are you. You know as well as any-body could know anything that Florence Almore didn't get up out of bed and walk down to that garage. You know she was carried. You know that was why Talley stole her slipper, the slipper that had never walked on a concrete path. You knew that Almore gave his wife a shot in the arm at Condy's place and that it was just enough and not any too much. He knew his shots in the arm the way you know how to rough up a bum that hasn't any money or any place to sleep. You know that Almore didn't murder his wife with morphine and that if he wanted to murder her, morphine would be the last thing in the world he would use. But you know that some-body else did, and that Almore carried her down to the garage and put her there – technically still alive to breathe in some monoxide, but medically just as dead as though she had stopped breathing. You know all that."

Degarmo said softly: "Brother, how did you ever manage to live so long?"

I said: "By not falling for too many gags and not getting too much afraid of professional hard guys. Only a heel would have done what Almore did, only a heel and a badly scared man who had things on his soul that wouldn't stand daylight. Technically he may even have been guilty of murder. I don't think the point has ever been settled. Certainly he would have a hell of a time proving that she was in such a deep coma that she was beyond any possibility of help. But as a practical matter of who killed her, you know the girl killed her."

Degarmo laughed. It was a grating unpleasant laugh, not only mirthless, but meaningless.

We reached Foothill Boulevard and turned east again. I thought it was still cool, but Degarmo was sweating. He couldn't take his coat off because of the gun under his arm.

I said: "The girl, Mildred Haviland, was playing house with Almore and his wife knew it. She had threatened him. I got that from her parents. The girl, Mildred Haviland, knew all about morphine and where to get all of it she needed and how much to use. She was alone in the house with Florence Almore, after she put her to bed. She was in a perfect spot to load a needle with four or five grains and shoot it into an unconscious woman through the same puncture Almore had already made. She would die, perhaps while Almore was still out of the house, and he would come home and find her dead. The problem would be his. He would have to solve it. Nobody would believe anybody else had doped his wife to death. Nobody that didn't know all the circumstances. But you knew. I'd have to think you much more of a damn fool than I think you are to believe you didn't know. You covered the girl up. You were in love with her still. You scared her out of town, out of danger, out of reach, but you covered up for her. You let the murder ride. She had you that way. Why did you go up to the mountains looking for her?"

"And how did I know where to look?" he said harshly. "It wouldn't bother you to add an explanation of that, would it?"

"Not at all," I said. "She got sick of Bill Chess and his boozing and his tempers and his down-at-heels living. But she had to have money to make a break. She thought she was safe now, that she had something on Almore that was safe to use. So she wrote him for money. He sent you up to talk to her. She didn't tell Almore what her present name was or any details or where or how she was living. A letter addressed to Mildred Haviland at Puma Point would reach her. All she had to do was ask for it. But no letter came and nobody connected her with Mildred Haviland. All you had was an old photo and your usual bad manners, and they didn't get you anywhere with those people."

Degarmo said gratingly: "Who told you she tried to get money from Almore?"

"Nobody. I had to think of something to fit what happened. If Lavery or Mrs. Kingsley had known who Muriel Chess had been, and had tipped it off, you would have known where to find her and what name she was using. You didn't know those things. Therefore the lead had to come from the only person up there who knew who she was, and that was herself. So I assume she wrote to Almore."

"Okay," he said at last. "Let's forget it. It doesn't make any difference any more now. If I'm in a jam, that's my business. I'd do it again, in the same circumstances."

"That's all right," I said. "I'm not planning to put the bite on anybody myself. Not even on you. I'm telling you this mostly so you won't try to hang any murders on Kingsley that don't belong on him. If there is one that does, let it hang."

"Is that why you're telling me?" he asked.

"Yeah."

"I thought maybe it was because you hated my guts," he said.

"I'm all done with hating you," I said. "It's all washed out of me. I hate people hard, but I don't hate them very long."

We were going through the grape country now, the open sandy grape country along the scarred flanks of the foothills.

We came in a little while to San Bernardino and I kept on through it without stopping.

37

AT CRESTLINE, ELEVATION 5000 feet, it had not yet started to warm up. We stopped for a beer. When we got back into the car, Degarmo took the gun from his underarm holster and looked it over. It was a .38 Smith and Wesson on a .44 frame, a wicked weapon with a kick like a .45 and a much greater effective range.

"You won't need that," I said. "He's big and strong, but he's not that kind of tough."

He put the gun back under his arm and grunted. We didn't talk any more now. We had no more to talk about. We rolled around the curves and along the sharp sheer edges walled with white guard rails and in some places with walls of field stone and heavy iron chains. We climbed through the tall oaks and on to the altitudes where the oaks are not so tall and the pines are taller and taller. We came at last to the dam at the end of Puma Lake.

I stopped the car and the sentry threw his piece across his body and stepped up to the window.

"Close all the windows of your car before proceeding across the dam, please."

I reached back to wind up the rear window on my side. Degarmo held his shield up. "Forget it, buddy. I'm a police officer," he said with his usual tact.

The sentry gave him a solid expressionless stare. "Close all windows, please," he said in the same tone he had used before.

"Nuts to you," Degarmo said. "Nuts to you, soldier boy."

"It's an order," the sentry said. His jaw muscles bulged very slightly. His dull grayish eyes stared at Degarmo. "And I didn't write the order, mister. Up with the windows."

"Suppose I told you to go jump in the lake," Degarmo sneered.

The sentry said: "I might do it. I scare easily." He patted the breech of his rifle with a leathery hand.

Degarmo turned and closed the windows on his side. We drove across the dam. There was a sentry in the middle and one at the far end. The first one must have flashed them some kind of signal. They looked at us with steady watchful eyes, without friendliness.

I drove on through the piled masses of granite and down through the meadows of coarse grass. The same gaudy slacks and short shorts and peasant handkerchiefs as the day before yesterday, the same light breeze and golden sun and clear blue sky, the same smell of pine needles, the same cool softness of a mountain summer. But that was a hundred years ago, something crystallized in time, like a fly in amber.

I turned off on the road to Little Fawn Lake and wound around the huge rocks and past the little gurgling waterfall. The gate into Kingsley's property was open and Patton's car was standing in the road pointing towards the lake, which was invisible from that point. There was nobody in it. The card sign on the windshield still read: "*Keep Jim Patton Constable. He Is Too Old to Go to Work.*"

Close to it and pointed the other way was a small battered coupe. Inside the coupe a lion hunter's hat. I stopped my car behind Patton's and locked it and got out. Andy got out of the coupe and stood staring at us woodenly.

I said: "This is Lieutenant Degarmo of the Bay City police."

Andy said: "Jim's just over the ridge. He's waiting for you. He ain't had any breakfast."

We walked up the road to the ridge as Andy got back into his coupe. Beyond it the road dropped to the tiny blue lake. Kingsley's cabin across the water seemed to be without life.

"That's the lake," I said.

Degarmo looked down at it silently. His shoulders moved in a heavy shrug. "Let's go get the bastard," was all he said.

We went on and Patton stood up from behind a rock. He was wearing the same old Stetson and khaki pants and shirt buttoned to his thick neck. The star on his left breast still had a bent point. His jaws moved slowly, munching.

"Nice to see you again," he said, not looking at me, but at Degarmo.

He put his hand out and shook Degarmo's hard paw. "Last time I seen you, lieutenant, you was wearing another name. Kind of undercover, I guess you'd call it. I guess I didn't treat you right neither. I apologize. Guess I knew who that photo of yours was all the time."

Degarmo nodded and said nothing.

"Likely if I'd of been on my toes and played the game right, a lot of trouble would have been saved," Patton said. "Maybe a life would have been saved. I feel kind of bad about it, but then again I ain't a fellow that feels too bad about anything very long. Suppose we sit down here and you tell me what it is we're supposed to be doing now."

Degarmo said: "Kingsley's wife was murdered in Bay City last night. I have to talk to him about it."

"You mean you suspect him?" Patton asked.

"And how," Degarmo grunted.

Patton rubbed his neck and looked across the lake. "He ain't showed outside the cabin at all. Likely he's still asleep. Early this morning I snuck around the cabin. There was a radio goin' then and I heard sounds like a man would make playing with a bottle and a glass. I stayed away from him. Was that right?"

"We'll go over there now," Degarmo said.

"You got a gun, lieutenant?"

Degarmo patted under his left arm. Patton looked at me. I shook my head, no gun.

"Kingsley might have one too," Patton said. "I don't hanker after no fast shooting around here, lieutenant. It wouldn't do me no good to have a gunfight. We don't have that kind of community up here. You look to me like a fellow who would jack his gun out kind of fast."

"I've got plenty of swift, if that's what you mean," Degarmo said. "But I want this guy talking."

Patton looked at Degarmo, looked at me, looked back at Degarmo and spat tobacco juice in a long stream to one side.

"I ain't heard enough to even approach him," he said stubbornly.

So we sat down on the ground and told him the story. He listened silently, not blinking an eye. At the end he said to me: "You got a funny way of working for people, seems to me. Personally I think you boys are plumb misinformed. We'll go over and see. I'll go in first — in case you would know what you are talking about and Kingsley would have a gun and would be a little desperate. I got a big belly. Makes a nice target."

We stood up off the ground and started around the lake the long way. When we came to the little pier I said:

"Did they autopsy her yet, sheriff ?"

Patton nodded. "She drowned all right. They say they're satisfied that's how she died. She wasn't knifed or shot or had her head cracked in or anything. There's marks on her body, but too many to mean anything. And it ain't a very nice body to work with."

Degarmo looked white and angry.

"I guess I oughtn't to have said that, lieutenant," Patton added mildly. "Kind of tough to take. Seeing you knew the lady pretty well."

Degarmo said: "Let's get it over and do what we have to do."

We went on along the shore of the lake and came to Kingsley's cabin. We went up the heavy steps. Patton went quietly across the porch to the door. He tried the screen. It was not hooked. He opened it and tried the door. That was unlocked also. He held the door shut, with the knob turned in his hand, and Degarmo took hold of the screen and pulled it wide. Patton opened the door and we walked into the room.

Derace Kingsley lay back in a deep chair by the cold fireplace with his eyes closed. There was an empty glass and an almost empty whiskey bottle on the table beside him. The room smelled of whiskey. A dish near the bottle was choked with cigarette stubs. Two crushed empty packs lay on top of the stubs.

All the windows in the room were shut. It was already close and hot in there. Kingsley was wearing a sweater and his face was flushed and heavy. He snored and his hands hung lax outside the arms of the chair, the fingertips touching the floor.

Patton moved to within a few feet of him and stood looking silently down at him for a long moment before he spoke.

"Mr. Kingsley," he said then, in a calm steady voice, "we got to talk to you a little."

38

KINGSLEY MOVED WITH a kind of jerk, and opened his eyes and moved them without moving his head. He looked at Patton, then at Degarmo, lastly at me. His eyes were heavy, but the light sharpened in them. He sat up slowly in the chair and rubbed his hands up and down the sides of his face.

"I was asleep," he said. "Fell asleep a couple of hours ago. I was as drunk as a skunk, I guess. Anyway, much drunker than I like to be." He dropped his hands and let them hang.

Patton said: "This is Lieutenant Degarmo of the Bay City police. He has to talk to you."

Kingsley looked briefly at Degarmo and his eyes came around to stare at me. His voice when he spoke again sounded sober and quiet and tired to death.

"So you let them get her?" he said.

I said: "I would have, but I didn't."

Kingsley thought about that, looking at Degarmo. Patton had left the front door open. He pulled the brown venetian blinds up at two front windows and pulled the windows up. He sat in a chair near one of them and clasped his hands over his stomach. Degarmo stood glowering down at Kingsley.

"Your wife is dead, Kingsley," he said brutally. "If it's any news to you."

Kingsley stared at him and moistened his lips.

"Takes it easy, don't he?" Degarmo said. "Show him the scarf."

I took the green and yellow scarf out and dangled it. Degarmo jerked a thumb. "Yours?"

Kingsley nodded. He moistened his lips again.

"Careless of you to leave it behind you," Degarmo said. He was breathing a little hard. His nose was pinched and deep lines ran from his nostrils to the corners of his mouth.

Kingsley said very quietly: "Leave it behind me where?" He had barely glanced at the scarf. He hadn't looked at all at me.

"In the Granada Apartments, on Eighth Street, in Bay City. Apartment 716. Am I telling you something?"

Kingsley now very slowly lifted his eyes to meet mine. "Is that where she was?" he breathed.

I nodded. "She didn't want me to go there. I wouldn't give her the money until she talked to me. She admitted she killed Lavery. She pulled a gun and planned to give me the same treatment. Somebody came from behind the curtain and knocked me out without letting me see him. When I came to she was dead." I told him how she was dead and how she looked. I told him what I had done and what had been done to me.

He listened without moving a muscle of his face. When I had done talking he made a vague gesture towards the scarf.

"What has that got to do with it?"

"The lieutenant regards it as evidence that you were the party hidden out in the apartment."

Kingsley thought that over. He didn't seem to get the implications of it very quickly. He leaned back in the chair and rested his head against the back. "Go on," he said at length. "I suppose you know what you're talking about. I'm sure I don't."

Degarmo said: "All right, play dumb. See what it gets you. You could begin by accounting for your time last night after you dropped your biddy at her apartment house."

Kingsley said evenly: "If you mean Miss Fromsett, I didn't. She went home in a taxi. I was going home myself, but I didn't. I came up here instead. I thought the trip and the night air and the quiet might help me to get straightened out."

"Just think of that," Degarmo jeered. "Straightened out from what, if I might ask?"

"Straightened out from all the worry I had been having."

"Hell," Degarmo said, "a little thing like strangling your wife and clawing her belly wouldn't worry you that much, would it?"

"Son, you hadn't ought to say things like that," Patton put in from the background. "That ain't no way to talk. You ain't produced anything yet that sounds like evidence."

"No?" Degarmo swung his hard head at him. "What about this scarf, fatty? Isn't that evidence?"

"You didn't fit it in to anything – not that I heard," Patton said peacefully. "And I ain't fat either, just well covered."

Degarmo swung away from him disgustedly. He jabbed his finger at Kingsley.

"I suppose you didn't go down to Bay City at all," he said harshly.

"No. Why should I? Marlowe was taking care of that. And I don't see why you are making a point of the scarf. Marlowe was wearing it."

Degarmo stood rooted and savage. He turned very slowly and gave me his bleak angry stare.

"I don't get this," he said. "Honest, I don't. It wouldn't be that somebody is kidding me, would it? Somebody like you?"

I said: "All I told about the scarf was that it was in the apartment and that I had seen Kingsley wearing it earlier this evening. That seemed to be all you wanted. I might have added that I had later worn the scarf myself, so the girl I was to meet could identify me that much easier."

Degarmo backed away from Kingsley and leaned against the wall at the end of the fireplace. He pulled his lower lip out with thumb and forefinger of his left hand. His right hand hung lax at his side, the fingers slightly curved.

I said: "I told you all I had ever seen of Mrs. Kingsley was a snapshot. One of us had to be sure of being able to identify the other. The scarf seemed obvious enough for identification. As a matter of fact I had seen her once before, although I didn't know it when I went to meet her. But I didn't recognize her at once." I turned to Kingsley. "Mrs. Fallbrook," I said.

"I thought you said Mrs. Fallbrook was the owner of the house," he answered slowly.

"That's what she said at the time. That's what I believed at the time. Why shouldn't I?"

Degarmo made a sound in his throat. His eyes were a little crazy. I told him about Mrs. Fallbrook and her purple hat and her fluttery manner and the empty gun she had been holding and how she gave it to me.

When I stopped, he said very carefully: "I didn't hear you tell Webber any of that."

"I didn't tell him. I didn't want to admit I had already been in the house three hours before. That I had gone to talk it over with Kingsley before I reported it to the police."

"That's something we're going to love you for," Degarmo said with a cold grin. "Jesus, what a sucker I've been. How much you paying this shamus to cover up your murders for you, Kingsley?"

"His usual rates," Kingsley told him emptily. "And a five-hundred-dollar bonus if he can prove my wife didn't murder Lavery."

"Too bad he can't earn that," Degarmo sneered.

"Don't be silly," I said. "I've already earned it."

There was a silence in the room. One of those charged silences which seem about to split apart with a peal of thunder. It didn't. It remained, hung heavy and solid, like a wall. Kingsley moved a little in his chair, and after a long moment, he nodded his head.

"Nobody could possibly know that better than you know it, Degarmo," I said.

Patton had as much expression on his face as a chunk of wood. He watched Degarmo quietly. He didn't look at Kingsley at all. Degarmo looked at a point between my eyes, but not as if that was anything in the room with him. Rather as if he was looking at something very far away, like a mountain across a valley.

After what seemed a very long time, Degarmo said quietly: "I don't see why. I don't know anything about Kingsley's wife. To the best of my knowledge I never laid eyes on her – until last night."

He lowered his eyelids a little and watched me broodingly. He knew perfectly well what I was going to say. I said it anyway.

"And you never saw her last night. Because she had already been dead for over a month. Because she had been drowned in Little Fawn Lake. Because the woman you saw dead in the Granada Apartments was Mildred Haviland, and Mildred Haviland was Muriel Chess. And since Mrs. Kingsley was dead long before Lavery was shot, it follows that Mrs. Kingsley did not shoot him."

Kingsley clenched his fists on the arms of his chair, but he made no sound, no sound at all.

39

THERE WAS ANOTHER heavy silence. Patton broke it by saying in his careful slow voice: "That's kind of a wild statement, ain't it? Don't you kind of think Bill Chess would know his own wife?"

I said: "After a month in the water? With his wife's clothes on her and some of his wife's trinkets? With water-soaked blond hair like his wife's hair and almost no recognizable face? Why would he even have a doubt about it? She left a note that might be a suicide note. She had gone away. They had quarreled. Her clothes and car had gone away. During the month she was gone, he had heard nothing from her. He had no idea where she had gone. And then this corpse comes up out of the water with Muriel's clothes on it. A blonde woman about his wife's size. Of course there would be differences and if any substitution had been suspected, they would have been found and checked. But there was no reason to suspect any such thing. Crystal Kingsley was still alive. She had gone off with Lavery. She had left her car in San Bernardino. She had sent a wire to her husband from El Paso. She was all taken care of, so far as Bill Chess was concerned. He had no thoughts about her at all. She didn't enter the picture anywhere for him. Why should she?"

Patton said: "I ought to of thought of it myself. But if I had, it would be one of those ideas a fellow would throw away almost as quick as he thought of it. It would look too kind of far-fetched."

"Superficially yes," I said. "But only superficially. Suppose the body had not come up out of the lake for a year, or not at all, unless the lake was dragged for it. Muriel Chess was gone and nobody was going to spend much time looking for her. We might never have heard of her again. Mrs. Kingsley was a different proposition. She had money and connections and an anxious husband. She would be searched for, as she was, eventually. But not very soon, unless something happened to start suspicion. It might have been a matter of months before anything was found out. The lake might have been dragged, but if a search along her trail seemed to indicate

THE LADY IN THE LAKE

that she had actually left the lake and gone down the hill, even as far as San Bernardino, and the train from there east, then the lake might never have been dragged. And even if it was and the body was found, there was rather better than an even chance that the body would not be correctly identified. Bill Chess was arrested for his wife's murder. For all I know he might even have been convicted of it, and that would have been that, as far as the body in the lake was concerned. Crystal Kingsley would still be missing, and it would be an unsolved mystery. Eventually it would be assumed that something had happened to her and that she was no longer alive. But nobody would know where or when or how it had happened. If it hadn't been for Lavery, we might not be here talking about it now. Lavery is the key to the whole thing. He was in the Prescott Hotel in San Bernardino the night Crystal Kingsley was supposed to have left here. He saw a woman there who had Crystal Kingsley's car, who was wearing Crystal Kingsley's clothes, and of course he knew who she was. But he didn't have to know there was anything wrong. He didn't have to know they were Crystal Kingsley's clothes or that the woman had put Crystal Kingsley's car in the hotel garage. All he had to know was that he met Muriel Chess. Muriel took care of the rest."

I stopped and waited for somebody to say anything. Nobody did. Patton sat immovable in his chair, his plump, hairless hands clasped comfortably across his stomach. Kingsley leaned his head back and he had his eyes half closed and he was not moving. Degarmo leaned against the wall by the fireplace, taut and white-faced and cold, a big hard solemn man whose thoughts were deeply hidden.

I went on talking.

"If Muriel Chess impersonated Crystal Kingsley, she murdered her. That's elementary. All right, let's look at it. We know who she was and what kind of woman she was. She had already murdered before she met and married Bill Chess. She

213

had been Dr. Almore's office nurse and his little pal and she had murdered Dr. Almore's wife in such a neat way that Almore had to cover up for her. And she had been married to a man in the Bay City police who also was sucker enough to cover up for her. She got the men that way, she could make them jump through hoops. I didn't know her long enough to see why, but her record proves it. What she was able to do with Lavery proves it. Very well, she killed people who got in her way, and Kingsley's wife got in her way too. I hadn't meant to talk about this, but it doesn't matter much now. Crystal Kingsley could make the men do a little jumping through hoops too. She made Bill Chess jump and Bill Chess's wife wasn't the girl to take that and smile. Also, she was sick to death of her life up here – she must have been – and she wanted to get away. But she needed money. She had tried to get it from Almore, and that sent Degarmo up here looking for her. That scared her a little. Degarmo is the sort of fellow you are never quite sure of. She was right not to be sure of him, wasn't she, Degarmo?"

Degarmo moved his foot on the ground. "The sands are running against you, fellow," he said grimly. "Speak your little piece while you can."

"Mildred didn't positively have to have Crystal Kingsley's car and clothes and credentials and what not, but they helped. What money she had must have helped a great deal, and Kingsley says she liked to have a good deal of money with her. Also she must have had jewelry which could eventually be turned into money. All this made killing her a rational as well as an agreeable thing to do. That disposes of motive, and we come to means and opportunity.

"The opportunity was made to order for her. She had quarreled with Bill and he had gone off to get drunk. She knew her Bill and how drunk he could get and how long he would stay away. She needed time. Time was of the essence. She had to assume that there was time. Otherwise the whole thing flopped. She had to pack her own clothes and take them in her car to Coon Lake and hide them there, because they had to be gone. She had to walk back. She had to murder Crystal Kingsley and dress her in Muriel's clothes and get her down in the lake. All that took time. As to the murder itself, I imagine she got her drunk or knocked her on the head and drowned her in the bathtub in this cabin. That would be logical and simple too. She was a nurse, she knew how to handle things like bodies. She knew how to swim — we have it from Bill that she was a fine swimmer. And a drowned body will sink. All she had to do was guide it down into the deep water where she wanted it. There is nothing in all this beyond the powers of one woman who could swim. She did it, she dressed in Crystal Kingsley's clothes, packed what else of hers she wanted, got into Crystal Kingsley's car and departed. And at San Bernardino she ran into her first snag, Lavery."

"Lavery knew her as Muriel Chess. We have no evidence and no reason whatever to assume that he knew her as any-thing else. He had seen her up here and he was probably on his way up here again when he met her. She wouldn't want that. All he would find would be a locked-up cabin but he might get talking to Bill and it was part of her plan that Bill should not know positively that she had ever left Little Fawn Lake. So that when, and if, the body was found, he would identify it. So she put her hooks into Lavery at once, and that wouldn't be too hard. If there is one thing we know for cer-tain about Lavery, it is that he couldn't keep his hands off the women. The more of them, the better. He would be easy for a smart girl like Mildred Haviland. So she played him and took him away with her. She took him to El Paso and there sent a wire he knew nothing about. Finally she played him back to Bay City. She probably couldn't help that. He wanted to go home and she couldn't let him get too far from her. Because Lavery was dangerous to her. Lavery alone could destroy all the indications that Crystal Kingsley had actually left Little Fawn Lake. When the search for Crystal Kingsley eventually began, it had to come to Lavery, and at that moment Lavery's life wasn't worth a plugged nickel. His first denials might not be believed, as they were not, but when he opened up with the whole story, that would be believed, because it could be checked. So the search began and immediately Lavery was shot dead in his bathroom, the very night after I went down to talk to him. That's about all there is to it, except why she went back to the house the next morning. That's just one of those things that murderers seem to do. She said he had taken her money, but I don't believe it. I think more likely she got to thinking he had some of his own hidden away, or that she had better edit the job with a cool head and make sure it was all in order and pointing the right way; or perhaps it was just what she said, and to take in the paper and the milk. Anything is possible. She went back and I found her there and she put on an act that left me with both feet in my mouth."

Patton said: "Who killed her, son? I gather you don't like Kingsley for that little job."

I looked at Kingsley and said: "You didn't talk to her on the phone, you said. What about Miss Fromsett? Did she think she was talking to your wife?"

Kingsley shook his head. "I doubt it. It would be pretty hard to fool her that way. All she said was that she seemed very changed and subdued. I had no suspicion then. I didn't have any until I got up here. When I walked into this cabin last night, I felt there was something wrong. It was too clean and neat and orderly. Crystal didn't leave things that way. There would have been clothes all over the bedroom, cigarette stubs all over the house, bottles and glasses all over the kitchen. There would have been unwashed dishes and ants and flies. I thought Bill's wife might have cleaned up, and then I remembered that Bill's wife wouldn't have, not on that particular day. She had been too busy quarreling with Bill and being murdered, or committing suicide, whichever it was. I thought about all this in a confused sort of way, but I don't claim I actually made anything of it."

Patton got up from his chair and went out on the porch. He came back wiping his lips with his tan handkerchief. He sat down again, and eased himself over on his left hip, on account of the hip holster on the other side. He looked thoughtfully at Degarmo. Degarmo stood against the wall, hard and rigid, a stone man. His right hand still hung down at his side, with the fingers curled.

Patton said: "I still ain't heard who killed Muriel. Is that part of the show or is that something that still has to be worked out?"

I said: "Somebody who thought she needed killing, somebody who had loved her and hated her, somebody who was too much of a cop to let her get away with any more murders, but not enough of a cop to pull her in and let the whole story come out. Somebody like Degarmo."

40

DEGARMO STRAIGHTENED AWAY from the wall and smiled bleakly. His right hand made a hard clean movement and was holding a gun. He held it with a lax wrist, so that it pointed down at the floor in front of him. He spoke to me without looking at me.

"I don't think you have a gun," he said. "Patton has a gun but I don't think he can get it out fast enough to do him any good. Maybe you have a little evidence to go with that last guess. Or wouldn't that be important enough for you to bother with?"

"A little evidence," I said. "Not very much. But it will grow. Somebody stood behind that green curtain in the Granada for more than half an hour and stood as silently as only a cop on a stake-out knows how to stand. Somebody who had a blackjack. Somebody who knew I had been hit with one without looking at the back of my head. You told Shorty, remember? Somebody who knew the dead girl had been hit with one too, although it wouldn't have showed and he wouldn't have been likely at that time to have handled the body enough to find out. Somebody who stripped her and raked her body with scratches in the kind of sadistic hate a man like you might feel for a woman who had made a small private hell for him. Somebody who has blood and cuticle under his fingernails right now, plenty enough for a chemist to work on. I bet you won't let Patton look at the fingernails of your right hand, Degarmo."

Degarmo lifted the gun a little and smiled. A wide white smile.

"And just how did I know where to find her?" he asked.

"Almore saw her – coming out of, or going into Lavery's house. That's what made him so nervous, that's why he called you when he saw me hanging around. As to how exactly you trailed her to the apartment, I don't know. I don't see anything difficult about it. You could have hid out in Almore's house and followed her, or followed Lavery. All that would be routine work for a copper."

Degarmo nodded and stood silent for a moment, thinking. His face was grim, but his metallic blue eyes held a light that was almost amusement. The room was hot and heavy with a disaster that could no longer be mended. He seemed to feel it less than any of us.

"I want to get out of here," he said at last. "Not very far maybe, but no hick cop is going to put the arm on me. Any objections?"

Patton said quietly: "Can't be done, son. You know I got to take you. None of this ain't proved, but I can't just let you walk out."

"You have a nice big belly, Patton. I'm a good shot. How do you figure to take me?"

"I been trying to figure," Patton said and rumpled his hair under his pushed-back hat. "I ain't got very far with it. I don't want no holes in my belly. But I can't let you make a monkey of me in my own territory either."

"Let him go," I said. "He can't get out of these mountains. That's why I brought him up here."

Patton said soberly: "Somebody might get hurt taking him. That wouldn't be right. If it's anybody, it's got to be me."

Degarmo grinned. "You're a nice boy, Patton," he said. "Look, I'll put the gun back under my arm and we'll start from scratch. I'm good enough for that too."

He tucked the gun under his arm. He stood with his arms hanging, his chin pushed forward a little, watching. Patton chewed softly, with his pale eyes on Degarmo's vivid eyes.

"I'm sitting down," he complained. "I ain't as fast as you anyways. I just don't like to look yellow." He looked at me sadly. "Why the hell did you have to bring this up here? It ain't any part of my troubles. Now look at the jam I'm in." He sounded hurt and confused and rather feeble.

Degarmo put his head back a little and laughed. While he was still laughing, his right hand jumped for his gun again.

I didn't see Patton move at all. The room throbbed with the roar of his frontier Colt.

Degarmo's arm shot straight out to one side and the heavy Smith and Wesson was torn out of his hand and thudded against the knotty pine wall behind him. He shook his numbed right hand and looked down at it with wonder in his eyes.

Patton stood up slowly. He walked slowly across the room and kicked the revolver under a chair. He looked at Degarmo sadly. Degarmo was sucking a little blood off his knuckles.

"You give me a break," Patton said sadly. "You hadn't ought ever to give a man like me a break. I been a shooter more years than you been alive, son."

Degarmo nodded to him and straightened his back and started for the door.

"Don't do that," Patton told him calmly.

Degarmo kept on going. He reached the door and pushed on the screen. He looked back at Patton and his face was very white now.

"I'm going out of here," he said. "There's only one way you can stop me. So long, fatty."

Patton didn't move a muscle.

Degarmo went out through the door. His feet made heavy sounds on the porch and then on the steps. I went to the front window and looked out. Patton still hadn't moved. Degarmo came down off the steps and started across the top of the little dam.

"He's crossing the dam," I said. "Has Andy got a gun?"

"I don't figure he'd use one if he had," Patton said calmly. "He don't know any reason why he should."

"Well, I'll be damned," I said.

Patton sighed. "He hadn't ought to have given me a break like that," he said. "Had me cold. I got to give it back to him. Kind of puny too. Won't do him a lot of good."

"He's a killer," I said.

"He ain't that kind of killer," Patton said. "You lock your car?"

I nodded. "Andy's coming down to the other end of the dam," I said. "Degarmo has stopped him. He's speaking to him."

"He'll take Andy's car maybe," Patton said sadly.

"Well, I'll be damned," I said again. I looked back at Kingsley. He had his head in his hands and he was staring at the floor. I turned back to the window. Degarmo was out of sight beyond the rise. Andy was half way across the dam, coming slowly, looking back over his shoulder now and then. The sound of a starting car came distantly. Andy looked up at the cabin, then turned back and started to run back along the dam.

The sound of the motor died away. When it was quite gone, Patton said: "Well, I guess we better go back to the office and do some telephoning."

Kingsley got up suddenly and went out to the kitchen and came back with a bottle of whiskey. He poured himself a stiff drink and drank it standing. He waved a hand at it and walked heavily out of the room. I heard bed springs creak.

Patton and I went quietly out of the cabin.

41

PATTON HAD JUST finished putting his calls through to block the highways when a call came through from the sergeant in charge of the guard detail at Puma Lake dam. We went out and got into Patton's car and Andy drove very fast along the lake road through the village and along the lake shore back to the big dam at the end. We were waved across the dam where the sergeant was waiting in a jeep beside the headquarters hut.

The sergeant waved his arm and started the jeep and we followed him a couple of hundred feet along the highway to where a few soldiers stood on the edge of the canyon looking down. Several cars had stopped there and a cluster of people was grouped near the soldiers. The sergeant got out of the jeep and Patton and Andy and I climbed out of the official car and went over by the sergeant.

"Guy didn't stop for the sentry," the sergeant said, and there was bitterness in his voice. "Damn near knocked him off the road. The sentry in the middle of the bridge had to jump fast to get missed. The one at this end had enough. He called the guy to halt. Guy kept going."

The sergeant chewed his gum and looked down into the canyon.

"Orders are to shoot in a case like that," he said. "The sentry shot." He pointed down to the grooves in the shoulder at the edge of the drop. "This is where he went off."

A hundred feet down in the canyon a small coupe was smashed against the side of a huge granite boulder. It was almost upside down, leaning a little. There were three men down there. They had moved the car enough to lift something out.

Something that had been a man.

THE LITTLE SISTER

1

THE PEBBLED GLASS door panel is lettered in flaked black paint: "*Philip Marlowe . . . Investigations.*" It is a reasonably shabby door at the end of a reasonably shabby corridor in the sort of building that was new about the year the all-tile bathroom became the basis of civilization. The door is locked, but next to it is another door with the same legend which is not locked. Come on in – there's nobody in here but me and a big bluebottle fly. But not if you're from Manhattan, Kansas.

★

It was one of those clear, bright summer mornings we get in the early spring in California before the high fog sets in. The rains are over. The hills are still green and in the valley across the Hollywood hills you can see snow on the high mountains. The fur stores are advertising their annual sales. The call houses that specialize in sixteen-year-old virgins are doing a land-office business. And in Beverly Hills the jacaranda trees are beginning to bloom.

I had been stalking the bluebottle fly for five minutes, waiting for him to sit down. He didn't want to sit down. He just wanted to do wing-overs and sing the prologue to *Pagliacci*. I had the fly swatter poised in midair and I was all set. There was a patch of bright sunlight on the corner of the desk and I knew that sooner or later that was where he was going to light. But when he did, I didn't even see him at first. The buzzing stopped and there he was. And then the phone rang.

I reached for it inch by inch with a slow and patient left hand. I lifted the phone slowly and spoke into it softly: "Hold the line a moment, please."

I laid the phone down gently on the brown blotter. He was still there, shining and blue-green and full of sin. I took a deep breath and swung. What was left of him sailed halfway across the room and dropped to the carpet. I went over and picked him up by his good wing and dropped him into the wastebasket.

"Thanks for waiting," I said into the phone.

"Is this Mr. Marlowe, the detective?" It was a small, rather hurried, little-girlish voice. I said it was Mr. Marlowe, the detective. "How much do you charge for your services, Mr. Marlowe?"

"What was it you wanted done?"

The voice sharpened a little. "I can't very well tell you that over the phone. It's — it's very confidential. Before I'd waste time coming to your office I'd have to have some idea —"

"Forty bucks a day and expenses. Unless it's the kind of job that can be done for a flat fee."

"That's far too much," the little voice said. "Why, it might cost hundreds of dollars and I only get a small salary and —"

"Where are you now?"

"Why, I'm in a drugstore. It's right next to the building where your office is."

"You could have saved a nickel. The elevator's free."

"I — I beg your pardon?"

I said it all over again. "Come on up and let's have a look at you," I added. "If you're in my kind of trouble, I can give you a pretty good idea —"

"I have to know something about you," the small voice said very firmly. "This is a very delicate matter, very personal. I couldn't talk to just anybody."

"If it's that delicate," I said, "maybe you need a lady detective."

"Goodness, I didn't know there were any." Pause. "But I don't think a lady detective would do at all. You see, Orrin was living in a very tough neighborhood, Mr. Marlowe. At least

226

I thought it was tough. The manager of the rooming house is a most unpleasant person. He smelled of liquor. Do you drink, Mr. Marlowe?"

"Well, now that you mention it –"

"I don't think I'd care to employ a detective that uses liquor in any form. I don't even approve of tobacco."

"Would it be all right if I peeled an orange?"

I caught the sharp intake of breath at the far end of the line. "You might at least talk like a gentleman," she said.

"Better try the University Club," I told her. "I heard they had a couple left over there, but I'm not sure they'll let you handle them." I hung up.

It was a step in the right direction, but it didn't go far enough. I ought to have locked the door and hid under the desk.

2

FIVE MINUTES LATER the buzzer sounded on the outer door of the half-office I use for a reception room. I heard the door close again. Then I didn't hear anything more. The door between me and there was half open. I listened and decided somebody had just looked in at the wrong office and left without entering. Then there was a small knocking on wood. Then the kind of cough you use for the same purpose. I got my feet off the desk, stood up and looked out. There she was. She didn't have to open her mouth for me to know who she was. And nobody ever looked less like Lady Macbeth. She was a small, neat, rather prissy-looking girl with primly smooth brown hair and rimless glasses. She was wearing a brown tailor-made and from a strap over her shoulder hung one of those awkward-looking square bags that make you think of a Sister of Mercy taking first aid to the wounded. On the smooth brown hair was a hat that had been taken from its mother too young. She had no make-up, no lipstick and no jewelry. The rimless glasses gave her that librarian's look.

"That's no way to talk to people over the telephone," she said sharply. "You ought to be ashamed of yourself."

"I'm just too proud to show it," I said. "Come on in." I held the door for her. Then I held the chair for her.

She sat down on about two inches of the edge. "If I talked like that to one of Dr. Zugsmith's patients," she said, "I'd lose my position. He's most particular how I speak to the patients – even the difficult ones."

"How is the old boy? I haven't seen him since that time I fell off the garage roof."

She looked surprised and quite serious. "Why surely you can't know Dr. Zugsmith." The tip of a rather anemic tongue came out between her lips and searched furtively for nothing.

"I know a Dr. George Zugsmith," I said, "in Santa Rosa."

"Oh no. This is Dr. Alfred Zugsmith, in Manhattan. Manhattan, Kansas, you know, not Manhattan, New York."

"Must be a different Dr. Zugsmith," I said. "And your name?"

"I'm not sure I'd care to tell you."

"Just window shopping, huh?"

"I suppose you could call it that. If I have to tell my family affairs to a total stranger, I at least have the right to decide whether he's the kind of person I could trust."

"Anybody ever tell you you're a cute little trick?"

The eyes behind the rimless cheaters flashed. "I should hope not."

I reached for a pipe and started to fill it. "Hope isn't exactly the word," I said. "Get rid of that hat and get yourself a pair of those slinky glasses with colored rims. You know, the ones that are all cockeyed and oriental –"

"Dr. Zugsmith wouldn't permit anything like that," she said quickly. Then, "Do you really think so?" she asked and blushed ever so slightly.

I put a match to the pipe and puffed smoke across the desk. She winced back.

"If you hire me," I said, "I'm the guy you hire. Me. Just as I am. If you think you're going to find any lay readers in this business, you're crazy. I hung up on you, but you came up here all the same. So you need help. What's your name and trouble?"

She just stared at me.

"Look," I said. "You come from Manhattan, Kansas. The last time I memorized the *World Almanac* that was a little town not far from Topeka. Population around twelve thousand. You work for Dr. Alfred Zugsmith and you're looking for somebody named Orrin. Manhattan is a small town. It has to be. Only half a dozen places in Kansas are anything else. I already have enough information about you to find out your whole family history.

"But why should you want to ? I'm fed up with people telling me histories. I'm just sitting here because I don't have any place to go. I don't want to work. I don't want anything."

"You talk too much."

"Yes," I said, "I talk too much. Lonely men always talk too much. Either that or they don't talk at all. Shall we get down to business? You don't look like the type that goes to see private detectives, and especially private detectives you don't know."

"I know that," she said quietly. "And Orrin would be absolutely livid. Mother would be furious too. I just picked your name out of the phone book –"

"What principle?" I asked. "And with the eyes closed or open?"

She stared at me for a moment as if I were some kind of freak. "Seven and thirteen," she said quietly.

"How?"

"Marlowe has seven letters," she said, "and Philip Marlowe has thirteen. Seven together with thirteen –"

"What's *your* name?" I almost snarled.

"Orfamay Quest." She crinkled her eyes as if she could cry. She spelled the first name out for me, all one word. "I live with my mother," she went on, her voice getting rapid now as if my time is costing her. "My father died four years ago. He was a doctor. My brother Orrin was going to be a surgeon, too, but he changed into engineering after two years of medical. Then a year ago Orrin came out to work for the Cal-Western Aircraft Company in Bay City. He didn't have to. He had a good job in Wichita. I guess he just sort of wanted to come out here to California. Most everybody does."

"*Almost* everybody," I said. "If you're going to wear those rimless glasses, you might at least try to live up to them."

She giggled and drew a line along the desk with her fingertip, looking down. "Did you mean those slanting kind of glasses that make you look kind of oriental?"

"Uh-huh. Now about Orrin. We've got him to California, and we've got him to Bay City. What do we do with him?"

She thought a moment and frowned. Then she studied my face as if making up her mind. Then her words came with a burst: "It wasn't like Orrin not to write to us regularly. He only wrote twice to mother and three times to me in the last six months. And the last letter was several months ago. Mother and I got worried. So it was my vacation and I came out to see him. He'd never been away from Kansas before." She stopped. "Aren't you going to take any notes?" she asked.

I grunted.

"I thought detectives always wrote things down in little notebooks."

"I'll make the gags," I said. "You tell the story. You came out on your vacation. Then what?"

"I'd written to Orrin that I was coming but I didn't get any answer. Then I sent a wire to him about Salt Lake City but he didn't answer that either. So all I could do was go down where he lived. It's an awful long way. I went in a bus. It's in Bay City. No. 449 Idaho Street."

She stopped again, then repeated the address, and I still didn't write it down. I just sat there looking at her glasses and

her smooth brown hair and the silly little hat and the fingernails with no color and her mouth with no lipstick and the
tip of the little tongue that came and went between the
pale lips.

"Maybe you don't know Bay City, Mr. Marlowe."

"Ha," I said. "All I know about Bay City is that every time
I go there I have to buy a new head. You want me to finish
your story for you?"

"Wha-a-at?" Her eyes opened so wide that the glasses
made them look like something you see in the deep-sea fish
tanks.

"He's moved," I said. "And you don't know where he's
moved to. And you're afraid he's living a life of sin in a penthouse on top of the Regency Towers with something in a
long mink coat and an interesting perfume."

"Well for goodness' sakes!"

"Or am I being coarse?" I asked.

"Please, Mr. Marlowe," she said at last, "I don't think anything of the sort about Orrin. And if Orrin heard you say that
you'd be sorry. He can be awfully mean. But I know something has happened. It was just a cheap rooming house, and
I didn't like the manager at all. A horrid kind of man. He said
Orrin had moved away a couple of weeks before and he didn't
know where to and he didn't care, and all he wanted was a
good slug of gin. I don't know why Orrin would even live in
a place like that."

"Did you say slug of gin?" I asked.

She blushed. "That's what the manager said. I'm just telling
you."

"All right," I said. "Go on."

"Well, I called the place where he worked. The Cal-
Western Company, you know. And they said he'd been laid off
like a lot of others and that was all they knew. So then I went
to the post office and asked if Orrin had put in a change of
address to anywhere. And they said they couldn't give me any

information. It was against the regulations. So I told them how it was and the man said, well if I was his sister he'd go look. So he went and looked and came back and said no. Orrin hadn't put in any change of address. So then I began to get a little frightened. He might have had an accident or something."

"Did it occur to you to ask the police about that?"

"I wouldn't dare ask the police. Orrin would never forgive me. He's difficult enough at the best of times. Our family —" She hesitated and there was something behind her eyes she tried not to have there. So she went on breathlessly: "Our family's not the kind of family —"

"Look," I said wearily, "I'm not talking about the guy lifting a wallet. I'm talking about him getting knocked down by a car and losing his memory or being too badly hurt to talk."

She gave me a level look which was not too admiring. "If it was anything like that, we'd know," she said. "Everybody has things in their pockets to tell who they are."

"Sometimes all they have left is pockets."

"Are you trying to scare me, Mr. Marlowe?"

"If I am, I'm certainly getting nowhere fast. Just what do you think might have happened?"

She put her slim forefinger to her lips and touched it very carefully with the tip of that tongue. "I guess if I knew that I wouldn't have to come and see you. How much would you charge to find him?"

I didn't answer for a long moment, then I said: "You mean alone, without telling anybody?"

"Yes. I mean alone, without telling anybody."

"Uh-huh. Well that depends. I told you what my rates were."

She clasped her hands on the edge of the desk and squeezed them together hard. She had about the most meaningless set of gestures I had ever laid eyes on. "I thought you being a detective and all you could find him right away," she said. "I couldn't possibly afford more than twenty dollars. I've got to buy my meals here and my hotel and the train going back and you know the hotel is so terribly expensive and the food on the train —"

"Which one are you staying at?"

"I — I'd rather not tell you, if you don't mind."

"Why?"

"I'd just rather not. I'm terribly afraid of Orrin's temper. And, well I can always call you up, can't I?"

"Uh-huh. Just what is it you're scared of, besides Orrin's temper, Miss Quest?" I had let my pipe go out. I struck a match and held it to the bowl, watching her over it.

"Isn't pipe-smoking a very dirty habit?" she asked.

"Probably," I said. "But it would take more than twenty bucks to have me drop it. And don't try to side-step my questions."

"You can't talk to me like that," she flared up. "Pipe-smoking *is* a dirty habit. Mother never let father smoke in the house, even the last two years after he had his stroke. He used to sit with that empty pipe in his mouth sometimes. But she didn't like him to do that really. We owed a lot of money too and she said she couldn't afford to give him money for useless things like tobacco. The church needed it much more than he did."

"I'm beginning to get it," I said slowly. "Take a family like yours and somebody in it has to be the dark meat."

She stood up sharply and clasped the first-aid kit to her body. "I don't like you," she said. "I don't think I'm going to employ you. If you're insinuating that Orrin has done something wrong, well I can assure you that it's not Orrin who's the black sheep of our family."

I didn't move an eyelash. She swung around and marched to the door and put her hand on the knob and then she swung around again and marched back and suddenly began to cry. I reacted to that just the way a stuffed fish reacts to cut bait. She got out her little handkerchief and tickled the corners of her eyes.

"And now I suppose you'll call the p-police," she said with a catch in her voice. "And the Manhattan p-paper will hear about it and they'll print something n-nasty about us."

"You don't suppose anything of the sort. Stop chipping at my emotions. Let's see a photo of him."

She put the handkerchief away in a hurry and dug something else out of her bag. She passed it across the desk. An envelope. Thin, but there could be a couple of snapshots in it. I didn't look inside.

"Describe him the way you see him," I said.

She concentrated. That gave her a chance to do something with her eyebrows. "He was twenty-eight years old last March. He has light brown hair, much lighter than mine, and lighter blue eyes, and he brushes his hair straight back. He's very tall, over six feet. But he only weighs about a hundred and forty pounds. He's sort of bony. He used to wear a little blond mustache but mother made him cut it off. She said –"

"Don't tell me. The minister needed it to stuff a cushion."

"You can't talk like that about my mother," she yelped getting pale with rage.

"Oh stop being silly. There's a lot of things about you I don't know. But you can stop pretending to be an Easter lily right now. Does Orrin have any distinguishing marks on him, like moles or scars, or a tattoo of the Twenty-third Psalm on his chest? And don't bother to blush."

"Well you don't have to yell at me. Why don't you look at the photograph?"

"He probably has his clothes on. After all, you're his sister. You ought to know."

"No he hasn't," she said tightly. "He has a little scar on his left hand where he had a wen removed."

"What about his habits? What does he do for fun – besides not smoking or drinking or going out with girls?"

"Why – how did you know that?"

"Your mother told me."

She smiled. I was beginning to wonder if she had one in her. She had very white teeth and she didn't wave her gums. That was something. "Aren't you silly," she said. "He studies a lot and he has a very expensive camera he likes to snap people with when they don't know. Sometimes it makes them mad. But Orrin says people ought to see themselves as they really are."

"Let's hope it never happens to him," I said. "What kind of camera is it?"

"One of those little cameras with a very fine lens. You can take snaps in almost any kind of light. A Leica."

I opened the envelope and took out a couple of small prints, very clear. "These weren't taken with anything like that," I said.

"Oh no. Philip took those, Philip Anderson. A boy I was going with for a while." She paused and sighed. "And I guess that's really why I came here, Mr. Marlowe. Just because your name's Philip too."

I just said: "Uh-huh," but I felt touched in some vague sort of way. "What happened to Philip Anderson?"

"But it's about Orrin –"

"I know," I interrupted. "But what happened to Philip Anderson?"

"He's still there in Manhattan." She looked away. "Mother doesn't like him very much. I guess you know how it is."

"Yes," I said, "I know how it is. You can cry if you want to. I won't hold it against you. I'm just a big soft slob myself."

I looked at the two prints. One of them was looking down and was no good to me. The other was a fairly good shot of a tall angular bird with narrow-set eyes and a thin straight mouth and a pointed chin. He had the expression I expected to see. If you forgot to wipe the mud off your shoes, he was the boy who would tell you. I laid the photos aside and looked at Orfamay Quest, trying to find something in her face even remotely like his. I couldn't. Not the slightest trace of family resemblance, which of course meant absolutely nothing. It never has.

"All right," I said. "I'll go down there and take a look. But you ought to be able to guess what's happened. He's in a strange city. He's made good money for a while. More than he's ever made in his life, perhaps. He's meeting a kind of people he never met before. And it's not the kind of town – believe me it isn't, I know Bay City – that Manhattan, Kansas, is. So he just broke training and he doesn't want his family to know about it. He'll straighten out."

She just stared at me for a moment in silence, then she shook her head. "No. Orrin's not the type to do that, Mr. Marlowe."

"Anyone is," I said. "Especially a fellow like Orrin. The small-town sanctimonious type of guy who's lived his entire life with his mother on his neck and the minister holding his hand. Out here he's lonely. He's got dough. He'd like to buy a little sweetness and light, and not the kind that comes through the east window of a church. Not that I have anything against that. I mean he already had enough of that, didn't he?"

She nodded her head silently.

"So he starts to play," I went on, "and he doesn't know how to play. That takes experience too. He's got himself all jammed up with some floozy and a bottle of hooch and what he's done looks to him as if he'd stolen the bishop's pants. After all, the guy's going on twenty-nine years old and if he wants to roll in the gutter that's his business. He'll find somebody to blame it on after a while."

"I hate to believe you, Mr. Marlowe," she said slowly. "I'd hate for mother –"

"Something was said about twenty dollars," I cut in.

She looked shocked. "Do I have to pay you now?"

"What would be the custom in Manhattan, Kansas?"

"We don't have any private detectives in Manhattan. Just the regular police. That is, I don't think we do."

She probed in the inside of her tool kit again and dragged out a red change purse and from that she took a number of bills, all neatly folded and separate. Three fives and five ones. There didn't seem to be much left. She kind of held the purse so I could see how empty it was. Then she straightened the bills out on the desk and put one on top of the other and pushed them across. Very slowly, very sadly, as if she was drowning a favorite kitten.

"I'll give you a receipt," I said.

"I don't need a receipt, Mr. Marlowe."

"I do. You won't give me your name and address, so I want something with your name on it."

"What for?"

"To show I'm representing you." I got the receipt book out and made the receipt and held the book for her to sign the duplicate. She didn't want to. After a moment reluctantly she took the hard pencil and wrote "Orfamay Quest" in a neat secretary's writing across the face of the duplicate.

"Still no address?" I asked.

"I'd rather not."

"Call me any time then. My home number is in the phone book, too. Bristol Apartments, Apartment 428."

"I shan't be very likely to visit you," she said coldly.

"I haven't asked you yet," I said. "Call me around four if you like. I might have something. And then again I might not."

She stood up. "I hope mother won't think I've done wrong," she said, picking at her lip now with a pale fingernail. "Coming here, I mean."

"Just don't tell me any more of the things your mother won't like," I said. "Just leave that part out."

"Well really!"

237

"And stop saying 'well really.' "

"I think you are a very offensive person," she said.

"No, you don't. You think I'm cute. And I think you're a fascinating little liar. You don't think I'm doing this for any twenty bucks, do you?"

She gave me a level, suddenly cool stare. "Then why?" Then when I didn't answer she added, "Because spring is in the air?"

I still didn't answer. She blushed a little. Then she giggled.

I didn't have the heart to tell her I was just plain bored with doing nothing. Perhaps it *was* the spring too. And something in her eyes that was much older than Manhattan, Kansas.

"I think you're very nice – really," she said softly. Then she turned quickly and almost ran out of the office. Her steps along the corridor outside made tiny, sharp pecky sounds, kind of like mother drumming on the edge of the dinner table when father tried to promote himself a second piece of pie. And him with no money any more. No nothing. Just sitting in a rocker on the front porch back there in Manhattan, Kansas, with his empty pipe in his mouth. Rocking on the front porch, slow and easy, because when you've had a stroke you have to take it slow and easy. And wait for the next one. And the empty pipe in his mouth. No tobacco. Nothing to do but wait.

I put Orfamay Quest's twenty hard-earned dollars in an envelope and wrote her name on it and dropped it in the desk drawer. I didn't like the idea of running around loose with that much currency on me.

3

YOU COULD KNOW Bay City a long time without knowing Idaho Street. And you could know a lot of Idaho Street without knowing Number 449. The block in front of it had a broken paving that had almost gone back to dirt. The warped fence of a lumberyard bordered the cracked sidewalk on the opposite side of the street. Halfway up the block the rusted rails of a spur track turned in to a pair of high, chained wooden gates that seemed not to have been opened for twenty years. Little boys with chalk had been writing and drawing pictures on the gates and all along the fence.

Number 449 had a shallow, paintless front porch on which five wood and cane rockers loafed dissolutely, held together with wire and the moisture of the beach air. The green shades over the lower windows of the house were two thirds down and full of cracks. Beside the front door there was a large printed sign "No Vacancies." That had been there a long time too. It had got faded and fly-specked. The door opened on a long hall from which stairs went up a third of the way back. To the right there was a narrow shelf with a chained, indelible pencil hanging beside it. There was a push button and a yellow and black sign above which read "Manager," and was held up by three thumbtacks no two of which matched. There was a pay phone on the opposite wall.

I pushed the bell. It rang somewhere near by but nothing happened. I rang it again. The same nothing happened. I prowled along to a door with a black and white metal sign on it – "Manager." I knocked on that. Then I kicked it. Nobody seemed to mind my kicking it.

I went back out of the house and down around the side where a narrow concrete walk led to the service entrance. It looked as if it was in the right place to belong to the manager's apartment. The rest of the house would be just rooms. There was a dirty garbage pail on the small porch and a wooden box full of liquor bottles. Behind the screen the back door of the house was open. It was gloomy inside. I put my face against the screen and peered in. Through the open inner door beyond the service porch I could see a straight chair with a man's coat hanging over it and in the chair a man in shirtsleeves with his hat on. He was a small man. I couldn't see what he was doing, but he seemed to be sitting at the end of the built-in breakfast table in the breakfast nook.

I banged on the screen door. The man paid no attention. I banged again, harder. This time he tilted his chair back and showed me a small pale face with a cigarette in it. "Whatcha want?" he barked.

"Manager."

"Not in, bub."

"Who are you?"

"What's it to you?"

"I want a room."

"No vacancies, bub. Can't you read large print?"

"I happen to have different information," I said.

"Yeah?" He shook ash from his cigarette by flicking it with a nail without removing it from his small sad mouth. "Go fry your head in it."

He tilted his chair forward again and went on doing whatever it was he was doing.

I made noise getting down off the porch and none whatever coming back up on it. I felt the screen door carefully. It was hooked. With the open blade of a penknife I lifted the hook and eased it out of the eye. It made a small tinkle but louder tinkling sounds were being made beyond, in the kitchen.

I stepped into the house, crossed the service porch, went through the door into the kitchen. The little man was too busy to notice me. The kitchen had a three-burner gas stove, a few shelves of greasy dishes, a chipped icebox and the break-fast nook. The table in the breakfast nook was covered with money. Most of it was paper, but there was silver also, in all sizes up to dollars. The little man was counting and stacking it and making entries in a small book. He wetted his pencil without bothering the cigarette that lived in his face.

There must have been several hundred dollars on that table.

"Rent day?" I asked genially.

The small man turned very suddenly. For a moment he smiled and said nothing. It was the smile of a man whose mind is not smiling. He removed the stub of cigarette from his mouth, dropped it on the floor and stepped on it. He reached a fresh one out of his shirt and put it in the same hole in his face and started fumbling for a match.

"You came in nice," he said pleasantly.

Finding no match, he turned casually in his chair and reached into a pocket of his coat. Something heavy knocked against the wood of the chair. I got hold of his wrist before the heavy thing came out of the pocket. He threw his weight backwards and the pocket of the coat started to lift towards me. I yanked the chair out from under him.

He sat down hard on the floor and knocked his head against the end of the breakfast table. That didn't keep him from trying to kick me in the groin. I stepped back with his coat and took a .38 out of the pocket he had been playing with.

"Don't sit on the floor just to be chummy," I said.

He got up slowly, pretending to be groggier than he was. His hand fumbled at the back of his collar and light winked on metal as his arm swept toward me. He was a game little rooster.

I sideswiped his jaw with his own gun and he sat down on the floor again. I stepped on the hand that held the knife. His faced twisted with pain but he didn't make a sound. So I kicked the knife into a corner. It was a long thin knife and it looked very sharp.

"You ought to be ashamed of yourself," I said. "Pulling guns and knives on people that are just looking for a place to live. Even for these times that's out of line."

He held his hurt hand between his knees and squeezed it and began to whistle through his teeth. The slap on the jaw didn't seem to have hurt him. "Okay," he said, "Okay I ain't supposed to be perfect. Take the dough and beat it. But don't ever think we won't catch up with you."

I looked at the collection of small bills and medium bills and silver on the table. "You must meet a lot of sales resistance, the weapons you carry," I told him. I walked across to the inner door and tried it. It was not locked. I turned back.

"I'll leave your gun in the mailbox," I said. "Next time ask to see the buzzer."

He was still whistling gently between his teeth and holding his hands. He gave me a narrow, thoughtful eye, then shoveled the money into a shabby briefcase and slipped its catch. He took his hat off, straightened it around, put it back jauntily on the back of his head and gave me a quiet efficient smile.

"Never mind about the heater," he said. "The town's full of old iron. But you could leave the skiv with Clausen. I've done quite a bit of work on it to get it in shape."

"And with it?" I said.

"Could be." He flicked a finger at me airily. "Maybe we meet again some day soon. When I got a friend with me."

"Tell him to wear a clean shirt," I said. "And lend you one."

"My, my," the little man said chidingly. "How tough we get how quick once we get that badge pinned on."

He went softly past me and down the wooden steps from the back porch. His footsteps tapped to the street and faded. They sounded very much like Orfamay's heels clicking along the corridor in my office building. And for some reason I had that empty feeling of having miscounted the trumps. No reason for it at all. Maybe it was the steely quality about the little man. No whimper, no bluster, just the smile, the whistling between the teeth, the light voice and the unforgetting eyes.

I went over and picked up the knife. The blade was long and round and thin, like a rat-tailed file that has been ground smooth. The handle and guard were lightweight plastic and seemed all one piece. I held the knife by the handle and gave it a quick flip at the table. The blade came loose and quivered in the wood.

I took a deep breath and slid the handle down over the end again and worked the blade loose from the table. A curious knife, with design and purpose in it, and neither of them agreeable.

I opened the door beyond the kitchen and went through it with the gun and knife in one hand.

It was a wall-bed living room, with the wall bed down and rumpled. There was an overstuffed chair with a hole burnt in the arm. A high oak desk with tilted doors like old-fashioned cellar doors stood against the wall by the front window. Near this there was a studio couch and on the studio couch lay a man. His feet hung over the end of the couch in knobby gray socks. His head had missed the pillow by two feet. It was nothing much to miss from the color of the slip on it. The upper part of him was contained in a colorless shirt and a threadbare gray coatsweater. His mouth was open and his face was shining with sweat and he breathed like an old Ford with a leaky head gasket. On a table beside him was a plate full of cigarette stubs, some of which had a homemade look. On the floor a near full gin bottle and a cup that seemed to have contained coffee but not at all recently. The room was full mostly of gin and bad air, but there was also a reminiscence of marihuana smoke.

I opened a window and leaned my forehead against the screen to get a little cleaner air into my lungs and looked out into the street. Two kids were wheeling bicycles along the lumberyard fence, stopping from time to time to study the examples of rest-room art on the boarding. Nothing else moved in the neighborhood. Not even a dog. Down at the corner was dust in the air as though a car had passed that way.

I went over to the desk. Inside it was the house register, so I leafed back until I came to the name "Orrin P. Quest," written in a sharp meticulous handwriting, and the number 214 added in pencil by another hand that was by no means sharp or meticulous. I followed on through to the end of the register but found no new registration for Room 214. A party named G. W. Hicks had Room 215. I shut the register in the desk and crossed to the couch. The man stopped his snoring and bubbling and threw his right arm across his body as if he thought he was making a speech. I leaned down and gripped his nose tight between my first and second fingers and stuffed a handful of his sweater into his mouth. He stopped snoring and jerked his eyes open. They were glazed and bloodshot. He struggled against my hand. When I was sure he was fully awake I let go of him, picked the bottle full of gin off the floor and poured some into a glass that lay on its side near the bottle. I showed the glass to the man.

His hand came out to it with the beautiful anxiety of a mother welcoming a lost child.

I moved it out of his reach and said: "You the manager?"

He licked his lips stickily and said: "Gr–r–r–r."

He made a grab for the glass. I put it on the table in front of him. He grasped it carefully in both hands and poured the gin into his face. Then he laughed heartily and threw the glass at me. I managed to catch it and up-end it on the table again. The man looked me over with a studied but unsuccessful attempt at sternness.

"What gives?" he croaked in an annoyed tone.

"Manager?"

He nodded and almost fell off the couch. "Must be I'm drunky," he said. "Kind of a bit of a little bit drunky."

"You're not bad," I said. "You're still breathing."

He put his feet on the ground and pushed himself upright. He cackled with sudden amusement, took three uneven steps, went down on his hands and knees and tried to bite the leg of a chair.

I pulled him up on his feet again, set him down in the overstuffed chair with the burned arm and poured him another slug of his medicine. He drank it, shuddered violently and all at once his eyes seemed to get sane and cunning. Drunks of his type have a certain balanced moment of reality. You never know when it will come or how long it will last.

"Who the hell are you?" he growled.

"I'm looking for a man named Orrin P. Quest."

"Huh?"

I said it again. He smeared his face with his hands and said tersely: "Moved away."

"Moved away when?"

He waved his hand, almost fell out of his chair and waved it again the other way to restore his balance. "Gimme a drink," he said.

I poured another slug of the gin and held it out of his reach.

"Gimme," the man said urgently. "I'm not happy."

"All I want is the present address of Orrin P. Quest."

"Just think of that," he said wittily and made a loose pass at the glass I was holding.

I put the glass down on the floor and got one of my business cards out for him. "This might help you to concentrate," I told him.

He peered at the card closely, sneered, bent it in half and bent it again. He held it on the flat of his hand, spit on it, and tossed it over his shoulder.

I handed him the glass of gin. He drank it to my health, nodded solemnly, and threw the glass over his shoulder too. It rolled along the floor and thumped the baseboard. The man stood up with surprising ease, jerked a thumb towards the ceiling, doubled the fingers of his hand under it and made a sharp noise with his tongue and teeth.

"Beat it," he said. "I got friends." He looked at the telephone on the wall and back at me with cunning. "A couple of boys to take care of you," he sneered. I said nothing. "Don't believe me, huh?" he snarled, suddenly angry. I shook my head.

He started for the telephone, clawed the receiver off the hook, and dialed the five digits of a number. I watched him. One-three-five-seven-two.

That took all he had for the time being. He let the receiver fall and bang against the wall and he sat down on the floor beside it. He put it to his ear and growled at the wall: "Lemme talk to the Doc." I listened silently. "Vince! The Doc!" he shouted angrily. He shook the receiver and threw it away from him. He put his hands down on the floor and started to crawl in a circle. When he saw me he looked surprised and annoyed. He got shakily to his feet again and held his hand out. "Gimme a drink."

I retrieved the fallen glass and milked the gin bottle into it. He accepted it with the dignity of an intoxicated dowager, drank it down with an airy flourish, walked calmly over to the couch and lay down, putting the glass under his head for a pillow. He went to sleep instantly.

I put the telephone receiver back on its hook, glanced out in the kitchen again, felt the man on the couch over and dug some keys out of his pocket. One of them was a passkey. The door to the hallway had a spring lock and I fixed it so that I could come in again and started up the stars. I paused on the way to write "Doc — Vince, 13572" on an envelope. Maybe it was a clue.

The house was quite silent as I went on up.

4

THE MANAGER'S MUCH filed passkey turned the lock of Room 214 without noise. I pushed the door open. The room was not empty. A chunky, strongly built man was bending over a suitcase on the bed, with his back to the door. Shirts and socks and underwear were laid out on the bed cover, and he was packing them leisurely and carefully, whistling between his teeth in a low monotone.

He stiffened as the door hinge creaked. His hand moved fast for the pillow on the bed.

"I beg your pardon," I said. "The manager told me this room was vacant."

He was as bald as a grapefruit. He wore dark gray flannel slacks and transparent plastic suspenders over a blue shirt. His hand came up from the pillow, went to his head, and down again. He turned and he had hair.

It looked as natural as hair ever looked, smooth, brown, not parted. He glared at me from under it.

"You can always try knocking," he said.

He had a thick voice and a broad careful face that had been around.

"Why would I? If the manager said the room was empty?"

He nodded, satisfied. The glare went out of his eyes.

I came further into the room without invitation. An open love-pulp magazine lay face down on the bed near the suitcase. A cigar smoked in a green glass ashtray. The room was careful and orderly, and, for that house, clean.

"He must have thought you had already moved out," I said, trying to look like a well-meaning party with some talent for the truth.

"Have it in half an hour," the man said.

"Okay if I look around?"

He smiled mirthlessly. "Ain't been in town long, have you?"

"Why?"

"New around here, ain't you?"

"Why?"

"Like the house and the neighborhood?"

"Not much," I said. "The room looks all right."

He grinned, showing a porcelain jacket crown that was too white for his other teeth. "How long you been looking?"

"Just started," I said. "Why all the questions?"

"You make me laugh," the man said, not laughing. "You don't look at rooms in this town. You grab them sight unseen.

247

This burg's so jam-packed even now that I could get ten bucks just for telling there's a vacancy here."

"That's too bad," I said. "A man named Orrin P. Quest told me about the room. So there's one sawbuck you don't get to spend."

"That so?" Not a flicker of an eye. Not a movement of a muscle. I might as well have been talking to a turtle.

"Don't get tough with me," the man said. "I'm a bad man to get tough with."

He picked his cigar out of the green glass ashtray and blew a little smoke. Through it he gave me the cold gray eye. I got a cigarette out and scratched my chin with it.

"What happens to people that get tough with you?" I asked him. "You make them hold your toupee?"

"You lay off my toupee," he said savagely.

"So sorry," I said.

"There's a 'No Vacancy' sign on the house," the man said. "So what makes you come here and find one?"

"You didn't catch the name," I said. "Orrin P. Quest." I spelled it for him. Even that didn't make him happy. There was a dead-air pause.

He turned abruptly and put a pile of handkerchiefs into his suitcase. I moved a little closer to him. When he turned back there was what might have been a watchful look on his face. But it had been a watchful face to start with.

"Friend of yours?" he asked casually.

"We grew up together," I said.

"Quiet sort of guy," the man said easily. "I used to pass the time of day with him. Works for Cal-Western, don't he?"

"He did," I said.

"Oh. He quit?"

"Let out."

We went on staring at each other. It didn't get either of us anywhere. We both had done too much of it in our lives to expect miracles.

The man put the cigar back in his face and sat down on the side of the bed beside the open suitcase. Glancing into it I saw the square butt of an automatic peeping out from under a pair of badly folded shorts.

"This Quest party's been out of here ten days," the man said thoughtfully. "So he still thinks the room is vacant, huh?"

"According to the register it *is* vacant," I said.

He made a contemptuous noise. "That rummy downstairs probably ain't looked at the register in a month. Say — wait a minute." His eyes sharpened and his hand wandered idly over the open suitcase and gave an idle pat to something close to the gun. When the hand moved away, the gun was no longer visible.

"I've been kind of dreamy all morning or I'd have wised up," he said. "You're a dick."

"All right. Say I'm a dick."

"What's the beef?"

"No beef at all. I just wondered why you had the room."

"I moved from 215 across the hall. This here is a better room. That's all. Simple. Satisfied?"

"Perfectly," I said, watching the hand that could be near the gun if it wanted to.

"What kind of dick? City? Let's see the buzzer."

I didn't say anything.

"I don't believe you got no buzzer."

"If I showed it to you, you're the type of guy would say it was counterfeit. So you're Hicks."

He looked surprised.

"George W. Hicks," I said. "It's in the register. Room 215. You just got through telling me you moved from 215." I glanced around the room. "If you had a blackboard here, I'd write it out for you."

"Strictly speaking, we don't have to get into no snarling match," he said. "Sure I'm Hicks. Pleased to meetcha. What's yours?"

He held his hand out. I shook hands with him, but not as if I had been longing for the moment to arrive.

"My name's Marlowe," I said. "Philip Marlowe."

"You know something," Hicks said politely, "you're a Goddamn liar."

I laughed in his face.

"You ain't getting no place with that breezy manner, bub. What's your connection?"

I got my wallet out and handed him one of my business cards. He read it thoughtfully and tapped the edge against his porcelain crown.

"He coulda went somewhere without telling me," he mused.

"Your grammar," I said, "is almost as loose as your toupee."

"You lay off my toupee, if you know what's good for you," he shouted.

"I wasn't going to eat it," I said. "I'm not that hungry."

He took a step towards me, and dropped his right shoulder. A scowl of fury dropped his lip almost as far.

"Don't hit me. I'm insured," I told him.

"Oh hell. Just another screwball." He shrugged and put his lip back up on his face. "What's the lay?"

"I have to find this Orrin P. Quest," I said.

"Why?"

I didn't answer that.

After a moment he said: "Okay. I'm a careful guy myself. That's why I'm movin' out."

"Maybe you don't like the reefer smoke."

"That," he said emptily, "and other things. That's why Quest left. Respectable type. Like me. I think a couple of hard boys threw a scare into him."

"I see," I said. "That would be why he left no forwarding address. And why did they throw a scare into him?"

"You just mentioned reefer smoke, didn't you? Wouldn't he be the type to go to headquarters about that?"

"In Bay City?" I asked. "Why would he bother? Well, thanks a lot, Mr. Hicks. Going far?"

"Not far," he said. "No. Not very far. Just far enough."

"What's your racket?" I asked him.

"Racket?" He looked hurt.

"Sure. What do you shake them for? How do you make your dibs?"

"You got me wrong, brother. I'm a retired optometrist."

"That why you have the .45 gun in there?" I pointed to the suitcase.

"Nothing to get cute about," he said sourly. "It's been in the family for years." He looked down at the card again. "Private investigator, huh?" he said thoughtfully. "What kind of work do you do mostly?"

"Anything that's reasonably honest," I said.

He nodded. "Reasonably is a word you could stretch. So is honest."

I gave him a shady leer. "You're so right," I agreed. "Let's get together some quiet afternoon and stretch them." I reached out and slipped the card from between his fingers and dropped it into my pocket. "Thanks for the time," I said.

I went out and closed the door, then stood against it listening. I don't know what I expected to hear. Whatever it was I didn't hear it. I had a feeling he was standing exactly where I had left him and looking at the spot where I had made my exit. I made noise going along the hall and stood at the head of the stairs.

A car drove away from in front of the house. Somewhere a door closed. I went quietly back to Room 215 and used the passkey to enter. I closed and locked its door silently, and waited just inside.

5

NOT MORE THAN two minutes passed before Mr. George W. Hicks was on his way. He came out so quietly that I wouldn't have heard him if I hadn't been listening for precisely that kind of movement. I heard the slight metallic sound of the doorknob turning. The slow steps. Then very gently the door was closed. The steps moved off. The faint distant creak of the stairs. Then nothing. I waited for the sound of the front door. It didn't come. I opened the door of 215 and moved along the hall to the stairhead again. Below there was the careful sound of a door being tried. I looked down to see Hicks going into the manager's apartment. The door closed behind him. I waited for the sound of voices. No voices.

I shrugged and went back to 215.

The room showed signs of occupancy. There was a small radio on a night table, an unmade bed with shoes under it, and an old bathrobe hung over the cracked, pull-down green shade to keep the glare out.

I looked at all this as if it meant something, then stepped back into the hall and relocked the door. Then I made another pilgrimage into Room 214. Its door was now unlocked. I searched the room with care and patience and found nothing that connected it in any way with Orrin P. Quest. I didn't expect to. There was no reason why I should. But you always have to look.

I went downstairs, listened outside the manager's door, heard nothing, went in and crossed to put the keys on the desk. Lester B. Clausen lay on his side on the couch with his face to the wall, dead to the world. I went through the desk, found an old account book that seemed to be concerned with rent taken in and expenses paid out and nothing else. I looked at the register again. It wasn't up to date but the party on the couch seemed enough explanation for that. Orrin P. Quest had moved away. Somebody had taken over his room. Somebody else had the room registered to Hicks. The little man counting money in the kitchen went nicely with the neighborhood. The fact that he carried a gun and a knife was a social eccentricity that would cause no comment at all on Idaho Street.

I reached the small Bay City telephone book off the hook beside the desk. I didn't think it would be much of a job to sift out the party that went by the name of "Doc" or "Vince" and the phone number one-three-five-seven-two. First of all I leafed back through the register. Something which I ought to have done first. The page with Orrin Quest's registration had been torn out. A careful man, Mr. George W. Hicks. Very careful.

I closed the register, glanced over at Lester B. Clausen again, wrinkled my nose at the stale air and the sickly sweetish smell of gin and of something else, and started back to the entrance door. As I reached it, something for the first time penetrated my mind. A drunk like Clausen ought to be snoring very loudly. He ought to be snoring his head off with a nice assortment of checks and gurgles and snorts. He wasn't making any sound at all. A brown army blanket was pulled up around his shoulders and the lower part of his head. He looked very comfortable, very calm. I stood over him and looked down. Something which was not an accidental fold held the army blanket away from the back of his neck. I moved it. A square yellow wooden handle was attached to the back of Lester B. Clausen's neck. On the side of the yellow handle were printed the words "Compliments of the Crumsen Hardware Company." The position of the handle was just below the occipital bulge.

It was the handle of an ice pick. . . .

I did a nice quiet thirty-five getting away from the neighborhood. On the edge of the city, a frog's jump from the line, I shut myself in an outdoor telephone booth and called the Police Department.

"Bay City Police. Moot talking," a furry voice said.

I said: "Number 449 Idaho Street. In the apartment of the manager. His name's Clausen."

"Yeah?" The voice said. "What do we do?"

"I don't know," I said. "It's a bit of a puzzle to me. But the man's name is Lester B. Clausen. Got that?"

"What makes it important?" the furry voice said without suspicion.

"The coroner will want to know," I said, and hung up.

6

I DROVE BACK to Hollywood and locked myself in the office with the Bay City telephone book. It took me a quarter-hour to find out that the party who went with the telephone number one-three-five-seven-two in Bay City was a Dr. Vincent Lagardie, who called himself a neurologist, had his home and offices on Wyoming Street, which according to my map was not quite in the best residential neighborhood and not quite out of it. I locked the Bay City telephone book up in my desk and went down to the corner drugstore for a sandwich and a cup of coffee and used a pay booth to call Dr. Vincent Lagardie. A woman answered and I had some trouble getting through to Dr. Lagardie himself. When I did his voice was impatient. He was very busy, in the middle of an examination he said. I never knew a doctor who wasn't. Did he know Lester B. Clausen? He never heard of him. What was the purpose of my inquiry?

"Mr. Clausen tried to telephone you this morning," I said. "He was too drunk to talk properly."

"But I don't know Mr. Clausen," the doctor's cool voice answered. He didn't seem to be in quite such a hurry now.

"Well that's all right then," I said. "Just wanted to make sure. Somebody stuck an ice pick into the back of his neck."

There was a quiet pause. Dr. Lagardie's voice was now almost unctuously polite. "Has this been reported to the police?"

"Naturally," I said. "But it shouldn't bother you – unless of course it was your ice pick."

He passed that one up. "And who is this speaking?" he inquired suavely.

"The name is Hicks," I said. "George W. Hicks. I just moved out of there. I don't want to get mixed up with that sort of thing. I just figured when Clausen tried to call you – this was before he was dead you understand – that you might be interested."

"I'm sorry, Mr. Hicks," Dr. Lagardie's voice said, "but I don't *know* Mr. Clausen. I have never *heard* of Mr. Clausen or had any contact with him whatsoever. And I have an excellent memory for names."

"Well, that's fine," I said. "And you won't meet him now. But somebody *may* want to know why he tried to telephone you – unless I forget to pass the information along."

There was a dead pause. Dr. Lagardie said: "I can't think of any comment to make on that."

I said: "Neither can I. I may call you again. Don't get me wrong, Dr. Lagardie. This isn't any kind of a shake. I'm just a mixed-up little man who needs a friend. I kind of felt that a doctor – like a clergyman –"

"I'm at your entire disposal," Dr. Lagardie said. "Please feel free to consult me."

"Thank you, doctor," I said fervently. "Thank you very very much."

I hung up. If Dr. Vincent Lagardie was on the level, he would now telephone the Bay City Police Department and tell them the story. If he didn't telephone the police, he wasn't on the level. Which might or might not be useful to know.

7

THE PHONE ON my desk rang at four o'clock sharp.

"Did you find Orrin yet, Mr. Marlowe?"

"Not yet. Where are you?"

"Why I'm in the drugstore next to –"

"Come on up and stop acting like Mata Hari," I said.

"Aren't you ever polite to anybody?" she snapped.

I hung up and fed myself a slug of Old Forester to brace my nerves for the interview. As I was inhaling it I heard her steps tripping along the corridor. I moved across and opened the door.

"Come in this way and miss the crowd," I said.

She seated herself demurely and waited.

"All I could find out," I told her, "is that the dump on Idaho Street is peddling reefers. That's marihuana cigarettes."

"Why, how disgusting," she said.

"We have to take the bad with the good in this life," I said. "Orrin must have got wise and threatened to report it to the police."

"You mean," she said in her little-girl manner, "that they might hurt him for doing that?"

"Well, most likely they'd just throw a scare into him first."

"Oh, they couldn't scare Orrin, Mr. Marlowe," she said decisively. "He just gets mean when people try to run him."

"Yeah," I said. "But we're not talking about the same things. You can scare anybody – with the right technique."

She set her mouth stubbornly. "No, Mr. Marlowe. They couldn't scare Orrin."

"Okay," I said. "So they didn't scare him. Say they just cut off one of his legs and beat him over the head with it. What would he do then – write to the Better Business Bureau?"

"You're making fun of me," she said politely. Her voice was as cool as boarding-house soup. "Is that all you did all day? Just find Orrin had moved and it was a bad neighborhood? Why I found that out for myself, Mr. Marlowe. I thought you being a detective and all –" She trailed off, leaving the rest of it in the air.

"I did a little more than that," I said. "I gave the landlord a little gin and went through the register and talked to a man named Hicks. George W. Hicks. He wears a toupee. I guess maybe you didn't meet him. He has, or had, Orrin's room. So I thought maybe –" It was my turn to do a little trailing in the air.

She fixed me with her pale blue eyes enlarged by the glasses. Her mouth was small and firm and tight, her hands clasped on the desk in front of her over her large square bag, her whole body stiff and erect and formal and disapproving.

"I paid you twenty dollars, Mr. Marlowe," she said coldly. "I understood that was in payment of a day's work. It doesn't seem to me that you've done a day's work."

"No," I said. "That's true. But the day isn't over yet. And don't bother about the twenty bucks. You can have it back if you like. I didn't even bruise it."

I opened the desk drawer and got out her money. I pushed it across the desk. She looked at it but didn't touch it. Her eyes came up slowly to meet mine.

"I didn't mean it like that. I know you're doing the best you can, Mr. Marlowe."

"With the facts I have."

"But I've told you all I know."

"I don't think so," I said.

"Well I'm sure I can't help what you think," she said tartly. "After all, if I knew what I wanted to know already, I wouldn't have come here and asked you to find it out, would I?"

"I'm not saying you know all you want to know," I answered. "The point is I don't know all I want to know in order to do a job for you. And what you tell me doesn't add up."

"What doesn't add up? I've told you the truth. I'm Orrin's sister. I guess I know what kind of person he is."

"How long did he work for Cal-Western?"

"I've told you that. He came out to California just about a year ago. He got work right away because he practically had the job before he left."

"He wrote home how often? Before he stopped writing."

"Every week. Sometimes oftener. He'd take turns writing to mother and me. Of course the letters were for both of us."

"About what?"

"You mean what did he write about?"

"What did you think I meant?"

"Well, you don't have to snap at me. He wrote about his work and the plant and the people there and sometimes about a show he'd been to. Or it was about California. He'd write about church too."

"Nothing about girls?"

"I don't think Orrin cared much for girls."

"And lived at the same address all this time?"

She nodded, looking puzzled.

"And he stopped writing how long ago?"

That took thought. She pressed her lips and pushed a fingertip around the middle of the lower one. "About three or four months," she said at last.

"What was the date of his last letter?"

"I — I'm afraid I can't tell you exactly the date. But it was like I said, three or four —"

I waved a hand at her. "Anything out of the ordinary in it? Anything unusual said or anything unusual unsaid?"

"Why no. It seemed just like all the rest."

"Don't you have any friends or relatives in this part of the country?"

She gave me a funny stare, started to say something, then shook her head sharply. "No."

"Okay. Now I'll tell you what's wrong. I'll skip over your not telling me where you're staying, because it might be just that you're afraid I'll show up with a quart of hooch under my arm and make a pass at you."

"That's not a very nice way to talk," she said.

"Nothing I say is nice. I'm not nice. By your standards nobody with less than three prayerbooks could be nice. But I *am* inquisitive. What's wrong with this picture is that you're not scared. Neither you personally nor your mother. And you ought to be scared as hell."

She clutched her bag to her bosom with tight little fingers. "You mean something has happened to him?" Her voice faded off into a sort of sad whisper, like a mortician asking for a down payment.

"I don't know that anything has. But in your position, knowing the kind of guy Orrin was, the way his letters came through and then didn't, I can't see myself waiting for my summer vacation to come around before I start asking questions. I can't see myself by-passing the police who have an organization for finding people. And going to a lone-wolf operator you never heard of, asking him to root around for you in the rubble. And I can't see your dear old mother just sitting there in Manhattan, Kansas, week after week darning the minister's winter underwear. No letter from Orrin. No news. And all she does about it is take a long breath and mend up another pair of pants."

She came to her feet with a lunge. "You're a horrid, disgusting person," she said angrily. "I think you're vile. Don't you dare say mother and I weren't worried. Just don't you dare."

I pushed the twenty dollars' worth of currency a little closer to the other side of the desk. "You were worried twenty dollars' worth, honey," I said. "But about what I wouldn't know. I guess I don't really want to know. Just put this hunk of folding back in your saddlebag and forget you ever met me. You might want to lend it to another detective tomorrow."

She snapped her bag shut viciously on the money. "I'm not very likely to forget your rudeness," she said between her teeth. "Nobody in the world's ever talked to me the way you have."

I stood up and wandered around the end of the desk. "Don't think about it too much. You might get to like it."

I reached up and twitched her glasses off. She took half a step back, almost stumbled, and I reached an arm around her by pure instinct. Her eyes widened and she put her hands

259

against my chest and pushed. I've been pushed harder by a kitten.

"Without the cheaters those eyes are really something," I said in an awed voice.

She relaxed and let her head go back and her lips open a little. "I suppose you do this to all the clients," she said softly. Her hands now had dropped to her sides. The bag whacked against my leg. She leaned her weight on my arm. If she wanted me to let go of her, she had her signals mixed.

"I just didn't want you to lose your balance," I said.

"I knew you were the thoughtful type." She relaxed still more. Her head went back now. Her upper lids drooped, fluttered a bit and her lips came open a little farther. On them appeared the faint provocative smile that nobody ever has to teach them. "I suppose you thought I did it on purpose," she said.

"Did what on purpose?"

"Stumbled, sort of."

"Wel-l-l-l."

She reached a quick arm around my neck and started to pull. So I kissed her. It was either that or slug her. She pushed her mouth hard at me for a long moment, then quietly and very comfortably wriggled around in my arms and nestled. She let out a long easy sigh.

"In Manhattan, Kansas, you could be arrested for this," she said.

"If there was any justice, I could be arrested just for being there," I said.

She giggled and poked the end of my nose with a fingertip. "I suppose you really prefer fast girls," she said, looking up at me sideways. "At least you won't have to wipe off any lip rouge. Maybe I'll wear some next time."

"Maybe we'd better sit down on the floor," I said. "My arm's getting tired."

She giggled again and disengaged herself gracefully. "I guess you think I've been kissed lots of times," she said.

"What girl hasn't?"

She nodded, gave me the up-from-under look that made her eyelashes cut across the iris. "Even at the church socials they play kissing games," she said.

"Or there wouldn't be any church socials," I said.

We looked at each other with no particular expression.

"Well-l-l —" she began at last. I handed her back her glasses. She put them on. She opened her bag, looked at herself in a small mirror, rooted around in her bag and came out with her hand clenched.

"I'm sorry I was mean," she said, and pushed something under the blotter of my desk. She gave me another little frail smile and marched to the door and opened it.

"I'll call you," she said intimately. And out she went, tap, tap, tap down the hall.

I went over and lifted the blotter and smoothed out the crumpled currency that lay under it. It hadn't been much of a kiss, but it looked like I had another chance at the twenty dollars.

The phone rang before I had quite started to worry about Mr. Lester B. Clausen. I reached for it absently. The voice I heard was an abrupt voice, but thick and clogged, as if it was being strained through a curtain or somebody's long white beard.

"You Marlowe?" it said.

"Speaking."

"You got a safe-deposit box, Marlowe?"

I had enough of being polite for one afternoon. "Stop asking and start telling," I said.

"I asked you a question, Marlowe."

"I didn't answer it," I said. "Like this." I reached over and pressed down the riser on the phone. Held it that way while I fumbled for a cigarette. I knew he would call right back. They always do when they think they're tough. They haven't used their exit line. When it rang again I started right in.

"If you have a proposition, state it. And I get called 'mister' until you give me some money."

"Don't let that temper ride you so hard, friend. I'm in a jam. I need something kept in a safe place. For a few days. Not longer. And for that you make a little quick money."

"How little?" I asked. "And how quick?"

"A C note. Right here and waiting. I'm warming it for you."

"I can hear it purr," I said. "Right where and waiting?" I was listening to the voice twice, once when I heard it and once when it echoed in my mind.

"Room 332, Van Nuys Hotel. Knock two quick ones and two slow ones. Not too loud. I got to have live action. How fast can you —"

"What is it you want me to keep?"

"That'll wait till you get here. I said I was in a hurry."

"What's your name?"

"Just Room 332."

"Thanks for the time," I said. "Goodbye."

"Hey. Wait a minute, dope. It's nothing hot like you think. No ice. No emerald pendants. It just happens to be worth a lot of money to me — and nothing at all to anybody else."

"The hotel has a safe."

"Do you want to die poor, Marlowe?"

"Why not? Rockefeller did. Goodbye again."

The voice changed. The furriness went out of it. It said sharply and swiftly: "How's every little thing in Bay City?"

I didn't speak. Just waited. There was a dim chuckle over the wire. "Thought that might interest you, Marlowe. Room 332 it is. Tramp on it friend. Make speed."

The phone clicked in my ear. I hung up. For no reason a pencil rolled off the desk and broke its point on the glass doohickey under one of the desk legs. I picked it up and slowly and carefully sharpened it in the Boston sharpener screwed to the edge of the window frame, turning the pencil around to get it nice and even. I laid it down in the tray on the desk and dusted off my hands. I had all the time in the world. I looked out of the window. I didn't see anything. I didn't hear anything.

And then, for even less reason, I saw Orfamay Quest's face without the glasses, and polished and painted and with blond hair piled up high on the forehead with a braid around the middle of it. And bedroom eyes. They all have to have bedroom eyes. I tried to imagine this face in a vast close-up being gnawed by some virile character from the wide-open spaces of Romanoff's bar.

It took me twenty-nine minutes to get to the Van Nuys Hotel.

8

ONCE, LONG AGO, it must have had a certain elegance. But no more. The memories of old cigars clung to its lobby like the dirty gilt on its ceiling and the sagging springs of its leather lounging chairs. The marble of the desk had turned a yellowish brown with age. But the floor carpet was new and had a hard look, like the room clerk. I passed him up and strolled over to the cigar counter in the corner and put down a quarter for a package of Camels. The girl behind the counter was a straw blonde with a long neck and tired eyes. She put the cigarettes in front of me, added a packet of matches, dropped my change into a slotted box marked "The Community Chest Thanks You."

"You'd want me to do that, wouldn't you," she said, smiling patiently. "You'd want to give your change to the poor little underprivileged kids with bent legs and stuff, wouldn't you?"

"Suppose I didn't," I said.

"I dig up seven cents," the girl said, "and it would be very painful." She had a low lingering voice with a sort of moist caress in it like a damp bath towel. I put a quarter after the seven cents. She gave me her big smile then. It showed more of her tonsils.

"You're nice," she said. "I can see you're nice. A lot of fellows would have come in here and made a pass at a girl. Just think. Over seven cents. A pass."

"Who's the house peeper here now?" I asked her, without taking up the option.

"There's two of them." She did something slow and elegant to the back of her head, exhibiting what seemed like more than one handful of blood-red fingernails in the process. "Mr. Hady is on nights and Mr. Flack is on days. It's day now so it would be Mr. Flack would be on."

"Where could I find him?"

She leaned over the counter and let me smell her hair, pointing with a half-inch fingernail toward the elevator bank. "It's down along that corridor there, next to the porter's room. You can't miss the porter's room on account of it has a half-door and says PORTER on the upper part in gold letters. Only that half is folded back like, so I guess maybe you can't see it."

"I'll see it," I said. "Even if I have to get a hinge screwed to my neck. What does this Flack look like?"

"Well," she said, "he's a little squatty number, with a bit of a mustache. A sort of chunky type. Thick-set like, only not tall." Her fingers moved languidly along the counter to where I could have touched them without jumping. "He's not interesting," she said. "Why bother?"

"Business," I said, and made off before she threw a half-nelson on me.

I looked back at her from the elevators. She was staring after me with an expression she probably would have said was thoughtful.

The porter's room was halfway down the corridor to the Spring Street entrance. The door beyond it was half open. I looked around its edge, then went in and closed it behind me.

A man was sitting at a small desk which had dust on it, a very large ashtray and very little else. He was short and thick-set. He had something dark and bristly under his nose about an inch long. I sat down across from him and put a card on the desk.

He reached for the card without excitement, read it, turned it over and read the back with as much care as the front. There was nothing on the back to read. He picked half of a cigar out of his ashtray and burned his nose lighting it.

"What's the gripe?" he growled at me.

"No gripe. You Flack?"

He didn't bother to answer. He gave me a steady look which may or may not have concealed his thoughts, depending on whether he had any to conceal.

"Like to get a line on one of the customers," I said.

"What name?" Flack asked, with no enthusiasm.

"I don't know what name he's using here. He's in Room 332."

"What name was he using before he came here?" Flack asked.

"I don't know that either."

"Well, what did he look like?" Flack was suspicious now. He reread my card but it added nothing to his knowledge.

"I never saw him, so far as I know."

Flack said: "I must be overworked. I don't get it."

"I had a call from him," I said. "He wanted to see me."

"Am I stopping you?"

"Look, Flack. A man in my business makes enemies at times. You ought to know that. This party wants something done. Tells me to come on over, forgets to give his name, and hangs up. I figured I'd do a little checking before I went up there."

Flack took the cigar out of his mouth and said patiently: "I'm in terrible shape. I still don't get it. Nothing makes sense to me any more."

I leaned over the desk and spoke to him slowly and distinctly: "The whole thing could be a nice way to get me into a hotel room and knock me off and then quietly check out. You wouldn't want anything like that to happen in your hotel, would you, Flack?"

"Supposing I cared," he said, "you figure you're that important?"

"Do you smoke that piece of rope because you like it or because you think it makes you look tough?"

"For forty-five bucks a week," Flack said, "would I smoke anything better?" He eyed me steadily.

"No expense account yet," I told him. "No deal yet."

He made a sad sound and got up wearily and went out of the room. I lit one of my cigarettes and waited. He came back in a short time and dropped a registration card on the desk. *Dr. G. W. Hambleton, El Centro, California* was written on it in a firm round hand in ink. The clerk had written other things on it, including the room number and daily rate. Flack pointed a finger that needed a manicure or failing that a nailbrush.

"Came in at 2.47 P.M.," he said. "Just today, that is. Nothing on his bill. One day's rent. No phone calls. No nothing. That what you want?"

"What does he look like?" I asked.

"I didn't see him. You think I stand out there by the desk and take pictures of them while they register?"

"Thanks," I said. "Dr. G. W. Hambleton, El Centro. Much obliged." I handed him back the registration card.

"Anything I ought to know," Flack said as I went out, "don't forget where I live. That is, if you call it living."

I nodded and went out. There are days like that. Everybody you meet is a dope. You begin to look at yourself in the glass and wonder.

9

ROOM 332 WAS at the back of the building near the door to the fire escape. The corridor which led to it had a smell of old carpet and furniture oil and the drab anonymity of a thousand shabby lives. The sand bucket under the racked fire hose was full of cigarette and cigar stubs, an accumulation of several days. A radio pounded brassy music through an open transom. Through another transom people were laughing fit to kill themselves. Down at the end by Room 332 it was quieter.

I knocked the two longs and two shorts as instructed. Nothing happened. I felt jaded and old. I felt as if I had spent my life knocking at doors in cheap hotels that nobody bothered to open. I tried again. Then turned the knob and walked in. A key with a red fiber tab hung in the inside keyhole.

There was a short hall with a bathroom on the right. Beyond the hall the upper half of a bed was in view and a man lay on it in shirt and pants.

I said: "Dr. Hambleton?"

The man didn't answer. I went past the bathroom door towards him. A whiff of perfume reached me and I started to turn, but not quickly enough. A woman who had been in the bathroom was standing there holding a towel in front of the lower part of her face. Dark glasses showed above the towel. And then the brim of a widebrimmed straw hat in a sort of dusty delphinium blue. Under that was fluffed-out pale blond hair. Blue earbuttons lurked somewhere back in the shadows. The sunglasses were in white frames with broad flat sidebows. Her dress matched her hat. An embroidered silk or rayon coat was open over the dress. She wore gauntleted gloves and there was an automatic in her right hand. White bone grip. Looked like a .32.

"Turn around and put your hands behind you," she said through the towel. The voice muffled by the towel meant as little to me as the dark glasses. It was not the voice which had talked to me on the telephone. I didn't move.

"Don't ever think I'm fooling," she said. "I'll give you exactly three seconds to do what I say."

"Couldn't you make it a minute? I like looking at you."

She made a threatening gesture with the little gun. "Turn around," she snapped. "But fast."

"I like the sound of your voice too."

"All right," she said, in a tight dangerous tone. "If that's the way you want it, that's the way you want it."

"Don't forget you're a lady," I said, and turned around and put my hands up to my shoulders. A gun muzzle poked into the back of my neck. Breath almost tickled my skin. The perfume was an elegant something or other, not strong, not decisive. The gun against my neck went away and a white flame burned for an instant behind my eyes. I grunted and fell forward on my hands and knees and reached back quickly. My hand touched a leg in a nylon stocking but slipped off, which seemed a pity. It felt like a nice leg. The jar of another blow on the head took the pleasure out of this and I made the hoarse sound of a man in desperate shape. I collapsed on the floor. The door opened. A key rattled. The door closed. The key turned. Silence.

I climbed up to my feet and went into the bathroom. I bathed my head with a towel from the rack soaked with cold water. It felt as if the heel of a shoe had hit me. Certainly it was not a gun butt. There was a little blood, not much. I rinsed the towel out and stood there patting the bruise and wondering why I didn't run after her screaming. But what I was doing was staring into the open medicine cabinet over the basin. The upper part of a can of talcum had been pried off the shoulder. There was talcum all over the shelf. A toothpaste tube had been cut open. Someone had been looking for something.

I went back to the little hallway and tried the room door. Locked from the outside. I bent down and looked through the keyhole. But it was an up-and-down lock, with the outer and inner keyholes on different levels. The girl in the dark glasses with the white rims didn't know much about hotels. I twisted the night latch, which opened the outside lock, opened the door, looked along the empty corridor, and closed the door again.

Then I went towards the man on the bed. He had not moved during all this time, for a somewhat obvious reason.

Beyond the little hallway the room widened towards a pair of windows through which the evening sun slanted in a shaft that reached almost across the bed and came to a stop under the neck of the man that lay there. What it stopped on was blue and white and shining and round. He lay quite comfortably half on his face with his hands down at his sides and his shoes off. The side of his face was on the pillow and he seemed relaxed. He was wearing a toupee. The last time I had talked to him his name had been George W. Hicks. Now it was Dr. G. W. Hambleton. Same initials. Not that it mattered any more. I wasn't going to be talking to him again. There was no blood. None at all, which is one of the few nice things about an expert ice-pick job.

I touched his neck. It was still warm. While I was doing it the shaft of sunlight moved away from the knob of the ice pick toward his left ear. I turned away and looked the room over. The telephone bell box had been opened and left open. The Gideon Bible was thrown in the corner. The desk had been searched. I went to a closet and looked into that. There were clothes in it and a suitcase I had seen before. I found nothing that seemed important. I picked a snap-brim hat off the floor and put it on the desk and went back to the bathroom. The point of interest now was whether the people who had icepicked Dr. Hambleton had found what they came for. They had had very little time.

I searched the bathroom carefully. I moved the top of the toilet tank and drained it. There was nothing in it. I peered down the overflow pipe. No thread hung there with a small object at the end of it. I searched the bureau. It was empty except for an old envelope. I unhooked the window screens and felt under the sills outside. I picked the Gideon Bible off the floor and leafed through it again. I examined the backs of three pictures and studied the edge of the carpet. It was tacked close to the wall and there were little pockets of dust in the depressions made by the tacks. I got down on the floor and examined the part under the bed. Just the same. I stood on a chair, looked into the bowl of the light fixture. It contained dust and dead moths. I looked the bed over. It had been made up by a professional and not touched since. I felt the pillow under the dead man's head, then got the extra pillow out of the closet and examined its edges. Nothing.

Dr. Hambleton's coat hung over a chair back. I went through that, knowing it was the least likely place to find anything. Somebody with a knife had worked on the lining and the shoulder padding. There were matches, a couple of cigars, a pair of dark glasses, a cheap handkerchief not used, a Bay City movie theater ticket stub, a small comb, an unopened package of cigarettes. I looked at it in the light. It showed no sign of having been disturbed. I disturbed it. I tore off the cover, went through it, found nothing but cigarettes.

That left Dr. Hambleton himself. I eased him over and got into his trouser pockets. Loose change, another handkerchief, a small tube of dental floss, more matches, a bunch of keys, a folder of bus schedules. In a pigskin wallet was a book of stamps, a second comb (here was a man who really took care of his toupee), three flat packages of white powder, seven printed cards reading *Dr. G. W. Hambleton, O. D. Tustin Building, El Centro, California, Hours 9–12 and 2–4, and by Appointment. Telephone El Centro 50406*. There was no driver's license, no social-security card, no insurance cards, no real identification at all. There was $164 in currency in the wallet. I put the wallet back where I found it.

I lifted Dr. Hambleton's hat off the desk and examined the sweatband and the ribbon. The ribbon bow had been picked loose with a knife point, leaving hanging threads. There was nothing hidden inside the bow. No evidence of any previous ripping and restitching.

This was the take. If the killers knew what they were look-ing for, it was something that could be hidden in a book, a telephone box, a tube of toothpaste, or a hatband. I went back into the bathroom and looked at my head again. It was still oozing a tiny trickle of blood. I gave it more cold water and dried the cut with toilet paper and flushed that down the bowl. I went back and stood a moment looking down on Dr. Hambleton, wondering what his mistake had been. He had seemed a fairly wise bird. The sunlight had moved over to the far edge of the room now, off the bed and down into a sad dusty corner.

I grinned suddenly, bent over and quickly and with the grin still on my face, out of place as it was, pulled off Dr. Hambleton's toupee and turned it inside out. As simple as all that. To the lining of the toupee a piece of orange-colored paper was fastened by Scotch tape, protected by a square of cellophane. I pulled it loose, turned it over, and saw that it was a numbered claim check belonging to the Bay City Camera Shop. I put it in my wallet and put the toupee carefully back on the dead egg-bald head.

I left the room unlocked because I had no way to lock it.

Down the hall the radio still blared through the transom and the exaggerated alcoholic laughter accompanied it from across the corridor.

10

OVER THE TELEPHONE the Bay City Camera Shop man said: "Yes, Mr. Hicks. We have them for you. Six enlarged prints on glossy from your negative."

"What time do you close?" I asked.

"Oh in about five minutes. We open at nine in the morning."

"I'll pick them up in the morning. Thanks."

I hung up, reached mechanically into the slot and found somebody else's nickel. I walked over to the lunch counter and bought myself a cup of coffee with it, and sat there sipping and listening to the auto horns complaining on the street outside. It was time to go home. Whistles blew. Motors raced. Old brake linings squeaked. There was a dull steady mutter of feet on the sidewalk outside. It was just after five-thirty. I finished the coffee, stuffed a pipe, and strolled a half-block back to the Van Nuys Hotel. In the writing room I folded the orange camera-shop check into a sheet of hotel stationery and addressed an envelope to myself. I put a special-delivery stamp on it and dropped it in the mail chute by the elevator bank. Then I went along to Flack's office again.

Again I closed his door and sat down across from him. Flack didn't seem to have moved an inch. He was chewing morosely on the same cigar butt and his eyes were still full of nothing. I relit my pipe by striking a match on the side of his desk. He frowned.

"Dr. Hambleton doesn't answer his door," I said.

"Huh?" Flack looked at me vacantly.

"Party in 332. Remember? He doesn't answer his door."

"What should I do – bust my girdle?" Flack asked.

"I knocked several times," I said. "No answer. Thought he might be taking a bath or something, although I couldn't hear anything. Went away for a while, then tried again. Same no answer again."

Flack looked at a turnip watch he got from his vest. "I'm off at seven," he said. "Jesus. A whole hour to go, and more. Boy, am I hungry."

"Working the way you do," I said, "you must be. You have to keep your strength up. Do I interest you at all in Room 332?"

"You said he wasn't in," Flack said irritably. "So what? He wasn't in."

"I didn't say he wasn't in. I said he didn't answer his door."

Flack leaned forward. Very slowly he removed the débris of the cigar from his mouth and put it in the glass tray. "Go on. Make me like it," he said, carefully.

"Maybe you'd like to run up and look," I said. "Maybe you didn't see a first-class ice-pick job lately."

Flack put his hands on the arms of his chair and squeezed the wood hard. "Aw," he said painfully, "aw." He got to his feet and opened the desk drawer. He took out a large black gun, flicked the gate open, studied the cartridges, squinted down the barrel, snapped the cylinder back into place. He unbuttoned his vest and tucked the gun down inside his waistband. In an emergency he could probably have got to it in less than a minute. He put his hat on firmly and jerked a thumb at the door.

We went up to the third floor in silence. We went down the corridor. Nothing had changed. No sound had increased or diminished. Flack hurried along to 332 and knocked from force of habit. Then tried the door. He looked back at me with a twisted mouth.

"You said the door wasn't locked," he complained.

"I didn't exactly say that. It *was* unlocked, though."

"It ain't now," Flack said, and unshipped a key on a long chain. He unlocked the door and glanced up and down the hall. He twisted the knob slowly without sound and eased the door a couple of inches. He listened. No sounds came from within. Flack stepped back, took the black gun out of his waistband. He removed the key from the door, kicked it wide open, and brought the gun up hard and straight, like the wicked foreman of the Lazy Q. "Let's go," he said out of the corner of his mouth.

Over his shoulder I could see that Dr. Hambleton lay exactly as before, but the ice-pick handle didn't show from the entrance. Flack leaned forward and edged cautiously into the room. He reached the bathroom door and put his eye to the crack, then pushed the door open until it bounded against the tub. He went in and came out, stepped down into the room, a tense and wary man who was taking no chances.

He tried the closet door, leveled his gun and jerked it wide open. No suspects in the closet.

"Look under the bed," I said.

Flack bent swiftly and looked under the bed.

"Look under the carpet," I said.

"You kidding me?" Flack asked nastily.

"I just like to watch you work."

He bent over the dead man and studied the ice pick.

"Somebody locked that door," he sneered. "Unless you're lying about its being unlocked."

I said nothing.

"Well I guess it's the cops," he said slowly. "No chance to cover up on this one."

"It's not your fault," I told him. "It happens even in good hotels."

11

THE REDHEADED INTERN filled out a DOA form and clipped his stylus to the outside pocket of his white jacket. He snapped the book shut with a faint grin on his face.

"Punctured spinal cord just below the occipital bulge, I'd say," he said carelessly. "A very vulnerable spot. If you know how to find it. And I suppose you do."

Detective Lieutenant Christy French growled. "Think it's the first time I've seen one?"

"No, I guess not," the intern said. He gave a last quick look at the dead man, turned and walked out of the room. "I'll call the coroner," he said over his shoulder. The door closed behind him.

"What a stiff means to those birds is what a plate of warmed-up cabbage means to me," Christy French said sourly to the closed door. His partner, a cop named Fred Beifus, was down on one knee by the telephone box. He had dusted it for fingerprints and blown off the loose powder. He was looking at the smudge through a small magnifying glass. He shook his head, then picked something off the screw with which the box had been fastened shut.

"Gray cotton undertaker's gloves," he said disgustedly. "Cost about four cents a pair wholesale. Fat lot of good printing this joint. They were looking for something in the telephone box, huh?"

"Evidently something that could be there," French said. "I didn't expect prints. These ice-pick jobs are a specialty. We'll get the experts after a while. This is just a quick-over."

He was stripping the dead man's pockets and laying what had been in them out on the bed beside the quiet and already waxy corpse. Flack was sitting in a chair by the window, looking out morosely. The assistant manager had been up, said nothing with a worried expression, and gone away. I was leaning against the bathroom wall and sorting out my fingers.

Flack said suddenly: "I figure an ice-pick job's a dame's work. You can buy them anywhere. Ten cents. If you want one fast, you can slip it down inside a garter and let it hang there."

Christy French gave him a brief glance which had a kind of wonder in it. Beifus said: "What kind of dames you been running around with, honey? The way stockings cost now-adays a dame would as soon stick a saw down her sock."

"I never thought of that," Flack said.

Beifus said: "Leave us do the thinking sweetheart. It takes equipment."

"No need to get tough," Flack said.

Beifus took his hat off and bowed. "You mustn't deny us our little pleasures, Mr. Flack."

Christy French said: "Besides, a woman would keep on jabbing. She wouldn't even know how much was enough. Lots of the punks don't. Whoever did this one was a per-former. He got the spinal cord the first try. And another thing – you have to have the guy quiet to do it. That means more than one guy, unless he was doped, or the killer was a friend of his."

I said: "I don't see how he could have been doped, if he's the party that called me on the phone."

French and Beifus both looked at me with the same expression of patient boredom. "If," French said, "and since you didn't know the guy – according to you – there's always the faint possibility that you wouldn't know his voice. Or am I being too subtle?"

"I don't know," I said. "I haven't read your fan mail."

French grinned.

"Don't waste it on him," Beifus told French. "Save it for when you talk to the Friday Morning Club. Some of them old ladies in the shiny-nose league go big for the nicer angles of murder."

French rolled himself a cigarette and lit it with a kitchen match he struck on the back of a chair. He sighed.

"They worked the technique out in Brooklyn," he explained. "Sunny Moe Stein's boys specialized in it, but they run it into the ground. It got so you couldn't walk across a vacant lot without finding some of their work. Then they came out here, what was left of them. I wonder why did they do that."

"Maybe we just got more vacant lots," Beifus said.

"Funny thing, though," French said, almost dreamily. "When Weepy Moyer had the chill put on Sunny Moe Stein over on Franklin Avenue last February, the killer used a gun. Moe wouldn't have liked that at all."

"I betcha that was why his face had that disappointed look, after they washed the blood off," Beifus remarked.

"Who's Weepy Moyer?" Flack asked.

"He was next to Moe in the organization," French told him. "This could easily be his work. Not that he'd have done it personal."

"Why not?" Flack asked sourly.

"Don't you guys ever read a paper? Moyer's a gentleman now. He knows the nicest people. Even has another name. And as for the Sunny Moe Stein job, it just happened we had him in jail on a gambling rap. We didn't get anywhere. But we did make him a very sweet alibi. Anyhow he's a gentleman like I said, and gentlemen don't go around sticking ice picks into people. They hire it done."

"Did you ever have anything on Moyer?" I asked.

French looked at me sharply. "Why?"

"I just had an idea. But it's very fragile," I said.

French eyed me slowly. "Just between us girls in the powder room," he said, "we never even proved the guy we had *was* Moyer. But don't broadcast it. Nobody's supposed to know but him and his lawyer and the D.A. and the police beat and the city hall and maybe two or three hundred other people."

He slapped the dead man's empty wallet against his thigh and sat down on the bed. He leaned casually against the corpse's leg, lit a cigarette and pointed with it.

"That's enough time on the vaudeville circuit. Here's what we got, Fred. First off, the customer here was not too bright. He was going by the name of Dr. G. W. Hambleton and had the cards printed with an El Centro address and a phone number. It took just two minutes to find out there ain't any such address or any such phone number. A bright boy doesn't lay open that easy. Next, the guy is definitely not in the chips. He has fourteen smackeroos folding in here and about two bucks loose change. On his key ring he don't have any car key or any safe-deposit key or any house key. All he's got is a suitcase key and seven filed Yale master keys. Filed fairly recently at that. I figure he was planning to sneak the hotel a little. Do you think these keys would work in your dump, Flack?"

Flack went over and stared at the keys. "Two of them are the right size," he said. "I couldn't tell if they'd work by just looking. If I want a master key I have to get it from the office. All I carry is a passkey. I can only use that if the guest is out." He took a key out of his pocket, a key on a long chain, and compared it. He shook his head. "They're no good without more work," he said. "Far too much metal on them."

French flicked ash into the palm of his hand and blew it off as dust. Flack went back to his chair by the window.

"Next point," Christy French announced. "He don't have a driver's license or any identification. None of his outside clothes were bought in El Centro. He had some kind of a grift, but he don't have the looks or personality to bounce checks."

"You didn't really see him at his best," Beifus put in.

"And this hotel is the wrong dump for that anyway," French went on. "It's got a crummy reputation."

"Now wait a minute!" Flack began.

French cut him short with a gesture. "I know every hotel in the metropolitan district, Flack. It's my business to know. For fifty bucks I could organize a double-strip act with French trimmings inside of an hour in any room in this hotel. Don't kid me. You earn your living and I'll earn mine. Just don't kid me. All right. The customer had something he was afraid to keep around. That means he knew somebody was after him and getting close. So he offers Marlowe a hundred bucks to keep it for him. But he doesn't have that much money on him. So what he must have been planning on was getting Marlowe to gamble with him. It couldn't have been hot jewelry then. It had to be something semi-legitimate. That right, Marlowe?"

"You could leave out the semi," I said.

French grinned faintly. "So what he had was something that could be kept flat or rolled up – in a phone box, a hat-band, a Bible, a can of talcum. We don't know whether it was found or not. But we do know there was very little time. Not much more than half an hour."

"If Dr. Hambleton did the phoning," I said. "You opened that can of beans yourself."

"It's kind of pointless any other way. The killers wouldn't be in a hurry to have him found. Why should they ask anybody to come over to his room?" He turned to Flack. "Any chance to check his visitors?"

Flack shook his head gloomily. "You don't even have to pass the desk to get to the elevators."

Beifus said: "Maybe that was one reason he came here. That, and the homey atmosphere."

"All right," French said. "Whoever knocked him off could come and go without any questions asked. All he had to know was his room number. And that's about all we know. Okay, Fred?"

Beifus nodded.

I said: "Not quite all. It's a nice toupee, but it's still a toupee."

French and Beifus both swung around quickly. French reached, carefully removed the dead man's hair, and whistled. "I wondered what that damn intern was grinning at," he said.

"The bastard didn't even mention it. See what I see, Fred?"

"All I see is a guy without no hair," Beifus answered.

"Maybe you never knew him at that. Mileaway Marston. Used to be a runner for Ace Devore."

"Why sure enough," Beifus chuckled. He leaned over and patted the dead bald head gently. "How you been all this time, Mileaway? I didn't see you in so long I forgot. But you know me, pal. Once a softy always a softy."

The man on the bed looked old and hard and shrunken without his toupee. The yellow mask of death was beginning to set his face into rigid lines.

French said calmly: "Well, that takes a load off my mind. This punk ain't going to be no twenty-four-hour-a-day job. The hell with him." He replaced the toupee over one eye and stood up off the bed. That's all for you two," he said to Flack and me.

Flack stood up.

"Thanks for the murder, honey," Beifus told him. "You get any more in your nice hotel, don't forget our service. Even when it ain't good, it's quick."

Flack went down the short hall and yanked the door open. I followed him out. On the way to the elevator we didn't

279

speak. Nor on the way down. I walked with him along to his little office, followed him in and shut the door. He seemed surprised.

He sat down at his desk and reached for his telephone. "I got to make a report to the Assistant Manager," he said. "Something you want?"

I rolled a cigarette around on my fingers, put a match to it and blew smoke softly across the desk. "One hundred and fifty dollars," I said.

Flack's small, intent eyes became round holes in a face washed clean of expression. "Don't get funny in the wrong place," he said.

"After those two comedians upstairs, you could hardly blame me if I did. But I'm not being funny." I beat a tattoo on the edge of the desk and waited.

Tiny beads of sweat showed on Flack's lip above his little mustache. "I got business to attend to," he said, more throatily this time. "Beat it and keep going."

"Such a tough little man," I said. "Dr. Hambleton had $164 currency in his wallet when I searched him. He promised me a hundred as retainer, remember? Now, in the same wallet, he has fourteen dollars. And I *did* leave the door of his room unlocked. And somebody else locked it. You locked it, Flack."

Flack took hold of the arms of his chair and squeezed. His voice came from the bottom of a well saying: "You can't prove a damn thing."

"Do I have to try?"

He took the gun out of his waistband and laid it on the desk in front of him. He stared down at it. It didn't have any message for him. He looked up at me again. "Fifty-fifty, huh?" he said brokenly.

There was a moment of silence between us. He got his old shabby wallet out and rooted in it. He came up with a handful of currency and spread bills out on the desk, sorted them into two piles and pushed one pile my way.

I said: "I want the whole hundred and fifty."

He hunched down in his chair and stared at a corner of the desk. After a long time, he sighed. He put the two piles together and pushed them over – to my side of the desk.

"It wasn't doing him any good," Flack said. "Take the dough and breeze. I'll remember you, buddy. All you guys make me sick to my stomach. How do I know you didn't take half a grand off him?"

"I'd take it all. So would the killer. Why leave fourteen dollars?"

"So why did I leave fourteen dollars?" Flack asked, in a tired voice, making vague movements along the desk edge with his fingers. I picked up the money, counted it and threw it back at him.

"Because you're in the business and could size him up. You knew he'd at least have room rent, and a few dollars for loose change. The cops would expect the same thing. Here, I don't want the money. I want something else."

He stared at me with his mouth open.

"Put that dough out of sight," I said.

He reached for it and crammed it back in his wallet. "What something else?" His eyes were small and thoughtful. His tongue pushed out his lower lip. "It don't seem to me *you're* in a very hot trading position either."

"You could be a little wrong about that. If I have to go back up there and tell Christy French and Beifus I was up there before and searched the body, I'd get a tongue-lashing all right. But he'd understand that I haven't been holding out just to be smart. He'd know that somewhere in the background I had a client I was trying to protect. I'd get tough talk and bluster. But that's not what *you'd* get." I stopped and watched the faint glisten of moisture forming on his forehead now. He swallowed hard. His eyes were sick.

"Cut out the wise talk and lay your deal on the deck," he said. He grinned suddenly, rather wolfishly. "Got here a little late to protect her, didn't you?" The fat sneer he lived with was coming home again, but slowly, but gladly.

I killed my cigarette and got another one out and went through all the slow futile face-saving motions of lighting it, getting rid of the match, blowing smoke off to one side, inhaling deeply as though that scrubby little office was a hilltop overlooking the bouncing ocean – all the tired clichéd mannerisms of my trade.

"All right," I said. "I'll admit it was a woman. I'll admit she must have been up there while he was dead, if that makes you happy. I guess it was just shock that made her run away."

"Oh sure," Flack said nastily. The fat sneer was all the way home now. "Or maybe she hadn't ice-picked a guy in a month. Kind of lost touch."

"But why would she take his key?" I said, talking to myself. "And why leave it at the desk? Why not just walk away and leave the whole thing? What if she did think she had to lock the door? Why not drop the key in a sand jar and cover it up? Or take it away with her and lose it? Why do anything with that key that would connect her with that room?" I brought my eyes down and gave Flack a thick leaden stare. "Unless of course she was seen to leave the room – with the key in her hand – and followed out of the hotel."

"What for would anybody do that?" Flack asked.

"Because whoever saw her could have got into that room at once. He had a passkey."

Flack's eyes flicked up at me and dropped all in one motion.

"So he must have followed her," I said. "He must have seen her dump the key at the desk and stroll out of the hotel and he must have followed her a little further than that."

Flack said derisively: "What makes you so wonderful?"

I leaned down and pulled the telephone towards me. "I'd better call Christy and get this over with," I said. "The more I think about it the scareder I get. Maybe she did kill him. I can't cover up for a murderer."

I took the receiver off the hook. Flack slammed his moist paw down hard on top of my hand. The phone jumped on the desk. "Lay off." His voice was almost a sob. "I followed her to a car parked down the street. Got the number. Christ sake, pal, give me some kind of a break." He was fumbling wildly in his pockets. "Know what I make on this job? Cigarette and cigar money and hardly a dime more. Wait a minute now. I think –" He looked down and played solitaire with some dirty envelopes, finally selected one and tossed it over to me. "License number," he said wearily, "and if it's any satisfaction to you, I can't even remember what it was."

I looked down at the envelope. There was a scrawled license number on it all right. Ill-written and faint and oblique, the way it would be written hastily on a paper held in a man's hand on the street. 6N 333. California 1947.

"Satisfied?" This was Flack's voice. Or it came out of his mouth. I tore the number off and tossed the envelope back to him.

"4P 327," I said, watching his eyes. Nothing flicked in them. No trace of derision or concealment. "But how do I know this isn't just some license number you had already?"

"You just got to take my word for it."

"Describe the car," I said.

"Caddy convertible, not new, top up. About 1942 model. Sort of dusty blue color."

"Describe the woman."

"Want a lot for your dough, don't you, peeper?"

"Dr. Hambleton's dough."

He winced. "All right. Blonde. White coat with some colored stitching on it. Wide blue straw hat. Dark glasses. Height about five two. Built like a Conover model."

"Would you know her again – without the glasses?" I asked carefully.

He pretended to think. Then shook his head, no.

"What was that license number again, Flackie?" I caught him off guard.

"Which one?" he said.

I leaned across the desk and dropped some cigarette ash on his gun. I did some more staring into his eyes. But I knew he was licked now. He seemed to know too. He reached for his gun, blew off the ash and put it back in the drawer of his desk.

"Go on. Beat it," he said between his teeth. "Tell the cops I frisked the stiff. So what? Maybe I lose a job. Maybe I get tossed in the fishbowl. So what? When I come out I'm solid. Little Flackie don't have to worry about coffee and crullers. Don't think for a minute those dark cheaters fool little Flackie. I've seen too many movies to miss that lovely puss. And if you ask me that babe'll be around for a long time. She's a comer – and who knows –" he leered at me triumphantly – "she'd need a bodyguard one of these days. A guy to have around, watch things, keep her out of jams. Somebody that knows the ropes and ain't unreasonable about dough. . . . What's the matter?"

I had put my head on one side and was leaning forward. I was listening. "I thought I heard a church bell," I said.

"There ain't any church around here," he said contemptuously. "It's that platinum brain of yours getting cracks in it."

"Just one bell," I said. "Very slow. Tolling is the word, I believe."

Flack listened with me. "I don't hear anything," he said sharply.

"Oh you wouldn't hear it," I said. "You'd be the one guy in the whole world who wouldn't hear it."

He just sat there and stared at me with his nasty little eyes half closed and his nasty little mustache shining. One of his hands twitched on the desk, an aimless movement.

I left him to his thoughts, which were probably as small, ugly and frightened as the man himself.

12

THE APARTMENT HOUSE was over on Doheny Drive, just down the hill from the Strip. It was really two buildings, one behind the other, loosely connected by a floored patio with a fountain, and a room built over the arch. There were mailboxes and bells in the imitation marble foyer. Three out of the sixteen had no names over them. The names that I read meant nothing to me. The job needed a little more work. I tried the front door, found it unlocked, and the job still needed more work.

Outside stood two Cadillacs, a Lincoln Continental and a Packard Clipper. Neither of the Cadillacs had the right color or license. Across the way a guy in riding breeches was sprawled with his legs over the door of a low-cut Lancia. He was smoking and looking up at the pale stars which know enough to keep their distance from Hollywood. I walked up the steep hill to the boulevard and a block east and smothered myself in an outdoor sweat-box phone booth. I dialed a man named Peoria Smith, who was so-called because he stuttered – another little mystery I hadn't had time to work out.

"Mavis Weld," I said. "Phone number. This is Marlowe."

"S-s-s-ure," he said. "M-M-Mavis Weld huh? You want h-h-her ph-ph-phone number?"

"How much?"

"Be-b-b-be ten b-b-b-bucks," he said.

"Just forget I called," I said.

"W-W-Wait a minute! I ain't supposed to give out with them b-b-babes' phone numbers. An assistant prop man is taking a hell of a chance."

I waited and breathed back my own breath.

"The address goes with it naturally," Peoria whined, forgetting to stutter.

"Five bucks," I said. "I've got the address already. And don't haggle. If you think you're the only studio grifter in the business of selling unlisted telephone numbers —"

"Hold it," he said wearily, and went to get his little red book. A left-handed stutterer. He only stuttered when he wasn't excited. He came back and gave it to me. A Crestview number of course. If you don't have a Crestview number in Hollywood you're a bum.

I opened up the steel-and-glass cell to let in some air while I dialed again. After two rings a drawling sexy voice answered. I pulled the door shut.

"Ye-e-e-s," the voice cooed.

"Miss Weld, please."

"And who is calling Miss Weld if you please?"

"I have some stills Whitey wants me to deliver tonight."

"Whitey? And who is Whitey, amigo?"

"The head still-photographer at the studio," I said. "Don't you know that much? I'll come up if you'll tell me which apartment. I'm only a couple of blocks away."

"Miss Weld is taking a bath." She laughed. I guess it was a silvery tinkle where she was. It sounded like somebody putting away saucepans where I was. "But of course bring up the photographs. I am sure she is dying to see them. The apartment number is fourteen."

"Will you be there too?"

"But of course. But naturally. Why do you ask that?"

I hung up and staggered out into the fresh air. I went down the hill. The guy in the riding breeches was still hanging out of the Lancia but one of the Cadillacs was gone and two Buick convertibles had joined the cars in front. I pushed the bell to number fourteen, went on through the patio where scarlet Chinese honeysuckle was lit by a peanut spotlight. Another light glowed down on the big ornamental pool full of fat goldfish and silent lily pads, the lilies folded tight for the night. There were a couple of stone seats and a lawn swing.

The place didn't look very expensive except that every place was expensive that year. The apartment was on the second floor, one of two doors facing across a wide landing.

The bell chimed and a tall dark girl in jodhpurs opened the door. Sexy was very faint praise for her. The jodhpurs, like her hair, were coal black. She wore a white silk shirt with a scarlet scarf loose around her throat. It was not as vivid as her mouth. She held a long brown cigarette in a pair of tiny golden tweezers. The fingers holding it were more than adequately jeweled. Her black hair was parted in the middle and a line of scalp as white as snow went over the top of her head and dropped out of sight behind. Two thick braids of her shining black hair lay one on each side of her slim brown neck. Each was tied with a small scarlet bow. But it was a long time since she was a little girl.

She looked sharply down at my empty hands. Studio stills are usually a little too big to put in your pocket.

I said: "Miss Weld please."

"You can give me the stills." The voice was cool, drawling and insolent, but the eyes were something else. She looked almost as hard to get as a haircut.

"For Miss Weld personally. Sorry."

"I told you she was taking a bath."

"I'll wait."

"Are you quite sure you have the stills, amigo?"

"As sure as I'll ever be. Why?"

"Your name?" Her voice froze on the second word, like a feather taking off in a sudden draft. Then it cooed and hovered and soared and eddied and the silent invitation of a smile picked delicately at the corners of her lips, very slowly, like a child trying to pick up a snowflake.

"Your last picture was wonderful, Miss Gonzales."

The smile flashed like lightning and changed her whole face. The body came erect and vibrant with delight. "But it was stinking," she glowed. "Positively God-damned stinking, you sweet lovely man. You know but positively God-damn well it was stinking."

"Nothing with you in it stinks for me, Miss Gonzales."

She stood away from the door and waved me in. "We will have a drink," she said. "The God-damnest drink we will have. I adore flattery, however dishonest."

I went in. A gun in the kidney wouldn't have surprised me a bit. She stood so that I had to practically push her mammaries out of the way to get through the door. She smelled the way the Taj Mahal looks by moonlight. She closed the door and danced over to a small portable bar.

"Scotch? Or would you prefer a mixed drink? I mix a perfectly loathsome Martini," she said.

"Scotch is fine, thanks."

She made a couple of drinks in a couple of glasses you could almost have stood umbrellas in. I sat down in a chintz chair and looked around. The place was old-fashioned. It had a false fireplace with gas logs and a marble mantel, cracks in the plaster, a couple of vigorously colored daubs on the walls that looked lousy enough to have cost money, an old black chipped Steinway and for once no Spanish shawl on it. There were a lot of new-looking books in bright jackets scattered around and a double-barreled shotgun with a handsomely carved stock stood in the corner with a white satin bow tied around the barrels. Hollywood wit.

The dark lady in the jodhpurs handed me a glass and perched on the arm of my chair. "You may call me Dolores if you wish," she said, taking a hearty swig out of her own tumbler.

"Thanks."

"And what may I call you?"

I grinned.

"Of course," she said, "I am most fully aware that you are a God-damn liar and that you have no stills in your pockets. Not that I wish to inquire into your no doubt very private business."

"Yeah?" I inhaled a couple of inches of my liquor. "Just what kind of bath is Miss Weld taking? An old-fashioned soap or something with Arabian spices in it?"

She waved the remains of the brown cigarette in the small gold clasp. "Perhaps you would like to help her. The bathroom is over there – through the arch and to the right. Most probably the door is not locked."

"Not if it's that easy," I said.

"Oh," she gave me the brilliant smile again. "You like to do the difficult things in life. I must remember to be less approachable, must I not?" She removed herself elegantly from the arm of my chair and ditched her cigarette, bending over enough so that I could trace the outline of her hips.

"Don't bother, Miss Gonzales. I'm just a guy who came here on business. I don't have any idea of raping anybody."

"No?" The smile became soft, lazy and, if you can't think of a better word, provocative.

"But I'm sure as hell working up to it," I said.

"You are an amusing son-of-a-bitch," she said with a shrug and went off through the arch, carrying her half-quart of Scotch and water with her. I heard a gentle tapping on a door and her voice: "Darling, there's a man here who says he has some stills from the studio. He says. Muy simpático. Muy guapo también. Con cojones."

A voice I had heard before said sharply: "Shut up, you little bitch. I'll be out in a second."

The Gonzales came back through the archway humming. Her glass was empty. She went to the bar again. "But you are not drinking," she cried, looking at my glass.

"I ate dinner. I only have a two-quart stomach anyway. I understand a little Spanish."

She tossed her head. "You are shocked?" Her eyes rolled. Her shoulders did a fan dance.

"I'm pretty hard to shock."

"But you heard what I said? Madre de Dios. I'm so terribly sorry."

"I'll bet," I said.

She finished making herself another highball.

"Yes. I am so sorry," she sighed. "That is, I think I am. Sometimes I am not sure. Sometimes I do not give a good goddamn. It is so confusing. All my friends tell me I am far too outspoken. I do shock you, don't I?" She was on the arm of my chair again.

"No. But if I wanted to be shocked I'd know right where to come." She reached her glass behind her indolently and leaned towards me.

"But I do not live here," she said. "I live at the Chateau Bercy."

"Alone?"

She slapped me delicately across the tip of my nose. The next thing I knew I had her in my lap and she was trying to bite a piece off my tongue. "You are a very sweet son-of-a-bitch," she said. Her mouth was as hot as ever a mouth was. Her lips burned like dry ice. Her tongue was driving hard against my teeth. Her eyes looked enormous and black and the whites showed under them.

"I am so tired," she whispered into my mouth. "I am so worn, so incredibly tired."

I felt her hand in my breast pocket. I shoved her off hard, but she had my wallet. She danced away with it laughing, flicked it open and went through it with fingers that darted like little snakes.

"So glad you two got acquainted," a voice off to one side said coolly. Mavis Weld stood in the archway.

Her hair was fluffed out carelessly and she hadn't bothered with make-up. She wore a hostess gown and very little else. Her legs ended in little green and silver slippers. Her eyes were empty, her lips contemptuous. But she was the same girl all right, dark glasses on or off.

The Gonzales gave her a quick darting glance, closed my wallet and tossed it. I caught it and put it away. She strolled to a table and picked up a black bag with a long strap, hooked it over her shoulder and moved towards the door.

Mavis Weld didn't move, didn't look at her. She looked at me. But there was no emotion of any kind in her face. The Gonzales opened the door and glanced outside and almost closed it and turned.

"The name is Philip Marlowe," she said to Mavis Weld. "Nice don't you think?"

"I didn't know you bothered to ask them their names," Mavis Weld said. "You so seldom know them long enough."

"I see," the Gonzales answered gently. She turned and smiled at me faintly. "Such a charming way to call a girl a whore, don't you think?"

Mavis Weld said nothing. Her face had no expression.

"At least," the Gonzales said smoothly as she pulled the door open again, "I haven't been sleeping with any gunmen lately."

"Are you sure you can remember?" Mavis Weld asked her in exactly the same tone. "Open the door, honey. This is the day we put the garbage out."

The Gonzales looked back at her slowly, levelly, and with a knife in her eyes. Then she made a faint sound with her lips and teeth and yanked the door wide. It closed behind her with a jarring smash. The noise didn't even flicker the steady dark-blue glare in Mavis Weld's eyes.

"Now suppose you do the same – but more quietly," she said.

I got out a handkerchief and scrubbed the lipstick over my face. It looked exactly the color of blood, fresh blood. "That could happen to anybody," I said. "I wasn't petting her. She was petting me."

She marched to the door and heaved it open. "On your way, dreamboat. Make with the feet."

"I came here on business, Miss Weld."

"Yes. I can imagine. Out. I don't know you. I don't want to know you. And if I did, this wouldn't be either the day or the hour."

"Never the time and place and the loved one all together," I said.

"What's that?" She tried to throw me out with the point of her chin, but even she wasn't that good.

"Browning. The poet, not the automatic. I feel sure you'd prefer the automatic."

"Look little man, do I have to call the manager to bounce you downstairs like a basketball?"

I went over and pushed the door shut. She held on to the last moment. She didn't quite kick me, but it cost her an effort not to. I tried to ease her away from the door without appearing to. She didn't ease worth a darn. She stood her ground, one hand still reaching for the doorknob, her eyes full of dark-blue rage.

If you're going to stand that close to me," I said, "maybe you'd better put some clothes on."

She took her hand back and swung it hard. The slap sounded like Miss Gonzales slamming the door, but it stung. And it reminded me of the sore place on the back of my head.

"Did I hurt you?" she said softly.

I nodded.

"That's fine." She hauled off and slapped me again, harder if anything. "I think you'd better kiss me," she breathed. Her eyes were clear and limpid and melting. I glanced down casually. Her right hand was balled into a very businesslike fist. It wasn't too small to work with, either.

"Believe me," I said. "There's only one reason I don't. Even if you had your little black gun with you. Or the brass knuckles you probably keep on your night table."

She smiled politely.

"I might just happen to be working for you," I said. "And I don't go whoring around after every pair of legs I see."

I looked down at hers. I could see them all right and the flag that marked the goal line was no larger than it had to be. She pulled the hostess gown together and turned and walked over to the little bar shaking her head.

"I'm free, white and twenty-one," she said. "I've seen all the approaches there are. I think I have. If I can't scare you, lick you, or seduce you, what the hell can I buy you with?"

"Well —"

"Don't tell me," she interrupted sharply and turned with a glass in her hand. She drank and tossed the loose hair around and smiled a thin little smile. "Money, of course. How damned stupid of me to overlook that."

"Money would help," I said.

Her mouth twisted in wry disgust but the voice was almost affectionate. "How much money?"

"Oh a hundred bucks would do to start with."

"You're cheap. It's a cheap little bastard, isn't it? A hundred bucks it says. Is a hundred bucks money in your circle, darling?"

"Make it two hundred then. I could retire on that."

"Still cheap. Every week of course. In a nice clean envelope?"

"You could skip the envelope. I'd only get it dirty."

"And just what would I get for this money, my charming little gum-shoe? I'm quite sure of what you are, of course."

"You'd get a receipt. Who told you I was a gum-shoe?"

She stared out of her own eyes for a brief instant before the act dropped over her again. "It must have been the smell." She sipped her drink and stared at me over it with a faint smile of contempt.

"I'm beginning to think you write your own dialogue," I said. "I've been wondering just what was the matter with it."

I ducked. A few drops splattered me. The glass splintered on the wall behind me. The broken pieces fell soundlessly.

293

"And with that," she said, completely calm, "I believe I must have used up my entire stock of girlish charm."

I went over and picked up my hat. "I never thought *you* killed him," I said. "But it would help to have some sort of reason for not telling you were there. It's a help to have enough money for a retainer just to establish myself. And enough information to justify my accepting the retainer."

She picked a cigarette out of a box, tossed it in the air, caught it between her lips effortlessly and lit it with a match that came from nowhere.

"My goodness. Am I supposed to have killed somebody?" she asked. I was still holding the hat. It made me feel foolish. I don't know why. I put it on and started for the door.

"I trust you have carfare home," the contemptuous voice said behind me.

I didn't answer. I just kept going. When I had the door ready to open she said: "I also trust Miss Gonzales gave you her address and phone number. You should be able to get almost anything out of her — including, I am told, money."

I let go of the doorknob and went back across the room fast. She stood her ground and the smile on her lips didn't slip a millimeter.

"Look," I said. "You're going to find this hard to believe. But I came over here with the quaint idea that you might be a girl who needed some help — and would find it rather hard to get anyone you could bank on. I figured you went to that hotel room to make some kind of a payoff. And the fact that you went by yourself and took chances on being recognized — and *were* recognized by a house dick whose standard of ethics would take about as much strain as a very tired old cobweb — all this made me think you might be in one of those Hollywood jams that really mean curtains. But you're not in any jam. You're right up front under the baby spot pulling every tired ham gesture you ever used in the most tired B-picture you ever acted in — if acting is the word —"

"Shut up," she said, between teeth so tight they grated. "Shut up, you slimy, blackmailing keyhole peeper."

"You don't need me," I said. "You don't need anybody. You're so God-damn smart you could talk your way out of a safe-deposit box. Okay. Go ahead and talk your way out. I won't stop you. Just don't make me listen to it. I'd burst out crying to think a mere slip of an innocent little girl like you should be so clever. You do things to me, honey. Just like Margaret O'Brien."

She didn't move or breathe when I reached the door, nor when I opened it. I don't know why. The stuff wasn't *that* good.

I went down the stairs and across the court and out of the front door, almost bumping into a slim dark-eyed man who was standing there lighting a cigarette.

"Excuse me," he said quietly, "I'm afraid I'm in your way."

I started to go around him, then I noticed that his lifted right hand held a key. I reached out and snapped it out of his hand for no reason at all. I looked at the number stamped on it. No. 14. Mavis Weld's apartment. I threw it off behind some bushes.

"You don't need that," I said. "The door isn't locked."

"Of course," he said. There was a peculiar smile on his face. "How stupid of me."

"Yeah," I said. "We're both stupid. Anybody's stupid that bothers with that tramp."

"I wouldn't quite say that," he answered quietly, his small sad eyes watching me without any particular expression.

"You don't have to," I said. "I just said it for you. I beg your pardon. I'll get your key." I went over behind the bushes, picked it up and handed it to him.

"Thank you very much," he said. "And by the way —" He stopped. I stopped. "I hope I don't interrupt an interesting quarrel," he said. "I should hate to do that. No?" He smiled. "Well, since Miss Weld is a friend in common, may I introduce myself. My name is Steelgrave. Haven't I seen you somewhere?"

"No you haven't seen me anywhere, Mr. Steelgrave," I said. "My name's Marlowe, Philip Marlowe. It's extremely unlikely that we've met. And, strange to relate, I never heard of you, Mr. Steelgrave. And I wouldn't give a damn, even if your name was Weepy Moyer." I never knew quite why I said that. There was nothing to make me say it, except that the name had been mentioned. A peculiar stillness came over his face. A peculiar fixed look in his silent black eyes. He took the cigarette out of his mouth, looked at the tip, flicked a little ash off it, although there was no ash to flick off, looking down as he said: "Weepy Moyer? Peculiar name. I don't think I ever heard that. Is he somebody I should know?"

"Not unless you're unusually fond of ice picks," I said, and left him. I went on down the steps, crossed to my car, looked back before I got in. He was standing there looking down at me, the cigarette between his lips. From that distance I couldn't see whether there was any expression on his face. He didn't move or make any kind of gesture when I looked back at him. He didn't even turn away. He just stood there. I got in and drove off.

13

I DROVE EAST on Sunset but I didn't go home. At La Brea I turned north and swung over to Highland, out over Cahuenga Pass and down on to Ventura Boulevard, past Studio City and Sherman Oaks and Encino. There was nothing lonely about the trip. There never is on that road. Fast boys in stripped-down Fords shot in and out of the traffic streams, missing fenders by a sixteenth of an inch, but somehow always missing them. Tired men in dusty coupes and sedans winced and tightened their grip on the wheel and plowed on north and west towards home and dinner, an evening with the sports page, the blatting of the radio, the whining of their spoiled children and the gabble of their silly wives. I drove on past the gaudy neons and the false fronts behind them, the sleazy hamburger joints that look like palaces under the colors, the circular drive-ins as gay as circuses with the chipper hard-eyed carhops, the brilliant counters, and the sweaty greasy kitchens that would have poisoned a toad. Great double trucks rumbled down over Sepulveda from Wilmington and San Pedro and crossed towards the Ridge Route, starting up in low-low from the traffic lights with a growl of lions in the zoo.

Behind Encino an occasional light winked from the hills through thick trees. The homes of screen stars. Screen stars, phooey. The veterans of a thousand beds. Hold it, Marlowe, you're not human tonight.

The air got cooler. The highway narrowed. The cars were so few now that the headlights hurt. The grade rose against chalk walls and at the top a breeze, unbroken from the ocean, danced casually across the night.

I ate dinner at a place near Thousand Oaks. Bad but quick. Feed 'em and throw 'em out. Lots of business. We can't bother with you sitting over your second cup of coffee, mister. You're using money space. See those people over there behind the rope? They want to eat. Anyway they think they have to. God knows why they want to eat here. They could do better home out of a can. They're just restless. Like you. They have to get the car out and go somewhere. Sucker-bait for the racketeers that have taken over the restaurants. Here we go again. You're not human tonight, Marlowe.

I paid off and stopped in a bar to drop a brandy on top of the New York cut. Why New York, I thought. It was Detroit where they made machine tools. I stepped out into the night air that nobody had yet found out how to option. But a lot of people were probably trying. They'd get around to it.

I drove on to the Oxnard cut-off and turned back along the ocean. The big eight-wheelers and sixteen-wheelers were streaming north, all hung over with orange lights. On the right the great fat solid Pacific trudging into shore like a scrubwoman going home. No moon, no fuss, hardly a sound of the surf. No smell. None of the harsh wild smell of the sea. A California ocean. California, the department-store state. The most of everything and the best of nothing. Here we go again. You're not human tonight, Marlowe.

All right. Why would I be? I'm sitting in that office, playing with a dead fly and in pops this dowdy little item from Manhattan, Kansas, and chisels me down to a shopworn twenty to find her brother. He sounds like a creep but she wants to find him. So with this fortune clasped to my chest, I trundle down to Bay City and the routine I go through is so tired I'm half asleep on my feet. I meet nice people, with and without ice picks in their necks. I leave, and I leave myself wide-open too. Then she comes in and takes the twenty away from me and gives me a kiss and gives it back to me because I didn't do a full day's work.

So I go see Dr. Hambleton, retired (and how) optometrist from El Centro, and meet again the new style in neckwear. And I don't tell the cops. I just frisk the customer's toupee and put on an act. Why? Who am I cutting my throat for this time? A blonde with sexy eyes and too many door keys? A girl from Manhattan, Kansas? I don't know. All I know is that something isn't what it seems and the old tired but always reliable hunch tells me that if the hand is played the way it is dealt the wrong person is going to lose the pot. Is that my business? Well, what is my business? Do I know? Did I ever know? Let's not go into that. You're not human tonight, Marlowe. Maybe I never was or ever will be. Maybe I'm an ectoplasm with a private license. Maybe we all get like this in the cold half-lit world where always the wrong thing happens and never the right.

Malibu. More movie stars. More pink and blue bathtubs. More tufted beds. More Chanel No. 5. More Lincoln Continentals and Cadillacs. More wind-blown hair and sunglasses and attitudes and pseudo-refined voices and waterfront morals. Now, wait a minute. Lots of nice people work in pictures. You've got the wrong attitude, Marlowe. You're not human tonight.

I smelled Los Angeles before I got to it. It smelled stale and old like a living room that had been closed too long. But the colored lights fooled you. The lights were wonderful. There ought to be a monument to the man who invented neon lights. Fifteen stories high, solid marble. There's a boy who really made something out of nothing.

So I went to a picture show and it had to have Mavis Weld in it. One of those glass-and-chromium deals where everybody smiled too much and talked too much and knew it. The women were always going up a long curving staircase to change their clothes. The men were always taking monogrammed cigarettes out of expensive cases and snapping expensive lighters at each other. And the help was round-shouldered from carrying trays with drinks across the terrace to a swimming pool about the size of Lake Huron but a lot neater.

The leading man was an amiable ham with a lot of charm, some of it turning a little yellow at the edges. The star was a bad-tempered brunette with contemptuous eyes and a couple of bad close-ups that showed her pushing forty-five backwards almost hard enough to break a wrist. Mavis Weld played second lead and she played it with wraps on. She was good, but she could have been ten times better. But if she had been ten times better half her scenes would have been yanked out to protect the star. It was as neat a bit of tightrope walking as I ever saw. Well it wouldn't be a tightrope she'd be walking from now on. It would be a piano wire. It would be very high. And there wouldn't be any net under it.

14

I HAD A reason for going back to the office. A special-delivery letter with an orange claim check ought to have arrived there by now. Most of the windows were dark in the building, but not all. People work nights in other businesses than mine. The elevator man said "Howdy" from the depths of his throat and trundled me up. The corridor had lighted open doors where the scrubwomen were still cleaning up the débris of the wasted hours. I turned a corner past the slobbery hum of a vacuum cleaner, let myself into my dark office and opened the windows. I sat there at the desk doing nothing, not even thinking. No special-delivery letter. All the noise of the building, except the vacuum cleaner, seemed to have flowed out into the street and lost itself among the turning wheels of innumerable cars. Then somewhere along the hall outside a man started whistling "Lili Marlene" with elegance and virtuosity. I knew who that was. The night man checking office doors. I switched the desk lamp on and he passed without trying mine. His steps went away, then came back with a different sound, more of a shuffle. The buzzer sounded in the other office which was still unlocked. That would be special delivery. I went out to get it, only it wasn't.

A fat man in sky-blue pants was closing the door with that beautiful leisure only fat men ever achieve. He wasn't alone, but I looked at him first. He was a large man and wide. Not young nor handsome, but he looked durable. Above the sky-blue gabardine slacks he wore a two-tone leisure jacket which would have been revolting on a zebra. The neck of his canary-yellow shirt was open wide, which it had to be if his neck was going to get out. He was hatless and his large head was deco-rated with a reasonable amount of pale salmon-colored hair. His nose had been broken but well set and it hadn't been a collector's item in the first place.

The creature with him was a weedy number with red eyes and sniffles. Age about twenty, five feet nine, thin as a broom straw. His nose twitched and his mouth twitched and his hands twitched and he looked very unhappy.

The big man smiled genially. "Mr. Marlowe, no doubt?"

I said: "Who else?"

"It's a little late for a business call," the big man said and hid half the office by spreading out his hands. "I hope you don't mind. Or do you already have all the business you can handle?"

"Don't kid me. My nerves are frayed," I said. "Who's the junky?"

"Come along, Alfred," the big man said to his companion. "And stop acting girlish."

"In a pig's valise," Alfred told him.

The big man turned to me placidly. "Why do all these punks keep saying that? It isn't funny. It isn't witty. It doesn't mean anything. Quite a problem, this Alfred. I got him off the stuff, you know, temporarily at least. Say 'how do you do' to Mr. Marlowe, Alfred."

"Screw him," Alfred said.

The big man sighed. "My name's Toad," he said. "Joseph P. Toad."

I didn't say anything.

"Go ahead and laugh," the big man said. "I'm used to it. Had the name all my life." He came towards me with his hand out. I took it. The big man smiled pleasantly into my eyes. "Okay Alfred," he said without looking back.

Alfred made what seemed to be a very slight and unimportant movement at the end of which a heavy automatic was pointing at me.

"Careful, Alfred," the big man said, holding my hand with a grip that would have bent a girder. "Not yet."

"In a pig's valise," Alfred said. The gun pointed at my chest. His finger tightened around the trigger. I watched it tighten. I knew at precisely what moment that tightening would release the hammer. It didn't seem to make any difference. This was happening somewhere else in a cheesy program picture. It wasn't happening to me.

301

The hammer of the automatic clicked dryly on nothing. Alfred lowered the gun with a grunt of annoyance and it disappeared whence it had come. He started to twitch again. There was nothing nervous about his movements with the gun. I wondered just what junk he was off of.

The big man let go of my hand, the genial smile still over his large healthy face.

He patted a pocket. "I got the magazine," he said. "Alfred ain't reliable lately. The little bastard might have shot you."

Alfred sat down in a chair and tilted it against the wall and breathed through his mouth.

I let my heels down on the floor again.

"I bet he scared you," Joseph P. Toad said.

I tasted salt on my tongue.

"You ain't so tough," Toad said, poking me in the stomach with a fat finger.

I stepped away from the finger and watched his eyes.

"What does it cost?" he asked almost gently.

"Let's go into my parlor," I said.

I turned my back on him and walked through the door into the other office. It was hard work but I made it. I sweated all the way. I went around behind the desk and stood there waiting. Mr. Toad followed me in placidly. The junky came twitching in behind him.

"You don't have a comic book around, do you?" Toad asked. "Keeps him quiet."

"Sit down," I said. "I'll look."

He reached for the chair arms. I jerked a drawer open and got my hand around the butt of a Luger. I brought it up slowly, looking at Alfred. Alfred didn't even look at me. He was studying the corner of the ceiling and trying to keep his mouth out of his eye.

"This is as comic as I get," I said.

"You won't need that," the big man said, genially.

"That's fine," I said, like somebody else talking, far away behind a wall. I could just barely hear the words. "But if

I do, here it is. And this one's loaded. Want me to prove it to you?"

The big man looked as near worried as he would ever look. "I'm sorry you take it like that," he said. "I'm so used to Alfred I hardly notice him. Maybe you're right. Maybe I ought to do something about him."

"Yeah," I said. "Do it this afternoon before you come up here. It's too late now."

"Now wait a minute, Mr. Marlowe." He put his hand out. I slashed at it with the Luger. He was fast, but not fast enough. I cut the back of his hand open with the sight on the gun. He grabbed at it and sucked at the cut. "Hey, please! Alfred's my nephew. My sister's kid. I kind of look after him. He wouldn't hurt a fly, really."

"Next time you come up I'll have one for him not to hurt," I said.

"Now don't be like that, mister. Please don't be like that. I've got quite a nice little proposition —"

"Shut up," I said. I sat down very slowly. My face burned. I had difficulty speaking clearly at all. I felt a little drunk. I said, slowly and thickly: "A friend of mine told me about a fellow that had something like this pulled on him. He was at a desk the way I am. He had a gun, just the way I have. There were two men on the other side of the desk, like you and Alfred. The man on my side began to get mad. He couldn't help himself. He began to shake. He couldn't speak a word. He just had this gun in his hand. So without a word he shot twice under the desk, right where your belly is."

The big man turned a sallow green color and started to get up. But he changed his mind. He got a violent-looking hand-kerchief out of his pocket and mopped his face. "You seen that in a picture," he said.

"That's right," I said. "But the man who made the picture told me where he got the idea. *That* wasn't in any picture." I put the Luger down on the desk in front of me and said in a more natural voice: "You've got to be careful about firearms, Mr. Toad. You never know but what it may upset a man to have an Army .45 snapped in his face — especially when he doesn't know it's not loaded. It made me kind of nervous for a minute. I haven't had a shot of morphine since lunch time."

Toad studied me carefully with narrow eyes. The junky got up and went to another chair and kicked it around and sat down and tilted his greasy head against the wall. But his nose and hands kept on twitching.

"I heard you were kind of hard-boiled," Toad said slowly, his eyes cool and watchful.

"You heard wrong. I'm a very sensitive guy. I go all to pieces over nothing."

"Yeah. I understand." He stared at me a long time without speaking. "Maybe we played this wrong. Mind if I put my hand in my pocket? I don't wear a gun."

"Go ahead," I said. "It would give me the greatest possible pleasure to see you try to pull a gun."

He frowned, then very slowly got out a flat pigskin wallet and drew out a crisp new one-hundred-dollar bill. He laid it on the edge of the glass top, drew out another just like it, then one by one three more. He laid them carefully in a row along the desk, end to end. Alfred let his chair settle to the floor and stared at the money with his mouth quivering.

"Five C's," the big man said. He folded his wallet and put it away. I watched every movement he made. "For nothing at all but keeping the nose clean. Check?"

I just looked at him.

"You ain't looking for nobody," the big man said. "You couldn't find nobody. You don't have time to work for nobody. You didn't hear a thing or see a thing. You're clean. Five C's clean. Okay?"

There was no sound in the office but Alfred's sniffling. The big man half turned his head. "Quiet Alfred. I'll give you a

shot when we leave," the big man told him. "Try to act nice."
He sucked again at the cut on the back of his hand.

"With you for a model that ought to be easy," I said.

"Screw you," Alfred said.

"Limited vocabulary," the big man told me. "Very limited.
Get the idea, chum?" He indicated the money. I fingered the
butt of the Luger. He leaned forward a little. "Relax, can't you.
It's simple. This is a retainer. You don't do a thing for it.
Nothing is what you do. If you keep on doing nothing for a
reasonable length of time you get the same amount later on.
That's simple, isn't it?"

"And who am I doing this nothing for?" I asked.

"Me. Joseph P. Toad."

"What's your racket?"

"Business representative, you might call me."

"What else could I call you? Besides what I could think
up myself?"

"You could call me a guy that wants to help out a guy that
don't want to make trouble for a guy."

"And what could I call that lovable character?" I asked.

Joseph P. Toad gathered the five hundred-dollar bills
together, lined up the edges neatly and pushed the packet
across the desk. "You can call him a guy that would rather spill
money than blood," he said. "But he don't mind spilling blood
if it looks like that's what he's got to do."

"How is he with an ice pick?" I asked. "I can see how lousy
he is with a .45."

The big man chewed his lower lip, then pulled it out with
a blunt forefinger and thumb and nibbled on the inside of it
softly, like a milch cow chewing her cud. "We're not talking
about ice picks," he said at length. "All we're talking about is
how you might get off on the wrong foot and do yourself a
lot of harm. Whereas if you don't get off on no foot at all,
you're sitting pretty and money coming in."

"Who is the blonde?" I asked.

He thought about that and nodded. "Maybe you're into this too far already," he sighed. "Maybe it's too late to do business."

After a moment he leaned forward and said gently: "Okay. I'll check back with my principal and see how far out he wants to come. Maybe we can still do business. Everything stands as it is until you hear from me. Check?"

I let him have that one. He put his hands on the desk and very slowly stood up, watching the gun I was pushing around on the blotter.

"You can keep the dough," he said. "Come on, Alfred." He turned and walked solidly out of the office.

Alfred's eyes crawled sideways watching him, then jerked to the money on the desk. The big automatic appeared with the same magic in his thin right hand. Dartingly as an eel he moved over to the desk. He kept the gun on me and reached for the money with his left hand. It disappeared into his pocket. He gave me a smooth cool empty grin, nodded and moved away, apparently not realizing for a moment that I was holding a gun too.

"Come on, Alfred," the big man called sharply from outside the door. Alfred slipped through the door and was gone.

The outer door opened and closed. Steps went along the hall. Then silence. I sat there thinking back over it, trying to make up my mind whether it was pure idiocy or just a new way to toss a scare.

Five minutes later the telephone rang.

A thick pleasant voice said: "Oh by the way, Mr. Marlowe, I guess you know Sherry Ballou, don't you?"

"Nope."

"Sheridan Ballou, Incorporated. The big agent? You ought to look him up sometime."

I held the phone silently for a moment. Then I said: "Is he her agent?"

"He might be," Joseph P. Toad said, and paused a moment. "I suppose you realize we're just a couple of bit players, Mr.

Marlowe. That's all. Just a couple of bit players. Somebody wanted to find out a little something about you. It seemed the simplest way to do it. Now, I'm not so sure."

I didn't answer. He hung up. Almost at once the phone rang again.

A seductive voice said: "You do not like me so well, do you, amigo?"

"Sure I do. Just don't keep biting me."

"I am at home at the Chateau Bercy. I am lonely."

"Call an escort bureau."

"But please. That is no way to talk. This is business of a great importance."

"I bet. But not the business I'm in."

"That slut — What does she say about me?" she hissed.

"Nothing. Oh, she might have called you a Tijuana hooker in riding pants. Would you mind?"

That amused her. The silvery giggle went on for a little while. "Always the wisecrack with you. Is it not so? But you see I did not then know you were a detective. That makes a very big difference."

I could have told her how wrong she was. I just said: "Miss Gonzales, you said something about business. What kind of business, if you're not kidding me?"

"Would you like to make a great deal of money? A very great deal of money?"

"You mean without getting shot?" I asked.

Her incaught breath came over the wire. "Sí," she said thoughtfully. "There is also that to consider. But you are so brave, so big, so —"

"I'll be at my office at nine in the morning, Miss Gonzales. I'll be a lot braver then. Now if you'll excuse me —"

"You have a date? Is she beautiful? More beautiful than I am?"

"For Christ's sake," I said. "Don't you ever think of anything but one thing?"

"The hell with you, darling," she said and hung up in my face.

I turned the lights out and left. Halfway down the hall I met a man looking at numbers. He had a special delivery in his hand. So I had to go back to the office and put it in the safe. And the phone rang again while I was doing this.

I let it ring. I had had enough for one day. I just didn't care. It could have been the Queen of Sheba with her cellophane pajamas on – or off – I was too tired to bother. My brain felt like a bucket of wet sand.

It was still ringing as I reached the door. No use. I had to go back. Instinct was stronger than weariness. I lifted the receiver.

Orfamay Quest's twittery little voice said: "Oh Mr. Marlowe I've been trying to get you for just the longest time. I'm so upset. I'm –"

"In the morning," I said. "The office is closed."

"Please, Mr. Marlowe – just because I lost my temper for a moment –"

"In the morning."

"But I tell you I have to see you." The voice didn't quite rise to a yell. "It's terribly important."

"Unhuh."

She sniffled. "You – you kissed me."

"I've kissed better since," I said. To hell with her. To hell with all women.

"I've heard from Orrin," she said.

That stopped me for a moment, then I laughed. "You're a nice little liar," I said. "Goodbye."

"But really I have. He called me. On the telephone. Right here where I'm staying."

"Fine," I said. "Then you don't need a detective at all. And if you did, you've got a better one than I am right in the family. I couldn't even find out where you were staying."

There was a little pause. She still had me talking to her anyway. She'd kept me from hanging up. I had to give her that much.

"I wrote to him where I'd be staying," she said at last.

"Unhuh. Only he didn't get the letter because he had moved and he didn't leave any forwarding address. Remember? Try again some time when I'm not so tired. Goodnight, Miss Quest. And you don't have to tell me where you are staying now. I'm not working for you."

"Very well, Mr. Marlowe. I'm ready to call the police now. But I don't think you'll like it. I don't think you'll like it at all."

"Why?"

"Because there's murder in it, Mr. Marlowe, and murder is a very nasty word — don't you think?"

"Come on up," I said. "I'll wait."

I hung up. I got the bottle of Old Forester out. There was nothing slow about the way I poured myself a drink and dropped it down my throat.

15

SHE CAME IN briskly enough this time. Her motions were small and quick and determined. There was one of those thin little, bright little smiles on her face. She put her bag down firmly, settled herself in the customer's chair and went on smiling.

"It's nice of you to wait for me," she said. "I bet you haven't had your dinner yet, either."

"Wrong," I said. "I have had my dinner. I am now drinking whiskey. You don't approve of whiskey-drinking do you?"

"I certainly do not."

"That's just dandy," I said. "I hoped you hadn't changed your mind." I put the bottle up on the desk and poured myself another slug. I drank a little of it and gave her a leer above the glass.

"If you keep on with that you won't be in any condition to listen to what I have to say," she snapped.

"About this murder," I said. "Anybody I know? I can see you're not murdered — yet."

"Please don't be unnecessarily horrid. It's not my fault. You doubted me over the telephone so I had to convince you. Orrin did call me up. But he wouldn't tell me where he was or what he was doing. I don't know why."

"He wanted you to find out for yourself," I said. "He's building your character."

"That's not funny. It's not even smart."

"But you've got to admit it's nasty," I said. "Who was murdered? Or is that a secret too?"

She fiddled a little with her bag, not enough to overcome her embarrassment, because she wasn't embarrassed. But enough to needle me into taking another drink.

"That horrid man in the rooming house was murdered. Mr. – Mr. – I forget his name."

"Let's both forget it," I said. "Let's do something together for once." I dropped the whiskey bottle into the desk drawer and stood up. "Look, Orfamay, I'm not asking you how you know all this. Or rather how Orrin knows it all. Or if he *does* know it. You've found him. That's what you wanted me to do. Or he's found you, which comes to the same thing."

"It's not the same thing," she cried. "I haven't really found him. He wouldn't tell me where he was living."

"Well if it is anything like the last place, I don't blame him."

She set her lips in a firm line of distaste. "He wouldn't tell me anything really."

"Just about murders," I said. "Trifles like that."

She laughed bubblingly. "I just said that to scare you. I don't really mean anybody was murdered, Mr. Marlowe. You sounded so cold and distant. I thought you wouldn't help me any more. And – well, I just made it up."

I took a couple of deep breaths and looked down at my hands. I straightened out the fingers slowly. Then I stood up. I didn't say anything.

"Are you mad at me?" she asked timidly, making a little circle on the desk with the point of a finger.

"I ought to slap your face off," I said. "And quit acting innocent. Or it mightn't be your face I'd slap."

Her breath caught with a jerk. "Why, how dare you!"

"You used that line," I said. "You used it too often. Shut up and get the hell out of here. Do you think I enjoy being dared to death? Oh – there's this." I yanked a drawer open, got out her twenty dollars and threw them down in front of her. "Take this money away. Endow a hospital or a research laboratory with it. It makes me nervous having it around."

Her hand reached automatically for the money. Her eyes behind the cheaters were round and wondering. "Goodness," she said, assembling her handbag with a nice dignity. "I'm sure I didn't know you scared that easy. I thought you were tough."

"That's just an act," I growled, moving around the desk. She leaned back in her chair away from me. "I'm only tough with little girls like you that don't let their fingernails grow too long. I'm all mush inside." I took hold of her arm and yanked her to her feet. Her head went back. Her lips parted. I was hell with the women that day.

"But you will find Orrin for me, won't you?" she whispered. "It was all a lie. Everything I've told you was a lie. He didn't call me up. I – I don't know anything."

"Perfume," I said sniffing. "Why, you little darling. You put perfume behind your ears – and all for me!"

She nodded her little chin half an inch. Her eyes were melting. "Take my glasses off," she whispered, "Philip. I don't mind if you take a little whiskey once in a while. Really I don't."

Our faces were about six inches apart. I was afraid to take her glasses off. I might have socked her on the nose.

"Yes," I said in a voice that sounded like Orson Welles with his mouth full of crackers. "I'll find him for you, honey, if he's still alive. And for free. Not a dime of expense involved. I only ask one thing."

"What, Philip?" she asked softly and opened her lips a little wider.

"Who was the black sheep in your family?"

She jerked away from me like a startled fawn might, if I had a startled fawn and it jerked away from me. She stared at me stony-faced.

"You said Orrin wasn't the black sheep in your family. Remember? With a very peculiar emphasis. And when you mentioned your sister Leila, you sort of passed on quickly as if the subject was distasteful."

"I – I don't remember saying anything like that," she said very slowly.

"So I was wondering," I said. "What name does your sister Leila use in pictures?"

"Pictures?" she sounded vague. "Oh you mean motion pictures? Why I never said she was in pictures. I never said anything about her like that."

I gave her my big homely lopsided grin. She suddenly flew into a rage.

"Mind your own business about my sister Leila," she spit at me. "You leave my sister Leila out of your dirty remarks."

"What dirty remarks?" I asked. "Or should I try to guess?"

"All you think about is liquor and women," she screamed. "I hate you!" She rushed to the door and yanked it open and went out. She practically ran down the hall.

I went back around my desk and slumped into the chair. A very strange little girl. Very strange indeed. After a while the phone started ringing again, as it would. On the fourth ring I leaned my head on my hand and groped for it, fumbled it to my face.

"Utter McKinley Funeral Parlors," I said.

A female voice said: "Wha-a-t?" and went off into a shriek of laughter. That one was a riot at the police smoker in 1921. What a wit. Like a hummingbird's beak. I put the lights out and went home.

16

EIGHT-FORTY-FIVE the next morning found me parked a couple of doors from the Bay City Camera Shop, breakfasted and peaceful and reading the local paper through a pair of sunglasses. I had already chewed my way through the Los Angeles paper, which contained no item about ice picks in the Van Nuys or any other hotel. Not even MYSTERIOUS DEATH IN DOWNTOWN HOTEL, with no names or weapons specified. The Bay City *News* wasn't too busy to write up a murder. They put it on the first page, right next to the price of meat.

LOCAL MAN FOUND STABBED
IN IDAHO STREET ROOMING HOUSE

An anonymous telephone call late yesterday sent police speeding to an address on Idaho Street opposite the Seamans and Jansing Company's lumber yard. Entering the unlocked door of his apartment, officers found Lester B. Clausen, 45, manager of the rooming house, dead on the couch. Clausen had been stabbed in the neck with an ice pick which was still in his body. After a preliminary examination, Coroner Frank L. Crowdy announced that Clausen had been drinking heavily and may have been unconscious at the time of his death. No signs of struggle were observed by the police.

Detective Lieutenant Moses Maglashan immediately took charge and questioned tenants of the rooming house on their return from work, but no light has so far been thrown on the circumstances of the crime. Interviewed by this reporter, Coroner Crowdy stated that Clausen's death might have been suicide but that the position of the wound made this unlikely. Examination of the rooming-house register disclosed that a page had recently been torn out. Lieutenant Maglashan, after questioning the tenants at length, stated that a thick-set middle-aged man with brown hair and heavy features had been noticed in the hallway of the rooming house on several occasions,

RAYMOND CHANDLER

*but that none of the tenants knew his name or occupation. After care-
fully checking all rooms, Maglashan further gave it as his opinion that
one of the roomers had left recently and in some haste. The mutila-
tion of the register, however, the character of the neighborhood, the lack
of an accurate description of the missing man, made the job of tracing
him extremely difficult.*

*"I have no idea at present why Clausen was murdered,"
Maglashan announced at a late hour last night. "But I have had my
eye on this man for some time. Many of his associates are known to
me. It's a tough case, but we'll crack it."*

It was a nice piece and only mentioned Maglashan's name
twelve times in the text and twice more in picture captions.
There was a photo of him on page three holding an ice pick
and looking at it with profound thought wrinkling his
brows. There was a photo of 449 Idaho Street which did it
more than justice, and a photo of something with a sheet
over it on a couch and Lieutenant Maglashan pointing at it
sternly. There was also a closeup of the mayor looking as
executive as hell behind his official desk and an interview
with him on the subject of post-war crime. He said just
what you would expect a mayor to say – a watered-down
shot of J. Edgar Hoover with some extra bad grammar
thrown in.

At three minutes to nine the door of the Bay City Camera
Shop opened and an elderly Negro began to sweep dirt across
the sidewalk into the gutter. At nine A.M. a neat-appearing
young guy in glasses fixed the lock on the door and I went in
there with the black-and-orange check Dr. G. W. Hambleton
had pasted to the inside of his toupee.

The neat-appearing young man gave me a searching
glance as I exchanged the check and some money for an
envelope containing a tiny negative and half a dozen shiny
prints blown up to eight times the size of the negative. He
didn't say anything, but the way he looked at me gave me the

314

impression that he remembered I was not the man who had left the negative.

I went out and sat in my car and looked over the catch. The prints showed a man and a blonde girl sitting in a rounded booth in a restaurant with food in front of them. They were looking up as though their attention had suddenly been attracted and they had only just had time to react before the camera had clicked. It was clear from the lighting that no flashbulb had been used.

The girl was Mavis Weld. The man was rather small, rather dark, rather expressionless. I didn't recognize him. There was no reason why I should. The padded leather seat was covered with tiny figures of dancing couples. That made the restaurant THE DANCERS. This added to the confusion. Any amateur camera hound that tried to flash a lens in there without getting an okay from the management would have been thrown out so hard that he would have bounced all the way down to Hollywood and Vine. I figured it must have been the hidden-camera trick, the way they took Ruth Snyder in the electric chair. He would have the little camera up hanging by a strap under his coat collar, the lens just peeping out from his open jacket, and he would have rigged a bulb release that he could hold in his pocket. It wasn't too hard for me to guess who had taken the picture. Mr. Orrin P. Quest must have moved fast and smooth to get out of there with his face still in front of his head.

I put the pictures in my vest pocket and my fingers touched a crumpled piece of paper. I got it out and read: "Doctor Vincent Lagardie, 965 Wyoming Street, Bay City." That was the Vince I had talked to on the phone, the one Lester B. Clausen might have been trying to call.

An elderly flatfoot was strolling down the line of parked cars, marking tires with yellow chalk. He told me where Wyoming Street was. I drove out there. It was a cross-town street well out beyond the business district, parallel with two numbered streets. Number 965, a gray-white frame house, was on a corner. On its door a brass plate said *Vincent Lagardie, M. D., Hours 10:00 to 12:00 and 2:30 to 4:00.*

The house looked quiet and decent. A woman with an unwilling small boy was going up the steps. She read the plate, looked at a watch pinned to her lapel and chewed irresolutely on her lip. The small boy looked around carefully, then kicked her on the ankle. She winced but her voice was patient. "Now, Johnny, you mustn't do that to Aunty Fern," she said mildly.

She opened the door and dragged the little ape in with her. Diagonally across the intersection was a big white colonial mansion with a portico which was roofed and much too small for the house. Floodlight reflectors were set into the front lawn. The walk was bordered by tree roses in bloom. A large black and silver sign over the portico said: "*The Garland Home of Peace.*" I wondered how Dr. Lagardie liked looking out of his front windows at a funeral parlor. Maybe it made him careful.

I turned around at the intersection and drove back to Los Angeles, and went up to the office to look at my mail and lock my catch from the Bay City Camera Shop up in the battered green safe – all but one print. I sat down at the desk and studied this through a magnifying glass. Even with that and the camera shop blow-up the detail was still clear. There was an evening paper, a *News-Chronicle*, lying on the table in front of the dark thin expressionless man who sat beside Mavis Weld. I could just read the headline. *LIGHT HEAVY-WEIGHT CONTENDER SUCCUMBS TO RING INJURIES.* Only a noon or late sports edition would use a headline like that. I pulled the phone towards me. It rang just as I got my hand on it.

"Marlowe? This is Christy French downtown. Any ideas this morning?"

"Not if your teletype's working. I've seen a Bay City paper."

"Yeah, we got that," he said casually. "Sounds like the same guy, don't it? Same initials, same description, same method of murder, and the time element seems to check. I hope to Christ this doesn't mean Sunny Moe Stein's mob have started in business again."

"If they have, they've changed their technique," I said. "I was reading up on it last night. The Stein mob used to jab their victims full of holes. One of them had over a hundred stab wounds in him."

"They could learn better," French said a little evasively, as if he didn't want to talk about it. "What I called you about was Flack. Seen anything of him since yesterday afternoon?"

"No."

"He skipped out. Didn't come to work. Hotel called his landlady. Packed up and left last night. Destination unknown."

"I haven't seen him or heard from him," I said.

"Didn't it strike you as kind of funny our stiff only had fourteen bucks in his kick?"

"It did a little. You answered that yourself."

"I was just talking. I don't buy that any more. Flack's either scared out or come into money. Either he saw something he didn't tell and got paid to breeze, or else he lifted the customer's case dough, leaving the fourteen bucks to make it look better."

I said: "I'll buy either one. Or both at the same time. Whoever searched that room so thoroughly wasn't looking for money."

"Why not?"

"Because when this Dr. Hambleton called me up I suggested the hotel safe to him. He wasn't interested."

"A type like that wouldn't have hired you to hold his dough anyway," French said. "He wouldn't have hired you to keep anything for him. He wanted protection or he wanted a sidekick – or maybe just a messenger."

"Sorry," I said. "He told me just what I told you."

"And seeing he was dead when you got over there," French said with a too casual drawl, "you couldn't hardly have given him one of your business cards."

I held the phone too tight and thought back rapidly over my talk with Hicks in the Idaho Street rooming house. I saw him holding my card between his fingers, looking down at it. And then I saw myself taking it out of his hand quickly, before he froze to it. I took a deep breath and let it out slowly.

"Hardly," I said. "And stop trying to scare me to death."

"He had one, chum. Folded twice across in his pants watch pocket. We missed it the first time."

"I gave Flack a card," I said, stiff-lipped.

There was silence. I could hear voices in the background and the clack of a typewriter. Finally French said dryly: "Fair enough. See you later." He hung up abruptly.

I put the phone down very slowly in its cradle and flexed my cramped fingers. I stared down at the photo lying on the desk in front of me. All it told me was that two people, one of whom I knew, were having lunch at The Dancers. The paper on the table told me the date, or would.

I dialed the *News-Chronicle* and asked for the sports section. Four minutes later I wrote on a pad: "Ritchy Belleau, popular young light heavyweight contender, died in the Sisters Hospital just before midnight February 19 as a result of ring injuries sustained the previous evening in the main event at the Hollywood Legion Stadium. The *News-Chronicle* Noon Sports Edition for February 20 carried the headlines."

I dialed the same number again and asked for Kenny Haste in the City Room. He was an ex-crime reporter I had known for years. We chatted around for a minute and then I said:

"Who covered the Sunny Moe Stein killing for you?"

"Tod Barrow. He's on the *Post-Despatch* now. Why?"

"I'd like the details, if any."

He said he would send to the morgue for the file and call me, which he did ten minutes later. "He was shot twice in the

318

head, in his car, about two blocks from the Chateau Bercy on Franklin. Time, about 11.15 P.M."

"Date, February 20," I said, "or was it?"

"Check, it was. No witnesses, no arrests except the usual police stock company of book-handlers, out-of-work fight managers and other professional suspects. What's in it?"

"Wasn't a pal of his supposed to be in town about that time?"

"Nothing here says so. What name?"

"Weepy Moyer. A cop friend of mine said something about a Hollywood money man being held on suspicion and then released for lack of evidence.

Kenny said: "Wait a minute. Something's coming back to me – yeah. Fellow named Steelgrave, owns The Dancers, supposed to be a gambler and so on. Nice guy. I've met him. That was a bust."

"How do you mean, a bust?"

"Some smart monkey tipped the cops he was Weepy Moyer and they held him for ten days on an open charge for Cleveland. Cleveland brushed it off. That didn't have anything to do with the Stein killing. Steelgrave was under glass all that week. No connection at all. Your cop friend has been reading pulp magazines."

"They all do," I said. "That's why they talk so tough. Thanks, Kenny."

We said goodbye and hung up and I sat leaning back in my chair and looking at my photograph. After a while I took scissors and cut out the piece that contained the folded newspaper with the headline. I put the two pieces in separate envelopes and put them in my pocket with the sheet from the pad.

I dialed Miss Mavis Weld's Crestview number. A woman's voice answered after several rings. It was a remote and formal voice that I might or might not have heard before. All it said was, "Hello?"

"This is Philip Marlowe. Is Miss Weld in?"

"Miss Weld will not be in until late this evening. Do you care to leave a message?"

"Very important. Where could I reach her?"

"I'm sorry. I have no information."

"Would her agent know?"

"Possibly."

"You're quite sure *you're* not Miss Weld?"

"Miss Weld is not in." She hung up.

I sat there and listened to the voice. At first I thought yes, then I thought no. The longer I thought the less I knew. I went down to the parking lot and got my car out.

17

ON THE TERRACE at The Dancers a few early birds were getting ready to drink their lunch. The glass-fronted upstairs room had the awning let down in front of it. I drove on past the curve that goes down into the Strip and stopped across the street from a square building of two stories of rose-red brick with small white leaded bay windows and a Greek porch over the front door and what looked, from across the street, like an antique pewter doorknob. Over the door was a fanlight and the name Sheridan Ballou, Inc., in black wooden letters severely stylized. I locked my car and crossed to the front door. It was white and tall and wide and had a keyhole big enough for a mouse to crawl through. Inside this keyhole was the real lock. I went for the knocker, but they had thought of that too. It was all in one piece and didn't knock.

So I patted one of the slim fluted white pillars and opened the door and walked directly into the reception room which filled the entire front of the building. It was furnished in dark antique-looking furniture and many chairs and settees of quilted chintz-like material. There were lace curtains at the windows and chintz boxes around them that matched the chintz of the furniture. There was a flowered carpet and a lot of people waiting to see Mr. Sheridan Ballou.

Some of them were bright and cheerful and full of hope. Some looked as if they had been there for days. One small dark girl was sniffling into her handkerchief in the corner. Nobody paid any attention to her. I got a couple of profiles at nice angles before the company decided I wasn't buying anything and didn't work there.

A dangerous-looking redhead sat languidly at an Adam desk talking into a pure-white telephone. I went over there and she put a couple of cold blue bullets into me with her eyes and then stared at the cornice that ran around the room.

"No," she said into the phone. "No. So sorry. I'm afraid it's no use. Far, far too busy." She hung up and ticked off something on a list and gave me some more of her steely glance.

"Good morning. I'd like to see Mr. Ballou," I said. I put my plain card on her desk. She lifted it by one corner, smiled at it amusedly.

"Today?" she inquired amiably. "This week?"

"How long does it usually take?"

"It *has* taken six months," she said cheerfully. "Can't somebody else help you?"

"No."

"So sorry. Not a chance. Drop in again won't you? Somewhere about Thanksgiving." She was wearing a white wool skirt, a burgundy silk blouse and a black velvet over-jacket with short sleeves. Her hair was a hot sunset. She wore a golden topaz bracelet and topaz earrings and a topaz dinner ring in the shape of a shield. Her fingernails matched her blouse exactly. She looked as if it would take a couple of weeks to get her dressed.

"I've got to see him," I said.

She read my card again. She smiled beautifully. "Everyone has," she said. "Why – er – Mr. Marlowe. Look at all these lovely people. Every one of them has been here since the office opened two hours ago."

"This is important."

"No doubt. In what way if I may ask?"

"I want to peddle a little dirt."

She picked a cigarette out of a crystal box and lit it with a crystal lighter. "Peddle? You mean for money – in Hollywood?"

"Could be."

"What kind of dirt? Don't be afraid to shock me."

"It's a bit obscene, Miss – Miss –" I screwed my head around to read the plaque on her desk.

"Helen Grady," she said. "Well, a little well-bred obscenity never did any harm, did it?"

"I didn't say it was well-bred."

She leaned back carefully and puffed smoke in my face.

"Blackmail in short." She sighed. "Why the hell don't you lam out of here, bud? Before I throw a handful of fat coppers in your lap?"

I sat on the corner of her desk, grabbed a double handful of her cigarette smoke and blew it into her hair. She dodged angrily. "Beat it, lug," she said in a voice that could have been used for paint remover.

"Oh oh. What happened to the Bryn Mawr accent?"

Without turning her head she said sharply: "Miss Vane."

A tall slim elegant dark girl with supercilious eyebrows looked up. She had just come through an inner door camouflaged as a stained-glass window. The dark girl came over. Miss Grady handed her my card: "Spink."

Miss Vane went back through the stained-glass window with the card.

"Sit down and rest your ankles, big stuff," Miss Grady informed me. "You may be here all week."

I sat down in a chintz winged chair, the back of which came eight inches above my head. It made me feel shrunken.

322

Miss Grady gave me her smile again, the one with the hand-honed edge, and bent to the telephone once more.

I looked around. The little girl in the corner had stopped crying and was making up her face with calm unconcern. A very tall distinguished-looking party swung up a graceful arm to stare at his elegant wrist watch and oozed gently to his feet. He set a pearl-gray homburg at a rakish angle on the side of his head, checked his yellow chamois gloves and his silver-knobbed cane, and strolled languidly over to the red-headed receptionist.

"I have been waiting two hours to see Mr. Ballou," he said icily in a rich sweet voice that had been modulated by a lot of training. "I'm not accustomed to waiting two hours to see anybody."

"So sorry, Mr. Fortescue. Mr. Ballou is just too busy for words this A.M."

"I'm sorry I cannot leave him a check," the elegant tall party remarked with a weary contempt. "Probably the only thing that would interest him. But in default of that —"

"Just a minute, kid." The redhead picked up a phone and said into it: "Yes? . . . Who says so besides Goldwyn? Can't you reach somebody that's not crazy? . . . Well try again." She slammed the telephone down. The tall party had not moved.

"In default of that," he resumed as if he had never stopped speaking, "I should like to leave a short personal message."

"Please do," Miss Grady told him. "I'll get it to him somehow."

"Tell him with my love that he is a dirty polecat."

"Make it skunk, darling," she said. "He doesn't know any English words."

"Make it skunk and double skunk," Fortescue told her. "With a slight added nuance of sulphurated hydrogen and a very cheap grade of whore-house perfume." He adjusted his hat and gave his profile the once over in a mirror. "I now bid you good morning and to hell with Sheridan Ballou, Incorporated."

The tall actor stalked out elegantly, using his cane to open the door.

"What's the matter with him?" I asked.

She looked at me pityingly. "Billy Fortescue? Nothing's the matter with him. He isn't getting any parts so he comes in every day and goes through that routine. He figures somebody might see him and like it."

I shut my mouth slowly. You can live a long time in Hollywood and never see the part they use in pictures.

Miss Vane appeared through the inner door and made a chin-jerk at me. I went in past her. "This way. Second on the right." She watched me while I went down the corridor to the second door which was open. I went in and closed the door.

A plump white-haired Jew sat at the desk smiling at me tenderly. "Greetings," he said. "I'm Moss Spink. What's on the thinker, pal? Park the body. Cigarette?" He opened a thing that looked like a trunk and presented me with a cigarette which was not more than a foot long. It was in an individual glass tube.

"No thanks," I said. "I smoke tobacco."

He sighed. "All right. Give. Let's see. Your name's Marlowe. Huh? Marlowe. Marlowe. Have I ever heard of anybody named Marlowe?"

"Probably not," I said. "I never heard of anybody named Spink. I asked to see a man named Ballou. Does that sound like Spink? I'm not looking for anybody named Spink. And just between you and me, the hell with people named Spink."

"Anti-Semitic huh?" Spink said. He waved a generous hand on which a canary-yellow diamond looked like an amber traffic light. "Don't be like that," he said. "Sit down and dust off the brains. You don't know me. You don't want to know me. Okay. I ain't offended. In a business like this you got to have somebody around that don't get offended."

"Ballou," I said.

"Now be reasonable, pal. Sherry Ballou's a very busy guy. He works twenty hours a day and even then he's way behind schedule. Sit down and talk it out with little Spinky."

"You're what around here?" I asked him.

"I'm his protection, pal. I gotta protect him. A guy like Sherry can't see everybody. I see people for him. I'm the same as him – up to a point you understand."

"Could be I'm past the point you're up to," I said.

"Could be," Spink agreed pleasantly. He peeled a thick tape off an aluminum individual cigar container, reached the cigar out tenderly and looked it over for birthmarks. "I don't say not. Why not demonstrate a little? Then we'll know. Up to now all you're doing is throwing a line. We get so much of that in here it don't mean a thing to us."

I watched him clip and light the expensive-looking cigar. "How do I know you wouldn't double-cross him?" I asked cunningly.

Spink's small tight eyes blinked and I wasn't sure but that there were tears in them. "Me cross Sherry Ballou?" he asked brokenly in a hushed voice, like a six-hundred-dollar funeral. "Me? I'd sooner double-cross my own mother."

"That doesn't mean anything to me either," I said. "I never met your mother."

Spink laid his cigar aside in an ashtray the size of a bird bath. He waved both his arms. Sorrow was eating into him. "Oh pal. What a way to talk," he wailed. "I love Sherry Ballou like he was my own father. Better. My father – well, skip it. Come on, pal. Be human. Give with a little of the old trust and friendliness. Spill the dirt to little Spinky, huh?"

I drew an envelope from my pocket and tossed it across the desk to him. He pulled the single photograph from it and stared at it solemnly. He laid it down on the desk. He looked up at me, down at the photo, up at me. "Well," he said woodenly, in a voice suddenly empty of the old trust and friendliness he had been talking about. "What's it got that's so wonderful?"

"Do I have to tell you who the girl is?"

"Who's the guy?" Spink snapped.

I said nothing.

"I said who's the guy?" Spink almost yelled at me. "Cough up, mug. Cough up."

I still didn't say anything. Spink reached slowly for his telephone, keeping his hard bright eyes on my face.

"Go on. Call them," I said. "Call downtown and ask for Lieutenant Christy French in the homicide bureau. There's another boy that's hard to convince."

Spink took his hand off the phone. He got up slowly and went out with the photograph. I waited. Outside on Sunset Boulevard traffic went by distantly, monotonously. The minutes dropped silently down a well. The smoke of Spink's freshly lit cigar played in the air for a moment, then was sucked through the vent of the air-conditioning apparatus. I looked at the innumerable inscribed photos on the walls, all inscribed to Sherry Ballou with somebody's eternal love. I figured they were back numbers if they were in Spink's office.

18

AFTER A WHILE Spink came back and gestured to me. I followed him along the corridor through double doors into an anteroom with two secretaries. Past them towards more double doors of heavy black glass with silver peacocks etched into the panels. As we neared the doors they opened of themselves.

We went down three carpeted steps into an office that had everything in it but a swimming pool. It was two stories high, surrounded by a balcony loaded with book shelves. There was a concert grand Steinway in the corner and a lot of glass and bleached-wood furniture and a desk about the size of a badminton court and chairs and couches and tables and a man lying on one of the couches with his coat off and his shirt open over a Charvet scarf you could have found in the dark by listening to it purr. A white cloth was over his eyes and forehead and a lissome blonde girl was wringing out another in a silver bowl of ice water at a table beside him.

The man was a big shapely guy with wavy dark hair and a strong brown face below the white cloth. An arm dropped to the carpet and a cigarette hung between fingers, wisping a tiny thread of smoke.

The blonde girl changed the cloth deftly. The man on the couch groaned. Spink said: "This is the boy, Sherry. Name of Marlowe."

The man on the couch groaned. "What does he want?"

Spink said: "Won't spill."

The man on the couch said: "What did you bring him in for then? I'm tired."

Spink said: "Well you know how it is, Sherry. Sometimes you kind of got to."

The man on the couch said: "What did you say his beautiful name was?"

Spink turned to me. "You can tell us what you want now. And make it snappy, Marlowe."

I said nothing.

After a moment the man on the couch slowly raised the arm with the cigarette at the end of it. He got the cigarette wearily into his mouth and drew on it with the infinite languor of a decadent aristocrat moldering in a ruined château.

"I'm talking to you pal," Spink said harshly. The blonde changed the cloth again, looking at nobody. The silence hung in the room as acrid as the smoke of the cigarette. "Come on, lug. Snap it up."

I got one of my Camels out and lit it and picked out a chair and sat down. I stretched my hand out and looked at it. The thumb twitched up and down slowly every few seconds.

Spink's voice cut into this furiously: "Sherry don't have all day, you."

"What would he do with the rest of the day?" I heard myself asking. "Sit on a white satin couch and have his toenails gilded?"

The blonde turned suddenly and stared at me. Spink's mouth fell open. He blinked. The man on the couch lifted a slow hand to the corner of the towel over his eyes. He removed enough so that one seal-brown eye looked at me. The towel fell softly back into place.

"You can't talk like that in here," Spink said in a tough voice.

I stood up. I said: "I forgot to bring my prayer book. This is the first time I knew God worked on commission."

Nobody said anything for a minute. The blonde changed the towel again.

From under it the man on the couch said calmly: "Get the Jesus out of here, darlings. All but the new chum."

Spink gave me a narrow glare of hate. The blonde left silently.

Spink said: "Why don't I just toss him out on his can?"

The tired voice under the towel said: "I've been wondering about that so long I've lost interest in the problem. Beat it."

"Okay, boss," Spink said. He withdrew reluctantly. He paused at the door, gave me one more silent snarl and disappeared.

The man on the couch listened to the door close and then said: "How much?"

"You don't want to buy anything."

He pushed the towel off his head, tossed it to one side and sat up slowly. He put his bench-made pebble-grain brogues on the carpet and passed a hand across his forehead. He looked tired but not dissipated. He fumbled another cigarette from somewhere, lit it and stared morosely through the smoke at the floor.

"Go on," he said.

"I don't know why you wasted all the build-up on me," I said, "but I credit you with enough brains to know you couldn't buy anything, and know it would stay bought."

Ballou picked up the photo that Spink had put down near him on a long low table. He reached out a languid hand. "The piece that's cut out would be the punch line, no doubt," he said.

I got the envelope out of my pocket and gave him the cut out corner, watched him fit the two pieces together. "With a glass you can read the headline," I said.

"There's one on my desk. Please."

I went over and got the magnifying glass off his desk. "You're used to a lot of service, aren't you, Mr. Ballou?"

"I pay for it." He studied the photograph through the glass and sighed. "Seems to me I saw that fight. They ought to take more care of these boys."

"Like you do of your clients," I said.

He laid down the magnifying glass and leaned back to stare at me with cool untroubled eyes.

"That's the chap that owns The Dancers. Name's Steelgrave. The girl is a client of mine, of course." He made a vague gesture towards a chair. I sat down in it. "What were you thinking of asking, Mr. Marlowe?"

"For what?"

"All the prints and the negative. The works."

"Ten grand," I said, and watched his mouth. The mouth smiled, rather pleasantly.

"It needs a little more explanation, doesn't it? All I see is two people having lunch in a public place. Hardly disastrous to the reputation of my client. I assume that was what you had in mind."

I grinned. "You can't buy anything, Mr. Ballou. I could have had a positive made from the negative and another negative from the positive. If that snap is evidence of something, you could never know you had suppressed it."

"Not much of a sales talk for a blackmailer," he said, still smiling.

"I always wonder why people pay blackmailers. They can't buy anything. Yet they do pay them, sometimes over and over and over again. And in the end are just where they started."

"The fear of today," he said, "always overrides the fear of tomorrow. It's a basic fact of the dramatic emotions that the part is greater than the whole. If you see a glamour star on the screen in a position of great danger, you fear for her with one part of your mind, the emotional part. Notwithstanding that your reasoning mind knows that she is the star of the picture and nothing very bad is going to happen to her. If suspense and menace didn't defeat reason, there would be very little drama."

I said: "Very true, I guess," and puffed some of my Camel smoke around.

His eyes narrowed a little. "As to really being able to buy anything, if I paid you a substantial price and didn't get what I bought, I'd have you taken care of. Beaten to a pulp. And when you got out of the hospital, if you felt agressive enough, you could try to get me arrested."

"It's happened to me," I said. "I'm a private eye. I know what you mean. Why are you talking to me?"

He laughed. He had a deep pleasant effortless laugh. "I'm an agent, sonny. I always tend to think traders have a little something in reserve. But we won't talk about any ten grand. She hasn't got it. She only makes a grand a week so far. I admit she's very close to the big money, though."

"That would stop her cold," I said, pointing to the photo. "No big money, no swimming pool with underwater lights, no platinum mink, no name in neons, no nothing. All blown away like dust."

He laughed contemptuously.

"Okay if I show this to the johns down town, then?" I said.

He stopped laughing. His eyes narrowed. Very quietly he asked:

"Why would they be interested?"

I stood up. "I don't think we're going to do any business, Mr Ballou. And you're a busy man. I'll take myself off."

He got up off the couch and stretched, all six feet two of him. He was a very fine hunk of man. He came over and stood close to me. His seal-brown eyes had little gold flecks in them. "Let's see who you are, sonny."

He put his hand out. I dropped my open wallet into it. He read the photostat of my license, poked a few more things out of the wallet and glanced at them. He handed it back.

"What would happen, if you did show your little picture to the cops?"

"I'd first of all have to connect it up with something they're working on – something that happened in the Van Nuys Hotel yesterday afternoon. I'd connect it up through the girl – who won't talk to me – that's why I'm talking to you."

"She told me about it last night," he sighed.

"Told you how much?" I asked.

"That a private detective named Marlowe had tried to force her to hire him, on the ground that she was seen in a downtown hotel inconveniently close to where a murder was committed."

"How close?" I asked.

"She didn't say."

"Nuts she didn't."

He walked away from me to a tall cylindrical jar in the corner. From this he took one of a number of short thin malacca canes. He began to walk up and down the carpet, swinging the cane deftly past his right shoe.

I sat down again and killed my cigarette and took a deep breath. "It could only happen in Hollywood," I grunted.

He made a neat about turn and glanced at me. "I beg your pardon."

"That an apparently sane man could walk up and down inside the house with a Piccadilly stroll and a monkey stick in his hand."

He nodded. "I caught the disease from a producer at MGM. Charming fellow. Or so I've been told." He stopped and pointed the cane at me. "You amuse the hell out of me, Marlowe. Really you do. You're so transparent. You're trying to use me for a shovel to dig yourself out of a jam."

"There's some truth in that. But the jam I'm in is nothing to the jam your client would be in if I hadn't done the thing that put me in the jam."

He stood quite still for a moment. Then he threw the cane away from him and walked over to a liquor cabinet and swung the two halves of it open. He poured something into a couple of pot-bellied glasses. He carried one of them over to me. Then went back and got his own. He sat down with it on the couch.

"Armagnac," he said. "If you knew me, you'd appreciate the compliment. This stuff is pretty scarce. The Krauts cleaned most of it out. Our brass got the rest. Here's to you."

He lifted the glass, sniffed and sipped a tiny sip. I put mine down in a lump. It tasted like good French brandy.

Ballou looked shocked. "My God, you sip that stuff, you don't swallow it whole."

"I swallow it whole," I said. "Sorry. She also told you that if somebody didn't shut my mouth, she would be in a lot of trouble."

He nodded.

"Did she suggest how to go about shutting my mouth?"

"I got the impression she was in favor of doing it with some kind of heavy blunt instrument. So I tried out a mixture of threat and bribery. We have an outfit down the street that specializes in protecting picture people. Apparently they didn't scare you and the bribe wasn't big enough."

"They scared me plenty," I said. "I damn near fanned a Luger at them. That junky with the .45 puts on a terrific act.

And as for the money not being big enough, it's all a question of how it's offered to me."

He sipped a little more of his Armagnac. He pointed at the photograph lying in front of him with the two pieces fitted together.

"We got to where you were taking that to the cops. What then?"

"I don't think we got that far. We got to why she took this up with you instead of with her boy friend. He arrived just as I left. He has his own key."

"Apparently she just didn't." He frowned and looked down into his Armagnac.

"I like that fine," I said. "I'd like it still better if the guy didn't have her doorkey."

He looked up rather sadly. "So would I. So would we all. But show busines has always been like that – any kind of show business. If these people didn't live intense and rather dis-ordered lives, if their emotions didn't ride them too hard – well, they wouldn't be able to catch those emotions in flight and imprint them on a few feet of celluloid or project them across the footlights."

"I'm not talking about her love life," I said. "She doesn't have to shack up with a redhot."

"There's no proof of that, Marlowe."

I pointed to the photograph. "The man that took that is missing and can't be found. He's probably dead. Two other men who lived at the same address are dead. One of them was trying to peddle those pictures just before he got dead. She went to his hotel in person to take delivery. So did whoever killed him. She didn't get delivery and neither did the killer. They didn't know where to look."

"And you did?"

"I was lucky. I'd seen him without his toupee. None of this is what I call proof, maybe. You could build an argument against it. Why bother? Two men have been killed, perhaps three. She took an awful chance. Why? She wanted that picture. Getting it was worth an awful chance. Why, again? It's just two people having lunch on a certain day. The day Moe Stein was shot to death on Franklin Avenue. The day a character named Steelgrave was in jail because the cops got a tip he was a Cleveland redhot named Weepy Moyer. That's what the record shows. But the photo says he was out of jail. And by saying that about him on that particular day it says who he is. And she knows it. And he still has her doorkey."

I paused and we eyed each other solidly for a while. I said:

"You don't really want the cops to have that picture, do you? Win, lose or draw, they'd crucify her. And when it was all over it wouldn't make a damn bit of difference whether Steelgrave was Moyer or whether Moyer killed Stein or had him killed or just happened to be out on a jail pass the day he was killed. If he got away with it, there'd always be enough people to think it was a fix. She wouldn't get away with anything. She's a gangster's girl in the public mind. And as far as your business is concerned, she's definitely and completely through."

Ballou was silent for a moment, staring at me without expression. "And where are you all this time?" he asked softly.

"That depends a good deal on you, Mr. Ballou."

"What do you really want?" His voice was thin and bitter now.

"What I wanted from her and couldn't get. Something that gives me a colorable right to act in her interests up to the point where I decided I can't go any farther."

"By suppressing evidence?" he asked tightly.

"If it *is* evidence. The cops couldn't find out without smearing Miss Weld. Maybe I can. They wouldn't be bothered to try; they don't care enough. I do."

"Why?"

"Let's say it's the way I earn my living. I might have other motives, but that one's enough."

"What's your price?"

334

"You sent it to me last night. I wouldn't take it then. I'll take it now. With a signed letter employing my services to investigate an attempt to blackmail one of your clients."

I got up with my empty glass and went over and put it down on the desk. As I bent down I heard a soft whirring noise. I went around behind the desk and yanked upon a drawer. A wire recorder slid out on a hinged shelf. The motor was running and the fine steel wire was moving steadily from one spool to the other. I looked across at Ballou.

"You can shut it off and take the record with you," he said. "You can't blame me for using it."

I moved the switch over to rewind and the wire reversed direction and picked up speed until the wire was winding so fast I couldn't see it. It made a sort of high keening noise, like a couple of pansies fighting for a piece of silk. The wire came loose and the machine stopped. I took the spool off and dropped it into my pocket.

"You might have another one," I said. "I'll have to chance that."

"Pretty sure of yourself, aren't you, Marlowe?"

"I only wish I was."

"Press that button on the end of the desk, will you?"

I pressed it. The black glass doors opened and a dark girl came in with a stenographer's notebook.

Without looking at her Ballou began to dictate. "Letter to Mr. Philip Marlowe, with his address, Dear Mr. Marlowe: This agency herewith employs you to investigate an attempt to blackmail one of my clients, particulars of which have been given to you verbally. Your fee is to be one hundred dollars a day with a retainer of five hundred dollars, receipt of which you acknowledge on the copy of this letter. Blah, blah, blah. That's all, Eileen. Right away please."

I gave the girl my address and she went out.

I took the wire spool out of my pocket and put it back in the drawer.

335

Ballou crossed his knees and danced the shiny tip of his shoe up and down staring at it. He ran his hand through crisp dark hair.

"One of these days," he said, "I'm going to make the mistake which a man in my business dreads above all other mistakes. I'm going to find myself doing business with a man I can trust and I'm going to be just too god-damn smart to trust him. Here, you'd better keep this." He held out the two pieces of the photograph.

Five minutes later I left. The glass doors opened when I was three feet from them. I went past the two secretaries and down the corridor past the open door of Spink's office. There was no sound in there, but I could smell his cigar smoke. In the reception room exactly the same people seemed to be sitting around in the chintzy chairs. Miss Helen Grady gave me her Saturday-night smile. Miss Vane beamed at me.

I had been forty minutes with the boss. That made me as gaudy as a chiropractor's chart.

19

THE STUDIO COP at the semicircular glassed-in desk put down his telephone and scribbled on a pad. He tore off the sheet and pushed it through the narrow slit not more than three quarters of an inch wide where the glass did not quite meet the top of his desk. His voice coming through the speaking device set into the glass panel had a metallic ring.

"Straight through to the end of the corridor," he said, "you'll find a drinking fountain in the middle of the patio. George Wilson will pick up there."

I said: "Thanks. Is this bullet-proof glass?"

"Sure. Why?"

"I just wondered," I said. "I never heard of anybody shooting his way into the picture business."

Behind me somebody snickered. I turned to look at a girl in slacks with a red carnation behind her ear. She was grinning.

"Oh brother, if a gun was all it took."

I went over to an olive-green door that didn't have any handle. It made a buzzing sound and let me push it open. Beyond was an olive-green corridor with bare walls and a door at the far end. A rat trap. If you got into that and something was wrong, they could still stop you. The far door made the same buzz and click. I wondered how the cop knew I was at it. So I looked up and found his eyes staring at me in a tilted mirror. As I touched the door the mirror went blank. They thought of everything.

Outside in the hot midday sun flowers rioted in a small patio with tiled walks and a pool in the middle and a marble seat. The drinking fountain was beside the marble seat. An elderly and beautifully dressed man was lounging on the marble seat watching three tan-colored boxers root up some tea-rose begonias. There was an expression of intense but quiet satisfaction on his face. He didn't glance at me as I came up. One of the boxers, the biggest one, came over and made a wet on the marble seat beside his pants leg. He leaned down and patted the dog's hard short-haired head.

"You Mr. Wilson?" I asked.

He looked up at me vaguely. The middle-sized boxer trotted up and sniffed and wet after the first one.

"Wilson?" He had a lazy voice with a touch of drawl to it. "Oh, no. My name's not Wilson. Should it be?"

"Sorry." I went over to the drinking fountain and hit myself in the face with a stream of water. While I was wiping it off with a handkerchief the smallest boxer did his duty on the marble bench.

The man whose name was not Wilson said lovingly, "Always do it in the exact same order. Fascinates me."

"Do what?" I asked.

"Pee," he said. "Question of seniority it seems. Very orderly. First Maisie. She's the mother. Then Mac. Year older than Jock, the baby. Always the same. Even in my office."

"In your office?" I said, and nobody ever looked stupider saying anything.

He lifted his whitish eyebrows at me, took a plain brown cigar out of his mouth, bit the end off and spit it into the pool.

"That won't do the fish any good," I said.

He gave me an up-from-under look. "I raise boxers. The hell with fish."

I figured it was just Hollywood. I lit a cigarette and sat down on the bench. "In your office," I said. "Well, every day has its new idea, hasn't it."

"Up against the corner of the desk. Do it all the time. Drives my secretaries crazy. Gets into the carpet, they say. What's the matter with women nowadays? Never bothers me. Rather like it. You get fond of dogs, you even like to watch them pee."

One of the dogs heaved a full-blown begonia plant into the middle of the tiled walk at his feet. He picked it up and threw it into the pool.

"Bothers the gardeners, I suppose," he remarked as he sat down again. "Oh well, if they're not satisfied, they can always —" He stopped dead and watched a slim mail girl in yellow slacks deliberately detour in order to pass through the patio. She gave him a quick side glance and went off making music with her hips.

"You know what's the matter with this business?" he asked me.

"Nobody does," I said.

"Too much sex," he said. "All right in its proper time and place. But we get it in carload lots. Wade through it. Stand up to our necks in it. Gets to be like flypaper." He stood up. "We have too many flies too. Nice to have met you, Mister —"

"Marlowe," I said. "I'm afraid you don't know me."

"Don't know anybody," he said. "Memory's going. Meet too many people. Name's Oppenheimer."

"Jules Oppenheimer?"

He nodded. "Right. Have a cigar." He held one out to me. I showed my cigarette. He threw the cigar into the pool, then frowned. "Memory's going," he said sadly. "Wasted fifty cents. Oughtn't to do that."

"You run this studio," I said.

He nodded absently. "Ought to have saved that cigar. Save fifty cents and what have you got?"

"Fifty cents," I said, wondering what the hell he was talking about.

"Not in this business. Save fifty cents in this business and all you have is five dollars' worth of bookkeeping." He paused and made a motion to the three boxers. They stopped whatever they were rooting at and watched him. "Just run the financial end," he said. "That's easy. Come on children, back to the brothel." He sighed. "Fifteen hundred theaters," he added.

I must have been wearing my stupid expression again. He waved a hand around the patio. "Fifteen hundred theaters is all you need. A damn sight easier than raising purebred boxers. The motion-picture business is the only business in the world in which you can make all the mistakes there are and still make money."

"Must be the only business in the world where you can have three dogs pee up against your office desk," I said.

"You have to have the fifteen hundred theaters."

"That makes it a little harder to get a start," I said.

He looked pleased. "Yes. That *is* the hard part." He looked across the green clipped lawn at a four-story building which made one side of the open square. "All offices over there," he said. "I never go there. Always redecorating. Makes me sick to look at the stuff some of these people put in their suites. Most expensive talent in the world. Give them anything they like, all the money they want. Why? No reason at all. Just habit. Doesn't matter a damn what they do or how they do it. Just give me fifteen hundred theaters."

"You wouldn't want to be quoted on that, Mr. Oppenheimer?"

"You a newspaper man?"

"No."

"Too bad. Just for the hell of it I'd like to see somebody try to get that simple elementary fact of life into the papers." He paused and snorted. "Nobody'd print it. Afraid to. Come on, children!"

The big one, Maisie, came over and stood beside him. The middle-sized one paused to ruin another begonia and then trotted up beside Maisie. The little one, Jock, lined up in order, then with a sudden inspiration, lifted a hind leg at the cuff of Oppenheimer's pants. Maisie blocked him off casually.

"See that?" Oppenheimer beamed. "Jock tried to get out of turn. Maisie wouldn't stand for it." He leaned down and patted Maisie's head. She looked up at him adoringly.

"The eyes of your dog," Oppenheimer mused. "The most unforgettable thing in the world."

He strolled off down the tiled path towards the executive building, the three boxers trotting sedately beside him.

"Mr. Marlowe?"

I turned to find that a tall sandy-haired man with a nose like a straphanger's elbow had sneaked up on me.

"I'm George Wilson. Glad to know you. I see you know Mr. Oppenheimer."

"Been talking to him. He told me how to run the picture business. Seems all it takes is fifteen hundred theaters."

"I've been working here five years. I've never even spoken to him."

"You just don't get pee'd on by the right dogs."

340

"You could be right. Just what can I do for you, Mr. Marlowe?"

"I want to see Mavis Weld."

"She's on the set. She's in a picture that's shooting."

"Could I see her on the set for a minute?"

He looked doubtful. "What kind of pass did they give you?"

"Just a pass, I guess," I held it out to him. He looked it over.

"Ballou sent you. He's her agent. I guess we can manage. Stage 12. Want to go over there now?"

"If you have time."

"I'm the unit publicity man. That's what my time is for." We walked along the tiled path towards the corners of two buildings. A concrete roadway went between them towards the back lot and the stages.

"You in Ballou's office?" Wilson asked.

"Just came from there."

"Quite an organization, I hear. I've thought of trying that business myself. There's nothing in this but a lot of grief."

We passed a couple of uniformed cops, then turned into a narrow alley between two stages. A red wigwag was swinging in the middle of the alley, a red light was on over a door marked 12, and a bell was ringing steadily above the red light. Wilson stopped beside the door. Another cop in a tilted-back chair nodded to him, and looked me over with that dead gray expression that grows on them like scum on a water tank.

The bell and the wigwag stopped and the red light went off. Wilson pulled a heavy door open and I went in past him. Inside was another door. Inside that what seemed after the sunlight to be pitch-darkness. Then I saw a concentration of lights in the far corner. The rest of the enormous sound stage seemed to be empty.

We went towards the lights. As we drew near the floor seemed to be covered with thick black cables. There were rows of folding chairs, a cluster of portable dressing rooms with names on the doors. We were wrong way on to the set and all I could see was the wooden backing and on either side a big screen. A couple of back-projection machines sizzled off to the side.

A voice shouted: "Roll 'em." A bell rang loudly. The two screens came alive with tossing waves. Another calmer voice said: "Watch your positions, please, we may have to end up matching this little vignette. All right, action."

Wilson stopped dead and touched my arm. The voices of the actors came out of nowhere, neither loud nor distinct, an unimportant murmur with no meaning.

One of the screens suddenly went blank. The smooth voice, without change of tone, said: "Cut."

The bell rang again and there was a general sound of movement. Wilson and I went on. He whispered in my ear: "If Ned Gammon doesn't get this take before lunch, he'll bust Torrance on the nose."

"Oh, Torrance in this?" Dick Torrance at the time was a ranking star of the second grade, a not uncommon type of Hollywood actor that nobody really wants but a lot of people in the end have to take for lack of better.

"Care to run over the scene again, Dick?" the calm voice asked, as we came around the corner of the set and saw what it was – the deck of a pleasure yacht near the stern. There were two girls and three men in the scene. One of the men was middle-aged, in sport clothes, lounging in a deck chair. One wore whites and had red hair and looked like the yacht's captain. The third was the amateur yachtsman, with the handsome cap, the blue jacket with gold buttons, the white shoes and slacks and the supercilious charm. This was Torrance. One of the girls was a dark beauty who had been younger; Susan Crawley. The other was Mavis Weld. She wore a wet white sharkskin swim suit, and had evidently just come aboard. A make-up man was spraying water on her face and arms and the edges of her blond hair.

Torrance hadn't answered. He turned suddenly and stared at the camera. "You think I don't know my lines?"

A gray-haired man in gray clothes came forward into the light from the shadowy background. He had hot black eyes, but there was no heat in his voice.

"Unless you changed them intentionally," he said, his eyes steady on Torrance.

"It's just possible that I'm not used to playing in front of a back projection screen that has a habit of running out of film only in the middle of a take."

"That's a fair complaint," Ned Gammon said. "Trouble is he only has two hundred and twelve feet of film, and that's my fault. If you could take the scene just a little faster —"

"Huh." Torrance snorted. "If *I* could take it a little faster. Perhaps Miss Weld could be prevailed upon to climb aboard this yacht in rather less time than it would take to build the damn boat."

Mavis Weld gave him a quick, contemptuous look.

"Weld's timing is just right," Gammon said. "Her performance is just right too."

Susan Crawley shrugged elegantly. "I had the impression she could speed it up a trifle, Ned. It's good, but it *could* be better."

"If it was any better, darling," Mavis Weld told her smoothly, "somebody might call it acting. You wouldn't want anything like that to happen in *your* picture, would you."

Torrance laughed. Susan Crawley turned and glared at him. "What's funny, Mister Thirteen?"

Torrance's face settled into an icy mask. "The name again?" he almost hissed.

"Good heavens, you mean you didn't know," Susan Crawley said wonderingly. "They call you Mister Thirteen because any time you play a part it means twelve other guys have turned it down."

"I see," Torrance said coolly, then burst out laughing again. He turned to Ned Gammon. "Okay, Ned. Now everybody's got the rat poison out of their system, maybe we can give it to you the way you want it."

Ned Gammon nodded. "Nothing like a little hamming to clear the air. All right here we go."

He went back beside the camera. The assistant shouted "roll 'em" and the scene went through without a hitch.

"Cut," Gammon said. "Print that one. Break for lunch everybody."

The actors came down a flight of rough wooden steps and nodded to Wilson. Mavis Weld came last, having stopped to put on a terry-cloth robe and a pair of beach sandals. She stopped dead when she saw me. Wilson stepped forward.

"Hello, George," Mavis Weld said, staring at me. "Want something from me?"

"Mr. Marlowe would like a few words with you. Okay?"

"Mr. Marlowe?"

Wilson gave me a quick sharp look. "From Ballou's office. I supposed you knew him."

"I may have seen him." She was still staring at me. "What is it?"

I didn't speak.

After a moment she said, "Thanks, George. Better come along to my dressing room, Mr. Marlowe."

She turned and walked off around the far side of the set. A green and white dressing room stood against the wall. The name on the door was Miss Weld. At the door she turned and looked around carefully. Then she fixed her lovely blue eyes on my face.

"And now, Mr. Marlowe?"

"You *do* remember me?"

"I believe so."

"Do we take up where we left off – or have a new deal with a clean deck?"

"Somebody let you in here. Who? Why? That takes explaining."

344

"I'm working for you. I've been paid a retainer and Ballou has the receipt."

"How very thoughtful. And suppose I don't want you to work for me? Whatever your work is."

"All right, be fancy," I said. I took the Dancers photo out of my pocket and held it out. She looked at me a long steady moment before she dropped her eyes. Then she looked at the snapshot of herself and Steelgrave in the booth. She looked at it gravely without movement. Then very slowly she reached up and touched the tendrils of damp hair at the side of her face. Ever so slightly she shivered. Her hand came out and she took the photograph. She stared at it. Her eyes came up again slowly, slowly.

"Well?" she asked.

"I have the negative and some other prints. You would have had them, if you had had more time and known where to look. Or if he had stayed alive to sell them to you."

"I'm a little chilly," she said. "And I have to eat some lunch." She held the photo out to me.

"You're a little chilly and you have to eat some lunch," I said.

I thought a pulse beat in her throat. But the light was not too good. She smiled very faintly. The bored-aristocrat touch.

"The significance of all this escapes me," she said.

"You're spending too much time on yachts. What you mean is I know you and I know Steelgrave, so what has this photo got that makes anybody give me a diamond dog collar?"

"All right," she said. "What?"

"I don't know," I said. "But if finding out is what it takes to shake you out of this duchess routine, I'll find out. And in the meantime you're still chilly and you still have to eat some lunch."

"And you've waited too long," she said quietly. "You haven't anything to sell. Except perhaps your life."

"I'd sell that cheap. For love of a pair of dark glasses and a delphinium-blue hat and a crack on the head from a high-heeled slipper."

Her mouth twitched as if she was going to laugh. But there was no laughter in her eyes.

"Not to mention three slaps in the face," she said. "Goodbye, Mr. Marlowe. You came too late. Much, much too late."

"For me – or for you?" She reached back and opened the door of the dressing room.

"I think for both of us." She went in quickly, leaving the door open.

"Come in and shut the door," her voice said from the dressing room.

I went in and shut the door. It was no fancy custom-built star's dressing room. Strictly utility only. There was a shabby couch, one easy chair, a small dressing table with mirror and two lights, a straight chair in front of it, a tray that had held coffee.

Mavis Weld reached down and plugged in a round electric heater. Then she grabbed up a towel and rubbed the damp edges of her hair. I sat down on the couch and waited.

"Give me a cigarette." She tossed the towel to one side. Her eyes came close to my face as I lit the cigarette for her. "How did you like that little scene we ad libbed on the yacht?"

"Bitchy."

"We're all bitches. Some smile more than others, that's all. Show business. There's something cheap about it. There always has been. There was a time when actors went in at the back door. Most of them still should. Great strain, great urgency, great hatred, and it comes out in nasty little scenes. They don't mean a thing."

"Cat talk," I said.

She reached up and pulled a fingertip down the side of my cheek. It burned like a hot iron. "How much money do you make, Marlowe?"

"Forty bucks a day and expenses. That's the asking price. I take twenty-five. I've taken less." I thought about Orfamay's worn twenty.

346

She did that with her finger again and I just didn't grab hold of her. She moved away from me and sat in the chair, drawing the robe close. The electric heater was making the little room warm.

"Twenty-five dollars a day," she said wonderingly.

"'Little lonely dollars."

"Are they very lonely?"

"Lonely as lighthouses."

She crossed her legs and the pale glow of her skin in the light seemed to fill the room.

"So ask me the questions," she said, making no attempt to cover her thighs.

"Who's Steelgrave?"

"A man I've known for years. And liked. He owns things. A restaurant or two. Where he comes from – that I don't know."

"But you know him very well."

"Why don't you ask me if I sleep with him?"

"I don't ask that kind of question."

She laughed and snapped ash from her cigarette. "Miss Gonzales would be glad to tell you. She's dark and lovely and passionate. And very, very kind."

"And exclusive as a mailbox," I said. "The hell with her. About Steelgrave – has he ever been in trouble?"

"Who hasn't?"

"With the police."

Her eyes widened a little too innocently. Her laugh was a little too silvery. "Don't be ridiculous. The man is worth a couple of million dollars."

"How did he get it?"

"How would I know?"

"All right. You wouldn't. That cigarette's going to burn your fingers." I leaned across and took the stub out of her hand. Her hand lay open on her bare leg. I touched the palm with a fingertip. She drew away from me and tightened the hand into a fist.

347

"Don't do that," she said sharply.

"Why? I used to do that to girls when I was a kid."

"I know." She was breathing a little fast. "It makes me feel very young and innocent and kind of naughty. And I'm far from being young and innocent any more."

"Then you don't really know anything about Steelgrave."

"I wish you'd make up your mind whether you are giving me a third degree or making love to me."

"My mind has nothing to do with it," I said.

After a silence she said: "I really do have to eat something, Marlowe. I'm working this afternoon. You wouldn't want me to collapse on the set, would you?"

"Only stars do that." I stood up. "Okay, I'll leave. Don't forget I'm working for you. I wouldn't be if I thought you'd killed anybody. But you were there. You took a big chance. There was something you wanted very badly."

She reached the photo out from somewhere and stared at it, biting her lip. Her eyes came up without her head moving.

"It could hardly have been this."

"That was the one thing he had so well hidden that it was not found. But what good is it? You and a man called Steelgrave in a booth at The Dancers. Nothing in that."

"Nothing at all," she said.

"So it has to be something about Steelgrave — or something about the date."

Her eyes snapped down to the picture again. "There's nothing to tell the date," she said quickly. "Even if it meant something. Unless the cut-out piece —"

"Here." I gave her the cut-out piece. "But you'll need a magnifier. Show it to Steelgrave. Ask *him* if it means anything. Or ask Ballou."

I started towards the exit of the dressing room. "Don't kid yourself the date can't be fixed," I said over my shoulder. "Steelgrave won't."

"You're just building a sand castle, Marlowe."

"Really?" I looked back at her, not grinning. "You really think that? Oh no you don't. You went there. The man was murdered. You had a gun. He was a known crook. And I found something the police would love to have me hide from them. Because it must be as full of motive as the ocean is full of salt. As long as the cops don't find it I have a license. And as long as somebody else doesn't find it I don't have an ice pick in the back of my neck. Would you say I was in an overpaid profession?"

She just sat there and looked at me, one hand on her kneecap, squeezing it. The other moving restlessly, finger by finger, on the arm of the chair.

All I had to do was turn the knob and go on out. I don't know why it had to be so hard to do.

20

THERE WAS THE usual coming and going in the corridor outside my office and when I opened the door and walked into the musty silence of the little waiting room there was the usual feeling of having been dropped down a well dried up twenty years ago to which no one would come back ever. The smell of old dust hung in the air as flat and stale as a football interview.

I opened the inner door and inside there it was the same dead air, the same dust along the veneer, the same broken promise of a life of ease. I opened the windows and turned on the radio. It came up too loud and when I had it tuned down to normal the phone sounded as if it had been ringing for some time. I took my hat off it and lifted the receiver.

It was high time I heard from her again. Her cool compact voice said: "This time I really mean it."

"Go on."

"I lied before. I'm not lying now. I really have heard from Orrin."

"Go on."

"You're not believing me. I can tell by your voice."

"You can't tell anything by my voice. I'm a detective. Heard from him how?"

"By phone from Bay City."

"Wait a minute." I put the receiver down on the stained brown blotter and lit my pipe. No hurry. Lies are always patient. I took it up again.

"We've been through that routine," I said. "You're pretty forgetful for your age. I don't think Dr. Zugsmith would like it."

"Please don't tease me. This is very serious. He got my letter. He went to the post office and asked for his mail. He knew where I'd be staying. And about when I'd be here. So he called up. He's staying with a doctor he got to know down there. Doing some kind of work for him. I told you he had two years medical."

"Doctor have a name?"

"Yes. A funny name. Dr. Vincent Lagardie."

"Just a minute. There's somebody at the door."

I laid the phone down very carefully. I might be brittle. I might be made of spun glass. I got a handkerchief out and wiped the palm of my hand, the one that had been holding it. I got up and went to the built-in wardrobe and looked at my face in the flawed mirror. It was me all right. I had a strained look. I'd been living too fast.

Dr. Vincent Lagardie, 965 Wyoming Street. Cattycorners from The Garland Home of Peace. Frame house on the corner. Quiet. Nice neighborhood. Friend of the extinct Clausen. Maybe. Not according to him. But still maybe.

I went back to the telephone and squeezed the jerks out of my voice. "How would you spell that?" I asked.

She spelled it – with ease and precision. "Nothing to do then, is there?" I said. "All jake to the angels – or whatever they say in Manhattan, Kansas."

"Stop sneering at me. Orrin's in a lot of trouble. Some —" her voice quivered a little and her breath came quickly, "some gangsters are after him."

"Don't be silly, Orfamay. They don't have gangsters in Bay City. They're all working in pictures. What's Dr. Lagardie's phone number?"

She gave it to me. It was right. I won't say the pieces were beginning to fall into place, but at least they were getting to look like parts of the same puzzle. Which is all I ever get or ask.

"Please go down there and see him and help him. He's afraid to leave the house. After all I did pay you."

"I gave it back."

"Well, I offered it to you again."

"You more or less offered me other things that are more than I'd care to take."

There was silence.

"All right," I said. "All right. If I can stay free that long. I'm in a lot of trouble myself."

"Why?"

"Telling lies and not telling the truth. It always catches up with me. I'm not as lucky as some people."

"But I'm not lying, Philip. I'm not lying. I'm frantic."

"Take a deep breath and get frantic so I can hear it."

"They might kill him," she said quietly.

"And what is Dr. Vincent Lagardie doing all this time?"

"He doesn't know, of course. Please, please go at once. I have the address here. Just a moment."

And the little bell rang, the one that rings far back at the end of the corridor, and is not loud, but you'd better hear it. No matter what other noises there are you'd better hear it.

"He'll be in the phone book," I said. "And by an odd coincidence I have a Bay City phone book. Call me around four. Or five. Better make it five."

I hung up quickly. I stood up and turned the radio off, not having heard a thing it said. I closed the windows again. I opened the drawer of my desk and took out the Luger and strapped it on. I fitted my hat on my head. On the way out I had another look at the face in the mirror.

I looked as if I had made up my mind to drive off a cliff.

21

THEY WERE JUST finishing a funeral service at The Garland Home of Peace. A big gray hearse was waiting at the side entrance. Cars were clotted along both sides of the street, three black sedans in a row at the side of Dr. Vincent Lagardie's establishment. People were coming sedately down the walk from the funeral chapel to the corner and getting into their cars. I stopped a third of a block away and waited. The cars didn't move. Then three people came out with a woman heavily veiled and all in black. They half carried her down to a big limousine. The boss mortician fluttered around making elegant little gestures and body movements as graceful as a Chopin ending. His composed gray face was long enough to wrap twice around his neck.

The amateur pallbearers carried the coffin out the side door and professionals eased the weight from them and slid it into the back of the hearse as smoothly as if it had no more weight than a pan of butter rolls. Flowers began to grow into a mound over it. The glass doors were closed and motors started all over the block.

A few moments later nothing was left but one sedan across the way and the boss mortician sniffing a tree-rose on his way back to count the take. With a beaming smile he faded into his neat colonial doorway and the world was still and empty again. The sedan that was left hadn't moved. I drove along and made a U-turn and came up behind it. The driver wore blue serge and a soft cap with a shiny peak. He was doing a crossword puzzle from the morning paper. I stuck a pair of those diaphanous mirror sunglasses on my nose and strolled past him toward Dr. Lagardie's place. He didn't look up. When I was a few yards ahead I took the glasses off and pretended to polish them on my handkerchief. I caught him in one of the mirror lenses. He still didn't look up. He was just a guy doing a crossword puzzle. I put the mirror glasses back on my nose, and went around to Dr. Lagardie's front door.

The sign over the door said: Ring and Enter. I rang, but the door wouldn't let me enter. I waited. I rang again. I waited again. There was silence inside. Then the door opened a crack very slowly, and the thin expressionless face over a white uniform looked out at me.

"I'm sorry. Doctor is not seeing any patients today." She blinked at the mirror glasses. She didn't like them. Her tongue moved restlessly inside her lips.

"I'm looking for a Mr. Quest. Orrin P. Quest."

"Who?" There was a dim reflection of shock behind her eyes.

"Quest. Q as in quintessential, U as in uninhibited, E as in Extrasensory, S as in Subliminal, T as in Toots. Put them all together and they spell Brother."

She looked at me as if I had just come up from the floor of the ocean with a drowned mermaid under my arm.

"I beg your pardon. Dr. Lagardie is not —"

She was pushed out of the way by invisible hands and a thin dark haunted man stood in the half-open doorway.

"I am Dr. Lagardie. What is it, please?"

I gave him a card. He read it. He looked at me. He had the white pinched look of a man who is waiting for a disaster to happen.

"We talked over the phone," I said. "About a man named Clausen."

"Please come in," he said quickly. "I don't remember, but come in."

353

I went in. The room was dark, the blinds drawn, the windows closed. It was dark, and it was cold.

The nurse backed away and sat down behind a small desk. It was an ordinary living room with light painted woodwork which had once been dark, judging by the probable age of the house. A square arch divided the living room from the dining room. There were easy chairs and a center table with magazines. It looked like what it was – the reception room of a doctor practicing in what had been a private home.

The telephone rang on the desk in front of the nurse. She started and her hand went out and then stopped. She stared at the telephone. After a while it stopped ringing.

"What was the name you mentioned?" Dr. Lagardie asked me softly.

"Orrin Quest. His sister told me he was doing some kind of work for you, Doctor. I've been looking for him for days. Last night he called her up. From here, she said."

"There is no one of that name here," Dr. Lagardie said politely. "There hasn't been."

"You don't know him at all?"

"I have never heard of him."

"I can't figure why he would say that to his sister."

The nurse dabbed at her eyes furtively. The telephone on her desk burred and made her jump again. "Don't answer it," Dr. Lagardie said without turning his head.

We waited while it rang. Everybody waits while a telephone rings. After a while it stopped.

"Why don't you go home, Miss Watson? There's nothing for you to do here."

"Thank you, Doctor." She sat without moving, looking down at the desk. She squeezed her eyes shut and blinked them open. She shook her head hopelessly.

Dr. Lagardie turned back to me. "Shall we go into my office?"

354

We went across through another door leading to the hall-way. I walked on eggs. The atmosphere of the house was charged with foreboding. He opened a door and ushered me into what must have once been a bedroom, but nothing suggested a bedroom. It was a small compact doctor's office. An open door showed a part of an examination room. A sterilizer was working in the corner. There were a lot of needles cooking in it.

"That's a lot of needles," I said, always quick with an idea.

"Sit down, Mr. Marlowe."

He went behind the desk and sat down and picked up a long thin letter-opening knife.

He looked at me levelly from his sorrowful eyes. "No, I don't know anyone named Orrin Quest, Mr. Marlowe. I can't imagine any reason in the world why a person of that name should say he was in my house."

"Hiding out," I said.

His eyebrows went up. "From what?"

"From some guys that might want to stick an ice pick in the back of his neck. On account of he is a little too quick with his little Leica. Taking people's photographs when they want to be private. Or it could be something else, like peddling reefers and he got wise. Am I talking in riddles?"

"It was you who sent the police here," he said coldly.

I didn't say anything.

"It was you who called up and reported Clausen's death."

I said the same as before.

"It was you who called me up and asked me if I knew Clausen. I said I did not."

"But it wasn't true."

"I was under no obligation to give you information, Mr. Marlowe."

I nodded and got a cigarette out and lit it. Dr. Lagardie glanced at his watch. He turned in his chair and switched off the sterilizer. I looked at the needles. A lot of needles. Once before I had had trouble in Bay City with a guy who cooked a lot of needles.

"What makes it?" I asked him. "The yacht harbor?" He picked up the wicked-looking paper knife with a silver handle in the shape of a nude woman. He pricked the ball of his thumb. A pearl of dark blood showed on it. He put it to his mouth and licked it. "I like the taste of blood," he said softly.

There was a distant sound as of the front door opening and closing. We both listened to it carefully. We listened to retreating steps on the front steps of the house. We listened hard.

"Miss Watson has gone home," Dr. Lagardie said. "We are all alone in the house." He mulled that over and licked his thumb again. He laid the knife down carefully on the desk blotter. "Ah, the question of the yacht harbor," he added. "The proximity of Mexico you are thinking of, no doubt. The ease with which marihuana —"

"I wasn't thinking so much of marihuana any more." I stared again at the needles. He followed my stare. He shrugged.

I said: "Why so many of them?"

"Is it any of your business?"

"Nothing's any of my business."

"But you seem to expect your questions to be answered."

"I'm just talking," I said. "Waiting for something to happen. Something's going to happen in this house. It's leering at me from corners."

Dr. Lagardie licked another pearl of blood off his thumb.

I looked hard at him. It didn't buy me a way into his soul. He was quiet, dark and shuttered and all the misery of life was in his eyes. But he was still gentle.

"Let me tell you about the needles," I said.

"By all means." He picked the long thin knife up again.

"Don't do that," I said sharply. "It gives me the creeps. Like petting snakes."

He put the knife down again gently and smiled. "We do seem to talk in circles," he suggested.

"We'll get there. About the needles. A couple of years back I had a case that brought me down here and mixed me up with a doctor named Almore. Lived over on Altair Street. He had a funny practice. Went out nights with a big case of hypodermic needles – all ready to go. Loaded with the stuff. He had a peculiar practice. Drunks, rich junkies, of whom there are far more than people think, overstimulated people who had driven themselves beyond the possibility of relaxing. Insomniacs – all the neurotic types that can't take it cold. Have to have their little pills and little shots in the arm. Have to have help over the humps. It gets to be all humps after a while. Good business for the doctor. Almore was the doctor for them. It's all right to say it now. He died a year or so back. Of his own medicine."

"And you think I may have inherited his practice?"

"Somebody would. As long as there are the patients, there will be the doctor."

He looked even more exhausted than before. "I think you are an ass, my friend. I did not know Dr. Almore. And I do not have the sort of practice you attribute to him. As for the needles – just to get that trifle out of the way – they are in somewhat constant use in the medical profession today, often for such innocent medicaments as vitamin injections. And needles get dull. And when they are dull they are painful. Therefore in the course of the day one may use a dozen or more. Without narcotics in a single one."

He raised his head slowly and stared at me with a fixed contempt.

"I can be wrong," I said. "Smelling that reefer smoke over at Clausen's place yesterday, and having him call your number on the telephone – and call you by your first name – all this probably made me jump to wrong conclusions."

"I have dealt with addicts," he said. "What doctor has not? It is a complete waste of time."

357

"They get cured sometimes."

"They can be deprived of their drug. Eventually after great suffering they can do without it. That is not curing them, my friend. That is not removing the nervous or emotional flaw which made them become addicts. It is making them dull negative people who sit in the sun and twirl their thumbs and die of sheer boredom and inanition."

"That's a pretty raw theory, Doctor."

"You raised the subject. I have disposed of it. I will raise another subject. You may have noticed a certain atmosphere and strain about this house. Even with those silly mirror glasses on. Which you may now remove. They don't make you look in the least like Cary Grant."

I took them off. I'd forgotten all about them.

"The police have been here, Mr. Marlowe. A certain Lieutenant Maglashan, who is investigating Clausen's death. He would be pleased to meet you. Shall I call him? I'm sure he would come back."

"Go ahead, call him," I said. "I just stopped off here on my way to commit suicide."

His hand went towards the telephone but was pulled to one side by the magnetism of the paper knife. He picked it up again. Couldn't leave it alone, it seemed.

"You could kill a man with that," I said.

"Very easily," and he smiled a little.

"An inch and a half in the back of the neck, square in the center, just under the occipital bulge."

"An ice pick would be better," he said. "Especially a short one, filed down very sharp. It would not bend. If you miss the spinal cord, you do no great damage."

"Takes a bit of medical knowledge then?" I got out a poor old package of Camels and untangled one from the cellophane.

He just kept on smiling. Very faintly, rather sadly. It was not the smile of a man in fear. "That would help," he said softly.

"But any reasonably dexterous person could acquire the technique in ten minutes."

"Orrin Quest had a couple of years medical," I said.

"I told you I did not know anybody of that name."

"Yeah, I know you did. I didn't quite believe you."

He shrugged his shoulders. But his eyes as always went to the knife in the end.

"We're a couple of sweethearts," I said. "We just sit here making with the old over-the-desk dialogue. As though we hadn't a care in the world. Because both of us are going to be in the clink by nightfall."

He raised his eyebrows again. I went on:

"You, because Clausen knew you by your first name. And you may have been the last man he talked to. Me, because I've been doing all the things a P.I. never gets away with. Hiding evidence, hiding information, finding bodies and not coming in with my hat in my hand to these lovely incorruptible Bay City cops. Oh, I'm through. Very much through. But there's a wild perfume in the air this afternoon. I don't seem to care. Or I'm in love. I just don't seem to care."

"You have been drinking," he said slowly.

"Only Chanel No. 5, and kisses, and the pale glow of lovely legs, and the mocking invitation in deep blue eyes. Innocent things like that."

He just looked sadder than ever. "Women can weaken a man terribly, can they not?" he said.

"Clausen."

"A hopeless alcoholic. You probably know how they are. They drink and drink and don't eat. And little by little the vitamin deficiency brings on the symptoms of delirium. There is only one thing to do for them." He turned and looked at the sterilizer. "Needles, and more needles. It makes me feel dirty. I am a graduate of the Sorbonne. But I practice among dirty little people in a dirty little town."

"Why?"

359

"Because of something that happened years ago – in another city. Don't ask me too much, Mr. Marlowe."

"He used your first name."

"It is a habit with people of a certain class. Onetime actors especially. And onetime crooks."

"Oh," I said. "That all there is to it?"

"All."

"Then the cops coming here doesn't bother you on account of Clausen. You're just afraid of this other thing that happened somewhere else long gone. Or it could even be love."

"Love?" He dropped the word slowly off the end of his tongue, tasting it to the last. A bitter little smile stayed after the word, like powder smell in the air after a gun is fired. He shrugged and pushed a desk cigarette box from behind a filing tray and over to my side of the desk.

"Not love then," I said. "I'm trying to read your mind. Here you are a guy with a Sorbonne degree and a cheap little practice in a cheap and nasty little town. I know it well. So what are you doing here? What are you doing with people like Clausen? What was the rap, Doctor? Narcotics, abortions, or were you by any chance a medic for the gang boys in some hot Eastern city?"

"As for instance?" he smiled thinly.

"As for instance Cleveland."

"A very wild suggestion, my friend." His voice was like ice now.

"Wild as all hell," I said. "But a fellow like me with very limited brain tends to fit the things he knows into a pattern. It's often wrong, but it's an occupational disease with me. It goes like this, if you want to listen."

"I am listening." He picked the knife up again and pricked lightly at the blotter on his desk.

"'You knew Clausen. Clausen was killed very skillfully with an ice pick, killed while I was in the house, upstairs talking to a grifter named Hicks. Hicks moved out fast taking a page of the register with him, the page that had Orrin Quest's name on it. Later that afternoon Hicks was killed with an ice pick in L.A. His room had been searched. There was a woman there who had come to buy something from him. She didn't get it. I had more time to search. I did get it. Presumption A: Clausen and Hicks killed by same man, not necessarily for same reason. Hicks killed because he muscled in on another guy's racket and muscled the other guy out. Clausen killed because he was a babbling drunk and might know who would be likely to kill Hicks. Any good so far?"

"Not the slightest interest to me," Dr. Lagardie said.

"But you *are* listening. Sheer good manners, I suppose. Okay. Now what did I find? A photo of a movie queen and an ex-Cleveland gangster, maybe, on a particular day. Day when the ex-Cleveland gangster was supposed to be in hock at the County Jail, also day when ex-Cleveland gangster's onetime sidekick was shot dead on Franklin Avenue in Los Angeles. Why was he in hock? Tip-off that he was who he was, and say what you like against the L.A. cops they do try to run back-East hot shots out of town. Who gave them the tip? The guy they pinched gave it to them himself, because his ex-partner was being troublesome and had to be rubbed out, and being in jail was a first-class alibi when it happened."

"All fantastic," Dr. Lagardie smiled wearily. "Utterly fantastic."

"Sure. It gets worse. Cops couldn't prove anything on ex-gangster. Cleveland police not interested. The L.A. cops turn him loose. But they wouldn't have turned him loose if they'd seen that photo. Photo therefore strong blackmail material, first against ex-Cleveland character, if he really is the guy; secondly against movie queen for being seen around with him in public. A good man could make a fortune out of that photo. Hicks not good enough. Paragraph. Presumption B: Orrin Quest, the boy I'm trying to find, took that photo. Taken with

Contax or Leica, without flashbulb, without subjects knowing they were being photographed. Quest had a Leica and liked to do things like that. In this case of course he had a more commercial motive. Question, how did he get a chance to take photo? Answer, the movie queen was his sister. She would let him come up and speak to her. He was out of work, needed money. Likely enough she gave him some and made it a condition he stay away from her. She wants no part of her family. Is it still utterly fantastic, Doctor?"

He stared at me moodily. "I don't know," he said slowly. "It begins to have possibilities. But why are you telling this rather dangerous story to me?"

He reached a cigarette out of the box and tossed me one casually. I caught it and looked it over. Egyptian, oval and fat, a little rich for my blood. I didn't light it, just sat holding it between my fingers, watching his dark unhappy eyes. He lit his own cigarette and puffed nervously.

"I'll tie you in on it now," I said. "You knew Clausen. Professionally, you said. I showed him I was a dick. He tried at once to call you up. He was too drunk to talk to you. I caught the number and later told you he was dead. Why? If you were on the level, you would call the cops. You didn't. Why? You knew Clausen, you could have known some of his roomers. No proof either way. Paragraph. Presumption C: you knew Hicks or Orrin Quest or both. The L.A. cops couldn't or didn't establish identity of ex-Cleveland character – let's give him his new name, call him Steelgrave. But *somebody* had to be able to – if that photo was worth killing people over. Did you ever practice medicine in Cleveland, Doctor?"

"Certainly not." His voice seemed to come from far off. His eyes were remote too. His lips opened barely enough to admit his cigarette. He was very still.

I said: "They have a whole roomful of directories over at the telephone office. From all over the country. I checked you up."

"A suite in a downtown office building," I said. "And now this – an almost furtive practice in a little beach town. You'd have liked to change your name – but you couldn't and keep your license. Somebody had to mastermind this deal, Doctor. Clausen was a bum. Hicks a stupid lout, Orrin Quest a nasty-minded creep. But they could be used. You couldn't go up against Steelgrave directly. You wouldn't have stayed alive long enough to brush your teeth. You had to work through pawns – expendable pawns. Well – are we getting anywhere?"

He smiled faintly and leaned back in his chair with a sigh. "Presumption D, Mr. Marlowe," he almost whispered. "You are an unmitigated idiot."

I grinned and reached for a match to light his fat Egyptian cigarette.

"Added to all the rest," I said, "Orrin's sister calls me up and tells me he is in your house. There are a lot of weak arguments taken one at a time, I admit. But they do seem to sort of focus on you." I puffed peacefully on the cigarette.

He watched me. His face seemed to fluctuate and become vague, to move far off and come back. I felt a tightness in my chest. My mind had slowed to a turtle's gallop.

"What's going on here?" I heard myself mumble.

I put my hands on the arms of the chair and pushed myself up. "Been dumb, haven't I?" I said, with the cigarette still in my mouth and me still smoking it. Dumb was hardly the word. Have to coin a new word.

I was out of the chair and my feet were stuck in two barrels of cement. When I spoke my voice seemed to come through cottonwool.

I let go of the arms of the chair and reached for the cigarette. I missed it clean a couple of times, then got my hand around it. It didn't feel like a cigarette. It felt like the hind leg of an elephant. With sharp toenails. They stuck into my hand. I shook my hand and the elephant took his leg away.

A vague but enormously tall figure swung around in front of me and a mule kicked me in the chest. I sat down on the floor.

"A little potassium hydrocyanide," a voice said, over the transatlantic telephone. "Not fatal, not even dangerous. Merely relaxing. . . ."

I started to get up off the floor. You ought to try it sometime. But have somebody nail the floor down first. This one looped the loop. After a while it steadied a little. I settled for an angle of forty-five degrees. I took hold of myself and started to go somewhere. There was a thing that might have been Napoleon's tomb on the horizon. That was a good enough objective. I started that way. My heart beat fast and thick and I was having trouble opening my lungs. Like after being winded at football. You think your breath will never come back. Never, never, never.

Then it wasn't Napoleon's tomb any more. It was a raft on a swell. There was a man on it. I'd seen him somewhere. Nice fellow. We'd got on fine. I started towards him and hit a wall with my shoulder. That spun me around. I started clawing for something to hold on to. There was nothing but the carpet. How did I get down there? No use asking. It's a secret. Every time you ask a question they just push the floor in your face. Okay, I started to crawl along the carpet. I was on what formerly had been my hands and knees. No sensation proved it. I crawled towards a dark wooden wall. Or it could have been black marble. Napoleon's tomb again. What did I ever do to Napoleon? What for should he keep shoving his tomb at me?

"Need a drink of water," I said.

I listened for the echo. No echo. Nobody said anything. Maybe I didn't say it. Maybe it was just an idea I thought better of. Potassium cyanide. That's a couple of long words to be worrying about when you're crawling through tunnels. Nothing fatal, he said. Okay, this is just fun. What you might call semi-fatal. Philip Marlowe, 38, a private license operator of shady reputation, was apprehended by police last night while crawling through the Ballona Storm Drain with a grand piano on his back. Questioned at the University Heights Police station Marlowe declared he was taking the piano to the Maharajah of Coot-Berar. Asked why he was wearing spurs Marlowe declared that a client's confidence was sacred. Marlowe is being held for investigation. Chief Hornside said police were not yet ready to say more. Asked if the piano was in tune Chief Hornside declared that he had played the Minute Waltz on it in thirty-five seconds and so far as he could tell there were no strings in the piano. He intimated that something else was. A complete statement to the press will be made within twelve hours, Chief Hornside said abruptly. Speculation is rife that Marlowe was attempting to dispose of a body.

A face swam towards me out of the darkness. I changed direction and started for the face. But it was too late in the afternoon. The sun was setting. It was getting dark rapidly. There was no face. There was no wall, no desk. Then there was no floor. There was nothing at all.

I wasn't even there.

22

A BIG BLACK gorilla with a big black paw had his big black paw over my face and was trying to push it through the back of my neck. I pushed back. Taking the weak side of an argument is my specialty. Then I realized that he was trying to keep me from opening my eyes.

I decided to open my eyes just the same. Others have done it, why not me? I gathered my strength and very slowly, keeping the back straight, flexing the thighs and knees, using the arms as ropes, I lifted the enormous weight of my eyelids.

I was looking at the ceiling, lying on my back on the floor, a position in which my calling has occasionally placed me.

I rolled my head. My lungs felt stiff and my mouth felt dry. The room was just Dr. Lagardie's consulting room. Same chair, same desk, same walls and window. There was a shuttered silence hanging around.

I got up on my haunches and braced myself on the floor and shook my head. It went into a flat spin. It spun down about five thousand feet and then I dragged it out and leveled off. I blinked. Same floor, same desk, same walls. But no Dr. Lagardie.

I wet my lips and made some kind of a vague noise to which nobody paid any attention. I got up on my feet. I was as dizzy as a dervish, as weak as a worn-out washer, as low as a badger's belly, as timid as a titmouse, and as unlikely to succeed as a ballet dancer with a wooden leg.

I groped my way over behind the desk and slumped into Lagardie's chair and began to paw fitfully through his equipment for a likely-looking bottle of liquid fertilizer. Nothing doing. I got up again. I was as hard to lift as a dead elephant. I staggered around looking into cabinets of shining white enamel which contained everything somebody else was in a hurry for. Finally, after what seemed like four years on the road gang, my little hand closed around six ounces of ethyl alcohol. I got the top off the bottle and sniffed. Grain alcohol. Just what the label said. All I needed now was a glass and some water. A good man ought to be able to get that far. I started through the door to the examination room. The air still had the aromatic perfume of overripe peaches. I hit both sides of the doorway going through and paused to take a fresh sighting.

At that moment I was aware that steps were coming down the hall. I leaned against the wall wearily and listened.

Slow, dragging steps with a long pause between each. At first they seemed furtive. Then they just seemed very, very tired. An old man trying to make it to his last armchair. That made two of us. And then I thought, for no reason at all, of

Orfamay's father back there on the porch in Manhattan, Kansas, moving quietly along to his rocking chair with his cold pipe in his hand, to sit down and look out over the front lawn and have himself a nice economical smoke that required no matches and no tobacco and didn't mess up the living-room carpet. I arranged his chair for him. In the shade at the end of the porch where the bougainvillea was thick I helped him sit down. He looked up and thanked me with the good side of his face. His fingernails scratched on the arms of the chair as he leaned back.

The fingernails scratched, but it wasn't on the arm of any chair. It was a real sound. It was close by, on the outside of a closed door that led from the examination room to the hall-way. A thin feeble scratch, possibly a young kitten wanting to be let in. Okay, Marlowe, you're an old animal lover. Go over and let the kitten in. I started. I made it with the help of the nice examination couch with the rings on the end and the nice clean towels. The scratching had stopped. Poor little kitten, outside and wanting in. A tear formed itself in my eye and trickled down my furrowed cheek. I let go of the examination table and made a smooth four yards to the door. The heart was bumping inside me. And the lungs still had that feeling of having been in storage for a couple of years. I took a deep breath and got hold of the doorknob and opened it. Just at the last moment it occurred to me to reach for a gun. It occurred to me but that's as far as I got. I'm a fellow that likes to take an idea over by the light and have a good look at it. I'd have had to let go of the doorknob. It seemed like too big an operation. I just twisted the knob and opened the door instead.

He was braced to the door frame by four hooked fingers made of white wax. He had eyes an eighth of an inch deep, pale gray-blue, wide open. They looked at me but they didn't see me. Our faces were inches apart. Our breathing met in midair. Mine was quick and harsh, his was the far-off whisper which has not yet begun to rattle. Blood bubbled from his mouth and ran down his chin. Something made me look down. Blood drained slowly down the inside of his trouser leg and out on his shoe and from his shoe it flowed without haste to the floor. It was already a small pool.

I couldn't see where he had been shot. His teeth clicked and I thought he was going to speak, or try to speak. But that was the only sound from him. He had stopped breathing. His jaw fell slack. Then the rattle started. It isn't a rattle at all, of course. It isn't anything like a rattle.

Rubber heels squeaked on the linoleum between the rug and the door sill. The white fingers slid away from the door frame. The man's body started to wind up on the legs. The legs refused to hold it. They scissored. His torso turned in midair, like a swimmer in a wave, and jumped at me.

In the same moment his other arm, the one that had been out of sight, came up and over in a galvanic sweep that seemed not to have any possible living impetus behind it. It fell across my left shoulder blade. Something besides the bottle of alcohol I had been holding thumped to the floor and rattled against the bottom of the wall.

I clamped my teeth hard and spread my feet and caught him under the arms. He weighed like five men. I took a step back and tried to hold him up. It was like trying to lift one end of a fallen tree. I went down with him. His head bumped the floor. I couldn't help it. There wasn't enough of me working to stop it. I straightened him out a bit and got away from him. I climbed up on my knees, and bent down and listened. The rattle stopped. There was a long silence. Then there was a muted sigh, very quiet and indolent and without urgency. Another silence. Another still slower sigh, languid and peaceful as a summer breeze drifting past the nodding roses.

Something happened to his face and behind his face, the indefinable thing that happens in that always baffling and inscrutable moment, the smoothing out, the going back over the years to the age of innocence. The face now had a vague inner amusement, an almost roguish lift at the corners of the mouth. All of which was very silly, because I knew damn well, if I ever knew anything at all, that Orrin P. Quest had not been that kind of boy.

In the distance a siren wailed. I stayed kneeling and listened. It wailed and went away. I got to my feet and went over and looked out of the side window. In front of The Garland Home of Peace another funeral was forming up. The street was thick with cars again. People walked slowly up the path past the tree roses. Very slowly, the men with their hats in their hands long before they reached the little colonial porch.

I dropped the curtain and went over and picked up the bottle of ethyl alcohol and wiped it off with my handkerchief and laid it aside. I was no longer interested in alcohol. I bent down again and the bee-sting between my shoulder blades reminded me that there was something else to pick up. A thing with a round white wooden handle that lay against the baseboard. An ice pick with a filed-down blade not more than three inches long. I held it against the light and looked at the needle-sharp tip. There might or might not have been a faint stain of my blood on it. I pulled a finger gently beside the point. No blood. The point was very sharp.

I did some more work with my handkerchief and then bent down and put the ice pick on the palm of his right hand, white and waxy against the dull nap of the carpet. It looked too arranged. I shook his arm enough to make it roll off his hand to the floor. I thought about going through his pockets, but a more ruthless hand than mine would have done that already.

In a flash of sudden panic I went through mine instead. Nothing had been taken. Even the Luger under my arm had been left. I dragged it out and sniffed at it. It had not been fired, something I should have known without looking. You don't walk around much after being shot with a Luger.

I stepped over the dark red pool in the doorway and looked along the hall. The house was still silent and waiting. The blood trail led me back and across to a room furnished like a den. There was a studio couch and a desk, some books and medical journals, an ashtray with five fat oval stubs in it. A metallic glitter near the leg of the studio couch turned out to be a used shell from an automatic – .32 caliber. I found another under the desk. I put them in my pocket.

I went back out and up the stairs. There were two bedrooms, both in use, one pretty thoroughly stripped of clothes. In an ashtray more of Dr. Lagardie's oval stubs. The other room contained Orrin Quest's meager wardrobe, his spare suit and overcoat neatly hung in the closet, his shirts and socks and underwear equally neat in the drawers of a chest. Under the shirts at the back I found a Leica with an F.2 lens.

I left all these things as they were and went back downstairs into the room where the dead man lay indifferent to these trifles. I wiped off a few more doorknobs out of sheer perverseness, hesitated over the phone in the front room, and left without touching it. The fact that I was still walking around was a pretty good indication that the good Dr. Lagardie hadn't killed anybody.

People were still crawling up the walk to the oddly undersized colonial porch of the funeral parlors across the street. An organ was moaning inside.

I went around the corner of the house and got into my car and left. I drove slowly and breathed deeply from the bottom of my lungs, but I still couldn't seem to get enough oxygen.

Bay City ends about four miles from the ocean. I stopped in front of the last drugstore. It was time for me to make one more of my anonymous phone calls. Come and pick up the body, fellows. Who am I? Just a lucky boy who keeps finding them for you. Modest too. Don't even want my name mentioned.

I looked at the drugstore and in through the plate-glass front. A girl with slanted cheaters was reading at a magazine. She looked something like Orfamay Quest. Something tightened up my throat.

I let the clutch in and drove on. She had a right to know first, law or no law. And I was far outside the law already.

23

I STOPPED AT the office door with the key in my hand. Then I went noiselessly along to the other door, the one that was always unlocked, and stood there and listened. She might be in there already, waiting, with her eyes shining behind the slanted cheaters and the small moist mouth willing to be kissed. I would have to tell her a harder thing than she dreamed of, and then after a while she would go and I would never see her again.

I didn't hear anything. I went back and unlocked the other door and picked the mail up and carried it over and dumped it on the desk. Nothing in it made me feel any taller. I left it and crossed to turn the latch in the other door and after a long slow moment I opened it and looked out. Silence and emptiness. A folded piece of paper lay at my feet. It had been pushed under the door. I picked it up and unfolded it.

"Please call me at the apartment house. Most urgent. I must see you." It was signed D.

I dialed the number of the Chateau Bercy and asked for Miss Gonzales. Who was calling, please? One moment please, Mr. Marlowe. Buzz, buzz. Buzz, buzz.

"'Allo?"

"The accent's a bit thick this afternoon."

"Ah, it is you, amigo. I waited so long in your funny little office. Can you come over here and talk to me?"

"Impossible. I'm waiting for a call."

"Well, may I come there?"

"What's it all about?"

"Nothing I could discuss on the telephone, amigo."

"Come ahead."

I sat there and waited for the telephone to ring. It didn't ring. I looked out of the window. The crowd was seething on the boulevard, the kitchen of the coffee shop next door was pouring the smell of Blue Plate Specials out of its ventilator shaft. Time passed and I sat there hunched over the desk, my chin in a hand, staring at the mustard-yellow plaster of the end wall, seeing on it the vague figure of a dying man with a short ice pick in his hand, and feeling the sting of its point between my shoulder blades. Wonderful what Hollywood will do to a nobody. It will make a radiant glamour queen out of a drab little wench who ought to be ironing a truck driver's shirts, a he-man hero with shining eyes and brilliant smile reeking of sexual charm out of some overgrown kid who was meant to go to work with a lunchbox. Out of a Texas car hop with the literacy of a character in a comic strip it will make an international courtesan, married six times to six millionaires and so blasé and decadent at the end of it that her idea of a thrill is to seduce a furniture mover in a sweaty undershirt.

And by remote control it might even take a small-town prig like Orrin Quest and make an ice-pick murderer out of him in a matter of months, elevating his simple meanness into the classic sadism of the multiple killer.

It took her a little over ten minutes to get there. I heard the door open and close and I went through to the waiting room and there she was, the All-American Gardenia. She hit me right between the eyes. Her own were deep and dark and unsmiling.

She was all in black, like the night before, but a tailor-made outfit this time, a wide black straw hat set at a rakish angle, the collar of a white silk shirt folded out over the collar of her jacket, and her throat brown and supple and her mouth as red as a new fire engine.

"I waited a long time," she said. "I have not had any lunch."

"I had mine," I said. "Cyanide. Very satisfying. I've only just stopped looking blue."

"I am not in an amusing mood this morning, amigo."

"You don't have to amuse me," I said. "I amuse myself. I do a brother act that has me rolling in the aisle. Let's go inside."

We went into my private thinking parlor and sat down.

"You always wear black?" I asked.

"But yes. It is more exciting when I take my clothes off."

"Do you have to talk like a whore?"

"You do not know much about whores, amigo. They are always most respectable. Except of course the very cheap ones."

"Yeah," I said. "Thanks for telling me. What is the urgent matter we have to talk about? Going to bed with you is not urgent. It can be done any day."

"You are in a nasty mood."

"Okay. I'm in a nasty mood."

She got one of her long brown cigarettes out of her bag and fitted it carefully into the golden tweezers. She waited for me to light it for her. I didn't so she lit it herself with a golden lighter.

She held this doohickey in a black gauntleted glove and stared at me out of depthless black eyes that had no laughter in them now.

"Would you like to go to bed with me?"

"Most anyone would. But let's leave sex out of it for now."

"I do not draw a very sharp line between business and sex," she said evenly. "And you cannot humiliate me. Sex is a net with which I catch fools. Some of these fools are useful and generous. Occasionally one is dangerous."

She paused thoughtfully.

I said: "If you're waiting for me to say something that lets on I know who a certain party is – okay, I know who he is."

373

"Can you prove it?"

"Probably not. The cops couldn't."

"The cops," she said contemptuously, "do not always tell all they know. They do not always prove everything they could prove. I suppose you know he was in jail for ten days last February."

"Yes."

"Did it not occur to you as strange that he did not get bail?"

"I don't know what charge they had him on. If it was as a material witness —"

"Do you not think he could get the charge changed to something bailable — if he really wanted to?"

"I haven't thought much about it," I lied. "I don't know the man."

"You have never spoken to him?" she asked idly, a little too idly.

I didn't answer.

She laughed shortly. "Last night, amigo. Outside Mavis Weld's apartment. I was sitting in a car across the street."

"I may have bumped into him accidentally. Was that the guy?"

"You do not fool me at all."

"Okay. Miss Weld was pretty rough with me. I went away sore. Then I meet this ginzo with her doorkey in his hand. I yank it out of his hand and toss it behind some bushes. Then I apologize and go get it for him. He seemed like a nice little guy too."

"Ver-ry nice," she drawled. "He was *my* boy friend also."

I grunted.

"Strange as it may seem I'm not a hell of a lot interested in your love life, Miss Gonzales. I assume it covers a wide field — all the way from Stein to Steelgrave."

"Stein?" she asked softly. "Who is Stein?"

"A Cleveland hot shot that got himself gunned in front of your apartment house last February. He had an apartment there. I thought perhaps you might have met him."

374

She let out a silvery little laugh. "Amigo, there are men I do not know. Even at the Chateau Bercy."

"Reports say he was gunned two blocks away," I said. "I like it better that it happened right in front. And you were looking out of the window and saw it happen. And saw the killer run away and just under a street light he turned back and the light caught his face and darned if it wasn't old man Steelgrave. You recognized him by his rubber nose and the fact that he was wearing his tall hat with the pigeons on it."

She didn't laugh.

"You like it better that way," she purred.

"We could make more money that way."

"But Steelgrave was in jail," she smiled. "And even if he was not in jail — even if, for example, I happened to be friendly with a certain Dr. Chalmers who was county jail physician at the time and he told me, in an intimate moment, that he had given Steelgrave a pass to go to the dentist — with a guard of course, but the guard was a reasonable man — on the very day Stein was shot — even if this happened to be true, would it not be a very poor way to use the information by blackmailing Steelgrave?"

"I hate to talk big," I said, "but I'm not afraid of Steelgrave — or a dozen like him in one package."

"But I am, amigo. A witness to a gang murder is not in a very safe position in this country. No, we will not blackmail Steelgrave. And we will not say anything about Mr. Stein, whom I may or may not have known. It is enough that Mavis Weld is a close friend of a known gangster and is seen in public with him."

"We'd have to prove he was a known gangster," I said.

"Can we not do that?"

"How?"

She made a disappointed mouth. "But I felt sure that was what you had been doing these last couple of days."

"Why?"

375

"I have private reasons."

"They mean nothing to me while you keep them private."

She got rid of the brown cigarette stub in my ashtray. I leaned over and squashed it out with the stub of a pencil. She touched my hand lightly with a gauntleted finger. Her smile was the reverse of anesthetic. She leaned back and crossed her legs. The little lights began to dance in her eyes. It was a long time between passes – for her.

"Love is such a dull word," she mused. "It amazes me that the English language so rich in the poetry of love can accept such a feeble word for it. It has no life, no resonance. It suggests to me little girls in ruffled summer dresses, with little pink smiles, and little shy voices, and probably the most unbecoming underwear."

I said nothing. With an effortless change of pace she became businesslike again.

"Mavis will get $75,000 a picture from now on, and eventually $150,000. She has started to climb and nothing will stop her. Except possibly a bad scandal."

"Then somebody ought to tell her who Steelgrave is," I said. "Why don't you? And incidentally, suppose we did have all this proof, what's Steelgrave doing all the time we're putting the bite on Weld?"

"Does he have to know? I hardly think she would tell him. In fact, I hardly think she would go on having anything to do with him. But that would not matter to us – if we had our proof. And if she knew we had it."

Her black gauntleted hand moved towards her black bag, stopped, drummed lightly on the edge of the desk, and so got back to where it could drop in her lap. She hadn't looked at the bag. I hadn't either.

I stood up. "I might happen to be under some obligation to Miss Weld. Ever think of that?"

She just smiled.

"And if that was so," I said, "don't you think it's about time you got the hell out of my office?"

She put her hands on the arms of her chair and started to get up, still smiling. I scooped the bag before she could change direction. Her eyes filled with glare. She made a spitting sound.

I opened the bag and went through it and found a white envelope that looked a little familiar. Out of it I shook the photo at The Dancers, the two pieces fitted together and pasted on another piece of paper.

I closed the bag and tossed it across to her.

She was on her feet now, her lips drawn back over her teeth. She was very silent.

"Interesting," I said and snapped a digit at the glazed surface of the print. "If it's not a fake. Is that Steelgrave?"

The silvery laugh bubbled up again. "You are a ridiculous character, amigo. You really are. I did not know they made such people any more."

"Prewar stock," I said. "We're getting scarcer every day. Where did you get this?"

"From Mavis Weld's purse in Mavis Weld's dressing room. While she was on the set."

"She know?"

"She does not know."

"I wonder where she got it."

"From you."

"Nonsense." I raised my eyebrows a few inches. "Where would *I* get it?"

She reached the gauntleted hand across the desk. Her voice was cold. "Give it back to me, please."

"I'll give it back to Mavis Weld. And I hate to tell you this, Miss Gonzales, but I'd never get anywhere as a blackmailer. I just don't have the engaging personality."

"Give it back to me!" she said sharply. "If you do not —"

She cut herself off. I waited for her to finish. A look of contempt showed on her smooth features.

"Very well," she said. "It is my mistake. I thought you were smart, I can see that you are just another dumb private eye.

This shabby little office," she waved a black gloved hand at it, "and the shabby little life that goes on here – they ought to tell me what sort of idiot you are."

"They do," I said.

She turned slowly and walked to the door. I got around the desk and she let me open it for her.

She went out slowly. The way she did it hadn't been learned at business college.

She went on down the hall without looking back. She had a beautiful walk.

The door bumped against the pneumatic doorcloser and very softly clicked shut. It seemed to take a long time to do that. I stood there watching it as if I had never seen it happen before. Then I turned and started back towards my desk and the phone rang.

I picked it up and answered it. It was Christy French. "Marlowe? We'd like to see you down at headquarters."

"Right away?"

"If not sooner," he said and hung up.

I slipped the pasted-together print from under the blotter and went over to put it in the safe with the others. I put my hat on and closed the window. There was nothing to wait for. I looked at the green tip on the sweep hand of my watch. It was a long time until five o'clock. The sweep hand went around and around the dial like a door-to-door salesman. The hands stood at four-ten. You'd think she'd have called up by now. I peeled my coat off and unstrapped the shoulder harness and locked it with the Luger in the desk drawer. The cops don't like you to be wearing a gun in their territory. Even if you have the right to wear one. They like you to come in properly humble, with your hat in your hand, and your voice low and polite, and your eyes full of nothing.

I looked at the watch again. I listened. The building seemed quiet this afternoon. After a while it would be silent and then the madonna of the dark-gray mop would come shuffling along the hall, trying doorknobs.

I put my coat back on and locked the communicating door and switched off the buzzer and let myself out into the hallway. And then the phone rang. I nearly took the door off its hinges getting back to it. It was her voice all right, but it had a tone I had never heard before. A cool balanced tone, not flat or empty or dead, or even childish. Just the voice of a girl I didn't know and yet did know. What was in that voice I knew before she said more than three words.

"I called you up because you told me to," she said. "But you don't have to tell me anything. I went down there."

I was holding the phone with both hands.

"You went down there," I said. "Yes, I heard that. So?"

"I – borrowed a car," she said. "I parked across the street. There were so many cars you would never have noticed me. There's a funeral home there. I wasn't following you. I tried to go after you when you came out but I don't know the streets down there at all. I lost you. So I went back."

"What did you go back for?"

"I don't really know. I thought you looked kind of funny when you came out of the house. Or maybe I just had a feeling. He being my brother and all. So I went back and rang the bell. And nobody answered the door. I thought that was funny too. Maybe I'm psychic or something. All of a sudden I seemed to have to get into that house. And I didn't know how to do it, but I had to."

"That's happened to me," I said, and it was my voice, but somebody had been using my tongue for sandpaper.

"I called the police and told them I had heard shots," she said. "They came and one of them got into the house through a window. And then he let the other one in. And after a while they let me in. And then they wouldn't let me go. I had to tell them all about it, who he was, and that I had lied about the shots, but I was afraid something had happened to Orrin. And I had to tell them about you too."

"That's all right," I said. "I'd have told them myself as soon as I could get a chance to tell *you*."

"It's kind of awkward for you, isn't it?"

"Yes."

"Will they arrest you or something?"

"They could."

"You left him lying there on the floor. Dead. You had to, I guess."

"I had my reasons," I said. "They won't sound too good, but I had them. It made no difference to him."

"Oh you'd have your reasons all right," she said. "You're very smart. You'd always have reasons for things. Well, I guess you'll have to tell the police your reasons too."

"Not necessarily."

"Oh yes, you will," the voice said, and there was a ring of pleasure in it I couldn't account for. "You certainly will. They'll make you."

"We won't argue about that," I said. "In my business a fellow does what he can to protect a client. Sometimes he goes a little too far. That's what I did. I've put myself where they can hurt me. But not entirely for you."

"You left him lying on the floor, dead," she said. "And I don't care what they do to you. If they put you in prison, I think I would like that. I bet you'll be awfully brave about it."

"Sure," I said. "Always a gay smile. Do you see what he had in his hand?"

"He didn't have anything in his hand."

"Well, lying near his hand."

"There wasn't anything. There wasn't anything at all. What sort of thing?"

"That's fine," I said. "I'm glad of that. Well, goodbye. I'm going down to headquarters now. They want to see me. Good luck, if I don't see you again."

"You'd better keep your good luck," she said. "You might need it. And I wouldn't want it."

"I did my best for you," I said. "Perhaps if you'd given me a little more information in the beginning —"

She hung up while I was saying it.

I put the phone down in its cradle as gently as if it was a baby. I got out a handkerchief and wiped the palms of my hands. I went over to the washbasin and washed my hands and face. I sloshed cold water on my face and dried off hard with the towel and looked at it in the mirror.

"You drove off a cliff all right," I said to the face.

24

IN THE CENTER of the room was a long yellow oak table. Its edges were unevenly grooved with cigarette burns. Behind it was a window with wire over the stippled glass. Also behind it with a mess of papers spread out untidily in front of him was Detective-Lieutenant Fred Beifus. At the end of the table leaning back on two legs of an armchair was a big burly man whose face had for me the vague familiarity of a face previously seen in a halftone on newsprint. He had a jaw like a park bench. He had the butt end of a carpenter's pencil between his teeth. He seemed to be awake and breathing, but apart from that he just sat.

There were two rolltop desks at the other side of the table and there was another window. One of the rolltop desks was backed to the window. A woman with orange-colored hair was typing out a report on a typewriter stand beside the desk. At the other desk, which was endways to the window, Christy French sat in a tilted-back swivel chair with his feet on the corner of the desk. He was looking out of the window, which was open and afforded a magnificent view of the police parking lot and the back of a billboard.

"Sit down there," Beifus said, pointing.

I sat down across from him in a straight oak chair without arms. It was far from new and when new had not been beautiful.

"This is Lieutenant Moses Maglashan of the Bay City police," Beifus said. "He don't like you any better than we do."

Lieutenant Moses Maglashan took the carpenter's pencil out of his mouth and looked at the teeth marks in the fat octagonal pencil butt. Then he looked at me. His eyes went over me slowly exploring me, noting me, cataloguing me. He said nothing. He put the pencil back in his mouth.

Beifus said: "Maybe I'm a queer, but for me you don't have no more sex appeal than a turtle." He half turned to the typing woman in the corner. "Millie."

She swung around from the typewriter to a shorthand notebook. "Name's Philip Marlowe," Beifus said. "With an 'e' on the end, if you're fussy. License number?"

He looked back at me. I told him. The orange queen wrote without looking up. To say she had a face that would have stopped a clock would have been to insult her. It would have stopped a runaway horse.

"Now if you're in the mood," Beifus told me, "you could start in at the beginning and give us all the stuff you left out yesterday. Don't try to sort it out. Just let it flow natural. We got enough stuff to check you as you go along."

"You want me to make a statement?"

"A very full statement," Beifus said. "Fun, huh?"

"This statement is to be voluntary and without coercion?"

"Yeah. They all are." Beifus grinned.

Maglashan looked at me steadily for a moment. The orange queen turned back to her typing. Nothing for her yet. Thirty years of it had perfected her timing.

Maglashan took a heavy worn pigskin glove out of his pocket and put it on his right hand and flexed his fingers.

"What's that for?" Beifus asked him.

"I bite my nails times," Maglashan said. "Funny. Only bite 'em on my right hand." He raised his slow eyes to stare at me. "Some guys are more voluntary than others," he said idly. "Something to do with the kidneys, they tell me. I've known guys of the not so voluntary type that had to go to the can every fifteen minutes for weeks after they got voluntary. Couldn't seem to hold water."

"Just think of that," Beifus said wonderingly.

"Then there's the guys can't talk above a husky whisper," Maglashan went on. "Like punch-drunk fighters that have stopped too many with their necks."

Maglashan looked at me. It seemed to be my turn.

"Then there's the type that won't go to the can at all," I said. "They try too hard. Sit in a chair like this for thirty hours straight. Then they fall down and rupture a spleen or burst a bladder. They overco-operate. And after sunrise court, when the tank is empty, you find them dead in a dark corner. Maybe they ought to have seen a doctor, but you can't figure everything, can you, Lieutenant?"

"We figure pretty close down in Bay City," he said. "When we got anything to figure with."

There were hard lumps of muscle at the corners of his jaws. His eyes had a reddish glare behind them.

"I could do lovely business with you," he said staring at me. "Just lovely."

"I'm sure you could, Lieutenant. I've always had a swell time in Bay City – while I stayed conscious."

"I'd keep you conscious a long long time, baby. I'd make a point of it. I'd give it my personal attention."

Christy French turned his head slowly and yawned. "What makes you Bay City cops so tough?" he asked. "You pickle your nuts in salt water or something?"

Beifus put his tongue out so that the tip showed and ran it along his lips.

"We've always been tough," Maglashan said, not looking at him. "We like to be tough. Jokers like this character here keep us tuned up." He turned back to me. "So you're the sweetheart that phoned in about Clausen. You're right handy with a pay phone, ain't you, sweetheart?"

I didn't say anything.

"I'm talking to you, sweetheart," Maglashan said. "I asked you a question, sweetheart. When I ask a question I get answered. Get that, sweetheart?"

"Keep on talking and you'll answer yourself," Christy French said. "And maybe you won't like the answer, and maybe you'll be so damn tough you'll have to knock yourself out with that glove. Just to prove it."

Maglashan straightened up. Red spots the size of half-dollars glowed dully on his cheeks.

"I come up here to get co-operation," he told French slowly. "The big razzoo I can get at home. From my wife. Here I don't expect the wise numbers to work out on me."

"You'll get co-operation," French said. "Just don't try to steal the picture with that nineteen-thirty dialogue." He swung his chair around and looked at me. "Let's take out a clean sheet of paper and play like we're just starting this investigation. I know all your arguments. I'm no judge of them. The point is do you want to talk or get booked as a material witness?"

"Ask the questions," I said. "If you don't like the answers, you can book me. If you book me, I get to make a phone call."

"Correct," French said, "*if* we book you. But we don't have to. We can ride the circuit with you. It might take days."

"And canned cornbeef hash to eat," Beifus put in cheerfully.

"Strictly speaking, it wouldn't be legal," French said. "But we do it all the time. Like you do a few things which you hadn't ought to do maybe. Would you say you were legal in this picture?"

"No."

Maglashan let out a deep-throated "Ha!"

I looked across at the orange queen who was back to her notebook, silent and indifferent.

"You got a client to protect," French said.

"Maybe."

"You mean you did have a client. She ratted on you."

I said nothing.

"Name's Orfamay Quest," French said, watching me.

"Ask your questions," I said.

"What happened down there in Idaho Street?"

"I went there looking for her brother. He'd moved away, she said, and she'd come out here to see him. She was worried. The manager, Clausen, was too drunk to talk sense. I looked at the register and saw another man had moved into Quest's room. I talked to this man. He told me nothing that helped."

French reached around and picked a pencil off the desk and tapped it against his teeth. "Ever see this man again?"

"Yes. I told him who I was. When I went back downstairs Clausen was dead. And somebody had torn a page out of the register. The page with Quest's name on it. I called the police."

"But you didn't stick around?"

"I had no information about Clausen's death."

"But you didn't stick around," French repeated. Maglashan made a savage noise in his throat and threw the carpenter's pencil clear across the room. I watched it bounce against the wall and floor and come to a stop.

"That's correct," I said.

"In Bay City," Maglashan said, "we could murder you for that."

"In Bay City you could murder me for wearing a blue tie," I said.

He started to get up. Beifus looked sideways at him and said: "Leave Christy handle it. There's always a second show."

385

"We could break you for that," French said to me without inflexion.

"Consider me broke," I said. "I never liked the business anyway."

"So you came back to your office. What then?"

"I reported to the client. Then a guy called me up and asked me over to the Van Nuys Hotel. He was the same guy I had talked to down on Idaho Street, but with a different name."

"You could have told us that, couldn't you?"

"If I had, I'd have had to tell you everything. That would have violated the conditions of my employment."

French nodded and tapped his pencil. He said slowly: "A murder wipes out agreements like that. Two murders ought to do it double. And two murders by the same method, treble. You don't look good, Marlowe. You don't look good at all."

"I don't even look good to the client," I said, "after today."

"What happened today?"

"She told me her brother had called her up from this doctor's house. Dr. Lagardie. The brother was in danger. I was to hurry on down and take care of him. I hurried on down. Dr. Lagardie and his nurse had the office closed. They acted scared. The police had been there." I looked at Maglashan.

"Another of his phone calls," Maglashan snarled.

"Not me this time," I said.

"All right. Go on," French said, after a pause.

"Lagardie denied knowing anything about Orrin Quest. He sent his nurse home. Then he slipped me a doped cigarette and I went away from there for a while. When I came to I was alone in the house. Then I wasn't. Orrin Quest, or what was left of him, was scratching at the door. He fell through it and died as I opened it. With his last ounce of strength he tried to stick me with an ice pick." I moved my shoulders. The place between them was a little stiff and sore, nothing more.

French looked hard at Maglashan. Maglashan shook his head, but French kept on looking at him. Beifus began to whistle under his breath. I couldn't make out the tune at first, and then I could. It was "Old Man Mose is Dead."

French turned his head and said slowly: "No ice pick was found by the body."

"I left it where it fell," I said.

Maglashan said: "Looks like I ought to be putting on my glove again." He stretched it between his fingers. "Somebody's a goddam liar and it ain't me."

"All right," French said. "All right. Let's not be theatrical. Suppose the kid did have an ice pick in his hand, that doesn't prove he was born holding one."

"Filed down," I said. "Short. Three inches from the handle to the tip of the point. That's not the way they come from the hardware store."

"Why would he want to stick you?" Beifus asked with his derisive grin. "You were his pal. You were down there to keep him safe for his sister."

"I was just something between him and the light," I said. "Something that moved and could have been a man and could have been the man that hurt him. He was dying on his feet. I'd never seen him before. If he ever saw me, I didn't know it."

"It could have been a beautiful friendship," Beifus said with a sigh. "Except for the ice pick, of course."

"And the fact that he had it in his hand and tried to stick me with it could mean something."

"For instance what?"

"A man in his condition acts from instinct. He doesn't invent new techniques. He got me between the shoulder blades, a sting, the feeble last effort of a dying man. Maybe it would have been a different place and a much deeper penetration if he had had his health."

Maglashan said: "How much longer we have to barber round with this monkey? You talk to him like he was human. Leave me talk to him my way."

"The captain doesn't like it," French said casually.

"Hell with the captain."

"The captain doesn't like small-town cops saying the hell with him," French said.

Maglashan clamped his teeth tight and the line of his jaw showed white. His eyes narrowed and glistened. He took a deep breath through his nose.

"Thanks for the co-operation," he said and stood up. "I'll be on my way." He rounded the corner of the table and stopped beside me. He put his left hand out and tilted my chin up again.

"See you again, sweetheart. In *my* town."

He lashed me across the face twice with the wrist end of the glove. The buttons stung sharply. I put my hand up and rubbed my lower lip.

French said: "For Chrissake, Maglashan, sit down and let the guy speak his piece. And keep your hands off him."

Maglashan looked back at him and said: "Think you can make me?"

French just shrugged. After a moment Maglashan rubbed his big hand across his mouth and strolled back to his chair. French said:

"Let's have your ideas about all this, Marlowe."

"Among other things Clausen was probably pushing reefers," I said. "I sniffed marihuana smoke in his apartment. A tough little guy was counting money in the kitchen when I got there. He had a gun and a sharpened rat-tail file, both of which he tried to use on me. I took them away from him and he left. He would be the runner. But Clausen was liquored to a point where you wouldn't want to trust him any more. They don't go for that in the organizations. The runner thought I was a dick. Those people wouldn't want Clausen picked up. He would be too easy to milk. The minute they smelled dick around the house Clausen would be missing."

French looked at Maglashan. "That make any sense to you?"

"It could happen," Maglashan said grudgingly.

French said: "Suppose it was so, what's it got to do with this Orrin Quest?"

"Anybody can smoke reefers," I said. "If you're dull and lonely and depressed and out of a job, they might be very attractive. But when you smoke them you get warped ideas and calloused emotions. And marihuana affects different people different ways. Some it makes very tough and some it just makes never-no-mind. Suppose Quest tried to put the bite on somebody and threatened to go to the police. Quite possibly all three murders are connected with the reefer gang."

"That don't jibe with Quest having a filed-down ice pick," Beifus said.

I said: "According to the lieutenant here he didn't have one. So I must have imagined that. Anyhow, he might just have picked it up. They might be standard equipment around Dr. Lagardie's house. Get anything on him?"

He shook his head, "Not so far."

"He didn't kill me, probably he didn't kill anybody," I said. "Quest told his sister – according to her – that he was working for Dr. Lagardie, but that some gangsters were after him."

"This Lagardie," French said, prodding at his blotter with a pen point, "what do you make of him?"

"He used to practice in Cleveland. Downtown in a large way. He must have had his reasons for hiding out in Bay City."

"Cleveland, huh?" French drawled and looked at a corner of the ceiling. Beifus looked down at his papers. Maglashan said:

"Probably an abortionist. I've had my eye on him for some time."

"Which eye?" Beifus asked him mildly.

Maglashan flushed.

French said: "Probably the one he didn't have on Idaho Street."

Maglashan stood up violently. "You boys think you're so goddam smart it might interest you to know that we're just a small town police force. We got to double in brass once in a while. Just the same I like that reefer angle. It might cut down my work considerable. I'm looking into it right now."

He marched solidly to the door and left. French looked after him. Beifus did the same. When the door closed they looked at each other.

"I betcha they pull that raid again tonight," Beifus said.

French nodded.

Beifus said: "In a flat over a laundry. They'll go down on the beach and pull in three or four vagrants and stash them in the flat and then they'll line them up for the camera boys after they pull the raid."

French said: "You're talking too much, Fred."

Beifus grinned and was silent. French said to me: "If you were guessing, what would you guess they were looking for in that room at the Van Nuys?"

"A claim check for a suitcase full of weed."

"Not bad," French said. "And still guessing, where would it have been?"

"I thought about that. When I talked to Hicks down at Bay City he wasn't wearing his muff. A man doesn't around the house. But he was wearing it on the bed at the Van Nuys. Maybe he didn't put it on himself."

French said: "So?"

I said: "Wouldn't be a bad place to stash a claim check."

French said: "You could pin it down with a piece of scotch tape. Quite an idea."

There was a silence. The orange queen went back to her typing. I looked at my nails. They weren't as clean as they might be. After the pause French said slowly:

"Don't think for a minute you're in the clear, Marlowe. Still guessing, how come Dr. Lagardie mentioned Cleveland to you?"

"I took the trouble to look him up. A doctor can't change his name if he wants to go on practicing. The ice pick made you think of Weepy Moyer. Weepy Moyer operated in Cleveland. Sunny Moe Stein operated in Cleveland. It's true the ice-pick technique was different, but it was an ice pick. You said yourself the boys might have learned. And always with these gangs there's a doctor somewhere in the background."

"Pretty wild," French said. "Pretty loose connection."

"Would I do myself any good if I tightened it up?"

"Can you?"

"I can try."

French sighed. "The little Quest girl is okay," he said. "I talked to her mother back in Kansas. She really did come out here to look for her brother. And she really did hire you to do it. She gives you a good write-up. Up to a point. She really did suspect her brother was mixed up in something wrong. You make any money on the deal?"

"Not much," I said. "I gave her back the fee. She didn't have much."

"That way you don't have to pay income tax on it," Beifus said.

French said, "Let's break this off. The next move is up to the D.A. And if I know Endicott, it will be a week from Tuesday before he decides how to play it." He made a gesture towards the door.

I stood up. "Will it be all right if I don't leave town?" I asked.

They didn't bother to answer that one.

I just stood there and looked at them. The ice-pick wound between my shoulders had a dry sting, and the flesh around the place was stiff. The side of my face and mouth smarted where Maglashan had sideswiped me with his well-used pigskin glove. I was in the deep water. It was dark and unclear and the taste of the salt was in my mouth.

They just sat there and looked back at me. The orange queen was clacking her typewriter. Cop talk was no more treat to her than legs to a dance director. They had the calm weathered faces of healthy men in hard condition. They had the eyes they always have, cloudy and gray like freezing water. The firm set mouth, the hard little wrinkles at the corners of the eyes, the hard hollow meaningless stare, not quite cruel and a thousand miles from kind. The dull ready-made clothes, worn without style, with a sort of contempt; the look of men who are poor and yet proud of their power, watching always for ways to make it felt, to shove it into you and twist it and grin and watch you squirm, ruthless without malice, cruel and yet not always unkind. What would you expect them to be? Civilization had no meaning for them. All they saw of it was the failures, the dirt, the dregs, the aberrations and the disgust.

"What you standing there for?" Beifus asked sharply. "You want us to give you a great big spitty kiss? No snappy comeback, huh? Too bad." His voice fell away into a dull drone. He frowned and reached a pencil off the desk. With a quick motion of his fingers he snapped it in half and held the two halves out on his palm.

"We're giving you that much break," he said thinly, the smile all gone. "Go on out and square things up. What the hell you think we're turning you loose for? Maglashan bought you a rain check. Use it."

I put my hand up and rubbed my lip. My mouth had too many teeth in it.

Beifus lowered his eyes to the table, picked up a paper and began to read it. Christy French swung around in his chair and put his feet on the desk and stared out of the open window at the parking lot. The orange queen stopped typing. The room was suddenly full of heavy silence, like a fallen cake.

I went on out, parting the silence as if I was pushing my way through water.

25

THE OFFICE WAS empty again. No leggy brunettes, no little girls with slanted glasses, no neat dark men with gangster's eyes.

I sat down at the desk and watched the light fade. The going-home sounds had died away. Outside the neon signs began to glare at one another across the boulevard. There was something to be done, but I didn't know what. Whatever it was it would be useless. I tidied up my desk, listening to the scrape of a bucket on the tiling of the corridor. I put my papers away in the drawer, straightened the pen stand, got out a duster and wiped off the glass and then the telephone. It was dark and sleek in the fading light. It wouldn't ring tonight. Nobody would call me again. Not now, not this time. Perhaps not ever.

I put the duster away folded with the dust in it, leaned back and just sat, not smoking, not even thinking. I was a blank man. I had no face, no meaning, no personality, hardly a name. I didn't want to eat. I didn't even want a drink. I was the page from yesterday's calendar crumpled at the bottom of the waste-basket.

So I pulled the phone towards me and dialed Mavis Weld's number. It rang and rang and rang. Nine times. That's a lot of ringing, Marlowe. I guess there's nobody home. Nobody home to you. I hung up. Who would you like to call now? You got a friend somewhere that might like to hear your voice? No. Nobody.

Let the telephone ring, please. Let there be somebody to call up and plug me into the human race again. Even a cop. Even a Maglashan. Nobody has to like me. I just want to get off this frozen star.

The telephone rang.

"Amigo," her voice said. "There is trouble. Bad trouble. She wants to see you. She likes you. She thinks you are an honest man."

"Where?" I asked. It wasn't really a question, just a sound I made. I sucked on a cold pipe and leaned my head on my hand, brooding at the telephone. It was a voice to talk to anyway.

"You will come?"

"I'd sit up with a sick parrot tonight. Where do I go?"

"I will come for you. I will be before your building in fifteen minutes. It is not easy to get where we go."

"How is it coming back," I asked, "or don't we care?"

But she had already hung up.

Down at the drugstore lunch counter I had time to inhale two cups of coffee and a melted-cheese sandwich with two slivers of ersatz bacon imbedded in it, like dead fish in the silt at the bottom of a drained pool.

I was crazy. I liked it.

26

IT WAS A black Mercury convertible with a light top. The top was up. When I leaned in at the door Dolores Gonzales slid over towards me along the leather seat.

"You drive please, amigo. I do not really ever like to drive."

The light from the drugstore caught her face. She had changed her clothes again, but it was still all black, save for a flame-colored shirt. Slacks and a kind of loose coat like a man's leisure jacket.

I leaned on the door of the car. "Why didn't she call me?"

"She couldn't. She did not have the number and she had very little time."

"Why?"

"It seemed to be while someone was out of the room for just a moment."

"And where is this place she called from?"

"I do not know the name of the street. But I can find the house. That is why I come. Please get into the car and let us hurry."

"Maybe," I said. "And again maybe I am not getting into the car. Old age and arthritis have made me cautious."

"Always the wisecrack," she said. "It is a very strange man."

"Always the wisecrack where possible," I said, "and it is a very ordinary guy with only one head – which has been rather harshly used at times. The times usually started out like this."

"Will you make love to me tonight?" she asked softly.

"That again is an open question. Probably not."

"You would not waste your time. I am not one of these synthetic blondes with a skin you could strike matches on. These ex-laundresses with large bony hands and sharp knees and unsuccessful breasts."

"Just for half an hour," I said, "let's leave the sex to one side. It's great stuff, like chocolate sundaes. But there comes a time you would rather cut your throat. I guess maybe I'd better cut mine."

I went around the car and slid under the wheel and started the motor.

"We go west," she said, "through the Beverly Hills and then farther on."

I let the clutch in and drifted around the corner to go south to Sunset. Dolores got one of her long brown cigarettes out.

"Did you bring a gun?" she asked.

"No. What would I want a gun for?" The inside of my left arm pressed against the Luger in the shoulder harness.

"It is better not perhaps." She fitted the cigarette into the little golden tweezer thing and lit it with the golden lighter. The light flaring in her face seemed to be swallowed up by her depthless black eyes.

I turned west on Sunset and swallowed myself up in three lanes of race-track drivers who were pushing their mounts hard to get nowhere and do nothing.

"What kind of trouble is Miss Weld in?"

"I do not know. She just said that it was trouble and she was much afraid and she needed you."

"You ought to be able to think up a better story than that."

She didn't answer. I stopped for a traffic signal and turned to look at her. She was crying softly in the dark.

"I would not hurt a hair of Mavis Weld's head," she said. "I do not quite expect that you would believe me."

"On the other hand," I said, "maybe the fact that you don't have a story helps."

She started to slide along the seat towards me.

"Keep to your own side of the car," I said. "I've got to drive this heap."

"You do not want my head on your shoulder?"

"Not in this traffic."

I stopped at Fairfax with the green light to let a man make a left turn. Horns blew violently behind. When I started again the car that had been right behind swung out and pulled level and a fat guy in a sweatshirt yelled:

"Aw go get yourself a hammock!"

He went on, cutting in so hard that I had to brake.

"I used to like this town," I said, just to be saying something and not to be thinking too hard. "A long time ago. There were trees along Wilshire Boulevard. Beverly Hills was a country town. Westwood was bare hills and lots offering at eleven hundred dollars and no takers. Hollywood was a bunch of frame houses on the interurban line. Los Angeles was just a big dry sunny place with ugly homes and no style, but goodhearted and peaceful. It had the climate they just yap about now. People used to sleep out on porches. Little groups who thought they were intellectual used to call it the Athens of America. It wasn't that, but it wasn't a neon-lighted slum either."

We crossed La Cienega and went into the curve of the Strip. The Dancers was a blaze of light. The terrace was packed. The parking lot was like ants on a piece of overripe fruit.

"Now we get characters like this Steelgrave owning restaurants. We get guys like that fat boy that bawled me out back there. We've got the big money, the sharp shooters, the percentage workers, the fast-dollar boys, the hoodlums out of New York and Chicago and Detroit – and Cleveland. We've got the flash restaurants and night clubs they run, and the hotels and apartment houses they own, and the grifters and con men and female bandits that live in them. The luxury trades, the pansy decorators, the lesbian dress designers, the riffraff of a big hard-boiled city with no more personality than a paper cup. Out in the fancy suburbs dear old Dad is reading the sports page in front of a picture window, with his shoes off, thinking he is high class because he has a three-car garage. Mom is in front of her princess dresser trying to paint the suitcases out from under her eyes. And Junior is clamped onto the telephone calling up a succession of high school girls that talk pigeon English and carry contraceptives in their make-up kit."

"It is the same in all big cities, amigo."

"Real cities have something else, some individual bony structure under the muck. Los Angeles has Hollywood – and hates it. It ought to consider itself damn lucky. Without Hollywood it would be a mail-order city. Everything in the catalogue you could get better somewhere else."

"You are bitter tonight, amigo."

"I've got a few troubles. The only reason I'm driving this car with you beside me is that I've got so much trouble a little more will seem like icing."

"You have done something wrong?" she asked and came close to me along the seat.

"Well, just collecting bodies," I said. "Depends on the point of view. The cops don't like the work done by us amateurs. They have their own service."

"What will they do to you?"

"They might run me out of town and I couldn't care less. Don't push me so hard. I need this arm to shift gears with."

She pulled away in a huff. "I think you are very nasty to get along with," she said. "Turn right at the Lost Canyon Road."

After a while we passed the University. All the lights of the city were on now, a vast carpet of them stretching down the slope to the south and on into the almost infinite distance. A plane droned overhead losing altitude, its two signal lights winking on and off alternately. At Lost Canyon I swung right skirting the big gates that led into Bel-Air. The road began to twist and climb. There were too many cars; the headlights glared angrily down the twisting white concrete. A little breeze blew down over the pass. There was the odor of wild sage, the acrid tang of eucalyptus, and the quiet smell of dust. Windows glowed on the hillside. We passed a big white two storied Monterey house that must have cost $70,000 and had a cut-out illuminated sign in front: "Cairn Terriers."

"The next to the right," Dolores said.

I made the turn. The road got steeper and narrower. There were houses behind walls and masses of shrubbery but you couldn't see anything. Then we came to the fork and there was a police car with a red spotlight parked at it and across the right side of the fork two cars parked at right angles. A torch waved up and down. I slowed the car and stopped level with the police car. Two cops sat in it smoking. They didn't move.

"What goes on?"

"Amigo, I have no idea at all." Her voice had a hushed withdrawn sound. She might have been a little scared. I didn't know what of.

A tall man, the one with the torch, came around the side of the car and poked the flash at me, then lowered it.

"We're not using this road tonight," he said. "Going any-where in particular?"

I set the brake, reached for a flash which Dolores got out of the glove compartment. I snapped the light on to the tall man. He wore expensive-looking slacks, a sport shirt with initials on the pocket and a polka-dot scarf knotted around his neck. He had horn-rimmed glasses and glossy wavy black hair. He looked as Hollywood as all hell.

I said: "Any explanation – or are you just making law?"

"The law is over there, if you want to talk to them." His voice held a tone of contempt. "We are merely private citizens. We live around here. This is a residential neighborhood. We mean to keep it that way."

A man with a sporting gun came out of the shadows and stood beside the tall man. He held the gun in the crook of his left arm, pointed muzzle down. But he didn't look as if he just had it for ballast.

"That's jake with me," I said. "I didn't have any other plans. We just want to go to a place."

"What place?" the tall man asked coolly.

I turned to Dolores. "What place?"

"It is a white house on the hill, high up," she said.

"And what did you plan to do up there?" the tall man asked.

"The man who lives there is my friend," she said tartly.

He shone the flash in her face for a moment. "You look swell," he said. "But we don't like your friend. We don't like characters that try to run gambling joints in this kind of neighborhood."

"I know nothing about a gambling joint," Dolores told him sharply.

"Neither do the cops," the tall man said. "They don't even want to find out. What's your friend's name, darling?"

"That is not of your business," Dolores spit at him.

"Go on home and knit socks, darling," the tall man said. He turned to me.

"The road's not in use tonight," he said. "Now you know why."

"Think you can make it stick?" I asked him.

"It will take more than you to change our plans. You ought to see our tax assessments. And those monkeys in the prowl car – and a lot more like them down at the City Hall – just sit on their hands when we ask for the law to be enforced."

I unlatched the car door and swung it open. He stepped back and let me get out. I walked over to the prowl car. The two cops in it were leaning back lazily. Their loudspeaker was turned low, just audibly muttering. One of them was chewing gum rhythmically.

"How's to break up this road block and let the citizens through?" I asked him.

"No orders, buddy. We're just here to keep the peace. Anybody starts anything, we finish it."

"They say there's a gambling house up the line."

"They say," the cop said.

"You don't believe them?"

"I don't even try, buddy," he said, and spit past my shoulder.

"Suppose I have urgent business up there."

He looked at me without expression and yawned.

"Thanks a lot, buddy," I said.

I went back to the Mercury, got my wallet out and handed the tall man a card. He put his flash on it, and said: "Well?"

He snapped the flash off and stood silent. His face began to take form palely in the darkness.

"I'm on business. To me it's important business. Let me through and perhaps you won't need this block tomorrow."

"You talk large, friend."

"Would I have the kind of money it takes to patronize a private gambling club?"

"*She* might," he flicked an eye at Dolores. "She might have brought you along for protection."

He turned to the shotgun man. "What do you think?"

"Chance it. Just two of them and both sober."

The tall one snapped his flash on again and made a side-sweep with it back and forth. A car motor started. One of the block cars backed around on to the shoulder. I got in and started the Mercury, went on through the gap and watched the block car in the mirror as it took up position again, then cut its high beam lights.

"Is this the only way in and out of here?"

"They think it is, amigo. There is another way, but it is a private road through an estate. We would have had to go around by the valley side."

"We nearly didn't get through," I told her. "This can't be very bad trouble anybody is in."

"I knew you would find a way, amigo."

"Something stinks," I said nastily. "And it isn't wild lilac."

"Such a suspicious man. Do you not even want to kiss me?"

"You ought to have used a little of that back at the road block. That tall guy looked lonely. You could have taken him off in the bushes."

She hit me across the mouth with the back of her hand. "You son of a bitch," she said casually. "The next driveway on the left, if you please."

We topped a rise and the road ended suddenly in a wide black circle edged with whitewashed stones. Directly ahead was a wire fence with a wide gate in it, and a sign on the gate: Private Road. No Trespassing. The gate was open and a padlock hung from one end of a loose chain on the posts. I turned the car around a white oleander bush and was in the motor yard of a long low white house with a tile roof and a four-car garage in the corner, under a walled balcony. Both the wide garage doors were closed. There was no light in the house. A high moon made a bluish radiance on the white stucco walls. Some of the lower windows were shuttered. Four packing cases full of trash stood in a row at the foot of the steps. There was a big garbage can up-ended and empty. There were two steel drums with papers in them.

There was no sound from the house, no sign of life. I stopped the Mercury, cut the lights and the motor, and just sat. Dolores moved in the corner. The seat seemed to be shaking. I reached across and touched her. She was shivering.

"What's the matter?"

"Get – get out, please," she said as if her teeth chattered.

"How about you?"

She opened the door on her side and jumped out. I got out my side and left the door hanging open, the keys in the lock. She came around the back of the car and as she got close to me I could almost feel her shaking before she touched me. Then she leaned up against me hard thigh to thigh and breast to breast. Her arms went around my neck.

"I am being very foolish," she said softly. "He will kill me for this – just as he killed Stein. Kiss me."

I kissed her. Her lips were hot and dry. "Is he in there?"

"Yes."

"Who else?"

"Nobody else – except Mavis. He will kill her too."

"Listen –"

"Kiss me again, I have not very long to live, amigo. When you are the finger for a man like that – you die young."

I pushed her away from me, but gently.

She stepped back and lifted her right hand quickly. There was a gun in it now.

I looked at the gun. There was a dull shine on it from the high moon. She held it level and her hand wasn't shaking now.

"What a friend I would make if I pulled this trigger," she said.

"They'd hear the shot down the road."

She shook her head. "No, there is a little hill between. I do not think they would hear, amigo."

I thought the gun would jump when she pulled the trigger. If I dropped just at the right moment –

I wasn't that good. I didn't say anything. My tongue felt large in my mouth.

She went on slowly, in a soft tired voice: "With Stein it did not matter. I would have killed him myself, gladly. That filth. To die is not much, to kill is not much. But to entice people to their deaths —" She broke off with what might have been a sob. "Amigo, I liked you for some strange reason. I should be far beyond such nonsense. Mavis took him away from me, but I did not want him to kill her. The world is full of men who have enough money."

"He seems like a nice little guy," I said, still watching the hand that held the gun. Not a quiver in it now.

She laughed contemptuously. "Of course he does. That is why he is what he is. You think you are tough, amigo. You are a very soft peach compared with Steelgrave." She lowered the gun and now it was my time to jump. I still wasn't good enough.

"He has killed a dozen men," she said. "With a smile for each one. I have known him for a long time. I knew him in Cleveland."

"With ice picks?" I asked.

"If I give you the gun, will you kill him for me?"

"Would you believe me if I promised?"

"Yes." Somewhere down the hill there was the sound of a car. But it seemed as remote as Mars, as meaningless as the chattering of monkeys in the Brazilian jungle. It had nothing to do with me.

"I'd kill him if I had to," I said licking along my lips.

I was leaning a little, knees bent, all set for a jump again.

"Good night, amigo. I wear black because I am beautiful and wicked — and lost."

She held the gun out to me. I took it. I just stood there holding it. For another silent moment neither of us moved. Then she smiled and tossed her head and jumped into the car. She started the motor and slammed the door shut. She idled the motor down and sat looking out at me. There was a smile on her face now.

"I was pretty good in there, no?" she said softly.

Then the car backed violently with a harsh tearing of the tires on the asphalt paving. The lights jumped on. The car curved away and was gone past the oleander bush. The lights turned left, into the private road. The lights drifted off among trees and the sound faded into the long-drawn whee of tree frogs. Then that stopped and for a moment there was no sound at all. And no light except the tired old moon.

I broke the magazine from the gun. It had seven shells in it. There was another in the breach. Two less than a full load. I sniffed at the muzzle. It had been fired since it was cleaned. Fired twice, perhaps.

I pushed the magazine into place again and held the gun on the flat of my hand. It had a white bone grip. .32 caliber.

Orrin Quest had been shot twice. The two exploded shells I picked up on the floor of the room were .32 caliber.

And yesterday afternoon, in Room 332 of the Hotel Van Nuys, a blonde girl with a towel in front of her face had pointed a .32-caliber automatic with a white bone grip at me.

You can get too fancy about these things. You can also not get fancy enough.

27

I WALKED ON rubber heels across to the garage and tried to open one of the two wide doors. There were no handles, so it must have been operated by a switch. I played a tiny pencil flash on the frame, but no switch looked at me.

I left that and prowled over to the trash barrels. Wooden steps went up to a service entrance. I didn't think the door would be unlocked for my convenience. Under the porch was another door. This was unlocked and gave on darkness and the smell of corded eucalyptus wood. I closed the door behind me and put the little flash on again. In the corner there was another staircase, with a thing like a dumb-waiter beside it. It wasn't dumb enough to let me work it. I started up the steps.

Somewhere remotely something buzzed. I stopped. The buzzing stopped. I started again. The buzzing didn't. I went on up to a door with no knob, set flush. Another gadget.

But I found the switch to this one. It was an oblong movable plate set into the door frame. Too many dusty hands had touched it. I pressed it and the door clicked and fell back off the latch. I pushed it open, with the tenderness of a young intern delivering his first baby.

Inside was a hallway. Through shuttered windows moonlight caught the white corner of a stove and the chromed griddle on top of it. The kitchen was big enough for a dancing class. An open arch led to a butler's pantry tiled to the ceiling. A sink, a huge icebox set into the wall, a lot of electrical stuff for making drinks without trying. You pick your poison, press a button, and four days later you wake up on the rubbing table in a reconditioning parlor.

Beyond the butler's pantry a swing door. Beyond the swing door a dark dining room with an open end to a glassed-in lounge into which the moonlight poured like water through the flood-gates of a dam.

A carpeted hall led off somewhere. From another flat arch a flying buttress of a staircase went up into more darkness, but shimmered as it went in what might have been glass brick and stainless steel.

At last I came to what should be the living room. It was curtained and quite dark, but it had the feel of great size. The darkness was heavy in it and my nose twitched at a lingering odor that said somebody had been there not too long ago. I stopped breathing and listened. Tigers could be in the darkness watching me. Or guys with large guns, standing flat-footed, breathing softly with their mouths open. Or nothing and nobody and too much imagination in the wrong place.

I edged back to the wall and felt around for a light switch. There's always a light switch. Everybody has light switches. Usually on the right side as you go in. You go into a dark room and you want light. Okay, you have a light switch in a natural place at a natural height. This room hadn't. This was a different kind of house. They had odd ways of handling doors and lights. The gadget this time might be something fancy like having to sing A above high C, or stepping on a flat button under the carpet, or maybe you just spoke and said: "Let there be light," and a mike picked it up and turned the voice vibration into a low-power electrical impulse and a transformer built that up to enough voltage to throw a silent mercury switch.

I was psychic that night. I was a fellow who wanted company in a dark place and was willing to pay a high price for it. The Luger under my arm and the .32 in my hand made me tough. Two-gun Marlowe, the kid from Cyanide Gulch.

I took the wrinkles out of my lips and said aloud:

"Hello again. Anybody here needing a detective?"

Nothing answered me, not even a stand-in for an echo. The sound of my voice fell on silence like a tired head on a swansdown pillow.

And then amber light began to grow high up behind the cornice that circumnavigated the huge room. It brightened very slowly, as if controlled by a rheostat panel in a theater. Heavy apricot-colored curtains covered the windows.

The walls were apricot too. At the far end was a bar off to one side, a little catty-corner, reaching back into the space by the butler's pantry. There was an alcove with small tables and padded seats. There were floor lamps and soft chairs and love seats and the usual paraphernalia of a living room, and there were long shrouded tables in the middle of the floor space.

The boys back at the road block had something after all. But the joint was dead. The room was empty of life. It was almost empty. Not quite empty.

A blonde in a pale cocoa fur coat stood leaning against the side of a grandfather's chair. Her hands were in the pockets of the coat. Her hair was fluffed out carelessly and her face was not chalk-white because the light was not white.

"Hello again yourself," she said in a dead voice. "I still think you came too late."

"Too late for what?"

I walked towards her, a movement which was always a pleasure. Even then, even in that too silent house.

"You're kind of cute," she said. "I didn't think you were cute. You found a way in. You –" Her voice clicked off and strangled itself in her throat.

"I need a drink," she said after a thick pause. "Or maybe I'll fall down."

"That's a lovely coat," I said. I was up to her now. I reached out and touched it. She didn't move. Her mouth moved in and out, trembling.

"Stone marten," she whispered. "Forty thousand dollars. Rented. For the picture."

"Is this part of the picture?" I gestured around the room.

"This is the picture to end all pictures – for me. I – I do need that drink. If I try to walk –" the clear voice whispered away into nothing. Her eyelids fluttered up and down.

"Go ahead and faint," I said. "I'll catch you on the first bounce."

A smile struggled to arrange her face for smiling. She pressed her lips together, fighting hard to stay on her feet.

"Why did I come too late?" I asked. "Too late for what?"

"Too late to be shot."

"Shucks, I've been looking forward to it all evening. Miss Gonzales brought me."

"I know."

I reached out and touched the fur again. Forty thousand dollars is nice to touch, even rented.

"Dolores will be disappointed as hell," she said, her mouth edged with white.

"No."

"She put you on the spot – just as she did Stein."

"She may have started out to. But she changed her mind."

She laughed. It was a silly pooped-out little laugh like a child trying to be supercilious at a playroom tea party.

"What a way you have with the girls," she whispered. "How the hell do you do it, wonderful? With doped cigarettes? It can't be your clothes or your money or your personality. You don't have any. You're not too young, nor too beautiful. You've seen your best days and —"

Her voice had been coming faster and faster, like a motor with a broken governor. At the end she was chattering. When she stopped a spent sigh drifted along the silence and she caved at the knees and fell straight forward into my arms.

If it was an act it worked perfectly. I might have had guns in all nine pockets and they would have been as much use to me as nine little pink candles on a birthday cake.

But nothing happened. No hard characters peeked at me with automatics in their hands. No Steelgrave smiled at me with the faint dry remote killer's smile. No stealthy footsteps crept up behind me.

She hung in my arms as limp as a wet tea towel and not as heavy as Orrin Quest, being less dead, but heavy enough to make the tendons in my knee joints ache. Her eyes were closed when I pushed her head away from my chest. Her breath was inaudible and she had that bluish look on the parted lips.

I got my right hand under her knees and carried her over to a gold couch and spread her out on it. I straightened up and went along to the bar. There was a telephone on the corner of it but I couldn't find the way through to the bottles. So I had to swing over the top. I got a likely-looking bottle with a blue and silver label and five stars on it. The cork had been loosened. I poured dark and pungent brandy into the wrong kind of glass and went back over the bar top, taking the bottle with me.

She was lying as I had left her, but her eyes were open.

"Can you hold a glass?"

She could, with a little help. She drank the brandy and pressed the edge of the glass hard against her lips as if she wanted to hold them still. I watched her breathe into the glass and cloud it. A slow smile formed itself on her mouth.

"It's cold tonight," she said.

She swung her legs over the edge of the couch and put her feet on the floor.

"More," she said, holding the glass out. I poured into it. "Where's yours?"

"Not drinking. My emotions are being worked on enough without that."

The second drink made her shudder. But the blue look had gone away from her mouth and her lips didn't glare like stop lights and the little etched lines at the corners of her eyes were not in relief any more.

"Who's working on your emotions?"

"Oh, a lot of women that keep throwing their arms around my neck and fainting on me and getting kissed and so forth. Quite a full couple of days for a beat-up gumshoe with no yacht."

"No yacht," she said. "I'd hate that. I was brought up rich."

"Yeah," I said. "You were born with a Cadillac in your mouth. And I could guess where."

Her eyes narrowed. "Could you?"

"Didn't think it was a very tight secret, did you?"

"I – I –" She broke off and made a helpless gesture. "I can't think of any lines tonight."

"It's the technicolor dialogue," I said. "It freezes up on you."

"Aren't we talking like a couple of nuts?"

"We could get sensible. Where's Steelgrave?"

She just looked at me. She held the empty glass out and I took it and put it somewhere or other without taking my eyes off her. Nor she hers off me. It seemed as if a long long minute went by.

"He was here," she said at last, as slowly as if she had to invent the words one at a time. "May I have a cigarette?"

409

"The old cigarette stall," I said. I got a couple out and put them in my mouth and lit them. I leaned across and tucked one between her ruby lips.

"Nothing's cornier than that," she said. "Except maybe butterfly kisses."

"Sex is a wonderful thing," I said. "When you don't want to answer questions."

She puffed loosely and blinked, then put her hand up to adjust the cigarette. After all these years I can never put a cigarette in a girl's mouth where she wants it.

She gave her head a toss and swung the soft loose hair around her cheeks and watched me to see how hard that hit me. All the whiteness had gone now. Her cheeks were a little flushed. But behind her eyes things watched and waited.

"You're rather nice," she said, when I didn't do anything sensational. "For the kind of guy you are."

I stood that well too.

"But I don't really know what kind of guy you are, do I?" She laughed suddenly and a tear came from nowhere and slid down her cheek. "For all I know you might be nice for any kind of guy." She snatched the cigarette loose and put her hand to her mouth and bit on it. "What's the matter with me? Am I drunk?"

"You're stalling for time," I said. "But I can't make up my mind whether it's to give someone time to get here – or to give somebody time to get far away from here. And again it could just be brandy on top of shock. You're a little girl and you want to cry into your mother's apron."

"Not my mother," she said. "I could get as far crying into a rain barrel."

"Dealt and passed. So where is Steelgrave?"

"You ought to be glad wherever he is. He had to kill you. Or thought he had."

"You wanted me here, didn't you? Were you that fond of him?"

She blew cigarette ash off the back of her hand. A flake of it went into my eye and made me blink.

"I must have been," she said, "once." She put a hand down on her knee and spread the fingers out, studying the nails. She brought her eyes up slowly without moving her head. "It seems like about a thousand years ago I met a nice quiet little guy who knew how to behave in public and didn't shoot his charm around every bistro in town. Yes, I liked him. I liked him a lot."

She put her hand up to her mouth and bit a knuckle. Then she put the same hand into the pocket of the fur coat and brought out a white-handled automatic, the brother of the one I had myself.

"And in the end I liked him with this," she said.

I went over and took it out of her hand. I sniffed the muzzle. Yes. That made two of them fired around.

"Aren't you going to wrap it up in a handkerchief, the way they do in the movies?"

I just dropped it into my other pocket, where it could pick up a few interesting crumbs of tobacco and some seeds that grow only on the southeast slope of the Beverly Hills City Hall. It might amuse a police chemist for a while.

28

I WATCHED HER for a minute, biting at the end of my lip. She watched me. I saw no change of expression. Then I started prowling the room with my eyes. I lifted up the dust cover on one of the long tables. Under it was a roulette layout but no wheel. Under the table was nothing.

"Try that chair with the magnolias on it," she said.

She didn't look towards it so I had to find it myself. Surprising how long it took me. It was a high-backed wing chair, covered in flowered chintz, the kind of chair that a long time ago was intended to keep the draft off while you sat crouched over a fire of cannel coal.

It was turned away from me. I went over there walking softly, in low gear. It almost faced the wall. Even at that it seemed ridiculous that I hadn't spotted him on my way back from the bar. He leaned in the corner of the chair with his head tilted back. His carnation was red and white and looked as fresh as though the flower girl had just pinned it into his lapel. His eyes were half open as such eyes usually are. They stared at a point in the corner of the ceiling. The bullet had gone through the outside pocket of his double-breasted jacket. It had been fired by someone who knew where the heart was.

I touched his cheek and it was still warm. I lifted his hand and let it fall. It was quite limp. It felt like the back of somebody's hand. I reached for the big artery in his neck. No blood moved in him and very little had stained his jacket. I wiped my hands off on my handkerchief and stood for a little longer looking down at his quiet little face. Everything I had done or not done, everything wrong and everything right – all wasted.

I went back and sat down near her and squeezed my kneecaps.

"What did you expect me to do?" she asked. "He killed my brother."

"Your brother was no angel."

"He didn't have to kill him."

"Somebody had to – and quick."

Her eyes widened suddenly.

I said: "Didn't you ever wonder why Steelgrave never went after me and why he let you go to the Van Nuys yesterday instead of going himself? Didn't you ever wonder why a fellow with his resources and experience never tried to get hold of those photographs, no matter what he had to do to get them?"

She didn't answer.

"How long have you known the photographs existed?" I asked.

"Weeks, nearly two months. I got one in the mail a couple of days after − after that time we had lunch together."

"After Stein was killed."

"Yes, of course."

"Did you think Steelgrave had killed Stein?"

"No. Why should I? Until tonight, that is."

"What happened after you got the photo?"

"My brother Orrin called me up and said he had lost his job and was broke. He wanted money. He didn't say anything about the photo. He didn't have to. There was only one time it could have been taken."

"How did he get your number?"

"Telephone? How did you?"

"Bought it."

"Well −" She made a vague movement with her hand. "Why not call the police and get it over with."

"Wait a minute. Then what? More prints of the photo?"

"One every week. I showed them to *him*." She gestured toward the chintzy chair. "He didn't like it. I didn't tell him about Orrin."

"He must have known. His kind find things out."

"I suppose so."

"But not where Orrin was hiding out," I said. "Or he wouldn't have waited this long. *When* did you tell Steelgrave?"

She looked away from me. Her fingers kneaded her arm. "Today," she said in a distant voice.

"Why today?"

Her breath caught in her throat. "Please," she said. "Don't ask me a lot of useless questions. Don't torment me. There's nothing you can do. I thought there was − when I called Dolores. There isn't now."

I said: "All right. There's something you don't seem to understand. Steelgrave knew that whoever was behind that photograph wanted money − a lot of money. He knew that sooner or later the blackmailer would have to show himself.

That was what Steelgrave was waiting for. He didn't care anything about the photo itself, except for your sake."

"He certainly proved that," she said wearily.

"In his own way," I said.

Her voice came to me with glacial calm. "He killed my brother. He told me so himself. The gangster showed through then all right. Funny people you meet in Hollywood, don't you – including me."

"You were fond of him once," I said brutally.

Red spots flared on her cheeks.

"I'm not fond of anybody," she said. "I'm all through being fond of people." She glanced briefly towards the highbacked chair. "I stopped being fond of him last night. He asked me about you, who you were and so on. I told him. I told him that I would have to admit that I was at the Van Nuys Hotel when that man was lying there dead."

"You were going to tell the police that?"

"I was going to tell Julius Oppenheimer. He would know how to handle it."

"If he didn't one of his dogs would," I said.

She didn't smile. I didn't either.

"If Oppenheimer couldn't handle it, I'd be through in pictures," she added without interest. "Now I'm through everywhere else as well."

I got a cigarette out and lit it. I offered her one. She didn't want one. I wasn't in any hurry. Time seemed to have lost its grip on me. And almost everything else. I was flat out.

"You're going too fast for me," I said, after a moment. "You didn't know when you went to the Van Nuys that Steelgrave was Weepy Moyer."

"No."

"Then what did you go there for?"

"To buy back those photographs."

"That doesn't check. The photographs didn't mean anything to you then. They were just you and him having lunch."

She stared at me and winked her eyes tight, then opened them wide. "I'm not going to cry," she said. "I said I didn't *know*. But when he was in jail that time, I had to know there was something about him that he didn't care to have known. I knew he had been in some kind of racket, I guess. But not killing people."

I said: "Uh-huh." I got up and walked around the high-backed chair again. Her eyes traveled slowly to watch me. I leaned over the dead Steelgrave and felt under his arm on the left side. There was a gun there in the holster. I didn't touch it. I went back and sat down opposite her again.

"It's going to cost a lot of money to fix this," I said.

For the first time she smiled. It was a very small smile, but it was a smile. "I don't have a lot of money," she said. "So that's out."

"Oppenheimer has. You're worth millions to him by now."

"He wouldn't chance it. Too many people have their knives into the picture business these days. He'll take his loss and forget it in six months."

"You said you'd go to him."

"I said if I got into a jam and hadn't really done anything, I'd go to him. But I have done something now."

"How about Ballou? You're worth a lot to him too."

"I'm not worth a plugged nickel to anybody. Forget it, Marlowe. You mean well, but I know these people."

"That puts it up to me," I said. "That would be why you sent for me."

"Wonderful," she said. "You fix it, darling. For free." Her voice was brittle and shallow again.

I went and sat beside her on the davenport. I took hold of her arm and pulled her hand out of the fur pocket and took hold of that. It was almost ice cold, in spite of the fur.

She turned her head and looked at me squarely. She shook her head a little. "Believe me, darling, I'm not worth it − even to sleep with."

415

I turned the hand over and opened the fingers out. They were stiff and resisted. I opened them out one by one. I smoothed the palm of her hand.

"Tell me why you had the gun with you."

"The gun?"

"Don't take time to think. Just tell me. Did you mean to kill him?"

"Why not, darling? I thought I meant something to him. I guess I'm a little vain. He fooled me. Nobody means anything to the Steelgraves of this world. And nobody means anything to the Mavis Welds of this world any more."

She pulled away from me and smiled thinly. "I oughtn't to have given you that gun. If I killed you I might get clear yet."

I took it out and held it towards her. She took it and stood up quickly. The gun pointed at me. The small tired smile moved her lips again. Her finger was very firm on the trigger.

"Shoot high," I said. "I'm wearing my bullet-proof underwear."

She dropped the gun to her side and for a moment she just stood staring at me. Then she tossed the gun down on the davenport.

"I guess I don't like the script," she said. "I don't like the lines. It just isn't me, if you know what I mean."

She laughed and looked down at the floor. The point of her shoe moved back and forth on the carpeting. "We've had a nice chat, darling. The phone's over there at the end of the bar."

"Thanks, do you remember Dolores's number?"

"Why Dolores?"

When I didn't answer she told me. I went along the room to the corner of the bar and dialed. The same routine as before. Good evening, the Chateau Bercy, who is calling Miss Gonzales please. One moment, please, buzz, buzz, and then a sultry voice saying: "Hello?"

"This is Marlowe. Did you really mean to put me on a spot?"

I could almost hear her breath catch. Not quite. You can't really hear it over the phone. Sometimes you think you can.

"Amigo, but I am glad to hear your voice," she said, "I am so very very glad."

"Did you or didn't you?"

"I – I don't know. I am very sad to think that I might have. I like you very much."

"I'm in a little trouble here."

"Is he –" Long pause. Apartment house phone. Careful. "Is he there?"

"Well – in a way. He is and yet he isn't."

I really did hear her breath this time. A long indrawn sigh that was almost a whistle.

"Who else is there?"

"Nobody. Just me and my homework. I want to ask you something. It is deadly important. Tell me the truth. Where did you get that thing you gave me tonight?"

"Why, from him. He gave it to me."

"When?"

"Early this evening. Why?"

"How early?"

"About six o'clock, I think."

"*Why* did he give it to you?"

"He asked me to keep it. He always carried one."

"Asked you to keep it why?"

"He did not say, amigo. He was a man that did things like that. He did not often explain himself."

"Notice anything unusual about it? About what he gave you?"

"Why – no, I did not."

"Yes, you did. You noticed that it had been fired and that it smelled of burned powder."

"But I did not –"

417

"Yes, you did. Just like that. You wondered about it. You didn't like to keep it. You didn't keep it. You gave it back to him. You don't like them around anyhow."

There was a long silence. She said at last, "But of course. But why did he want me to have it? I mean, if that was what happened."

"He didn't tell you why. He just tried to ditch a gun on you and you weren't having any. Remember?"

"That is something I have to tell?"

"Sí."

"Will it be safe for me to do that?"

"When did you ever try to be safe?"

She laughed softly. "Amigo, you understand me very well."

"Goodnight," I said.

"One moment, you have not told me what happened."

"I haven't even telephoned you."

I hung up and turned.

Mavis Weld was standing in the middle of the floor watching me.

"You have your car here?" I asked.

"Yes."

"Get going."

"And do what?"

"Just go home. That's all."

"You can't get away with it," she said softly.

"You're my client."

"I can't let you. I killed him. Why should you be dragged into it?"

"Don't stall. And when you leave go the back way. Not the way Dolores brought me."

She stared me straight in the eyes and repeated in a tense voice, "But I killed him."

"I can't hear a word you say."

Her teeth took hold of her lower lip and held it cruelly. She seemed hardly to breathe. She stood rigid. I went over close to her and touched her cheek with a fingertip. I pressed it hard and watched the white spot turn red.

"If you want to know my motive," I said, "it has nothing to do with you. I owe it to the johns. I haven't played clean cards in this game. They know. I know. I'm just giving them a chance to use the loud pedal."

"As if anyone ever had to give them that," she said, and turned abruptly and walked away. I watched her to the arch and waited for her to look back. She went on through without turning. After a long time I heard a whirring noise. Then the bump of something heavy – the garage door going up. A car started a long way off. It idled down and after another pause the whirring noise again.

When that stopped the motor faded off into the distance. I heard nothing now. The silence of the house hung around me in thick loose folds like that fur coat around the shoulders of Mavis Weld.

I carried the glass and bottle of brandy over to the bar and climbed over it. I rinsed the glass in a little sink and set the bottle back on the shelf. I found the trick catch this time and swung the door open at the end opposite the telephone. I went back to Steelgrave.

I took out the gun Dolores had given me and wiped it off and put his small limp hand around the butt, held it there and let go. The gun thudded to the carpet. The position looked natural. I wasn't thinking about fingerprints. He would have learned long ago not to leave them on any gun.

That left me with three guns. The weapon in his holster I took out and went and put it on the bar shelf under the counter, wrapped in a towel. The Luger I didn't touch. The other white-handled automatic was left. I tried to decide about how far away from him it had been fired. Beyond scorching distance, but probably very close beyond. I stood about three feet from him and fired two shots past him. They nicked peacefully into the wall. I dragged the chair around until it faced into the room. I laid the small automatic down on the dust cover of one of the roulette tables. I touched the big muscle in the side of his neck, usually the first to harden. I couldn't tell whether it had begun to set or not. But his skin was colder than it had been.

There was not a hell of a lot of time to play around with.

I went to the telephone and dialed the number of the Los Angeles Police Department. I asked the police operator for Christy French. A voice from homicide came on, said he had gone home and what was it. I said it was a personal call he was expecting. They gave me his phone number at home, reluctantly, not because they cared, but because they hate to give anybody anything any time.

I dialed and a woman answered and screamed his name. He sounded rested and calm.

"This is Marlowe. What were you doing?"

"Reading the funnies to my kid. He ought to be in bed. What's doing?"

"Remember over at the Van Nuys yesterday you said a man could make a friend if he got you something on Weepy Moyer?"

"Yeah."

"I need a friend."

He didn't sound very interested. "What you got on him?"

"I'm assuming it's the same guy. Steelgrave."

"Too much assuming, kid. We had him in the fishbowl because we thought the same. It didn't pan any gold."

"You got a tip. He set that tip up himself. So the night Stein was squibbed off he would be where you knew."

"You just making this up – or got evidence?" He sounded a little less relaxed.

"If a man got out of jail on a pass from the jail doctor, could you prove that?"

There was a silence. I heard a child's voice complaining and a woman's voice speaking to the child.

"It's happened," French said heavily. "I dunno. That's a tough order to fill. They'd send him under guard. Did he get to the guard?"

"That's my theory."

"Better sleep on it. Anything else?"

"I'm out at Stillwood Heights. In a big house where they were setting up for gambling and the local residents didn't like it."

"Read about it. Steelgrave there?"

"He's here. I'm here alone with him."

Another silence. The kid yelled and I thought I heard a slap. The kid yelled louder. French yelled at somebody.

"Put him on the phone," French said at last.

"You're not bright tonight, Christy. Why would I call you?"

"Yeah," he said. "Stupid of me. What's the address there?"

"I don't know. But it's up at the end of Tower Road in Stillwood Heights and the phone number is Halldale 9-5033. I'll be waiting for you."

He repeated the number and said slowly: "This time you wait, huh?"

"It had to come sometime."

The phone clicked and I hung up.

I went back through the house putting on lights as I found them and came out at the back door at the top of the stairs. There was a floodlight for the motor yard. I put that on. I went down the steps and walked along to the oleander bush. The private gate stood open as before. I swung it shut, hooked up the chain and clicked the padlock. I went back, walking slowly, looking up at the moon, sniffing the night air, listening to the tree frogs and the crickets. I went into the house and found the front door and put the light on over that. There was a big parking space in front and a circular lawn with roses. But you had to slide back around the house to the rear to get away.

The place was a dead end except for the driveway through the neighboring grounds. I wondered who lived there. A long way off through trees I could see the lights of a big house. Some Hollywood big shot, probably, some wizard of the slobbery kiss, and the pornographic dissolve.

I went back in and felt the gun I had just fired. It was cold enough. And Mr. Steelgrave was beginning to look as if he meant to stay dead.

No siren. But the sound of a car coming up the hill at last. I went out to meet it, me and my beautiful dream.

29

THEY CAME IN as they should, big, tough and quiet, their eyes flickering with watchfulness and cautious with disbelief.

"Nice place," French said. "Where's the customer?"

"In there," Beifus said, without waiting for me to answer.

They went along the room without haste and stood in front of him looking down solemnly.

"Dead, wouldn't you say?" Beifus remarked, opening up the act.

French leaned down and took the gun that lay on the floor with thumb and finger on the trigger guard. His eyes flicked sideways and he jerked his chin. Beifus took the other white-handled gun by sliding a pencil into the end of the barrel.

"Fingerprints all in the right places, I hope," Beifus said. He sniffed. "Oh yeah, this baby's been working. How's yours, Christy?"

"Fired," French said. He sniffed again. "But not recently." He took a clip flash from his pocket and shone it into the barrel of the black gun. "Hours ago."

"Down at Bay City, in a house on Wyoming Street," I said.

Their heads swung around to me in unison.

"Guessing?" French asked slowly.

"Yes."

He walked over to the covered table and laid the gun down some distance from the other. "Better tag them right away, Fred. They're twins. We'll both sign the tags."

Beifus nodded and rooted around in his pockets. He came up with a couple of tie-on tags. The things cops carry around with them.

French moved back to me. "Let's stop guessing and get to the part you know."

"A girl I know called me this evening and said a client of mine was in danger up here – from him." I pointed with my chin at the dead man in the chair. "This girl rode me up here. We passed the road block. A number of people saw us both. She left me in back of the house and went home."

"Somebody with a name?" French asked.

"Dolores Gonzales, Chateau Bercy Apartments. On Franklin. She's in pictures."

"Oh-ho," Beifus said and rolled his eyes.

"Who's your client? Same one?" French asked.

"No. This is another party altogether."

"She have a name?"

"Not yet."

They stared at me with hard bright faces. French's jaw moved almost with a jerk. Knots of muscles showed at the sides of his jaw bone.

"New rules, huh?" he said softly.

I said, "There has to be some agreement about publicity. The D.A. ought to be willing."

Beifus said, "You don't know the D.A. good, Marlowe. He eats publicity like I eat tender young garden peas."

French said, "We don't give you any undertaking whatsoever."

"She hasn't any name," I said.

"There's a dozen ways we can find out, kid," Beifus said. "Why go into this routine that makes it tough for all of us?"

"No publicity," I said, "unless charges are actually filed."

423

"You can't get away with it, Marlowe."

"God damn it," I said, "this man killed Orrin Quest. You take that gun downtown and check it against the bullets in Quest. Give me that much at least, before you force me into an impossible position."

"I wouldn't give you the dirty end of a burnt match," French said.

I didn't say anything. He stared at me with cold hate in his eyes. His lips moved slowly and his voice was thick saying, "You here when he got it?"

"No."

"Who was?"

"He was," I said looking across at the dead Steelgrave.

"Who else?"

"I won't lie to you," I said. "And I won't tell you anything I don't want to tell – except on the terms I stated. I don't know who was here when he got it."

"Who was here when you got here?"

I didn't answer. He turned his head slowly and said to Beifus: "Put the cuffs on him. Behind."

Beifus hesitated. Then he took a pair of steel handcuffs out of his left hip pocket and came over to me. "Put your hands behind you," he said in an uncomfortable voice.

I did. He clicked the cuffs on. French walked over slowly and stood in front of me. His eyes were half closed. The skin around them was grayish with fatigue.

"I'm going to make a little speech," he said. "You're not going to like it."

I didn't say anything.

French said: "It's like this with us, baby. We're coppers and everybody hates our guts. And as if we didn't have enough trouble, we have to have you. As if we didn't get pushed around enough by the guys in the corner offices, the City Hall gang, the day chief, the night chief, the Chamber of Commerce, His Honor the Mayor in his paneled office four times as big as the three lousy rooms the whole homicide staff has to work out of. As if we didn't have to handle one hundred and fourteen homicides last year out of three rooms that don't have enough chairs for the whole duty squad to sit down in at once. We spend our lives turning over dirty underwear and sniffing rotten teeth. We go up dark stairways to get a gun punk with a skinful of hop and sometimes we don't get all the way up, and our wives wait dinner that night and all the other nights. We don't come home any more. And nights we do come home, we come home so goddam tired we can't eat or sleep or even read the lies the papers print about us. So we lie awake in the dark in a cheap house on a cheap street and listen to the drunks down the block having fun. And just about the time we drop off the phone rings and we get up and start all over again. Nothing we do is right, not ever. Not once. If we get a confession, we beat it out of the guy, they say, and some shyster calls us Gestapo in court and sneers at us when we muddle our grammar. If we make a mistake they put us back in uniform on Skid Row and we spend the nice cool summer evenings picking drunks out of the gutter and being yelled at by whores and taking knives away from greaseballs in zoot suits. But all that ain't enough to make us entirely happy. We got to have you."

He stopped and drew in his breath. His face glistened a little as if with sweat. He leaned forward from his hips.

"We got to have you," he repeated. "We got to have sharpers with private licenses hiding information and dodging around corners and stirring up dust for us to breathe in. We got to have you suppressing evidence and framing set-ups that wouldn't fool a sick baby. You wouldn't mind me calling you a goddam cheap double-crossing keyhole peeper, would you, baby?"

"You want me to mind?" I asked him.

He straightened up. "I'd love it," he said. "In spades redoubled."

"Some of what you say is true," I said. "Not all. Any private eye wants to play ball with the police. Sometimes it's a little hard to find out who's making the rules of the ball game. Sometimes he doesn't trust the police, and with cause. Sometimes he just gets in a jam without meaning to and has to play his hand out the way it's dealt. He'd usually rather have a new deal. He'd like to keep on earning a living."

"Your license is dead," French said. "As of now. That problem won't bother you any more."

"It's dead when the commission that gave it to me says so. Not before."

Beifus said quietly, "Let's get on with it, Christy. This could wait."

"I'm getting on with it," French said. "My way. This bird hasn't cracked wise yet. I'm waiting for him to crack wise. The bright repartee. Don't tell me you're all out of the quick stuff, Marlowe."

"Just what is it you want me to say?" I asked him.

"Guess," he said.

"You're a man eater tonight," I said. "You want to break me in half. But you want an excuse. And you want me to give it to you?"

"That might help," he said between his teeth.

"What would you have done in my place?" I asked him.

"I couldn't imagine myself getting that low."

He licked at the point of his upper lip. His right hand was hanging loose at his side. He was clenching and unclenching the fingers without knowing it.

"Take it easy, Christy," Beifus said. "Lay off."

French didn't move. Beifus came over and stepped between us. French said, "Get out of there, Fred."

"No."

French doubled his fist and slugged him hard on the point of the jaw. Beifus stumbled back and knocked me out of the way. His knees wobbled. He bent forward and coughed.

He shook his head slowly in a bent-over position. After a while he straightened up with a grunt. He turned and looked at me. He grinned.

"It's a new kind of third degree," he said. "The cops beat hell out of each other and the suspect cracks up from the agony of watching."

His hand went up and felt the angle of his jaw. It already showed swelling. His mouth grinned but his eyes were still a little vague. French stood rooted and silent.

Beifus got out a pack of cigarettes and shook one loose and held the pack out to French. French looked at the cigarette, looked at Beifus.

"Seventeen years of it," he said. "Even my wife hates me."

He lifted his open hand and slapped Beifus across the cheek with it lightly. Beifus kept on grinning.

French said: "Was it you I hit, Fred?"

Beifus said: "Nobody hit me, Christy. Nobody that I can remember."

French said: "Take the cuffs off him and take him out to the car. He's under arrest. Cuff him to the rail if you think it's necessary."

"Okay." Beifus went around behind me. The cuffs came loose. "Come along, baby," Beifus said.

I stared hard at French. He looked at me as if I was the wallpaper. His eyes didn't seem to see me at all.

I went out under the archway and out of the house.

30

I NEVER KNEW his name, but he was rather short and thin for a cop, which was what he must have been, partly because he was there, and partly because when he leaned across the table to reach a card I could see the leather underarm holster and the butt end of a police .38.

He didn't speak much, but when he did he had a nice voice, a soft-water voice. And he had a smile that warmed the whole room.

"Wonderful casting," I said, looking at him across the cards. We were playing double Canfield. Or he was. I was just there, watching him, watching his small and very neat and very clean hands go out across the table and touch a card and lift it delicately and put it somewhere else. When he did this he pursed his lips a little and whistled without tune, a low soft whistle, like a very young engine that is not yet sure of itself.

He smiled and put a red nine on a black ten.

"What do you do in your spare time?" I asked him.

"I play the piano a good deal," he said. "I have a seven-foot Steinway. Mozart and Bach mostly. I'm a bit old-fashioned. Most people find it dull stuff. I don't."

"Perfect casting," I said, and put a card somewhere.

"You'd be surprised how difficult some of that Mozart is," he said. "It sounds so simple when you hear it played well."

"Who can play it well?" I asked.

"Schnabel."

"Rubinstein?"

He shook his head. "Too heavy. Too emotional. Mozart is just music. No comment needed from the performer."

"I bet you get a lot of them in the confession mood," I said. "Like the job?"

He moved another card and flexed his fingers lightly. His nails were bright but short. You could see he was a man who loved to move his hands, to make little neat inconspicuous motions with them, motions without any special meaning, but smooth and flowing and light as swansdown. They gave him a feel of delicate things delicately done, but not weak. Mozart, all right. I could see that.

It was about five-thirty, and the sky behind the screened window was getting light. The rolltop desk in the corner was rolled shut. The room was the same room I had been in the afternoon before. Down at the end of the table the square carpenter's pencil was lying where somebody had picked it up and put it back after Lieutenant Maglashan of Bay City threw it against the wall. The flat desk at which Christy French had sat was littered with ash. An old cigar butt clung to the extreme edge of a glass ashtray. A moth circled around the overhead light on a drop cord that had one of those green and white glass shades they still have in country hotels.

"Tired?" he asked.

"Pooped."

"You oughtn't to get yourself involved in these elaborate messes. No point in it that I can see."

"No point in shooting a man?"

He smiled the warm smile. "You never shot anybody."

"What makes you say that?"

"Common sense – and a lot of experience sitting here with people."

"I guess you do like the job," I said.

"It's night work. Gives me the days to practice. I've had it for twelve years now. Seen a lot of funny ones come and go."

He got another ace out, just in time. We were almost blocked.

"Get many confessions?"

"I don't take confessions," he said. "I just establish a mood."

"Why give it all away?"

He leaned back and tapped lightly with the edge of a card on the edge of the table. The smile came again. "I'm not giving anything away. We got you figured long ago."

"Then what are they holding me for?"

He wouldn't answer that. He looked around at the clock on the wall. "I think we could get some food now." He got up and went to the door. He half opened it and spoke softly to someone outside. Then he came back and sat down again and looked at what we had in the way of cards.

"No use," he said. "Three more up and we're blocked. Okay with you to start over?"

"Okay with me if we never started at all. I don't play cards. Chess."

He looked up at me quickly. "Why didn't you say so? I'd rather have played chess too."

"I'd rather drink some hot black coffee as bitter as sin."

"Any minute now. But I won't promise the coffee's what you're used to."

"Hell, I eat anywhere. . . . Well, if I didn't shoot him, who did?"

"Guess that's what is annoying them."

"They ought to be glad to have him shot."

"They probably are," he said. "But they don't like the way it was done."

"Personally I thought it was as neat a job as you could find."

He looked at me in silence. He had the cards between his hands, all in a lump. He smoothed them out and flicked them over on their faces and dealt them rapidly into the two decks. The cards seemed to pour from his hands in a stream, in a blur.

"If you were that fast with a gun," I began.

The stream of cards stopped. Without apparent motion a gun took their place. He held it lightly in his right hand pointed at a distant corner of the room. It went away and the cards started flowing again.

"You're wasted in here," I said. "You ought to be in Las Vegas."

He picked up one of the packs and shuffled it slightly and quickly, cut it, and dealt me a king high flush in spades.

"I'm safer with a Steinway," he said.

The door opened and a uniformed man came in with a tray.

We ate canned cornbeef hash and drank hot but weak coffee. By that time it was full morning.

At eight-fifteen Christy French came in and stood with his hat on the back of his head and dark smudges under his eyes.

I looked from him to the little man across the table. But he wasn't there any more. The cards weren't there either. Nothing was there but a chair pushed in neatly to the table and the dishes we had eaten off gathered on a tray. For a moment I had that creepy feeling.

Then Christy French walked around the table and jerked the chair out and sat down and leaned his chin on his hand. He took his hat off and rumpled his hair. He stared at me with hard morose eyes. I was back in coptown again.

31

"THE D.A. WANTS to see you at nine o'clock," he said. "After that I guess you can go on home. That is, if he doesn't hang a pinch on you. I'm sorry you had to sit up in that chair all night."

"It's all right," I said. "I needed the exercise."

"Yeah, back in the groove again," he said. He stared moodily at the dishes on the tray.

"Got Lagardie?" I asked him.

"No. He's a doctor all right, though." His eyes moved to mine. "He practiced in Cleveland."

I said: "I hate it to be that tidy."

"How do you mean?"

"Young Quest wants to put the bite on Steelgrave. So he just by pure accident runs into the one guy in Bay City that could prove who Steelgrave was. *That's* too tidy."

"Aren't you forgetting something?"

"I'm tired enough to forget my name. What?"

"Me too," French said. "*Somebody* had to tell him who Steelgrave was. When that photo was taken Moe Stein hadn't been squibbed off. So what good was the photo unless somebody knew who Steelgrave was?"

"I guess Miss Weld knew," I said. "And Quest was her brother."

"You're not making much sense, chum." He grinned a tired grin. "Would she help her brother put the bite on her boy friend and on her too?"

"I give up. Maybe the photo was just a fluke. His other sister — my client that was — said he liked to take candid camera shots. The candider the better. If he'd lived long enough you'd have had him up for mopery."

"For murder," French said indifferently.

"Oh?"

"Maglashan found that ice pick all right. He just wouldn't give out to you."

"There'd have to be more than that."

"There is, but it's a dead issue. Clausen and Mileaway Marston both had records. The kid's dead. His family's respectable. He had an off streak in him and he got in with the wrong people. No point in smearing his family just to prove the police can solve a case."

"That's white of you. How about Steelgrave?"

"That's out of my hands." He started to get up. "When a gangster gets his how long does the investigation last?"

"Just as long as it's front-page stuff," I said. "But there's a question of identity involved here."

"No."

I stared at him. "How do you mean, no?"

"Just no. We're sure." He was on his feet now. He combed his hair with his fingers and rearranged his tie and hat. Out of the corner of his mouth he said in a low voice: "Off the record — we were always sure. We just didn't have a thing on him."

"Thanks," I said, "I'll keep it to myself. How about the guns?"

He stopped and stared down at the table. His eyes came up to mine rather slowly. "They both belonged to Steelgrave.

What's more he had a permit to carry a gun. From the sheriff's office in another county. Don't ask me why. One of them —" he paused and looked up at the wall over my head — "one of them killed Quest. . . . The same gun killed Stein."

"Which one?"

He smiled faintly. "It would be hell if the ballistics man got them mixed up and we didn't know," he said.

He waited for me to say something. I didn't have anything to say. He made a gesture with his hand.

"Well, so long. Nothing personal you know, but I hope the D.A. takes your hide off — in long thin strips."

He turned and went out.

I could have done the same, but I just sat there and stared across the table at the wall, as if I had forgotten how to get up. After a while the door opened and the orange queen came in. She unlocked her rolltop desk and took her hat off of her impossible hair and hung her jacket on a bare hook in the bare wall. She opened the window near her and uncovered her typewriter and put paper in it. Then she looked across at me. "Waiting for somebody?"

"I room here," I said. "Been here all night."

She looked at me steadily for a moment. "You were here yesterday afternoon. I remember."

She turned to her typewriter and her fingers began to fly. From the open window behind her came the growl of cars filling up the parking lot. The sky had a white glare and there was not much smog. It was going to be a hot day.

The telephone rang on the orange queen's desk. She talked into it inaudibly, and hung up. She looked across at me again.

"Mr. Endicott's in his office," she said. "Know the way?"

"I worked there once. Not for him, though. I got fired."

She looked at me with that City Hall look they have. A voice that seemed to come from anywhere but her mouth said:

"Hit him in the face with a wet glove."

433

I went over near her and stood looking down at the orange hair. There was plenty of gray at the roots.

"Who said that?"

"It's the wall," she said. "It talks. The voices of the dead men who have passed through on the way to hell."

I went out of the room walking softly and shut the door against the closer so that it wouldn't make any noise.

32

YOU GO IN through double swing doors. Inside the double doors there is a combination PBX and information desk at which sits one of those ageless women you see around municipal offices everywhere in the world. They were never young and will never be old. They have no beauty, no charm, no style. They don't have to please anybody. They are safe. They are civil without ever quite being polite and intelligent and knowledgeable without any real interest in anything. They are what human beings turn into when they trade life for existence and ambition for security.

Beyond this desk there is a row of glassed-in cubicles stretching along one side of a very long room. On the other side is the waiting room, a row of hard chairs all facing one way, towards the cubicles.

About half of the chairs were filled with people waiting and the look of long waiting on their faces and the expectation of still longer waiting to come. Most of them were shabby. One was from the jail, in denim, with a guard. A white-faced kid built like a tackle, with sick, empty eyes.

At the back of the line of cubicles a door was lettered SEWELL ENDICOTT DISTRICT ATTORNEY. I knocked and went on into a big airy corner room. A nice enough room, old-fashioned with padded black leather chairs and pictures of former D.A.'s and governors on the walls. Breeze fluttered the net curtains at four windows. A fan on a high shelf purred and swung slowly in a languid arc.

Sewell Endicott sat behind a flat dark desk and watched me come. He pointed to a chair across from him. I sat down. He was tall, thin and dark with loose black hair and long delicate fingers.

"You're Marlowe?" he said in a voice that had a touch of the soft South.

I didn't think he really needed an answer to that. I just waited.

"You're in a bad spot, Marlowe. You don't look good at all. You've been caught suppressing evidence helpful to the solution of a murder. That is obstructing justice. You could go up for it."

"Suppressing what evidence?" I asked.

He picked a photo off his desk and frowned at it. I looked across at the other two people in the room. They sat in chairs side by side. One of them was Mavis Weld. She wore the dark glasses with the wide white bows. I couldn't see her eyes, but I thought she was looking at me. She didn't smile. She sat very still.

By her side sat a man in an angelic pale-gray flannel suit with a carnation the size of a dahlia in his lapel. He was smoking a monogrammed cigarette and flicking the ashes on the floor, ignoring the smoking stand at his elbow. I knew him by pictures I had seen in the papers. Lee Farrell, one of the hottest trouble-shooting lawyers in the country. His hair was white but his eyes were bright and young. He had a deep outdoor tan. He looked as if it would cost a thousand dollars to shake hands with him.

Endicott leaned back and tapped the arm of his chair with his long fingers. He turned with polite deference to Mavis Weld.

"And how well did you know Steelgrave, Miss Weld?"

"Intimately. He was very charming in some ways. I can hardly believe –" She broke off and shrugged.

"And you are prepared to take the stand and swear as to the time and place when this photograph was taken?" He turned the photograph over and showed it to her.

Farrell said indifferently, "Just a moment. Is that the evidence Mr. Marlowe is supposed to have suppressed?"

"I ask the questions," Endicott said sharply.

Farrell smiled. "Well, in case the answer is yes, that photo isn't evidence of anything."

Endicott said softly: "Will you answer my question, Miss Weld?"

She said quietly and easily: "No, Mr. Endicott, I couldn't swear when that picture was taken or where. I didn't know it was being taken."

"All you have to do is look at it," Endicott suggested.

"And all I know is what I get from looking at it," she told him.

I grinned. Farrell looked at me with a twinkle. Endicott caught the grin out of the corner of his eye. "Something you find amusing?" he snapped at me.

"I've been up all night. My face keeps slipping," I said.

He gave me a stern look and turned to Mavis Weld again. "Will you amplify that, Miss Weld?"

"I've had a lot of photos taken of me, Mr. Endicott. In a lot of different places and with a lot of different people. I have had lunch and dinner at The Dancers with Mr. Steelgrave and with various other men. I don't know what you want me to say."

Farrell put in smoothly, "If I understand your point, you would like Miss Weld to be your witness to connect this photo up. In what kind of proceeding?"

"That's my business," Endicott said shortly. "Somebody shot Steelgrave to death last night. It could have been a woman. It could even have been Miss Weld. I'm sorry to say that, but it seems to be in the cards."

Mavis Weld looked down at her hands. She twisted a white glove between her fingers.

"Well, let's assume a proceeding," Farrell said. "One in which that photo is part of your evidence – if you can get it

436

in. But you can't get it in. Miss Weld won't get it in for you. All she knows about the photo is what she sees by looking at it. What anybody can see. You'd have to connect it up with a witness who could swear as to when, how and where it was taken. Otherwise I'd object – if I happened to be on the other side. I could even introduce experts to swear the photo was faked."

"I'm sure you could," Endicott said dryly.

"The only man who could connect it up for you is the man who took it," Farrell went on without haste or heat. "I understand he's dead. I suspect that was why he was killed."

Endicott said: "This photo is clear evidence of itself that at a certain time and place Steelgrave was not in jail and therefore had no alibi for the killing of Stein."

Farrell said: "It's evidence when and if you get it introduced in evidence, Endicott. For Pete's sake, I'm not trying to tell you the law. You know it. Forget that picture. It proves nothing whatsoever. No paper would dare print it. No judge would admit it in evidence, because no competent witness can connect it up. And if that's the evidence Marlowe suppressed, then he didn't in a legal sense suppress evidence at all."

"I wasn't thinking of trying Steelgrave for murder," Endicott said dryly. "But I *am* a little interested in who killed him. The police department, fantastically enough, also has an interest in that. I hope our interest doesn't offend you."

Farrell said: "Nothing offends me. That's why I'm where I am. Are you sure Steelgrave was murdered?"

Endicott just stared at him. Farrell said easily: "I understand two guns were found, both the property of Steelgrave."

"Who told you?" Endicott asked sharply. He leaned forward frowning.

Farrell dropped his cigarette into the smoking stand and shrugged. "Hell, these things come out. One of these guns had killed Quest and also Stein. The other had killed Steelgrave.

437

Fired at close quarters too. I admit those boys don't as a rule take that way out. But it could happen."

Endicott said gravely: "No doubt. Thanks for the suggestion. It happens to be wrong."

Farrell smiled a little and was silent. Endicott turned slowly to Mavis Weld.

"Miss Weld, this office – or the present incumbent of it at least – doesn't believe in seeking publicity at the expense of people to whom a certain kind of publicity might be fatal. It is my duty to determine whether anyone should be brought to trial for any of these murders, and to prosecute them, if the evidence warrants it. It is not my duty to ruin your career by exploiting the fact that you had the bad luck or bad judgment to be the friend of a man who, although never convicted or even indicted for any crime, was undoubtedly a member of a criminal mob at one time. I don't think you have been quite candid with me about this photograph, but I won't press the matter now. There is not much point in my asking you whether you shot Steelgrave. But I do ask you whether you have any knowledge that would point to who may have or might have killed him."

Farrell said quickly: "Knowledge, Miss Weld – not mere suspicion."

She faced Endicott squarely. "No."

He stood up and bowed. "That will be all for now then. Thanks for coming in."

Farrell and Mavis Weld stood up. I didn't move. Farrell said: "Are you calling a press conference?"

"I think I'll leave that to you, Mr. Farrell. You have always been very skillful in handling the press."

Farrell nodded and went to open the door. They went out. She didn't seem to look at me when she went out, but something touched the back of my neck lightly. Probably accidental. Her sleeve.

Endicott watched the door close. He looked across the desk at me. "Is Farrell representing you? I forgot to ask him."

"I can't afford him. So I'm vulnerable."

He smiled thinly. "I let them take all the tricks and then salve my dignity by working out on you, eh?"

"I couldn't stop you."

"You're not exactly proud of the way you have handled things, are you, Marlowe?"

"I got off on the wrong foot. After that I just had to take my lumps."

"Don't you think you owe a certain obligation to the law?"

"I would – if the law was like you."

He ran his long pale fingers through his tousled black hair.

"I could make a lot of answers to that," he said. "They'd all sound about the same. The citizen is the law. In this country we haven't got around to understanding that. We think of the law as an enemy. We're a nation of cop-haters."

"It'll take a lot to change that," I said. "On both sides."

He leaned forward and pressed a buzzer. "Yes," he said quietly. "It will. But somebody has to make a beginning. Thanks for coming in."

As I went out a secretary came in at another door with a fat file in her hand.

33

A SHAVE AND a second breakfast made me feel a little less like the box of shavings the cat had had kittens in. I went up to the office and unlocked the door and sniffed in the twice-breathed air and the smell of dust. I opened a window and inhaled the fry-cook smell from the coffee shop next door. I sat down at my desk and felt the grit on it with fingertips. I filled a pipe and lit it and leaned back and looked around.

"Hello," I said.

I was just talking to the office equipment, the three green filing cases, the threadbare piece of carpet, the customer's chair across from me, and the light fixture in the ceiling with three dead moths in it that had been there for at least six months. I was talking to the pebbled glass panel and the grimy woodwork and the pen set on the desk and tired, tired telephone. I was talking to the scales on an alligator, the name of the alligator being Marlowe, a private detective in our thriving little community. Not the brainiest guy in the world, but cheap. He started out cheap and he ended cheaper still.

I reached down and put the bottle of Old Forester up on the desk. It was about a third full. Old Forester. Now who gave you that, pal? That's green-label stuff. Out of your class entirely. Must have been a client. I had a client once.

And that got me thinking about her, and maybe I have stronger thoughts than I know. The telephone rang, and the funny little precise voice sounded just as it had the first time she called me up.

"I'm in that telephone booth," she said. "If you're alone, I'm coming up."

"Uh-huh."

"I suppose you're mad at me," she said.

"I'm not mad at anybody. Just tired."

"Oh yes you are," her tight little voice said. "But I'm coming up anyway. I don't care if you *are* mad at me."

She hung up. I took the cork out of the bottle of Old Forester and gave a sniff at it. I shuddered. That settled it. Any time I couldn't smell whiskey without shuddering I was through.

I put the bottle away and got up to unlock the communicating door. Then I heard her tripping along the hall. I'd know those tight little footsteps anywhere. I opened the door and she came up to me and looked at me shyly.

It was all gone. The slanted cheaters, and the new hair-do and the smart little hat and the perfume and the prettied-up touch. The costume jewelry, the rouge, the everything. All gone. She was right back where she started the first morning.

Same brown tailor-made, same square bag, same rimless glasses, same prim little narrow-minded smile.

"It's me," she said. "I'm going home."

She followed me into my private thinking parlor and sat down primly and I sat down just any old way and stared at her.

"Back to Manhattan," I said. "I'm surprised they let you."

"I may have to come back."

"Can you afford it?"

She gave a quick little half-embarrassed laugh. "It won't cost me anything," she said. She reached up and touched the rimless glasses. "These feel all wrong now," she said. "I liked the others. But Dr. Zugsmith wouldn't like them at all." She put her bag on the desk and drew a line along the desk with her fingertip. That was just like the first time too.

"I can't remember whether I gave you back your twenty dollars or not," I said. "We kept passing it back and forth until I lost count."

"Oh, you gave it to me," she said. "Thank you."

"Sure?"

"I never make mistakes about money. Are you all right? Did they hurt you?"

"The police? No. And it was as tough a job as they ever didn't do."

She looked innocently surprised. Then her eyes glowed. "You must be awfully brave," she said.

"Just luck," I said. I picked up a pencil and felt the point. It was a good sharp point, if anybody wanted to write anything. I didn't. I reached across and slipped the pencil through the strap of her bag and pulled it towards me.

"Don't touch my bag," she said quickly and reached for it.

I grinned and drew it out of her reach. "All right. But it's such a cute little bag. It's so like you."

She leaned back. There was a vague worry behind her eyes, but she smiled. "You think I'm cute – Philip? I'm so ordinary."

441

"I wouldn't say so."

"You wouldn't?"

"Hell no, I think you're one of the most unusual girls I ever met." I swung the bag by its strap and set it down on the corner of the desk. Her eyes fastened on it quickly, but she licked her lip and kept on smiling at me.

"And I bet you've known an awful lot of girls," she said. "Why —" she looked down and did that with her fingertip on the desk again — "why didn't you ever get married?"

I thought of all the ways you answer that. I thought of all the women I had liked that much. No, not all. But some of them.

"I suppose I know the answer," I said. "But it would just sound corny. The ones I'd maybe like to marry — well, I haven't what they need. The others you don't have to marry. You just seduce them — if they don't beat you to it."

She flushed to the roots of her mousy hair.

"You're horrid when you talk like that."

"That goes for some of the nice ones too," I said. "Not what you said. What I said. You wouldn't have been so hard to take yourself."

"Don't talk like that, please!"

"Well, would you?"

She looked down at the desk. "I wish you'd tell me," she said slowly, "what happened to Orrin. I'm all confused."

"I told you he probably went off the rails. The first time you came in. Remember?"

She nodded slowly, still blushing.

"Abnormal sort of home life," I said. "Very inhibited sort of guy and with a very highly developed sense of his own importance. It looked at you out of the picture you gave me. I don't want to go psychological on you, but I figure he was just the type to go very completely haywire, if he went haywire at all. Then there's that awful money hunger that runs in your family — all except one."

442

She smiled at me now. If she thought I meant her, that was jake with me.

"There's one question I want to ask you," I said. "Was your father married before?"

She nodded, yes.

"That helps. Leila had another mother. That suits me fine. Tell me some more. After all I did a lot of work for you, for a very low fee of no dollars net."

"You got paid," she said sharply. "Well paid. By Leila. And don't expect me to call her Mavis Weld. I won't do it."

"You didn't know I was going to get paid."

"Well –" there was a long pause, during which her eyes went to her bag again – "you did get paid."

"Okay, pass that. Why wouldn't you tell me who she was?"

"I was ashamed. Mother and I were both ashamed."

"Orrin wasn't. He loved it."

"Orrin?" There was a tidy little silence while she looked at her bag again. I was beginning to get curious about that bag. "But he had been out here and I suppose he'd got used to it."

"Being in pictures isn't that bad, surely."

"It wasn't just that," she said swiftly, and her tooth came down on the outer edge of her lower lip and something flared in her eyes and very slowly died away. I just put another match to my pipe. I was too tired to show emotions, even if I felt any.

"I know. Or anyway I kind of guessed. How did Orrin find out something about Steelgrave that the cops didn't know?"

"I – I don't know," she said slowly, picking her way among her words like a cat on a fence. "Could it have been that doctor?"

"Oh sure," I said, with a big warm smile. "He and Orrin got to be friends somehow. A common interest in sharp tools maybe."

She leaned back in her chair. Her little face was thin and angular now. Her eyes had a watchful look.

443

"Now you're just being nasty," she said. "Every so often you have to be that way."

"Such a pity," I said. "I'd be a lovable character if I'd let myself alone. Nice bag." I reached for it and pulled it in front of me and snapped it open.

She came up out of her chair and lunged.

"You let my bag alone!"

I looked her straight in the rimless glasses. "You want to go home to Manhattan, Kansas, don't you? Today? You got your ticket and everything?"

She worked her lips and slowly sat down again.

"Okay," I said. "I'm not stopping you. I just wondered how much dough you squeezed out of the deal."

She began to cry. I opened the bag and went through it. Nothing until I came to the zipper pocket at the back. I unzipped and reached in. There was a flat packet of new bills in there. I took them out and riffled them. Ten centuries. All new. All nice. An even thousand dollars. Nice traveling money.

I leaned back and tapped the edge of the packet on my desk. She sat silent now, staring at me with wet eyes. I got a handkerchief out of her bag and tossed it across to her. She dabbed at her eyes. She watched me around the handkerchief. Once in a while she made a nice little appealing sob in her throat.

"Leila gave the money to me," she said softly.

"What size chisel did you use?"

She just opened her mouth and a tear ran down her cheek into it.

"Skip it," I said. I dropped the pack of money back into the bag, snapped the bag shut and pushed it across the desk to her. "I guess you and Orrin belong to that class of people that can convince themselves that everything they do is right. He can blackmail his sister and then when a couple of small-time crooks get wise to his racket and take it away from him, he can sneak up on them and knock them off with an ice pick

444

in the back of the neck. Probably didn't even keep him awake that night. You can do much the same. Leila didn't give you that money. Steelgrave gave it to you. For what?"

"You're filthy," she said. "You're vile. How dare you say such things to me?"

"Who tipped off the law that Dr. Lagardie knew Clausen? Lagardie thought I did. I didn't. So you did. Why? To smoke out your brother who was not cutting you in – because right then he had lost his deck of cards and was hiding out. I'd like to see some of those letters he wrote home. I bet they're meaty. I can see him working at it, watching his sister, trying to get her lined up for his Leica, with the good Doctor Lagardie waiting quietly in the background for his share of the take. What did you hire me for?"

"I didn't know," she said evenly. She wiped her eyes again and put the handkerchief away in the bag and got herself all collected and ready to leave. "Orrin never mentioned any names. I didn't even know Orrin had lost his pictures. But I knew he had taken them and that they were very valuable. I came out to make sure."

"Sure of what?"

"That Orrin treated me right. He could be awfully mean sometimes. He might have kept all the money himself."

"Why did he call you up night before last?"

"He was scared. Dr. Lagardie wasn't pleased with him any more. He didn't have the pictures. Somebody else had them. Orrin didn't know who. But he was scared."

"I had them. I still have," I said. "They're in that safe."

She turned her head very slowly to look at the safe. She ran a fingertip questioningly along her lip. She turned back.

"I don't believe you," she said, and her eyes watched me like a cat watching a mousehole.

"How's to split that grand with me. You get the pictures."

She thought about it. "I could hardly give you all that money for something that doesn't belong to you," she said and smiled. "Please give them to me. Please, Philip. Leila ought to have them back.

"For how much dough?"

She frowned and looked hurt.

"She's my client now," I said. "But double-crossing her wouldn't be bad business – at the right price."

"I don't believe you have them."

"Okay." I got up and went to the safe. In a moment I was back with the envelope. I poured the prints and the negative out on the desk – my side of the desk. She looked down at them and started to reach.

I picked them up and shuffled them together and held one so that she could look at it. When she reached for it I moved it back.

"But I can't see it so far away," she complained.

"It costs money to get closer."

"I never thought you were a crook," she said with dignity. I didn't say anything. I relit my pipe.

"I could make you give them to the police," she said.

"You could try."

Suddenly she spoke rapidly. "I couldn't give you this money I have, really I couldn't. We – well mother and I owe money still on account of father and the house isn't clear and –"

"What did you sell Steelgrave for the grand?"

Her mouth fell open and she looked ugly. She closed her lips and pressed them together. It was a tight hard little face that I was looking at.

"You had one thing to sell," I said. "You knew where Orrin was. To Steelgrave that information was worth a grand. Easy. It's a question of connecting up evidence. You wouldn't understand. Steelgrave went down there and killed him. He paid you the money for the address."

"Leila told him," she said in a faraway voice.

"Leila told me she told him," I said. "If necessary Leila would tell the world she told him. Just as she would tell the world she killed Steelgrave – if that was the only way out.

446

Leila is a sort of free-and-easy Hollywood babe that doesn't have very good morals. But when it comes to bedrock guts – she has what it takes. She's not the icepick type. And she's not the blood-money type."

The color flowed away from her face and left her as pale as ice. Her mouth quivered, then tightened up hard into a little knot. She pushed her chair back and leaned forward to get up.

"Blood money," I said quietly. "Your own brother. And you set him up so they could kill him. A thousand dollars blood money. I hope you'll be happy with it."

She stood away from the chair and took a couple of steps backward. Then suddenly she giggled.

"Who could prove it?" she half squealed. "Who's alive to prove it? You? Who are you? A cheap shyster, a nobody." She went off into a shrill peal of laughter. "Why even twenty dollars buys you."

I was still holding the packet of photos. I struck a match and dropped the negative into the ashtray and watched it flare up.

She stopped dead, frozen in a kind of horror. I started to tear the pictures up into strips. I grinned at her.

"A cheap shyster," I said. "Well, what would you expect. I don't have any brothers or sisters to sell out. So I sell out my clients."

She stood rigid and glaring. I finished my tearing-up job and lit the scraps of paper in the tray.

"One thing I regret," I said. "Not seeing your meeting back in Manhattan, Kansas, with dear old Mom. Not seeing the fight over how to split that grand. I bet that would be something to watch."

I poked at the paper with a pencil to keep it burning. She came slowly, step by step, to the desk and her eyes were fixed on the little smoldering heap of torn prints.

"I could tell the police," she whispered. "I could tell them a lot of things. They'd believe me."

"I could tell them who shot Steelgrave," I said. "Because I know who didn't. They might believe *me*."

447

The small head jerked up. The light glinted on the glasses. There were no eyes behind them.

"Don't worry," I said. "I'm not going to. It wouldn't cost me enough. And it would cost somebody else too much."

The telephone rang and she jumped a foot. I turned and reached for it and put my face against it and said, "Hello."

"Amigo, are you all right?"

There was a sound in the background. I swung around and saw the door click shut. I was alone in the room.

"Are you all right, amigo?"

"I'm tired. I've been up all night. Apart from —"

"Has the little one called you up?"

"The little sister? She was just in here. She's on her way back to Manhattan with the swag."

"The swag?"

"The pocket money she got from Steelgrave for fingering her brother."

There was a silence, then she said gravely, "You cannot know that, amigo."

"Like I know I'm sitting leaning on this desk holding on to this telephone. Like I know I hear your voice. And not quite so certainly, but certainly enough like I know who shot Steelgrave."

"You are somewhat foolish to say that to me, amigo. I am not above reproach. You should not trust me too much."

"I make mistakes, but this won't be one. I've burned all the photographs. I tried to sell them to Orfamay. She wouldn't bid high enough."

"Surely you are making fun, amigo."

"Am I? Who of ?"

She tinkled her laugh over the wire. "Would you like to take me to lunch?"

"I might. Are you home?"

"Sí."

"I'll come over in a little while."

448

"But I shall be delighted."

I hung up.

★

The play was over. I was sitting in the empty theater. The curtain was down and projected on it dimly I could see the action. But already some of the actors were getting vague and unreal. The little sister above all. In a couple of days I would forget what she looked like. Because in a way she *was* so unreal. I thought of her tripping back to Manhattan, Kansas, and dear old Mom, with that fat little new little thousand dollars in her purse. A few people had been killed so she could get it, but I didn't think that would bother her for long. I thought of her getting down to the office in the morning – what was the man's name? Oh yes. Dr. Zugsmith – and dusting off his desk before he arrived and arranging the magazines in the waiting room. She'd have her rimless cheaters on and a plain dress and her face would be without make-up and her manners to the patients would be most correct.

"Dr. Zugsmith will see you now, Mrs. Whosis."

She would hold the door open with a little smile and Mrs. Whosis would go in past her and Dr. Zugsmith would be sitting behind his desk as professional as hell with a white coat on and his stethoscope hanging around his neck. A case file would be in front of him and his note pad and prescription pad would be neatly squared off. Nothing that Dr. Zugsmith didn't know. You couldn't fool him. He had it all at his fingertips. When he looked at a patient he knew the answers to all the questions he was going to ask just as a matter of form.

When he looked at his receptionist, Miss Orfamay Quest, he saw a nice quiet young lady, properly dressed for a doctor's office, no red nails, no loud make-up, nothing to offend the old-fashioned type of customer. An ideal receptionist, Miss Quest.

Dr. Zugsmith, when he thought about her at all, thought of her with self-satisfaction. He had made her what she was. She was just what the doctor ordered.

Most probably he hadn't made a pass at her yet. Maybe they don't in those small towns. Ha, ha! I grew up in one.

I changed position and looked at my watch and got that bottle of Old Forester up out of the drawer after all. I sniffed it. It smelled good. I poured myself a good stiff jolt and held it up against the light.

"Well, Dr. Zugsmith," I said out loud, just as if he was sitting there on the other side of the desk with a drink in his hand, "I don't know you very well and you don't know me at all. Ordinarily I don't believe in giving advice to strangers, but I've had a short intensive course of Miss Orfamay Quest and I'm breaking my rule. If ever that little girl wants anything from you, give it to her quick. Don't stall around or gobble about your income tax and your overhead. Just wrap youself in a smile and shell out. Don't get involved in any discussions about what belongs to who. Keep the little girl happy, that's the main thing. Good luck to you, Doctor, and don't leave any harpoons lying around the office."

I drank off half of my drink and waited for it to warm me up. When it did that I drank the rest and put the bottle away.

I knocked the cold ashes out of my pipe and refilled it from the leather humidor an admirer had given me for Christmas, the admirer by an odd coincidence having the same name as mine.

When I had the pipe filled I lit it carefully, without haste, and went on out and down the hall, as breezy as a Britisher coming in from a tiger hunt.

34

THE CHATEAU BERCY was old but made over. It had the sort of lobby that asks for plush and india-rubber plants, but gets glass brick, cornice lighting, three-cornered glass tables, and a general air of having been redecorated by a parolee from a nut hatch. Its color scheme was bile green, linseed-poultice brown, sidewalk gray and monkey-bottom blue. It was as restful as a split lip.

The small desk was empty but the mirror behind it could be diaphanous, so I didn't try to sneak up the stairs. I rang a bell and a large soft man oozed out from behind a wall and smiled at me with moist soft lips and bluish-white teeth and unnaturally bright eyes.

"Miss Gonzales," I said. "Name's Marlowe. She's expecting me."

"Why, yes of course," he said, fluttering his hands. "Yes, of course. I'll telephone up at once." He had a voice that fluttered too.

He picked up the telephone and gurgled into it and put it down.

"Yes, Mr. Marlowe. Miss Gonzales says to come right up. Apartment 412." He giggled. "But I suppose you know."

"I know now," I said. "By the way were you here last February?"

"Last February? Last February? Oh yes, I was here last February." He pronounced it exactly as spelled.

"Remember the night Stein got chilled out front?"

The smile went away from the fat face in a hurry. "Are you a police officer?" His voice was now thin and reedy.

"No. But your pants are unzipped, if you care."

He looked down with horror and zipped them up with hands that almost trembled.

"Why thank you," he said. "Thank you." He leaned across the low desk. "It was not exactly out front," he said. "That is not exactly. It was almost to the next corner."

"Living here, wasn't he?"

"I'd really rather not talk about it. Really I'd rather not talk about it." He paused and ran his pinkie along his lower lip. "Why do you ask?"

"Just to keep you talking. You want to be more careful, bud. I can smell it on your breath."

The pink flowed all over him right down to his neck. "If you suggest I have been drinking —"

"Only tea," I said. "And not from a cup."

I turned away. He was silent. As I reached the elevator I looked back. He stood with his hands flat on the desk and his head strained around to watch me. Even from a distance he seemed to be trembling.

The elevator was self-service. The fourth floor was cool gray, the carpet thick. There was a small bell push beside Apartment 412. It chimed softly inside. The door was swung open instantly. The beautiful deep dark eyes looked at me and the red red mouth smiled at me. Black slacks and the flame-colored shirt, just like last night.

"Amigo," she said softly. She put her arms out. I took hold of her wrists and brought them together and made her palms touch. I played patacake with her for a moment. The expression in her eyes was languorous and fiery at the same time.

I let go of her wrists, closed the door with my elbow and slid past her. It was like the first time.

"You ought to carry insurance on those," I said touching one. It was real enough. The nipple was as hard as a ruby.

She went into her joyous laugh. I went on in and looked the place over. It was French gray and dusty blue. Not her colors, but very nice. There was a false fireplace with gas logs, and enough chairs and tables and lamps, but not too many. There was a neat little cellarette in the corner.

"You like my little apartment, amigo?"

"Don't say little apartment. That sounds like a whore too."

I didn't look at her. I didn't want to look at her. I sat down on a davenport and rubbed a hand across my forehead.

"Four hours' sleep and a couple of drinks," I said. "And I'd be able to talk nonsense to you again. Right now I've barely strength to talk sense. But I've got to."

452

She came to sit close to me. I shook my head. "Over there. I really do have to talk sense."

She sat down opposite and looked at me with grave dark eyes. "But yes, amigo, whatever you wish. I am your girl – at least I would gladly be your girl."

"Where did you live in Cleveland?"

"In Cleveland?" Her voice was very soft, almost cooing. "Did I say I had lived in Cleveland?"

"You said you knew him there."

She thought back and then nodded. "I was married then, amigo. What is the matter?"

"You did live in Cleveland then?"

"Yes," she said softly.

"You got to know Steelgrave how?"

"It was just that in those days it was fun to know a gangster. A form of inverted snobbery, I suppose. One went to the places where they were said to go and if one was lucky, perhaps some evening –"

"You let him pick you up."

She nodded brightly. "Let us say I picked *him* up. He was a very nice little man. Really, he was."

"What about the husband? *Your* husband. Or don't you remember?"

She smiled. "The streets of the world are paved with discarded husbands," she said.

"Isn't it the truth? You find them everywhere. Even in Bay City."

That bought me nothing. She shrugged politely. "I would not doubt it."

"Might even be a graduate of the Sorbonne. Might even be mooning away in a measly small-town practice. Waiting and hoping. That's one coincidence I'd like to eat. It has a touch of poetry."

The polite smile stayed in place on her lovely face.

"We've slipped far apart," I said. "Ever so far. And we got to be pretty clubby there for a while."

453

I looked down at my fingers. My head ached. I wasn't even forty per cent of what I ought to be. She reached me a crystal cigarette box and I took one. She fitted one for herself into the golden tweezers. She took it from a different box.

"I'd like to try one of yours," I said.

"But Mexican tobacco is so harsh to most people."

"As long as it's tobacco," I said, watching her. I made up my mind. "No, you're right. I wouldn't like it."

"What," she asked carefully, "is the meaning of this by-play?"

"Desk clerk's a muggle-smoker."

She nodded slowly. "I have warned him," she said. "Several times."

"Amigo," I said.

"What?"

"You don't use much Spanish do you? Perhaps you don't know much Spanish. Amigo gets worn to shreds."

"We are not going to be like yesterday afternoon, I hope," she said slowly.

"We're not. The only thing Mexican about you is a few words and a careful way of talking that's supposed to give the impression of a person speaking a language they had to learn. Like saying 'do not' instead of 'don't.' That sort of thing."

She didn't answer. She puffed gently on her cigarette and smiled.

"I'm in bad trouble downtown," I went on. "Apparently Miss Weld had the good sense to tell it to her boss – Julius Oppenheimer – and he came through. Got Lee Farrell for her. I don't think they think she shot Steelgrave. But they think I know who did, and they don't love me any more."

"And do you know, amigo?"

"Told you over the phone I did."

She looked at me steadily for a longish moment. "I was there." Her voice had a dry serious sound for once.

"It was very curious, really. The little girl wanted to see the gambling house. She had never seen anything like that and there had been in the papers –"

"She was staying here – with you?"

"Not in my apartment, amigo. In a room I got for her here."

"No wonder she wouldn't tell me," I said. "But I guess you didn't have time to teach her the business."

She frowned very slightly and made a motion in the air with the brown cigarette. I watched its smoke write something unreadable in the still air.

"Please. As I was saying she wanted to go to that house. So I called him up and he said to come along. When we got there he was drunk. I have never seen him drunk before. He laughed and put his arm around little Orfamay and told her she had earned her money well. He said he had something for her, then he took from his pocket a billfold wrapped in a cloth of some kind and gave it to her. When she unwrapped it there was a hole in the middle of it and the hole was stained with blood."

"That wasn't nice," I said. "I wouldn't even call it characteristic."

"You did not know him very well."

"True. Go on."

"Little Orfamay took the billfold and stared at it and then stared at him and her white little face was very still. Then she thanked him and opened her bag to put the billfold in it, as I thought – it was all very curious –"

"A scream," I said. "It would have had me gasping on the floor."

" – but instead she took a gun out of her bag. It was a gun he had given Mavis, I think. It was like the one –"

"I know exactly what it was like," I said. "I played with it some."

"She turned around and shot him dead with one shot. It was very dramatic."

455

She put the brown cigarette back in her mouth and smiled at me. A curious, rather distant smile, as if she was thinking of something far away.

"You made her confess to Mavis Weld," I said.

She nodded.

"Mavis wouldn't have believed *you*, I guess."

"I did not care to risk it."

"It wasn't you gave Orfamay the thousand bucks, was it, darling? To make her tell? She's a little girl who would go a long way for a thousand bucks."

"I do not care to answer that," she said with dignity.

"No. So last night when you rushed me out there, you already knew he was dead and there wasn't anything to be afraid of and all that act with the gun was just an act."

"I do not like to play God," she said softly. "There was a situation and I knew that somehow or other you would get Mavis out of it. There was no one else who would. Mavis was determined to take the blame."

"I better have a drink," I said. "I'm sunk."

She jumped up and went to the little cellarette. She came back with a couple of huge glasses of Scotch and water. She handed me one and watched me over her glass as I tried it out. It was wonderful. I drank some more. She sank down into her chair again, and reached for the golden tweezers.

"I chased her out," I said, finally. "Mavis, I'm talking about. She told me she had shot him. She had the gun. The twin of the one you gave me. You didn't probably notice that yours had been fired."

"I know very little about guns," she said softly.

"Sure. I counted the shells in it, and assuming it had been full to start with, two had been fired. Quest was killed with two shots from a .32 automatic. Same caliber. I picked up the empty shells in the den down there."

"Down where, amigo?"

It was beginning to grate. Too much amigo, far too much.

"Of course I couldn't know it was the same gun, but it seemed worth trying out. Only confuse things up a little anyhow, and give Mavis that much break. So I switched guns on him, and put his behind the bar. His was a black .38. More like what he would carry, if he carried one at all. Even with a checked grip you can leave prints, but with an ivory grip you're apt to leave a fair set of finger marks on the left side. Steelgrave couldn't carry that kind of gun."

Her eyes were round and empty and puzzled. "I am afraid I am not following you too well."

"And if he killed a man he would kill him dead, and be sure of it. This guy got up and walked a bit."

A flash of something showed in her eyes and was gone.

"I'd like to say he talked a bit," I went on. "But he didn't. His lungs were full of blood. He died at my feet. Down there."

"But down where? You have not told me where it was that this —"

"Do I have to?"

She sipped from her glass. She smiled. She put the glass down. I said:

"You were present when little Orfamay told him where to go."

"Oh yes, of course." Nice recovery. Fast and clean. But her smile looked a little more tired.

"Only he didn't go," I said.

Her cigarette stopped in midair. That was all. Nothing else. It went on slowly to her lips. She puffed elegantly.

"That's what's been the matter all along," I said. "I just wouldn't buy what was staring me in the face. Steelgrave is Weepy Moyer. That's solid, isn't it?"

"Most certainly. And it can be proved."

"Steelgrave is a reformed character and doing fine. Then this Stein comes out bothering him, wanting to cut in. I'm guessing, but that's about how it would happen. Okay, Stein has to go. Steelgrave doesn't want to kill anybody — and he has never been accused of killing anybody. The Cleveland cops wouldn't come out and get him. No charges pending. No mystery – except that he had been connected with a mob in some capacity. But he has to get rid of Stein. So he gets himself pinched. And then he gets out of jail by bribing the jail doctor, and he kills Stein and goes back into jail at once. When the killing shows up whoever let him out of jail is going to run like hell and destroy any records there might be of his going out. Because the cops will come over and ask questions."

"Very naturally, amigo."

I looked her over for cracks, but there weren't any yet.

"So far so good. But we've got to give this lad credit for a few brains. Why did he let them hold him in jail for ten days? Answer One, to make himself an alibi. Answer Two, because he knew that sooner or later this question of him being Moyer was going to get aired, so why not give them the time and get it over with? That way any time a racket boy gets blown down around here they're not going to keep pulling Steelgrave in and trying to hang the rap on him."

"You like that idea, amigo?"

"Yes. Look at it this way. Why would he have lunch in a public place the very day he was out of the cooler to knock Stein off? And if he did, why would young Quest happen around to snap that picture? Stein hadn't been killed, so the picture wasn't evidence of anything. I like people to be lucky, but that's *too* lucky. Again, even if Steelgrave didn't know his picture had been taken, he knew who Quest was. Must have. Quest had been tapping his sister for eating money since he lost his job, maybe before. Steelgrave had a key to her apartment. He must have known something about this brother of hers. Which simply adds up to the result, that *that* night of all nights Steelgrave would *not* have shot Stein – even if he had planned to."

"It is now for me to ask you who did," she said politely.

"Somebody who knew Stein and could get close to him. Somebody who already knew that photo had been taken, knew who Steelgrave was, knew that Mavis Weld was on the edge of becoming a big star, knew that her association with Steelgrave was dangerous, but would be a thousand times more dangerous if Steelgrave could be framed for the murder of Stein. Knew Quest, because he had been to Mavis Weld's apartment, and had met him there and given him the works, and he was a boy that could be knocked clean out of his mind by that sort of treatment. Knew that those bone-handled .32's were registered to Steelgrave, although he had only bought them to give to a couple of girls, and if he carried a gun himself, it would be one that was not registered and could not be traced to him. Knew —"

"Stop!" Her voice was a sharp stab of sound, but neither frightened nor even angry. "You will stop at once, please! I will not tolerate this another minute. You will now go!"

I stood up. She leaned back and a pulse beat in her throat. She was exquisite, she was dark, she was deadly. And nothing would ever touch her, not even the law.

"Why did you kill Quest?" I asked her.

She stood up and came close to me, smiling again. "For two reasons, amigo. He was more than a little crazy and in the end he would have killed me. And the other reason is that none of this — absolutely none of it — was for money. It was for love."

I started to laugh in her face. I didn't. She was dead serious. It was out of this world.

"No matter how many lovers a woman may have," she said softly, "there is always one she cannot bear to lose to another woman. Steelgrave was the one."

I just stared into her lovely dark eyes. "I believe you," I said at last.

"Kiss me, amigo."

"Good God!"

459

"I must have men, amigo. But the man I loved is dead. I killed him. That man I would not share."

"You waited a long time."

"I can be patient – as long as there is hope."

"Oh, nuts."

She smiled a free, beautiful and perfectly natural smile. "And you cannot do a damn thing about all this, darling, unless you destroy Mavis Weld utterly and finally."

"Last night she proved she was willing to destroy herself."

"If she was not acting." She looked at me sharply and laughed. "That hurt, did it not? You are in love with her."

I said slowly, "That would be kind of silly. I could sit in the dark with her and hold hands, but for how long? In a little while she will drift off into a haze of glamour and expensive clothes and froth and unreality and muted sex. She won't be a real person any more. Just a voice from a sound track, a face on a screen. I'd want more than that."

I moved towards the door without putting my back to her. I didn't really expect a slug. I thought she liked better having me the way I was – and not being able to do a damn thing about any of it.

I looked back as I opened the door. Slim, dark and lovely and smiling. Reeking with sex. Utterly beyond the moral laws of this or any world I could imagine.

She was one for the book all right. I went out quietly. Very softly her voice came to me as I closed the door.

"Querido – I have liked you very much. It is too bad."

I shut the door.

35

AS THE ELEVATOR opened at the lobby a man stood there waiting for it. He was tall and thin and his hat was pulled low over his eyes. It was a warm day but he wore a thin topcoat with the collar up. He kept his chin low.

"Dr. Lagardie," I said softly.

He glanced at me with no trace of recognition. He moved into the elevator. It started up.

I went across to the desk and banged the bell. The large fat soft man came out and stood with a pained smile on his loose mouth. His eyes were not quite so bright.

"Give me the phone."

He reached down and put it on the desk. I dialed Madison 7911. The voice said: "Police." This was the Emergency Board.

"Chateau Bercy Apartments, Franklin and Girard in Hollywood. A man named Dr. Vincent Lagardie wanted for questioning by homicide, Lieutenants French and Beifus, has just gone up to Apartment 412. This is Philip Marlowe, a private detective."

"Franklin and Girard. Wait there please. Are you armed?"

"Yes."

"Hold him if he tries to leave."

I hung up and wiped my mouth off. The fat softy was leaning against the counter, white around the eyes.

★

They came fast – but not fast enough. Perhaps I ought to have stopped him. Perhaps I had a hunch what he would do, and deliberately let him do it. Sometimes when I'm low I try to reason it out. But it gets too complicated. The whole damn case was that way. There was never a point where I could do the natural obvious thing without stopping to rack my head dizzy with figuring how it would affect somebody I owed something to.

★

When they cracked the door he was sitting on the couch holding her pressed against his heart. His eyes were blind and there was bloody foam on his lips. He had bitten through his tongue.

461

Under her left breast and tight against the flame-colored shirt lay the silver handle of a knife I had seen before. The handle was in the shape of a naked woman. The eyes of Miss Dolores Gonzales were half open and on her lips there was the dim ghost of a provocative smile.

"The Hippocrates smile," the ambulance intern said, and sighed. "On her it looks good."

He glanced across at Dr. Lagardie who saw nothing and heard nothing, if you could judge by his face.

"I guess somebody lost a dream," the intern said. He bent over and closed her eyes.

THE LONG GOODBYE

1

THE FIRST TIME I laid eyes on Terry Lennox he was drunk in a Rolls-Royce Silver Wraith outside the terrace of The Dancers. The parking lot attendant had brought the car out and he was still holding the door open because Terry Lennox's left foot was still dangling outside, as if he had forgotten he had one. He had a young-looking face but his hair was bone white. You could tell by his eyes that he was plastered to the hairline, but otherwise he looked like any other nice young guy in a dinner jacket who had been spending too much money in a joint that exists for that purpose and for no other.

There was a girl beside him. Her hair was a lovely shade of dark red and she had a distant smile on her lips and over her shoulders she had a blue mink that almost made the Rolls-Royce look like just another automobile. It didn't quite. Nothing can.

The attendant was the usual half-tough character in a white coat with the name of the restaurant stitched across the front of it in red. He was getting fed up.

"Look, mister," he said with an edge to his voice, "would you mind a whole lot pulling your leg into the car so I can kind of shut the door? Or should I open it all the way so you can fall out?"

The girl gave him a look which ought to have stuck at least four inches out of his back. It didn't bother him enough to give him the shakes. At The Dancers they get the sort of people that disillusion you about what a lot of golfing money can do for the personality.

A low-swung foreign speedster with no top drifted into the parking lot and a man got out of it and used the dash lighter on a long cigarette. He was wearing a pullover check shirt, yellow slacks, and riding boots. He strolled off trailing clouds of incense, not even bothering to look towards the Rolls-Royce. He probably thought it was corny. At the foot of the steps up to the terrace he paused to stick a monocle in his eye.

The girl said with a nice burst of charm: "I have a wonderful idea, darling. Why don't we just take a cab to your place and get your convertible out? It's such a wonderful night for a run up the coast to Montecito. I know some people there who are throwing a dance around the pool."

The white-haired lad said politely: "Awfully sorry, but I don't have it any more. I was compelled to sell it." From his voice and articulation you wouldn't have known he had had anything stronger than orange juice to drink.

"Sold it, darling? How do you mean?" She slid away from him along the seat but her voice slid away a lot farther than that.

"I mean I had to," he said. "For eating money."

"Oh, I see." A slice of spumoni wouldn't have melted on her now.

The attendant had the white-haired boy right where he could reach him – in a low-income bracket. "Look, buster," he said, "I've got to put a car away. See you some more some other time – maybe."

He let the door swing open. The drunk promptly slid off the seat and landed on the blacktop on the seat of his pants. So I went over and dropped my nickel. I guess it's always a mistake to interfere with a drunk. Even if he knows and likes you he is always liable to haul off and poke you in the teeth. I got him under the arms and got him up on his feet.

"Thank you so very much," he said politely.

The girl slid under the wheel. "He gets so goddam English when he's loaded," she said in a stainless-steel voice. "Thanks for catching him."

"I'll get him in the back of the car," I said.

"I'm terribly sorry. I'm late for an engagement." She let the clutch in and the Rolls started to glide. "He's just a lost dog," she added with a cool smile. "Perhaps you can find a home for him. He's housebroken – more or less."

And the Rolls ticked down the entrance driveway onto Sunset Boulevard, made a right turn, and was gone. I was looking after her when the attendant came back. And I was still holding the man up and he was now sound asleep.

"Well, that's one way of doing it," I told the white coat.

"Sure," he said cynically. "Why waste it on a lush? Them curves and all."

"You know him?"

"I heard the dame call him Terry. Otherwise I don't know him from a cow's caboose. But I only been here two weeks."

"Get my car, will you?" I gave him the ticket.

By the time he brought my Olds over I felt as if I was holding up a sack of lead. The white coat helped me get him into the front seat. The customer opened an eye and thanked us and went to sleep again.

"He's the politest drunk I ever met," I said to the white coat.

"They come all sizes and shapes and all kinds of manners," he said. "And they're all bums. Looks like this one had a plastic job one time."

"Yeah." I gave him a dollar and he thanked me. He was right about the plastic job. The right side of my new friend's face was frozen and whitish and seamed with thin fine scars. The skin had a glossy look along the scars. A plastic job and a pretty drastic one.

"Whatcha aim to do with him?"

"Take him home and sober him up enough to tell me where he lives."

The white coat grinned at me. "Okay, sucker. If it was me, I'd just drop him in the gutter and keep going. Them booze hounds just make a man a lot of trouble for no fun. I got a philosophy about them things. The way the competition is nowadays a guy has to save his strength to protect hisself in the clinches."

"I can see you've made a big success out of it," I said.

He looked puzzled and then he started to get mad, but by that time I was in the car and moving.

He was partly right of course. Terry Lennox made me plenty of trouble. But after all that's my line of work.

★

I was living that year in a house on Yucca Avenue in the Laurel Canyon district. It was a small hillside house on a dead-end street with a long flight of redwood steps to the front door and a grove of eucalyptus trees across the way. It was furnished, and it belonged to a woman who had gone to Idaho to live with her widowed daughter for a while. The rent was low, partly because the owner wanted to be able to come back on short notice, and partly because of the steps. She was getting too old to face them every time she came home.

I got the drunk up them somehow. He was eager to help but his legs were rubber and he kept falling asleep in the middle of an apologetic sentence. I got the door unlocked and dragged him inside and spread him on the long couch, threw a rug over him and let him go back to sleep. He snored like a grampus for an hour. Then he came awake all of a sudden and wanted to go to the bathroom. When he came back he looked at me peeringly, squinting his eyes, and wanted to know where the hell he was. I told him. He said his name was Terry Lennox and that he lived in an apartment in Westwood and no one was waiting up for him. His voice was clear and unslurred.

He said he could handle a cup of black coffee. When I brought it he sipped it carefully holding the saucer close under the cup.

"How come I'm here?" he asked, looking around.

"You squiffed out at The Dancers in a Rolls. Your girl friend ditched you."

"Quite," he said. "No doubt she was entirely justified."

"You English?"

"I've lived there. I wasn't born there. If I might call a taxi, I'll take myself off."

"You've got one waiting."

He made the steps on his own going down. He didn't say much on the way to Westwood, except that it was very kind of me and he was sorry to be such a nuisance. He had probably said it so often and to so many people that it was automatic.

His apartment was small and stuffy and impersonal. He might have moved in that afternoon. On a coffee table in front of a hard green davenport there was a half empty Scotch bottle and melted ice in a bowl and three empty fizz-water bottles and two glasses and a glass ashtray loaded with stubs with and without lipstick. There wasn't a photograph or a personal article of any kind in the place. It might have been a hotel room rented for a meeting or a farewell, for a few drinks and a talk, for a roll in the hay. It didn't look like a place where anyone lived.

He offered me a drink. I said no thanks. I didn't sit down. When I left he thanked me some more, but not as if I had climbed a mountain for him, nor as if it was nothing at all. He was a little shaky and a little shy but polite as hell. He stood in the open door until the automatic elevator came up and I got into it. Whatever he didn't have he had manners.

He hadn't mentioned the girl again. Also, he hadn't mentioned that he had no job and no prospects and that almost his last dollar had gone into paying the check at The Dancers for a bit of high class fluff that couldn't stick around long enough to make sure he didn't get tossed in the sneezer by some prowl car boys, or rolled by a tough hackie and dumped out in a vacant lot.

On the way down in the elevator I had an impulse to go back up and take the Scotch bottle away from him. But it wasn't any of my business and it never does any good anyway. They always find a way to get it if they have to have it.

I drove home chewing my lip. I'm supposed to be tough but there was something about the guy that got me. I didn't know what it was unless it was the white hair and the scarred face and the clear voice and the politeness. Maybe that was enough. There was no reason why I should ever see him again. He was just a lost dog, like the girl said.

2

IT WAS THE week after Thanksgiving when I saw him again. The stores along Hollywood Boulevard were already beginning to fill up with overpriced Christmas junk, and the daily papers were beginning to scream about how terrible it would be if you didn't get your Christmas shopping done early. It would be terrible anyway; it always is.

It was about three blocks from my office building that I saw a cop car double-parked and the two buttons in it staring at something over by a shop window on the sidewalk. The something was Terry Lennox – or what was left of him – and that little was not too attractive.

He was leaning against a store front. He had to lean against something. His shirt was dirty and open at the neck and partly outside his jacket and partly not. He hadn't shaved for four or five days. His nose was pinched. His skin was so pale that the long thin scars hardly showed. And his eyes were like holes poked in a snowbank. It was pretty obvious that the buttons in the prowl car were about ready to drop the hook on him, so I went over there fast and took hold of his arm.

"Straighten up and walk," I said, putting on the tough. I winked at him from the side. "Can you make it? Are you stinko?"

He looked me over vaguely and then smiled his little one-sided smile. "I have been," he breathed. "Right now I guess I'm just a little – empty."

"Okay, but make with the feet. You're halfway into the drunk tank already."

He made the effort and let me walk him through the side-walk loafers to the edge of the curb. There was a taxi stand there and I yanked open the door.

"He goes first," the hackie said, jerking a thumb at the cab ahead. He swung his head around and saw Terry. "If at all," he added.

"This is an emergency. My friend is sick."

"Yeah," the hackie said. "He could get sick somewheres else."

"Five bucks," I said, "and let's see that beautiful smile."

"Oh well," he said, and stuck a magazine with a Martian on the cover behind his mirror. I reached in and got the door open. I got Terry Lennox in and the shadow of the prowl car blocked the far window. A gray-haired cop got out and came over. I went around the taxi and met him.

"Just a minute, Mac. What have we got here? Is the gentle-man in the soiled laundry a real close friend of yours?"

"Close enough for me to know he needs a friend. He's not drunk."

"For financial reasons, no doubt," the cop said. He put his hand out and I put my license in it. He looked at it and handed it back. "Oh-oh," he said. "A P.I. picking up a client." His voice changed and got tough. "That tells a little some-thing about you, Mr. Marlowe. What about him?"

"His name's Terry Lennox. He works in pictures."

"That's nice." He leaned into the taxi and stared at Terry back in the corner. "I'd say he didn't work too lately. I'd say he didn't sleep indoors too lately. I'd even say he was a vag and so maybe we ought to take him in."

"Your arrest record can't be that low," I said. "Not in Hollywood."

He was still looking in at Terry. "What's your friend's name, buddy?"

"Philip Marlowe," Terry said slowly. "He lives on Yucca Avenue, Laurel Canyon."

The cop pulled his head out of the window space. He turned, and made a gesture with his hand. "You could of just told him."

"I could have, but I didn't."

He stared at me for a second or two. "I'll buy it this time," he said. "But get him off the street." He got into the police car and the police car went away.

I got into the taxi and we went the three-odd blocks to my parking lot and shifted to my car. I held out the five-spot to the hackie. He gave me a stiff look and shook his head.

"Just what's on the meter, Jack, or an even buck if you feel like it. I been down and out myself. In Frisco. Nobody picked me up in no taxi either. There's one stony-hearted town."

"San Francisco," I said mechanically.

"I call it Frisco," he said. "The hell with them minority groups. Thanks." He took the dollar and went away.

We went to a drive-in where they made hamburgers that didn't taste like something the dog wouldn't eat. I fed Terry Lennox a couple and a bottle of beer and drove him home. The steps were still tough on him but he grinned and panted and made the climb. An hour later he was shaved and bathed and he looked human again. We sat down over a couple of very mild drinks.

"Lucky you remembered my name," I said.

"I made a point of it," he said. "I looked you up too. Could I do less?"

"So why not give me a ring? I live here all the time. I have an office as well."

"Why should I bother you?"

"Looks like you had to bother somebody. Looks like you don't have many friends."

472

"Oh I have friends," he said, "of a sort." He turned his glass on the table top. "Asking for help doesn't come easy — especially when it's all your own fault." He looked up with a tired smile. "Maybe I can quit drinking one of these days. They all say that, don't they?"

"It takes about three years."

"Three years?" He looked shocked.

"Usually it does. It's a different world. You have to get used to a paler set of colors, a quieter lot of sounds. You have to allow for relapses. All the people you used to know well will get to be just a little strange. You won't even like most of them, and they won't like you too well."

"That wouldn't be much of a change," he said. He turned and looked at the clock. "I have a two-hundred-dollar suitcase checked at the Hollywood bus station. If I could bail it out I could buy a cheap one and pawn the one that's checked for enough to get to Vegas on the bus. I can get a job there."

I didn't say anything. I just nodded and sat there nursing my drink.

"You're thinking that idea might have come to me a little sooner," he said quietly.

"I'm thinking there's something behind all this that's none of my business. Is the job for sure or just a hope?"

"It's for sure. Fellow I knew very well in the army runs a big club there, the Terrapin Club. He's part racketeer, of course, they all are — but the other part is a nice guy."

"I can manage the bus fare and something over. But I'd just as soon it bought something that would stay bought for a while. Better talk to him on the phone."

"Thank you, but it's not necessary. Randy Starr won't let me down. He never has. And the suitcase will pawn for fifty dollars. I know from experience."

"Look," I said, "I'd put up what you need. I'm no big soft-hearted slob. So you take what's offered and be good. I want you out of my hair because I've got a feeling about you."

473

"Really?" He looked down into his glass. He was only sipping the stuff. "We've only met twice and you've been more than white to me both times. What sort of feeling?"

"A feeling that next time I'll find you in worse trouble than I can get you out of. I don't know just why I have the feeling, but I have it."

He touched the right side of his face gently with two fingertips. "Maybe it's this. It does make me look a little sinister, I suppose. But it's an honorable wound – or anyhow the result of one."

"It's not that. That doesn't bother me at all. I'm a private dick. You're a problem that I don't have to solve. But the problem is there. Call it a hunch. If you want to be extra polite, call it a sense of character. Maybe that girl didn't walk out on you at The Dancers just because you were drunk. Maybe she had a feeling too."

He smiled faintly. "I was married to her once. Her name is Sylvia Lennox. I married her for her money."

I stood up scowling at him. "I'll fix you some scrambled eggs. You need food."

"Wait a minute, Marlowe. You're wondering why if I was down and out and Sylvia had plenty I couldn't ask her for a few bucks. Did you ever hear of pride?"

"You're killing me, Lennox."

"Am I? My kind of pride is different. It's the pride of a man who has nothing else. I'm sorry if I annoy you."

I went out to my kitchen and cooked up some Canadian bacon and scrambled eggs and coffee and toast. We ate in the breakfast nook. The house belonged to the period that always had one.

I said I had to go to the office and would pick up his suitcase on the way back. He gave me the check ticket. His face now had a little color and the eyes were not so far back in his head that you had to grope for them.

Before I went out I put the whiskey bottle on the table in front of the couch. "Use your pride on that," I said. "And call Vegas, if only as a favor to me."

He just smiled and shrugged his shoulders. I was still sore going down the steps. I didn't know why, any more than I knew why a man would starve and walk the streets rather than pawn his wardrobe. Whatever his rules were he played by them.

★

The suitcase was the damnedest thing you ever saw. It was bleached pigskin and when new had been a pale cream color. The fittings were gold. It was English made and if you could buy it here at all, it would cost more like eight hundred than two.

I planked it down in front of him. I looked at the bottle on the cocktail table. He hadn't touched it. He was as sober as I was. He was smoking, but not liking that very well.

"I called Randy," he said. "He was sore because I hadn't called him before."

"It takes a stranger to help you," I said. "A present from Sylvia?" I pointed at the suitcase.

He looked out of the window. "No. That was given to me in England, long before I met her. Very long ago indeed. I'd like to leave it with you if you could lend me an old one."

I got five double sawbucks out of my wallet and dropped them in front of him. "I don't need security."

"That wasn't the idea at all. You're no pawnbroker. I just don't want it with me in Vegas. And I don't need this much money."

"Okay. You keep the money and I'll keep the suitcase. But this house is easy to burgle."

"It wouldn't matter," he said indifferently. "It wouldn't matter at all."

He changed his clothes and we ate dinner at Musso's about five-thirty. No drinks. He caught the bus on Cahuenga and

I drove home thinking about this and that. His empty suitcase was on my bed where he had unpacked it and put his stuff in a lightweight job of mine. His had a gold key which was in one of the locks. I locked the suitcase up empty and tied the key to the handle and put it on the high shelf in my clothes closet. It didn't feel quite empty, but what was in it was no business of mine.

It was a quiet night and the house seemed emptier than usual. I set out the chessmen and played a French defense against Steinitz. He beat me in forty-four moves, but I had him sweating a couple of times.

The phone rang at nine-thirty and the voice that spoke was one I had heard before.

"Is this Mr. Philip Marlowe?"

"Yeah. I'm Marlowe."

"This is Sylvia Lennox, Mr. Marlowe. We met very briefly in front of The Dancers one night last month. I heard afterwards that you had been kind enough to see that Terry got home."

"I did that."

"I suppose you know that we are not married any more, but I've been a little worried about him. He gave up the apartment he had in Westwood and nobody seems to know where he is."

"I noticed how worried you were the night we met."

"Look, Mr. Marlowe, I've been married to the man. I'm not very sympathetic to drunks. Perhaps I was a little unfeeling and perhaps I had something rather important to do. You're a private detective and this can be put on a professional basis, if you prefer it."

"It doesn't have to be put on any basis at all, Mrs. Lennox. He's on a bus going to Las Vegas. He has a friend there who will give him a job."

She brightened up very suddenly. "Oh – to Las Vegas? How sentimental of him. That's where we were married."

"I guess he forgot," I said, "or he would have gone somewhere else."

Instead of hanging up on me she laughed. It was a cute little laugh. "Are you always as rude as this to your clients?"

"You're not a client, Mrs. Lennox."

"I might be someday. Who knows? Let's say to your lady friends, then."

"Same answer. The guy was down and out, starving, dirty, without a bean. You could have found him if it had been worth your time. He didn't want anything from you then and he probably doesn't want anything from you now."

"That," she said coolly, "is something you couldn't possibly know anything about. Good night." And she hung up.

She was dead right, of course, and I was dead wrong. But I didn't feel wrong. I just felt sore. If she had called up half an hour earlier I might have been sore enough to beat the hell out of Steinitz – except that he had been dead for fifty years and the chess game was out of a book.

3

THREE DAYS BEFORE Christmas I got a cashier's check on a Las Vegas bank for $100. A note written on hotel paper came with it. He thanked me, wished me a Merry Christmas and all kinds of luck and said he hoped to see me again soon. The kick was in a postscript. "Sylvia and I are starting a second honeymoon. She says please don't be sore at her for wanting to try again."

I caught the rest of it in one of those snob columns in the society section of the paper. I don't read them often, only when I run out of things to dislike.

"Your correspondent is all fluttery at the news that Terry and Sylvia Lennox have rehitched at Las Vegas, the dears. She's the younger daughter of multimillionaire Harlan Potter of San Francisco and Pebble Beach, of course. Sylvia is having Marcel and Jeanne Duhaux redecorate the entire mansion in Encino from basement to roof in the most *devastatingly* dernier cri. Curt Westerheym, Sylvia's last but one, my dears, gave her the little eighteen-room shack for a wedding present, you may remember. And whatever happened to Curt, you ask? Or do you? St. Tropez has the answer, and permanently I hear. Also a certain very, *very* blue-blooded French duchess with two perfectly adorable children. And what does Harlan Potter think of the remarriage, you may also ask? One can only guess. Mr. Potter is one person who but *never* gives an interview. How exclusive can you get darlings?"

I threw the paper into the corner and turned on the TV set. After the society page dog vomit even the wrestlers looked good. But the facts were probably right. On the society page they better be.

I had a mental picture of the kind of eighteen-room shack that would go with a few of the Potter millions, not to mention decorations by Duhaux in the last subphallic symbolism. But I had no mental picture at all of Terry Lennox loafing around one of the swimming pools in Bermuda shorts and phoning the butler by R/T to ice the champagne and get the grouse atoasting. There was no reason why I should have. If the guy wanted to be somebody's woolly bear, it was no skin off my teeth. I just didn't want to see him again. But I knew I would – if only on account of his goddam gold-plated pigskin suitcase.

It was five o'clock of a wet March evening when he walked into my down-at-heels brain emporium. He looked changed. Older, very sober and severe and beautifully calm. He looked like a guy who had learned to roll with a punch. He wore an oyster-white raincoat and gloves and no hat and his white hair was as smooth as a bird's breast.

"Let's go to some quiet bar and have a drink," he said, as if he had been in ten minutes before. "If you have the time, that is."

We didn't shake hands. We never did. Englishmen don't shake hands all the time like Americans and although he wasn't English he had some of the mannerisms.

I said: "Let's go by my place and pick up your fancy suit-case. It kind of worries me."

He shook his head. "It would be kind of you to keep it for me."

"Why?"

"I just feel that way. Do you mind? It's a sort of link with a time when I wasn't a no-good waster."

"Nuts to that," I said. "But it's your business."

"If it bothers you because you think it might be stolen —"

"That's your business too. Let's go get that drink."

We went to Victor's. He drove me in a rust-colored Jupiter-Jowett with a flimsy canvas rain top under which there was only just room for the two of us. It had pale leather uphol-stery and what looked like silver fittings. I'm not too fussy about cars, but the damn thing did make my mouth water a little. He said it would do sixty-five in second. It had a squatty little gear shift that barely came up to his knee.

"Four speeds," he said. "They haven't invented an auto-matic shift that will work for one of these jobs yet. You don't really need one. You can start it in third even uphill and that's as high as you can shift in traffic anyway."

"Wedding present?"

"Just a casual 'I happened to see this gadget in a window' sort of present. I'm a very pampered guy."

"Nice," I said. "If there's no price tag."

He glanced at me quickly and then put his eyes back on the wet pavement. Double wipers swished gently over the little windscreen. "Price tag? There's always a price tag, chum. You think I'm not happy maybe?"

"Sorry, I was out of line."

"I'm rich. Who the hell wants to be happy?" There was a bitterness in his voice that was new to me.

"How's your drinking?"

"Perfectly elegant, old top. For some strange reason I seem to be able to handle the stuff. But you never know, do you?"

479

"Perhaps you were never really a drunk."

We sat in a corner of the bar at Victor's and drank gimlets. "They don't know how to make them here," he said. "What they call a gimlet is just some lime or lemon juice and gin with a dash of sugar and bitters. A real gimlet is half gin and half Rose's Lime Juice and nothing else. It beats martinis hollow."

"I was never fussy about drinks. How did you get on with Randy Starr? Down my street he's called a tough number."

He leaned back and looked thoughtful. "I guess he is. I guess they all are. But it doesn't show on him. I could name you a couple of lads in the same racket in Hollywood that act the part. Randy doesn't bother. In Las Vegas he's a legitimate businessman. You look him up next time you're there. He'll be your pal."

"Not too likely. I don't like hoodlums."

"That's just a word, Marlowe. We have that kind of world. Two wars gave it to us and we are going to keep it. Randy and I and another fellow were in a jam once. It made a sort of bond between us."

"Then why didn't you ask him for help when you needed it?"

He drank up his drink and signaled the waiter. "Because he couldn't refuse."

The waiter brought fresh drinks and I said: "That's just talk to me. If by any chance the guy owed you something, think of *his* end. He'd like a chance to pay something back."

He shook his head slowly. "I know you're right. Of course I did ask him for a job. But I worked at it while I had it. As for asking favors or handouts, no."

"But you'll take them from a stranger."

He looked me straight in the eye. "The stranger can keep going and pretend not to hear."

We had three gimlets, not doubles, and it didn't do a thing to him. That much would just get a real souse started. So I guess maybe he was cured at that.

480

Then he drove me back to the office.

"We have dinner at eight-fifteen," he said. "Only millionaires can afford it. Only millionaires' servants will stand for it nowadays. Lots of lovely people coming."

★

From then on it got to be a sort of habit with him to drop in around five o'clock. We didn't always go to the same bar, but oftener to Victor's than anywhere else. It may have had some association for him that I didn't know about. He never drank too much, and that surprised him.

"It must be something like the tertian ague," he said. "When it hits you it's bad. When you don't have it, it's as though you never did have it."

"What I don't get is why a guy with your privileges would want to drink with a private eye."

"Are you being modest?"

"Nope. I'm just puzzled. I'm a reasonably friendly type but we don't live in the same world. I don't even know where you hang out except that it's Encino. I should guess your home life is adequate."

"I don't have any home life."

We were drinking gimlets again. The place was almost empty. There was the usual light scattering of compulsive drinkers getting tuned up at the bar on the stools, the kind that reach very slowly for the first one and watch their hands so they won't knock anything over.

"I don't get that. Am I supposed to?"

"Big production, no story, as they say around the movie lots. I guess Sylvia is happy enough, though not necessarily with me. In our circle that's not too important. There's always something to do if you don't have to work or consider the cost. It's no real fun but the rich don't know that. They never had any. They never want anything very hard except maybe somebody else's wife and that's a pretty pale desire compared with the way a plumber's wife wants new curtains for the living room."

I didn't say anything. I let him carry the ball.

"Mostly I just kill time," he said, "and it dies hard. A little tennis, a little golf, a little swimming and horseback riding, and the exquisite pleasure of watching Sylvia's friends trying to hold out to lunch time before they start killing their hangovers."

"The night you went to Vegas she said she didn't like drunks."

He grinned crookedly. I was getting so used to his scarred face that I only noticed it when some change of expression emphasized its one-sided woodenness.

"She meant drunks without money. With money they are just heavy drinkers. If they vomit in the lanai, that's for the butler to handle."

"You didn't have to have it the way it is."

He finished his drink at a gulp and stood up. "I've got to run, Marlowe. Besides I'm boring you and God knows I'm boring myself."

"You're not boring me. I'm a trained listener. Sooner or later I may figure out why you like being a kept poodle."

He touched his scars gently with a fingertip. He had a remote little smile. "You should wonder why she wants me around, not why I want to be there, waiting patiently on my satin cushion to have my head patted."

"You like satin cushions," I said, as I stood up to leave with him. "You like silk sheets and bells to ring and the butler to come with his deferential smile."

"Could be. I was raised in an orphanage in Salt Lake City."

We went out into the tired evening and he said he wanted to walk. We had come in my car, and for once I had been fast enough to grab the check. I watched him out of sight. The light from a store window caught the gleam of his white hair for a moment as he faded into the light mist.

I liked him better drunk, down and out, hungry and beaten and proud. Or did I? Maybe I just liked being top man. His reasons for things were hard to figure. In my business there's a time to ask questions and a time to let your man simmer until he boils over. Every good cop knows that. It's a good deal like chess or boxing. Some people you have to crowd and keep off balance. Some you just box and they will end up beating themselves.

He would have told me the story of his life if I had asked him. But I never even asked him how he got his face smashed. If I had and he told me, it just possibly might have saved a couple of lives. Just possibly, no more.

4

THE LAST TIME we had a drink in a bar was in May and it was earlier than usual, just after four o'clock. He looked tired and thinner but he looked around with a slow smile of pleasure.

"I like bars just after they open for the evening. When the air inside is still cool and clean and everything is shiny and the barkeep is giving himself that last look in the mirror to see if his tie is straight and his hair is smooth. I like the neat bottles on the bar back and the lovely shining glasses and the anticipation. I like to watch the man mix the first one of the evening and put it down on a crisp mat and put the little folded napkin beside it. I like to taste it slowly. The first quiet drink of the evening in a quiet bar – that's wonderful."

I agreed with him.

"Alcohol is like love," he said. "The first kiss is magic, the second is intimate, the third is routine. After that you take the girl's clothes off."

"Is that bad?" I asked him.

"It's excitement of a high order, but it's an impure emotion – impure in the aesthetic sense. I'm not sneering at sex. It's necessary and it doesn't have to be ugly. But it always has to

483

be managed. Making it glamorous is a billion-dollar industry and it costs every cent of it."

He looked around and yawned. "I haven't been sleeping well. It's nice in here. But after a while the lushes will fill the place up and talk loud and laugh and the goddam women will start waving their hands and screwing up their faces and tinkling their goddam bracelets and making with the packaged charm which will later on in the evening have a slight but unmistakable odor of sweat."

"Take it easy," I said. "So they're human, they sweat, they get dirty, they have to go to the bathroom. What did you expect — golden butterflies hovering in a rosy mist?"

He emptied his glass and held it upside down and watched a slow drop form on the rim and then tremble and fall.

"I'm sorry for her," he said slowly. "She's such an absolute bitch. Could be I'm fond of her too in a remote sort of way. Some day she'll need me and I'll be the only guy around not holding a chisel. Likely enough then I'll flunk out."

I just looked at him. "You do a great job of selling yourself," I said after a moment.

"Yeah, I know. I'm a weak character, without guts or ambition. I caught the brass ring and it shocked me to find out it wasn't gold. A guy like me has one big moment in his life, one perfect swing on the high trapeze. Then he spends the rest of his time trying not to fall off the sidewalk into the gutter."

"What's this in favor of?" I got out a pipe and started to fill it.

"She's scared. She's scared stiff."

"What of?"

"I don't know. We don't talk much any more. Maybe of the old man. Harlan Potter is a coldhearted son of a bitch. All Victorian dignity on the outside. Inside he's as ruthless as a Gestapo thug. Sylvia is a tramp. He knows it and he hates it and there's nothing he can do about it. But he waits and he watches and if Sylvia ever gets into a big mess of scandal he'll break her in half and bury the two halves a thousand miles apart."

"You're her husband."

He lifted the empty glass and brought it down hard on the edge of the table. It smashed with a sharp ping. The barman stared, but didn't say anything.

"Like that, chum. Like that. Oh sure, I'm her husband. That's what the record says. I'm the three white steps and the big green front door and the brass knocker you rap one long and two short and the maid lets you into the hundred-dollar whorehouse."

I stood up and dropped some money on the table. "You talk too damn much," I said, "and it's too damn much about you. See you later."

I walked out leaving him sitting there shocked and white-faced as well as I could tell by the kind of light they have in bars. He called something after me, but I kept going.

Ten minutes later I was sorry. But ten minutes later I was somewhere else. He didn't come to the office any more. Not at all, not once. I had got to him where it hurt.

I didn't see him again for a month. When I did it was five o'clock in the morning and just beginning to get light. The persistent ringing of the doorbell yanked me out of bed. I plowed down the hall and across the living room and opened up. He stood there looking as if he hadn't slept for a week. He had a light topcoat on with the collar turned up and he seemed to be shivering. A dark felt hat was pulled down over his eyes.

He had a gun in his hand.

5

THE GUN WASN'T pointed at me, he was just holding it. It was a medium-caliber automatic, foreign made, certainly not a Colt or a Savage. With the white tired face and the scars and the turned-up collar and the pulled-down hat and the gun he could have stepped right out of an old-fashioned kick-'em-in-the-teeth gangster movie.

"You're driving me to Tijuana to get a plane at ten-fifteen," he said. "I have a passport and visa and I'm all set except for transportation. For certain reasons I can't take a train or a bus or a plane from L.A. Would five hundred bucks be a reasonable taxi fare?"

I stood in the doorway and didn't move to let him in. "Five hundred plus the gat?" I asked.

He looked down at it rather absently. Then he dropped it into his pocket.

"It might be a protection," he said, "for you. Not for me."

"Come on in then." I stood to one side and he came in with an exhausted lunge and fell into a chair.

The living room was still dark, because of the heavy growth of shrubbery the owner had allowed to mask the windows. I put a lamp on and mooched a cigarette. I lit it. I stared down at him. I rumpled my hair which was already rumpled. I put the old tired grin on my face.

"What the hell's the matter with me sleeping such a lovely morning away? Ten-fifteen, huh? Well, there's plenty of time. Let's go out to the kitchen and I'll brew some coffee."

"I'm in a great deal of trouble, shamus." Shamus, it was the first time he had called me that. But it kind of went with his style of entry, the way he was dressed, the gun and all.

"It's going to be a peach of a day. Light breeze. You can hear those tough old eucalyptus trees across the street whispering to each other. Talking about old times in Australia when the wallabies hopped about underneath the branches and the koala bears rode piggyback on each other. Yes, I got the general idea you were in some trouble. Let's talk about it after I've had a couple of cups of coffee. I'm always a little lightheaded when I first wake up. Let us confer with Mr. Huggins and Mr. Young."

"Look, Marlowe, this is not the time —"

"Fear nothing, old boy. Mr. Huggins and Mr. Young are two of the best. They make Huggins-Young coffee. It's their life work, their pride and joy. One of these days I'm going to see that they get the recognition they deserve. So far all they're making is money. You couldn't expect that to satisfy them."

I left him with that bright chatter and went out to the kitchen at the back. I turned the hot water on and got the coffee maker down off the shelf. I wet the rod and measured the stuff into the top and by that time the water was steaming. I filled the lower half of the dingus and set it on the flame. I set the upper part on top and gave it a twist so it would bind.

By that time he had come in after me. He leaned in the doorway a moment and then edged across to the breakfast nook and slid into the seat. He was still shaking. I got a bottle of Old Grand-Dad off the shelf and poured him a shot in a big glass. I knew he would need a big glass. Even with that he had to use both hands to get it to his mouth. He swallowed, put the glass down with a thud, and hit the back of the seat with a jar.

"Almost passed out," he muttered. "Seems like I've been up for a week. Didn't sleep at all last night."

The coffee maker was almost ready to bubble. I turned the flame low and watched the water rise. It hung a little at the bottom of the glass tube. I turned the flame up just enough to get it over the hump and then turned it low again quickly. I stirred the coffee and covered it. I set my timer for three minutes. Very methodical guy, Marlowe. Nothing must interfere with his coffee technique. Not even a gun in the hand of a desperate character.

I poured him another slug. "Just sit there," I said. "Don't say a word. Just sit."

He handled the second slug with one hand. I did a fast wash-up in the bathroom and the bell of the timer went just as I got back. I cut the flame and set the coffee maker on a straw mat on the table. Why did I go into such detail? Because the charged atmosphere made every little thing stand out as a performance, a movement distinct and vastly important. It was one of those hypersensitive moments when all your automatic movements, however long established, however habitual, become separate acts of will. You are like a man learning to walk after polio. You take nothing for granted, absolutely nothing at all.

The coffee was all down and the air rushed in with its usual fuss and the coffee bubbled and then became quiet. I removed the top of the maker and set it on the drainboard in the socket of the cover.

I poured two cups and added a slug to his. "Black for you, Terry." I added two lumps of sugar and some cream to mine. I was coming out of it by now. I wasn't conscious of how I opened the Frig and got the cream carton.

I sat down across from him. He hadn't moved. He was propped in the corner of the nook, rigid. Then without warning his head came down on the table and he was sobbing.

He didn't pay any attention when I reached across and dug the gun out of his pocket. It was a Mauser 7.65, a beauty. I sniffed it. I sprang the magazine loose. It was full. Nothing in the breach.

He lifted his head and saw the coffee and drank some slowly, not looking at me. "I didn't shoot anybody," he said.

"Well – not recently anyhow. And the gun would have had to be cleaned. I hardly think you shot anybody with this."

"I'll tell you about it," he said.

"Wait just a minute." I drank my coffee as quickly as the heat would let me. I refilled my cup. "It's like this," I said. "Be very careful what you tell me. If you really want me to ride you down to Tijuana, there are two things I must not be told. One – are you listening?"

He nodded very slightly. He was looking blank-eyed at the wall over my head. The scars were very livid this morning. His skin was almost dead white but the scars seemed to shine out of it just the same.

"One," I repeated slowly, "if you have committed a crime or anything the law calls a crime – a serious crime, I mean – I can't be told about it. Two, if you have essential knowledge that such a crime has been committed, I can't be told about that either. Not if you want me to drive you to Tijuana. That clear?"

He looked me in the eye. His eyes focused, but they were lifeless. He had the coffee inside him. He had no color, but he was steady. I poured him some more and loaded it the same way.

"I told you I was in a jam," he said.

"I heard you. I don't want to know what kind of jam. I have a living to earn, a license to protect."

"I could hold the gun on you," he said.

I grinned and pushed the gun across the table. He looked down at it but didn't touch it.

"Not to Tijuana you couldn't hold it on me, Terry. Not across the border, not up the steps into a plane. I'm a man who occasionally has business with guns. We'll forget about the gun. I'd look great telling the cops I was so scared I just had to do what you told me to. Supposing, of course, which I don't know, that there was anything to tell the cops."

"Listen," he said, "it will be noon or even later before anybody knocks at the door. The help knows better than to disturb her when she sleeps late. But by about noon her maid would knock and go in. She wouldn't be in her room."

I sipped my coffee and said nothing.

"The maid would see that her bed hadn't been slept in," he went on. "Then she would think of another place to look. There's a big guest house pretty far back from the main house. It has its own driveway and garage and so on. Sylvia spent the night there. The maid would eventually find her there."

I frowned. "I've got to be very careful what questions I ask you, Terry. Couldn't she have spent the night away from home?"

"Her clothes would be thrown all over her room. She never hangs anything up. The maid would know she had put a robe over her pajamas and gone out that way. So it would only be to the guest house."

489

"Not necessarily," I said.

"It would be to the guest house. Hell, do you think they don't know what goes on in the guest house? Servants always know."

"Pass it," I said.

He ran a finger down the side of his good cheek hard enough to leave a red streak. "And in the guest house," he went on slowly, "the maid would find –"

"Sylvia dead drunk, paralyzed, spifflicated, iced to the eyebrows," I said harshly.

"Oh." He thought about it. Big think. "Of course," he added, "that's how it would be. Sylvia is not a souse. When she does get over the edge it's pretty drastic."

"That's the end of the story," I said. "Or almost. Let me improvise. The last time we drank together I was a bit rough with you, walked out if you recall. You irritated the hell out of me. Thinking it over afterwards I could see that you were just trying to sneer yourself out of a feeling of disaster. You say you have a passport and a visa. It takes a little time to get a visa to Mexico. They don't let just anybody in. So you've been planning to blow for some time. I was wondering how long you would stick."

"I guess I felt some vague kind of obligation to be around, some idea she might need me for something more than a front to keep the old man from nosing around too hard. By the way, I tried to call you in the middle of the night."

"I sleep hard. I didn't hear."

"Then I went to a Turkish bath place. I stayed a couple of hours, had a steam bath, a plunge, a needle shower, a rubdown and made a couple of phone calls from there. I left the car at La Brea and Fountain. I walked from there. Nobody saw me turn into your street."

"Do these phone calls concern me?"

"One was to Harlan Potter. The old man flew down to Pasadena yesterday, some business. He hadn't been to the house. I had a lot of trouble getting him. But he finally talked to me. I told him I was sorry, but I was leaving." He was looking a little sideways when he said this, towards the window over the sink and the tecoma bush that fretted against the screen.

"How did he take it?"

"He was sorry. He wished me luck. Asked if I needed any money." Terry laughed harshly. "Money. Those are the first five letters of his alphabet. I said I had plenty. Then I called Sylvia's sister. Much the same story there. That's all."

"I want to ask this," I said. "Did you ever find her with a man in that guest house?"

He shook his head. "I never tried. It would not have been difficult. It never has been."

"Your coffee's getting cold."

"I don't want any more."

"Lots of men, huh? But you went back and married her again. I realize that she's quite a dish, but all the same —"

"I told you I was no good. Hell, why did I leave her the first time? Why after that did I get stinking every time I saw her? Why did I roll in the gutter rather than ask her for money? She's been married five times, not including me. Any one of them would go back at the crook of her finger. And not just for a million bucks."

"She's quite a dish," I said. I looked at my watch. "Just why does it have to be the ten-fifteen at Tijuana?"

"There's always space on that flight. Nobody from L.A. wants to ride a DC-3 over mountains when he can take a Connie and make it in seven hours to Mexico City. And the Connies don't stop where I want to go."

I stood up and leaned against the sink. "Now let's add it up and don't interrupt me. You came to me this morning in a highly emotional condition and wanted to be driven to Tijuana to catch an early plane. You had a gun in your pocket, but I needn't have seen it. You told me you had stood things as long as you could but last night you blew up. You found your wife dead drunk and a man had been with her. You got out and went to a Turkish bath to pass the time until morning and you phoned your wife's two closest relatives and told them what you were doing. Where you went was none of my business. You had the necessary documents to enter Mexico. How you went was none of my business either. We are friends and I did what you asked me without much thought. Why wouldn't I? You're not paying me anything. You had your car but you felt too upset to drive yourself. That's your business too. You're an emotional guy and you got yourself a bad wound in the war. I think I ought to pick up your car and shove it in a garage somewhere for storage."

He reached into his clothes and pushed a leather keyholder across the table.

"How does it sound?" he asked.

"Depends who's listening. I haven't finished. You took nothing but the clothes you stood up in and some money you had from your father-in-law. You left everything she had given you including that beautiful piece of machinery you parked at La Brea and Fountain. You wanted to go away as clean as it was possible for you to go and still go. All right. I'll buy it. Now I shave and get dressed."

"Why are you doing it, Marlowe?"

"Buy yourself a drink while I shave."

I walked out and left him sitting there hunched in the corner of the nook. He still had his hat and light topcoat on. But he looked a lot more alive.

I went into the bathroom and shaved. I was back in the bedroom knotting my tie when he came and stood in the doorway. "I washed the cups just in case," he said. "But I got thinking. Maybe it would be better if you called the police."

"Call them yourself. I haven't anything to tell them."

"You want me to?"

I turned around sharply and gave him a hard stare. "God damn it!" I almost yelled at him. "Can't you for Chrissake just leave it lay?"

"I'm sorry."

"Sure you're sorry. Guys like you are always sorry, and always too late."

He turned and walked back along the hall to the living room.

I finished dressing and locked up the back part of the house. When I got to the living room he had fallen asleep in a chair, his head on one side, his face drained of color, his whole body slack with exhaustion. He looked pitiful. When I touched his shoulder he came awake slowly as if it was a long way from where he was to where I was.

When I had his attention I said, "What about a suitcase? I still got that white pigskin job on the top shelf in my closet."

"It's empty," he said without interest. "Also it's too conspicuous."

"You'd be more conspicuous without any baggage."

I walked back to the bedroom and stood up on the steps in the clothes closet and pulled the white pigskin job down off the high shelf. The square ceiling trap was right over my head, so I pushed that up and reached in as far as I could and dropped his leather keyholder behind one of the dusty tie beams or whatever they were.

I climbed down with the suitcase, dusted it off, and shoved some things into it, a pair of pajamas never worn, toothpaste, an extra toothbrush, a couple of cheap towels and washcloths, a package of cotton handkerchiefs, a fifteen-cent tube of shaving cream, and one of the razors they give away with a package of blades. Nothing used, nothing marked, nothing conspicuous, except that his own stuff would be better. I added a pint of bourbon still in its wrapping paper. I locked the suitcase and left the key in one of the locks and carried it up front. He had gone to sleep again. I opened the door

493

without waking him and carried the suitcase down to the garage and put it in the convertible behind the front seat. I got the car out and locked the garage and went back up the steps to wake him. I finished locking up and we left.

I drove fast but not fast enough to get tagged. We hardly spoke on the way down. We didn't stop to eat either. There wasn't that much time.

The border people had nothing to say to us. Up on the windy mesa where the Tijuana Airport is I parked close to the office and just sat while Terry got his ticket. The propellers of the DC-3 were already turning over slowly, just enough to keep warm. A tall dreamboat of a pilot in a gray uniform was chatting with a group of four people. One was about six feet four and carried a gun case. There was a girl in slacks beside him, and a smallish middle-aged man and a gray-haired woman so tall that she made him look puny. Three or four obvious Mexicans were standing around as well. That seemed to be the load. The steps were at the door but nobody seemed anxious to get in. Then a Mexican flight steward came down the steps and stood waiting. There didn't seem to be any loudspeaker equipment. The Mexicans climbed into the plane but the pilot was still chatting with the Americans.

There was a big Packard parked next to me. I got out and took a gander at the license on the post. Maybe someday I'll learn to mind my own business. As I pulled my head out I saw the tall woman staring in my direction.

Then Terry came across the dusty gravel.

"I'm all set," he said. "This is where I say goodbye."

He put his hand out. I shook it. He looked pretty good now, just tired, just tired as all hell.

I lifted the pigskin suitcase out of the Olds and put it down on the gravel. He stared at it angrily.

"I told you I didn't want it," he said snappishly.

"There's a nice pint of hooch in it, Terry. Also some pajamas and stuff. And it's all anonymous. If you don't want it, check it. Or throw it away."

"I have reasons," he said stiffly.

"So have I."

He smiled suddenly. He picked up the suitcase and squeezed my arm with his free hand. "Okay, pal. You're the boss. And remember, if things get tough, you have a blank check. You don't owe me a thing. We had a few drinks together and got to be friendly and I talked too much about me. I left five C notes in your coffee can. Don't be sore at me."

"I'd rather you hadn't."

"I'll never spend half of what I have."

"Good luck, Terry."

The two Americans were going up the steps into the plane. A squatty guy with a wide dark face came out of the door of the office building and waved and pointed.

"Climb aboard," I said. "I know you didn't kill her. That's why I'm here."

He braced himself. His whole body got stiff. He turned slowly, then looked back.

"I'm sorry," he said quietly. "But you're wrong about that. I'm going to walk quite slowly to the plane. You have plenty of time to stop me."

He walked. I watched him. The guy in the doorway of the office was waiting, but not too impatient. Mexicans seldom are. He reached down and patted the pigskin suitcase and grinned at Terry. Then he stood aside and Terry went through the door. In a little while Terry came out through the door on the other side, where the customs people are when you're coming in. He walked, still slowly, across the gravel to the steps. He stopped there and looked towards me. He didn't signal or wave. Neither did I. Then he went up into the plane, and the steps were pulled back.

495

I got into the Olds and started it and backed and turned and moved halfway across the parking space. The tall woman and the short man were still out on the field. The woman had a handkerchief out to wave. The plane began to taxi down to the end of the field raising plenty of dust. It turned at the far end and the motors revved up in a thundering roar. It began to move forward picking up speed slowly.

The dust rose in clouds behind it. Then it was airborne. I watched it lift slowly into the gusty air and fade off into the naked blue sky to the southeast.

Then I left. Nobody at the border gate looked at me as if my face meant as much as the hands on a clock.

6

IT's A LONG drag back from Tijuana and one of the dullest drives in the state. Tijuana is nothing; all they want there is the buck. The kid who sidles over to your car and looks at you with big wistful eyes and says, "One dime, please, mister," will try to sell you his sister in the next sentence. Tijuana is not Mexico. No border town is anything but a border town, just as no waterfront is anything but a waterfront. San Diego? One of the most beautiful harbors in the world and nothing in it but navy and a few fishing boats. At night it is fairyland. The swell is as gentle as an old lady singing hymns. But Marlowe has to get home and count the spoons.

The road north is as monotonous as a sailor's chantey. You go through a town, down a hill, along a stretch of beach, through a town, down a hill, along a stretch of beach.

It was two o'clock when I got back and they were waiting for me in a dark sedan with no police tags, no red light, only the double antenna, and not only police cars have those. I was halfway up the steps before they came out of it and yelled at me, the usual couple in the usual suits, with the usual stony leisure of movement, as if the world was waiting hushed and silent for them to tell it what to do.

"Your name Marlowe? We want to talk to you."

He let me see the glint of a badge. For all I caught of it he might have been Pest Control. He was gray blond and looked sticky. His partner was tall, good-looking, neat, and had a precise nastiness about him, a goon with an education. They had watching and waiting eyes, patient and careful eyes, cool disdainful eyes, cops' eyes. They get them at the passing-out parade at the police school.

"Sergeant Green, Central Homicide. This is Detective Dayton."

I went on up and unlocked the door. You don't shake hands with big city cops. That close is too close.

They sat in the living room. I opened the windows and the breeze whispered. Green did the talking.

"Man named Terry Lennox. Know him, huh?"

"We have a drink together once in a while. He lives in Encino, married money. I've never been where he lives."

"Once in a while," Green said. "How often would that be?"

"It's a vague expression. I meant it that way. It could be once a week or once in two months."

"Met his wife?"

"Once, very briefly, before they were married."

"You saw him last when and where?"

I took a pipe off the end table and filled it. Green leaned forward close to me. The tall lad sat farther back holding a ballpoint poised over a red-edged pad.

"This is where I say, 'What's this all about?' and you say, 'We ask the questions.' "

"So you just answer them, huh?"

I lit the pipe. The tobacco was a little too moist. It took me some time to light it properly and three matches.

"I got time," Green said, "but I already used up a lot of it waiting around. So snap it up, mister. We know who you are. And you know we ain't here to work up an appetite."

"I was just thinking," I said. "We used to go to Victor's fairly often, and not so often to The Green Lantern and The Bull and Bear – that's the place down at the end of the Strip that tries to look like an English inn –"

"Quit stalling."

"Who's dead?" I asked.

Detective Dayton spoke up. He had a hard, mature, don't-try-to-fool-with-me voice. "Just answer the questions, Marlowe. We are conducting a routine investigation. That's all you need to know."

Maybe I was tired and irritable. Maybe I felt a little guilty. I could learn to hate this guy without even knowing him. I could just look at him across the width of a cafeteria and want to kick his teeth in.

"Shove it, Jack," I said. "Keep that guff for the juvenile bureau. It's a horse laugh even to them."

Green chuckled. Nothing changed in Dayton's face that you could put a finger on but he suddenly looked ten years older and twenty years nastier. The breath going through his nose whistled faintly.

"He passed the bar examination," Green said. "You can't fool around with Dayton."

I got up slowly and went over to the bookshelves. I took down the bound copy of the California Penal Code. I held it out to Dayton.

"Would you kindly find me the section that says I have to answer the questions?"

He was holding himself very still. He was going to slug me and we both knew it. But he was going to wait for the break. Which meant that he didn't trust Green to back him up if he got out of line.

498

He said: "Every citizen has to co-operate with the police. In all ways, even by physical action, and especially by answering any questions of a non-incriminating nature the police think it necessary to ask." His voice saying this was hard and bright and smooth.

"It works out that way," I said. "Mostly by a process of direct or indirect intimidation. In law no such obligation exists. Nobody has to tell the police anything, any time, anywhere."

"Aw shut up," Green said impatiently. "You're crawfishing and you know it. Sit down. Lennox's wife has been murdered. In a guest house at their place in Encino. Lennox has skipped out. Anyway he can't be found. So we're looking for a suspect in a murder case. That satisfy you?"

I threw the book in a chair and went back to the couch across the table from Green. "So why come to me?" I asked. "I've never been near the house. I told you that."

Green patted his thighs, up and down, up and down. He grinned at me quietly. Dayton was motionless in the chair. His eyes ate me.

"On account of your phone number was written on a pad in his room during the past twenty-four hours," Green said. "It's a date pad and yesterday was torn off but you could see the impression on today's page. We don't know when he called you up. We don't know where he went or why or when. But we got to ask, natch."

"Why in the guest house?" I asked, not expecting him to answer, but he did.

He blushed a little. "Seems she went there pretty often. At night. Had visitors. The help can see down through the trees where the lights show. Cars come and go, sometimes late, sometimes very late. Too much is enough, huh? Don't kid yourself. Lennox is our boy. He went down that way about one in the A.M. The butler happened to see. He come back alone, maybe twenty minutes later. After that nothing. The

499

lights stayed on. This morning no Lennox. The butler goes down by the guest house. The dame is as naked as a mermaid on the bed and let me tell you he don't recognize her by her face. She practically ain't got one. Beat to pieces with a bronze statuette of a monkey."

"Terry Lennox wouldn't do anything like that," I said. "Sure she cheated on him. Old stuff. She always had. They'd been divorced and remarried. I don't suppose it made him happy but why should he go crazy over it now?"

"Nobody knows that answer," Green said patiently. "It happens all the time. Men and women both. A guy takes it and takes it and takes it. Then he don't. He probably don't know why himself, why at that particular instant he goes berserk. Only he does, and somebody's dead. So we got business to do. So we ask you one simple question. So quit horsing around or we take you in."

"He's not going to tell you, Sergeant," Dayton said acidly. "He read that law book. Like a lot of people that read a law book he thinks the law is in it."

"You make the notes," Green said, "and leave your brains alone. If you're real good we'll let you sing 'Mother Machree' at the police smoker."

"The hell with you, Sarge, if I may say so with proper respect for your rank."

"Let's you and him fight," I said to Green. "I'll catch him when he drops."

Dayton laid his note pad and ballpoint aside very carefully. He stood up with a bright gleam in his eyes. He walked over and stood in front of me.

"On your feet, bright boy. Just because I went to college don't make me take any guff from a nit like you."

I started to get up. I was still off balance when he hit me. He hooked me with a neat left and crossed it. Bells rang, but not for dinner. I sat down hard and shook my head. Dayton was still there. He was smiling now.

"Let's try again," he said. "You weren't set that time. It wasn't really kosher."

I looked at Green. He was looking at his thumb as if studying a hangnail. I didn't move or speak, waiting for him to look up. If I stood up again, Dayton would slug me again. He might slug me again anyhow. But if I stood up and he slugged me, I would take him to pieces, because the blows proved he was strictly a boxer. He put them in the right place but it would take a lot of them to wear me down.

Green said almost absently: "Smart work, Billy boy. You gave the man exactly what he wanted. Clam juice."

Then he looked up and said mildly: "Once more, for the record, Marlowe. Last time you saw Terry Lennox, where and how and what was talked about, and where did you come from just now. Yes − or no?"

Dayton was standing loosely, nicely balanced. There was a soft sweet sheen in his eyes.

"How about the other guy?" I asked, ignoring him.

"What other guy was that?"

"In the hay, in the guest house. No clothes on. You're not saying she had to go down there to play solitaire."

"That comes later − when we get the husband."

"Fine. If it's not too much trouble when you already have a patsy."

"You don't talk, we take you in, Marlowe."

"As a material witness?"

"As a material my foot. As a suspect. Suspicion of accessory after the fact of murder. Helping a suspect escape. My guess is you took the guy somewhere. And right now a guess is all I need. The skipper is tough these days. He knows the rule book but he gets absent-minded. This could be a misery for you. One way or another we get a statement from you. The harder it is to get, the surer we are we need it."

"That's a lot of crap to him," Dayton said. "He knows the book."

"It's a lot of crap to everybody," Green said calmly. "But it still works. Come on, Marlowe. I'm blowing the whistle on you."

"Okay," I said. "Blow it. Terry Lennox was my friend. I've got a reasonable amount of sentiment invested in him. Enough not to spoil it just because a cop says come through. You've got a case against him, maybe far more than I hear from you. Motive, opportunity, and the fact that he skipped out. The motive is old stuff, long neutralized, almost part of the deal. I don't admire that kind of deal, but that's the kind of guy he is – a little weak and very gentle. The rest of it means nothing except that if he knew she was dead he knew he was a sitting duck for you. At the inquest if they have one and if they call me, I'll have to answer questions. I don't have to answer yours. I can see you're a nice guy, Green. Just as I can see your partner is just another goddam badge flasher with a power complex. If you want to get me in a real jam, let him hit me again. I'll break his goddam pencil for him."

Green stood up and looked at me sadly. Dayton hadn't moved. He was a one-shot tough guy. He had to have time out to pat his back.

"I'll use the phone," Green said. "But I know what answer I'll get. You're a sick chicken, Marlowe. A very sick chicken. Get the hell outa my way." This last to Dayton. Dayton turned and went back and picked up his pad.

Green crossed to the phone and lifted it slowly, his plain face creased with the long slow thankless grind. That's the trouble with cops. You're all set to hate their guts and then you meet one that goes human on you.

The Captain said to bring me in, and rough.

They put handcuffs on me. They didn't search the house, which seemed careless of them. Possibly they figured I would be too experienced to have anything there that could be dangerous to me. In which they were wrong. Because if they had made any kind of job of it they would have found Terry

Lennox's car keys. And when the car was found, as it would be sooner or later, they would fit the keys to it and know he had been in my company.

Actually, as it turned out, that meant nothing. The car was never found by any police. It was stolen sometime in the night, driven most probably to El Paso, fitted with new keys and forged papers, and put on the market eventually in Mexico City. The procedure is routine. Mostly the money comes back in the form of heroin. Part of the good-neighbor policy, as the hoodlums see it.

7

THE HOMICIDE SKIPPER that year was a Captain Gregorius, a type of copper that is getting rarer but by no means extinct, the kind that solves crimes with the bright light, the soft sap, the kick to the kidneys, the knee to the groin, the fist to the solar plexus, the night stick to the base of the spine. Six months later he was indicted for perjury before a grand jury, booted without trial, and later stamped to death by a big stallion on his ranch in Wyoming.

Right now I was his raw meat. He sat behind his desk with his coat off and his sleeves rolled almost to his shoulders. He was as bald as a brick and getting heavy around the waist like all hard-muscled men in middle age. His eyes were fish gray. His big nose was a network of burst capillaries. He was drinking coffee and not quietly. His blunt strong hands had hairs thick on their backs. Grizzled tufts stuck out of his ears. He pawed something on his desk and looked at Green.

Green said: "All we got on him is he won't tell us nothing, skipper. The phone number makes us look him up. He's out riding and don't say where. He knows Lennox pretty well and don't say when he saw him last."

"Thinks he's tough," Gregorius said indifferently. "We could change that." He said it as if he didn't care one way or another. He probably didn't. Nobody was tough to him. "Point is the D.A. smells a lot of headlines on this one. Can't blame him, seeing who the girl's old man is. I guess we better pick this fellow's nose for him."

He looked at me as if I was a cigarette stub, or an empty chair. Just something in his line of vision, without interest for him.

Dayton said respectfully: "It's pretty obvious that his whole attitude was designed to create a situation where he could refuse to talk. He quoted law at us and needles me into socking him. I was out of line there, Captain."

Gregorius eyed him bleakly. "You must needle easy if this punk can do it. Who took the cuffs off?"

Green said he did. "Put them back on," Gregorius said. "Tight. Give him something to brace him up."

Green put the cuffs back on or started to. "Behind the back," Gregorius barked. Green cuffed my hands behind my back. I was sitting in a hard chair.

"Tighter," Gregorius said. "Make them bite."

Green made them tighter. My hands started to feel numb.

Gregorius looked at me finally. "You can talk now. Make it snappy."

I didn't answer him. He leaned back and grinned. His hand went out slowly for his coffee cup and went around it. He leaned forward a little. The cup jerked but I beat it by going sideways out of the chair. I landed hard on my shoulder, rolled over and got up slowly. My hands were quite numb now. They didn't feel anything. The arms above the cuffs were beginning to ache.

Green helped me back into the chair. The wet smear of the coffee was over the back and some of the seat, but most of it was on the floor.

"He don't like coffee," Gregorius said. "He's a swifty. He moves fast. Good reflexes."

Nobody said anything. Gregorius looked me over with fish eyes.

"In here, mister, a dick license don't mean any more than a calling card. Now let's have your statement, verbal at first. We'll take it down later. Make it complete. Let's have, say, a full account of your movements since ten P.M. last night. I mean full. This office is investigating a murder and the prime suspect is missing. You connect with him. Guy catches his wife cheating and beats her head to raw flesh and bone and bloodsoaked hair. Our old friend the bronze statuette. Not original but it works. You think any goddam private eye is going to quote law at me over this, mister, you got a hell of a tough time coming your way. There ain't a police force in the country could do its job with a law book. You got information and I want it. You could of said no and I could of not believed you. But you didn't even say no. You're not dummying up on me, my friend. Not six cents' worth. Let's go."

"Would you take the cuffs off, Captain?" I asked. "I mean if I made a statement?"

"I might. Make it short."

"If I told you I hadn't seen Lennox within the last twenty-four hours, hadn't talked to him and had no idea where he might be – would that satisfy you, Captain?"

"It might – if I believed it."

"If I told you I had seen him and where and when, but had no idea he had murdered anyone or that any crime had been committed, and further had no idea where he might be at this moment, that wouldn't satisfy you at all, would it?"

"With more detail I might listen. Things like where, when, what he looked like, what was talked about, where he was headed. It might grow into something."

"With your treatment," I said, "it would probably grow into making me an accessory."

His jaw muscles bulged. His eyes were dirty ice. "So?"

"I don't know," I said. "I need legal advice. I'd like to co-operate. How would it be if we had somebody from the D.A.'s office here?"

He let out a short raucous laugh. It was over very soon. He got up slowly and walked around the desk. He leaned down close to me, one big hand on the wood, and smiled. Then without change of expression he hit me on the side of the neck with a fist like a piece of iron.

The blow traveled eight or ten inches, no more. It nearly took my head off. Bile seeped into my mouth. I tasted blood mixed with it. I heard nothing but a roaring in my head. He leaned over me still smiling, his left hand still on the desk. His voice seemed to come from a long way off.

"I used to be tough but I'm getting old. You take a good punch, mister, and that's all you get from me. We got boys over at the City Jail that ought to be working in the stockyards. Maybe we hadn't ought to have them because they ain't nice clean powderpuff punchers like Dayton here. They don't have four kids and a rose garden like Green. They live for different amusements. It takes all kinds and labor's scarce. You got any more funny little ideas about what you might say, if you bothered to say it?"

"Not with the cuffs on, Captain." It hurt even to say that much.

He leaned farther towards me and I smelled his sweat and the gas of corruption. Then he straightened and went back around the desk and planted his solid buttocks in his chair. He picked up a three-cornered ruler and ran his thumb along one edge as if it was a knife. He looked at Green.

"What are you waiting for, Sergeant?"

"Orders." Green ground out the word as if he hated the sound of his own voice.

"You got to be told? You're an experienced man, it says in the records. I want a detailed statement of this man's movements for the past twenty-four hours. Maybe longer, but that much at first. I want to know what he did every minute of the time. I want it signed and witnessed and checked. I want it in two hours. Then I want him back

506

here clean, tidy, and unmarked. And one thing more, Sergeant."

He paused and gave Green a stare that would have frozen a fresh-baked potato.

"– next time I ask a suspect a few civil questions I don't want you standing there looking as if I had torn his ear off."

"Yes, sir." Green turned to me. "Let's go," he said gruffly.

Gregorius bared his teeth at me. They needed cleaning – badly. "Let's have the exit line, chum."

"Yes, sir," I said politely. "You probably didn't intend it, but you've done me a favor. With an assist from Detective Dayton. You've solved a problem for me. No man likes to betray a friend but I wouldn't betray an enemy into your hands. You're not only a gorilla, you're an incompetent. You don't know how to operate a simple investigation. I was balanced on a knife edge and you could have swung me either way. But you had to abuse me, throw coffee in my face, and use your fists on me when I was in a spot where all I could do was take it. From now on I wouldn't tell you the time by the clock on your own wall."

For some strange reason he sat there perfectly still and let me say it. Then he grinned. "You're just a little old cop-hater, friend. That's all you are, shamus, just a little old cop-hater."

"There are places where cops are not hated, Captain. But in those places you wouldn't be a cop."

He took that too. I guess he could afford it. He'd probably taken worse many times. Then the phone rang on his desk. He looked at it and gestured. Dayton stepped smartly around the desk and lifted the receiver.

"Captain Gregorius' office. Detective Dayton speaking."

He listened. A tiny frown drew his handsome eyebrows together. He said softly: "One moment, please, sir."

He held the phone out to Gregorius. "Commissioner Allbright, sir."

Gregorius scowled. "Yeah? What's that snotty bastard want?" He took the phone, held it a moment and smoothed his face out. "Gregorius, Commissioner."

He listened. "Yeah, he's here in my office, Commissioner. I been asking him a few questions. Not co-operative. Not co-operative at all . . . How's that again?" A sudden ferocious scowl twisted his face into dark knots. The blood darkened his forehead. But his voice didn't change in tone by a fraction. "If that's a direct order, it ought to come through the Chief of Detectives, Commissioner . . . Sure, I'll act on it until it's confirmed. Sure . . . Hell, no. Nobody laid a glove on him . . . Yes, sir. Right away."

He put the phone back in its cradle. I thought his hand shook a little. His eyes moved up and across my face and then to Green. "Take the cuffs off," he said tonelessly.

Green unlocked the cuffs. I rubbed my hands together, waiting for the pins and needles of circulation.

"Book him in the county jail," Gregorius said slowly. "Suspicion of murder. The D.A. has glommed the case right out of our hands. Lovely system we got around here."

Nobody moved. Green was close to me, breathing hard. Gregorius looked up at Dayton.

"Whatcha waiting for, cream puff? An ice-cream cone maybe?"

Dayton almost choked. "You didn't give me any orders, skipper."

"Say sir to me, damn you! I'm skipper to sergeants and better. Not to you, kiddo. Not to you. Out."

"Yes, sir." Dayton walked quickly to the door and went out. Gregorius heaved himself to his feet and moved to the window and stood with his back to the room.

"Come on, let's drift," Green muttered in my ear.

"Get him out of here before I kick his face in," Gregorius said to the window.

Green went to the door and opened it. I started through. Gregorius barked suddenly: "Hold it! Shut that door!"

Green shut it and leaned his back to it.

"Come here, you!" Gregorius barked at me.

I didn't move. I stood and looked at him. Green didn't move either. There was a grim pause. Then very slowly Gregorius walked across the room and stood facing me toe to toe. He put his big hard hands in his pockets. He rocked on his heels.

"Never laid a glove on him," he said under his breath, as if talking to himself. His eyes were remote and expressionless. His mouth worked convulsively.

Then he spat in my face.

He stepped back. "That will be all, thank you."

He turned and went back to the window. Green opened the door again.

I went through it reaching for my handkerchief.

8

CELL NO. 3 in the felony tank has two bunks, Pullman style, but the tank was not very full and I had the cell to myself. In the felony tank they treat you pretty well. You get two blankets, neither dirty nor clean, and a lumpy mattress two inches thick which goes over crisscrossed metal slats. There is a flush toilet, a washbasin, paper towels and gritty gray soap. The cell block is clean and doesn't smell of disinfectant. The trusties do the work. The supply of trusties is always ample.

The jail deputies look you over and they have wise eyes. Unless you are a drunk or a psycho or act like one you get to keep your matches and cigarettes. Until preliminary you wear your own clothes. After that you wear the jail denim, no tie, no belt, no shoelaces. You sit on the bunk and wait. There is nothing else to do.

In the drunk tank it is not so good. No bunk, no chair, no blankets, no nothing. You lie on the concrete floor. You sit on the toilet and vomit in your own lap. That is the depth of misery. I've seen it.

Although it was still daylight the lights were on in the ceiling. Inside the steel door of the cell block was a basket of steel bars around the Judas window. The lights were controlled from outside the steel door. They went out at nine P.M. Nobody came through the door or said anything. You might be in the middle of a sentence in a newspaper or magazine. Without any sound of a click or any warning – darkness. And there you were until the summer dawn with nothing to do but sleep if you could, smoke if you had anything to smoke, and think if you had anything to think about that didn't make you feel worse than not thinking at all.

In jail a man has no personality. He is a minor disposal problem and a few entries on reports. Nobody cares who loves or hates him, what he looks like, what he did with his life. Nobody reacts to him unless he gives trouble. Nobody abuses him. All that is asked of him is that he go quietly to the right cell and remain quiet when he gets there. There is nothing to fight against, nothing to be mad at. The jailers are quiet men without animosity or sadism. All this stuff you read about men yelling and screaming, beating against the bars, running spoons along them, guards rushing in with clubs – all that is for the big house. A good jail is one of the quietest places in the world. You could walk through the average cell block at night and look in through the bars and see a huddle of brown blanket, or a head of hair, or a pair of eyes looking at nothing. You might hear a snore. Once in a long while you might hear a nightmare. The life in a jail is in suspension, without purpose or meaning. In another cell you might see a man who cannot sleep or even try to sleep. He is sitting on the edge of his bunk doing nothing. He looks at you or doesn't. You look at him. He says nothing and you say nothing. There is nothing to communicate.

In the corner of the cell block there may be a second steel door that leads to the show-up box. One of its walls is wire mesh painted black. On the back wall are ruled lines for height. Overhead are floodlights. You go in there in the morning as a rule, just before the night captain goes off duty. You stand against the measuring lines and the lights glare at you and there is no light behind the wire mesh. But plenty of people are out there: cops, detectives, citizens who have been robbed or assaulted or swindled or kicked out of their cars at gun point or conned out of their life savings. You don't see or hear them. You hear the voice of the night captain. You receive him loud and clear. He puts you through your paces as if you were a performing dog. He is tired and cynical and competent. He is the stage manager of a play that has had the longest run in history, but it no longer interests him.

"All right, you. Stand straight. Pull your belly in. Pull your chin in. Keep your shoulders back. Hold your head level. Look straight front. Turn left. Turn right. Face front again and hold your hands out. Palms up. Palms down. Pull your sleeves back. No visible scars. Hair dark brown, some gray. Eyes brown. Height six feet, one half inch. Weight about one ninety. Name Philip Marlowe. Occupation private detective. Well, well, nice to see you, Marlowe. That's all. Next man."

Much obliged, Captain. Thanks for the time. You forgot to have me open my mouth. I have some nice inlays and one very high-class porcelain jacket crown. Eighty-seven dollars' worth of porcelain jacket crown. You forgot to look inside my nose too, Captain. A lot of scar tissue in there for you. Septum operation and was that guy a butcher! Two hours of it in those days. I hear they do it in twenty minutes now. I got it playing football, Captain, a slight miscalculation in an attempt to block a punt. I blocked the guy's foot instead – after he kicked the ball. Fifteen yards penalty, and that's about how much stiff bloody tape they pulled out of my nose an inch at a time the day after the operation. I'm not bragging, Captain. I'm just telling you. It's the little things that count.

On the third day a deputy unlocked my cell in the middle of the morning.

"Your lawyer's here. Kill the butt – and not on the floor."

I flushed it down the toilet. He took me to the conference room. A tall pale dark-haired man was standing there looking out of the window. There was a fat brown briefcase on the table. He turned. He waited for the door to close. Then he sat down near his briefcase on the far side of a scarred oak table that came out of the Ark. Noah bought it secondhand. The lawyer opened a hammered silver cigarette case and put it in front of him and looked me over.

"Sit down, Marlowe. Care for a cigarette? My name is Endicott. Sewell Endicott. I've been instructed to represent you without cost or expense to you. I guess you'd like to get out of here, wouldn't you?"

I sat down and took one of the cigarettes. He held a lighter for me.

"Nice to see you again, Mr. Endicott. We've met before – while you were D.A."

He nodded. "I don't remember, but it's quite possible." He smiled faintly. "That position was not quite in my line. I guess I don't have enough tiger in me."

"Who sent you?"

"I'm not at liberty to say. If you accept me as your attorney, the fee will be taken care of."

"I guess that means they've got him."

He just stared at me. I puffed at the cigarette. It was one of those things with filters in them. It tasted like a high fog strained through cotton wool.

"If you mean Lennox," he said, "and of course you do, no – they haven't got him."

"Why the mystery, Mr. Endicott? About who sent you."

"My principal wishes to remain anonymous. That is the privilege of my principal. Do you accept me?"

"I don't know," I said. "If they haven't got Terry, why are they holding me? Nobody has asked me anything, nobody has been near me."

He frowned and looked down at his long white delicate fingers. "District Attorney Springer has taken personal charge of this matter. He may have been too busy to question you yet. But you are entitled to arraignment and a preliminary hearing. I can get you out on bail on a habeas corpus proceeding. You probably know what the law is."

"I'm booked on suspicion of murder."

He shrugged impatiently. "That's just a catch-all. You could have been booked in transit to Pittsburgh, or any one of a dozen charges. What they probably mean is accessory after the fact. You took Lennox somewhere, didn't you?"

I didn't answer. I dropped the tasteless cigarette on the floor and stepped on it. Endicott shrugged again and frowned.

"Assume you did then, just for the sake of argument. To make you an accessory they have to prove intent. In this case that would mean knowledge that a crime had been committed and that Lennox was a fugitive. It's bailable in any case. Of course what you really are is a material witness. But a man can't be held in prison as a material witness in this state except by court order. He's not a material witness unless a judge so declares. But the law enforcement people can always find a way to do what they want to do."

"Yeah," I said. "A detective named Dayton slugged me. A homicide captain named Gregorius threw a cup of coffee at me, hit me in the neck hard enough to bust an artery – you can see it's still swollen, and when a call from Police Commissioner Allbright kept him from turning me over to the wrecking crew, he spat in my face. You're quite right, Mr. Endicott. The law boys can always do what they want to do."

He looked at his wrist watch rather pointedly. "You want out on bail or don't you?"

"Thanks. I don't think I do. A guy out on bail is already half guilty in the public mind. If he gets off later on, he had a smart lawyer."

"That's silly," he said impatiently.

"Okay, it's silly. I'm silly. Otherwise I wouldn't be here. If you're in touch with Lennox, tell him to quit bothering about me. I'm not in here for him. I'm in here for me. No complaints. It's part of the deal. I'm in a business where people come to me with troubles. Big troubles, little troubles, but always troubles they don't want to take to the cops. How long would they come if any bruiser with a police shield could hold me upside down and drain my guts?"

"I see your point," he said slowly. "But let me correct you on one thing. I am not in touch with Lennox. I scarcely know him. I'm an officer of the court, as all lawyers are. If I knew where Lennox was, I couldn't conceal the information from the District Attorney. The most I could do would be to agree to surrender him at a specified time and place after I had had an interview with him."

"Nobody else would bother to send you here to help me."

"Are you calling me a liar?" He reached down to rub out his cigarette stub on the underside of the table.

"I seem to remember that you're a Virginian, Mr. Endicott. In this country we have a sort of historical fixation about Virginians. We think of them as the flower of southern chivalry and honor."

He smiled. "That was nicely said. I only wish it was true. But we're wasting time. If you had had a grain of sense you'd have told the police you hadn't seen Lennox for a week. It didn't have to be true. Under oath you could always have told the real story. There's no law against lying to the cops. They expect it. They feel much happier when you lie to them than when you refuse to talk to them. That's a direct challenge to their authority. What do you expect to gain by it?"

I didn't answer. I didn't really have an answer. He stood up and reached for his hat and snapped his cigarette case shut and put it in his pocket.

"You had to play the big scene," he said coldly. "Stand on your rights, talk about the law. How ingenuous can a man get,

Marlowe? A man like you who is supposed to know his way around. The law isn't justice. It's a very imperfect mechanism. If you press exactly the right buttons and are also lucky, justice may show up in the answer. A mechanism is all the law was ever intended to be. I guess you're not in any mood to be helped. So I'll take myself off. You can reach me if you change your mind."

"I'll stick it out for a day or two longer. If they catch Terry they won't care how he got away. All they'll care about is the circus they can make of the trial. The murder of Mr. Harlan Potter's daughter is headline material all over the country. A crowd-pleaser like Springer could ride himself right into Attorney General on that show, and from there into the governor's chair and from there —" I stopped talking and let the rest of it float in the air.

Endicott smiled a slow derisive smile. "I don't think you know very much about Mr. Harlan Potter," he said.

"And if they don't get Lennox, they won't *want* to know how he got away, Mr. Endicott. They'll just want to forget the whole thing fast."

"Got it all figured out, haven't you, Marlowe?"

"I've had the time. All I know about Mr. Harlan Potter is that he is supposed to be worth a hundred million bucks, and that he owns nine or ten newspapers. How's the publicity going?"

"The publicity?" His voice was ice cold saying it.

"Yeah. Nobody's interviewed me from the press. I expected to make a big noise in the papers out of this. Get lots of business. Private eye goes to jail rather than split on a pal."

He walked to the door and turned with his hand on the knob. "You amuse me, Marlowe. You're childish in some ways. True, a hundred million dollars can buy a great deal of publicity. It can also, my friend, if shrewdly employed, buy a great deal of silence."

He opened the door and went out. Then a deputy came in and took me back to Cell No. 3 in the felony block.

"Guess you won't be with us long, if you've got Endicott," he said pleasantly as he locked me in. I said I hoped he was right.

9

THE DEPUTY ON the early night shift was a big blond guy with meaty shoulders and a friendly grin. He was middle-aged and had long since outlived both pity and anger. He wanted to put in eight easy hours and he looked as if almost anything would be easy down his street. He unlocked my door.

"Company for you. Guy from the D.A.'s office. No sleep, huh?"

"It's a little early for me. What time is it?"

"Ten-fourteen." He stood in the doorway and looked over the cell. One blanket was spread on the lower bunk, one was folded for a pillow. There were a couple of used paper towels in the trash bucket and a small wad of toilet paper on the edge of the washbasin. He nodded approval. "Anything personal in here?"

"Just me."

He left the cell door open. We walked along a quiet corridor to the elevator and rode down to the booking desk. A fat man in a gray suit stood by the desk smoking a corncob. His fingernails were dirty and he smelled.

"I'm Spranklin from the D.A.'s office," he told me in a tough voice. "Mr. Grenz wants you upstairs." He reached behind his hip and came up with a pair of bracelets. "Let's try these for size."

The jail deputy and the booking clerk grinned at him with deep enjoyment. "What's the matter, Sprank? Afraid he'll mug you in the elevator?"

"I don't want no trouble," he growled. "Had a guy break from me once. They ate my ass off. Let's go, boy."

The booking clerk pushed a form at him and he signed it with a flourish. "I never take no unnecessary chances," he said. "Man never knows what he's up against in this town."

A prowl car cop brought in a drunk with a bloody ear. We went towards the elevator. "You're in trouble, boy," Spranklin told me in the elevator. "Heap bad trouble." It seemed to give him a vague satisfaction. "A guy can get hisself in a lot of trouble in this town."

The elevator man turned his head and winked at me. I grinned.

"Don't try nothing, boy," Spranklin told me severely. "I shot a man once. Tried to break. They ate my ass off."

"You get it coming and going, don't you?"

He thought it over. "Yeah," he said. "Either way they eat your ass off. It's a tough town. No respect."

We got out and went in through the double doors of the D.A.'s office. The switchboard was dead, with lines plugged in for the night. There was nobody in the waiting chairs. Lights were on in a couple of offices. Spranklin opened the door of a small lighted room which contained a desk, a filing case, a hard chair or two, and a thick-set man with a hard chin and stupid eyes. His face was red and he was just pushing something into the drawer of his desk.

"You could knock," he barked at Spranklin.

"Sorry, Mr. Grenz," Spranklin bumbled. "I was thinkin' about the prisoner."

He pushed me into the office. "Should I take the cuffs off, Mr. Grenz?"

"I don't know what the hell you put them on for," Grenz said sourly. He watched Spranklin unlock the cuffs on my wrist. He had the key on a bunch the size of a grapefruit and it troubled him to find it.

"Okay, scram," Grenz said. "Wait outside to take him back."

"I'm kind of off duty, Mr. Grenz."

"You're off duty when I say you're off duty."

Spranklin flushed and edged his fat bottom out through the door. Grenz looked after him savagely, then when the door closed he moved the same look to me. I pulled a chair over and sat down.

"I didn't tell you to sit down," Grenz barked.

I got a loose cigarette out of my pocket and stuck it in my mouth. "And I didn't say you could smoke," Grenz roared.

"I'm allowed to smoke in the cell block. Why not here?"

"Because this is my office. *I* make the rules here." A raw smell of whiskey floated across the desk.

"Take another quick one," I said. "It'll calm you down. You got kind of interrupted when we came in."

His back hit the back of the chair hard. His face went dark red. I struck a match and lit my cigarette.

After a long minute Grenz said softly. "Okay, tough boy. Quite a man, aren't you? You know something? They're all sizes and shapes when they come in here, but they all go out the same size – small. And the same shape – bent."

"What did you want to see me about, Mr. Grenz? And don't mind me if you feel like hitting that bottle. I'm a fellow that will take a snort myself, if I'm tired and nervous and overworked."

"You don't seem much impressed by the jam you're in."

"I don't figure I'm in any jam."

"We'll see about that. Meantime I want a very full statement from you." He flicked a finger at a recording set on a stand beside his desk. "We'll take it now and have it transcribed tomorrow. If the Chief Deputy is satisfied with your statement, he may release you on your own undertaking not to leave town. Let's go." He switched on the recorder. His voice was cold, decisive, and as nasty as he knew how to make it. But his right hand kept edging towards the desk drawer. He was too young to have veins in his nose, but he had them, and the whites of his eyes were a bad color.

"I get so tired of it," I said.

"Tired of what?" he snapped.

"Hard little men in hard little offices talking hard little words that don't mean a goddam thing. I've had fifty-six hours in the felony block. Nobody pushed me around, nobody tried to prove he was tough. They didn't have to. They had it on ice for when they needed it. And why was I in there? I was booked on suspicion. What the hell kind of legal system lets a man be shoved in a felony tank because some cop didn't get an answer to some questions? What evidence did he have? A telephone number on a pad. And what was he trying to prove by locking me up? Not a damn thing except that he had the power to do it. Now you're on the same pitch – trying to make me feel what a lot of power you generate in this cigar box you call your office. You send this scared baby-sitter over late at night to bring me in here. You think maybe sitting alone with my thoughts for fifty-six hours has made gruel out of my brains? You think I'm going to cry in your lap and ask you to stroke my head because I'm so awful god-dam lonely in the great big jail? Come off it, Grenz. Take your drink and get human; I'm willing to assume you are just doing your job. But take the brass knuckles off before you start. If you're big enough you don't need them, and if you need them you're not big enough to push me around."

He sat there and listened and looked at me. Then he grinned sourly. "Nice speech," he said. "Now you've got the crap out of your system, let's get that statement. You want to answer specific questions or just tell it your own way?"

"I was talking to the birds," I said. "Just to hear the breeze blow. I'm not making any statement. You're a lawyer and you know I don't have to."

"That's right," he said coolly. "I know the law. I know police work. I'm offering you a chance to clear yourself. If you don't want it, that's jake with me too. I can arraign you tomorrow morning at ten A.M. and have you set for a preliminary hearing. You may get bail, although I'll fight it, but if you do, it will be stiff. It'll cost you plenty. That's one way we can do it."

He looked down at a paper on his desk, read it, and turned it face down.

"On what charge?" I asked him

"Section thirty-two. Accessory after the fact. A felony. It rates up to a five-spot in Quentin."

"Better catch Lennox first," I said carefully. Grenz had something and I sensed it in his manner. I didn't know how much, but he had something all right.

He leaned back in his chair and picked up a pen and twirled it slowly between his palms. Then he smiled. He was enjoying himself.

"Lennox is a hard man to hide, Marlowe. With most people you need a photo and a good clear photo. Not with a guy that has scars all over one side of his face. Not to mention white hair, and not over thirty-five years old. We got four witnesses, maybe more."

"Witnesses to what?" I was tasting something bitter in my mouth, like the bile I had tasted after Captain Gregorius slugged me. That reminded me that my neck was still sore and swollen. I rubbed it gently.

"Don't be a chump, Marlowe. A San Diego superior court judge and his wife happened to be seeing their son and daughter-in-law off on that plane. All four saw Lennox and the judge's wife saw the car he came in and who came with him. You don't have a prayer."

"That's nice," I said. "How did you get to them?"

"Special bulletin on radio and TV. A full description was all it took. The judge called in."

"Sounds good," I said judicially. "But it takes a little more than that, Grenz. You have to catch him and prove he committed a murder. Then you have to prove I knew it."

He snapped a finger at the back of the telegram. "I think I will take that drink," he said. "Been working nights too much." He opened the drawer and put a bottle and a shot glass on the desk. He poured it full to the brim and knocked it back in a lump. "Better," he said. "Much better. Sorry I can't offer you one while you're in custody." He corked the bottle and pushed it away from him, but not out of reach. "Oh yeah, we got to prove something, you said. Well, it could be we already got a confession, chum. Too bad, huh?"

A small but very cold finger moved the whole length of my spine, like an icy insect crawling.

"So why do you need a statement from me?"

He grinned. "We like a tidy record. Lennox will be brought back and tried. We need everything we can get. It's not so much what we want from you as what we might be willing to let you get away with – if you co-operate."

I stared at him. He did a little paper-fiddling. He moved around in his chair, looked at his bottle, and had to use up a lot of will power not grabbing for it. "Maybe you'd like the whole libretto," he said suddenly with an off-key leer. "Well, smart guy, just to show you I'm not kidding, here it is."

I leaned across his desk and he thought I was reaching for his bottle. He grabbed it away and put it back in the drawer. I just wanted to drop a stub in his ashtray. I leaned back again and lit another pill. He spoke rapidly.

"Lennox got off the plane at Mazatlán, an airline junction point and a town of about thirty-five thousand. He disappeared for two or three hours. Then a tall man with black hair and a dark skin and what might have been a lot of knife scars booked to Torreón under the name of Silvano Rodriguez. His Spanish was good but not good enough for a man of his name. He was too tall for a Mexican with such dark skin. The pilot turned in a report on him. The cops were too slow at Torreón. Mex cops are no balls of fire. What they do best is shoot people. By the time they got going the man had chartered a plane and gone on to a little mountain town called Otatoclán, a small time summer resort with a lake. The pilot of the charter plane had trained as a combat pilot in Texas. He spoke good English. Lennox pretended not to catch what he said."

"If it *was* Lennox," I put in.

"Wait a while, chum. It was Lennox all right. Okay, he gets off at Otatoclán and registers at the hotel there, this time as Mario de Cerva. He was wearing a gun, a Mauser 7.65, which doesn't mean too much in Mexico, of course. But the charter pilot thought the guy didn't seem kosher, so he had a word with the local law. They put Lennox under surveillance. They did some checking with Mexico City and then they moved in."

Grenz picked up a ruler and sighted along it, a meaningless gesture which kept him from looking at me.

I said, "Uh-huh. Smart boy, your charter pilot, and nice to his customers. The story stinks."

He looked up at me suddenly. "What we want," he said dryly, "is a quick trial, a plea of second degree which we will accept. There are some angles we'd rather not go into. After all, the family is pretty influential."

"Meaning Harlan Potter."

He nodded briefly. "For my money the whole idea is all wet. Springer could have a field day with it. It's got everything. Sex, scandal, money, beautiful unfaithful wife, wounded war hero husband – I suppose that's where he got the scars – hell, it would be front-page stuff for weeks. Every rag in the country would eat it up. So we shuffle it off to a fast fade." He shrugged. "Okay, if the chief wants it that way, it's up to him. Do I get that statement?" He turned to the recording machine which had been humming away softly all this time, with the light showing in front.

"Turn it off," I said.

He swung around and gave me a vicious look. "You like it in jail?"

"It's not too bad. You don't meet the best people, but who the hell wants to? Be reasonable, Grenz. You're trying to make a fink out of me. Maybe I'm obstinate, or even sentimental, but I'm practical too. Suppose you had to hire a private eye — yeah, yeah, I know how you would hate the idea — but just suppose you were where it was your only out. Would you want one that finked on his friends?"

He stared at me with hate.

"A couple more points. Doesn't it strike you that Lennox's evasion tactics were just a little too transparent? If he wanted to be caught, he didn't have to go to all that trouble. If he didn't want to be caught, he had brains enough not to disguise himself as a Mexican in Mexico."

"Meaning what?" Grenz was snarling at me now.

"Meaning you could just be filling me up with a lot of hooey you made up, that there wasn't any Rodriguez with dyed hair and there wasn't any Mario de Cerva at Otatoclán, and you don't know any more about where Lennox is than where Black Beard the Pirate buried his treasure."

He got his bottle out again. He poured himself a shot and drank it down quickly, as before. He relaxed slowly. He turned in his chair and switched off the recording machine.

"I'd like to have tried you," he said gratingly. "You're the kind of wise guy I like to work over. This rap will be hanging over you for a long long time, cutie. You'll walk with it and eat with it and sleep with it. And next time you step out of line we'll murder you with it. Right now I got to do something that turns my guts inside out."

He pawed on his desk and pulled the face-down paper to him, turned it over and signed it. You can always tell when a man is writing his own name. He has a special way of moving. Then he stood up and marched around the desk and threw the door of his shoe box open and yelled for Spranklin.

The fat man came in with his B.O. Grenz gave him the paper.

"I've just signed your release order," he said. "I'm a public servant and sometimes I have unpleasant duties. Would you care to know why I signed it?"

I stood up. "If you want to tell me."

"The Lennox case is closed, mister. There ain't any Lennox case. He wrote out a full confession this afternoon in his hotel room and shot himself. In Otatoclán, just like I said."

I stood there looking at nothing. Out of the corner of my eye I saw Grenz back away slowly as if he thought I might be going to slug him. I must have looked pretty nasty for a moment. Then he was behind his desk again and Spranklin had grabbed onto my arm.

"Come on, move," he said in a whining kind of voice. "Man likes to get home nights once in a while."

I went out with him and closed the door. I closed it quietly as if on a room where someone had just died.

10

I DUG OUT the carbon of my property slip and turned it over and receipted on the original. I put my belongings back in my pockets. There was a man draped over the end of the booking desk and as I turned away he straightened up and spoke to me. He was about six feet four inches tall and as thin as a wire.

"Need a ride home?"

In the bleak light he looked young-old, tired and cynical, but he didn't look like a grifter. "For how much?"

"For free. I'm Lonnie Morgan of the *Journal*. I'm knocking off."

"Oh, police beat," I said.

"Just this week. The City Hall is my regular beat."

We walked out of the building and found his car in the parking lot. I looked up at the sky. There were stars but there was too much glare. It was a cool pleasant night. I breathed it in. Then I got into his car and he drove away from there.

"I live way out in Laurel Canyon," I said. "Just drop me anywhere."

"They ride you in," he said, "but they don't worry how you get home. This case interests me, in a repulsive sort of way."

"It seems there isn't any case," I said. "Terry Lennox shot himself this afternoon. So they say. So they say."

"Very convenient," Lonnie Morgan said, staring ahead through the windshield. His car drifted quietly along quiet streets. "It helps them build their wall."

"What wall?"

"Somebody's building a wall around the Lennox case, Marlowe. You're smart enough to see that, aren't you? It's not getting the kind of play it rates. The D.A. left town tonight for Washington. Some kind of convention. He walked out on the sweetest hunk of publicity he's had in years. Why?"

"No use to ask me. I've been in cold storage."

"Because somebody made it worth his while, that's why. I don't mean anything crude like a wad of dough. Somebody promised him something important to him and there's only one man connected with the case in a position to do that. The girl's father."

I leaned my head back in a corner of the car. "Sounds a little unlikely," I said. "What about the press? Harlan Potter owns a few papers, but what about the competition?"

He gave me a brief amused glance and then concentrated on his driving. "Ever been a newspaperman?"

"No."

"Newspapers are owned and published by rich men. Rich men all belong to the same club. Sure, there's competition – hard tough competition for circulation, for newsbeats, for exclusive stories. Just so long as it doesn't damage the prestige and privilege and position of the owners. If it does, down comes the lid. The lid, my friend, is down on the Lennox case. The Lennox case, my friend, properly built up, could have sold a hell of a lot of papers. It has everything. The trial would have drawn feature writers from all over the country. But there ain't going to be no trial. On account of Lennox checked out before it could get moving. Like I said – very convenient – for Harlan Potter and his family."

I straightened up and gave him a hard stare.

"You calling the whole thing a fix?"

He twisted his mouth sardonically. "Could just be Lennox had some help committing suicide. Resisting arrest a little. Mexican cops have very itchy trigger fingers. If you want to lay a little bet, I'll give you nice odds that nobody gets to count the bullet holes."

"I think you're wrong," I said. "I knew Terry Lennox pretty well. He wrote himself off a long time ago. If they brought him back alive, he would have let them have it their way. He'd have copped a manslaughter plea."

Lonnie Morgan shook his head. I knew what he was going to say and he said it. "Not a chance. If he had shot her or cracked her skull, maybe yes. But there was too much brutality. Her face was beaten to a pulp. Second degree murder would be the best he could get, and even that would raise a stink."

I said: "You could be right."

He looked at me again. "You say you knew the guy. Do you go for the setup?"

"I'm tired. I'm not in a thinking mood tonight."

There was a long pause. Then Lonnie Morgan said quietly: "If I was a real bright guy instead of a hack newspaperman, I'd think maybe he didn't kill her at all."

"It's a thought."

He stuck a cigarette in his mouth and lit it by scratching a match on the dashboard. He smoked silently with a fixed frown on his thin face. We reached Laurel Canyon and I told him where to turn off the boulevard and where to turn into my street. His car churned up the hill and stopped at the foot of my redwood steps.

I got out. "Thanks for the ride, Morgan. Care for a drink?"

"I'll take a rain check. I figure you'd rather be alone."

"I've got lots of time to be alone. Too damn much."

"You've got a friend to say goodbye to," he said. "He must have been that if you let them toss you into the can on his account."

"Who said I did that?"

He smiled faintly. "Just because I can't print it don't mean I didn't know it, chum. So long. See you around."

I shut the car door and he turned and drove off down the hill. When his tail lights vanished around the corner I climbed the steps, picked up newspapers, and let myself into the empty house. I put all the lamps on and opened all the windows. The place was stuffy.

I made some coffee and drank it and took the five C notes out of the coffee can. They were rolled tight and pushed down into the coffee at the side. I walked up and down with a cup of coffee in my hand, turned the TV on, turned it off, sat, stood, and sat again. I read through the papers that had piled up on the front steps. The Lennox case started out big, but by that morning it was a Part Two item. There was a photo of Sylvia, but none of Terry. There was a snap of me that I didn't know existed. "L.A. Private Detective Held for Questioning." There was a large photo of the Lennox home in Encino. It was pseudo English with a lot of peaked roof and it would have cost a hundred bucks to wash the windows. It stood on a knoll in a big two acres, which is a lot of real estate for the Los Angeles area. There was a photo of the guest house, which was a miniature of the main building. It was hedged in with trees. Both photos had obviously been taken from some distance off and then blown up and trimmed. There was no photo of what the papers called the "death room."

I had seen all this stuff before, in jail, but I read it and looked at it again with different eyes. It told me nothing except that a rich and beautiful girl had been murdered and the press had been pretty thoroughly excluded. So the influence had started to work very early. The crime beat boys must have gnashed their teeth and gnashed them in vain. It figured. If Terry talked to his father-in-law in Pasadena the very night she was killed, there would have been a dozen guards on the estate before the police were even notified.

But there was something that didn't figure at all – the way she had been beaten up. Nobody could sell me that Terry had done that.

I put the lamps out and sat by an open window. Outside in a bush a mockingbird ran through a few trills and admired himself before settling down for the night. My neck itched, so I shaved and showered and went to bed and lay on my back listening, as if far off in the dark I might hear a voice, the kind of calm and patient voice that makes everything clear. I didn't hear it and I knew I wasn't going to. Nobody was going to explain the Lennox case to me. No explanation was necessary. The murderer had confessed and he was dead. There wouldn't even be an inquest.

As Lonnie Morgan of the *Journal* had remarked – very convenient. If Terry Lennox had killed his wife, that was fine. There was no need to try him and bring out all the unpleasant details. If he hadn't killed her, that was fine too. A dead man is the best fall guy in the world. He never talks back.

11

IN THE MORNING I shaved again and dressed and drove downtown in the usual way and parked in the usual place and if the parking lot attendant happened to know that I was an important public character he did a top job in hiding it. I went upstairs and along the corridor and got keys out to unlock my door. A dark smooth-looking guy watched me.

"You Marlowe?"

"So?"

"Stick around," he said. "A guy wants to see you." He unplastered his back from the wall and strolled off languidly.

I stepped inside the office and picked up the mail. There was more of it on the desk where the night cleaning woman had put it. I slit the envelopes after I opened windows, and threw away what I didn't want, which was practically all of it. I switched on the buzzer to the other door and filled a pipe and lit it and then just sat there waiting for somebody to scream for help.

I thought about Terry Lennox in a detached sort of way. He was already receding into the distance, white hair and scarred face and weak charm and his peculiar brand of pride. I didn't judge him or analyze him, just as I had never asked him questions about how he got wounded or how he ever happened to get himself married to anyone like Sylvia. He was like somebody you meet on board ship and get to know very well and never really know at all. He was gone like the same fellow when he says goodbye at the pier and let's keep in touch, old man, and you know you won't and he won't. Likely enough you'll never even see the guy again. If you do he will be an entirely different person, just another Rotarian in a club car. How's business? Oh, not too bad. You look good. So do you. I've put on too much weight. Don't we all? Remember that trip in the *Franconia* (or whatever it was)? Oh sure, swell trip, wasn't it?

The hell it was a swell trip. You were bored stiff. You only talked to the guy because there wasn't anybody around that interested you. Maybe it was like that with Terry Lennox and me. No, not quite. I owned a piece of him. I had invested time and money in him, and three days in the icehouse, not to mention a slug on the jaw and a punch in the neck that I felt every time I swallowed. Now he was dead and I couldn't even give him back his five hundred bucks. That made me sore. It is always the little things that make you sore.

The door buzzer and the telephone rang at the same time. I answered the phone first because the buzzer meant only that somebody had walked into my pint-size waiting room.

"Is this Mr. Marlowe? Mr. Endicott is calling you. One moment please."

He came on the line. "This is Sewell Endicott," he said, as if he didn't know his goddam secretary had already fed me his name.

"Good morning, Mr. Endicott."

"Glad to hear they turned you loose. I think possibly you had the right idea not to build any resistance."

"It wasn't an idea. It was just mulishness."

"I doubt if you'll hear any more about it. But if you do and need help, let me hear from you."

"Why would I? The man is dead. They'd have a hell of a time proving he ever came near me. Then they'd have to prove I had guilty knowledge. And then they'd have to prove he had committed a crime or was a fugitive."

He cleared his throat. "Perhaps," he said carefully, "you haven't been told he left a full confession."

"I was told, Mr. Endicott. I'm talking to a lawyer. Would I be out of line in suggesting that the confession would have to be proved too, both as to genuineness and as to veracity?"

"I'm afraid I have no time for a legal discussion," he said sharply. "I'm flying to Mexico with a rather melancholy duty to perform. You can probably guess what it is?"

"Uh-huh. Depends who you're representing. You didn't tell me, remember."

"I remember very well. Well, goodbye, Marlowe. My offer of help is still good. But let me also offer you a little advice. Don't be too certain you're in the clear. You're in a pretty vulnerable business."

He hung up. I put the phone back in its cradle carefully. I sat for a moment with my hand on it, scowling. Then I

wiped the scowl off my face and got up to open the communicating door into my waiting room.

A man was sitting by the window ruffling a magazine.
He wore a bluish-gray suit with an almost invisible pale blue
check. On his crossed feet were black moccasin-type ties, the
kind with two eyelets that are almost as comfortable as strollers
and don't wear your socks out every time you walk a block.
His white handkerchief was folded square and the end of a pair
of sunglasses showed behind it. He had thick dark wavy hair.
He was tanned very dark. He looked up with bird-bright eyes
and smiled under a hairline mustache. His tie was a dark
maroon tied in a pointed bow over a sparkling white shirt.

He threw the magazine aside. "The crap these rags go for,"
he said. "I been reading a piece about Costello. Yeah, they
know all about Costello. Like I know all about Helen of Troy."

"What can I do for you?"

He looked me over unhurriedly. "Tarzan on a big red
scooter," he said.

"What?"

"You. Marlowe. Tarzan on a big red scooter. They rough
you up much?"

"Here and there. What makes it your business?"

"After Allbright talked to Gregorius?"

"No. Not after that."

He nodded shortly. "You got a crust asking Allbright to use
ammunition on that slob."

"I asked you what made it your business. Incidentally
I don't know Commissioner Allbright and I didn't ask him to
do anything. Why would he do anything for me?"

He stared at me morosely. He stood up slowly, graceful as
a panther. He walked across the room and looked into my
office. He jerked his head at me and went in. He was a guy
who owned the place where he happened to be. I went in
after him and shut the door. He stood by the desk looking
around, amused.

"You're small time," he said. "Very small time."

I went behind my desk and waited.

"How much you make in a month, Marlowe?"

I let it ride, and lit my pipe.

"Seven-fifty would be tops," he said.

I dropped a burnt match into a tray and puffed tobacco smoke.

"You're a piker, Marlowe. You're a peanut grifter. You're so little it takes a magnifying glass to see you."

I didn't say anything at all.

"You got cheap emotions. You're cheap all over. You pal around with a guy, eat a few drinks, talk a few gags, slip him a little dough when he's strapped, and you're sold out to him. Just like some school kid that read *Frank Merriwell*. You got no guts, no brains, no connections, no savvy, so you throw out a phony attitude and expect people to cry over you. Tarzan on a big red scooter." He smiled a small weary smile. "In my book you're a nickel's worth of nothing."

He leaned across the desk and flicked me across the face back-handed, casually and contemptuously, not meaning to hurt me, and the small smile stayed on his face. Then when I didn't even move for that he sat down slowly and leaned an elbow on the desk and cupped his brown chin in his brown hand. The bird-bright eyes stared at me without anything in them but brightness.

"Know who I am, cheapie?"

"Your name's Menendez. The boys call you Mendy. You operate on the Strip."

"Yeah? How did I get so big?"

"I wouldn't know. You probably started out as a pimp in a Mexican whorehouse."

He took a gold cigarette case out of his pocket and lit a brown cigarette with a gold lighter. He blew acrid smoke and nodded. He put the gold cigarette case on the desk and caressed it with his fingertips.

"I'm a big bad man, Marlowe. I make lots of dough. I got to make lots of dough to juice the guys I got to juice in order to make lots of dough to juice the guys I got to juice. I got a place in Bel-Air that cost ninety grand and I already spent more than that to fix it up. I got a lovely platinum-blonde wife and two kids in private schools back east. My wife's got a hundred and fifty grand in rocks and another seventy-five in furs and clothes. I got a butler, two maids, a cook, a chauffeur, not counting the monkey that walks behind me. Everywhere I go I'm a darling. The best of everything, the best food, the best drinks, the best hotel suites. I got a place in Florida and a seagoing yacht with a crew of five men. I got a Bentley, two Cadillacs, a Chrysler station wagon, and an MG for my boy. Couple of years my girl gets one too. What you got?"

"Not much," I said. "This year I have a house to live in — all to myself."

"No woman?"

"Just me. In addition to that I have what you see here and twelve hundred dollars in the bank and a few thousand in bonds. That answer your question?"

"What's the most you ever made on a single job?"

"Eight-fifty."

"Jesus, how cheap can a guy get?"

"Stop hamming and tell me what you want."

He killed his cigarette half smoked and immediately lit another. He leaned back in his chair. His lip curled at me.

"We were three guys in a foxhole eating," he said. "It was cold as hell, snow all around. We eat out of cans. Cold food. A little shelling, more mortar fire. We are blue with the cold, and I mean blue, Randy Starr and me and this Terry Lennox. A mortar shell plops right in the middle of us and for some reason it don't go off. Those jerries have a lot of tricks. They got a twisted sense of humor. Sometimes you think it's a dud and three seconds later it ain't a dud. Terry grabs it and he's out of the foxhole before Randy and me can even start to get

533

unstuck. But I mean quick, brother. Like a good ball handler. He throws himself face down and throws the thing away from him and it goes off in the air. Most of it goes over his head but a hunk gets the side of his face. Right then the krauts mount an attack and the next thing we know we ain't there any more."

Menendez stopped talking and gave me the bright steady glare of his dark eyes.

"Thanks for telling me," I said.

"You take a good ribbing, Marlowe. You're okay. Randy and me talked things over and we decided that what happened to Terry Lennox was enough to screw up any guy's brains. For a long time we figured he was dead but he wasn't. The krauts got him. They worked him over for about a year and a half. They did a good job but they hurt him too much. It cost us money to find out, and it cost us money to find him. But we made plenty in the black market after the war. We could afford it. All Terry gets out of saving our lives is half of a new face, white hair, and a bad case of nerves. Back east he hits the bottle, gets picked up here and there, kind of goes to pieces. There's something on his mind but we never know what. The next thing we know he's married to this rich dame and riding high. He unmarries her, hits bottom again, marries her again, and she gets dead. Randy and me can't do a thing for him. He won't let us except for that short job in Vegas. And when he gets in a real jam he don't come to us, he goes to a cheapie like you, a guy that cops can push around. So then *he* gets dead, and without telling us goodbye, and without giving us a chance to pay off. I could have got him out of the country faster than a card sharp can stack a deck. But he goes crying to you. It makes me sore. A cheapie, a guy cops can push around."

"The cops can push anybody around. What do you want me to do about it?"

"Just lay off," Menendez said tightly.

"Lay off what?"

"Trying to make yourself dough or publicity out of the Lennox case. It's finished, wrapped up. Terry's dead and we don't want him bothered any more. The guy suffered too much."

"A hoodlum with sentiment," I said. "That slays me."

"Watch your lip, cheapie. Watch your lip. Mendy Menendez don't argue with guys. He tells them. Find yourself another way to grab a buck. Get me?"

He stood up. The interview was finished. He picked up his gloves. They were snow-white pigskin. They didn't look as if he ever had them on. A dressy type, Mr. Menendez. But very tough behind it all.

"I'm not looking for publicity," I said. "And nobody's offered me any dough. Why would they and for what?"

"Don't kid me, Marlowe. You didn't spend three days in the freezer just because you're a sweetheart. You got paid off. I ain't saying who by but I got a notion. And the party I'm thinking about has plenty more of the stuff. The Lennox case is closed and it stays closed even if —" He stopped dead and flipped his gloves at the desk edge.

"Even if Terry didn't kill her," I said.

His surprise was as thin as the gold on a weekend wedding ring. "I'd like to go along with you on that, cheapie. But it don't make any sense. But if it did make sense — and Terry wanted it the way it is — then that's how it stays."

I didn't say anything. After a moment he grinned slowly.

"Tarzan on a big red scooter," he drawled. "A tough guy. Lets me come in here and walk all over him. A guy that gets hired for nickels and dimes and gets pushed around by anybody. No dough, no family, no prospects, no nothing. See you around, cheapie."

I sat still with my jaws clamped, staring at the glitter of his gold cigarette case on the desk corner. I felt old and tired. I got up slowly and reached for the case.

"You forgot this," I said, going around the desk.

"I got half a dozen of them," he sneered.

When I was near enough to him I held it out. His hand reached for it casually. "How about half a dozen of these?" I asked him and hit him as hard as I could in the middle of his belly.

He doubled up mewling. The cigarette case fell to the floor. He backed against the wall and his hands jerked back and forth convulsively. His breath fought to get into his lungs. He was sweating. Very slowly and with an intense effort he straightened up and we were eye to eye again. I reached out and ran a finger along the bone of his jaw. He held still for it. Finally he worked a smile onto his brown face.

"I didn't think you had it in you," he said.

"Next time bring a gun – or don't call me cheapie."

"I got a guy to carry the gun."

"Bring him with you. You'll need him."

"You're a hard guy to get sore, Marlowe."

I moved the gold cigarette case to one side with my foot and bent and picked it up and handed it to him. He took it and dropped it into his pocket.

"I couldn't figure you," I said. "Why it was worth your time to come up here and ride me. Then it got monotonous. All tough guys are monotonous. Like playing cards with a deck that's all aces. You've got everything and you've got nothing. You're just sitting there looking at yourself. No wonder Terry didn't come to you for help. It would be like borrowing money from a whore."

He pressed delicately on his stomach with two fingers. "I'm sorry you said that, cheapie. You could crack wise once too often."

He walked to the door and opened it. Outside the bodyguard straightened from the opposite wall and turned. Menendez jerked his head. The bodyguard came into the office and stood there looking me over without expression.

"Take a good look at him, Chick," Menendez said. "Make sure you know him just in case. You and him might have business one of these days."

"I already saw him, Chief," the smooth dark tight-lipped guy said in the tight-lipped voice they all affect. "He wouldn't bother me none."

"Don't let him hit you in the guts," Menendez said with a sour grin. "His right hook ain't funny."

The bodyguard just sneered at me. "He wouldn't get that close."

"Well, so long, cheapie," Menendez told me and went out.

"See you around," the bodyguard told me coolly. "The name's Chick Agostino. I guess you'll know me."

"Like a dirty newspaper," I said. "Remind me not to step on your face."

His jaw muscles bulged. Then he turned suddenly and went out after his boss.

The door closed slowly on the pneumatic gadget. I listened but I didn't hear their steps going down the hall. They walked as softly as cats. Just to make sure, I opened the door again after a minute and looked out. But the hall was quite empty.

I went back to my desk and sat down and spent a little time wondering why a fairly important local racketeer like Menendez would think it worth his time to come in person to my office and warn me to keep my nose clean, just minutes after I had received a similiar though differently expressed warning from Sewell Endicott.

I didn't get anywhere with that, so I thought I might as well make it a perfect score. I lifted the phone and put in a call to the Terrapin Club at Las Vegas, person to person, Philip Marlowe calling Mr. Randy Starr. No soap. Mr. Starr was out of town, and would I talk to anyone else? I would not. I didn't even want to talk to Starr very badly. It was just a passing fancy. He was too far away to hit me.

After that nothing happened for three days. Nobody slugged me or shot at me or called me up on the phone and warned me to keep my nose clean. Nobody hired me to find the wandering daughter, the erring wife, the lost pearl necklace, or the missing will. I just sat there and looked at the wall. The Lennox case died almost as suddenly as it had been born. There was a brief inquest to which I was not summoned. It was held at an odd hour, without previous announcement and without a jury. The coroner entered his own verdict, which was that the death of Sylvia Potter Westerheym di Giorgio Lennox had been caused with homicidal intent by her husband, Terence William Lennox, since deceased outside the jurisdiction of the coroner's office. Presumably a confession was read into the record. Presumably it was verified enough to satisfy the coroner.

The body was released for burial. It was flown north and buried in the family vault. The press was not invited. Nobody gave any interviews, least of all Mr. Harlan Potter, who never gave interviews. He was about as hard to see as the Dalai Lama. Guys with a hundred million dollars live a peculiar life, behind a screen of servants, bodyguards, secretaries, lawyers, and tame executives. Presumably they eat, sleep, get their hair cut, and wear clothes. But you never know for sure. Everything you read or hear about them has been processed by a public relations gang of guys who are paid big money to create and maintain a usable personality, something simple and clean and sharp, like a sterilized needle. It doesn't have to be true. It just has to be consistent with the known facts, and the known facts you could count on your fingers.

Late afternoon of the third day the telephone rang and I was talking to a man who said his name was Howard Spencer, that he was a representative of a New York publishing house in California on a brief business trip, that he had a problem he would like to discuss with me and would I meet him in the bar of the Ritz-Beverly Hotel at eleven A.M. the next morning.

I asked him what sort of problem.

"Rather a delicate one," he said, "but entirely ethical. If we don't agree, I shall expect to pay you for your time, naturally."

"Thank you, Mr. Spencer, but that won't be necessary. Did someone I know recommend me to you?"

"Someone who knows about you — including your recent brush with the law, Mr. Marlowe. I might say that that was what interested me. My business, however, has nothing to do with that tragic affair. It's just that — well, let's discuss it over a drink, rather than over the telephone."

"You sure you want to mix it with a guy who has been in the cooler?"

He laughed. His laugh and his voice were both pleasant. He talked the way New Yorkers used to talk before they learned to talk Flatbush.

"From my point of view, Mr. Marlowe, that is a recommendation. Not, let me add, the fact that you were, as you put it, in the cooler, but the fact, shall I say, that you appear to be extremely reticent, even under pressure."

He was a guy who talked with commas, like a heavy novel. Over the phone anyway.

"Okay, Mr. Spencer, I'll be there in the morning."

He thanked me and hung up. I wondered who could have given me the plug. I thought it might be Sewell Endicott and called him to find out. But he had been out of town all week, and still was. It didn't matter much. Even in my business you occasionally get a satisfied customer. And I needed a job because I needed the money — or thought I did, until I got home that night and found the letter with a portrait of Madison in it.

12

THE LETTER WAS in the red and white birdhouse mailbox at the foot of my steps. A woodpecker on top of the box attached to the swing arm was raised and even at that I might not have looked inside because I never got mail at the house. But the woodpecker had lost the point of his beak quite recently. The wood was fresh broken. Some smart kid shooting off his atom gun.

The letter had Correo Aéreo on it and a flock of Mexican stamps and writing that I might or might not have recognized if Mexico hadn't been on my mind pretty constantly lately. I couldn't read the postmark. It was hand-stamped and the ink pad was pretty far gone. The letter was thick. I climbed my steps and sat down in the living room to read it. The evening seemed very silent. Perhaps a letter from a dead man brings its own silence with it.

It began without date and without preamble.

I'm sitting beside a second-floor window in a room in a not too clean hotel in a town called Otatoclán, a mountain town with a lake. There's a mailbox just below the window and when the mozo comes in with some coffee I've ordered he is going to mail the letter for me and hold it up so that I can see it before he puts it in the slot. When he does that he gets a hundred-peso note, which is a hell of a lot of money for him.

Why all the finagling? There's a swarthy character with pointed shoes and a dirty shirt outside the door watching it. He's waiting for something, I don't know what, but he won't let me out. It doesn't matter too much as long as the letter gets posted. I want you to have this money because I don't need it and the local gendarmerie would swipe it for sure. It is not intended to buy anything. Call it an apology for making you so much trouble and a token of esteem for a pretty decent guy. I've done everything wrong as usual, but I still have the gun. My hunch is that you have probably made up your mind on a certain point. I might have killed her and perhaps I did, but

I never could have done the other thing. That kind of brutality is not in my line. So something is very sour. But it doesn't matter, not in the least. The main thing now is to save an unnecessary and useless scandal. Her father and her sister never did me any harm. They have their lives to live and I'm up to here in disgust with mine. Sylvia didn't make a bum out of me, I was one already. I can't give you any very clean answer about why she married me. I suppose it was just a whim. At least she died young and beautiful. They say lust makes a man old, but keeps a woman young. They say a lot of nonsense. They say the rich can always protect themselves and that in their world it is always summer. I've lived with them and they are bored and lonely people.

I have written a confession. I feel a little sick and more than a little scared. You read about these situations in books, but you don't read the truth. When it happens to you, when all you have left is the gun in your pocket, when you are cornered in a dirty little hotel in a strange country, and have only one way out – believe me, pal, there is nothing elevating or dramatic about it. It is just plain nasty and sordid and gray and grim.

So forget it and me. But first drink a gimlet for me at Victor's. And the next time you make coffee, pour me a cup and put some bourbon in it and light me a cigarette and put it beside the cup. And after that forget the whole thing. Terry Lennox over and out. And so goodbye.

A knock at the door. I guess it will be the mozo with coffee. If it isn't, there will be some shooting. I like Mexicans, as a rule, but I don't like their jails. So long.

TERRY

That was all. I refolded the letter and put it back in the envelope. It had been the mozo with the coffee all right.

Otherwise I would never have had the letter. Not with a portrait of Madison in it. A portrait of Madison is a $5000 bill.

It lay in front of me green and crisp on the table top. I had never even seen one before. Lots of people who work in banks haven't either. Very likely characters like Randy Starr and Menendez wear them for folding money. If you went to a bank and asked for one, they wouldn't have it. They'd have to get it for you from the Federal Reserve. It might take several days. There are only about a thousand of them in circulation in the whole U.S.A. Mine had a nice glow around it. It created a little private sunshine all its own.

I sat there and looked at it for a long time. At last I put it away in my letter case and went out to the kitchen to make that coffee. I did what he asked me to, sentimental or not. I poured two cups and added some bourbon to his and set it down on the side of the table where he had sat the morning I took him to the plane. I lit a cigarette for him and set it in an ashtray beside the cup. I watched the steam rise from the coffee and the thin thread of smoke rise from the cigarette. Outside in the tecoma a bird was gussing around, talking to himself in low chirps, with an occasional brief flutter of wings.

Then the coffee didn't steam any more and the cigarette stopped smoking and was just a dead butt on the edge of an ashtray. I dropped it into the garbage can under the sink. I poured the coffee out and washed the cup and put it away.

That was that. It didn't seem quite enough to do for five thousand dollars.

I went to a late movie after a while. It meant nothing. I hardly saw what went on. It was just noise and big faces. When I got home again I set out a very dull Ruy Lopez and that didn't mean anything either. So I went to bed.

But not to sleep. At three A.M. I was walking the floor and listening to Khachaturyan working in a tractor factory. He called it a violin concerto. I called it a loose fan belt and the hell with it.

A white night for me is as rare as a fat postman. If it hadn't been for Mr. Howard Spencer at the Ritz-Beverly I would have killed a bottle and knocked myself out. And the next time I saw a polite character drunk in a Rolls-Royce Silver Wraith, I would depart rapidly in several directions. There is no trap so deadly as the trap you set for yourself.

13

AT ELEVEN O'CLOCK I was sitting in the third booth on the right-hand side as you go in from the dining-room annex. I had my back against the wall and I could see anyone who came in or went out. It was a clear morning, no smog, no high fog even, and the sun dazzled the surface of the swimming pool which began just outside the plateglass wall of the bar and stretched to the far end of the dining room. A girl in a white sharkskin suit and a luscious figure was climbing the ladder to the high board. I watched the band of white that showed between the tan of her thighs and the suit. I watched it carnally. Then she was out of sight, cut off by the deep overhang of the roof. A moment later I saw her flash down in a one and a half. Spray came high enough to catch the sun and make rainbows that were almost as pretty as the girl. Then she came up the ladder and unstrapped her white helmet and shook her bleach job loose. She wobbled her bottom over to a small white table and sat down beside a lumberjack in white drill pants and dark glasses and a tan so evenly dark that he couldn't have been anything but the hired man around the pool. He reached over and patted her thigh. She opened a mouth like a firebucket and laughed. That terminated my interest in her. I couldn't hear the laugh but the hole in her face when she unzipped her teeth was all I needed.

The bar was pretty empty. Three booths down a couple of sharpies were selling each other pieces of Twentieth Century-Fox, using double-arm gestures instead of money. They had a telephone on the table between them and every two or three minutes they would play the match game to see who called Zanuck with a hot idea. They were young, dark, eager and full of vitality. They put as much muscular activity into a telephone conversation as I would put into carrying a fat man up four flights of stairs. There was a sad fellow over on a bar stool talking to the bartender, who was polishing a glass and listening with that plastic smile people wear when they are trying not to scream. The customer was middle-aged, handsomely dressed, and drunk. He wanted to talk and he couldn't have stopped even if he hadn't really wanted to talk. He was polite and friendly and when I heard him he didn't seem to slur his words much, but you knew that he got up on the bottle and only let go of it when he fell asleep at night. He would be like that for the rest of his life and that was what his life was. You would never know how he got that way because even if he told you it would not be the truth. At the very best a distorted memory of the truth as he knew it. There is a sad man like that in every quiet bar in the world.

I looked at my watch and this high-powered publisher man was already twenty minutes late. I would wait half an hour and then I would leave. It never pays to let the customer make all the rules. If he can push you around, he will assume other people can too, and that is not what he hires you for. And right now I didn't need the work badly enough to let some fathead from back east use me for a horse-holder, some executive character in a paneled office on the eighty-fifth floor, with a row of pushbuttons and an intercom and a secretary in a Hattie Carnegie Career Girl's Special and a pair of those big beautiful promising eyes. This was the kind of operator who would tell you to be there at nine sharp and if you weren't sitting quietly with a pleased smile on your pan when he floated in two hours later on a double Gibson, he would have a paroxysm of outraged executive ability which would necessitate five weeks at Acapulco before he got back the hop on his high hard one.

The old bar waiter came drifting by and glanced softly at my weak Scotch and water. I shook my head and he bobbed his white thatch, and right then a dream walked in. It seemed to me for an instant that there was no sound in the bar, that the sharpies stopped sharping and the drunk on the stool stopped burbling away, and it was like just after the conductor taps on his music stand and raises his arms and holds them poised.

She was slim and quite tall in a white linen tailormade with a black and white polka-dotted scarf around her throat. Her hair was the pale gold of a fairy princess. There was a small hat on it into which the pale gold hair nestled like a bird in its nest. Her eyes were cornflower blue, a rare color, and the lashes were long and almost too pale. She reached the table across the way and was pulling off a white gauntleted glove and the old waiter had the table pulled out in a way no waiter ever will pull a table out for me. She sat down and slipped the gloves under the strap of her bag and thanked him with a smile so gentle, so exquisitely pure, that he was damn near paralyzed by it. She said something to him in a very low voice. He hurried away, bending forward. There was a guy who really had a mission in life.

I stared. She caught me staring. She lifted her glance half an inch and I wasn't there any more. But wherever I was I was holding my breath.

There are blondes and blondes and it is almost a joke word nowadays. All blondes have their points, except perhaps the metallic ones who are as blond as a Zulu under the bleach and as to disposition as soft as a sidewalk. There is the small cute blonde who cheeps and twitters, and the big statuesque blonde who straight-arms you with an ice-blue glare. There is the blonde who gives you the up-from-under look and smells lovely and shimmers and hangs on your arm and is always very very tired when you take her home. She makes that helpless gesture and has that goddamned headache and you would like to slug her except that you are glad you found out about the headache before you invested too much time and money and hope in her. Because the headache will always be there, a weapon that never wears out and is as deadly as the bravo's rapier or Lucrezia's poison vial.

There is the soft and willing and alcoholic blonde who doesn't care what she wears as long as it is mink or where she goes as long as it is the Starlight Roof and there is plenty of dry champagne. There is the small perky blonde who is a little pal and wants to pay her own way and is full of sunshine and common sense and knows judo from the ground up and can toss a truck driver over her shoulder without missing more than one sentence out of the editorial in the *Saturday Review*. There is the pale, pale blonde with anemia of some non-fatal but incurable type. She is very languid and very shadowy and she speaks softly out of nowhere and you can't lay a finger on her because in the first place you don't want to and in the second place she is reading *The Waste Land* or Dante in the original, or Kafka or Kierkegaard or studying Provençal. She adores music and when the New York Philharmonic is playing Hindemith she can tell you which one of the six bass viols came in a quarter of a beat too late. I hear Toscanini can also. That makes two of them.

And lastly there is the gorgeous show piece who will out-last three kingpin racketeers and then marry a couple of millionaires at a million a head and end up with a pale rose villa at Cap Antibes, an Alfa-Romeo town car complete with pilot and co-pilot, and a stable of shopworn aristocrats, all of whom she will treat with the affectionate absent-mindedness of an elderly duke saying goodnight to his butler.

The dream across the way was none of these, not even of that kind of world. She was unclassifiable, as remote and clear as mountain water, as elusive as its color. I was still staring when a voice close to my elbow said:

"I'm shockingly late. I apologize. You must blame it on this. My name's Howard Spencer. You're Marlowe, of course."

I turned my head and looked at him. He was middle-aged, rather plump, dressed as if he didn't give any thought to it, but well shaved and with thin hair smoothed back carefully over a head that was wide between the ears. He wore a flashy double-breasted vest, the sort of thing you hardly ever see in California except perhaps on a visiting Bostonian. His glasses were rimless and he was patting a shabby old dog of a brief-case which was evidently the "this."

"Three brand new book-length manuscripts. Fiction. It would be embarrassing to lose them before we have a chance to reject them." He made a signal to the old waiter who had just stepped back from placing a tall green something or other in front of the dream. "I have a weakness for gin and orange. A silly sort of drink really. Will you join me? Good."

I nodded and the old waiter drifted away.

Pointing to the briefcase I said: "How do you know you are going to reject them?"

"If they were any good, they wouldn't be dropped at my hotel by the writers in person. Some New York agent would have them."

"Then why take them at all?"

"Partly not to hurt feelings. Partly the thousand-to-one chance all publishers live for. But mostly you're at a cocktail party and get introduced to all sorts of people, and some of them have novels written and you are just liquored up enough to be benevolent and full of love for the human race, so you say you'd love to see the script. It is then dropped at your hotel with such sickening speed that you are forced to go through the motions of reading it. But I don't suppose you are much interested in publishers and their problems."

The waiter brought the drinks. Spencer grabbed for his and took a healthy swig. He wasn't noticing the golden girl across the way. I had all his attention. He was a good contact man.

"If it's part of the job," I said. "I can read a book once in a while."

"One of our most important authors lives around here," he said casually. "Maybe you've read his stuff. Roger Wade."

"Uh-huh."

"I see your point." He smiled sadly. "You don't care for historical romances. But they sell brutally."

"I don't have any point, Mr. Spencer. I looked at one of his books once. I thought it was tripe. Is that the wrong thing for me to say?"

He grinned. "Oh no. There are many people who agree with you. But the point is at the moment that he's an automatic best seller. And every publisher has to have a couple with the way costs are now."

I looked across at the golden girl. She had finished her limeade or whatever it was and was glancing at a microscopic wrist watch. The bar was filling up a little, but not yet noisy. The two sharpies were still waving their hands and the solo drinker on the bar stool had a couple of pals with him. I looked back at Howard Spencer.

"Something to do with your problem?" I asked him. "This fellow Wade, I mean."

He nodded. He was giving me a careful once over. "Tell me a little about yourself, Mr. Marlowe. That is, if you don't find the request objectionable."

"What sort of thing? I'm a licensed private investigator and have been for quite a while. I'm a lone wolf, unmarried, getting middle-aged, and not rich. I've been in jail more than once and I don't do divorce business. I like liquor and women and chess and a few other things. The cops don't like me too well, but I know a couple I get along with. I'm a native son, born in Santa Rosa, both parents dead, no brothers or sisters, and when I get knocked off in a dark alley sometime, if it happens, as it could to anyone in my business, and to plenty of people in any business or no business at all these days, nobody will feel that the bottom has dropped out of his or her life."

"I see," he said. "But all that doesn't exactly tell me what I want to know."

I finished the gin and orange. I didn't like it. I grinned at him. "I left out one item, Mr. Spencer. I have a portrait of Madison in my pocket."

"A portrait of Madison? I'm afraid I don't —"

"A five-thousand-dollar bill," I said. "Always carry it. My lucky piece."

"Good God," he said in a hushed voice. "Isn't that terribly dangerous?"

"Who was it said that beyond a certain point all dangers are equal?"

"I think it was Walter Bagehot. He was talking about a steeplejack." Then he grinned. "Sorry, but I am a publisher. You're all right, Marlowe. I'll take a chance on you. If I didn't you would tell me to go to hell. Right?"

I grinned back at him. He called the waiter and ordered another pair of drinks.

"Here it is," he said carefully. "We are in bad trouble over Roger Wade. He can't finish a book. He's losing his grip and there's something behind it. The man seems to be going to pieces. Wild fits of drinking and temper. Every once in a while he disappears for days on end. Not very long ago he threw his wife downstairs and put her in the hospital with five broken ribs. There's no trouble between them in the usual sense, none at all. The man just goes nuts when he drinks." Spencer leaned back and looked at me gloomily. "We have to have that book finished. We need it badly. To a certain extent my job depends on it. But we need more than that. We want to save a very able writer who is capable of much better things than he has ever done. Something is very wrong. This trip he won't even see me. I realize this sounds like a job for a psychiatrist. Mrs. Wade disagrees. She is convinced that he is perfectly sane but that something is worrying him to death. A blackmailer, for instance. The Wades have been married five years. Something from his past may have caught up with him. It might even be — just as a wild guess — a fatal hit-and-run accident and someone has the goods on him. We don't know what it is. We want to know. And we are willing to pay well to correct the trouble. If it turns out to be a medical matter, well — that's that. If not, there has to be an answer. And in the meantime Mrs. Wade has to be protected. He might kill her the next time. You never know."

The second round of drinks came. I left mine untouched and watched him gobble half of his in one swallow. I lit a cigarette and just stared at him.

"You don't want a detective," I said. "You want a magician. What the hell could I do? If I happened to be there at exactly the right time, and if he isn't too tough for me to handle, I might knock him out and put him to bed. But I'd have to *be* there. It's a hundred to one against. You know that."

"He's about your size," Spencer said, "but he's not in your condition. And you could be there all the time."

"Hardly. And drunks are cunning. He'd be certain to pick a time when I wasn't around to throw his wingding. I'm not in the market for a job as a male nurse."

"A male nurse wouldn't be any use. Roger Wade is not the kind of man to accept one. He is a very talented guy who has been jarred loose from his self-control. He has made too much money writing junk for halfwits. But the only salvation for a writer is to write. If there is anything good in him, it will come out."

"Okay, I'm sold on him," I said wearily. "He's terrific. Also he's damn dangerous. He has a guilty secret and he tries to drown it in alcohol. It's not my kind of problem, Mr. Spencer."

"I see." He looked at his wrist watch with a worried frown that knotted his face and made it look older and smaller. "Well, you can't blame me for trying."

He reached for his fat briefcase. I looked across at the golden girl. She was getting ready to leave. The white-haired waiter was hovering over her with the check. She gave him some money and a lovely smile and he looked as if he had shaken hands with God. She touched up her lips and put her white gauntlets on and the waiter pulled the table halfway across the room for her to stroll out.

I glanced at Spencer. He was frowning down at the empty glass on the table edge. He had the briefcase on his knees.

"Look," I said. "I'll go see the man and try to size him up, if you want me to. I'll talk to his wife. But my guess is he'll throw me out of the house."

A voice that was not Spencer's said: "No, Mr. Marlowe, I don't think he would do that. On the contrary I think he might like you."

I looked up into the pair of violet eyes. She was standing at the end of the table. I got up and canted myself against the back of the booth in that awkward way you have to stand when you can't slide out.

"Please don't get up," she said in a voice like the stuff they use to line summer clouds with. "I know I owe you an apology, but it seemed important for me to have a chance to observe you before I introduced myself. I am Eileen Wade."

Spencer said grumpily: "He's not interested, Eileen."

She smiled gently. "I disagree."

I pulled myself together. I had been standing there off balance with my mouth open and me breathing through it like a sweet girl graduate. This was really a dish. Seen close up she was almost paralyzing.

"I didn't say I wasn't interested, Mrs. Wade. What I said or meant to say was that I didn't think I could do any good, and it might be a hell of a mistake for me to try. It might do a lot of harm."

She was very serious now. The smile had gone. "You are deciding too soon. You can't judge people by what they do. If you judge them at all, it must be by what they are."

I nodded vaguely. Because that was exactly the way I had thought about Terry Lennox. On the facts he was no bargain, except for that one brief flash of glory in the foxhole – if Menendez told the truth about that – but the facts didn't tell the whole story by any means. He had been a man it was impossible to dislike. How many do you meet in a lifetime that you can say that about?

"And you have to know them for that," she added gently. "Goodbye, Mr. Marlowe. If you should change your mind –" She opened her bag quickly and gave me a card – "and thank you for being here."

She nodded to Spencer and walked away. I watched her out of the bar, down the glassed-in annex to the dining room. She carried herself beautifully. I watched her turn under the archway that led to the lobby. I saw the last flicker of her white linen skirt as she turned the corner. Then I eased myself down into the booth and grabbed the gin and orange.

Spencer was watching me. There was something hard in his eyes.

"Nice work," I said, "but you ought to have looked at her once in a while. A dream like that doesn't sit across the room from you for twenty minutes without your even noticing."

"Stupid of me, wasn't it?" He was trying to smile, but he didn't really want to. He didn't like the way I had looked at her. "People have such queer ideas about private detectives. When you think of having one in your home –"

"Don't think of having this one in your home," I said. "Anyhow, think up another story first. You can do better than trying to make me believe anybody, drunk or sober, would throw that gorgeous downstairs and break five ribs for her."

He reddened. His hands tightened on the briefcase. "You think I'm a liar?"

"What's the difference? You've made your play. You're a little hot for the lady yourself, maybe."

He stood up suddenly. "I don't like your tone," he said. "I'm not sure I like *you*. Do me a favor and forget the whole idea. I think this ought to pay you for your time."

He threw a twenty on the table, and then added some ones for the waiter. He stood a moment staring down at me. His eyes were bright and his face was still red. "I'm married and have four children," he said abruptly.

"Congratulations."

He made a swift noise in his throat and turned and went. He went pretty fast. I watched him for a while and then I didn't. I drank the rest of my drink and got out my cigarettes and shook one loose and stuck it in my mouth and lit it. The old waiter came up and looked at the money.

"Can I get you anything else, sir?"

"Nope. The dough is all yours."

He picked it up slowly. "This is a twenty-dollar bill, sir. The gentleman made a mistake."

"He can read. The dough is all yours, I said."

"I'm sure I'm very grateful. If you are quite sure, sir —"

"Quite sure."

He bobbed his head and went away, still looking worried. The bar was filling up. A couple of streamlined demi-virgins went by caroling and waving. They knew the two hotshots in the booth farther on. The air began to be spattered with darlings and crimson fingernails.

I smoked half of my cigarette, scowling at nothing, and then got up to leave. I turned to reach back for my cigarettes and something bumped into me hard from behind. It was just what I needed. I swung around and I was looking at the profile of a broad-beamed crowd-pleaser in an overdraped oxford flannel. He had the outstretched arm of the popular character and the two-by-six grin of the guy who never loses a sale.

I took hold of the outstretched arm and spun him around. "What's the matter, Jack? Don't they make the aisles wide enough for your personality?"

He shook his arm loose and got tough. "Don't get fancy, buster. I might loosen your jaw for you."

"Ha, ha," I said. "You might play center field for the Yankees and hit a home run with a breadstick."

He doubled a meaty fist.

"Darling, think of your manicure," I told him.

He controlled his emotions. "Nuts to you, wise guy," he sneered. "Some other time, when I have less on my mind."

"Could there be less?"

"G'wan, beat it," he snarled. "One more crack and you'll need new bridgework."

I grinned at him. "Call me up, Jack. But with better dialogue."

His expression changed. He laughed. "You in pictures, chum?"

"Only the kind they pin up in the post office."

"See you in the mug book," he said, and walked away, still grinning.

It was all very silly, but it got rid of the feeling. I went along the annex and across the lobby of the hotel to the main entrance. I paused inside to put on my sunglasses. It wasn't until I got into my car that I remembered to look at the card Eileen Wade had given me. It was an engraved card, but not a formal calling card, because it had an address and a telephone number on it. Mrs. Roger Stearns Wade, 1247 Idle Valley Road. Tel. Idle Valley 5-6324.

I knew a good deal about Idle Valley, and I knew it had changed a great deal from the days when they had the gatehouse at the entrance and the private police force, and the gambling casino on the lake, and the fifty-dollar joy girls. Quiet money had taken over the tract after the casino was closed out. Quiet money had made it a subdivider's dream.

A club owned the lake and the lake frontage and if they didn't want you in the club, you didn't get to play in the water. It was exclusive in the only remaining sense of the word that doesn't mean merely expensive.

I belonged in Idle Valley like a pearl onion on a banana split.

Howard Spencer called me up late in the afternoon. He had got over his mad and wanted to say he was sorry and he hadn't handled the situation very well, and had I perhaps any second thoughts.

"I'll go see him if he asks me to. Not otherwise."

"I see. There would be a substantial bonus —"

"Look, Mr. Spencer," I said impatiently, "you can't hire destiny. If Mrs. Wade is afraid of the guy, she can move out. That's *her* problem. Nobody could protect her twenty-four hours a day from her own husband. There isn't that much protection in the world. But that's not all you want. You want to know why and how and when the guy jumped the rails, and then fix it so that he doesn't do it again — at least until he finishes the book. And that's up to him. If he wants to write the damn book bad enough, he'll lay off the hooch until he does it. You want too damn much."

"They all go together," he said. "It's all one problem. But I guess I understand. It's a little oversubtle for your kind of operation. Well, goodbye. I'm flying back to New York tonight."

"Have a smooth trip."

He thanked me and hung up. I forgot to tell him I had given his twenty to the waiter. I thought of calling back to tell him, then I thought he was miserable enough already.

I closed the office and started off in the direction of Victor's to drink a gimlet, as Terry had asked me to in his letter. I changed my mind. I wasn't feeling sentimental enough. I went to Lowry's and had a martini and some prime ribs and Yorkshire pudding instead.

When I got home I turned on the TV set and looked at the fights. They were no good, just a bunch of dancing masters who ought to have been working for Arthur Murray. All they did was jab and bob up and down and feint one another off balance. Not one of them could hit hard enough to wake his grandmother out of a light doze. The crowd was booing and the referee kept clapping his hands for action, but they went right on swaying and jittering and jabbing long lefts. I turned to another channel and looked at a crime show. The action took place in a clothes closet and the faces were tired and over familiar and not beautiful. The dialogue was stuff even Monogram wouldn't have used. The dick had a colored houseboy for comic relief. He didn't need it, he was plenty comical all by himself. And the commercials would have sickened a goat raised on barbed wire and broken beer bottles.

I cut it off and smoked a long cool tightly packed cigarette. It was kind to my throat. It was made of fine tobacco. I forgot to notice what brand it was. I was about ready to hit the hay when Detective-Sergeant Green of homicide called me up.

"Thought you might like to know they buried your friend Lennox a couple of days ago right in that Mexican town where he died. A lawyer representing the family went down there and attended to it. You were pretty lucky this time, Marlowe. Next time you think of helping a pal skip the country, don't."

"How many bullet holes did he have in him?"

"What's that?" he barked. Then he was silent for a space. Then he said rather too carefully: "One, I should say. It's usually enough when it blows a guy's head off. The lawyer is bringing back a set of prints and whatever was in his pockets. Anything more you'd like to know?"

"Yeah, but you can't tell me. I'd like to know who killed Lennox's wife."

"Cripes, didn't Grenz tell you he left a full confession? It was in the papers, anyway. Don't you read the papers any more?"

"Thanks for calling me, Sergeant. It was real kind of you."

"Look, Marlowe," he said raspingly. "You got any funny ideas about this case, you could buy yourself a lot of grief talking about them. The case is closed, finalized, and laid away in mothballs. Damn lucky for you it is. Accessory after the fact is good for five years in this state. And let me tell you something else. I've been a cop a long time and one thing I've learned for sure is it ain't always what you do that gets you sent up. It's what it can be made to look like when it comes in to court. Goodnight."

He hung up in my ear. I replaced the phone thinking that an honest cop with a bad conscience always acts tough. So does a dishonest cop. So does almost anyone, including me.

14

NEXT MORNING THE bell rang as I was wiping the talcum off an earlobe. When I got to the door and opened up I looked into a pair of violet-blue eyes. She was in brown linen this time, with a pimento-colored scarf, and no earrings or hat. She looked a little pale, but not as though anyone had been throwing her downstairs. She gave me a hesitant little smile.

"I know I shouldn't have come here to bother you, Mr. Marlowe. You probably haven't even had breakfast. But I had a reluctance to go to your office and I hate telephoning about personal matters."

"Sure. Come in, Mrs. Wade. Would you go for a cup of coffee?"

She came into the living room and sat on the davenport without looking at anything. She balanced her bag on her lap and sat with her feet close together. She looked rather prim. I opened windows and pulled up venetian blinds and lifted a dirty ashtray off the cocktail table in front of her.

"Thank you. Black coffee, please. No sugar."

I went out to the kitchen and spread a paper napkin on a green metal tray. It looked as cheesy as a celluloid collar. I crumpled it up and got out one of those fringed things that come in sets with little triangular napkins. They came with the house, like most of the furniture. I set out two Desert Rose coffee cups and filled them and carried the tray in.

She sipped. "This is very nice," she said. "You make good coffee."

"Last time anyone drank coffee with me was just before I went to jail," I said. "I guess you knew I'd been in the cooler, Mrs. Wade."

She nodded. "Of course. You were suspected of having helped him escape, wasn't it?"

"They didn't say. They found my telephone number on a pad in his room. They asked me questions I didn't answer – mostly because of the way they were asked. But I don't suppose you are interested in that."

She put her cup down carefully and leaned back and smiled at me. I offered her a cigarette.

"I don't smoke, thank you. Of course I'm interested. A neighbor of ours knew the Lennoxes. He must have been insane. He doesn't sound at all like that kind of man."

I filled a bulldog pipe and lit it. "I guess so," I said. "He must have been. He was badly wounded in the war. But he's dead and it's all done with. And I don't think you came here to talk about that."

She shook her head slowly. "He was a friend of yours, Mr. Marlowe. You must have a pretty strong opinion. And I think you are a pretty determined man."

I tamped the tobacco in my pipe and lit it again. I took my time and stared at her over the pipe bowl while I was doing it.

"Look, Mrs. Wade," I said finally. "My opinion means nothing. It happens every day. The most unlikely people commit the most unlikely crimes. Nice old ladies poison whole families. Clean-cut kids commit multiple holdups and shootings. Bank managers with spotless records going back twenty years are found out to be long-term embezzlers. And successful and popular and supposedly happy novelists get drunk and put their wives in the hospital. We know damn little about what makes even our best friends tick."

I thought it would burn her up, but she didn't do much more than press her lips together and narrow her eyes.

"Howard Spencer shouldn't have told you that," she said. "It was my own fault. I didn't know enough to keep away from him. I've learned since that the one thing you can never do to a man who is drinking too much is to try to stop him. You probably know that much better than I do."

"You certainly can't stop him with words," I said. "If you're lucky, and *if* you have the strength, you can sometimes keep him from hurting himself or someone else. Even that takes luck."

She reached quietly for her coffee cup and saucer. Her hands were lovely, like the rest of her. The nails were beautifully shaped and polished and only very slightly tinted.

"Did Howard tell you he hadn't seen my husband this time?"

"Yeah."

She finished her coffee and put the cup carefully back on the tray. She fiddled with the spoon for a few seconds. Then she spoke without looking up at me.

"He didn't tell you why, because he didn't know. I am very fond of Howard but he is the managing type, wants to take charge of everything. He thinks he is very executive."

I waited, not saying anything. There was another silence. She looked at me quickly then looked away again. Very softly she said: "My husband has been missing for three days. I don't know where he is. I came here to ask you to find him and bring him home. Oh, it has happened before. One time he drove himself all the way to Portland and got sick in a hotel

559

there and had to get a doctor to sober him up. It's a wonder how he ever got that far without getting into trouble. He hadn't eaten anything for three days. Another time he was in a Turkish bath in Long Beach, one of those Swedish places where they give high colonics. And the last time it was some sort of small private and probably not very reputable sanitarium. This was less than three weeks ago. He wouldn't tell me the name of it or where it was, just said he had been taking a cure and was all right. But he looked deadly pale and weak. I got a brief glimpse of the man who brought him home. A tall young man dressed in the sort of overelaborate cowboy outfit you would only see on the stage or in a technicolor musical film. He let Roger out in the driveway and backed out and drove away at once."

"Could have been a dude ranch," I said. "Some of these tame cowpunchers spend every dime they make on a fancy outfit like that. The women go crazy over them. That's what they're there for."

She opened her bag and took out a folded paper. "I've brought you a check for five hundred dollars, Mr. Marlowe. Will you accept it as a retainer?"

She put the folded check down on the table. I looked at it, but didn't touch it. "Why?" I asked her. "You say he has been gone three days. It takes three or four to sober a man up and get some food into him. Won't he come back the way he did before? Or does something make this time different?"

"He can't stand much more of it, Mr. Marlowe. It will kill him. The intervals are getting shorter. I'm badly worried. I'm more than worried, I'm scared. It's unnatural. We've been married for five years. Roger was always a drinker, but not a psychopathic drinker. Something is all wrong. I want him found. I didn't sleep more than an hour last night."

"Any idea *why* he drinks?"

The violet eyes were looking at me steadily. She seemed a bit fragile this morning, but certainly not helpless. She bit her lower lip and shook her head. "Unless it's me," she said at last, almost in a whisper. "Men fall out of love with their wives."

"I'm only an amateur psychologist, Mrs. Wade. A man in my racket has to be a little of that. I'd say it's more likely he has fallen out of love with the kind of stuff he writes."

"It's quite possible," she said quietly. "I imagine all writers have spells like that. It's true that he can't seem to finish a book he is working on. But it isn't as if he had to finish it for the rent money. I don't think that is quite enough reason."

"What sort of guy is he sober?"

She smiled. "Well, I'm rather prejudiced. I think he is a very nice guy indeed."

"And how is he drunk?"

"Horrible. Bright and hard and cruel. He thinks he is being witty when he is only being nasty."

"You left out violent."

She raised her tawny eyebrows. "Just once, Mr. Marlowe. And too much has been made of that. I'd never have told Howard Spencer. Roger told him himself."

I got up and walked around in the room. It was going to be a hot day. It already was hot. I turned the blinds on one of the windows to keep the sun out. Then I gave it to her straight.

"I looked him up in *Who's Who* yesterday afternoon. He's forty-two years old, yours is his only marriage, no children. His people are New Englanders, he went to Andover and Princeton. He has a war record and a good one. He has written twelve of these fat sex-and-swordplay historical novels and every damn one of them has been on the best-seller lists. He must have made plenty of the folding. If he had fallen out of love with his wife, he sounds like the type who would say so and get a divorce. If he was haring around with another woman, you would probably know about it, and anyway he wouldn't have to get drunk just to prove he felt bad. If you've been married five years, then he was thirty-seven when that happened. I'd say he knew most of what there is to know about women by that time. I say most, because nobody ever knows all of it."

I stopped and looked at her and she smiled at me. I wasn't hurting her feelings. I went on.

"Howard Spencer suggested – on what grounds I have no idea – that what's the matter with Roger Wade is something that happened a long time ago before you were married and that it has caught up with him now, and is hitting him harder than he can take. Spencer thought of blackmail. Would you know?"

She shook her head slowly. "If you mean would I know if Roger had been paying out a lot of money to someone – no, I wouldn't know that. I don't meddle with his bookkeeping affairs. He could give away a lot of money without my knowing it."

"Okay then. Not knowing Mr. Wade I can't have much idea how he would react to having the bite put on him. If he has a violent temper, he might break somebody's neck. If the secret, whatever it is, might damage his social or professional standing or even, to take an extreme case, made the law boys drop around, he might pay off – for a while anyhow. But none of this gets us anywhere. You want him found, you're worried, you're more than worried. So how do I go about finding him? I don't want your money, Mrs. Wade. Not now anyway."

She reached into her bag again and came up with a couple of pieces of yellow paper. They looked like second sheets, folded, and one of them looked crumpled. She smoothed them out and handed them to me.

"One I found on his desk," she said. "It was very late, or rather early in the morning. I knew he had been drinking and I knew he hadn't come upstairs. About two o'clock I went down to see if he was all right – or comparatively all right, passed out on the floor or the couch or something. He was gone. The other paper was in the wastebasket or rather caught on the edge, so that it hadn't fallen in."

I looked at the first piece, the one not crumpled. There was a short typewritten paragraph on it, no more. It read: "I do not care to be in love with myself and there is no longer anyone else for me to be in love with. Signed: Roger (F. Scott Fitzgerald) Wade. P.S. This is why I never finished *The Last Tycoon.*"

"That mean anything to you, Mrs. Wade?"

"Just attitudinizing. He has always been a great admirer of Scott Fitzgerald. He says Fitzgerald is the best drunken writer since Coleridge, who took dope. Notice the typing, Mr. Marlowe. Clear, even, and no mistakes."

"I did. Most people can't even write their names properly when soused." I opened the crumpled paper. More typing, also without any errors or unevenness. This one read: "I do not like you, Dr. V. But right now you're the man for me."

She spoke while I was still looking at it. "I have no idea who Dr. V. is. We don't know any doctor with a name beginning that way. I suppose he is the one who has that place where Roger was the last time."

"When the cowpoke brought him home? Your husband didn't mention any names at all – even place names?"

She shook her head. "Nothing. I've looked in the directory. There are dozens of doctors of one sort or another whose names begin with V. Also, it may not be his surname."

"Quite likely he's not even a doctor," I said. "That brings up the question of ready cash. A legitimate man would take a check, but a quack wouldn't. It might turn into evidence. And a guy like that wouldn't be cheap. Room and board at his house would come high. Not to mention the needle."

She looked puzzled. "The needle?"

"All the shady ones use dope on their clients. Easiest way to handle them. Knock them out for ten or twelve hours and when they come out of it, they're good boys. But using narcotics without a license can get you room and board with Uncle Sam. And that comes very high indeed."

"I see. Roger probably would have several hundred dollars. He always keeps that much in his desk. I don't know why. I suppose it's just a whim. There's none there now."

"Okay," I said. "I'll try to find Dr. V. I don't know just how, but I'll do my best. Take the check with you, Mrs. Wade."

"But why? Aren't you entitled —"

"Later on, thanks. And I'd rather have it from Mr. Wade. He's not going to like what I do in any case."

"But if he's sick and helpless —"

"He could have called his own doctor or asked you to. He didn't. That means he didn't want to."

She put the check back in her bag and stood up. She looked very forlorn. "Our doctor refused to treat him," she said bitterly.

"There are hundreds of doctors, Mrs. Wade. Any one of them would handle him once. Most of them would stay with him for some time. Medicine is a pretty competitive affair nowadays."

"I see. Of course you must be right." She walked slowly to the door and I walked with her. I opened it.

"You could have called a doctor on your own. Why didn't you?"

She faced me squarely. Her eyes were bright. There might have been a hint of tears in them. A lovely dish and no mistake.

"Because I love my husband, Mr. Marlowe. I'd do anything in the world to help him. But I know what sort of man he is too. If I called a doctor every time he took too many drinks, I wouldn't have a husband very long. You can't treat a grown man like a child with a sore throat."

"You can if he's a drunk. Often you damn well have to."

She was standing close to me. I smelled her perfume. Or thought I did. It hadn't been put on with a spray gun. Perhaps it was just the summer day.

"Suppose there *is* something shameful in his past," she said, dragging the words out one by one as if each of them had a bitter taste. "Even something criminal. It would make no difference to me. But I'm not going to be the means of its being found out."

"But it's all right if Howard Spencer hires me to find out?"

She smiled very slowly. "Do you really think I expected you to give Howard any answer but the one you did – a man who went to jail rather than betray a friend?"

"Thanks for the plug, but that wasn't why I got jugged."

She nodded after a moment of silence, said goodbye, and started down the redwood steps. I watched her get into her car, a slim gray Jaguar, very new looking. She drove it up to the end of the street and swung around in the turning circle there. Her glove waved at me as she went by down the hill. The little car whisked around the corner and was gone.

There was a red oleander bush against part of the front wall of the house. I heard a flutter in it and a baby mockingbird started cheeping anxiously. I spotted him hanging on to one of the top branches, flapping his wings as if he was having trouble keeping his balance. From the cypress trees at the corner of the wall there was a single harsh warning chirp. The cheeping stopped at once and the little fat bird was silent.

I went inside and shut the door and left him to his flying lesson. Birds have to learn too.

15

NO MATTER HOW smart you think you are, you have to have a place to start from: a name, an address, a neighborhood, a background, an atmosphere, a point of reference of some sort. All I had was typing on a crumpled yellow page that said, "I do not like you, Dr. V. But right now you're the man for me." With that I could pinpoint the Pacific Ocean, spend a month wading through the lists of half a dozen county medical associations, and end up with the big round 0. In our town quacks breed like guinea pigs. There are eight counties within a hundred miles of the City Hall and in every town in every single one of them there are doctors, some genuine medical men, some just mail-order mechanics with a license to cut corns or jump up and down on your spine. Of the real doctors some are prosperous and some poor, some ethical, others not sure they can afford it. A well-heeled patient with incipient D.T.'s could be money from home to plenty of old geezers who have fallen behind in the vitamin and antibiotic trade. But without a clue there was no place to start. I didn't have the clue and Eileen Wade either didn't have it or didn't know she had it. And even if I found some-body that fitted and had the right initial, he might turn out to be a myth, so far as Roger Wade was concerned. The jingle might be something that just happened to run through his head while he was getting himself stewed up. Just as the Scott Fitzgerald allusion might be merely an offbeat way of saying goodbye.

In a situation like that the small man tries to pick the big man's brains. So I called up a man I knew in The Carne Organization, a flossy agency in Beverly Hills that specialized in protection for the carriage trade – protection meaning almost anything with one foot inside the law. The man's name was George Peters and he said he could give me ten minutes if I made it fast.

They had half the second floor of one of these candy-pink four-storied buildings where the elevator doors open all by themselves with an electric eye, where the corridors are cool and quiet, and the parking lot has a name on every stall, and the druggist off the front lobby has a sprained wrist from fill-ing bottles of sleeping pills.

The door was French gray outside with raised metal let-tering, as clean and sharp as a new knife. THE CARNE ORGANIZATION, INC. GERALD C. CARNE, PRESIDENT.

Below and smaller: *Entrance*. It might have been an investment trust.

Inside was a small and ugly reception room, but the ugliness was deliberate and expensive. The furniture was scarlet and dark green, the walls were a flat Brunswick green, and the pictures hung on them were framed in a green about three shades darker than that. The pictures were guys in red coats on big horses that were just crazy to jump over high fences. There were two frameless mirrors tinted a slight but disgusting shade of rose pink. The magazines on the table of polished primavera were of the latest issue and each one was enclosed in a clear plastic cover. The fellow who decorated that room was not a man to let colors scare him. He probably wore a pimento shirt, mulberry slacks, zebra shoes, and vermilion drawers with his initials on them in a nice Mandarin orange.

The whole thing was just window-dressing. The clients of The Carne Organization were charged a minimum of one hundred fish *per diem* and they expected service in their homes. They didn't go sit in no waiting rooms. Carne was an ex-colonel of military police, a big pink and white guy as hard as a board. He had offered me a job once, but I never got desperate enough to take it. There are one hundred and ninety ways of being a bastard and Carne knew all of them.

A rubbed glass partition slid open and a receptionist looked out at me. She had an iron smile and eyes that could count the money in your hip wallet.

"Good morning. May I help you?"

"George Peters, please. My name is Marlowe."

She put a green leather book on the ledge. "Is he expecting you, Mr. Marlowe? I don't see your name on the appointment list."

"It's a personal matter. I just talked to him on the phone."

"I see. How do you spell your name, Mr. Marlowe? And your first name, please?"

I told her. She wrote it down on a long narrow form, then slipped the edge under a clock punch.

"Who's that supposed to impress?" I asked her.

"We are very particular about details here," she said coldly. "Colonel Carne says you never know when the most trivial fact may turn out to be vital."

"Or the other way around," I said, but she didn't get it. When she had finished her book work she looked up and said:

"I will announce you to Mr. Peters."

I told her that made me very happy. A minute later a door in the paneling opened and Peters beckoned me into a battleship-gray corridor lined with little offices that looked like cells. His office had soundproofing on the ceiling, a gray steel desk with two matching chairs, a gray dictating machine on a gray stand, a telephone and pen set of the same color as the walls and floor. There were a couple of framed photographs on the walls, one of Carne in uniform, with his snowdrop helmet on, and one of Carne as a civilian seated behind a desk and looking inscrutable. Also framed on the wall was a small inspirational legend in steely letters on a gray background. It read:

A CARNE OPERATIVE DRESSES, SPEAKS AND BEHAVES LIKE A GENTLEMAN AT ALL TIMES AND IN ALL PLACES. THERE ARE NO EXCEPTIONS TO THIS RULE.

Peters crossed the room in two long steps and pushed one of the pictures aside. Set into the gray wall behind it was a gray microphone pickup. He pulled it out, unclipped a wire, and pushed it back in place. He moved the picture in front of it again.

"Right now I'd be out of a job," he said, "except that the son of a bitch is out fixing a drunk-driving rap for some actor. All the mike switches are in his office. He has the whole joint wired. The other morning I suggested to him that he have a microfilm camera installed with infra red light behind a diaphanous mirror in the reception room. He didn't like the idea too well. Maybe because somebody else had it."

He sat down in one of the hard gray chairs. I stared at him. He was a gawky long-legged man with a bony face and receding hair. His skin had the worn weathered look of a man who has been out of doors a great deal, in all kinds of weather. He had deep-set eyes and an upper lip almost as long as his nose. When he grinned the bottom half of his face disappeared into two enormous ditches that ran from his nostrils to the ends of his wide mouth.

"How can you take it?" I asked him.

"Sit down, pal. Breathe quietly, keep your voice down, and remember that a Carne operative is to a cheap shamus like you what Toscanini is to an organ grinder's monkey." He paused and grinned. "I take it because I don't give a damn. It's good money and any time Carne starts acting like he thought I was doing time in that maximum-security prison he ran in England during the war, I'll pick up my check and blow. What's your trouble? I hear you had it rough a while back."

"No complaints about that. I'd like to look at your file on the barred-window boys. I know you have one. Eddie Dowst told me after he quit here."

He nodded. "Eddie was just a mite too sensitive for The Carne Organization. The file you mention is top secret. In no circumstances must any confidential information be disclosed to outsiders. I'll get it at once."

He went out and I stared at the gray wastebasket and the gray linoleum and the gray leather corners of the desk blotter. Peters came back with a gray cardboard file in his hand. He put it down and opened it.

"For Chrissake, haven't you got anything in this place that isn't gray?"

"The school colors, my lad. The spirit of the organization. Yeah, I have something that isn't gray."

He pulled a desk drawer open and took out a cigar about eight inches long.

"An Upman Thirty," he said. "Presented to me by an elderly gent from England who has been forty years in California and still says 'wireless.' Sober he is just an old swish with a good deal of superficial charm, which is all right with me, because most people don't have any, superficial or otherwise, including Carne. He has as much charm as a steel puddler's underpants. Not sober, the client has a strange habit of writing checks on banks which never heard of him. He always makes good and with my fond help he has so far stayed out of the icebox. He gave me this. Should we smoke it together, like a couple of Indian chiefs planning a massacre?"

"I can't smoke cigars."

Peters looked at the huge cigar sadly. "Same here," he said. "I thought of giving it to Carne. But it's not really a one-man cigar, even when the one man is Carne." He frowned. "You know something? I'm talking too much about Carne. I must be edgy." He dropped the cigar back in the drawer and looked at the open file. "Just what do we want from this?"

"I'm looking for a well-heeled alcoholic with expensive tastes and money to gratify them. So far he hasn't gone in for check-bouncing. I haven't heard so anyway. He has a streak of violence and his wife is worried about him. She thinks he's hid out in some sobering-up joint but she can't be sure. The only clue we have is a jingle mentioning a Dr. V. Just the initial. My man is gone three days now."

Peters stared at me thoughtfully. "That's not too long," he said. "What's to worry about?"

"If I find him first, I get paid."

He looked at me some more and shook his head. "I don't get it, but that's okay. We'll see." He began to turn the pages of the file. "It's not too easy," he said. "These people come and go. A single letter ain't much of a lead." He pulled a page out of the folder, turned some more pages, pulled another, and finally a third. "Three of them here," he said. "Dr. Amos Varley, an osteopath. Big place in Altadena. Makes or used to make night calls for fifty bucks. Two registered nurses. Was in a hassle with the State Narcotics people a couple of years back, and turned in his prescription book. This information is not really up to date."

I wrote down the name and address in Altadena.

"Then we have Dr. Lester Vukanich. Ear, Nose, and Throat, Stockwell Building, on Hollywood Boulevard. This one's a dilly. Office practice mostly, and seems to sort of specialize in chronic sinus infections. Rather a neat routine. You go in and complain of a sinus headache and he washes out your antrums for you. First of course he has to anesthetize with Novocain. But if he likes your looks it don't have to be Novocain. Catch?"

"Sure." I wrote that one down.

"This is good," Peters went on, reading some more. "Obviously his trouble would be supplies. So our Dr. Vukanich does a lot of fishing off Ensenada and flies down in his own plane."

"I wouldn't think he'd last long if he brings the dope in himself," I said.

Peters thought about that and shook his head. "I don't think I agree. He could last forever if he's not too greedy. His only real danger is a discontented customer – pardon me, I mean patient – but he probably knows how to handle that. He's had fifteen years in the same office."

"Where the hell do you get this stuff?" I asked him.

"We're an organization, my boy. Not a lone wolf like you. Some we get from the clients themselves, some we get from the inside. Carne's not afraid to spend money. He's a good mixer when he wants to be."

"He'd love this conversation."

"Screw him. Our last offering today is a man named Verringer. The operative who filed on him is long gone.

Seems a lady poet suicided at Verringer's ranch in Sepulveda Canyon one time. He runs a sort of art colony for writers and such who want seclusion and a congenial atmosphere. Rates moderate. He sounds legit. He calls himself doctor, but doesn't practice medicine. Could be a Ph.D. Frankly, I don't know why he's in here. Unless there was something about this suicide." He picked up a newspaper clipping pasted to a blank sheet. "Yeah, overdose of morphine. No suggestion Verringer knew anything about it."

"I like Verringer," I said. "I like him very much."

Peters closed the file and slapped it. "You haven't seen this," he said. He got up and left the room. When he came back I was standing up to leave. I started to thank him, but he shook it off.

"Look," he said, "there must be hundreds of places where your man could be."

I said I knew that.

"And by the way, I heard something about your friend Lennox that might interest you. One of our boys ran across a fellow in New York five or six years ago that answers the description exactly. But the guy's name was not Lennox, he says. It was Marston. Of course he could be wrong. The guy was drunk all the time, so you couldn't really be sure."

I said: "I doubt if it was the same man. Why would he change his name? He had a war record that could be checked."

"I didn't know that. Our man's in Seattle right now. You can talk to him when he gets back, if it means anything to you. His name is Ashterfelt."

"Thanks for everything, George. It was a pretty long ten minutes."

"I might need *your* help some day."

"The Carne Organization," I said, "never needs anything from anybody."

He made a rude gesture with his thumb. I left him in his metallic gray cell and departed through the waiting room. It looked fine now. The loud colors made sense after the cell block.

16

BACK FROM THE highway at the bottom of Sepulveda Canyon were two square yellow gateposts. A five-barred gate hung open from one of them. Over the entrance was a sign hung on wire: PRIVATE ROAD. NO ADMITTANCE. The air was warm and quiet and full of the tomcat smell of eucalyptus trees.

I turned in and followed a graveled road around the shoulder of a hill, up a gentle slope, over a ridge and down the other side into a shallow valley. It was hot in the valley, ten or fifteen degrees hotter than on the highway. I could see now that the graveled road ended in a loop around some grass edged with stones that had been limewashed. Off to my left there was an empty swimming pool, and nothing ever looks emptier than an empty swimming pool. Around three sides of it there was what remained of a lawn dotted with redwood lounging chairs with badly faded pads on them. The pads had been of many colors, blue, green, yellow, orange, rust red. Their edge bindings had come loose in spots, the buttons had popped, and the pads were bloated where this had happened. On the fourth side there was the high wire fence of a tennis court. The diving board over the empty pool looked knee-sprung and tired. Its matting covering hung in shreds and its metal fittings were flaked with rust.

I came to the turning loop and stopped in front of a redwood building with a shake roof and a wide front porch. The entrance had double screen doors. Large black flies dozed on the screens. Paths led off among the ever green and always dusty California oaks and among the oaks there were rustic cabins scattered loosely over the side of the hill, some almost completely hidden. Those I could see had that desolate out-of-season look. Their doors were shut, their windows were blanked by drawn curtains of monk's cloth or something on that order. You could almost feel the thick dust on their sills.

I switched off the ignition and sat there with my hands on the wheel listening. There was no sound. The place seemed to be as dead as Pharaoh, except that the doors behind the double screens were open and something moved in the dimness of the room beyond. Then I heard a light accurate whistling and a man's figure showed against the screen, pushed it open and strolled down the steps. He was something to see.

He wore a flat black gaucho hat with the woven strap under his chin. He wore a white silk shirt, spotlessly clean, open at the throat, with tight wristlets and loose puffed sleeves above. Around his neck a black fringed scarf was knotted unevenly so that one end was short and the other dropped almost to his waist. He wore a wide black sash and black pants, skin-tight at the hips, coal black, and stitched with gold thread down the side to where they were slashed and belled out loosely with gold buttons along both sides of the slash. On his feet he wore patent-leather dancing pumps.

He stopped at the foot of the steps and looked at me, still whistling. He was as lithe as a whip. He had the largest and emptiest smoke-colored eyes I had ever seen, under long silky lashes. His features were delicate and perfect without being weak. His nose was straight and almost but not quite thin, his mouth was a handsome pout, there was a dimple in his chin, and his small ears nestled gracefully against his head. His skin had that heavy pallor which the sun never touches.

He struck an attitude with his left hand on a hip and his right made a graceful curve in the air.

"Greetings," he said. "Lovely day, isn't it?"

"Pretty hot in here for me."

"I like it hot." The statement was flat and final and closed the discussion. What I liked was beneath his notice. He sat down on a step, produced a long file from somewhere, and began to file his fingernails. "You from the bank?" he asked without looking up.

"I'm looking for Dr. Verringer."

He stopped working with the file and looked off into the warm distance. "Who's he?" he asked with no possible interest.

"He owns the place. Laconic as hell, aren't you? As if you didn't know."

He went back to his file and fingernails. "You got told wrong, sweetie. The bank owns the place. They done foreclosed it or it's in escrow or something. I forget the details."

He looked up at me with the expression of a man to whom details mean nothing. I got out of the Olds and leaned against the hot door, then I moved away from that to where there was some air.

"Which bank would that be?"

"You don't know, you don't come from there. You don't come from there, you don't have any business here. Hit the trail, sweetie. Buzz off but fast."

"I have to find Dr. Verringer."

"The joint's not operating, sweetie. Like it says on the sign, this is a private road. Some gopher forgot to lock the gate."

"You the caretaker?"

"Sort of. Don't ask any more questions, sweetie. My temper's not reliable."

"What do you do when you get mad – dance a tango with a ground squirrel?"

He stood up suddenly and gracefully. He smiled a minute, an empty smile. "Looks like I got to toss you back in your little old convertible," he said.

"Later. Where would I find Dr. Verringer about now?"

He pocketed his file in his shirt and something else took its place in his right hand. A brief motion and he had a fist with shining brass knuckles on it. The skin over his cheekbones was tighter and there was a flame deep in his large smoky eyes.

He strolled towards me. I stepped back to get more room. He went on whistling but the whistle was high and shrill.

"We don't have to fight," I told him. "We don't have anything to fight about. And you might split those lovely britches."

He was as quick as a flash. He came at me with a smooth leap and his left hand snaked out very fast. I expected a jab and moved my head well enough but what he wanted was my right wrist and he got it. He had a grip too. He jerked me off balance and the hand with the brass knucks came around in a looping bolo punch. A crack on the back of the head with those and I would be a sick man. If I pulled he would catch me on the side of the face or on the upper arm below the point of the shoulder. It would have been a dead arm or a dead face, whichever it happened to be. In a spot like that there is only one thing to do.

I went with the pull. In passing I blocked his left foot from behind, grabbed his shirt and heard it tear. Something hit me on the back of the neck, but it wasn't the metal. I spun to the left and he went over sideways and landed catlike and was on his feet again before I had any kind of balance. He was grinning now. He was delighted with everything. He loved his work. He came for me fast.

A strong beefy voice yelled from somewhere: "Earl! Stop that at once! At once, do you hear me?"

The gaucho boy stopped. There was a sort of sick grin on his face. He made a quick motion and the brass knucks disappeared into the wide sash around the top of his pants.

I turned and looked at a solid chunk of man in a Hawaiian shirt hurrying towards us down one of the paths waving his arms. He came up breathing a little fast.

"Are you crazy, Earl?"

"Don't ever say that, Doc," Earl said softly. Then he smiled, turned away, and went to sit on the steps of the house. He took off the flat-crowned hat, produced a comb, and began to

576

comb his thick dark hair with an absent expression. In a second or two he started to whistle softly.

The heavy man in the loud shirt stood and looked at me. I stood and looked at him.

"What's going on here?" he growled. "Who are you, sir?"

"Name's Marlowe. I was asking for Dr. Verringer. The lad you call Earl wanted to play games. I figure it's too hot."

"I am Dr. Verringer," he said with dignity. He turned his head. "Go in the house, Earl."

Earl stood up slowly. He gave Dr. Verringer a thoughtful studying look, his large smoky eyes blank of expression. Then he went up the steps and pulled the screen door open. A cloud of flies buzzed angrily and then settled on the screen again as the door closed.

"Marlowe?" Dr. Verringer gave me his attention again. "And what can I do for you, Mr. Marlowe?"

"Earl says you are out of business here."

"That is correct. I am just waiting for certain legal formalities before moving out. Earl and I are alone here."

"I'm disappointed," I said, looking disappointed. "I thought you had a man named Wade staying with you."

He hoisted a couple of eyebrows that would have interested a Fuller Brush man. "Wade? I might possibly know somebody of that name – it's a common enough name – but why should he be staying with me?"

"Taking the cure."

He frowned. When a guy has eyebrows like that he can really do you a frown. "I am a medical man, sir, but no longer in practice. What sort of cure did you have in mind?"

"The guy's a wino. He goes off his rocker from time to time and disappears. Sometimes he comes home under his own power, sometimes he gets brought home, and sometimes he takes a bit of finding." I got a business card out and handed it to him.

He read it with no pleasure.

"What goes with Earl?" I asked him. "He think he's Valentino or something?"

He made with the eyebrows again. They fascinated me. Parts of them curled off all by themselves as much as an inch and a half. He shrugged his meaty shoulders.

"Earl is quite harmless, Mr. Marlowe. He is — at times — a little dreamy. Lives in a play world, shall we say?"

"You say it, Doc. From where I stand he plays rough."

"Tut, tut, Mr. Marlowe. You exaggerate surely. Earl likes to dress himself up. He is childlike in that respect."

"You mean he's a nut," I said. "This place some kind of sanitarium, isn't it? Or was?"

"Certainly not. When it was in operation it was an artists' colony. I provided meals, lodging, facilities for exercise and entertainment, and above all seclusion. And for moderate fees. Artists, as you probably know, are seldom wealthy people. In the term artists I of course include writers, musicians, and so on. It was a rewarding occupation for me — while it lasted."

He looked sad when he said this. The eyebrows drooped at the outer corners to match his mouth. Give them a little more growth and they would be *in* his mouth.

"I know that," I said. "It's in the file. Also the suicide you had here a while back. A dope case, wasn't it?"

He stopped drooping and bristled. "What file?" he asked sharply.

"We've got a file on what we call the barred-window boys, Doctor. Places where you can't jump out of when the French fits take over. Small private sanitariums or what have you that treat alcoholics and dopers and mild cases of mania."

"Such places must be licensed by law," Dr. Verringer said harshly.

"Yeah. In theory anyway. Sometimes they kind of forget about that."

He drew himself up stiffly. The guy had a kind of dignity, at that. "The suggestion is insulting, Mr. Marlowe. I have no knowledge of why my name should be on any such list as you mention. I must ask you to leave."

"Let's get back to Wade. Could he be here under another name, maybe?"

"There is no one here but Earl and myself. We are quite alone. Now if you will excuse me –"

"I'd like to look around."

Sometimes you can get them mad enough to say something off key. But not Dr. Verringer. He remained dignified. His eyebrows went all the way with him. I looked towards the house. From inside there came a sound of music, dance music. And very faintly the snapping of fingers.

"I bet he's in there dancing," I said. "That's a tango. I bet you he's dancing all by himself in there. Some kid."

"Are you going to leave, Mr. Marlowe? Or shall I have to ask Earl to assist me in putting you off my property?"

"Okay, I'll leave. No hard feelings, Doctor. There were only three names beginning with V and you seemed the most promising of them. That's the only real clue we had – Dr. V. He scrawled it on a piece of paper before he left: Dr. V."

"There must be dozens," Dr. Verringer said evenly.

"Oh sure. But not dozens in our file of the barred-window boys. Thanks for the time, Doctor. Earl bothers me a little."

I turned and went over to my car and got into it. By the time I had the door shut Dr. Verringer was beside me. He leaned in with a pleasant expression.

"We need not quarrel, Mr. Marlowe. I realize that in your occupation you often have to be rather intrusive. Just what bothers you about Earl?"

"He's so obviously a phony. Where you find one thing phony you're apt to expect others. The guy's a manic-depressive, isn't he? Right now he's on the upswing."

He stared at me in silence. He looked grave and polite. "Many interesting and talented people have stayed with me, Mr. Marlowe. Not all of them were as level-headed as you may be. Talented people are often neurotic. But I have no facilities for the care of lunatics or alcoholics, even if I had the taste for that sort of work. I have no staff except Earl, and he is hardly the type to care for the sick."

"Just what would you say he is the type for, Doctor? Apart from bubble-dancing and stuff?"

He leaned on the door. His voice got low and confidential. "Earl's parents were dear friends of mine, Mr. Marlowe. Someone has to look after Earl and they are no longer with us. Earl has to live a quiet life, away from the noise and temptations of the city. He is unstable but fundamentally harmless. I control him with absolute ease, as you saw."

"You've got a lot of courage," I said.

He sighed. His eyebrows waved gently, like the antennae of some suspicious insect. "It has been a sacrifice," he said. "A rather heavy one. I thought Earl could help me with my work here. He plays beautiful tennis, swims and dives like a champion, and can dance all night. Almost always he is amiability itself. But from time to time there were – incidents." He waved a broad hand as if pushing painful memories into the background. "In the end it was either give up Earl or give up my place here."

He held both hands palms up, spread them apart, turned them over and let them fall to his sides. His eyes looked moist with unshed tears.

"I sold out," he said. "This peaceful little valley will become a real estate development. There will be sidewalks and lampposts and children with scooters and blasting radios. There will even" – he heaved a forlorn sigh – "be Television." He waved his hand in a sweeping gesture. "I hope they will spare the trees," he said, "but I'm afraid they won't. Along the ridges there will be television aerials instead. But Earl and I will be far away, I trust."

"Goodbye, Doctor. My heart bleeds for you."

He put out his hand. It was moist but very firm. "I appreciate your sympathy and understanding, Mr. Marlowe. And I regret I am unable to help you in your quest for Mr. Slade."

"Wade," I said.

"Pardon me, Wade, of course. Goodbye and good luck, sir."

I started up and drove back along the graveled road by the way I had come. I felt sad, but not quite as sad as Dr. Verringer would have liked me to feel.

I came out through the gates and drove far enough around the curve of the highway to park out of sight of the entrance. I got out and walked back along the edge of the paving to where I could just see the gates from the barbed-wire boundary fence. I stood there under a eucalyptus and waited.

Five minutes or so passed. Then a car came down the private road churning gravel. It stopped out of sight from where I was. I pulled back still farther into the brush. I heard a creaking noise, then the click of a heavy catch and the rattle of a chain. The car motor revved up and the car went back up the road.

When the sound of it had died I went back to my Olds and did a U turn to face back towards town. As I drove past the entrance to Dr. Verringer's private road I saw that the gate was fastened with a padlocked chain. No more visitors today, thank you.

17

I DROVE THE twenty-odd miles back to town and ate lunch. While I ate I felt more and more silly over the whole deal. You just don't find people the way I was going about it. You meet interesting characters like Earl and Dr. Verringer, but you don't meet the man you are looking for. You waste tires, gasoline, words, and nervous energy in a game with no pay-off. You're not even betting table limit four ways on Black 28.

With three names that started with V, I had as much chance of paging my man as I had of breaking Nick the Greek in a crap game.

Anyway the first one is always wrong, a dead end, a promising lead that blows up in your face with no music. But he shouldn't have said Slade instead of Wade. He was an intelligent man. He wouldn't forget that easy, and if he did he would just forget.

Maybe, and maybe not. It had not been a long acquaintance. Over my coffee I thought about Drs. Vukanich and Varley. Yes or no? They would kill most of the afternoon. By then I could call the Wade mansion in Idle Valley and be told the head of the household had returned to his domicile and all was gleaming bright for the time being.

Dr. Vukanich was easy. He was only half a dozen blocks down the line. But Dr. Varley was away to hell and gone in the Altadena hills, a long, hot, boring drive. Yes or no?

The final answer was yes. For three good reasons. One was that you can never know too much about the shadow line and the people who walk it. The second was that anything I could add to the file Peters had got out for me was just that much thanks and goodwill. The third reason was that I didn't have anything else to do.

I paid my check, left my car where it was, and walked the north side of the street to the Stockwell Building. It was an antique with a cigar counter in the entrance and a manually operated elevator that lurched and hated to level off. The corridor of the sixth floor was narrow and the doors had frosted glass panels. It was older and much dirtier than my own building. It was loaded with doctors, dentists, Christian Science practitioners not doing too good, the kind of lawyers you hope the other fellow has, the kind of doctors and dentists who just scrape along. Not too skillful, not too clean, not too much on the ball, three dollars and please pay the nurse; tired, discouraged men who know just exactly where they stand, what kind of patients they can get and how much money they can be squeezed into paying. Please Do Not Ask For Credit. Doctor is In, Doctor is Out. That's a pretty shaky molar you have there, Mrs. Kazinski. Now if you want this new acrylic filling, every bit as good as a gold inlay, I can do it for you for $14. Novocain will be two dollars extra, if you wish it. Doctor is In, Doctor is Out. That will be Three Dollars. Please Pay the Nurse.

In a building like that there will always be a few guys making real money, but they don't look it. They fit into the shabby background, which is protective coloring for them. Shyster lawyers who are partners in a bail-bond racket on the side (only about two per cent of all forfeited bail bonds are ever collected). Abortionists posing as anything you like that explains their furnishings. Dope pushers posing as urologists, dermatologists, or any branch of medicine in which the treatment can be frequent, and the regular use of local anesthetics is normal.

Dr. Lester Vukanich had a small and ill-furnished waiting room in which there were a dozen people, all uncomfortable. They looked like anybody else. They had no signs on them. Anyway you can't tell a doper well under control from a vegetarian bookkeeper. I had to wait three quarters of an hour. The patients went in through two doors. An active ear, nose, and throat man can handle four sufferers at once, if he has enough room.

Finally I got in. I got to sit in a brown leather chair beside a table covered with a white towel on which was a set of tools. A sterilizing cabinet bubbled against the wall. Dr. Vukanich came in briskly with his white smock and his round mirror strapped to his forehead. He sat down in front of me on a stool.

"A sinus headache, is it? Very severe?" He looked at a folder the nurse had given him.

I said it was awful. Blinding. Especially when I first got up in the morning. He nodded sagely.

"Characteristic," he said, and fitted a glass cap over a thing that looked like a fountain pen.

He pushed it into my mouth. "Close the lips but not the teeth, please." While he said it he reached out and switched off the light. There was no window. A ventilating fan purred somewhere.

Dr. Vukanich withdrew his glass tube and put the lights back up. He looked at me carefully.

"No congestion at all, Mr. Marlowe. If you have a headache, it is not from a sinus condition. I'd hazard a guess that you never had sinus trouble in your life. You had a septum operation sometime in the past, I see."

"Yes, Doctor. Got a kick playing football."

He nodded. "There is a slight shelf of bone which should have been cut away. Hardly enough to interfere with breathing, however."

He leaned back on the stool and held his knee. "Just what did you expect me to do for you?" he asked. He was a thin-faced man with an uninteresting pallor. He looked like a tubercular white rat.

"I wanted to talk to you about a friend of mine. He's in bad shape. He's a writer. Plenty of dough, but bad nerves. Needs help. He lives on the sauce for days on end. He needs that little extra something. His own doctor won't co-operate any more."

"Exactly what do you mean by co-operate?" Dr. Vukanich asked.

"All the guy needs is an occasional shot to calm him down. I thought maybe we could work something out. The money would be solid."

"Sorry, Mr. Marlowe. It is not my sort of problem." He stood up. "Rather a crude approach, if I may say so. Your friend may consult me, if he chooses. But he'd better have something wrong with him that requires treatment. That will be ten dollars, Mr. Marlowe."

"Come off it, Doc. You're on the list."

Dr. Vukanich leaned against the wall and lit a cigarette. He was giving me time. He blew smoke and looked at it. I gave him one of my cards to look at instead. He looked at it.

"What list would that be?" he inquired.

"The barred-window boys. I figure you might know my friend already. His name's Wade. I figure you might have him stashed away somewhere in a little white room. The guy is missing from home."

"You are an ass," Dr. Vukanich told me. "I don't go in for penny ante stuff like four-day liquor cures. They cure nothing in any case. I have no little white rooms and I am not acquainted with the friend you mention — even if he exists. That will be ten dollars — cash — right now. Or would you rather I called the police and make a complaint that you solicited me for narcotics?"

"That would be dandy," I said. "Let's."

"Get out of here, you cheap grifter."

I stood up off the chair. "I guess I made a mistake, Doctor. The last time the guy broke parole he holed up with a doctor whose name began with V. It was strictly an undercover operation. They fetched him late at night and brought him back the same way when he was over the jumps. Didn't even wait long enough to see him go in the house. So when he hops the coop again and don't come back for quite a piece, naturally we check over our files for a lead. We come up with three doctors whose names begin with V."

"Interesting," he said with a bleak smile. He was still giving me time. "What is the basis of your selection?"

I stared at him. His right hand was moving softly up and down the upper part of his left arm on the inside of it. His face was covered with a light sweat.

"Sorry, Doctor. We operate very confidential."

"Excuse me a moment. I have another patient that —"

585

He left the rest of it hanging in the air and went out. While he was gone a nurse poked her head through the doorway, looked at me briefly and withdrew.

Then Dr. Vukanich came back in strolling happily. He was smiling and relaxed. His eyes were bright.

"What? Are you still here?" He looked very surprised or pretended to. "I thought our little visit had been brought to an end."

"I'm leaving. I thought you wanted me to wait."

He chuckled. "You know something, Mr. Marlowe? We live in extraordinary times. For a mere five hundred dollars I could have you put in the hospital with several broken bones. Comical, isn't it?"

"Hilarious," I said. "Shoot yourself in the vein, don't you, Doc? Boy, do you brighten up!"

I started out. "Hasta luego, amigo," he chirped. "Don't forget my ten bucks. Pay the nurse."

He moved to an intercom and was speaking into it as I left. In the waiting room the same twelve people or twelve just like them were being uncomfortable. The nurse was right on the job.

"That will be ten dollars, please, Mr. Marlowe. This office requires immediate cash payment."

I stepped among the crowded feet to the door. She bounded out of her chair and ran around the desk. I pulled the door open.

"What happens when you don't get it?" I asked her.

"You'll find out what happens," she said angrily.

"Sure. You're just doing your job. So am I. Take a gander at the card I left and you'll see what my job is."

I went on out. The waiting patients looked at me with disapproving eyes. That was no way to treat Doctor.

18

DR. AMOS VARLEY was a very different proposition. He had a big old house in a big old garden with big old oak trees shading it. It was a massive frame structure with elaborate scrollwork along the overhang of the porches and the white porch railings had turned and fluted uprights like the legs of an old-fashioned grand piano. A few frail elderly people sat in long chairs on the porches with rugs tucked around them.

The entrance doors were double and had stained-glass panels. The hall inside was wide and cool and the parquetry floor was polished and without a single rug. Altadena is a hot place in summer. It is pushed back against the hills and the breeze jumps clear over it. Eighty years ago people knew how to build houses for this climate.

A nurse in crisp white took my card and after a wait Dr. Amos Varley condescended to see me. He was a big bald-headed guy with a cheery smile. His long white coat was spotless, he walked noiselessly on crepe rubber soles.

"What can I do for you, Mr. Marlowe?" He had a rich soft voice to soothe the pain and comfort the anxious heart. Doctor is here, there is nothing to worry about, everything will be fine. He had that bedside manner, thick, honeyed layers of it. He was wonderful – and he was as tough as armor plate.

"Doctor, I am looking for a man named Wade, a well-to-do alcoholic who has disappeared from his home. His past history suggests that he is holed up in some discreet joint that can handle him with skill. My only lead is a reference to a Dr. V. You're my third Dr. V. and I'm getting discouraged."

He smiled benignly. "Only your third, Mr. Marlowe? Surely there must be a hundred doctors in and around the Los Angeles area whose names begin with V."

"Sure, but not many of them would have rooms with barred windows. I noticed a few upstairs here, on the side of the house."

"Old people," Dr. Varley said sadly, but it was a rich full sadness. "Lonely old people, depressed and unhappy old people, Mr. Marlowe. Sometimes –" He made an expressive gesture with his hand, a curving motion outwards, a pause, then a gentle falling, like a dead leaf fluttering to the ground. "I don't treat alcoholics here," he added precisely. "Now if you will excuse me –"

"Sorry, Doctor. You just happened to be on our list. Probably a mistake. Something about a run-in with the narcotics people a couple of years ago."

"Is that so?" He looked puzzled, then the light broke. "Ah, yes, an assistant I was unwise enough to employ. For a very short time. He abused my confidence badly. Yes, indeed."

"Not the way I heard it," I said. "I guess I heard it wrong."

"And how did you hear it, Mr. Marlowe?" He was still giving me the full treatment with his smile and his mellow tones.

"That you had to turn in your narcotic prescription book."

That got to him a little. He didn't quite scowl but he peeled off a few layers of the charm. His blue eyes had a chilly glint. "And the source of this fantastic information?"

"A large detective agency that has facilities for building files on that sort of thing."

"A collection of cheap blackmailers, no doubt."

"Not cheap, Doctor. Their base rate is a hundred dollars a day. It's run by a former colonel of miltary police. No nickel grabber, Doctor. He rates way up."

"I shall give him a piece of my mind," Dr. Varley said with cool distaste. "His name?" The sun had set in Dr. Varley's manner. It was getting to be a chilly evening.

"Confidential, Doctor. But don't give it a thought. All in the day's work. Name of Wade doesn't ring a bell at all, huh?"

"I believe you know your way out, Mr. Marlowe."

The door of a small elevator opened behind him. A nurse pushed a wheel chair out. The chair contained what was left of a broken old man. His eyes were closed, his skin had a bluish tinge. He was well wrapped up. The nurse wheeled him silently across the polished floor and out of a side door. Dr. Varley said softly:

"Old people. Sick old people. Lonely old people. Do not come back, Mr. Marlowe. You might annoy me. When annoyed I can be rather unpleasant. I might even say *very* unpleasant."

"Okay by me, Doctor. Thanks for the time. Nice little dying-in home you got here."

"What was that?" He took a step towards me and peeled off the remaining layers of honey. The soft lines of his face set themselves into hard ridges.

"What's the matter?" I asked him. "I can see my man wouldn't be here. I wouldn't look for anybody here that wasn't too frail to fight back. Sick old people. Lonely old people. You said it yourself, Doctor. Unwanted old people, but with money and hungry heirs. Most of them probably judged incompetent by the court."

"I am getting annoyed," Dr. Varley said.

"Light food, light sedation, firm treatment. Put them out in the sun, put them back in the bed. Bar some of the windows in case there's a little spunk left. They love you, Doctor, one and all. They die holding your hand and seeing the sadness in your eyes. It's genuine too."

"It certainly is," he said in a low throaty growl. His hands were fists now. I ought to knock it off. But he had begun to nauseate me.

"Sure it is," I said. "Nobody likes to lose a good paying customer. Especially one you don't even have to please."

"Somebody has to do it," he said. "Somebody has to care for these sad old people, Mr. Marlowe."

"Somebody has to clean out cesspools. Come to think of it that's a clean honest job. So long, Dr. Varley. When my job makes me feel dirty I'll think of you. It will cheer me up no end."

"You filthy louse," Dr. Varley said between his wide white teeth. "I ought to break your back. Mine is an honorable branch of an honorable profession."

"Yeah." I looked at him wearily. "I know it is. Only it smells of death."

He didn't slug me, so I walked away from him and out. I looked back from the wide double doors. He hadn't moved. He had a job to do, putting back the layers of honey.

19

I DROVE BACK to Hollywood feeling like a short length of chewed string. It was too early to eat, and too hot. I turned on the fan in my office. It didn't make the air any cooler, just a little more lively. Outside on the boulevard the traffic brawled endlessly. Inside my head thoughts stuck together like flies on flypaper.

Three shots, three misses. All I had been doing was seeing too many doctors.

I called the Wade home. A Mexican sort of accent answered and said that Mrs. Wade was not at home. I asked for Mr. Wade. The voice said Mr. Wade was not home either. I left my name. He seemed to catch it without any trouble. He said he was the houseboy.

I called George Peters at The Carne Organization. Maybe he knew some more doctors. He wasn't in. I left a phony name and a right telephone number. An hour crawled by like a sick cockroach. I was a grain of sand on the desert of oblivion. I was a two-gun cowpoke fresh out of bullets. Three shots, three misses. I hate it when they come in threes. You call on Mr. A. Nothing. You call on Mr. B. Nothing. You call on Mr. C. More of the same. A week later you find out it should have been Mr. D. Only you didn't know he existed and by the time you found out, the client had changed his mind and killed the investigation.

Drs. Vukanich and Varley were scratched. Varley had it too rich to fool with hooch cases. Vukanich was a punk, a high-wire performer who hit the main line in his own office. The help must know. At least some of the patients must know. All it took to finish him was one sorehead and one telephone call. Wade wouldn't have gone within blocks of him, drunk or sober. He might not be the brightest guy in the world — plenty of successful people are far from mental giants — but he couldn't be dumb enough to fool with Vukanich.

The only possible was Dr. Verringer. He had the space and the seclusion. He probably had the patience. But Sepulveda Canyon was a long way from Idle Valley. Where was the point of contact, how did they know each other, and if Verringer owned that property and had a buyer for it, he was halfway to being pretty well heeled. That gave me an idea. I called a man I knew in a title company to find out the status of the property. No answer. The title company had closed for the day.

I closed for the day too, and drove over to La Cienaga to Rudy's Bar-B-Q, gave my name to the master of ceremonies, and waited for the big moment on a bar stool with a whiskey sour in front of me and Marek Weber's waltz music in my ears. After a while I got in past the velvet rope and ate one of Rudy's "world-famous" Salisbury steaks, which is hamburger on a slab of burnt wood, ringed with browned-over mashed potato, supported by fried onion rings and one of those mixed up salads which men will eat with complete docility in restaurants, although they would probably start yelling if their wives tried to feed them one at home.

After that I drove home. As I opened the front door the phone started to ring.

"This is Eileen Wade, Mr. Marlowe. You wanted me to call you."

"Just to find out if anything had happened at your end. I have been seeing doctors all day and have made no friends."

"No, I'm sorry. He still hasn't showed up. I can't help being rather anxious. Then you have nothing to tell me, I suppose." Her voice was low and dispirited.

"It's a big crowded county, Mrs. Wade."

"It will be four whole days tonight."

"Sure, but that's not too long."

"For me it is." She was silent for a while. "I've been doing a lot of thinking, trying to remember something," she went on. "There must be something, some kind of hint or memory. Roger talks a great deal about all sorts of things."

"Does the name Verringer mean anything to you, Mrs. Wade?"

"No, I'm afraid not. Should it?"

"You mentioned that Mr. Wade was brought home one time by a tall young man dressed in a cowboy outfit. Would you recognize this tall young man if you saw him again, Mrs. Wade?"

"I suppose I might," she said hesitantly, "if the conditions were the same. But I only caught the merest glimpse of him. Was his name Verringer?"

"No, Mrs. Wade. Verringer is a heavily built, middle-aged man who runs, or more accurately has run, some kind of guest ranch in Sepulveda Canyon. He has a dressed up fancy boy named Earl working for him. And Verringer calls himself a doctor."

"That's wonderful," she said warmly. "Don't you feel that you're on the right track?"

"I could be wetter than a drowned kitten. I'll call you when I know. I just wanted to make sure Roger hadn't come home and that you hadn't recalled anything definite."

"I'm afraid I haven't been of much help to you," she said sadly. "Please call me at any time, no matter how late it is."

I said I would do that and we hung up. I took a gun and a three-cell flashlight with me this time. The gun was a tough little short-barreled .32 with flat-point cartridges. Dr. Verringer's boy Earl might have other toys than brass knuckles. If he had, he was plenty goofy enough to play with them.

I hit the highway again and drove as fast as I dared. It was a moonless night, and would be getting dark by the time

I reached the entrance to Dr. Verringer's estate. Darkness was what I needed.

The gates were still locked with the chain and padlock. I drove on past and parked well off the highway. There was still some light under the trees but it wouldn't last long. I climbed the gate and went up the side of the hill looking for a hiking path. Far back in the valley I thought I heard a quail. A mourning dove exclaimed against the miseries of life. There wasn't any hiking path or I couldn't find one, so I went back to the road and walked along the edge of the gravel. The eucalyptus trees gave way to the oaks and I crossed the ridge and far off I could see a few lights. It took me three quarters of an hour to work up behind the swimming pool and the tennis courts to a spot where I could look down on the main building at the end of the road. It was lighted up and I could hear music coming from it. And farther off in the trees another cabin showed light. There were small dark cabins dotted all over the place in the trees. I went along a path now and suddenly a floodlight went on at the back of the main cabin. I stopped dead. The floodlight was not looking for anything. It pointed straight down and made a wide pool of light on the back porch and the ground beyond. Then a door banged open and Earl came out. Then I knew I was in the right place.

Earl was a cowpoke tonight, and it had been a cowpoke who brought Roger Wade home the time before. Earl was spinning a rope. He wore a dark shirt stitched with white and a polka-dot scarf knotted loosely around his neck. He wore a wide leather belt with a load of silver on it and a pair of tooled leather holsters with ivory-handled guns in them. He wore elegant riding pants and boots cross-stitched in white and glistening new. On the back of his head was a white sombrero and what looked like a woven silver cord hanging loosely down his shirt, the ends not fastened.

He stood there alone under the white floodlight, spinning his rope around him, stepping in and out of it, an actor

593

without an audience, a tall, slender, handsome dude wrangler putting on a show all by himself and loving every minute of it. Two-Gun Earl, the Terror of Cochise County. He belonged on one of those guest ranches that are so all-fired horsy the telephone girl wears riding boots to work.

All at once he heard a sound, or pretended to. The rope dropped, his hands swept the two guns from the holsters, and the crook of his thumbs was over the hammers as they came level. He peered into the darkness. I didn't dare move. The damn guns could be loaded. But the floodlight had blinded him and he didn't see anything. He slipped his guns back in the holsters, picked up the rope and gathered it loosely, went back into the house. The light went off, and so did I.

I moved around through the trees and got close to the small lighted cabin on the slope. No sound came from it. I reached a screened window and looked in. The light came from a lamp on a night table beside a bed. A man lay flat on his back in the bed, his body relaxed, his arms in pajama sleeves outside the covers, his eyes wide open and staring at the ceiling. He looked big. His face was partly shadowed, but I could see that he was pale and that he needed a shave and had needed one for just about the right length of time. The spread fingers of his hands lay motionless on the outside of the bed. He looked as if he hadn't moved for hours.

I heard steps coming along the path at the far side of the cabin. A screen door creaked and then the solid shape of Dr. Verringer showed in the doorway. He was carrying what looked like a large glass of tomato juice. He switched on a standing lamp. His Hawaiian shirt gleamed yellowly. The man in the bed didn't even look at him.

Dr. Verringer put the glass down on the night table and pulled a chair close and sat down. He reached for one of the wrists and felt a pulse. "How are you feeling now, Mr. Wade?" His voice was kindly and solicitous.

The man on the bed didn't answer him or look at him. He went on staring at the ceiling.

"Come, come, Mr. Wade. Let us not be moody. Your pulse is only slightly faster than normal. You are weak, but otherwise —"

"Tejjy," the man on the bed said suddenly, "tell the man that if he knows how I am, the son of a bitch needn't bother to ask me." He had a nice clear voice, but the tone was bitter.

"Who is Tejjy?" Dr. Verringer said patiently.

"My mouthpiece. She's up there in the corner."

Dr. Verringer looked up. "I see a small spider," he said. "Stop acting, Mr. Wade. It is not necessary with me."

"*Tegenaria domestica*, the common jumping spider, pal. I like spiders. They practically never wear Hawaiian shirts."

Dr. Verringer moistened his lips. "I have no time for playfulness, Mr. Wade."

"Nothing playful about Tejjy." Wade turned his head slowly, as if it weighed very heavy, and stared at Dr. Verringer contemptuously. "Tejjy is dead serious. She creeps up on you. When you're not looking she makes a quick silent hop. After a while she's near enough. She makes the last jump. You get sucked dry, Doctor. Very dry. Tejjy doesn't eat you. She just sucks the juice until there's nothing left but the skin. If you plan to wear that shirt much longer, Doctor, I'd say it couldn't happen too soon."

Dr. Verringer leaned back in the chair. "I need five thousand dollars," he said calmly. "How soon could that happen?"

"You got six hundred and fifty bucks," Wade said nastily. "As well as my loose change. How the hell much does it cost in this bordello?"

"Chicken feed," Dr. Verringer said. "I told you my rates had gone up."

"You didn't say they had moved to Mount Wilson."

"Don't fence with me, Wade," Dr. Verringer said curtly. "You are in no position to get funny. Also you have betrayed my confidence."

"I didn't know you had any."

Dr. Verringer tapped slowly on the arms of the chair. "You called me up in the middle of the night," he said. "You were in a desperate condition. You said you would kill yourself if I didn't come. I didn't want to do it and you know why. I have no license to practice medicine in this state. I am trying to get rid of this property without losing it all. I have Earl to look after and he was about due for a bad spell. I told you it would cost you a lot of money. You still insisted and I went. I want five thousand dollars."

"I was foul with strong drink," Wade said. "You can't hold a man to that kind of bargain. You're damn well paid already."

"Also," Dr. Verringer said slowly, "you mentioned my name to your wife. You told her I was coming for you."

Wade looked surprised. "I didn't do anything of the sort," he said. "I didn't even see her. She was asleep."

"Some other time then. A private detective has been here asking about you. He couldn't possibly have known where to come, unless he was told. I stalled him off, but he may come back. You have to go home, Mr. Wade. But first I want my five thousand dollars."

"You're not the brightest guy in the world, are you, Doc? If my wife knew where I was, why would she need a detective? She could have come herself – supposing she cared that much. She could have brought Candy, our houseboy. Candy would cut your Blue Boy into thin strips while Blue Boy was making up his mind what picture he was starring in today."

"You have a nasty tongue, Wade. And a nasty mind."

"I have a nasty five thousand bucks too, Doc. Try and get it."

"You will write me a check," Dr. Verringer said firmly. "Now, at once. Then you will get dressed and Earl will take you home."

"A check?" Wade was almost laughing. "Sure I'll give you a check. Fine. How will you cash it?"

Dr. Verringer smiled quietly. "You think you will stop payment, Mr. Wade. But you won't. I assure you that you won't."

"You fat crook!" Wade yelled at him.

Dr. Verringer shook his head. "In some things, yes. Not in all. I am a mixed character like most people. Earl will drive you home."

"Nix. That lad makes my skin crawl," Wade said.

Dr. Verringer stood up gently and reached over and patted the shoulder of the man on the bed. "To me Earl is quite harmless, Mr. Wade. I have ways of controlling him."

"Name one," a new voice said, and Earl came through the door in his Roy Rogers outfit. Dr. Verringer turned smiling.

"Keep that psycho away from me," Wade yelled, showing fear for the first time.

Earl put his hands on his ornamented belt. His face was deadpan. A light whistling noise came from between his teeth. He moved slowly into the room.

"You shouldn't have said that," Dr. Verringer said quickly, and turned towards Earl. "All right, Earl. I'll handle Mr. Wade myself. I'll help him get dressed while you bring the car up here as close to the cabin as possible. Mr. Wade is quite weak."

"And he's going to be a lot weaker," Earl said in a whistling kind of voice. "Out of my way, fatso."

"Now, Earl —" he reached out and grabbed the handsome young man's arm — "you don't want to go back to Camarillo, do you? One word from me and —"

That was as far as he got. Earl jerked his arm loose and his right hand came up with a flash of metal. The armored fist crashed against Dr. Verringer's jaw. He went down as if shot through the heart. The fall shook the cabin. I started running.

I reached the door and yanked it open. Earl spun around, leaning forward a little, staring at me without recognition. There was a bubbling sound behind his lips. He started for me fast.

I jerked the gun out and showed it to him. It meant nothing. Either his own guns were not loaded or he had forgotten all about them. The brass knuckles were all he needed. He kept coming.

I fired through the open window across the bed. The crash of the gun in the small room seemed much louder than it should have been. Earl stopped dead. His head slewed around and he looked at the hole in the window screen. He looked back at me. Slowly his face came alive and he grinned.

"Wha' happen?" he asked brightly.

"Get rid of the knucks," I said, watching his eyes.

He looked surprised down at his hand. He slipped the mauler off and threw it casually in the corner.

"Now the gun belt," I said. "Don't touch the guns, just the buckle."

"They're not loaded," he said smiling. "Hell, they're not even guns, just stage money."

"The belt. Hurry it."

He looked at the short-barreled .32. "That a real one? Oh sure it is. The screen. Yeah, the screen."

The man on the bed wasn't on the bed any more. He was behind Earl. He reached swiftly and pulled one of the bright guns loose. Earl didn't like this. His face showed it.

"Lay off him," I said angrily. "Put that back where you got it."

"He's right," Wade said. "They're cap guns." He backed away and put the shiny pistol on the table. "Christ, I'm as weak as a broken arm."

"Take the belt off," I said for the third time. When you start something with a type like Earl you have to finish it. Keep it simple and don't change your mind.

He did it at last, quite amiably. Then, holding the belt, he walked over to the table and got his other gun and put it in the holster and put the belt right back on again. I let him do it. It wasn't until then that he saw Dr. Verringer crumpled on the floor against the wall. He made a sound of concern, went quickly across the room into the bathroom, and came back with a glass jug of water. He dumped the water on Dr. Verringer's head. Dr. Verringer sputtered and rolled over. Then he groaned. Then he clapped a hand to his jaw. Then he started to get up. Earl helped him.

"Sorry, Doc. I must have just let fly without seeing who it was."

"It's all right, nothing broken," Verringer said, waving him away. "Get the car up here, Earl. And don't forget the key for the padlock down below."

"Car up here, sure. Right away. Key for the padlock. I got it. Right away, Doc."

He went out of the room whistling.

Wade was sitting on the side of the bed, looking shaky. "You the dick he was talking about?" he asked me. "How did you find me?"

"Just asking around from people who know about these things," I said. "If you want to get home, you might get clothes on."

Dr. Verringer was leaning against the wall, massaging his jaw. "I'll help him," he said thickly. "All I do is help people and all they do is kick me in the teeth."

"I know just how you feel," I said.

I went out and left them to work at it.

20

THE CAR WAS close by when they came out, but Earl was gone. He had stopped the car, cut the lights, and walked back towards the big cabin without saying anything to me. He was still whistling, groping for some half-remembered tune.

Wade climbed carefully into the back seat and I got in beside him. Dr. Verringer drove. If his jaw hurt badly and his head ached, he didn't show it or mention it. We went over the ridge and down to the end of the graveled drive. Earl had already been down and unlocked the gate and pulled it open.

I told Verringer where my car was and he pulled up close to it. Wade got into it and sat silent, staring at nothing. Verringer got out and went round beside him. He spoke to Wade gently.

"About my five thousand dollars, Mr. Wade. The check you promised me."

Wade slid down and rested his head on the back of the seat. "I'll think about it."

"You promised it. I need it."

"Duress, the word is, Verringer, a threat of harm. I have protection now."

"I fed and washed you," Verringer persisted. "I came in the night. I protected you, I cured you — for the time being, at least."

"Not five grand worth," Wade sneered. "You got plenty out of my pockets."

Verringer wouldn't let go. "I have a promise of a connection in Cuba, Mr. Wade. You are a rich man. You should help others in their need. I have Earl to look after. To avail myself of this opportunity I need the money. I will pay it back in full."

I began to squirm. I wanted to smoke, but I was afraid it would make Wade sick.

"Like hell you'd pay it back," Wade said wearily. "You won't live long enough. One of these nights Blue Boy will kill you in your sleep."

Verringer stepped back. I couldn't see his expression, but his voice hardened. "There are more unpleasant ways to die," he said. "I think yours will be one of them."

He walked back to his car and got into it. He drove in through his gates and was gone. I backed and turned and headed towards the city. After a mile or two Wade muttered: "Why should I give that fat slob five thousand dollars?"

"No reason at all."

"Then why do I feel like a bastard for not giving it to him?"

"No reason at all."

He turned his head just enough to look at me. "He handled me like a baby," Wade said. "He hardly left me alone for fear Earl would come in and beat me up. He took every dime I had in my pockets."

"You probably told him to."

"You on his side?"

"Skip it," I said. "This is just a job to me."

Silence for a couple of miles more. We went past the fringe of one of the outlying suburbs. Wade spoke again.

"Maybe I'll give it to him. He's broke. The property is foreclosed. He won't get a dime out of it. All on account of that psycho. Why does he do it?"

"I wouldn't know."

"I'm a writer," Wade said. "I'm supposed to understand what makes people tick. I don't understand one damn thing about anybody."

I turned over the pass and after a climb the lights of the valley spread out endlessly in front of us. We dipped down to the highway north and west that goes to Ventura. After a while we passed through Encino. I stopped for a light and looked up towards the lights high on the hill where the big houses were. In one of them the Lennoxes had lived. We went on.

"The turn-off is pretty close now," Wade said. "Or do you know it?"

"I know it."

"By the way, you haven't told me your name."

"Philip Marlowe."

"Nice name." His voice changed sharply, saying: "Wait a minute. You the guy that was mixed up with Lennox?"

"Yeah."

He was staring at me in the darkness of the car. We passed the last building on the main drag of Encino.

"I knew her," Wade said. "A little. Him I never saw. Queer business, that. The law boys gave you the rough edge, didn't they?"

I didn't answer him.

"Maybe you don't like to talk about it," he said.

"Could be. Why would it interest you?"

"Hell, I'm a writer. It must be quite a story."

"Take tonight off. You must be feeling pretty weak."

"Okay, Marlowe. Okay. You don't like me. I get it."

We reached the turn-off and I swung the car into it and towards the low hills and the gap between them that was Idle Valley.

"I don't either like you or dislike you," I said. "I don't know you. Your wife asked me to find you and bring you home. When I deliver you at your house I'm through. Why she picked on me I couldn't say. Like I said, it's just a job."

We turned the flank of a hill and hit a wider, more firmly paved road. He said his house was a mile farther on, on the right side. He told me the number, which I already knew. For a guy in his shape he was a pretty persistent talker.

"How much is she paying you?" he asked.

"We didn't discuss it."

"Whatever it is, it's not enough. I owe you a lot of thanks. You did a great job, chum. I wasn't worth the trouble."

"That's just the way you feel tonight."

He laughed. "You know something, Marlowe? I could get to like you. You're a bit of a bastard – like me."

We reached the house. It was a two-story over-all shingle house with a small pillared portico and a long lawn from the entrance to a thick row of shrubs inside the white fence. There was a light in the portico. I pulled into the driveway and stopped close to the garage.

"Can you make it without help?"

"Of course." He got out of the car. "Aren't you coming in for a drink or something?"

"Not tonight, thanks; I'll wait here until you're in the house."

He stood there breathing hard. "Okay," he said shortly.

He turned and walked carefully along a flagged path to the front door. He held on to a white pillar for a moment, then tried the door. It opened, he went in. The door stayed open and light washed across the green lawn. There was a sudden flutter of voices. I started backing from the driveway, following the back-up light. Somebody called out.

I looked and saw Eileen Wade standing in the open doorway. I kept going and she started to run. So I had to stop. I cut the lights and got out of the car. When she came up I said:

"I ought to have called you, but I was afraid to leave him."

"Of course. Did you have a lot of trouble?"

"Well – a little more than ringing a doorbell."

"Please come in the house and tell me all about it."

"He should be in bed. By tomorrow he'll be as good as new."

"Candy will put him to bed," she said. "He won't drink tonight, if that's what you are thinking of."

"Never occurred to me. Goodnight, Mrs. Wade."

"You must be tired. Don't you want a drink yourself?"

I lit a cigarette. It seemed like a couple of weeks since I had tasted tobacco. I drank in the smoke.

"May I have just one puff?"

She came close to me and I handed her the cigarette. She drew on it and coughed. She handed it back laughing. "Strictly an amateur, as you see."

"So you knew Sylvia Lennox," I said. "Was that why you wanted to hire me?"

"I knew who?" She sounded puzzled.

"Sylvia Lennox." I had the cigarette back now. I was eating it pretty fast.

"Oh," she said, startled. "That girl that was – murdered. No, I didn't know her personally. I knew who she was. Didn't I tell you that?"

"Sorry, I'd forgotten just what you did tell me."

She was still standing there quietly, close to me, slim and tall in a white dress of some sort. The light from the open door touched the fringe of her hair and made it glow softly.

"Why did you ask me if that had anything to do with my wanting to, as you put it, hire you?" When I didn't answer at once she added, "Did Roger tell you he knew her?"

"He said something about the case when I told him my name. He didn't connect me with it immediately, then he did. He talked so damn much I don't remember half of what he said."

"I see. I must go in, Mr. Marlowe, and see if my husband needs anything. And if you won't come in —"

"I'll leave this with you," I said.

I took hold of her and pulled her towards me and tilted her head back. I kissed her hard on the lips. She didn't fight me and she didn't respond. She pulled herself away quietly and stood there looking at me.

"You shouldn't have done that," she said. "That was wrong. You're too nice a person."

"Sure. Very wrong." I agreed. "But I've been such a nice faithful well-behaved gun dog all day long, I got charmed into one of the silliest ventures I ever tackled, and damned if it didn't turn out just as though somebody had written a script for it. You know something? I believe you knew where he was all along – or at least knew the name of Dr. Verringer. You just wanted to get me involved with him, tangled up with him so I'd feel a sense of responsibility to look after him. Or am I crazy?"

"Of course you're crazy," she said coldly. "That is the most outrageous nonsense I ever listened to." She started to turn away.

"Wait a minute," I said. "That kiss won't leave a scar. You just think it will. And don't tell me I'm too nice a person. I'd rather be a heel."

She looked back. "Why?"

"If I hadn't been a nice guy to Terry Lennox, he would still be alive."

"Yes?" she said quietly. "How can you be so sure? Goodnight, Mr. Marlowe. And thank you so very much for almost everything."

She walked back along the edge of the grass. I watched her go into the house. The door closed. The porch light went off. I waved at nothing and drove away.

21

NEXT MORNING I got up late on account of the big fee I had earned the night before. I drank an extra cup of coffee, smoked an extra cigarette, ate an extra slice of Canadian bacon, and for the three hundredth time I swore I would never again use an electric razor. That made the day normal. I hit the office about ten, picked up some odds and ends of mail, slit the envelopes and let the stuff lie on the desk. I opened the windows wide to let out the smell of dust and dinginess that collected in the night and hung in the still air, in the corners of the room, in the slats of the venetian blinds. A dead moth was spread-eagled on a corner of the desk. On the window sill a bee with tattered wings was crawling along the woodwork, buzzing in a tired remote sort of way, as if she knew it wasn't any use, she was finished, she had flown too many missions and would never get back to the hive again.

I knew it was going to be one of those crazy days. Everyone has them. Days when nobody rolls in but the loose wheels, the dingoes who park their brains with their gum, the squirrels who can't find their nuts, the mechanics who always have a gear wheel left over.

The first was a big blond roughneck named Kuissenen or something Finnish like that. He jammed his massive bottom in the customer's chair and planted two wide horny hands on my desk and said he was a power-shovel operator, that he lived in Culver City, and the goddam woman who lived next door to him was trying to poison his dog. Every morning before he let the dog out for a run in the back yard he had to search the place from fence to fence for meatballs thrown over the potato vine from next door. He'd found nine of them so far and they were loaded with a greenish powder he knew was an arsenic weed killer.

"How much to watch out and catch her at it?" He stared at me as unblinkingly as a fish in a tank.

"Why not do it yourself?"

"I got to work for a living, mister. I'm losing four twenty-five an hour just coming up here to ask."

"Try the police?"

"I try the police. They might get around to it some time next year. Right now they're busy sucking up to MGM."

"S.P.C.A.? The Tailwaggers?"

"What's them?"

I told him about the Tailwaggers. He was far from interested. He knew about the S.P.C.A. The S.P.C.A. could take a running jump. They couldn't see nothing smaller than a horse.

"It says on the door you're an investigator," he said truculently. "Okay, go the hell out and investigate. Fifty bucks if you catch her."

"Sorry," I said. "I'm tied up. Spending a couple of weeks hiding in a gopher hole in your back yard would be out of my line anyway – even for fifty bucks."

He stood up glowering. "Big shot," he said. "Don't need the dough, huh? Can't be bothered saving the life of an itty-bitty dog. Nuts to you, big shot."

"I've got troubles, too, Mr. Kuissenen."

"I'll twist her goddam neck if I catch her," he said, and I didn't doubt he could have done it. He could have twisted the hind leg off of an elephant. "That's what makes it I want somebody else. Just because the little tike barks when a car goes by the house. Sour-faced old bitch."

He started for the door. "Are you sure it's the dog she's try-ing to poison?" I asked his back.

"Sure I'm sure." He was halfway to the door before the nickel dropped. He swung around fast then. "Say that again, buster."

I just shook my head. I didn't want to fight him. He might hit me on the head with my desk. He snorted and went out, almost taking the door with him.

The next cookie in the dish was a woman, not old, not young, not clean, not too dirty, obviously poor, shabby, queru-lous and stupid. The girl she roomed with – in her set any woman who works out is a girl – was taking money out of her purse. A dollar here, four bits there, but it added up. She figured she was out close to twenty dollars in all. She couldn't afford it. She couldn't afford to move either. She couldn't afford a detective. She thought I ought to be willing to throw a scare into the roommate just on the tele-phone like, not mentioning any names.

It took her twenty minutes or more to tell me this. She kneaded her bag incessantly while telling it.

"Anybody you know could do that," I said.

"Yeah, but you being a dick and all."

"I don't have a license to threaten people I know nothing about."

"I'm goin' to tell her I been in to see you. I don't have to say it's her. Just that you're workin' on it."

"I wouldn't if I were you. If you mention my name she may call me up. If she does that, I'll tell her the facts."

She stood up and slammed her shabby bag against her stomach. "You're no gentleman," she said shrilly.

"Where does it say I have to be?"

She went out mumbling.

After lunch I had Mr. Simpson W. Edelweiss. He had a card to prove it. He was manager of a sewing machine agency. He was a small tired-looking man about forty-eight to fifty, small hands and feet, wearing a brown suit with sleeves too long, and a stiff white collar behind a purple tie with black diamonds on it. He sat on the edge of the chair without fidgeting and looked at me out of sad black eyes. His hair was black too and thick and rough without a sign of gray in it that I could see. He had a clipped mustache with a reddish tone. He could have passed for thirty-five if you didn't look at the backs of his hands.

"Call me Simp," he said. "Everybody else does. I got it coming. I'm a Jewish man married to a Gentile woman, twenty-four years of age, beautiful. She run away a couple of times before."

He got out a photo of her and showed it to me. She might have been beautiful to him. To me she was a big sloppy-looking cow of a woman with a weak mouth.

"What's your trouble, Mr. Edelweiss? I don't do divorce business." I tried to give him back the photo. He waved it away. "The client is always mister to me," I added. "Until he has told me a few dozen lies anyway."

He smiled. "Lies I got no use for. It's not a divorce matter. I just want Mabel back again. But she don't come back until I find her. Maybe it's a kind of game with her."

He told me about her, patiently, without rancor. She drank, she played around, she wasn't a very good wife by his standards, but he could have been brought up too strict. She had a heart as big as a house, he said, and he loved her. He didn't kid himself he was any dreamboat, just a steady worker bringing home the pay check. They had a joint bank account. She had drawn it all out, but he was prepared for that. He had a pretty good idea who she had lit out with, and if he was right the man would clean her out and leave her stranded.

"Name of Kerrigan," he said. "Monroe Kerrigan. I don't aim to knock the Catholics. There is plenty of bad Jews too. This Kerrigan is a barber when he works. I ain't knocking barbers either. But a lot of them are drifters and horse players. Not real steady."

"Won't you hear from her when she is cleaned out?"

"She gets awful ashamed. She might hurt herself."

"It's a Missing Persons job, Mr. Edelweiss. You should go down and make a report."

"No. I'm not knocking the police, but I don't want it that way. Mabel would be humiliated."

The world seemed to be full of people Mr. Edelweiss was not knocking. He put some money on the desk.

"Two hundred dollars," he said. "Down payment. I'd rather do it my way."

"It will happen again," I said.

"Sure." He shrugged and spread his hands gently. "But twenty-four years old and me almost fifty. How could it be different? She'll settle down after a while. Trouble is, no kids. She can't have kids. A Jew likes to have a family. So Mabel knows that. She's humiliated."

"You're a very forgiving man, Mr. Edelweiss."

"Well I ain't a Christian," he said. "And I'm not knocking Christians, you understand. But with me it's real. I don't just say it. I do it. Oh, I almost forgot the most important."

He got out a picture postcard and pushed it across the desk after the money. "From Honolulu she sends it. Money goes fast in Honolulu. One of my uncles had a jewelry business there. Retired now. Lives in Seattle."

I picked the photo up again. "I'll have to farm this one out," I told him. "And I'll have to have this copied."

"I could hear you saying that, Mr. Marlowe, before I got here. So I come prepared." He took out an envelope and it contained five more prints. "I got Kerrigan too, but only a snapshot." He went into another pocket and gave me another envelope. I looked at Kerrigan. He had a smooth dishonest face that did not surprise me. Three copies of Kerrigan.

Mr. Simpson W. Edelweiss gave me another card which had on it his name, his residence, his telephone number. He said he hoped it would not cost too much but that he would respond at once to any demand for further funds and he hoped to hear from me.

"Two hundred ought to pretty near do it if she's still in Honolulu," I said. "What I need now is a detailed physical description of both parties that I can put into a telegram. Height, weight, age, coloring, any noticeable scars or other identifying marks, what clothes she was wearing and had with her, and how much money was in the account she cleaned out. If you've been through this before, Mr. Edelweiss, you will know what I want."

"I got a peculiar feeling about this Kerrigan. Uneasy."

I spent another half hour milking him and writing things down. Then he stood up quietly, shook hands quietly, bowed and left the office quietly.

"Tell Mabel everything is fine," he said as he went out.

It turned out to be routine. I sent a wire to an agency in Honolulu and followed it with an airmail containing the photos and whatever information I had left out of the wire. They found her working as a chambermaid's helper in a luxury hotel, scrubbing bathtubs and bathroom floors and so on. Kerrigan had done just what Mr. Edelweiss expected, cleaned her out while she was asleep and skipped, leaving her stuck with the hotel bill. She pawned a ring which Kerrigan couldn't have taken without violence, and got enough out of it to pay the hotel but not enough to buy her way home. So Edelweiss hopped a plane and went after her.

He was too good for her. I sent him a bill for twenty dollars and the cost of a long telegram. The Honolulu agency grabbed the two hundred. With a portrait of Madison in my office safe I could afford to be underpriced.

So passed a day in the life of a P.I. Not exactly a typical day but not totally untypical either. What makes a man stay with it nobody knows. You don't get rich, you don't often have much fun. Sometimes you get beaten up or shot at or tossed into the jailhouse. Once in a long while you get dead. Every other month you decide to give it up and find some sensible occupation while you can still walk without shaking your head. Then the door buzzer rings and you open the inner door to the waiting room and there stands a new face with a new problem, a new load of grief, and a small piece of money.

"Come in, Mr. Thingummy. What can I do for you?"

There must be a reason.

Three days later in the shank of the afternoon Eileen Wade called me up, and asked me to come around to the house for a drink the next evening. They were having a few friends in for cocktails. Roger would like to see me and thank me adequately. And would I please send in a bill?

"You don't owe me anything, Mrs. Wade. What little I did I got paid for."

"I must have looked very silly acting Victorian about it," she said. "A kiss doesn't seem to mean much nowadays. You will come, won't you?"

"I guess so. Against my better judgment."

"Roger is quite well again. He's working."

"Good."

"You sound very solemn today. I guess you take life pretty seriously."

"Now and then. Why?"

She laughed very gently and said goodbye and hung up. I sat there for a while taking life seriously. Then I tried to think of something funny so that I could have a great big laugh. Neither way worked, so I got Terry Lennox's letter of farewell out of the safe and reread it. It reminded me that I had never gone to Victor's for that gimlet he asked me to drink for him. It was just about the right time of day for the bar to be quiet, the way he would have liked it himself, if he had been around to go with me. I thought of him with a vague sadness and with a puckering bitterness too. When I got to Victor's I almost kept going. Almost, but not quite. I had too much of his money. He had made a fool of me but he had paid well for the privilege.

22

IT WAS SO quiet in Victor's that you almost heard the temperature drop as you came in at the door. On a bar stool a woman in a black tailormade, which couldn't at that time of year have been anything but some synthetic fabric like orlon, was sitting alone with a pale greenish-colored drink in front of her and smoking a cigarette in a long jade holder. She had that fine-drawn intense look that is sometimes neurotic, sometimes sex-hungry, and sometimes just the result of drastic dieting.

I sat down two stools away and the barkeep nodded to me, but didn't smile.

"A gimlet," I said. "No bitters."

He put the little napkin in front of me and kept looking at me. "You know something," he said in a pleased voice. "I heard you and your friend talking one night and I got me in a bottle of that Rose's Lime Juice. Then you didn't come back any more and I only opened it tonight."

"My friend left town," I said. "A double if it's all right with you. And thanks for taking the trouble."

He went away. The woman in black gave me a quick glance, then looked down into her glass. "So few people drink them around here," she said so quietly that I didn't realize at first that she was speaking to me. Then she looked my way again. She had very large dark eyes. She had the reddest fingernails I had ever seen. But she didn't look like a pickup and there was no trace of come-on in her voice. "Gimlets I mean."

"A fellow taught me to like them," I said.

"He must be English."

"Why?"

"The lime juice. It's as English as boiled fish with that awful anchovy sauce that looks as if the cook had bled into it. That's how they got called limeys. The English – not the fish."

"I thought it was more a tropical drink, hot weather stuff. Malaya or some place like that."

"You may be right." She turned away again.

The bartender set the drink in front of me. With the lime juice it has a sort of pale greenish yellowish misty look. I tasted it. It was both sweet and sharp at the same time. The woman in black watched me. Then she lifted her own glass towards me. We both drank. Then I knew hers was the same drink.

The next move was routine, so I didn't make it. I just sat there. "He wasn't English," I said after a moment. "I guess maybe he had been there during the war. We used to come in here once in a while, early like now. Before the mob started boiling."

"It's a pleasant hour," she said. "In a bar almost the only pleasant hour." She emptied her glass. "Perhaps I knew your friend," she said. "What was his name?"

I didn't answer her right away. I lit a cigarette and watched her tap the stub of hers out of the jade holder and fit another in its place. I reached across with a lighter. "Lennox," I said.

She thanked me for the light and gave me a brief searching glance. Then she nodded. "Yes, I knew him very well. Perhaps a little too well."

The barkeep drifted over and glanced at my glass. "A couple more of the same," I said. "In a booth."

I got down off the stool and stood waiting. She might or might not blow me down. I didn't particularly care. Once in a while in this much too sex-conscious country a man and a woman can meet and talk without dragging bedrooms into it. This could be it, or she could just think I was on the make. If so, the hell with her.

She hesitated, but not for long. She gathered up a pair of black gloves and a black suede bag with a gold frame and clasp and walked across into a corner booth and sat down without a word. I sat down across the small table.

"My name is Marlowe."

"Mine is Linda Loring," she said calmly. "A bit of a sentimentalist, aren't you, Mr. Marlowe?"

"Because I came in here to drink a gimlet? How about yourself?"

"I might have a taste for them."

"So might I. But it would be a little too much coincidence."

She smiled at me vaguely. She had emerald earrings and an emerald lapel pin. They looked like real stones because of the way they were cut – flat with beveled edges. And even in the dim light of a bar they had an inner glow.

"So you're the man," she said.

The bar waiter brought the drinks over and set them down. When he went away I said: "I'm a fellow who knew Terry Lennox, liked him, and had an occasional drink with him. It was kind of a side deal, an accidental friendship. I never went to his home or knew his wife. I saw her once in a parking lot."

"There was a little more to it than that, wasn't there?"

She reached for her glass. She had an emerald ring set in a nest of diamonds. Beside it a thin platinum band said she was married. I put her in the second half of the thirties, early in the second half.

"Maybe," I said. "The guy bothered me. He still does. How about you?"

She leaned on an elbow and looked up at me without any particular expression. "I said I knew him rather too well. Too well to think it mattered much what happened to him. He had a rich wife who gave him all the luxuries. All she asked in return was to be let alone."

"Seems reasonable," I said.

"Don't be sarcastic, Mr. Marlowe. Some women are like that. They can't help it. It wasn't as if he didn't know in the beginning. If he had to get proud, the door was open. He didn't have to kill her."

"I agree with you."

She straightened up and looked hard at me. Her lip curled. "So he ran away and, if what I hear is true, you helped him. I suppose you feel proud about that."

"Not me," I said. "I just did it for the money."

"That is not amusing, Mr. Marlowe. Frankly I don't know why I sit here drinking with you."

"That's easily changed, Mrs. Loring." I reached for my glass and dropped the contents down the hatch. "I thought perhaps you could tell me something about Terry that I didn't know. I'm not interested in speculating why Terry Lennox beat his wife's face to a bloody sponge."

"That's a pretty brutal way to put it," she said angrily.

"You don't like the words? Neither do I. And I wouldn't be here drinking a gimlet if I believed he did anything of the sort."

She stared. After a moment she said slowly: "He killed himself and left a full confession. What more do you want?"

"He had a gun," I said. "In Mexico that might be enough excuse for some jittery cop to pour lead into him. Plenty of American police have done their killings the same way – some of them through doors that didn't open fast enough to suit them. As for the confession, I haven't seen it."

"No doubt the Mexican police faked it," she said tartly.

"They wouldn't know how, not in a little place like Otatoclán. No, the confession is probably real enough, but it doesn't prove he killed his wife. Not to me anyway. All it proves to me is that he didn't see any way out. In a spot like that a certain sort of man – you can call him weak or soft or sentimental if it amuses you – might decide to save some other people from a lot of very painful publicity."

"That's fantastic," she said. "A man doesn't kill himself or deliberately get himself killed to save a little scandal. Sylvia was already dead. As for her sister and her father — they could take care of themselves very efficiently. People with enough money, Mr. Marlowe, can always protect themselves."

"Okay, I'm wrong about the motive. Maybe I'm wrong all down the line. A minute ago you were mad at me. You want me to leave now — so you can drink *your* gimlet?"

Suddenly she smiled. "I'm sorry. I'm beginning to think you are sincere. What I thought then was that you were trying to justify yourself, far more than Terry. I don't think you are, somehow."

"I'm not. I did something foolish and I got the works for it. Up to a point anyway. I don't deny that his confession saved me a lot worse. If they had brought him back and tried him, I guess they would have hung one on me too. The least it would have cost me would have been far more money than I could afford."

"Not to mention your license," she said dryly.

"Maybe. There was a time when any cop with a hangover could get me busted. It's a little different now. You get a hearing before a commission of the state licensing authority. Those people are not too crazy about the city police."

She tasted her drink and said slowly: "All things considered, don't you think it was best the way it was? No trial, no sensational headlines, no mud-slinging just to sell newspapers without the slightest regard for truth or fair play or for the feelings of innocent people."

"Didn't I just say so? And you said it was fantastic."

She leaned back and put her head against the upper curve of the padding on the back of the booth. "Fantastic that Terry Lennox should have killed himself just to achieve that. Not fantastic that it was better for all parties that there should be no trial."

"I need another drink," I said, and waved at the waiter. "I feel an icy breath on the back of my neck. Could you by any chance be related to the Potter family, Mrs. Loring?"

"Sylvia Lennox was my sister," she said simply. "I thought you would know."

The waiter drifted over and I gave him an urgent message. Mrs. Loring shook her head and said she didn't want anything more. When the waiter took off I said:

"With the hush old man Potter – excuse me, Mr. Harlan Potter – put on this affair, I would be lucky to know for sure that Terry's wife even had a sister."

"Surely you exaggerate. My father is hardly that powerful, Mr. Marlowe – and certainly not that ruthless. I'll admit he does have very old-fashioned ideas about his personal privacy. He never gives interviews even to his own newspapers. He is never photographed, he never makes speeches, he travels mostly by car or in his own plane with his own crew. But he is quite human for all that. He liked Terry. He said Terry was a gentleman twenty-four hours a day instead of for the fifteen minutes between the time the guests arrive and the time they feel their first cocktail."

"He slipped a little at the end. Terry did."

The waiter trotted up with my third gimlet. I tried it for flavor and then sat there with a finger on the edge of the round base of the glass.

"Terry's death was quite a blow to him, Mr. Marlowe. And you're getting sarcastic again. Please don't. Father knew it would all look far too neat to some people. He would much rather Terry had just disappeared. If Terry had asked him for help, I think he would have given it."

"Oh no, Mrs. Loring. His own daughter had been murdered."

She made an irritable motion and eyed me coldly.

"This is going to sound pretty blunt, I'm afraid. Father had written my sister off long ago. When they met he barely spoke to her. If he expressed himself, which he hasn't and won't, I feel sure he would be just as doubtful about Terry as you are. But once Terry was dead, what did it matter? They could have been killed in a plane crash or a fire or a highway accident. If she had to die, it was the best possible time for her to die. In another ten years she would have been a sex-ridden hag like some of these frightful women you see at Hollywood parties, or used to a few years back. The dregs of the international set."

All of a sudden I got mad, for no good reason. I stood up and looked over the booth. The next one was still empty. In the one beyond a guy was reading a paper all by himself, quietly. I sat down with a bump, pushed my glass out of the way, and leaned across the table. I had sense enough to keep my voice down.

"For hell's sake, Mrs. Loring, what are you trying to sell me? That Harlan Potter is such a sweet lovely character he wouldn't dream of using his influence on a political D.A. to drop the blanket on a murder investigation so that the murder was never really investigated at all? That he had doubts about Terry's guilt but didn't let anyone lift a finger to find out who was really the killer? That he didn't use the political power of his newspapers and his bank account and the nine hundred guys who would trip over their chins trying to guess what he wanted done before he knew himself? That he didn't arrange it so that a tame lawyer and nobody else, nobody from the D.A.'s office or the city cops, went down to Mexico to make sure Terry actually had put a slug in his head instead of being knocked off by some Indian with a hot gun just for kicks? Your old man is worth a hundred million bucks, Mrs. Loring. I wouldn't know just how he got it, but I know damn well he didn't get it without building himself a pretty far-reaching organization. He's no softie. He's a hard tough man. You've got to be in these days to make that kind of money. And you do business with some funny people. You may not meet them or shake hands with them, but they are there on the fringe doing business with you."

"You're a fool," she said angrily. "I've had enough of you."

"Oh sure. I don't make the kind of music you like to hear. Let me tell you something. Terry talked to your old man the night Sylvia died. What about? What did your old man say to him? 'Just run on down to Mexico and shoot yourself, old boy. Let's keep this in the family. I know my daughter is a tramp and that any one of a dozen drunken bastards might have blown his top and pushed her pretty face down her throat for her. But that's incidental, old boy. The guy will be sorry when he sobers up. You've had it soft and now is the time you pay back. What we want is to keep the fair Potter name as sweet as mountain lilac. She married you because she needed a front. She needs it worse than ever now she's dead. And you're it. If you can get lost and stay lost, fine. But if you get found, you check out. See you in the morgue."

"Do you really think," the woman in black asked with dry ice in her voice, "that my father talks like that?"

I leaned back and laughed unpleasantly. "We could polish up the dialogue a little if that helps."

She gathered her stuff together and slid along the seat. "I'd like to give you a word of warning," she said slowly and very carefully, "a very simple word of warning. If you think my father is that kind of man and if you go around broadcasting the kind of thoughts you have just expressed to me, your career in this city in your business or in any business is apt to be extremely short and terminated very suddenly."

"Perfect, Mrs. Loring. Perfect. I get it from the law, I get it from the hoodlum element, I get it from the carriage trade. The words change, but the meaning is the same. Lay off. I came in here to drink a gimlet because a man asked me to. Now look at me. I'm practically in the boneyard."

She stood up and nodded briefly. "Three gimlets. Doubles. Perhaps you're drunk."

I dropped too much money on the table and stood up beside her. "You had one and a half, Mrs. Loring. Why even that much? Did a man ask you too, or was it all your own idea? Your own tongue got a little loose."

"Who knows, Mr. Marlowe? Who knows? Who really knows anything? There's a man over there at the bar watching us. Would it be anyone you know?"

I looked around, surprised that she had noticed. A lean dark character sat on the end stool nearest the door.

"His name is Chick Agostino," I said. "He's a gun toter for a gambling boy named Menendez. Let's knock him down and jump on him."

"You certainly are drunk," she said quickly and started to walk. I went after her. The man on the stool swung around and looked to his front. When I came abreast I stepped up behind him and reached in under both his arms quickly. Maybe I *was* a little drunk.

He swung around angrily and slid off the stool. "Watch it, kiddo," he snarled. Out of the corner of my eye I saw that she had stopped just inside the door to glance back.

"No guns, Mr. Agostino? How reckless of you. It's almost dark. What if you should run into a tough midget?"

"Scram!" he said savagely.

"Aw, you stole that line from the *New Yorker*."

His mouth worked but he didn't move. I left him and followed Mrs. Loring out through the door into the space under the awning. A gray-haired colored chauffeur stood there talking to the kid from the parking lot. He touched his cap and went off and came back with a flossy Cadillac limousine. He opened the door and Mrs. Loring got in. He shut the door as though he was putting down the lid of a jewel box. He went around the car to the driver's seat.

She ran the window down and looked out at me, half smiling.

"Goodnight, Mr. Marlowe. It's been nice – or has it?"

"We had quite a fight."

"You mean you had – and mostly with yourself."

"It usually is. Goodnight, Mrs. Loring. You don't live around here, do you?"

"Not exactly. I live in Idle Valley. At the far end of the lake. My husband is a doctor."

"Would you happen to know any people named Wade?"

She frowned. "Yes, I know the Wades. Why?"

"Why do I ask? They're the only people in Idle Valley that I know."

"I see. Well, goodnight again, Mr. Marlowe."

She leaned back in the seat and the Cadillac purred politely and slid away into the traffic along the Strip.

Turning I almost bumped into Chick Agostino.

"Who's the doll?" he sneered. "And next time you crack wise, be missing."

"Nobody that would want to know you," I said.

"Okay, bright boy. I got the license number. Mendy likes to know little things like that."

The door of a car banged open and a man about seven feet high and four feet wide jumped out of it, took one look at Agostino, then one long stride, and grabbed him by the throat with one hand.

"How many times I gotta tell you cheap hoods not to hang around where I eat?" he roared.

He shook Agostino and hurled him across the sidewalk against the wall. Chick crumpled up coughing.

"Next time," the enormous man yelled, "I sure as hell put the blast on you, and believe me, boy, you'll be holding a gun when they pick you up."

Chick shook his head and said nothing. The big man gave me a raking glance and grinned. "Nice night," he said, and strolled into Victor's.

I watched Chick straighten himself out and regain some of his composure. "Who's your buddy?" I asked him.

621

"Big Willie Magoon," he said thickly. "A vice squad bimbo. He thinks he's tough."

"You mean he isn't sure?" I asked him politely.

He looked at me emptily and walked away. I got my car out of the lot and drove home. In Hollywood anything can happen, anything at all.

23

A LOW-SWUNG JAGUAR swept around the hill in front of me and slowed down so as not to bathe me in the granite dust from the half mile of neglected paving at the entrance to Idle Valley. It seemed they wanted it left that way to discourage the Sunday drivers spoiled by drifting along on superhighways. I caught a glimpse of a bright scarf and a pair of sun goggles. A hand waved at me casually, neighbor to neighbor. Then the dust slid across the road and added itself to the white film already well spread over the scrub and the sunbaked grass. Then I was around the outcrop and the paving started up in proper shape and everything was smooth and cared for. Live oaks clustered towards the road, as if they were curious to see who went by, and sparrows with rosy heads hopped about pecking at things only a sparrow would think worth pecking at.

Then there were a few cottonwoods but no eucalyptus. Then a thick growth of Carolina poplars screening a white house. Then a girl walking a horse along the shoulder of the road. She had Levis on and a loud shirt and she was chewing on a twig. The horse looked hot but not lathered and the girl was crooning to him gently. Beyond a fieldstone wall a gardener was guiding a power lawnmower over a huge undulating lawn that ended far back in the portico of a Williamsburg Colonial mansion, the large de luxe size. Somewhere someone was playing left-handed exercises on a grand piano.

Then all this wheeled away and the glisten of the lake showed hot and bright and I began to watch numbers on gateposts. I had seen the Wades' house only once and in the dark. It wasn't as big as it had looked by night. The driveway was full of cars, so I parked on the side of the road and walked in. A Mexican butler in a white coat opened the door for me. He was a slender neat good-looking Mexican and his coat fitted him elegantly and he looked like a Mexican who was getting fifty a week and not killing himself with hard work.

He said: "Buenas tardes, señor," and grinned as if he had put one over. "Su nombre de Usted, por favor?"

"Marlowe," I said, "and who are you trying to upstage, Candy? We talked on the phone, remember?"

He grinned and I went in. It was the same old cocktail party, everybody talking too loud, nobody listening, everybody hanging on for dear life to a mug of the juice, eyes very bright, cheeks flushed or pale and sweaty according to the amount of alcohol consumed and the capacity of the individual to handle it. Then Eileen Wade materialized beside me in a pale blue something which did her no harm. She had a glass in her hand but it didn't look as if it was more than a prop.

"I'm so glad you could come," she said gravely. "Roger wants to see you in his study. He hates cocktail parties. He's working."

"With this racket going on?"

"It never seems to bother him. Candy will get you a drink – or if you'd rather go to the bar –"

"I'll do that," I said. "Sorry about the other night."

She smiled. "I think you apologized already. It was nothing."

"The hell it was nothing."

She kept the smile long enough to nod and turn and walk away. I spotted the bar over in the corner by some very large french windows. It was one of those things you push around. I was halfway across the room, trying not to bump anybody, when a voice said: "Oh, Mr. Marlowe."

I turned and saw Mrs. Loring on a couch beside a prissy-looking man in rimless cheaters with a smear on his chin that might have been a goatee. She had a drink in her hand and looked bored. He sat still with his arms folded and scowled.

I went over there. She smiled at me and gave me her hand. "This is my husband, Dr. Loring. Mr. Philip Marlowe, Edward."

The guy with the goatee gave me a brief look and a still briefer nod. He didn't move otherwise. He seemed to be saving his energy for better things.

"Edward is very tired," Linda Loring said. "Edward is always very tired."

"Doctors often are," I said. "Can I get you a drink, Mrs. Loring? Or you, Doctor?"

"She's had enough," the man said without looking at either of us. "I don't drink. The more I see of people who do, the more glad I am that I don't."

"Come back, little Sheba," Mrs. Loring said dreamily.

He swung around and did a take. I got away from there and made it to the bar. In the company of her husband Linda Loring seemed like a different person. There was an edge to her voice and a sneer in her expression which she hadn't used on me even when she was angry.

Candy was behind the bar. He asked me what I would drink.

"Nothing right now, thanks. Mr. Wade wants to see me."

"Es muy occupado, señor. Very busy."

I didn't think I was going to like Candy. When I just looked at him he added: "But I go see. De pronto, señor."

He threaded his way delicately through the mob and was back in no time at all. "Okay, chum, let's go," he said cheerfully.

I followed him across the room the long way of the house. He opened a door, I went through, he shut it behind me, and a lot of the noise was dimmed. It was a corner room, big and cool and quiet, with french windows and roses outside and an air conditioner set in a window to one side. I could see the lake, and I could see Wade lying flat out on a long blond leather couch. A big bleached wood desk had a typewriter on it and there was a pile of yellow paper beside the typewriter.

"Good of you to come, Marlowe," he said lazily. "Park yourself. Did you have a drink or two?"

"Not yet." I sat down and looked at him. He still looked a bit pale and pinched. "How's the work going?"

"Fine, except that I get tired too quick. Pity a four-day drunk is so painful to get over. I often do my best work after one. In my racket it's so easy to tighten up and get all stiff and wooden. Then the stuff is no good. When it's good it comes easy. Anything you have read or heard to the contrary is a lot of mishmash."

"Depends who the writer is, maybe," I said. "It didn't come easy to Flaubert, and his stuff is good."

"Okay," Wade said, sitting up. "So you have read Flaubert, so that makes you an intellectual, a critic, a savant of the literary world." He rubbed his forehead. "I'm on the wagon and I hate it. I hate everybody with a drink in his hand. I've got to go out there and smile at those creeps. Every damn one of them knows I'm an alcoholic. So they wonder what I'm running away from. Some Freudian bastard has made that a commonplace. Every ten-year-old kid knows it by now. If I had a ten-year-old kid, which God forbid, the brat would be asking me, 'What are you running away from when you get drunk, Daddy?' "

"The way I got it, all this was rather recent," I said.

"It's got worse, but I was always a hard man with a bottle. When you're young and in hard condition you can absorb a lot of punishment. When you are pushing forty you don't snap back the same way."

I leaned back and lit a cigarette. "What did you want to see me about?"

"What do *you* think I'm running away from, Marlowe?"

"No idea. I don't have enough information. Besides, everybody is running away from something."

"Not everybody gets drunk. What are *you* running away from? Your youth or a guilty conscience or the knowledge that you're a small time operator in a small time business?"

"I get it," I said. "You need somebody to insult. Fire away, chum. When it begins to hurt I'll let you know."

He grinned and rumpled his thick curly hair. He speared his chest with a forefinger. "You're looking right at a small time operator in a small time business, Marlowe. All writers are punks and I am one of the punkest. I've written twelve best-sellers, and if I ever finish that stack of magoozlum on the desk there I may possibly have written thirteen. And not a damn one of them worth the powder to blow it to hell. I have a lovely home in a highly restricted residential neighborhood that belongs to a highly restricted multimillionaire. I have a lovely wife who loves me and a lovely publisher who loves me and I love me the best of all. I'm an egotistical son of a bitch, a literary prostitute or pimp – choose your own word – and an all-round heel. So what can you do for me?"

"Well, what?"

"Why don't you get sore?"

"Nothing to get sore about. I'm just listening to you hate yourself. It's boring but it doesn't hurt my feelings."

He laughed roughly. "I like you," he said. "Let's have a drink."

"Not in here, chum. Not you and me alone. I don't care to watch you take the first one. Nobody can stop you and I don't guess anyone would try. But I don't have to help."

He stood up. "We don't have to drink in here. Let's go outside and glance at a choice selection of the sort of people you get to know when you make enough lousy money to live where they live."

"Look," I said. "Shove it. Knock it off. They're no different from anybody else."

"Yeah," he said tightly, "but they ought to be. If they're not, what use are they? They're the class of the county and they're no better than a bunch of truckdrivers full of cheap whiskey. Not as good."

"Knock it off," I said again. "You want to get boiled, get boiled. But don't take it out on a crowd that can get boiled without having to lie up with Dr. Verringer or get loose in the head and throw their wives down the stairs."

"Yeah," he said, and he was suddenly calm and thoughtful. "You pass the test, chum. How about coming to live here for a while? You could do me a lot of good just being here."

"I don't see how."

"But I do. Just by being here. Would a thousand a month interest you? I'm dangerous when I'm drunk. I don't want to be dangerous and I don't want to be drunk."

"I couldn't stop you."

"Try it for three months. I'd finish the damn book and then go far off for a while. Lie up some place in the Swiss mountains and get clean."

"The book, huh? Do you have to have the money?"

"No. I just have to finish something I started. If I don't I'm through. I'm asking you as a friend. You did more than that for Lennox."

I stood up and walked over close to him and gave him a hard stare. "I got Lennox killed, mister. I got him killed."

"Phooey. Don't go soft on me, Marlowe." He put the edge of his hand against his throat. "I'm up to here in the soft babies."

"Soft?" I asked. "Or just kind?"

He stepped back and stumbled against the edge of the couch, but didn't lose his balance.

"The hell with you," he said smoothly. "No deal. I don't blame you, of course. There's something I want to know, that

I have to know. You don't know what it is and I'm not sure I know myself. All I'm positive of is that there is something, and I have to know it."

"About who? Your wife?"

He moved his lips one over the other. "I think it's about me," he said. "Let's go get that drink."

He walked to the door and threw it open and we went out.

If he had been trying to make me uncomfortable, he had done a first-class job.

24

WHEN HE OPENED the door the buzz from the living room exploded into our faces. It seemed louder than before, if possible. About two drinks louder. Wade said hello here and there and people seemed glad to see him. But by that time they would have been glad to see Pittsburgh Phil with his custom-built icepick. Life was just one great big vaudeville show.

On the way to the bar we came face to face with Dr. Loring and his wife. The doctor stood up and stepped forward to face Wade. He had a look on his face that was almost sick with hatred.

"Nice to see you, Doctor," Wade said amiably. "Hi, Linda. Where have you been keeping yourself lately? No, I guess that was a stupid question. I —"

"Mr. Wade," Loring said in a voice that had a tremor to it, "I have something to say to you. Something very simple, and I hope very conclusive. Stay away from my wife."

Wade looked at him curiously. "Doctor, you're tired. And you don't have a drink. Let me get you one."

"I don't drink, Mr. Wade. As you very well know. I am here for one purpose and I have expressed that purpose."

"Well, I guess I get your point," Wade said, still amiable. "And since you are a guest in my house, I have nothing to say except that I think you are a little off the beam."

There had been a drop in the talk near by. The boys and girls were all ears. Big production. Dr. Loring took a pair of gloves out of his pocket, straightened them, took hold of one by the finger end, and swung it hard against Wade's face.

Wade didn't bat an eye. "Pistols and coffee at dawn?" he asked quietly.

I looked at Linda Loring. She was flushed with anger. She stood up slowly and faced the doctor.

"Dear God, what a ham you are, darling. Stop acting like a damn fool, will you, darling? Or would you rather stick around until somebody slaps *your* face?"

Loring swung around to her and raised the gloves. Wade stepped in front of him. "Take it easy, Doc. Around here we only hit our wives in private."

"If you are speaking for yourself, I am well aware of it," Loring sneered. "And I don't need lessons in manners from you."

"I only take promising pupils," Wade said. "Sorry you have to leave so soon." He raised his voice. "Candy! Que el Doctor Loring salga de aqui en el acto!" He swung back to Loring. "In case you don't know Spanish, Doctor, that means the door is over there." He pointed.

Loring stared at him without moving. "I have warned you, Mr. Wade," he said icily. "And a number of people have heard me. I shall not warn you again."

"Don't," Wade said curtly. "But if you do, make it on neutral territory. Gives me a little more freedom of action. Sorry, Linda. But you married him." He rubbed his cheek gently where the heavy end of the glove had hit him. Linda Loring was smiling bitterly. She shrugged.

"We are leaving," Loring said. "Come, Linda."

She sat down again and reached for her glass. She gave her husband a glance of quiet contempt. "You are," she said. "You have a number of calls to make, remember."

"You are leaving with me," he said furiously.

She turned her back on him. He reached suddenly and took hold of her arm. Wade took him by the shoulder and spun him around.

"Take it easy, Doc. You can't win them all."

"Take your hand off me!"

"Sure, just relax," Wade said. "I have a good idea, Doctor. Why don't you see a good doctor?"

Somebody laughed loudly. Loring tensed like an animal all set to spring. Wade sensed it and neatly turned his back and moved away. Which left Dr. Loring holding the bag. If he went after Wade, he would look sillier than he looked now. There was nothing for him to do but leave, and he did it. He marched quickly across the room staring straight in front of him to where Candy was holding the door open. He went out. Candy shut the door, wooden-faced, and went back to the bar. I went over there and asked for some Scotch. I didn't see where Wade went. He just disappeared. I didn't see Eileen either. I turned my back on the room and let them sizzle while I drank my Scotch.

A small girl with mud-colored hair and a band around her forehead popped up beside me and put a glass on the bar and bleated. Candy nodded and made her another drink.

The small girl turned to me. "Are you interested in Communism?" she asked me. She was glassy-eyed and she was running a small red tongue along her lips as if looking for a crumb of chocolate. "I think everyone ought to be," she went on. "But when you ask any of the men here they just want to paw you."

I nodded and looked over my glass at her snub nose and sun-coarsened skin.

"Not that I mind too much if it's done nicely," she told me, reaching for the fresh drink. She showed me her molars while she inhaled half of it.

"Don't rely on me," I said.

"What's your name?"

"Marlowe."

"With an 'e' or not?"

"With."

"Ah, Marlowe," she intoned. "Such a sad beautiful name." She put her glass down damn nearly empty and closed her eyes and threw her head back and her arms out, almost hitting me in the eye. Her voice throbbed with emotion, saying:

"Was this the face that launch'd a thousand ships
    And burnt the topless towers of Ilium?
    Sweet Helen, make me immortal with a kiss."

She opened her eyes, grabbed her glass, and winked at me. "You were pretty good in there, chum. Been writing any poetry lately?"

"Not very much."

"You can kiss me if you like," she said coyly.

A guy in a shantung jacket and an open neck shirt came up behind her and grinned at me over the top of her head. He had short red hair and a face like a collapsed lung. He was as ugly a guy as I ever saw. He patted the top of the girl's head.

"Come on, kitten. Time to go home."

She rounded on him furiously. "You mean you got to water those goddamned tuberous begonias again?" she yelled.

"Aw listen, kitten —"

"Take your hands off me, you goddamned rapist," she screamed, and threw the rest of her drink in his face. The rest wasn't more than a teaspoonful and two lumps of ice.

"For Chrissake, baby, I'm your husband," he yelled back, grabbing for a handkerchief and mopping his face. "Get it? Your husband."

She sobbed violently and threw herself into his arms. I stepped around them and got out of there. Every cocktail party is the same, even the dialogue.

The house was leaking guests out into the evening air now. Voices were fading, cars were starting, goodbyes were bouncing around like rubber balls. I went to the french windows and out onto a flagged terrace. The ground sloped towards the lake, which was as motionless as a sleeping cat. There was a short wooden pier down there with a rowboat tied to it by a white painter. Towards the far shore, which wasn't very far, a black waterhen was doing lazy curves, like a skater. They didn't seem to cause as much as a shallow ripple.

I stretched out on a padded aluminum chaise and lit a pipe and smoked peacefully and wondered what the hell I was doing there. Roger Wade seemed to have enough control to handle himself if he really wanted to. He had done all right with Loring. I wouldn't have been too surprised if he had hung one on Loring's sharp little chin. He would have been out of line by the rules, but Loring was much farther out of line.

If the rules mean anything at all any more, they mean that you don't pick a roomful of people as the spot to threaten a man and hit him across the face with a glove when your wife is standing right beside you and you are practically accusing her of a little double time. For a man still shaky from a hard bout with the hard stuff Wade had done all right. He had done more than all right. Of course I hadn't seen him drunk. I didn't know what he would be like drunk. I didn't even know that he was an alcoholic. There's a big difference. A man who drinks too much on occasion is still the same man as he was sober. An alcoholic, a real alcoholic, is not the same man at all. You can't predict anything about him for sure except that he will be someone you never met before.

Light steps sounded behind me and Eileen Wade came across the terrace and sat down beside me on the edge of a chaise.

"Well, what did you think?" she asked quietly.

"About the gentleman with the loose gloves?"

"Oh no." She frowned. Then she laughed. "I hate people who make stagy scenes like that. Not that he isn't a fine doctor. He has played that scene with half the men in the valley.

Linda Loring is no tramp. She doesn't look like one, talk like one, or behave like one. I don't know what makes Dr. Loring behave as if she was."

"Maybe he's a reformed drunk," I said. "A lot of them grow pretty puritanical."

"It's possible," she said, and looked towards the lake. "This is a very peaceful place. One would think a writer would be happy here – if a writer is ever happy anywhere." She turned to look at me. "So you won't be persuaded to do what Roger asked."

"There's no point in it, Mrs. Wade. Nothing I could do. I've said all this before. I couldn't be sure of being around at the right time. I'd have to be around *all* the time. That's impossible, even if I had nothing else to do. If he went wild, for example, it would happen in a flash. And I haven't seen any indications that he does get wild. He seems pretty solid to me."

She looked down at her hands. "If he could finish his book, I think things would be much better."

"I can't help him do that."

She looked up and put her hands on the edge of the chaise beside her. She leaned forward a little. "You can if he thinks you can. That's the whole point. Is it that you would find it distasteful to be a guest in our house and be paid for it?"

"He needs a psychiatrist, Mrs. Wade. If you know one that isn't a quack."

She looked startled. "A psychiatrist? Why?"

I knocked the ashes out of my pipe and sat holding it, waiting for the bowl to get cooler before I put it away.

"You want an amateur opinion, here it is. He thinks he has a secret buried in his mind and he can't get at it. It may be a guilty secret about himself, it may be about someone else. He thinks that's what makes him drink, because he can't get at this thing. He probably thinks that whatever happened, happened while he was drunk and he ought to find it wherever

633

people go when they're drunk – really bad drunk, the way he gets. That's a job for a psychiatrist. So far, so good. If that is wrong, then he gets drunk because he wants to or can't help it, and the idea about the secret is just his excuse. He can't write his book, or anyway can't finish it. Because he gets drunk. That is, the assumption seems to be that he can't finish his book because he knocks himself out by drinking. It could be the other way around."

"Oh no," she said. "No. Roger has a great deal of talent. I feel quite sure that his best work is still to come."

"I told you it was an amateur opinion. You said the other morning that he might have fallen out of love with his wife. That's something else that could go the other way around."

She looked towards the house, then turned so that she had her back to it. I looked the same way. Wade was standing inside the doors, looking out at us. As I watched he moved behind the bar and reached for a bottle.

"There's no use interfering," she said quickly. "I never do. Never. I suppose you're right, Mr. Marlowe. There just isn't anything to do but let him work it out of his system."

The pipe was cool now and I put it away. "Since we're groping around in the back of the drawer, how about that other way around?"

"I love my husband," she said simply. "Not as a young girl loves, perhaps. But I love him. A woman is only a young girl once. The man I loved then is dead. He died in the war. His name, strangely enough, had the same initials as yours. It doesn't matter now – except that sometimes I can't quite believe that he is dead. His body was never found. But that happened to many men."

She gave me a long searching look. "Sometimes – not often, of course – when I go into a quiet cocktail lounge or the lobby of a good hotel at a dead hour, or along the deck of a liner early in the morning or very late at night, I think I may see him waiting for me in some shadowy corner." She paused and dropped her eyes. "It's very silly. I'm ashamed of it. We were very much in love – the wild, mysterious, improbable kind of love that never comes but once."

She stopped talking and sat there half in a trance looking out over the lake. I looked back at the house again. Wade was standing just inside the open french windows with a glass in his hand. I looked back at Eileen. For her I wasn't there any more. I got up and went into the house. Wade stood there with the drink and the drink looked pretty heavy. And his eyes looked wrong.

"How you making out with my wife, Marlowe?" It was said with a twist of the mouth.

"No passes, if you mean it that way."

"That's exactly the way I mean it. You got to kiss her the other night. Probably fancy yourself as a fast worker, but you're wasting your time, bud. Even if you had the right kind of polish."

I tried to move around him but he blocked me with a solid shoulder. "Don't hurry away, old man. We like you around. We get so few private dicks in our house."

"I'm the one too many," I said.

He hoisted the glass and drank from it. When he lowered it he leered at me.

"You ought to give yourself a little more time to build resistance," I told him. "Empty words, huh?"

"Okay, coach. Some little character builder, aren't you? You ought to have more sense than to try educating a drunk. Drunks don't educate, my friend. They disintegrate. And part of the process is a lot of fun." He drank from the glass again, leaving it nearly empty. "And part of it is damned awful. But if I may quote the scintillating words of the good Dr. Loring, a bastardly bastard with a little black bag, stay away from my wife, Marlowe. Sure you go for her. They all do. You'd like to sleep with her. They all would. You'd like to share her dreams and sniff the rose of her memories. Maybe I would too. But there is nothing to share, chum – nothing, nothing, nothing. You're all alone in the dark."

He finished his drink and turned the glass upside down.

"Empty like that, Marlowe. Nothing there at all. I'm the guy that knows."

He put the glass on the edge of the bar and walked stiffy to the foot of the stairs. He made about a dozen steps up, holding on to the rail, and stopped and leaned against it. He looked down at me with a sour grin.

"Forgive the corny sarcasm, Marlowe. You're a nice guy. I wouldn't want anything to happen to you."

"Anything like what?"

"Perhaps she didn't get around yet to that haunting magic of her first love, the guy that went missing in Norway. You wouldn't want to be missing, would you, chum? You're my own special private eye. You find me when I'm lost in the savage splendor of Sepulveda Canyon." He moved the palm of his hand in a circular motion on the polished wood banister. "It would hurt me to the quick if you got lost yourself. Like that character who hitched up with the limeys. He got so lost a man sometimes wonders if he ever existed. You figure she could have maybe just invented him to have a toy to play with?"

"How would I know?"

He looked down at me. There were deep lines between his eyes now and his mouth was twisted with bitterness.

"How would anybody know? Maybe she don't know herself. Baby's tired. Baby been playing too long with broken toys. Baby wants to go bye-bye."

He went on up the stairs.

I stood there until Candy came in and started tidying up around the bar, putting glasses on a tray, examining bottles to see what was left, paying no attention to me. Or so I thought. Then he said: "Señor. One good drink left. Pity to waste him." He held up a bottle.

"You drink it."

"Gracias, señor, no me gusta. Un vaso de Cerveza, no más. A glass of beer is my limit."

"Wise man."

"One lush in the house is enough," he said, staring at me. "I speak good English, not?"

"Sure, fine."

"But I think Spanish. Sometimes I think with a knife. The boss is my guy. He don't need any help, hombre. I take care of him, see."

"A great job you're doing, punk."

"Hijo de la flauta," he said between his white teeth. He picked up a loaded tray and swung it up on the edge of his shoulder and the flat of his hand, bus boy style.

I walked to the door and let myself out, wondering how an expression meaning 'son of a flute' had come to be an insult in Spanish. I didn't wonder very long. I had too many other things to wonder about. Something more than alcohol was the matter with the Wade family. Alcohol was no more than a disguised reaction.

Later that night, between nine-thirty and ten, I called the Wades' number. After eight rings I hung up, but I had only just taken my hand off the instrument when it started to ring me. It was Eileen Wade.

"Someone just rang here," she said. "I had a sort of hunch it might be you. I was just getting ready to take a shower."

"It was me, but it wasn't important, Mrs. Wade. He seemed a little woolly-headed when I left – Roger did. I guess maybe I feel a little responsibility for him by now."

"He's quite all right," she said. "Fast asleep in bed. I think Dr. Loring upset him more than he showed. No doubt he talked a lot of nonsense to you."

"He said he was tired and wanted to go to bed. Pretty sensible, I thought."

"If that is all he said, yes. Well, goodnight and thank you for calling, Mr. Marlowe."

"I didn't say it was all he said. I said he said it."

There was a pause, then: "Everyone gets fantastic ideas once in a while. Don't take Roger too seriously, Mr. Marlowe. After all, his imagination is rather highly developed. Naturally it would be. He shouldn't have had anything to drink so soon after the last time. Please try to forget all about it. I suppose he was rude to you among other things."

"He wasn't rude to me. He made quite a lot of sense. Your husband is a guy who can take a long hard look at himself and see what is there. It's not a very common gift. Most people go through life using up half their energy trying to protect a dignity they never had. Goodnight, Mrs. Wade."

She hung up and I set out the chess board. I filled a pipe, paraded the chessmen and inspected them for French shaves and loose buttons, and played a championship tournament game between Gortchakoff and Meninkin, seventy-two moves to a draw, a prize specimen of the irresistible force meeting the immovable object, a battle without armor, a war without blood, and as elaborate a waste of human intelligence as you could find anywhere outside an advertising agency.

25

NOTHING HAPPENED FOR a week except that I went about my business which just then didn't happen to be very much business. One morning George Peters of The Carne Organization called me up and told me he had happened to be down Sepulveda Canyon way and had looked in on Dr. Verringer's place just out of curiosity. But Dr. Verringer was no longer there. Half a dozen teams of surveyors were mapping the tract for a subdivision. Those he spoke to had never even heard of Dr. Verringer.

"The poor sucker got closed out on a trust deed," Peters said. "I checked. They gave him a grand for a quitclaim just to save time and expense, and now somebody is going to make a million bucks clear, out of cutting the place up for residential property. That's the difference between crime and business. For business you gotta have capital. Sometimes I think it's the only difference."

"A properly cynical remark," I said, "but big time crime takes capital too."

"And where does it come from, chum? Not from guys that hold up liquor stores. So long. See you soon."

It was ten minutes to eleven on a Thursday night when Wade called me up. His voice was thick, almost gurgling, but I recognized it somehow. And I could hear short hard rapid breathing over the telephone.

"I'm in bad shape, Marlowe. Very bad. I'm slipping my anchor. Could you make it out here in a hurry?"

"Sure — but let me talk to Mrs. Wade a minute."

He didn't answer. There was a crashing sound, then a dead silence, then in a short while a kind of banging around. I yelled something into the phone without getting any answer. Time passed. Finally the light click of the receiver being replaced and the buzz of an open line.

In five minutes I was on the way. I made it in slightly over half an hour and I still don't know how. I went over the pass on wings and hit Ventura Boulevard with the light against me and made a left turn anyhow and dodged between trucks and generally made a damn fool of myself. I went through Encino at close to sixty with a spotlight on the outer edge of the parked cars so that it would freeze anyone with a notion to step out suddenly. I had the kind of luck you only get when you don't care. No cops, no sirens, no red flashers. Just visions of what might be happening in the Wade residence and not very pleasant visions. She was alone in the house with a drunken maniac, she was lying at the bottom of the stairs with her neck broken, she was behind a locked door and somebody was howling outside and trying to break it in, she was running down a moonlit road barefoot and a big buck Negro with a meat cleaver was chasing her.

It wasn't like that at all. When I swung the Olds into their driveway lights were on all over the house and she was standing in the open doorway with a cigarette in her mouth. I got out and walked over the flagstones to her. She had slacks on and a shirt with an open collar. She looked at me calmly. If there was any excitement around there I had brought it with me.

The first thing I said was as loony as the rest of my behavior. "I thought you didn't smoke."

"What? No, I don't usually." She took the cigarette out and looked at it and dropped it and stepped on it. "Once in a long while. He called Dr. Verringer."

It was a remote placid voice, a voice heard at night over water. Completely relaxed.

"He couldn't," I said. "Dr. Verringer doesn't live there any more. He called me."

"Oh really? I just heard him telephoning and asking someone to come in a hurry. I thought it must be Dr. Verringer."

"Where is he now?"

"He fell down," she said. "He must have tipped the chair too far back. He's done it before. He cut his head on something. There's a little blood, not much."

"Well, that's fine," I said. "We wouldn't want a whole lot of blood. Where is he now, I asked you."

She looked at me solemnly. Then she pointed. "Out there somewhere. By the edge of the road or in the bushes along the fence."

I leaned forward and peered at her. "Chrissake, didn't you look?" I decided by this time that she was in shock. Then I looked back across the lawn. I didn't see anything but there was heavy shadow near the fence.

"No, I didn't look," she said quite calmly. "You find him. I've had all of it I can take. I've had more than I can take. You find him."

She turned and walked back into the house, leaving the door open. She didn't walk very far. About a yard inside the door she just crumpled to the floor and lay there. I scooped her up and spread her out on one of the two big davenports that faced each other across a long blond cocktail table. I felt her pulse. It didn't seem very weak or unsteady. Her eyes were closed and the lids were blue. I left her there and went back out.

He was there all right, just as she had said. He was lying on his side in the shadow of the hibiscus. He had a fast thumping pulse and his breathing was unnatural. Something on the back of his head was sticky. I spoke to him and shook him a little. I slapped his face a couple of times. He mumbled but didn't come to. I dragged him up into a sitting position and dragged one of his arms over my shoulder and heaved him up with my back turned to him and grabbed for a leg. I lost. He was as heavy as a block of cement. We both sat down on the grass and I took a short breather and tried again. Finally I got him hoisted into a fireman's lift position and plowed across the lawn in the direction of the open front door. It seemed about the same distance as a round trip to Siam. The two steps of the porch were ten feet high. I staggered over to the couch and went down on my knees and rolled him off. When I straightened up again my spine felt as if it had cracked in at least three places.

Eileen Wade wasn't there any more. I had the room to myself. I was too bushed at the moment to care where anybody was. I sat down and looked at him and waited for some breath. Then I looked at his head. It was smeared with blood. His hair was sticky with it. It didn't look very bad but you never know with a head wound.

Then Eileen Wade was standing beside me, quietly looking down at him with that same remote expression.

"I'm sorry I fainted," she said. "I don't know why."

"I guess we'd better call a doctor."

"I telephoned Dr. Loring. He is my doctor, you know. He didn't want to come."

"Try somebody else then."

"Oh he's coming," she said. "He didn't want to. But he's coming as soon as he can manage."

"Where's Candy?"

"This is his day off. Thursday. The cook and Candy have Thursdays off. It's the usual thing around here. Can you get him up to bed?"

"Not without help. Better get a rug or blanket. It's a warm night, but cases like this get pneumonia very easily."

She said she would get a rug. I thought it was damn nice of her. But I wasn't thinking very intelligently. I was too bushed from carrying him.

We spread a steamer rug over him and in fifteen minutes Dr. Loring came, complete with starched collar and rimless cheaters and the expression of a man who has been asked to clean up after the dog got sick.

He examined Wade's head. "A superficial cut and bruise," he said. "No chance of concussion. I should say his breath would indicate his condition rather obviously."

He reached for his hat. He picked up his bag.

"Keep him warm," he said. "You might bathe his head gently and get rid of the blood. He'll sleep it off."

"I can't get him upstairs alone, Doctor," I said.

"Then leave him where he is." He looked at me without interest. "Goodnight, Mrs. Wade. As you know I don't treat alcoholics. Even if I did, your husband would not be one of my patients. I'm sure you understand that."

"Nobody's asking you to treat him," I said. "I'm asking for some help to get him into his bedroom so that I can undress him."

"And just who are you?" Dr. Loring asked me freezingly.

"My name's Marlowe. I was here a week ago. Your wife introduced me."

"Interesting," he said. "In what connection do you know my wife?"

"What the hell does that matter? All I want is —"

"I'm not interested in what you want," he cut in on me. He turned to Eileen, nodded briefly, and started out. I got between him and the door and put my back to it.

"Just a minute, Doc. Must be a long time since you glanced at that little piece of prose called the Hippocratic Oath. This man called me on the phone and I live some way off. He sounded bad and I broke every traffic law in the state getting over here. I found him lying on the ground and I carried him in here and believe me he isn't any bunch of feathers. The houseboy is away and there's nobody here to help me upstairs with Wade. How does it look to you?"

"Get out of my way," he said between his teeth. "Or I shall call the sheriff's substation and have them send over a deputy. As a professional man —"

"As a professional man you're a handful of flea dirt," I said, and moved out of his way.

He turned red — slowly but distinctly. He choked on his own bile. Then he opened the door and went out. He shut it carefully. As he pulled it shut he looked in at me. It was as nasty a look as I ever got and on as nasty a face as I ever saw.

When I turned away from the door Eileen was smiling.

"What's funny?" I snarled.

"You. You don't care what you say to people, do you? Don't you know who Dr. Loring is?"

"Yeah — and I know what he is."

She glanced at her wrist watch. "Candy ought to be home by now," she said. "I'll go see. He has a room behind the garage."

She went out through an archway and I sat down and looked at Wade. The great big writer man went on snoring.

His face was sweaty but I left the rug over him. In a minute or two Eileen came back and she had Candy with her.

26

THE MEX HAD a black and white checked sport shirt, heavily pleated black slacks without a belt, two-tone black and white buckskin shoes, spotlessly clean. His thick black hair was brushed straight back and shining with some kind of hair oil or cream.

"Señor," he said, and sketched a brief sarcastic bow.

"Help Mr. Marlowe carry my husband upstairs, Candy. He fell and hurt himself a little. I'm sorry to trouble you."

"De nada, señora," Candy said smiling.

"I think I'll say goodnight," she said to me. "I'm tired out. Candy will get you anything you want."

She went slowly up the stairs. Candy and I watched her.

"Some doll," he said confidentially. "You stay the night?"

"Hardly."

"Es lástima. She is very lonely, that one."

"Get that gleam out of your eyes, kid. Let's put this to bed."

He looked sadly at Wade snoring on the couch. "Pobrecito," he murmured as if he meant it. "Borracho como una cuba."

"He may be drunk as a sow but he sure ain't little," I said. "You take the feet."

We carried him and even for two he was as heavy as a lead coffin. At the top of the stairs we went along an open balcony past a closed door. Candy pointed to it with his chin.

"La señora," he whispered. "You knock very light maybe she let you in."

I didn't say anything because I needed him. We went on with the carcass and turned in at another door and dumped him on the bed. Then I took hold of Candy's arm high up near the shoulder where dug-in fingers can hurt. I made mine hurt him. He winced a little and then his face set hard.

"What's your name, cholo?"

"Take your hand off me," he snapped. "And don't call me a cholo. I'm no wetback. My name is Juan García de Soto yo Soto-mayor. I am Chileno."

"Okay, Don Juan. Just don't get out of line around here. Keep your nose and mouth clean when you talk about the people you work for."

He jerked loose and stepped back, his black eyes hot with anger. His hand slipped inside his shirt and came out with a long thin knife. He balanced it by the point on the heel of his hand, hardly even glancing at it. Then he dropped the hand and caught the handle of the knife while it hung in the air. It was done very fast and without any apparent effort. His hand went up to shoulder height, then snapped forward and the knife sailed through the air and hung quivering in the wood of the window frame.

"Cuidado, señor!" he said with a sharp sneer. "And keep your paws to yourself. Nobody fools with me."

He walked lithely across the room and plucked the knife out of the wood, tossed it in the air, spun on his toes and caught it behind him. With a snap it disappeared under his shirt.

"Neat," I said, "but just a little on the gaudy side."

He strolled up to me smiling derisively.

"And it might get you a broken elbow," I said. "Like this."

I took hold of his right wrist, jerked him off balance, swung to one side and a little behind him, and brought my bent forearm up under the back of his elbow joint. I bore down on it, using my forearm as a fulcrum.

"One hard jerk," I said, "and your elbow joint cracks. A crack is enough. You'd be out of commission as a knife thrower for several months. Make the jerk a little harder and you'd be through permanently. Take Mr. Wade's shoes off."

I let go of him and he grinned at me. "Good trick," he said. "I will remember."

He turned to Wade and reached for one of his shoes, then stopped. There was a smear of blood on the pillow.

"Who cut the boss?"

"Not me, chum. He fell and cut his head on something. It's only a shallow cut. The doctor has been here."

Candy let his breath out slowly. "You see him fall?"

"Before I got here. You like this guy, don't you?"

He didn't answer me. He took the shoes off. We got Wade undressed little by little and Candy dug out a pair of green and silver pajamas. We got Wade into those and got him inside the bed and well covered up. He was still sweaty and still snoring. Candy looked down at him sadly, shaking his sleek head from side to side, slowly.

"Somebody's got to take care of him," he said. "I go change my clothes."

"Get some sleep. I'll take care of him. I can call you if I need you."

He faced me. "You better take care of him good," he said in a quiet voice. "Very good."

He went out of the room. I went into the bathroom and got a wet washcloth and a heavy towel. I turned Wade over a little and spread the towel on the pillow and washed the blood off his head gently so as not to start the bleeding again. Then I could see a sharp shallow cut about two inches long. It was nothing. Dr. Loring had been right that much. It wouldn't have hurt to stitch it but it probably was not really necessary. I found a pair of scissors and cut the hair away enough so that I could put on a strip of adhesive. Then I turned him on his back and washed his face. I guess that was a mistake.

He opened his eyes. They were vague and unfocused at first, then they cleared and he saw me standing beside the bed. His hand moved and went up to his head and felt the adhesive. His lips mumbled something, then his voice cleared up also.

"Who hit me? You?" His hand felt for the adhesive.

"Nobody hit you. You took a fall."

"Took a fall? When? Where?"

"Wherever you telephoned from. You called me. I heard you fall. Over the wire."

"I called you?" He grinned slowly. "Always available, aren't you, fella? What time is it?"

"After one A.M."

"Where's Eileen?"

"Gone to bed. She had it rough."

He thought that over silently. His eyes were full of pain. "Did I —" He stopped and winced.

"You didn't touch her as far as I know. If that's what you mean. You just wandered outdoors and passed out near the fence. Quit talking. Go to sleep."

"Sleep," he said quietly and slowly, like a child reciting its lesson. "What would that be?"

"Maybe a pill would help. Got any?"

"In the drawer. Night table."

I opened it and found a plastic bottle with red capsules in it. Seconal, 1½ grains. Prescription by Dr. Loring. That nice Dr. Loring. Mrs. Roger Wade's prescription.

I shook two of them loose and put the bottle back and poured a glass of water from a thermos jug on the night table. He said one capsule would be enough. He took it and drank some water and lay back and stared at the ceiling again. Time passed. I sat in a chair and watched him. He didn't seem to get sleepy. Then he said slowly:

"I remember something. Do me a favor, Marlowe. I wrote some crazy stuff I don't want Eileen to see. It's on top of the typewriter under the cover. Tear it up for me."

"Sure. That all you remember?"

"Eileen is all right? Positive about that?"

"Yes. She's just tired. Let it ride, Wade. Stop thinking. I shouldn't have asked you."

647

"Stop thinking, the man says." His voice was a little drowsy now. He was talking as if to himself. "Stop thinking, stop dreaming, stop loving, stop hating. Goodnight, sweet prince. I'll take that other pill."

I gave it to him with some more water. He lay back again, this time with his head turned so that he could see me. "Look, Marlowe, I wrote some stuff I don't want Eileen —"

"You told me already. I'll attend to it when you go to sleep."

"Oh. Thanks. Nice to have you around. Very nice."

Another longish pause. His eyelids were getting heavy.

"Ever kill a man, Marlowe?"

"Yes."

"Nasty feeling, isn't it?"

"Some people like it."

His eyes went shut all the way. Then they opened again, but they looked vague. "How could they?"

I didn't answer. The eyelids came down again, very gradually, like a slow curtain in the theater. He began to snore. I waited a little longer. Then I dimmed the light in the room and went out.

27

I STOPPED OUTSIDE Eileen's door and listened. I didn't hear any sound of movement inside, so I didn't knock. If she wanted to know how he was, it was up to her. Downstairs the living room looked bright and empty. I put out some of the lights. From over near the front door I looked up at the balcony. The middle part of the living room rose to the full height of the house walls and was crossed by open beams that also supported the balcony. The balcony was wide and edged on two sides by a solid railing which looked to be about three and a half feet high. The top and the uprights were cut square to match the cross beams. The dining room was through a

648

square arch closed off by double louvered doors. Above it I guessed there were servants' quarters. This part of the second floor was walled off so there would be another stairway reaching it from the kitchen part of the house. Wade's room was in the corner over his study. I could see the light from his open door reflected against the high ceiling and I could see the top foot of his doorway.

I cut all the lights except in one standing lamp and crossed to the study. The door was shut but two lamps were lit, a standing lamp at the end of the leather couch and a cowled desk lamp. The typewriter was on a heavy stand under this and beside it on the desk there was a disorderly mess of yellow paper. I sat in a padded chair and studied the layout. What I wanted to know was how he had cut his head. I sat in his desk chair with the phone at my left hand. The spring was set very weak. If I tilted back and went over, my head might have caught the corner of the desk. I moistened my handkerchief and rubbed the wood. No blood, nothing there. There was a lot of stuff on the desk, including a row of books between bronze elephants, and an old-fashioned square glass inkwell. I tried that without result. Not much point to it anyway, because if someone else had slugged him, the weapon didn't have to be in the room. And there wasn't anyone else to do it. I stood up and switched on the cornice lights. They reached into the shadowy corners and of course the answer was simple enough after all. A square metal wastebasket was lying on its side over against the wall, with paper spilled. It couldn't have walked there, so it had been thrown or kicked. I tried its sharp corners with my moistened handkerchief. I got the red-brown smear of blood this time. No mystery at all. Wade had fallen over and struck his head on the sharp corner of the wastebasket – a glancing blow most likely – picked himself up and booted the damn thing across the room. Easy.

Then he would have another quick drink. The drinking liquor was on the cocktail table in front of the couch. An empty bottle, another three quarters full, a thermos jug of water and a silver bowl containing water which had been ice cubes. There was only one glass and it was the large economy size.

Having taken his drink he felt a little better. He noticed the phone off the hook in a bleary sort of way and very likely didn't remember any more what he had been doing with it. So he just walked across and put it back in its cradle. The time had been just about right. There is something compulsive about a telephone. The gadget-ridden man of our age loves it, loathes it, and is afraid of it. But he always treats it with respect, even when he is drunk. The telephone is a fetish.

Any normal man would have said hello into the mouthpiece before hanging up, just to be sure. But not necessarily a man who was bleary with drink and had just taken a fall. It didn't matter anyhow. His wife might have done it, she might have heard the fall and the bang as the wastebasket bounced against the wall and come into the study. About that time the last drink would kick him in the face and he would stagger out of the house and across the front lawn and pass out where I had found him. Somebody was coming for him. By this time he didn't know who it was. Maybe the good Dr. Verringer.

So far, so good. So what would his wife do? She couldn't handle him or reason with him and she might well be afraid to try. So she would call somebody to come and help. The servants were out, so it would have to be by the telephone. Well, she *had* called somebody. She had called that nice Dr. Loring. I'd just assumed she called him after I got there. She hadn't said so.

From here on it didn't quite add up. You'd expect her to look for him and find him and make sure he wasn't hurt. It wouldn't hurt him to lie out on the ground on a warm summer night for a while. She couldn't move him. It had taken all I had to do that. But you wouldn't quite expect to find her standing in the open doorway smoking a cigarette, not knowing except very vaguely where he was. Or would you? I didn't know what she had been through with him, how dangerous he was in that condition, how much afraid she might be to go near him. "I've had all of it I can take," she had said to me when I arrived. "You find him." Then she had gone inside and pulled a faint.

It still bothered me, but I had to leave it at that. I had to assume that when she had been up against the situation often enough to know there was nothing she could do about it except to let it ride, then that would be what she would do. Just that. Let it ride. Let him lie out there on the ground until somebody came around with the physical equipment to handle him.

It still bothered me. It bothered me also that she had checked out and gone into her own room while Candy and I got him upstairs to bed. She said she loved the guy. He was her husband, they had been married for five years, he was a very nice guy indeed when sober – those were her own words. Drunk, he was something else, something to stay away from because he was dangerous. All right, forget it. But somehow it still bothered me. If she was really scared, she wouldn't have been standing there in the open door smoking a cigarette. If she was just bitter and withdrawn and disgusted, she wouldn't have fainted.

There was something else. Another woman, perhaps. Then she had only just found out. Linda Loring? Maybe. Dr. Loring thought so and said so in a very public manner.

I stopped thinking about it and took the cover off the typewriter. The stuff was there, several loose sheets of typed yellow paper that I was supposed to destroy so Eileen wouldn't see them. I took them over to the couch and decided I deserved a drink to go with the reading matter. There was a half bath off the study. I rinsed the tall glass out and poured a libation and sat down with it to read. And what I read was really wild. Like this:

28

THE MOON'S FOUR days off the full and there's a square patch of moonlight on the wall and it's looking at me like a big blind milky eye, a wall eye. Joke. Goddam silly simile. Writers. Everything has to be like something else. My head is as fluffy as whipped cream but not as sweet. More similes. I could vomit just thinking about the lousy racket. I could vomit anyway. I probably will. Don't push me. Give me time. The worms in my solar plexus crawl and crawl and crawl. I would be better off in bed but there would be a dark animal underneath the bed and the dark animal would crawl around rustling and hump himself and bump the underside of the bed, then I would let out a yell that wouldn't make any sound except to me. A dream yell, a yell in a nightmare. There is nothing to be afraid of and I am not afraid because there is nothing to be afraid of, but just the same I was lying like that once in bed and the dark animal was doing it to me, bumping himself against the underside of the bed, and I had an orgasm. That disgusted me more than any other of the nasty things I have done.

I'm dirty. I need a shave. My hands are shaking. I'm sweating. I smell foul to myself. The shirt under my arms is wet and on the chest and back. The sleeves are wet in the folds of the elbows. The glass on the table is empty. It would take both hands to pour the stuff now. I could get one out of the bottle maybe to brace me. The taste of the stuff is sickening. And it wouldn't get me anywhere. In the end I won't be able to sleep even and the whole world will moan in the horror of tortured nerves. Good stuff, huh, Wade? More.

It's all right for the first two or three days and then it is negative. You suffer and you take a drink and for a little while it is better, but the price keeps getting higher and higher and what you get for it is less and less and then there is always the point where you get nothing but nausea. Then you call Verringer. All right, Verringer, here I come. There isn't any Verringer any more. He's gone to Cuba or he is dead. The queen has killed him. Poor old Verringer, what a fate, to die in bed with a queen – that kind of queen. Come on, Wade, let's get up and go places. Places where we haven't ever been and aren't ever going back to when we have been. Does this sentence make sense? No. Okay, I'm not asking any money for it. A short pause here for a long commercial.

Well, I did it. I got up. What a man. I went over to the couch and here I am kneeling beside the couch with my hands down on it and my face in my hands, crying. Then I prayed and despised myself for praying. Grade Three drunk despising himself. What the hell are you praying to, you fool? If a well man prays, that's faith. A sick man prays and he is just scared. Nuts to prayer. This is the world you made and you make it all by yourself and what little outside help you got – well you made that too. Stop praying, you jerk. Get up on your feet and take that drink. It's too late for anything else now.

Well, I took it. Both hands. Poured it in the glass too. Hardly spilled a drop. Now if I can hold it without vomiting. Better add some water. Now lift it slow. Easy, not too much at a time. It gets warm. It gets hot. If I could stop sweating. The glass is empty. It's down on the table again.

There's a haze over the moonlight but I set that glass down in spite of it, carefully, carefully, like a spray of roses in a tall vase. The roses nod their heads with dew. Maybe I'm a rose. Brother, have I got dew. Now to get upstairs. Maybe a short one straight for the journey. No? Okay, whatever you say. Take it upstairs when I get there. If I get there, something to look forward to. If I make it upstairs I am entitled to compensation. A token of regard from me to me. I have such a beautiful love for myself – and the sweet part of it – no rivals.

Double space. Been up and came down. Didn't like it upstairs. The altitude makes my heart flutter. But I keep hitting these typewriter keys. What a magician is the subconscious. If only it would work regular hours. There was moonlight upstairs too. Probably the same moon. No variety about the moon. It comes and goes like the milkman and the moon's milk is always the same. The milk's moon is always – hold it chum. You've got your feet crossed. This is no time to get involved in the case history of the moon. You got enough case history to take care of the whole damn valley.

She was sleeping on her side without sound. Her knees drawn up. Too still I thought. You always make some sound when you sleep. Maybe not asleep, maybe just trying to sleep. If I went closer I would know. Might fall down too. One of her eyes opened – or did it? She looked at me or did she? No. Would have sat up and said, Are you sick, darling? Yes, I am sick, darling. But don't give it a thought, darling, because this sick is my sick and not your sick, and let you sleep still and lovely and never remember and no slime from me to you and nothing come near you that is grim and gray and ugly.

You're a louse, Wade. Three adjectives, you lousy writer. Can't you even stream-of-consciousness you louse without getting it in three adjectives for Chrissake? I came downstairs again holding on to the rail. My guts lurched with the steps and I held them together with a promise. I made the main floor and I made the study and I made the couch and I waited for my heart to slow down. The bottle is handy. One thing you can say about

Wade's arrangements the bottle is always handy. Nobody hides it, nobody locks it up. Nobody says, Don't you think you've had enough, darling? You'll make yourself sick, darling. Nobody says that. Just sleep on side softly like roses.

I gave Candy too much money. Mistake. Should have started him with a bag of peanuts and worked up to a banana. Then a little real change, slow and easy, always keep him eager. You give him a big slug of the stuff to begin with and pretty soon he has a stake. He can live in Mexico for a month, live high wide and nasty, on what it costs here for a day. So when he gets that stake, what does he do? Well, does a man ever have enough money, if he thinks he can get more? Maybe it's all right. Maybe I ought to kill the shiny-eyed bastard. A good man died for me once, why not a cockroach in a white jacket?

Forget Candy. There's always a way to blunt a needle. The other I shall never forget. It's carved on my liver in green fire.

Better telephone. Losing control. Feel them jumping, jumping, jumping. Better call someone quick before the pink things crawl on my face. Better call, call, call. Call Sioux City Sue. Hello, Operator, give me Long Distance. Hello, Long Distance, get me Sioux City Sue. What's her number? No have number, just name, Operator. You'll find her walking along Tenth Street, on the shady side, under the tall corn trees with their spreading ears . . . All right, Operator, all right. Just cancel the whole program and let me tell you something, I mean, ask you some- thing. Who's going to pay for all those snazzy parties Gifford is throwing in London, if you cancel my long distance call? Yeah, you think your job is solid. You think. Here, I better talk to Gifford direct. Get him on the line. His valet just brought in his tea. If he can't talk we'll send over somebody that can.

Now what did I write that for? What was I trying not to think about? Telephone. Better telephone now. Getting very bad, very very . . .

That was all. I folded the sheets up small and pushed them down into my inside breast pocket behind the note case. I went over to the french windows and opened them wide and stepped out onto the terrace. The moonlight was a little spoiled. But it was summer in Idle Valley and summer is never quite spoiled. I stood there looking at the motionless colorless lake and thought and wondered. Then I heard a shot.

29

ON THE BALCONY two lighted doors were open now – Eileen's and his. Her room was empty. There was a sound of struggling from his and I came through the door in a jump to find her bending over the bed wrestling with him. The black gleam of a gun shot up into the air, two hands, a large male hand and a woman's small hand were both holding it, neither by the butt. Roger was sitting up in bed and leaning forward pushing. She was in a pale blue house coat, one of those quilted things, her hair was all over her face and now she had both hands on the gun and with a quick jerk she got it away from him. I was surprised that she had the strength, even dopey as he was. He fell back glaring and panting and she stepped away and bumped into me.

She stood there leaning against me, holding the gun with both hands pressed hard against her body. She was racked with panting sobs. I reached around her body and put my hand on the gun.

She spun around as if it took that to make her realize I was there. Her eyes widened and her body sagged against me. She let go of the gun. It was a heavy clumsy weapon, a Webley double-action hammerless. The barrel was warm. I held her with one arm, dropped the gun in my pocket, and looked past her head at him. Nobody said anything.

Then he opened his eyes and that weary smile played on his lips. "Nobody hurt," he muttered. "Just a wild shot into the ceiling."

I felt her go stiff. Then she pulled away. Her eyes were focused and clear. I let her go.

"Roger," she said in a voice not much more than a sick whisper, "did it have to be that?"

He stared owlishly, licked his lip, and said nothing. She went and leaned against the dressing table. Her hand moved mechanically and threw the hair back from her face. She shuddered once from head to foot, shaking her head from side to side. "Roger," she whispered again. "Poor Roger. Poor miserable Roger."

He was staring straight up at the ceiling now. "I had a nightmare," he said slowly. "Somebody with a knife was leaning over the bed. I don't know who. Looked a little like Candy. Couldn't of been Candy."

"Of course not, darling," she said softly. She left the dressing table and sat down on the side of the bed. She put her hand out and began to stroke his forehead. "Candy has gone to bed long ago. And why would Candy have a knife?"

"He's a Mex. They all have knives," Roger said in the same remote impersonal voice. "They like knives. And he doesn't like me."

"Nobody likes you," I said brutally.

She turned her head swiftly. "Please – please don't talk like that. He didn't know. He had a dream –"

"Where was the gun?" I growled, watching her, not paying any attention to him.

"Night table. In the drawer." He turned his head and met my stare. There hadn't been any gun in the drawer, and he knew I knew it. The pills had been in there and some odds and ends, but no gun.

"Or under the pillow," he added. "I'm vague about it. I shot once —" he lifted a heavy hand and pointed — "up there."

I looked up. There seemed to be a hole in the ceiling plaster all right. I went where I could look up at it. Yes. The kind of hole a bullet might make. From that gun it would go on through, into the attic. I went back close to the bed and stood looking down at him, giving him the hard eye.

"Nuts. You meant to kill yourself. You didn't have any nightmare. You were swimming in a sea of self-pity. You didn't have any gun in the drawer or under your pillow either. You got up and got the gun and got back into bed and there you were all ready to wipe out the whole messy business. But I don't think you had the nerve. You fired a shot not meant to hit anything. And your wife came running — that's what you wanted. Just pity and sympathy, pal. Nothing else. Even the struggle was mostly fake. She couldn't take a gun away from you if you didn't want her to."

"I'm sick," he said. "But you could be right. Does it matter?"

"It matters like this. They'd put you in the psycho ward, and believe me, the people who run that place are about as sympathetic as Georgia chain-gang guards."

Eileen stood up suddenly. "That's enough," she said sharply. "He *is* sick, and you know it."

"He wants to be sick. I'm just reminding him of what it would cost him."

"This is not the time to tell him."

"Go on back to your room."

Her blue eyes flashed. "How dare you —"

"Go on back to your room. Unless you want me to call the police. These things are supposed to be reported."

He almost grinned. "Yeah, call the police," he said, "like you did on Terry Lennox."

I didn't pay any attention to that. I was still watching her. She looked exhausted now, and frail, and very beautiful. The moment of flashing anger was gone. I put a hand out and touched her arm. "It's all right," I said. "He won't do it again. Go back to bed."

She gave him a long look and went out of the room. When the open door was empty of her I sat down on the side of the bed where she had been sitting.

"More pills?"

"No thanks. It doesn't matter whether I sleep. I feel a lot better."

"Did I hit right about that shot? It was just a crazy bit of acting?"

"More or less." He turned his head away. "I guess I was lightheaded."

"Nobody can stop you from killing yourself, if you really want to. I realize that. So do you."

"Yes." He was still looking away. "Did you do what I asked you – that stuff in the typewriter?"

"Uh huh. I'm surprised you remember. It's pretty crazy writing. Funny thing, it's clearly typed."

"I can always do that – drunk or sober – up to a point anyway."

"Don't worry about Candy," I said. "You're wrong about his not liking you. And I was wrong to say nobody did. I was trying to jar Eileen, make her mad."

"Why?"

"She pulled one faint already tonight."

He shook his head slightly. "Eileen never faints."

"Then it was a phony."

He didn't like that either.

"What did you mean – a good man died for you?" I asked.

He frowned, thinking about it. "Just rubbish. I told you I had a dream –"

"I'm talking about that guff you typed out."

He looked at me now, turning his head on the pillow as if it had enormous weight. "Another dream."

"I'll try again. What's Candy got on you?"

"Shove it, Jack," he said, and closed his eyes.

I got up and closed the door. "You can't run forever, Wade. Candy could be a blackmailer, sure. Easy. He could even be nice about it – like you and lift your dough at the same time. What is it – a woman?"

"You believe that fool, Loring," he said with his eyes closed.

"Not exactly. What about the sister – the one that's dead?"

It was a wild pitch in a sense but it happened to split the plate. His eyes snapped wide open. A bubble of saliva showed on his lips.

"Is that – why you're here?" he asked slowly, and in a whispering voice.

"You know better, I was invited. You invited me."

His head rolled back and forth on the pillow. In spite of the Seconal he was eaten up by his nerves. His face was covered with sweat.

"I'm not the first loving husband who has been an adulterer. Leave me alone, damn you. Leave me alone."

I went into the bathroom and got a face towel and wiped his face off. I grinned at him sneeringly. I was the heel to end all heels. Wait until the man is down, then kick him and kick him again. He's weak. He can't resist or kick back.

"One of these days we'll get together on it," I said.

"I'm not crazy," he said.

"You just hope you're not crazy."

"I've been living in hell."

"Oh sure. That's obvious. The interesting point is why. Here – take this." I had another Seconal out of the night table and another glass of water. He got up on one elbow and grabbed for the glass and missed it by a good four inches. I put it in his hand. He managed to drink and swallow his pill. Then he lay back flat and deflated, his face drained of emotion. His nose had that pinched look. He could almost have been a dead man. He wasn't throwing anybody down any stairs tonight. Most likely not any night.

When his eyelids got heavy I went out of the room. The weight of the Webley was against my hip, dragging at my pocket. I started back downstairs again. Eileen's door was open. Her room was dark but there was enough light from the moon to frame her standing just inside the door. She called out something that sounded like a name, but it wasn't mine. I stepped close to her.

"Keep your voice down," I said. "He's gone back to sleep."

"I always knew you would come back," she said softly. "Even after ten years."

I peered at her. One of us was goofy.

"Shut the door," she said in the same caressing voice. "All these years I have kept myself for you."

I turned and shut the door. It seemed like a good idea at the moment. When I faced her she was already falling towards me. So I caught her. I damn well had to. She pressed herself hard against me and her hair brushed my face. Her mouth came up to be kissed. She was trembling. Her lips opened and her teeth opened and her tongue darted. Then her hands dropped and jerked at something and the robe she was wearing came open and underneath it she was as naked as September Morn but a darn sight less coy.

"Put me on the bed," she breathed.

I did that. Putting my arms around her I touched bare skin, soft skin, soft yielding flesh. I lifted her and carried her the few steps to the bed and lowered her. She kept her arms around my neck. She was making some kind of a whistling noise in her throat. Then she thrashed about and moaned. This was murder. I was as erotic as a stallion. I was losing control. You don't get that sort of invitation from that sort of woman very often anywhere.

Candy saved me. There was a thin squeak and I swung around to see the doorknob moving. I jerked loose and jumped for the door. I got it open and barged out through it and the Mex was tearing along the hall and down the stairs. Halfway down he stopped and turned and leered at me. Then he was gone.

I went back to the door and shut it – from the outside this time. Some kind of weird noises were coming from the woman on the bed, but that's all they were now. Weird noises. The spell was broken.

I went down the stairs fast and crossed into the study and grabbed the bottle of Scotch and tilted it. When I couldn't swallow any more I leaned against the wall and panted and let the stuff burn in me until the fumes reached my brain.

It was a long time since dinner. It was a long time since anything that was normal. The whiskey hit me hard and fast and I kept guzzling it until the room started to get hazy and the furniture was all in the wrong places and the lamplight was like wildfire or summer lightning. Then I was flat out on the leather couch, trying to balance the bottle on my chest. It seemed to be empty. It rolled away and thumped on the floor.

That was the last incident of which I took any precise notice.

30

A SHAFT OF sunlight tickled one of my ankles. I opened my eyes and saw the crown of a tree moving gently against a hazed blue sky. I rolled over and leather touched my cheek. An axe split my head. I sat up. There was a rug over me. I threw that off and got my feet on the floor. I scowled at a clock. The clock said a minute short of six-thirty.

I got up on my feet and it took character. It took will power. It took a lot out of me, and there wasn't as much to spare as there once had been. The hard heavy years had worked me over.

I plowed across to the half bath and stripped off my tie and shirt and sloshed cold water on my face with both hands

and sloshed it on my head. When I was dripping wet I tow-
eled myself off savagely. I put my shirt and tie back on and
reached for my jacket and the gun in the pocket banged
against the wall. I took it out and swung the cylinder away
from the frame and tipped the cartridges into my hand, five
full, one just a blackened shell. Then I thought, what's the use,
there are always more of them. So I put them back where they
had been before and carried the gun into the study and put it
away in one of the drawers of the desk.

When I looked up Candy was standing in the doorway,
spick and span in his white coat, his hair brushed back and
shining black, his eyes bitter.

"You want some coffee?"

"Thanks."

"I put the lamps out. The boss is okay. Asleep. I shut his
door. Why you get drunk?"

"I had to."

He sneered at me. "Didn't make her, huh? Got tossed out
on your can, shamus."

"Have it your own way."

"You ain't tough this morning, shamus. You ain't tough at all."

"Get the goddam coffee," I yelled at him.

"Hijo de la puta!"

In one jump I had him by the arm. He didn't move. He just
looked at me contemptuously. I laughed and let go of his arm.

"You're right, Candy. I'm not tough at all."

He turned and went out. In no time at all he was back with
a silver tray and a small silver pot of coffee on it and sugar and
cream and a neat triangular napkin. He set it down on the
cocktail table and removed the empty bottle and the rest of
the drinking materials. He picked another bottle off the floor.

"Fresh. Just made," he said, and went out.

I drank two cups black. Then I tried a cigarette. It was all
right. I still belonged to the human race. Then Candy was
back in the room again.

"You want breakfast?" he asked morosely.

"No, thanks."

"Okay, scram out of here. We don't want you around."

"Who's we?"

He lifted the lid of a box and helped himself to a cigarette. He lit it and blew smoke at me insolently.

"I take care of the boss," he said.

"You making it pay?"

He frowned, then nodded. "Oh yes. Good money."

"How much on the side – for not spilling what you know?"

He went back to Spanish. "No entendido."

"You understand all right. How much you shake him for? I bet it's not more than a couple of yards."

"What's that? Couple of yards."

"Two hundred bucks."

He grinned. "You give me couple of yards, shamus. So I don't tell the boss you come out of her room last night."

"That would buy a whole busload of wetbacks like you."

He shrugged that off. "The boss gets pretty rough when he blows his top. Better pay up, shamus."

"Pachuco stuff," I said contemptuously. "All you're touching is the small money. Lots of men play around when they're lit. Anyhow she knows all about it. You don't have anything to sell."

There was a gleam in his eye. "Just don't come round any more, tough boy."

"I'm leaving."

I stood up and walked around the table. He moved enough to keep facing towards me. I watched his hand but he evidently wasn't wearing a knife this morning. When I was close enough I slapped a hand across his face.

"I don't get called a son of a whore by the help, greaseball. I've got business here and I come around whenever I feel like it. Watch your lip from now on. You might get pistol-whipped. That pretty face of yours would never look the same again."

He didn't react at all, not even to the slap. That and being called a greaseball must have been deadly insults to him. But this time he just stood there wooden-faced, motionless. Then without a word he picked up the coffee tray and carried it out.

"Thanks for the coffee," I said to his back.

He kept going. When he was gone I felt the bristles on my chin, shook myself, and decided to be on my way. I had had a skinful of the Wade family.

As I crossed the living room Eileen was coming down the stairs in white slacks and open-toed sandals and a pale blue shirt. She looked at me with complete surprise. "I didn't know you were here, Mr. Marlowe," she said, as though she hadn't seen me for a week and at that time I had just dropped in for tea.

"I put his gun in the desk," I said.

"Gun?" Then it seemed to dawn on her. "Oh, last night was a little hectic, wasn't it? But I thought you had gone home."

I walked over closer to her. She had a thin gold chain around her neck and some kind of fancy pendant in gold and blue on white enamel. The blue enameled part looked like a pair of wings, but not spread out. Against these there was a broad white enamel and gold dagger that pierced a scroll. I couldn't read the words. It was some kind of military insigne.

"I got drunk," I said. "Deliberately and not elegantly. I was a little lonely."

"You didn't have to be," she said, and her eyes were as clear as water. There wasn't a trace of guile in them.

"A matter of opinion," I said. "I'm leaving now and I'm not sure I'll be back. You heard what I said about the gun?"

"You put it in his desk. It might be a good idea to put it somewhere else. But he didn't really mean to shoot himself, did he?"

"I can't answer that. But next time he might."

She shook her head. "I don't think so. I really don't. You were a wonderful help last night, Mr. Marlowe. I don't know how to thank you."

665

"You made a pretty good try."

She got pink. Then she laughed. "I had a very curious dream in the night," she said slowly, looking off over my shoulder. "Someone I used to know was here in the house. Someone who has been dead for ten years." Her fingers went up and touched the gold and enamel pendant. "That's why I am wearing this today. He gave it to me."

"I had a curious dream myself," I said. "But I'm not telling mine. Let me know how Roger gets on and if there is anything I can do."

She lowered her eyes and looked into mine. "You said you were not coming back."

"I said I wasn't sure. I may have to come back. I hope I won't. There is something very wrong in this house. And only part of it came out of a bottle."

She stared at me, frowning. "What does that mean?"

"I think you know what I'm talking about."

She thought it over carefully. Her fingers were still touching the pendant gently. She let out a slow patient sigh. "There's always another woman," she said quietly. "At some time or other. It's not necessarily fatal. We're talking at cross purposes, aren't we? We are not even talking about the same thing, perhaps?"

"Could be," I said. She was still standing on the steps, the third step from the bottom. She still had her fingers on the pendant. She still looked like a golden dream. "Especially if you have in mind that the other woman is Linda Loring."

She dropped her hand from the pendant and came down one more step of the stairs.

"Dr. Loring seems to agree with me," she said indifferently. "He must have some source of information."

"You said he had played that scene with half the males in the valley."

"Did I? Well — it was the conventional sort of thing to say at the time." She came down another step.

"I haven't shaved," I said.

That startled her. Then she laughed. "Oh, I wasn't expecting you to make love to me."

"Just what did you expect of me, Mrs. Wade – in the beginning, when you first persuaded me to go hunting? Why me – what have I got to offer?"

"You kept faith," she said quietly. "When it couldn't have been very easy."

"I'm touched. But I don't think that was the reason."

She came down the last step and then she was looking up at me. "Then what was the reason?"

"Or if it was – it was a damn poor reason. Just about the worst reason in the world."

She frowned a tiny frown. "Why?"

"Because what I did – this keeping faith – is something even a fool doesn't do twice."

"You know," she said lightly, "this is getting to be a very enigmatic conversation."

"You're a very enigmatic person, Mrs. Wade. So long and good luck and if you really care anything about Roger, you'd better find him the right kind of doctor – and quick."

She laughed again. "Oh, that was a mild attack last night. You ought to see him in a bad one. He'll be up and working by this afternoon."

"Like hell he will."

"But believe me he will. I know him so well."

I gave her the last shot right in the teeth and it sounded pretty nasty.

"You don't really want to save him, do you? You just want to look as if you are trying to save him."

"That," she said deliberately, "was a very beastly thing to say to me."

She stepped past me and walked through the dining room doors and then the big room was empty and I crossed to the front door and let myself out. It was a perfect summer morning in that bright secluded valley. It was too far from the city to get any smog and cut off by the low mountains from the dampness of the ocean. It was going to be hot later, but in a nice refined exclusive sort of way, nothing brutal like the heat of the desert, not sticky and rank like the heat of the city. Idle Valley was a perfect place to live. Perfect. Nice people with nice homes, nice cars, nice horses, nice dogs, possibly even nice children.

But all a man named Marlowe wanted from it was out. And fast.

31

I WENT HOME and showered and shaved and changed clothes and began to feel clean again. I cooked some breakfast, ate it, washed up, swept the kitchen and the service porch, filled a pipe and called the phone answering service. I shot a blank. Why go to the office? There would be nothing there but another dead moth and another layer of dust. In the safe would be my portrait of Madison. I could go down and play with that, and with the five crisp hundred-dollar bills that still smelled of coffee. I could do that, but I didn't want to. Something inside me had gone sour. None of it really belonged to me. What was it supposed to buy? How much loyalty can a dead man use? Phooey: I was looking at life through the mists of a hangover.

It was the kind of morning that seems to go on forever. I was flat and tired and dull and the passing minutes seemed to fall into a void, with a soft whirring sound, like spent rockets. Birds chirped in the shrubbery outside and the cars went up and down Laurel Canyon Boulevard endlessly. Usually I wouldn't even hear them. But I was brooding and irritable and mean and oversensitive. I decided to kill the hangover.

Ordinarily I was not a morning drinker. The Southern California climate is too soft for it. You don't metabolize fast enough. But I mixed a tall cold one this time and sat in an easy chair with my shirt open and pecked at a magazine, reading a crazy story about a guy that had two lives and two psychiatrists, one was human and one was some kind of insect in a hive. The guy kept going from one to the other and the whole thing was as crazy as a crumpet, but funny in an offbeat sort of way. I was handling the drink carefully, a sip at a time, watching myself.

It was about noon when the telephone rang and the voice said: "This is Linda Loring. I called your office and your phone service told me to try your home. I'd like to see you."

"Why?"

"I'd rather explain that in person. You go to your office from time to time, I suppose."

"Yeah. From time to time. Is there any money in it?"

"I hadn't thought of it that way. But I have no objection, if you want to be paid. I could be at your office in about an hour."

"Goody."

"What's the matter with you?" she asked sharply.

"Hangover. But I'm not paralyzed. I'll be there. Unless you'd rather come here."

"Your office would suit me better."

"I've got a nice quiet place here. Dead-end street, no near neighbors."

"The implication does not attract me – if I understand you."

"Nobody understands me, Mrs. Loring. I'm enigmatic. Okay, I'll struggle down to the coop."

"Thank you so much." She hung up.

I was slow getting down there because I stopped on the way for a sandwich. I aired out the office and switched on the buzzer and poked my head through the communicating door and she was there already, sitting in the same chair where Mendy Menendez had sat and looking through what could have been the same magazine. She had a tan gabardine suit on today and she looked pretty elegant. She put the magazine aside, gave me a serious look, and said:

"Your Boston fern needs watering. I think it needs repotting too. Too many air roots."

I held the door open for her. The hell with the Boston fern. When she was inside and I had let the door swing shut I held the customer's chair for her and she gave the office the usual once over. I got around to my side of the desk.

"Your establishment isn't exactly palatial," she said. "Don't you even have a secretary?"

"It's a sordid life, but I'm used to it."

"And I shouldn't think very lucrative," she said.

"Oh I don't know. Depends. Want to see a portrait of Madison?"

"A what?"

"A five-thousand-dollar bill. Retainer. I've got it in the safe." I got up and started over there. I spun the knob and opened it and unlocked a drawer inside, opened an envelope, and dropped it in front of her. She stared at it in something like amazement.

"Don't let the office fool you," I said. "I worked for an old boy one time that would cash in at about twenty millions. Even your old man would say hello to him. His office was no better than mine, except he was a bit deaf and had that soundproofing stuff on the ceiling. On the floor brown linoleum, no carpet."

She picked the portrait of Madison up and pulled it between her fingers and turned it over. She put it down again.

"You got this from Terry, didn't you?"

"Gosh, you know everything, don't you Mrs. Loring?"

She pushed the bill away from her, frowning. "He had one. He carried it on him ever since he and Sylvia were married the second time. He called it his mad money. It was not found on his body."

"There could be other reasons for that."

"I know. But how many people carry a five-thousand-dollar bill around with them? How many who could afford to give you that much money would give it to you in this form?"

It wasn't worth answering. I just nodded. She went on brusquely.

"And what were you supposed to do for it, Mr. Marlowe? Or would you tell me? On that last ride down to Tijuana he had plenty of time to talk. You made it very clear the other evening that you didn't believe his confession. Did he give you a list of his wife's lovers so that you might find a murderer among them?"

I didn't answer that either, but for different reasons.

"And would the name of Roger Wade appear on that list by any chance?" she asked harshly. "If Terry didn't kill his wife, the murderer would have to be some violent and irresponsible man, a lunatic or a savage drunk. Only that sort of man could, to use your own repulsive phrase, beat her face into a bloody sponge. Is that why you are making yourself so very useful to the Wades — a regular mother's helper who comes on call to nurse him when he is drunk, to find him when he is lost, to bring him home when he is helpless?"

"Let me set you right on a couple of points, Mrs. Loring. Terry may or may not have given me that beautiful piece of engraving. But he gave me no list and mentioned no names. There was nothing he asked me to do except what you seem to feel sure I did do, drive him to Tijuana. My getting involved with the Wades was the work of a New York publisher who is desperate to have Roger Wade finish his book, which involves keeping him fairly sober, which in turn involves finding out if there is any special trouble that makes him get drunk. If there is and it can be found out, then the next step would be an effort to remove it. I say effort, because the chances are you couldn't do it. But you could try."

"I could tell you in one simple sentence why he gets drunk," she said contemptuously. "That anemic blonde show piece he's married to."

"Oh I don't know," I said. "I wouldn't call her anemic."

"Really? How interesting." Her eyes glittered.

I picked up my portrait of Madison. "Don't chew too long on that one, Mrs. Loring. I am not sleeping with the lady. Sorry to disappoint you."

I went over to the safe and put my money away in the locked compartment. I shut the safe and spun the dial.

"On second thought," she said to my back, "I doubt very much that anyone is sleeping with her."

I went back and sat on the corner of the desk. "You're getting bitchy, Mrs. Loring. Why? Are you carrying a torch for our alcoholic friend?"

"I hate remarks like that," she said bitingly. "I hate them. I suppose that idiotic scene my husband made makes you think you have the right to insult me. No, I am not carrying a torch for Roger Wade. I never did – even when he was a sober man who behaved himself. Still less now that he is what he is."

I flopped into my chair, reached for a matchbox, and stared at her. She looked at her watch.

"You people with a lot of money are really something," I said. "You think anything you choose to say, however nasty, is perfectly all right. You can make sneering remarks about Wade and his wife to a man you hardly know, but if I hand you back a little change, that's an insult. Okay, let's play it low down. Any drunk will eventually turn up with a loose woman. Wade is a drunk, but you're not a loose woman. That's just a casual suggestion your high-bred husband drops to brighten up a cocktail party. He doesn't mean it, he's just saying it for laughs. So we rule you out, and look for a loose woman elsewhere. How far do we have to look, Mrs. Loring – to find one that would involve you enough to bring you down here trading sneers with me? It has to be somebody rather special, doesn't it – otherwise why should you care?"

She sat perfectly silent, just looking. A long half minute went by. The corners of her mouth were white and her hands were rigid on her gabardine bag that matched her suit.

"You haven't exactly wasted your time, have you?" she said at last. "How convenient that this publisher should have thought of employing you! So Terry named no names to you! Not a name. But it really didn't matter, did it, Mr. Marlowe? Your instinct was unerring. May I ask what you propose to do next?"

"Nothing."

"Why, what a waste of talent! How can you reconcile it with your obligation to your portrait of Madison? Surely there must be something you can do."

"Just between the two of us," I said, "you're getting pretty corny. So Wade knew your sister. Thanks for telling me, however indirectly. I already guessed it. So what? He's just one of what was most likely a fairly rich collection. Let's leave it there. And let's get around to why you wanted to see me. That kind of got lost in the shuffle didn't it?"

She stood up. She glanced at her watch once more. "I have a car downstairs. Could I prevail upon you to drive home with me and drink a cup of tea?"

"Go on," I said. "Let's have it."

"Do I sound so suspicious? I have a guest who would like to make your acquaintance."

"The old man?"

"I don't call him that," she said evenly.

I stood up and leaned across the desk. "Honey, you're awful cute sometimes. You really are. Is it all right if I carry a gun?"

"Surely you're not afraid of an old man." She wrinkled her lip at me.

"Why not? I'll bet you are – plenty."

She sighed. "Yes, I'm afraid I am. I always have been. He can be rather terrifying."

"Maybe I'd better take two guns," I said, then wished I hadn't.

32

IT WAS THE damnedest-looking house I ever saw. It was a square gray box three stories high, with a mansard roof, steeply sloped and broken by twenty or thirty double dormer windows with a lot of wedding cake decoration around them and between them. The entrance had double stone pillars on each side but the cream of the joint was an outside spiral stair-case with a stone railing, topped by a tower room from which there must have been a view of the whole length of the lake.

The motor yard was paved with stone. What the place really seemed to need was a half mile of poplar-lined drive-way and a deer park and a wild garden and a terrace on three levels and a few hundred roses outside the library window and a long green vista from every window ending in forest and silence and quiet emptiness. What it had was a wall of field-stone around a comfortable ten or fifteen acres, which is a fair hunk of real estate in our crowded little country. The drive-way was lined with a cypress hedge trimmed round. There were all sorts of ornamental trees in clumps here and there and they didn't look like California trees. Imported stuff. Whoever built that place was trying to drag the Atlantic seaboard over the Rockies. He was trying hard, but he hadn't made it.

Amos, the middle-aged colored chauffeur, stopped the Caddy gently in front of the pillared entrance, hopped out, and came around to hold the door open for Mrs. Loring. I got out first and helped him hold it. I helped her get out. She had hardly spoken to me since we got into the car in front of my building. She looked tired and nervous. Maybe this idiotic hunk of architecture depressed her. It would have depressed a laughing jackass and made it coo like a mourning dove.

"Who built this place?" I asked her. "And who was he mad at?"

She finally smiled. "Hadn't you seen it before?"

"Never been this far into the valley."

She walked me over to the other side of the driveway and pointed up. "The man who built it jumped out of that tower room and landed about where you are standing. He was a French count named La Tourelle and unlike most French counts he had a lot of money. His wife was Ramona Desborough, who was not exactly threadbare herself. In the silent-picture days she made thirty thousand a week. La Tourelle built this place for their home. It's supposed to be a miniature of the Château de Blois. You know that, of course."

"Like the back of my hand," I said. "I remember now. It was one of those Sunday paper stories once. She left him and he killed himself. There was some kind of queer will too, wasn't there?"

She nodded. "He left his ex-wife a few millions for carfare and tied the rest up in a trust. The estate was to be kept on just as it was. Nothing was to be changed, the dining table was to be laid in style every night, and nobody was to be allowed inside the grounds except the servants and the lawyers. The will was broken, of course. Eventually the estate was carved up to some extent and when I married Dr. Loring my father gave it to me for a wedding present. It must have cost him a fortune merely to make it fit to live in again. I loathe it. I always have."

"You don't have to stay here, do you?"

She shrugged in a tired sort of way. "Part of the time, at least. One of his daughters has to show him some sign of stability. Dr. Loring likes it here."

"He would. Any guy who could make the kind of scene he made at Wade's house ought to wear spats with his pajamas."

She arched her eyebrows. "Why, thank you for taking such an interest, Mr. Marlowe. But I think enough has been said on that subject. Shall we go in? My father doesn't like to be kept waiting."

We crossed the driveway again and went up the stone steps and half of the big double doors swung open noiselessly and an expensive and very snooty-looking character stood aside for us to enter. The hallway was bigger than all the floor space in the house I was living in. It had a tesselated floor and there seemed to be stained-glass windows at the back and if there had been any light coming through them I might have been able to see what else was there. From the hallway we went through some more double carved doors into a dim room that couldn't have been less than seventy feet long. A man was sitting there waiting, silent. He stared at us coldly.

"Am I late, Father?" Mrs. Loring asked hurriedly. "This is Mr. Philip Marlowe. Mr. Harlan Potter."

The man just looked at me and moved his chin down about half an inch.

"Ring for tea," he said. "Sit down, Mr. Marlowe."

I sat down and looked at him. He looked at me like an entomologist looking at a beetle. Nobody said anything. There was complete silence until the tea came. It was put down on a huge silver tray on a Chinese table. Linda sat at a table and poured.

"Two cups," Harlan Potter said. "You can have your tea in another room, Linda."

"Yes, Father. How do you like your tea, Mr. Marlowe?"

"Any way at all," I said. My voice seemed to echo off into the distance and get small and lonely.

She gave the old man a cup and then gave me a cup. Then she stood up silently and went out of the room. I watched her go. I took a sip of tea and got a cigarette out.

"Don't smoke, please. I am subject to asthma."

I put the cigarette back in the pack. I stared at him. I don't know how it feels to be worth a hundred million or so, but he didn't look as if he was having any fun. He was an enormous man, all of six feet five and built to scale. He wore a gray tweed suit with no padding. His shoulders didn't need any. He wore a white shirt and a dark tie and no display handkerchief. A spectacle case showed in the outside breast pocket. It was black, like his shoes. His hair was black too, no gray at all. It was brushed sideways across his skull in a MacArthur sweep. And I had a hunch there was nothing under it but bare skull. His eyebrows were thick and black. His voice seemed to come from a long way off. He drank his tea as if he hated it.

"It will save time, Mr. Marlowe, if I put my position before you. I believe you are interfering in my affairs. If I am correct, I propose to stop it."

"I don't know enough about your affairs to interfere in them, Mr. Potter."

"I disagree."

He drank some more tea and put the cup aside. He leaned back in the big chair he was sitting in and took me to pieces with his hard gray eyes.

"I know who you are, naturally. And how you make your living — if you make one — and how you became involved with Terry Lennox. It has been reported to me that you helped Terry get out of the country, that you have doubts about his guilt, and that you have since made contact with a man who was known to my dead daughter. For what purpose has not been explained to me. Explain it."

"If the man has a name," I said, "name it."

He smiled very slightly, but not as if he was falling for me. "Wade. Roger Wade. Some sort of writer, I believe. A writer, they tell me, of rather prurient books which I should not be interested to read. I further understand that this man is a dangerous alcoholic. That may have given you a strange notion."

"Maybe you had better let me have my own notions, Mr. Potter. They are not important, naturally, but they're all I have. First, I do not believe Terry killed his wife, because of the way it was done and because I don't think he was that kind of man. Second, I didn't make contact with Wade. I was asked to live in his house and do what I could to keep him sober while he finished a job of writing. Third, if he is a dangerous alcoholic, I haven't seen any sign of it. Fourth, my first contact was at the request of his New York publisher and I didn't at that time have any idea that Roger Wade even knew your daughter. Fifth, I refused this offer of employment and then Mrs. Wade asked me to find her husband who was away somewhere taking a cure. I found him and took him home."

"Very methodical," he said dryly.

"I'm not finished being methodical, Mr. Potter. Sixth, you or someone on your instructions sent a lawyer named Sewell Endicott to get me out of jail. He didn't say who sent him, but there wasn't anyone else in the picture. Seventh, when I got out of jail a hoodlum named Mendy Menendez pushed me around and warned me to keep my nose clean and gave me a song and dance about how Terry had saved his life and the life of a gambler at Las Vegas named Randy Starr. The story could be true for all I know. Menendez pretended to be sore that Terry hadn't asked him for help getting to Mexico and had asked a punk like me instead. He, Menendez, could have done it two ways from the jack by lifting one finger, and done it much better."

"Surely," Harlan Potter said with a bleak smile, "you are not under the impression that I number Mr. Menendez and Mr. Starr among my acquaintances."

"I wouldn't know, Mr. Potter. A man doesn't make your kind of money in any way I can understand. The next person to warn me off the courthouse lawn was your daughter, Mrs. Loring. We met by accident at a bar and we spoke because we were both drinking gimlets, Terry's favorite drink, but an uncommon one around here. I didn't know who she was until she told me. I told her a little of how I felt about Terry and she gave me the idea that I would have a short unhappy career if I got you mad. Are you mad, Mr. Potter?"

"When I am," he said coldly, "you will not have to ask me. You will be in no uncertainty about it."

"What I thought. I've been kind of expecting the goon squad to drop around, but they haven't shown so far. I haven't been bothered by the cops either. I could have been. I could have been given a rough time. I think all you wanted, Mr. Potter, was quiet. Just what have I done to disturb you?"

He grinned. It was a sour kind of grin, but it was a grin. He put his long yellow fingers together and crossed a leg over his knee and leaned back comfortably.

"A pretty good pitch, Mr. Marlowe, and I have let you make it. Now listen to me. You are exactly right in thinking all I want is quiet. It's quite possible that your connection with the Wades may be incidental, accidental, and coincidental. Let it remain so. I am a family man in an age when it means almost nothing. One of my daughters married a Bostonian prig and the other made a number of foolish marriages, the last being with a complaisant pauper who allowed her to live a worthless and immoral life until he suddenly and for no good reason lost his self-control and murdered her. You think that impossible to accept because of the brutality with which it was done. You are wrong. He shot her with a Mauser automatic, the very gun he took with him to Mexico. And after he shot her he did what he did in order to cover the bullet wound. I admit the brutality of this, but remember the man had been in a war, had been badly wounded, had suffered a great deal and seen others suffer. He may not have intended to kill her. There may have been some sort of scuffle, since the gun belonged to my daughter. It was a small but powerful gun, 7.65 m/m caliber, a model called P.P.K. The bullet went completely through her head and lodged in the wall behind a chintz curtain. It was not found immediately and the fact was not published at all. Now let us consider the situation." He broke off and stared at me. "Are you very badly in need of a cigarette?"

"Sorry, Mr. Potter. I took it out without thinking. Force of habit." I put the cigarette back for the second time.

"Terry had just killed his wife. He had ample motive from the rather limited police point of view. But he also had an excellent defense – that it was her gun in her possession and that he tried to take it away from her and failed and she shot herself with it. A good trial lawyer could have done a lot with that. He would probably have been acquitted. If he had called me up then, I would have helped him. But by making the murder a brutal affair to cover the traces of the bullet, he made it impossible. He had to run away and even that he did clumsily."

"He certainly did, Mr. Potter. But he called you up in Pasadena first, didn't he? He told me he did."

The big man nodded. "I told him to disappear and I would still see what I could do. I didn't want to know where he was. That was imperative. I could not hide a criminal."

"Sounds good, Mr. Potter."

"Do I detect a note of sarcasm? No matter. When I learned the details there was nothing to be done. I could not permit the sort of trial that kind of killing would result in. To be frank, I was very glad when I learned that he had shot himself in Mexico and left a confession."

"I can understand that, Mr. Potter."

He beetled his eyebrows at me. "Be careful, young man. I don't like irony. Can you understand now that I cannot tolerate any further investigation of any sort by any person? And why I have used all my influence to make what investigation there was as brief as possible and as little publicized as possible?"

"Sure – if you're convinced he killed her."

"Of course he killed her. With what intent is another matter. It is no longer important. I am not a public character and I do not intend to be. I have always gone to a great deal of trouble to avoid any kind of publicity. I have influence but I don't abuse it. The District Attorney of Los Angeles County is an ambitious man who has too much good sense to wreck his career for the notoriety of the moment. I see a glint in your eye, Marlowe. Get rid of it. We live in what is called a democracy, rule by the majority of the people. A fine ideal if it could be made to work. The people elect, but the party machines nominate, and the party machines to be effective must spend a great deal of money. Somebody has to give it to them, and that somebody, whether it be an individual, a financial group, a trade union or what have you, expects some consideration in return. What I and people of my kind expect is to be allowed to live our lives in decent privacy. I own newspapers, but I don't like them. I regard them as a constant menace to whatever privacy we have left. Their constant yelping about a free press means, with a few honorable exceptions, freedom to peddle scandal, crime, sex, sensationalism, hate, innuendo, and the political and financial uses of propaganda. A newspaper is a business out to make money through advertising revenue. That is predicated on its circulation and you know what the circulation depends on."

I got up and walked around my chair. He eyed me with cold attention. I sat down again. I needed a little luck. Hell, I needed it in carload lots.

"Okay, Mr. Potter, what goes from here?"

He wasn't listening. He was frowning at his own thoughts. "There's a peculiar thing about money," he went on. "In large quantities it tends to have a life of its own, even a conscience of its own. The power of money becomes very difficult to control. Man has always been a venal animal. The growth of populations, the huge costs of wars, the incessant pressure of confiscatory taxation – all these things make him more and more venal. The average man is tired and scared, and a tired, scared man can't afford ideals. He has to buy food for his family. In our time we have seen a shocking decline in both public and private morals. You can't expect quality from people whose lives are a subjection to a lack of quality. You can't have quality with mass production. You don't want it because it lasts too long. So you substitute styling, which is a commercial swindle intended to produce artificial obsolescence. Mass production couldn't sell its goods next year unless it made what it sold this year look unfashionable a year from now. We have the whitest kitchens and the most shining bathrooms in the world. But in the lovely white kitchen the average American housewife can't produce a meal fit to eat, and the lovely shining bathroom is mostly a receptacle for deodorants, laxatives, sleeping pills, and the products of that confidence racket called the cosmetic industry. We make the finest packages in the world, Mr. Marlowe. The stuff inside is mostly junk."

He took out a large white handkerchief and touched his temples with it. I was sitting there with my mouth open, wondering what made the guy tick. He hated everything.

"It's a little too warm for me in these parts," he said. "I'm used to a cooler climate. I'm beginning to sound like an editorial that has forgotten the point it wanted to make."

"I got your point all right, Mr. Potter. You don't like the way the world is going so you use what power you have to close off a private corner to live in as near as possible to the way you remember people lived fifty years ago before the age of mass production. You've got a hundred million dollars and all it has bought you is a pain in the neck."

He pulled the handkerchief taut by two opposite corners, then crumpled it into a ball and stuffed it in a pocket.

"And then?" he asked shortly.

"That's all there is, there isn't any more. You don't care who murdered your daughter, Mr. Potter. You wrote her off as a bad job long ago. Even if Terry Lennox didn't kill her, and the real murderer is still walking around free, you don't care. You wouldn't want him caught, because that would revive the scandal and there would have to be a trial and his defense would blow your privacy as high as the Empire State Building. Unless, of course, he was obliging enough to commit suicide, before there was any trial. Preferably in Tahiti or Guatemala or the middle of the Sahara Desert. Anywhere where the County would hate the expense of sending a man to verify what had happened."

He smiled suddenly, a big rugged smile with a reasonable amount of friendliness in it.

"What do you want from me, Marlowe?"

"If you mean how much money, nothing. I didn't ask myself here. I was brought. I told the truth about how I met Roger Wade. But he did know your daughter and he does have a record of violence, although I haven't seen any of it. Last night the guy tried to shoot himself. He's a haunted man. He has a massive guilt complex. If I happened to be looking for a good suspect, he might do. I realize he's only one of many, but he happens to be the only one I've met."

He stood up and standing up he was really big. Tough too. He came over and stood in front of me.

"A telephone call, Mr. Marlowe, would deprive you of your license. Don't fence with me. I won't put up with it."

"Two telephone calls and I'd wake up kissing the gutter – with the back of my head missing."

He laughed harshly. "I don't operate that way. I suppose in your quaint line of business it is natural for you to think so. I've given you too much of my time. I'll ring for the butler to show you out."

"Not necessary," I said, and stood up myself. "I came here and got told. Thanks for the time."

He held his hand out. "Thank you for coming. I think you're a pretty honest sort of fellow. Don't be a hero, young man. There's no percentage in it."

I shook hands with him. He had a grip like a pipe wrench. He smiled at me benignantly now. He was Mr. Big, the winner, everything under control.

"One of these days I might be able to throw some business your way," he said. "And don't go away thinking that I buy politicians or law enforcement officers. I don't have to. Goodbye, Mr. Marlowe. And thank you again for coming."

He stood there and watched me out of the room. I had my hand on the front door when Linda Loring popped out of a shadow somewhere.

"Well?" she asked me quietly. "How did you get on with Father?"

"Fine. He explained civilization to me. I mean how it looks to him. He's going to let it go on for a little while longer. But it better be careful and not interfere with his private life. If it does, he's apt to make a phone call to God and cancel the order."

"You're hopeless," she said.

"Me? I'm hopeless? Lady, take a look at your old man. Compared with him I'm a blue-eyed baby with a brand new rattle."

I went on out and Amos had the Caddy there waiting. He drove me back to Hollywood. I offered him a buck but he wouldn't take it. I offered to buy him the poems of T. S. Eliot. He said he already had them.

33

A WEEK WENT by and I heard nothing from the Wades. The weather was hot and sticky and the acid sting of the smog had crept as far west as Beverly Hills. From the top of Mulholland Drive you could see it leveled out all over the city like a ground mist. When you were in it you could taste it and smell it and it made your eyes smart. Everybody was griping about it. In Pasadena, where the stuffy millionaires holed up after Beverly Hills was spoiled for them by the movie crowd, the city fathers screamed with rage. Everything was the fault of the smog. If the canary wouldn't sing, if the milkman was late, if the Pekinese had fleas, if an old coot in a starched collar had a heart attack on the way to church, that was the smog. Where I lived it was usually clear in the early morning and nearly always at night. Once in a while a whole day would be clear, nobody quite knew why.

It was on a day like that – it happened to be a Thursday – that Roger Wade called me up. "How are you? This is Wade." He sounded fine.

"Fine, and you?"

"Sober, I'm afraid. Scratching a hard buck. We ought to have a talk. And I think I owe you some dough."

"Nope."

"Well, how about lunch today? Could you make it here somewhere around one?"

"I guess so. How's Candy?"

"Candy?" He sounded puzzled. He must have blacked out plenty that night. "Oh, he helped you put me to bed that night."

"Yeah. He's a helpful little guy – in spots. And Mrs. Wade?"

"She's fine too. She's in town shopping today."

We hung up and I sat and rocked in my swivel chair. I ought to have asked him how the book was going. Maybe you always ought to ask a writer how the book is going. And then again maybe he gets damned tired of that question.

I had another call in a little while, a strange voice.

"This is Roy Ashterfelt. George Peters told me to call you up, Marlowe."

"Oh yes, thanks. You're the fellow that knew Terry Lennox in New York. Called himself Marston then."

"That's right. He was sure on the sauce. But it's the same guy all right. You couldn't very well mistake him. Out here I saw him in Chasen's one night with his wife. I was with a client. The client knew them. Can't tell you the client's name, I'm afraid."

"I understand. It's not very important now, I guess. What was his first name?"

"Wait a minute while I bite my thumb. Oh yeah, Paul. Paul Marston. And there was one thing more, if it interests you. He was wearing a British Army service badge. Their version of the ruptured duck."

"I see. What happened to him?"

"I don't know. I came west. Next time I saw him he was here too – married to Harlan Potter's somewhat wild daughter. But you know all that."

"They're both dead now. But thanks for telling me."

"Not at all. Glad to help. Does it mean anything to you?"

"Not a thing," I said, and I was a liar. "I never asked him about himself. He told me once he had been brought up in an orphanage. Isn't it just possible you made a mistake?"

"With that white hair and that scarred face, brother? Not a chance. I won't say I never forget a face, but not that one."

"Did he see you?"

"If he did, he didn't let on. Hardly expect him to in the circumstances. Anyhow he might not have remembered me. Like I said, he was always pretty well lit back in New York."

I thanked him some more and he said it was a pleasure and we hung up.

I thought about it for a while. The noise of the traffic outside the building on the boulevard made an unmusical obbligato to my thinking. It was too loud. In summer in hot weather everything is too loud. I got up and shut the lower part of the window and called Detective-Sergeant Green at Homicide. He was obliging enough to be in.

"Look," I said, after the preliminaries, "I heard something about Terry Lennox that puzzles me. A fellow I know used to know him in New York under another name. You check his war record?"

"You guys never learn," Green said harshly. "You just never learn to stay on your own side of the street. That matter is closed, locked up, weighted with lead and dropped in the ocean. Get it?"

"I spent part of an afternoon with Harlan Potter last week at his daughter's house in Idle Valley. Want to check?"

"Doing what?" he asked sourly. "Supposing I believe you."

"Talking things over. I was invited. He likes me. Incidentally, he told me the girl was shot with a Mauser P.P.K. 7.65 m/m. That news to you?"

"Go on."

"Her own gun, chum. Makes a little difference, maybe. But don't get me wrong. I'm not looking into any dark corners. This is a personal matter. Where did he get that wound?"

Green was silent. I heard a door close in the background. Then he said quietly, "Probably in a knife fight south of the border."

"Aw hell, Green, you had his prints. You sent them to Washington like always. You got a report back — like always. All I asked was something about his service record."

"Who said he had one?"

"Well, Mendy Menendez for one. Seems Lennox saved his life one time and that's how he got the wound. He was captured by the Germans and they gave him the face he had."

"Menendez, huh? You believe that son of a bitch? You got a hole in your own head. Lennox didn't have any war record. Didn't have any record of any kind under any name. You satisfied?"

"If you say so," I said. "But I don't see why Menendez would bother to come up here and tell me a yarn and warn me to keep my nose clean on account of Lennox was a pal of him and Randy Starr in Vegas and they didn't want anybody fooling around. After all Lennox was already dead."

"Who knows what a hoodlum figures?" Green asked bitterly. "Or why? Maybe Lennox was in a racket with them before he married all that money, and got respectable. He was a floor manager at Starr's place in Vegas for a while. That's where he met the girl. A smile and a bow and a dinner jacket. Keep the customers happy and keep an eye on the house players. I guess he had class for the job."

"He had charm," I said. "They don't use it in police business. Much obliged, Sergeant. How is Captain Gregorius these days?"

"Retirement leave. Don't you read the papers?"

"Not the crime news, Sergeant. Too sordid."

I started to say goodbye but he chopped me off. "What did Mr. Money want with you?"

"We just had a cup of tea together. A social call. He said he might put some business my way. He also hinted – just hinted, not in so many words – that any cop that looked cross-eyed at me would be facing a grimy future."

"He don't run the police department," Green said.

"He admits it. Doesn't even buy commissioners or D.A.'s, he said. They just kind of curl up in his lap when he's having a doze."

"Go to hell," Green said, and hung up in my ear.

A difficult thing, being a cop. You never know whose stomach it's safe to jump up and down on.

34

THE STRETCH OF broken-paved road from the highway to the curve of the hill was dancing in the noon heat and the scrub that dotted the parched land on both sides of it was flour-white with granite dust by this time. The weedy smell was almost nauseating. A thin hot acrid breeze was blowing. I had my coat off and my sleeves rolled up, but the door was too hot to rest an arm on. A tethered horse dozed wearily under a clump of live oaks. A brown Mexican sat on the ground and ate something out of a newspaper. A tumbleweed rolled lazily across the road and came to rest against a piece of granite outcrop, and a lizard that had been there an instant before disappeared without seeming to move at all.

Then I was around the hill on the blacktop and in another country. In five minutes I turned into the driveway of the Wades' house, parked and walked across the flagstones and rang the bell. Wade answered the door himself, in a brown and white checked shirt with short sleeves, pale blue denim slacks, and house slippers. He looked tanned and he looked good. There was an inkstain on his hand and a smear of cigarette ash on one side of his nose.

He led the way into his study and parked himself behind his desk. On it there was a thick pile of yellow typescript. I put my coat on a chair and sat on the couch.

"Thanks for coming, Marlowe. Drink?"

I got that look on my face you get when a drunk asks you to have a drink. I could feel it. He grinned.

"I'll have a Coke," he said.

"You pick up fast," I said. "I don't think I want a drink right now. I'll take a Coke with you."

He pressed something with his foot and after a while Candy came. He looked surly. He had a blue shirt on and an orange scarf and no white coat. Two-tone black and white shoes, elegant high-waisted gabardine pants.

Wade ordered the Cokes. Candy gave me a hard stare and went away.

"Book?" I said, pointing to the stack of paper.

"Yeah. Stinks."

"I don't believe it. How far along?"

"About two thirds of the way – for what it's worth. Which is damn little. You know how a writer can tell when he's washed up?"

"Don't know anything about writers." I filled my pipe.

"When he starts reading his old stuff for inspiration. That's absolute. I've got five hundred pages of typescript here, well over a hundred thousand words. My books run long. The public likes long books. The damn fool public thinks if there's a lot of pages there must be a lot of gold. I don't dare read it over. And I can't remember half of what's in it. I'm just plain scared to look at my own work."

"You look good yourself," I said. "From the other night I wouldn't have believed it. You've got more guts than you think you have."

"What I need right now is more than guts. Something you don't get by wishing for it. A belief in yourself. I'm a spoiled writer who doesn't believe any more. I have a beautiful home, a beautiful wife, and a beautiful sales record. But all I really want is to get drunk and forget."

He leaned his chin in his cupped hands and stared across the desk.

"Eileen said I tried to shoot myself. Was it that bad?"

"You don't remember?"

He shook his head. "Not a damn thing except that I fell down and cut my head. And after a while I was in bed. And you were there. Did Eileen call you?"

"Yeah. Didn't she say?"

"She hasn't been talking to me very much this week. I guess she's had it. Up to here." He put the edge of one hand against his neck just under his chin. "That show Loring put on here didn't help any."

"Mrs. Wade said it meant nothing."

"Well, she would, wouldn't she? It happened to be the truth, but I don't suppose she believed it when she said it. The guy is just abnormally jealous. You have a drink or two with his wife in the corner and laugh a little and kiss her goodbye and right off he assumes you are sleeping with her. One reason being that he isn't."

"What I like about Idle Valley," I said, "is that everybody is living just a comfortable normal life."

He frowned and then the door opened and Candy came in with two Cokes and glasses and poured the Cokes. He set one in front of me without looking at me.

"Lunch in half an hour," Wade said, "and where's the white coat?"

"This is my day off," Candy said, deadpan. "I ain't the cook, boss."

"Cold cuts or sandwiches and beer will do," Wade said. "The cook's off today, Candy. I've got a friend to lunch."

690

"You think he is your friend?" Candy sneered. "Better ask your wife."

Wade leaned back in his chair and smiled at him. "Watch your lip, little man. You've got it soft here. I don't often ask a favor of you, do I?"

Candy looked down at the floor. After a moment he looked up and grinned. "Okay, boss. I put the white coat on. I get the lunch, I guess."

He turned softly and went out. Wade watched the door close. Then he shrugged and looked at me.

"We used to call them servants. Now we call them domestic help. I wonder how long it will be before we have to give them breakfast in bed. I'm paying the guy too much money. He's spoiled."

"Wages – or something on the side?"

"Such as what?" he asked sharply.

I got up and handed him some folded yellow sheets. "You'd better read it. Evidently you don't remember asking me to tear it up. It was in your typewriter, under the cover."

He unfolded the yellow pages and leaned back to read them. The glass of Coke fizzed unnoticed on the desk in front of him. He read slowly, frowning. When he came to the end he refolded the sheets and ran a finger along the edge.

"Did Eileen see this?" he asked carefully.

"I wouldn't know. She might have."

"Pretty wild, isn't it?"

"I liked it. Especially the part about a good man dying for you."

He opened the paper again and tore it into long strips viciously and dumped the strips into his wastebasket.

"I suppose a drunk will write or say or do anything," he said slowly. "It's meaningless to me. Candy's not blackmailing me. He likes me."

"Maybe you'd better get drunk again. You might remember what you meant. You might remember a lot of things.

We've been through this before — that night when the gun went off. I suppose the Seconal blanked you out too. You sounded sober enough. But now you pretend not to remember writing that stuff I just gave you. No wonder you can't write your book, Wade. It's a wonder you can stay alive."

He reached sideways and opened a drawer of his desk. His hand fumbled in it and came out with a three-decker check book. He opened it and reached for a pen.

"I owe you a thousand dollars," he said quietly. He wrote in the book. Then on the counterfoil. He tore the check out, came around the desk with it, and dropped it in front of me. "Is that all right?"

I leaned back and looked up at him and didn't touch the check and didn't answer him. His face was tight and drawn. His eyes were deep and empty.

"I suppose you think I killed her and let Lennox take the rap," he said slowly. "She was a tramp all right. But you don't beat a woman's head in just because she's a tramp. Candy knows I went there sometimes. The funny part of it is I don't think he would tell. I could be wrong, but I don't think so."

"Wouldn't matter if he did," I said. "Harlan Potter's friends wouldn't listen to him. Also, she wasn't killed with that bronze thing. She was shot through the head with her own gun."

"She maybe had a gun," he said almost dreamily. "But I didn't know she had been shot. It wasn't published."

"Didn't know or didn't remember?" I asked him. "No, it wasn't published."

"What are you trying to do to me, Marlowe?" His voice was still creamy, almost gentle. "What do you want me to do? Tell my wife? Tell the police? What good would it do?"

"You said a good man died for you."

"All I meant was that if there had been any real investigation I might have been identified as one — but only one — of the possible suspects. It would have finished me in several ways."

"I didn't come here to accuse you of a murder, Wade. What's eating you is that you're not sure yourself. You have a record of violence to your wife. You black out when you're drunk. It's no argument to say you don't beat a woman's head in just because she's a tramp. That is exactly what somebody did do. And the guy who got credit for the job seemed to me a lot less likely than you."

He walked to the open french windows and stood looking out at the shimmer of heat over the lake. He didn't answer me. He hadn't moved or spoken a couple of minutes later when there was a light knock at the door and Candy came in wheeling a tea wagon, with a crisp white cloth, silver-covered dishes, a pot of coffee, and two bottles of beer.

"Open the beer, boss?" he asked Wade's back.

"Bring me a bottle of whiskey." Wade didn't turn around.

"Sorry, boss. No whiskey."

Wade spun around and yelled at him, but Candy didn't budge. He looked down at the check lying on the cocktail table and his head twisted as he read it. Then he looked up at me and hissed something between his teeth. Then he looked at Wade.

"I go now. This my day off."

He turned and went. Wade laughed.

"So I get it myself," he said sharply, and went.

I lifted one of the covers and saw some neatly trimmed three cornered sandwiches. I took one and poured some beer and ate the sandwich standing up. Wade came back with a bottle and a glass. He sat down on the couch and poured a stiff jolt and sucked it down. There was the sound of a car going away from the house, probably Candy leaving by the service driveway. I took another sandwich.

"Sit down and make yourself comfortable," Wade said. "We have all afternoon to kill." He had a glow on already. His voice was vibrant and cheerful. "You don't like me, do you, Marlowe?"

"That question has already been asked and answered."

"Know something? You're a pretty ruthless son of a bitch. You'd do anything to find what you want. You'd even make love to my wife while I was helpless drunk in the next room."

"You believe everything that knife thrower tells you?"

He poured some more whiskey into his glass and held it up against the light. "Not everything, no. A pretty color whiskey is, isn't it? To drown in a golden flood – that's not so bad. 'To cease upon the midnight with no pain.' How does that go on? Oh, sorry, you wouldn't know. Too literary. You're some kind of a dick, aren't you? Mind telling me why you're here?"

He drank some more whiskey and grinned at me. Then he spotted the check lying on the table. He reached for it and read it over his glass.

"Seems to be made out to somebody named Marlowe. I wonder why, what for. Seems I signed it. Foolish of me. I'm a gullible chap."

"Stop acting," I said roughly. "Where's your wife?"

He looked up politely. "My wife will be home in due course. No doubt by that time I shall be passed out and she can entertain you at her leisure. The house will be yours."

"Where's the gun?" I asked suddenly.

He looked blank. I told him I had put it in his desk. "Not there now, I'm sure," he said. "You may search if it pleases you. Just don't steal any rubber bands."

I went to the desk and frisked it. No gun. That was something. Probably Eileen had hidden it.

"Look, Wade, I asked you where your wife was. I think she ought to come home. Not for my benefit, friend, for yours. Somebody has to look out for you, and I'll be goddamned if it's going to be me."

He stared vaguely. He was still holding the check. He put his glass down and tore the check across, then again and again, and let the pieces fall to the floor.

"Evidently the amount was too small," he said. "Your ser-vices come very high. Even a thousand dollars *and* my wife fail to satisfy you. Too bad, but I can't go any higher. Except on this." He patted the bottle.

"I'm leaving," I said.

"But why? You wanted me to remember. Well – here in the bottle is my memory. Stick around, pal. When I get lit enough I'll tell you about all the women I have murdered."

"All right, Wade. I'll stick around for a while. But not in here. If you need me, just smash a chair against the wall."

I went out and left the door open. I walked across the big living room and out to the patio and pulled one of the chaises into the shadow of the overhang and stretched out on it. Across the lake there was a blue haze against the hills. The ocean breeze had begun to filter through the low mountains to the west. It wiped the air clean and it wiped away just enough of the heat. Idle Valley was having a perfect summer. Somebody had planned it that way. Paradise Incorporated, and also Highly Restricted. Only the nicest people. Absolutely no Central Europeans. Just the cream, the top drawer crowd, the lovely, lovely people. Like the Lorings and the Wades. Pure gold.

35

I LAY THERE for half an hour trying to make up my mind what to do. Part of me wanted to let him get good and drunk and see if anything came out. I didn't think anything much would happen to him in his own study in his own house. He might fall down again but it would be a long time. The guy had capacity. And somehow a drunk never hurts himself very badly. He might get back his mood of guilt. More likely, this time he would just go to sleep.

The other part of me wanted to get out and stay out, but this was the part I never listened to. Because if I ever had

I would have stayed in the town where I was born and worked in the hardware store and married the boss's daughter and had five kids and read them the funny paper on Sunday morning and smacked their heads when they got out of line and squabbled with the wife about how much spending money they were to get and what programs they could have on the radio or TV set. I might even have got rich – small-town rich, an eight-room house, two cars in the garage, chicken every Sunday and the *Reader's Digest* on the living room table, the wife with a cast-iron permanent and me with a brain like a sack of Portland cement. You take it, friend. I'll take the big sordid dirty crooked city.

I got up and went back to the study. He was just sitting there staring at nothing, the Scotch bottle more than half empty, a loose frown on his face and a dull glitter in his eyes. He looked at me like a horse looking over a fence.

"What d'you want?"

"Nothing. You all right?"

"Don't bother me. I have a little man on my shoulder telling me stories."

I got another sandwich off the tea wagon and another glass of beer. I munched the sandwich and drank the beer, leaning against his desk.

"Know something?" he asked suddenly, and his voice suddenly seemed much more clear. "I had a male secretary once. Used to dictate to him. Let him go. He bothered me sitting there waiting for me to create. Mistake. Ought to have kept him. Word would have got around I was a homo. The clever boys that write book reviews because they can't write anything else would have caught on and started giving me the buildup. Have to take care of their own, you know. They're all queers, every damn one of them. The queer is the artistic arbiter of our age, chum. The pervert is the top guy now."

"That so? Always been around, hasn't he?"

He wasn't looking at me. He was just talking. But he heard what I said.

"Sure, thousands of years. And especially in all the great ages of art. Athens, Rome, the Renaissance, the Elizabethan Age, the Romantic Movement in France – loaded with them. Queers all over the place. Ever read *The Golden Bough*? No, too long for you. Shorter version though. Ought to read it. Proves our sexual habits are pure conventions like – wearing a black tie with a dinner jacket. Me. I'm a sex writer, but with frills and straight."

He looked up at me and sneered. "You know something? I'm a liar. My heroes are eight feet tall and my heroines have calluses on their bottoms from lying in bed with their knees up. Lace and ruffles, swords and coaches, elegance and leisure, duels and gallant death. All lies. They used perfume instead of soap, their teeth rotted because they never cleaned them, their fingernails smelled of stale gravy. The nobility of France urinated against the walls in the marble corridors of Versailles, and when you finally got several sets of underclothes off the lovely marquise the first thing you noticed was that she needed a bath. I ought to write it that way."

"Why don't you?"

He chuckled. "Sure, and live in a five-room house in Compton – if I was that lucky." He reached down and patted the whiskey bottle. "You're lonely, pal. You need company."

He got up and walked fairly steadily out of the room. I waited, thinking about nothing. A speedboat came racketing down the lake. When it came in sight I could see that it was high out of the water on its step and towing a surfboard with a husky sunburned lad on it. I went over to the french windows and watched it make a sweeping turn. Too fast, the speedboat almost turned over. The surfboard rider danced on one foot trying to hold his balance, then went shooting off into the water. The speedboat drifted to a stop and the man in the water came up to it in a lazy crawl, then went

697

back along the tow rope and rolled himself on to the surf-board.

Wade came back with another bottle of whiskey. The speedboat picked up and went off into the distance. Wade put his fresh bottle down beside the other. He sat down and brooded.

"Christ, you're not going to drink all that, are you?"

He squinted his eyes at me. "Take off, buster. Go on home and mop the kitchen floor or something. You're in my light." His voice was thick again. He had taken a couple in the kitchen, as usual.

"If you want me, holler."

"I couldn't get low enough to want you."

"Yeah, thanks. I'll be around until Mrs. Wade comes home. Ever hear of anybody named Paul Marston?"

His head came up slowly. His eyes focused, but with effort. I could see him fighting for control. He won the fight for the moment. His face became expressionless.

"Never did," he said carefully, speaking very slowly. "Who's he?"

The next time I looked in on him he was asleep, with his mouth open, his hair damp with sweat, and reeking of Scotch. His lips were pulled back from his teeth in a loose grimace and the furred surface of his tongue looked dry.

One of the whiskey bottles was empty. A glass on the table had about two inches in it and the other bottle was about three quarters full. I put the empty on the tea wagon and rolled it out of the room, then went back to close the french windows and turn the slats of the blinds. The speedboat might come back and wake him. I shut the study door.

I wheeled the tea wagon out to the kitchen, which was blue and white and large and airy and empty. I was still hungry. I ate another sandwich and drank what was left of the beer, then poured a cup of coffee and drank that. The beer was flat but the coffee was still hot. Then I went back to the patio. It was quite a long time before the speedboat came tearing down the lake again. It was almost four o'clock when I heard its distant roar swell into an ear-splitting howl of noise. There ought to be a law. Probably was and the guy in the speedboat didn't give a damn. He enjoyed making a nuisance of himself, like other people I was meeting. I walked down to the edge of the lake.

He made it this time. The driver slowed just enough on the turn and the brown lad on the surfboard leaned far out against the centrifugal pull. The surfboard was almost out of the water, but one edge stayed in and then the speedboat straightened out and the surfboard still had a rider and they went back the way they had come and that was that. The waves stirred up by the boat came charging in towards the shore of the lake at my feet. They slapped hard against the piles of the short landing and jumped the tied boat up and down. They were still slapping it around when I turned back to the house.

As I reached the patio I heard a bell chiming from the direction of the kitchen. When it sounded again I decided that only the front door would have chimes. I crossed to it and opened it.

Eileen Wade was standing there looking away from the house. As she turned she said: "I'm sorry, I forgot my key." Then she saw me. "Oh — I thought it was Roger or Candy."

"Candy isn't here. It's Thursday."

She came in and I shut the door. She put a bag down on the table between the two davenports. She looked cool and also distant. She pulled off a pair of white pigskin gloves.

"Is anything wrong?"

"Well, there's a little drinking being done. Not bad. He's asleep on the couch in his study."

"He called you?"

"Yes, but not for that. He asked me to lunch. I'm afraid he didn't have any himself."

"Oh." She sat down slowly on a davenport. "You know, I completely forgot it was Thursday. The cook's away too. How stupid."

"Candy got the lunch before he left. I guess I'll blow now. I hope my car wasn't in your way."

She smiled. "No. There was plenty of room. Won't you have some tea? I'm going to have some."

"All right." I didn't know why I said that. I didn't want any tea. I just said it.

She slipped off a linen jacket. She hadn't worn a hat. "I'll just look in and see if Roger is all right."

I watched her cross to the study door and open it. She stood there a moment and closed the door and came back.

"He's still asleep. Very soundly. I have to go upstairs for a moment. I'll be right down."

I watched her pick up her jacket and gloves and bag and go up the stairs and into her room. The door closed. I crossed to the study with the idea of removing the bottle of hooch. If he was still asleep, he wouldn't need it.

36

THE SHUTTING OF the french windows had made the room stuffy and the turning of the venetian blinds had made it dim. There was an acrid smell on the air and there was too heavy a silence. It was not more than sixteen feet from the door to the couch and I didn't need more than half of that to know a dead man lay on that couch.

He was on his side with his face to the back of the couch, one arm crooked under him and the forearm of the other lying almost across his eyes. Between his chest and the back of the couch there was a pool of blood and in that pool lay the Webley Hammerless. The side of his face was a smeared mask.

I bent over him, peering at the edge of the wide open eye, the bare and gaudy arm, at the inner curve of which I could see the puffed and blackened hole in his head from which the blood oozed still.

I left him like that. His wrist was warm but there was no doubt he was quite dead. I looked around for some kind of note or scribble. There was nothing but the pile of script on the desk. They don't always leave notes. The typewriter was uncovered on its stand. There was nothing in that. Otherwise everything looked natural enough. Suicides prepare themselves in all sorts of ways, some with liquor, some with elaborate champagne dinners. Some in evening clothes, some in no clothes. People have killed themselves on the tops of walls, in ditches, in bathrooms, in the water, over the water, on the water. They have hanged themselves in bars and gassed themselves in garages. This one looked simple. I hadn't heard the shot but it must have gone off when I was down by the lake watching the surfboard rider make his turn. There was plenty of noise. Why that should have mattered to Roger Wade I didn't know. Perhaps it hadn't. The final impulse had coincided with the run of the speedboat. I didn't like it, but nobody cared what I liked.

The torn pieces of the check were still on the floor but I left them. The torn strips of that stuff he had written that other night were in the wastebasket. These I did not leave. I picked them out and made sure I had them all and stuffed them into my pocket. The basket was almost empty, which made it easy. No use wondering where the gun had been. There were too many places to hide it in. It could have been in a chair or in the couch, under one of the cushions. It could have been on the floor, behind the books, anywhere.

I went out and shut the door. I listened. From the kitchen, sounds. I went out there. Eileen had a blue apron on and the kettle was just beginning to whistle. She turned the flame down and gave me a brief impersonal glance.

"How do you like your tea, Mr. Marlowe?"

"Just out of the pot as it comes."

I leaned against the wall and got a cigarette out just to have something to do with my fingers. I pinched and squeezed it and broke it in half and threw one half on the floor. Her eyes followed it down. I bent and picked it up. I squeezed the two halves together into a little ball.

She made the tea. "I always take cream and sugar," she said over her shoulder. "Strange, when I drink my coffee black. I learned tea drinking in England. They were using saccharin instead of sugar. When the war came they had no cream, of course."

"You lived in England?"

"I worked there. I stayed all through the Blitz. I met a man – but I told you about that."

"Where did you meet Roger?"

"In New York."

"Married there?"

She swung around, frowning. "No, we were not married in New York. Why?"

"Just talking while the tea draws."

She looked out of the window over the sink. She could see down to the lake from there. She leaned against the edge of the drainboard and her fingers fiddled with a folded tea towel.

"It has to be stopped," she said, "and I don't know how. Perhaps he'll have to be committed to an institution. Somehow I can't quite see myself doing that. I'd have to sign something, wouldn't I?"

She turned around when she asked that.

"He could do it himself," I said. "That is, he could have up to now."

The tea timer rang its bell. She turned back to the sink and poured the tea from one pot into another. Then she put the fresh pot on the tray she had already fixed up with cups. I went over and got the tray and carried it to the table between the two davenports in the living room. She sat down opposite me and poured two cups. I reached for mine and set it down in front of me for it to cool. I watched her fix hers with two lumps of sugar and the cream. She tasted it.

"What did you mean by that last remark?" she asked suddenly. "That he could have up to now – committed himself to some institution, you meant, didn't you?"

"I guess it was a wild pitch. Did you hide the gun I told you about? You know, the morning after he made that play upstairs."

"Hide it?" she repeated frowning. "No. I never do anything like that. I don't believe in it. Why are you asking?"

"And you forgot your house keys today?"

"I told you I did."

"But not the garage key. Usually in this kind of house the outside keys are mastered."

"I don't need a key for the garage," she said sharply. "It opens by a switch. There's a relay switch inside the front door you push up as you go out. Then another switch beside the garage operates that door. Often we leave the garage open. Or Candy goes out and closes it."

"I see."

"You are making some rather strange remarks," she said with acid in her voice. "You did the other morning."

"I've had some rather strange experiences in this house. Guns going off in the night, drunks lying out on the front lawn and doctors coming that won't do anything. Lovely women wrapping their arms around me and talking as if they thought I was someone else, Mexican houseboys throwing knives. It's a pity about that gun. But you don't really love your husband, do you? I guess I said that before too."

She stood up slowly. She was as calm as a custard, but her violet eyes didn't seem quite the same color, nor of quite the same softness. Then her mouth began to tremble.

"Is – is something wrong in there?" she asked very slowly, and looked towards the study.

I barely had time to nod before she was running. She was at the door in a flash. She threw it open and darted in. If I expected a wild scream I was fooled. I didn't hear anything.

I felt lousy. I ought to have kept her out and eased into that corny routine about bad news, prepare yourself, won't you sit down, I'm afraid something rather serious has happened. Blah, blah, blah. And when you have worked your way through it you haven't saved anybody a thing. Often enough you have made it worse.

I got up and followed her into the study. She was kneeling beside the couch with his head pulled against her breast, smearing herself with his blood. She wasn't making a sound of any kind. Her eyes were shut. She was rocking back and forth on her knees as far as she could, holding him tight.

I went back and found a telephone and a book. I called the sheriff's substation that seemed to be nearest. Didn't matter, they'd relay it by radio in any case. Then I went out to the kitchen and turned the water on and fed the strips of yellow paper from my pocket down the electric garbage grinder. I dumped the tea leaves from the other pot after it. In a matter of seconds the stuff was gone. I shut off the water and switched off the motor. I went back to the living room and opened the front door and stepped outside.

There must have been a deputy cruising close by because he was there in about six minutes. When I took him into the study she was still kneeling by the couch. He went over to her at once.

"I'm sorry, ma'am. I understand how you must feel, but you shouldn't be touching anything."

She turned her head, then scrambled to her feet. "It's my husband. He's been shot."

He took his cap off and put it on the desk. He reached for the telephone.

"His name is Roger Wade," she said in a high brittle voice. "He's the famous novelist."

"I know who he is, ma'am," the deputy said, and dialed.

She looked down at the front of her blouse. "May I go upstairs and change this?"

"Sure." He nodded to her and spoke into the phone, then hung up and turned. "You say he's been shot. That mean somebody else shot him?"

"I think this man murdered him," she said without looking at me, and went quickly out of the room.

The deputy looked at me. He got a notebook out. He wrote something in it. "I better have your name," he said casually, "and address. You the one called in?"

"Yes." I told him my name and address.

"Just take it easy until Lieutenant Ohls gets here."

"Bernie Ohls?"

"Yeah. You know him?"

"Sure. I've known him a long time. He used to work out of the D.A.'s office."

"Not lately," the deputy said. "He's Assistant Chief of Homicide, working out of the L.A. Sheriff's office. You a friend of the family, Mr. Marlowe?"

"Mrs. Wade didn't make it sound that way."

He shrugged and half smiled. "Just take it easy, Mr. Marlowe. Not carrying a gun, are you?"

"Not today."

"I better make sure." He did. He looked towards the couch then. "In spots like this you can't expect the wife to make much sense. We better wait outside."

37

OHLS WAS A medium-sized thick man with short-cropped faded blond hair and faded blue eyes. He had stiff white eyebrows and in the days before he stopped wearing a hat you were always a little surprised when he took it off – there was so much more head than you expected. He was a hard tough cop with a grim outlook on life but a very decent guy underneath. He ought to have made captain years ago. He had passed the examination among the top three half a dozen times. But the Sheriff didn't like him and he didn't like the Sheriff.

He came down the stairs rubbing the side of his jaw. Flash bulbs had been going off in the study for a long time. Men had gone in and out. I had just sat in the living room with a plainclothes dick and waited.

Ohls sat down on the edge of a chair and dangled his hands. He was chewing on an unlit cigarette. He looked at me broodingly.

"Remember the old days when they had a gatehouse and a private police force in Idle Valley?"

I nodded. "And gambling also."

"Sure. You can't stop it. This whole valley is still private property. Like Arrowhead used to be, and Emerald Bay. Long time since I was on a case with no reporters jumping around. Somebody must have whispered in Sheriff Petersen's ear. They kept it off the teletype."

"Real considerate of them," I said. "How is Mrs. Wade?"

"Too relaxed. She must of grabbed some pills. There's a dozen kinds up there – even Demerol. That's bad stuff. Your friends don't have a lot of luck lately, do they? They get dead."

I didn't have anything to say to that.

"Gunshot suicides always interest me," Ohls said loosely. "So easy to fake. The wife says you killed him. Why would she say that?"

"She doesn't mean it literally."

"Nobody else was here. She says you knew where the gun was, knew he was getting drunk, knew he had fired off the gun the other night when she had to fight with him to get the gun away from him. You were there that night too. Don't seem to help much, do you?"

"I searched his desk this afternoon. No gun. I'd told her where it was and to put it away. She says now she didn't believe in that sort of thing."

"Just when would 'now' be?" Ohls asked gruffly.

"After she came home and before I phoned the substation."

"You searched the desk. Why?" Ohls lifted his hands and put them on his knees. He was looking at me indifferently, as if he didn't care what I said.

"He was getting drunk. I thought it just as well to have the gun somewhere else. But he didn't try to kill himself the other night. It was just show-off."

Ohls nodded. He took the chewed cigarette out of his mouth, dropped it into a tray, and put a fresh one in place of it.

"I quit smoking," he said. "Got me coughing too much. But the goddam things still ride me. Can't feel right without one in my mouth. You supposed to watch the guy when he's alone?"

"Certainly not. He asked me to come out and have lunch. We talked and he was kind of depressed about his writing not going well. He decided to hit the bottle. Think I should have taken it away from him?"

"I'm not thinking yet. I'm just trying to get a picture. How much drinking did you do?"

"Beer."

"It's your tough luck you were here, Marlowe. What was the check for? The one he wrote and signed and tore up?"

"They all wanted me to come and live here and keep him in line. All means himself, his wife, and his publisher, a man named Howard Spencer. He's in New York, I guess. You can check with him. I turned it down. Afterwards she came to me and said her husband was off on a toot and she was worried and would I find him and bring him home. I did that. Next thing I knew I was carrying him in off his front lawn and putting him to bed. I didn't want any part of it, Bernie. It just kind of grew up around me."

"Nothing to do with the Lennox case, huh?"

"Aw, for Pete's sake. There isn't any Lennox case."

"How true," Ohls said dryly. He squeezed his kneecaps. A man came in at the front door and spoke to the other dick. Then came across to Ohls.

"There's a Dr. Loring outside, Lieutenant. Says he was called. He's the lady's doctor."

"Let him in."

The dick went back and Dr. Loring came in with his neat black bag. He was cool and elegant in a tropical worsted suit. He went past me without looking at me.

"Upstairs?" he asked Ohls.

"Yeah – in her room." Ohls stood up. "What you give her that Demerol for, Doc?"

Dr. Loring frowned at him. "I prescribe for my patient as I think proper," he said coldly. "I am not required to explain why. Who says I gave Mrs. Wade Demerol?"

"I do. The bottle's up there with your name on it. She's got a regular drugstore in her bathroom. Maybe you don't know it, Doc, but we have a pretty complete exhibit of the little pills downtown. Bluejays, redbirds, yellow jackets, goofballs, and all the rest of the list. Demerol's about the worst of the lot. That's the stuff Goering lived on, I heard somewhere. Took eighteen a day when they caught him. Took the army doctors three months to cut him down."

"I don't know what those words mean," Dr. Loring said frigidly.

"You don't? Pity. Bluejays are sodium amytal. Redbirds are Seconal. Yellow jackets are Nembutal. Goofballs are one of the barbiturates laced with Benzedrine. Demerol is a synthetic narcotic that is very habit forming. You just hand 'em out, huh? Is the lady suffering from something serious?"

"A drunken husband can be a very serious complaint indeed for a sensitive woman," Dr. Loring said.

"You didn't get around to him, huh? Pity. Mrs. Wade's upstairs, Doc. Thanks for the time."

"You are impertinent, sir. I shall report you."

708

"Yeah, do that," Ohls said. "But before you report me, do something else. Keep the lady clear in her head. I've got questions to ask."

"I shall do exactly what I think best for her condition. Do you know who I am, by any chance? And just to make matters clear, Mr. Wade was not my patient. I don't treat alcoholics."

"Just their wives, huh?" Ohls snarled at him. "Yeah, I know who you are, Doc. I'm bleeding internally. My name is Ohls. Lieutenant Ohls."

Dr. Loring went on up the stairs. Ohls sat down again and grinned at me.

"You got to be diplomatic with this kind of people," he said.

A man came out of the study and came up to Ohls. A thin serious-looking man with glasses and a brainy forehead.

"Lieutenant."

"Shoot."

"The wound is contact, typically suicidal, with a good deal of distention from gas pressure. The eyes are exophthalmic from the same cause. I don't think there will be any prints on the outside of the gun. It's been bled on too freely."

"Could it be homicide if the guy was asleep or passed out drunk?" Ohls asked him.

"Of course, but there's no indication of it. The gun's a Webley Hammerless. Typically, this gun takes a very stiff pull to cock it, but a very light pull to discharge it. The recoil explains the position of the gun. I see nothing against suicide so far. I expect a high figure on alcoholic concentration. If it's high enough —" the man stopped and shrugged meaningly — "I might be inclined to doubt suicide."

"Thanks. Somebody call the coroner?"

The man nodded and went away. Ohls yawned and looked at his watch. Then he looked at me.

"You want to blow?"

"Sure, if you'll let me. I thought I was a suspect."

"We might oblige you later on. Stick around where you can be found, that's all. You were a dick once, you know how they go. Some you got to work fast before the evidence gets away from you. This one is just the opposite. If it was a homicide, who wanted him dead? His wife? She wasn't here. You? Fine, you had the house to yourself and knew where the gun was. A perfect setup. Everything but a motive, and we might perhaps give some weight to your experience. I figure if you wanted to kill a guy, you could maybe do it a little less obviously."

"Thanks, Bernie. I could at that."

"The help wasn't here. They're out. So it must have been somebody that just happened to drop by. That somebody had to know where Wade's gun was, had to find him drunk enough to be asleep or passed out, and had to pull the trigger when that speedboat was making enough noise to drown the shot, and had to get away before you came back into the house. That I don't buy on any knowledge I have now. The only person who had the means and opportunity was the one guy who wouldn't have used them – for the simple reason he *was* the one guy who had them."

I stood up to go. "Okay, Bernie. I'll be home all evening."

"There's just one thing," Ohls said musingly. "This man Wade was a big time writer. Lots of dough, lots of reputation. I don't go for his sort of crap myself. You might find nicer people than his characters in a whorehouse. That's a matter of taste and none of my business as a cop. With all this money he had a beautiful home in one of the best places to live in in the country. He had a beautiful wife, lots of friends, and no troubles at all. What I want to know is what made all that so tough that he had to pull a trigger? Sure as hell something did. If you know, you better get ready to lay it on the line. See you."

I went to the door. The man on the door looked back at Ohls, got the sign, and let me out. I got into my car and had to edge over on the lawn to get around the various official

710

cars that jammed the driveway. At the gate another deputy looked me over but didn't say anything. I slipped my dark glasses on and drove back towards the main highway. The road was empty and peaceful. The afternoon sun beat down on the manicured lawns and the large roomy expensive houses behind them.

A man not unknown to the world had died in a pool of blood in a house in Idle Valley, but the lazy quiet had not been disturbed. So far as the newspapers were concerned it might have happened in Tibet.

At a turn of the road the walls of two estates came down to the shoulder and a dark green Sheriff's car was parked there. A deputy got out and held up his hand. I stopped. He came to the window.

"May I see your driver's license, please?"

I took out my wallet and handed it to him open.

"Just the license, please. I'm not allowed to touch your wallet."

I took it out and gave it to him. "What's the trouble?"

He glanced into my car and handed me back my license.

"No trouble," he said. "Just a routine check. Sorry to have troubled you."

He waved me on and went back to the parked car. Just like a cop. They never tell you why they are doing anything. That way you don't find out they don't know themselves.

I drove home, bought myself a couple of cold drinks, went out to dinner, came back, opened the windows and my shirt and waited for something to happen. I waited a long time. It was nine o'clock when Bernie Ohls called up and told me to come in and not stop on the way to pick any flowers.

38

THEY HAD CANDY in a hard chair against the wall of the Sheriff's anteroom. He hated me with his eyes as I went by him into the big square room where Sheriff Petersen held court in the middle of a collection of testimonials from a grateful public to his twenty years of faithful public service. The walls were loaded with photographs of horses and Sheriff Petersen made a personal appearance in every photograph. The corners of his carved desk were horses' heads. His inkwell was a mounted polished horse's hoof and his pens were planted in the mate to it filled with white sand. A gold plate on each of these said something or other about a date. In the middle of a spotless desk blotter lay a bag of Bull Durham and a pack of brown cigarette papers. Petersen rolled his own. He could roll one with one hand on horseback and often did, especially when leading a parade on a big white horse with a Mexican saddle loaded with beautiful Mexican silverwork. On horseback he wore a flat-crowned Mexican sombrero. He rode beautifully and his horse always knew exactly when to be quiet, when to act up so that the Sheriff with his calm inscrutable smile could bring the horse back under control with one hand. The Sheriff had a good act. He had a hand-some hawklike profile, getting a little saggy under the chin by now, but he knew how to hold his head so it wouldn't show too much. He put a lot of hard work into having his picture taken. He was in his middle fifties and his father, a Dane, had left him a lot of money. The Sheriff didn't look like a Dane, because his hair was dark and his skin was brown and he had the impassive poise of a cigar store Indian and about the same kind of brains. But nobody had ever called him a crook. There had been crooks in his department and they had fooled him as well as they had fooled the public, but none of the crookedness rubbed off on Sheriff Petersen. He just went right on getting elected without even trying, riding white horses at the head of parades, and questioning suspects in front of cameras. That's what the captions said. As a mat-ter of fact he never questioned anybody. He wouldn't have known how. He just sat at his desk looking sternly at the suspect, showing his profile to the camera. The flash bulbs would go off, the camera men would thank the Sheriff deferentially, the suspect would be removed not having opened his mouth, and the Sheriff would go home to his ranch in the San Fernando Valley. There he could always be reached. If you couldn't reach him in person, you could talk to one of his horses.

Once in a while, come election time, some misguided politician would try to get Sheriff Petersen's job, and would be apt to call him things like The Guy With The Built-In Profile or The Ham That Smokes Itself, but it didn't get him anywhere. Sheriff Petersen just went right on getting re-elected, a living testimonial to the fact that you can hold an important public office forever in our country with no qualifications for it but a clean nose, a photogenic face, and a closed mouth. If on top of that you look good on a horse, you are unbeatable.

As Ohls and I went in, Sheriff Petersen was standing behind his desk and the camera boys were filing out by another door. The Sheriff had his white Stetson on. He was rolling a cigarette. He was all set to go home. He looked at me sternly.

"Who's this?" he asked in a rich baritone voice.

"Name's Philip Marlowe, Chief," Ohls said. "Only person in the house when Wade shot himself. You want a picture?"

The Sheriff studied me. "I don't think so," he said, and turned to a big tired-looking man with iron-gray hair. "If you need me, I'll be at the ranch, Captain Hernandez."

"Yes, sir."

Petersen lit his cigarette with a kitchen match. He lit it on his thumbnail. No lighters for Sheriff Petersen. He was strictly a roll-your-own-and-light-'em-with-one-hand type.

He said goodnight and went out. A deadpan character with hard black eyes went with him, his personal bodyguard. The door closed. When he was gone Captain Hernandez moved to the desk and sat in the Sheriff's enormous chair and a stenotype operator in the corner moved his stand out from the wall to get elbow room. Ohls sat at the end of the desk and looked amused.

"All right, Marlowe," Hernandez said briskly. "Let's have it."

"How come I don't get my photo taken?"

"You heard what the Sheriff said."

"Yeah, but why?" I whined.

Ohls laughed. "You know damn well why."

"You mean on account of I'm tall, dark, and handsome and somebody might look at me?"

"Cut it," Hernandez said coldly. "Let's get on with your statement. Start from the beginning."

I gave it to them from the beginning: my interview with Howard Spencer, my meeting with Eileen Wade, her asking me to find Roger, my finding him, her asking me to the house, what Wade asked me to do and how I found him passed out near the hibiscus bushes and the rest of it. The stenotype operator took it down. Nobody interrupted me. All of it was true. The truth and nothing but the truth. But not quite all the truth. What I left out was my business.

"Nice," Hernandez said at the end. "But not quite complete." This was a cool competent dangerous guy, this Hernandez. Somebody in the Sheriff's office had to be. "The night Wade shot off the gun in his bedroom you went into Mrs. Wade's room and were in there for some time with the door shut. What were you doing in there?"

"She called me in and asked me how he was."

"Why shut the door?"

"Wade was half asleep and I didn't want to make any noise. Also the houseboy was hanging around with his ear out. Also she asked me to shut the door. I didn't realize it was going to be important."

"How long were you in there?"

"I don't know. Three minutes maybe."

"I suggest you were in there a couple of hours," Hernandez said coldly. "Do I make myself clear?"

I looked at Ohls. Ohls didn't look at anything. He was chewing on an unlighted cigarette as usual.

"You are misinformed, Captain."

"We'll see. After you left the room you went downstairs to the study and spent the night on the couch. Perhaps I should say the rest of the night."

"It was ten minutes to eleven when he called me at home. It was long past two o'clock when I went into the study for the last time that night. Call it the rest of the night if you like."

"Get the houseboy in here," Hernandez said.

Ohls went out and came back with Candy. They put Candy in a chair. Hernandez asked him a few questions to establish who he was and so on. Then he said: "All right, Candy — we'll call you that for convenience — after you helped Marlowe put Roger Wade to bed, what happened?"

I knew what was coming more or less. Candy told his story in a quiet savage voice with very little accent. It seemed as if he could turn that on and off at will. His story was that he had hung around downstairs in case he was wanted again, part of the time in the kitchen where he got himself some food, part of the time in the living room. While in the living room sitting in a chair near the front door he had seen Eileen Wade standing in the door of her room and he had seen her take her clothes off. He had seen her put a robe on with nothing under it and he had seen me go into her room and I shut the door and stayed in there a long time, a couple of hours he thought. He had gone up the stairs and listened. He had heard the bedsprings making sounds. He had heard whispering. He made his meaning very obvious. When he had finished he gave me a corrosive look and his mouth was twisted tight with hatred.

"Take him out," Hernandez said.

"Just a minute," I said. "I want to question him."

"I ask the questions here," Hernandez said sharply.

"You don't know how, Captain. You weren't there. He's lying and he knows it and I know it."

Hernandez leaned back and picked up one of the Sheriff's pens. He bent the handle of the pen. It was long and pointed and made of stiffened horsehair. When he let go of the point it sprang back.

"Shoot," he said at last.

I faced Candy. "Where were you when you saw Mrs. Wade take her clothes off?"

"I was sitting down in a chair near the front door," he said in a surly tone.

"Between the front door and the two facing davenports?"

"What I said."

"Where was Mrs. Wade?"

"Just inside the door of her room. The door was open."

"What light was there in the living room?"

"One lamp. Tall lamp what they call a bridge lamp."

"What light was on the balcony?"

"No light. Light in her bedroom."

"What kind of light in her bedroom?"

"Not much light. Night table lamp, maybe."

"Not a ceiling light?"

"No."

"After she took her clothes off – standing just inside the door of her room, you said – she put on a robe. What kind of robe?"

"Blue robe. Long thing like a house coat. She tie it with a sash."

"So if you hadn't actually seen her take her clothes off you wouldn't know what she had on under the robe?"

He shrugged. He looked vaguely worried. "Sí. That's right. But I see her take her clothes off."

"You're a liar. There isn't any place in the living room from which you could see her take her clothes off right bang in her doorway, much less inside her room. She would have to come

716

out to the edge of the balcony. If she had done that she would have seen you."

He just glared at me. I turned to Ohls. "You've seen the house. Captain Hernandez hasn't – or has he?"

Ohls shook his head slightly. Hernandez frowned and said nothing.

"There is no spot in that living room, Captain Hernandez, from which he could see even the top of Mrs. Wade's head – even if he was standing up – and he says he was sitting down – provided she was as far back as her own doorway or inside it. I'm four inches taller than he is and I could only see the top foot of an open door when I was standing just inside the front door of the house. She would have to come out to the edge of the balcony for him to see what he says he saw. Why would she do that? Why would she undress in her doorway even? There's no sense to it."

Hernandez just looked at me. Then he looked at Candy. "How about the time element?" he asked softly, speaking to me.

"That's his word against mine. I'm talking about what can be proved."

Hernandez spit Spanish at Candy too fast for me to understand. Candy just stared at him sulkily.

"Take him out," Hernandez said.

Ohls jerked a thumb and opened the door. Candy went out. Hernandez brought out a box of cigarettes, stuck one on his lip, and lit it with a gold lighter.

Ohls came back into the room. Hernandez said calmly: "I just told him that if there was an inquest and he told that story on the stand, he'd find himself doing a one-to-three up in Q for perjury. Didn't seem to impress him much. It's obvious what's eating him. An old-fashioned case of hot pants. If he'd been around and we had any reason to suspect murder, he'd make a pretty good pigeon – except that he would have used a knife. I got the impression earlier that he felt pretty bad about Wade's death. Any questions you want to ask, Ohls?"

Ohls shook his head. Hernandez looked at me and said: "Come back in the morning and sign your statement. We'll have it typed out by then. We ought to have a P.M. report by ten o'clock, preliminary anyway. Anything you don't like about this setup, Marlowe?"

"Would you mind rephrasing the question? The way you put it suggests there might be something I do like about it."

"Okay," he said wearily. "Take off. I'm going home."

I stood up.

"Of course I never did believe that stuff Candy pulled on us," he said. "Just used it for a corkscrew. No hard feelings, I hope."

"No feelings at all, Captain. No feelings at all."

They watched me go out and didn't say goodnight. I walked down the long corridor to the Hill Street entrance and got into my car and drove home.

No feelings at all was exactly right. I was as hollow and empty as the spaces between the stars. When I got home I mixed a stiff one and stood by the open window in the living room and sipped it and listened to the groundswell of the traffic on Laurel Canyon Boulevard and looked at the glare of the big angry city hanging over the shoulder of the hills through which the boulevard had been cut. Far off the banshee wail of police or fire sirens rose and fell, never for very long completely silent. Twenty-four hours a day somebody is running, somebody else is trying to catch him. Out there in the night of a thousand crimes people were dying, being maimed, cut by flying glass, crushed against steering wheels or under heavy tires. People were being beaten, robbed, strangled, raped, and murdered. People were hungry, sick, bored, desperate with loneliness or remorse or fear, angry, cruel, feverish, shaken by sobs. A city no worse than others, a city rich and vigorous and full of pride, a city lost and beaten and full of emptiness.

It all depends on where you sit and what your own private score is. I didn't have one. I didn't care.

I finished the drink and went to bed.

39

THE INQUEST WAS a flop. The coroner sailed into it before the medical evidence was complete, for fear the publicity would die on him. He needn't have worried. The death of a writer – even a loud writer – is not news for long, and that summer there was too much to compete. A king abdicated and another was assassinated. In one week three large passenger planes crashed. The head man of a big wire service was shot to pieces in Chicago in his own automobile. Twenty-four convicts were burned to death in a prison fire. The Coroner of Los Angeles County was out of luck. He was missing the good things in life.

As I left the stand I saw Candy. He had a bright malicious grin on his face – I had no idea why – and as usual he was dressed just a little too well, in a cocoa brown gabardine suit with a white nylon shirt and a midnight blue bow tie. On the witness stand he was quiet and made a good impression. Yes, the boss had been pretty drunk lately a lot of times. Yes, he had helped put him to bed the night the gun went off upstairs. Yes, the boss had demanded whiskey before he, Candy, left on the last day, but he had refused to get it. No, he didn't know anything about Mr. Wade's literary work, but he knew the boss had been discouraged. He kept throwing it away and then getting it out of the wastebasket again. No, he had never heard Mr. Wade quarreling with anyone. And so on. The coroner milked him but it was thin stuff. Somebody had done a good coaching job on Candy.

Eileen Wade wore black and white. She was pale and spoke in a low clear voice which even the amplifier could not spoil. The coroner handled her with two pairs of velvet gloves. He talked to her as if he had trouble keeping the sobs out of his voice. When she left the stand he stood up and bowed and she gave him a faint fugitive smile that nearly made him choke on his saliva.

She almost passed me without a glance on the way out, then at the last moment turned her head a couple of inches and nodded very slightly, as if I was somebody she must have met somewhere a long time ago, but couldn't quite place in her memory.

Outside on the steps when it was all over I ran into Ohls. He was watching the traffic down below, or pretending to.

"Nice job," he said without turning his head. "Congratulations."

"You did all right on Candy."

"Not me, kid. The D.A. decided the sexy stuff was irrelevant."

"What sexy stuff was that?"

He looked at me then. "Ha, ha, ha," he said. "And I don't mean you." Then his expression got remote. "I been looking at them for too many years. It wearies a man. This one came out of the special bottle. Old private stock. Strictly for the carriage trade. So long, sucker. Call me when you start wearing twenty-dollar shirts. I'll drop around and hold your coat for you."

People eddied around us going up and down the steps. We just stood there. Ohls took a cigarette out of his pocket and looked at it and dropped it on the concrete and ground it to nothing with his heel.

"Wasteful," I said.

"Only a cigarette, pal. It's not a life. After a while maybe you marry the girl, huh?"

"Shove it."

He laughed sourly. "I been talking to the right people about the wrong things," he said acidly. "Any objection?"

"No objection, Lieutenant," I said, and went on down the steps. He said something behind me but I kept going.

I went over to a corn-beef joint on Flower. It suited my mood. A rude sign over the entrance said: "Men Only. Dogs and Women Not Admitted." The service inside was equally polished. The waiter who tossed your food at you needed a shave and deducted his tip without being invited. The food was simple but very good and they had a brown Swedish beer which could hit as hard as a martini.

When I got back to the office the phone was ringing. Ohls said: "I'm coming by your place. I've got things to say."

He must have been at or near the Hollywood substation because he was in the office inside twenty minutes. He planted himself in the customer's chair and crossed his legs and growled:

"I was out of line. Sorry. Forget it."

"Why forget it? Let's open up the wound."

"Suits me. Under the hat, though. To some people you're a wrong gee. I never knew you to do anything too crooked."

"What was the crack about twenty-dollar shirts?"

"Aw hell, I was just sore," Ohls said. "I was thinking of old man Potter. Like he told a secretary to tell a lawyer to tell District Attorney Springer to tell Captain Hernandez you were a personal friend of his."

"He wouldn't take the trouble."

"You met him. He gave you time."

"I met him, period. I didn't like him, but perhaps it was only envy. He sent for me to give me some advice. He's big and he's tough and I don't know what else. I don't figure he's a crook."

"There ain't no clean way to make a hundred million bucks," Ohls said. "Maybe the head man thinks his hands are clean but somewhere along the line guys got pushed to the wall, nice little businesses got the ground cut from under them and had to sell out for nickels, decent people lost their jobs, stocks got rigged on the market, proxies got bought up like a pennyweight of old gold, and the five per centers and the big law firms got paid hundred-grand fees for beating some law the people wanted but the rich guys didn't, on account of it cut into their profits. Big money is big power and big power gets used wrong. It's the system. Maybe it's the best we can get, but it still ain't any Ivory Soap deal."

"You sound like a Red," I said, just to needle him.

"I wouldn't know," he said contemptuously. "I ain't been investigated yet. You liked the suicide verdict, didn't you?"

"What else could it be?"

"Nothing else, I guess." He put his hard blunt hands on the desk and looked at the big brown freckles on the backs of them. "I'm getting old. Keratosis, they call those brown spots. You don't get them until you're past fifty. I'm an old cop and an old cop is an old bastard. I don't like a few things about this Wade death."

"Such as?" I leaned back and watched the tight sun wrinkles around his eyes.

"You get so you can smell a wrong setup, even when you know you can't do a damn thing about it. Then you just sit and talk like now. I don't like that he left no note."

"He was drunk. Probably just a sudden crazy impulse."

Ohls lifted his pale eyes and dropped his hands off the desk. "I went through his desk. He wrote letters to himself. He wrote and wrote and wrote. Drunk or sober he hit that type-writer. Some of it is wild, some of it is kind of funny, and some of it is sad. The guy had something on his mind. He wrote all around it but he never quite touched it. That guy would have left a two-page letter if he knocked himself off."

"He was drunk," I said again.

"With him that didn't matter," Ohls said wearily. "The next thing I don't like is he did it there in that room and left his wife to find him. Okay, he was drunk. I still don't like it. The next thing I don't like is he pulled the trigger just when the noise of that speedboat could drown out the shot. What difference would it make to him? More coincidence, huh? More coincidence still that the wife forgot her door keys on the help's day off and had to ring the bell to get into the house."

"She could have walked around to the back," I said.

"Yeah, I know. What I'm talking about is a situation. Nobody to answer the door but you, and she said on the stand she didn't know you were there. Wade wouldn't have heard the bell if he had been alive and working in his study. His door is sound-proofed. The help was away. That was Thursday. That she forgot. Like she forgot her keys."

"You're forgetting something yourself, Bernie. My car was in the driveway. So she knew I was there – or that somebody was there – before she rang the bell."

He grinned. "I forgot that, didn't I? All right, here's the picture. You were down at the lake, the speedboat was making all that racket – incidentally it was a couple of guys from Lake Arrowhead just visiting, had their boat on a trailer – Wade was asleep in his study or passed out, somebody took the gun out of his desk already, and she knew you had put it there because you told her that other time. Now suppose she didn't forget her keys, that she goes into the house, looks across and sees you down at the water, looks into the study and sees Wade asleep, knows where the gun is, gets it, waits for the right moment, plugs him, drops the gun where it was found, goes back outside the house, waits a little while for the speedboat to go away, and then rings the doorbell and waits for you to open it. Any objections?"

"With what motive?"

"Yeah," he said sourly. "That knocks it. If she wanted to slough the guy, it was easy. She had him over a barrel, habitual drunk, record of violence to her. Plenty alimony, nice fat property settlement. No motive at all. Anyhow the timing was too neat. Five minutes earlier and she couldn't have done it unless you were in on it."

I started to say something but he put his hand up. "Take it easy. I'm not accusing anybody, just speculating. Five minutes later and you get the same answer. She had ten minutes to pull it off."

"Ten minutes," I said irritably, "that couldn't possibly have been foreseen, much less planned."

He leaned back in the chair and sighed. "I know. You've got all the answers, I've got all the answers. And I still don't like it. What the hell were you doing with these people anyway? The guy writes you a check for a grand, then tears it up. Got mad at you, you say. You didn't want it anyway, wouldn't have taken it, you say. Maybe. Did he think you were sleeping with his wife?"

"Lay off, Bernie."

"I didn't ask were you, I asked did he think you were."

"Same answer."

"Okay, try this. What did the Mex have on him?"

"Nothing that I know of."

"The Mex has too much money. Over fifteen hundred in the banks, all kinds of clothes, a brand new Chevvy."

"Maybe he peddles dope," I said.

Ohls pushed himself up out of the chair and scowled down at me.

"You're an awful lucky boy, Marlowe. Twice you've slid out from under a heavy one. You could get overconfident. You were pretty helpful to those people and you didn't make a dime. You were pretty helpful to a guy named Lennox too, the way I hear it. And you didn't make a dime out of that one either. What do you do for eating money, pal? You got a lot saved so you don't have to work any more?"

I stood up and walked around the desk and faced him. "I'm a romantic, Bernie. I hear voices crying in the night and I go see what's the matter. You don't make a dime that way. You got sense, you shut your windows and turn up more sound on the TV set. Or you shove down on the gas and get far away from there. Stay out of other people's troubles. All it can get you is the smear. The last time I saw Terry Lennox we had a cup of coffee together that I made myself in my house, and we smoked a cigarette. So when I heard he was dead I went out to the kitchen and made some coffee and poured a cup for him and lit a cigarette for him and when the coffee was cold and the cigarette was burned down I said goodnight to him. You don't make a dime that way. *You* wouldn't do it. That's why you're a good cop and I'm a private eye. Eileen Wade is worried about her husband, so I go out and find him and bring him home. Another time he's in trouble and calls me up and I go out and carry him in off the lawn and put him to bed and I don't make a dime out of it. No percentage at all. No nothing, except sometimes I get my face pushed in or get tossed in the can or get threatened by some fast money boy like Mendy Menendez. But no money, not a dime. I've got a five-thousand-dollar bill in my safe but I'll never spend a nickel of it. Because there was something wrong with the way I got it. I played with it a little at first and I still get it out once in a while and look at it. But that's all – not a dime of spending money."

"Must be a phony," Ohls said dryly, "except they don't make them that big. So what's your point with all this yap?"

"No point. I told you I was a romantic."

"I heard you. And you don't make a dime at it. I heard that too."

"But I can always tell a cop to go to hell. Go to hell, Bernie."

"You wouldn't tell me to go to hell if I had you in the back room under the light, chum."

"Maybe we'll find out about that some day."

He walked to the door and yanked it open. "You know something, kid? You think you're cute but you're just stupid. You're a shadow on the wall. I've got twenty years on the cops without a mark against me. I know when I'm being kidded and I know when a guy is holding out on me. The wise guy never fools anybody but himself. Take it from me, chum. I know."

He pulled his head back out of the doorway and let the door close. His heels hammered down the corridor. I could still hear them when the phone on my desk started to sound. The voice said in that clear professional tone:

"New York is calling Mr. Philip Marlowe."

"I'm Philip Marlowe."

"Thank you. One moment, please, Mr. Marlowe. Here is your party."

The next voice I knew. "Howard Spencer, Mr. Marlowe. We've heard about Roger Wade. It was a pretty hard blow. We haven't the full details, but your name seems to be involved."

"I was there when it happened. He just got drunk and shot himself. Mrs. Wade came home a little later. The servants were away — Thursday's the day off."

"You were alone with him?"

"I wasn't with him. I was outside the house, just hanging around waiting for his wife to come home."

"I see. Well, I suppose there will be an inquest."

"It's all over, Mr. Spencer. Suicide. And remarkably little publicity."

"Really? That's curious." He didn't exactly sound disappointed — more like puzzled and surprised. "He was so well known. I would have thought — well, never mind what I thought. I guess I'd better fly out there, but I can't make it before the end of next week. I'll send a wire to Mrs. Wade. There may be something I could do for her — and also about the book. I mean there may be enough of it so that we could get someone to finish it. I assume you did take the job after all."

"No. Although he asked me to himself. I told him right out I couldn't stop him from drinking."

"Apparently you didn't even try."

"Look, Mr. Spencer, you don't know the first damn thing about this situation. Why not wait until you do before jumping to conclusions? Not that I don't blame myself a little.

I guess that's inevitable when something like this happens, and you're the guy on the spot."

"Of course," he said. "I'm sorry I made that remark. Most uncalled for. Will Eileen Wade be at her home now – or wouldn't you know?"

"I wouldn't know, Mr. Spencer. Why don't you just call her up?"

"I hardly think she would want to speak to anyone yet," he said slowly.

"Why not? She talked to the coroner and never batted an eye."

He cleared his throat. "You don't sound exactly sympathetic."

"Roger Wade is dead, Spencer. He was a bit of a bastard and maybe a bit of a genius too. That's over my head. He was an egotistical drunk and he hated his own guts. He made me a lot of trouble and in the end a lot of grief. Why the hell should I be sympathetic?"

"I was talking about Mrs. Wade," he said shortly.

"So was I."

"I'll call you when I get in," he said abruptly. "Goodbye."

He hung up. I hung up. I stared at the telephone for a couple of minutes without moving. Then I got the phone book up on the desk and looked for a number.

40

I CALLED SEWELL Endicott's office. Somebody said he was in court and would not be available until late in the afternoon. Would I care to leave my name? No.

I dialed the number of Mendy Menendez's joint on the Strip. It was called El Tapado this year, not a bad name either. In American Spanish that means buried treasure among other things. It had been called other names in the past, quite a few other names. One year it was just a blue neon number on a blank high wall facing south on the Strip, with its back against the hill and a driveway curving around one side out of sight of the street. Very exclusive. Nobody knew much about it except vice cops and mobsters and people who could afford thirty bucks for a good dinner and any amount up to fifty grand in the big quiet room upstairs.

I got a woman who didn't know from nothing. Then I got a captain with a Mex accent.

"You wish to speak with Mr. Menendez? Who is calling?"

"No names, amigo. Private matter."

"Un momento, por favor."

There was a longish wait. I got a hard boy this time. He sounded as if he was talking through the slit in an armored car. It was probably just the slit in his face.

"Talk it up. Who wants him?"

"The name's Marlowe."

"Who's Marlowe?"

"This Chick Agostino?"

"No, this ain't Chick. Come on, let's have the password."

"Go fry your face."

There was a chuckle. "Hold the line."

Finally another voice said: "Hello, cheapie. What's the time by you?"

"You alone?"

"You can talk, cheapie. I been looking over some acts for the floor show."

"You could cut your throat for one."

"What would I do for an encore?"

I laughed. He laughed. "Been keeping your nose clean?" he asked.

"Haven't you heard? I got to be friends with another guy who suicided. They're going to call me the 'Kiss-of-Death Kid' from now on."

"That's funny, huh?"

"No, it isn't funny. Also the other afternoon I had tea with Harlan Potter."

"Nice going. I never drink the stuff myself."

"He said for you to be nice to me."

"I never met the guy and I don't figure to."

"He casts a long shadow. All I want is a little information, Mendy. Like about Paul Marston."

"Never heard of him."

"You said that too quick. Paul Marston was the name Terry Lennox used one time in New York before he came west."

"So?"

"His prints were checked through the F.B.I. files. No record. That means he never served in the Armed Forces."

"So?"

"Do I have to draw you a picture? Either that foxhole yarn of yours was all spaghetti or it happened somewhere else."

"I didn't say where it happened, cheapie. Take a kind word and forget the whole thing. You got told, you better stay told."

"Oh sure. I do something you don't like and I'm swimming to Catalina with a streetcar on my back. Don't try to scare me, Mendy. I've been up against the pros. You ever been in England?"

"Be smart, cheapie. Things can happen to a guy in this town. Things can happen to big strong boys like Big Willie Magoon. Take a look at the evening paper."

"I'll get one if you say so. It might even have my picture in it. What about Magoon?"

"Like I said – things can happen. I wouldn't know how except what I read. Seems Magoon tried to shake down four boys in a car with Nevada plates. Was parked right by his house. Nevada plates with big numbers like they don't have. Must have been some kind of a rib. Only Magoon ain't feeling funny, what with both arms in casts, and his jaw wired in three places, and one leg in high traction. Magoon ain't tough any more. It could happen to you."

"He bothered you, huh? I saw him bounce your boy Chick off the wall in front of Victor's. Should I ring up a friend in the Sheriff's office and tell him?"

"You do that, cheapie," he said very slowly. "You do that."

"And I'll mention that at the time I was just through having a drink with Harlan Potter's daughter. Corroborative evidence, in a sense, don't you think? You figure to smash her up too?"

"Listen to me careful, cheapie —"

"Were you ever in England, Mendy? You and Randy Starr and Paul Marston or Terry Lennox or whatever his name was? In the British Army perhaps? Had a little racket in Soho and got hot and figured the army was a cooling-off spot?"

"Hold the line."

I held it. Nothing happened except that I waited and my arm got tired. I switched the receiver to the other side. Finally he came back.

"Now listen careful, Marlowe. You stir up that Lennox case and you're dead. Terry was a pal and I got feelings too. So you got feelings. I'll go along with you just this far. It was a Commando outfit. It was British. It happened in Norway, one of those islands off the coast. They got a million of them. November 1942. Now will you lie down and rest that tired brain of yours?"

"Thank you, Mendy. I will do that. Your secret is safe with me. I'm not telling it to anybody but the people I know."

"Buy yourself a paper, cheapie. Read and remember. Big tough Willie Magoon. Beat up in front of his own house. Boy, was he surprised when he come out of the ether!"

He hung up. I went downstairs and bought a paper and it was just as Menendez had said. There was a picture of Big Willie Magoon in his hospital bed. You could see half his face and one eye. The rest of him was bandages. Seriously but not critically injured. The boys had been very careful about that. They wanted him to live. After all he was a cop. In our town the mobs don't kill a cop. They leave that to the juveniles. And a live cop who has been put through the meat grinder is a much better advertisement. He gets well eventually and goes back to work. But from that time on something is missing – the last inch of steel that makes all the difference. He's a walking lesson that it is a mistake to push the racket boys too hard – especially if you are on the vice squad and eating at the best places and driving a Cadillac.

I sat there and brooded about it for a while and then I dialed the number of The Carne Organization and asked for George Peters. He was out. I left my name and said it was urgent. He was expected in about five-thirty.

I went over to the Hollywood Public Library and asked questions in the reference room, but couldn't find what I wanted. So I had to go back for my Olds and drive downtown to the Main Library. I found it there, in a smallish red-bound book published in England. I copied what I wanted from it and drove home. I called The Carne Organization again. Peters was still out, so I asked the girl to reroute the call to me at home.

I put the chess board on the coffee table and set out a problem called The Sphynx. It is printed on the end papers of a book on chess by Blackburn, the English chess wizard, probably the most dynamic chess player who ever lived, although he wouldn't get to first base in the cold war type of chess they play nowadays. The Sphynx is an eleven-mover and it justifies its name. Chess problems seldom run to more than four or five moves. Beyond that the difficulty of solving them rises in almost geometrical progression. An eleven-mover is sheer unadulterated torture.

Once in a long while when I feel mean enough I set it out and look for a new way to solve it. It's a nice quiet way to go crazy. You don't even scream, but you come awfully close.

George Peters called me at five-forty. We exchanged pleasantries and condolences.

"You've got yourself in another jam, I see," he said cheerfully. "Why don't you try some quiet business like embalming?"

"Takes too long to learn. Listen, I want to become a client of your agency, if it doesn't cost too much."

"Depends on what you want done, old boy. And you'd have to talk to Carne."

"No."

"Well, tell me."

"London is full of guys like me, but I wouldn't know one from the other. They call them private enquiry agents. Your outfit would have connections. I'd just have to pick a name at random and probably get hornswoggled. I want some information that should be easy enough to get, and I want it quick. Must have it before the end of next week."

"Spill."

"I want to know something about the war service of Terry Lennox or Paul Marston, whatever name he used. He was in the Commandos over there. He was captured wounded in November 1942 in a raid on some Norwegian island. I want to know what outfit he was posted from and what happened to him. The War Office will have all that. It's not secret information, or I wouldn't think so. Let's say a question of inheritance is involved."

"You don't need a P.I. for that. You could get it direct. Write them a letter."

"Shove it, George. I might get an answer in three months. I want one in five days."

"You have a thought there, pal. Anything else?"

"One thing more. They keep all their vital records over there in a place they call Somerset House. I want to know if he figures there in any connection – birth, marriage, naturalization, anything at all."

"Why?"

"What do you mean, why? Who's paying the bill?"

"Suppose the names don't show?"

"Then I'm stuck. If they do, I want certified copies of anything your man turns up. How much you soaking me?"

"I'll have to ask Carne. He may thumb it out altogether. We don't want the kind of publicity you get. If he lets me handle it, and you agree not to mention the connection, I'd say three hundred bucks. Those guys over there don't get much by dollar standards. He might hit us for ten guineas, less than thirty bucks. On top of that any expenses he might have. Say fifty bucks altogether and Carne wouldn't open a file for less than two-fifty."

"Professional rates."

"Ha, ha. He never heard of them."

"Call me, George. Want to eat dinner?"

"Romanoff's?"

"All right," I growled, "if they'll give me a reservation — which I doubt."

"We can have Carne's table. I happen to know he's dining privately. He's a regular at Romanoff's. It pays off in the upper brackets of the business. Carne is a pretty big boy in this town."

"Yeah, sure. I know somebody — and know him personally — who could lose Carne under his little fingernail."

"Good work, kid. I always knew you would come through in the clutch. See you about seven o'clock in the bar at Romanoff's. Tell the head thief you're waiting for Colonel Carne. He'll clear a space around you so you don't get elbowed by any riffraff like screenwriters or television actors."

"See you at seven," I said.

We hung up and I went back to the chess board. But The Sphynx didn't seem to interest me any more. In a little while Peters called me back and said it was all right with Carne provided the name of their agency was not connected with my problems. Peters said he would get a night letter off to London at once.

41

HOWARD SPENCER CALLED me on the following Friday morning. He was at the Ritz-Beverly and suggested I drop over for a drink in the bar.

"Better make it in your room," I said.

"Very well, if you prefer it. Room 828. I've just talked to Eileen Wade. She seems quite resigned. She has read the script Roger left and says she thinks it can be finished off very easily. It will be a good deal shorter than his other books, but that is balanced by the publicity value. I guess you think we publishers are a pretty callous bunch. Eileen will be home all afternoon. Naturally she wants to see me and I want to see her."

"I'll be over in half an hour, Mr. Spencer."

He had a nice roomy suite on the west side of the hotel. The living room had tall windows opening on a narrow iron-railed balcony. The furniture was upholstered in some candy-striped material and that with the heavily flowered design of the carpet gave it an old-fashioned air, except that everything you could put a drink down on had a plate glass top and there were nineteen ashtrays spotted around. A hotel room is a pretty sharp indication of the manners of the guests. The Ritz-Beverly wasn't expecting them to have any.

Spencer shook hands. "Sit down," he said. "What will you drink?"

"Anything or nothing. I don't have to have a drink."

"I fancy a glass of Amontillado. California is poor drinking country in the summer. In New York you can handle four times as much for one half the hangover."

"I'll take a rye whiskey sour."

He went to the phone and ordered. Then he sat down on

one of the candy-striped chairs and took off his rimless glasses to polish them on a handkerchief. He put them back on, adjusted them carefully, and looked at me.

"I take it you have something on your mind. That's why you wanted to see me up here rather than in the bar."

"I'll drive you out to Idle Valley. I'd like to see Mrs. Wade too."

He looked a little uncomfortable. "I'm not sure that she wants to see you," he said.

"I know she doesn't. I can get in on your ticket."

"That would not be very diplomatic of me, would it?"

"She tell you she didn't want to see me?"

"Not exactly, not in so many words." He cleared his throat. "I get the impression that she blames you for Roger's death."

"Yeah. She said that right out — to the deputy who came the afternoon he died. She probably said it to the Sheriff's homicide lieutenant that investigated the death. She didn't say it to the coroner, however."

He leaned back and scratched the inside of his hand with a finger, slowly. It was just a sort of doodling gesture.

"What good would it do for you to see her, Marlowe? It was a pretty dreadful experience for her. I imagine her whole life had been pretty dreadful for some time. Why make her live it over? Do you expect to convince her that you didn't miss out a little?"

"She told the deputy I killed him."

"She couldn't have meant that literally. Otherwise —"

The door buzzer rang. He got up to go to the door and open it. The room service waiter came in with the drinks and put them down with as much flourish as if he was serving a seven course dinner. Spencer signed the check and gave him four bits. The guy went away. Spencer picked up his glass of sherry and walked away as if he didn't want to hand me my drink. I let it stay where it was.

"Otherwise what?" I asked him.

735

"Otherwise she *would* have said something to the coroner, wouldn't she?" He frowned at me. "I think we are talking nonsense. Just what did you want to see me about?"

"You wanted to see me."

"Only," he said coldly, "because when I talked to you from New York you said I was jumping to conclusions. That implied to me that you had something to explain. Well, what is it?"

"I'd like to explain it in front of Mrs. Wade."

"I don't care for the idea. I think you had better make your own arrangements. I have a great regard for Eileen Wade. As a businessman I'd like to salvage Roger's work if it can be done. If Eileen feels about you as you suggest, I can't be the means of getting you into her house. Be reasonable."

"That's all right," I said. "Forget it. I can get to see her without any trouble. I just thought I'd like to have somebody along with me as a witness."

"Witness to what?" he almost snapped at me.

"You'll hear it in front of her or you won't hear it at all."

"Then I won't hear it at all."

I stood up. "You're probably doing the right thing, Spencer. You want that book of Wade's — if it can be used. And you want to be a nice guy. Both laudable ambitions. I don't share either of them. The best of luck to you and goodbye."

He stood up suddenly and started towards me. "Now just a minute, Marlowe. I don't know what's on your mind but you seem to take it hard. Is there some mystery about Roger Wade's death?"

"No mystery at all. He was shot through the head with a Webley Hammerless revolver. Didn't you see a report of the inquest?"

"Certainly." He was standing close to me now and he looked bothered. "That was in the eastern papers and a couple of days later a much fuller account in the Los Angeles papers. He was alone in the house, although you were not far away.

The servants were away, Candy and the cook, and Eileen had been uptown shopping and arrived home just after it happened. At the moment it happened a very noisy motorboat on the lake drowned the sound of the shot, so that even you didn't hear it."

"That's correct," I said. "Then the motorboat went away, and I walked back from the lake edge and into the house, heard the doorbell ringing, and opened it to find Eileen Wade had forgotten her keys. Roger was already dead. She looked into the study from the doorway, thought he was asleep on the couch, went up to her room, then out to the kitchen to make some tea. A little later than she did I also looked into the study, noticed there was no sound of breathing, and found out why. In due course I called the law."

"I see no mystery," Spencer said quietly, all the sharpness gone from his voice. "It was Roger's own gun, and only the week before he had shot it off in his own room. You found Eileen struggling to get it away from him. His state of mind, his behavior, his depressions over his work — all that was brought out."

"She told you the stuff is good. Why should he be depressed over it?"

"That's just her opinion, you know. It may be very bad. Or he may have thought it worse than it was. Go on. I'm not a fool. I can see there is more."

"The homicide dick who investigated the case is an old friend of mine. He's a bulldog and a bloodhound and an old wise cop. He doesn't like a few things. Why did Roger leave no note — when he was a writing fool? Why did he shoot himself in such a way as to leave the shock of discovery to his wife? Why did he bother to pick the moment when I couldn't hear the gun go off? Why did she forget her house keys so that she had to be let in to the house? Why did she leave him alone on the day the help got off? Remember, she said she didn't know I would be there. If she did, those two cancel out."

"My God," Spencer bleated, "are you telling me the damn fool cop suspects Eileen?"

"He would if he could think of a motive."

"That's ridiculous. Why not suspect you? You had all afternoon. There could have been only a few minutes when she could have done it — and she had forgotten her house keys."

"What motive could I have?"

He reached back and grabbed my whiskey sour and swallowed it whole. He put the glass down carefully and got a handkerchief out and wiped his lips and his fingers where the chilled glass had moistened them. He put the handkerchief away. He stared at me.

"Is the investigation still going on?"

"Couldn't say. One thing is sure. They know by now whether he had drunk enough hooch to pass him out. If he had, there may still be trouble."

"And you want to talk to her," he said slowly, "in the presence of a witness."

"That's right."

"That means only one of two things to me, Marlowe. Either you are badly scared or you think she ought to be."

I nodded.

"Which one?" he asked grimly.

"I'm not scared."

He looked at his watch. "I hope to God you're crazy."

We looked at each other in silence.

42

NORTH THROUGH COLDWATER Canyon it began to get hot. When we topped the rise and started to wind down towards the San Fernando Valley it was breathless and blazing. I looked sideways at Spencer. He had a vest on, but the heat didn't seem to bother him. He had something else to bother him a lot more. He looked straight ahead through the windshield and said nothing. The valley had a thick layer of smog nuzzling down on it. From above it looked like a ground mist and then we were in it and it jerked Spencer out of his silence.

"My God, I thought Southern California had a climate," he said. "What are they doing – burning old truck tires?"

"It'll be all right in Idle Valley," I told him soothingly. "They get an ocean breeze in there."

"I'm glad they get something besides drunk," he said. "From what I've seen of the local crowd in the rich suburbs I think Roger made a tragic mistake in coming out here to live. A writer needs stimulation – and not the kind they bottle. There's nothing around here but one great big suntanned hangover. I'm referring to the upper crust people of course."

I turned off and slowed down for the dusty stretch to the entrance of Idle Valley, then hit the paving again and in a little while the ocean breeze made itself felt, drifting down through the gap in the hills at the far end of the lake. High sprinklers revolved over the big smooth lawns and the water made a swishing sound as it licked at the grass. By this time most of the well-heeled people were away somewhere else. You could tell by the shuttered look of the houses and the way the gardener's truck was parked smack in the middle of the driveway. Then we reached the Wades' place and I swung through the gateposts and stopped behind Eileen's Jaguar. Spencer got out and marched stolidly across the flagstones to the portico of the house. He rang the bell and the door opened almost at once. Candy was there in the white jacket and the dark good-looking face and the sharp black eyes. Everything was in order.

Spencer went in. Candy gave me a brief look and nearly shut the door in my face. I waited and nothing happened. I leaned on the bell and heard the chimes. The door swung wide and Candy came out snarling.

"Beat it! Turn blue. You want a knife in the belly?"

"I came to see Mrs. Wade."

"She don't want any part of you."

"Out of my way, peasant. I got business here."

"Candy!" It was her voice, and it was sharp.

He gave me a final scowl and backed into the house. I went in and shut the door. She was standing at the end of one of the facing davenports, and Spencer was standing beside her. She looked like a million. She had white slacks on, very high-waisted, and a white sport shirt with half sleeves, and a lilac-colored handkerchief budding from the pocket over her left breast.

"Candy is getting rather dictatorial lately," she said to Spencer. "It's so good to see you, Howard. And so nice of you to come all this way. I didn't realize you were bringing someone with you."

"Marlowe drove me out," Spencer said. "Also he wanted to see you."

"I can't imagine why," she said coolly. Finally she looked at me, but not as if not seeing me for a week had left an emptiness in her life. "Well?"

"It's going to take a little time," I said.

She sat down slowly. I sat down on the other davenport. Spencer was frowning. He took his glasses off and polished them. That gave him a chance to frown more naturally. Then he sat on the other end of the davenport from me.

"I was sure you would come in time for lunch," she told him, smiling.

"Not today, thanks."

"No? Well, of course if you are too busy. Then you just want to see that script."

"If I may."

"Of course. Candy! Oh, he's gone. It's on the desk in Roger's study. I'll get it."

Spencer stood up. "May I get it?"

Without waiting for an answer he started across the room. Ten feet behind her he stopped and gave me a strained look. Then he went on. I just sat there and waited until her head came around and her eyes gave me a cool impersonal stare.

"What was it you wanted to see me about?" she asked curtly.

"This and that. I see you are wearing that pendant again."

"I often wear it. It was given to me by a very dear friend a long time ago."

"Yeah. You told me. It's a British military badge of some sort, isn't it?"

She held it out at the end of the thin chain. "It's a jeweler's reproduction of one. Smaller than the original and in gold and enamel."

Spencer came back across the room and sat down again and put a thick pile of yellow paper on the corner of the cocktail table in front of him. He glanced at it idly, then his eyes were watching Eileen.

"Could I look at it a little closer?" I asked her.

She pulled the chain around until she could unfasten the clasp. She handed the pendant to me, or rather she dropped it in my hand. Then she folded her hands in her lap and just looked curious. "Why are you so interested? It's the badge of a regiment called the Artists Rifles, a Territorial regiment. The man who gave it to me was lost soon afterwards. At Andalsnes in Norway, in the spring of that terrible year – 1940." She smiled and made a brief gesture with one hand. "He was in love with me."

"Eileen was in London all through the Blitz," Spencer said in an empty voice. "She couldn't get away."

We both ignored Spencer. "And you were in love with him," I said.

She looked down and then raised her head and our glances locked. "It was a long time ago," she said. "And there was a war. Strange things happen."

741

"There was a little more to it than that, Mrs. Wade. I guess you forget how much you opened up about him. 'The wild mysterious improbable kind of love that never comes but once.' I'm quoting you. In a way you're still in love with him. It's darn nice of me to have the same initials. I suppose that had something to do with your picking me out."

"His name was nothing like yours," she said coldly. "And he is dead, dead, dead."

I held the gold and enamel pendant out to Spencer. He took it reluctantly. "I've seen it before," he muttered.

"Check me on the design," I said. "It consists of a broad dagger in white enamel with a gold edge. The dagger points downwards and the flat of the blade crosses in front of a pair of upward-curling pale blue enamel wings. Then it crosses in back of a scroll. On the scroll are the words: WHO DARES WINS."

"That seems to be correct," he said. "What makes it important?"

"She says it's a badge of the Artists Rifles, a Territorial outfit. She says it was given to her by a man who was in that outfit and was lost in the Norwegian campaign with the British Army in the spring of 1940 at Andalsnes."

I had their attention. Spencer watched me steadily. I wasn't talking to the birds and he knew it. Eileen knew it too. Her tawny eyebrows were crimped in a puzzled frown which could have been genuine. It was also unfriendly.

"This is a sleeve badge," I said. "It came into existence because the Artists Rifles were made over or attached or seconded or whatever the correct term is into a Special Air Service Outfit. They had originally been a Territorial regiment of infantry. This badge didn't even exist until 1947. Therefore nobody gave it to Mrs. Wade in 1940. Also, no Artists Rifles were landed at Andalsnes in Norway in 1940. Sherwood Foresters and Leicestershires, yes. Both Territorial. Artists Rifles, no. Am I being nasty?"

Spencer put the pendant down on the coffee table and pushed it slowly across until it was in front of Eileen. He said nothing.

"Do you think I wouldn't know?" Eileen asked me contemptuously.

"Do you think the British War Office wouldn't know?" I asked her right back.

"Obviously there must be some mistake," Spencer said mildly.

I swung around and gave him a hard stare. "That's one way of putting it."

"Another way of putting it is that I am a liar," Eileen said icily. "I never knew anyone named Paul Marston, never loved him or he me. He never gave me a reproduction of his regimental badge, he was never missing in action, he never existed. I bought this badge myself in a shop in New York where they specialize in imported British luxuries, things like leather goods, hand-made brogues, regimental and school ties and cricket blazers, knickknacks with coats of arms on them and so on. Would an explanation like that satisfy you, Mr. Marlowe?"

"The last part would. Not the first. No doubt somebody told you it was an Artists Rifles badge and forgot to mention what kind, or didn't know. But you did know Paul Marston and he did serve in that outfit, and he was missing in action in Norway. But it didn't happen in 1940, Mrs. Wade. It happened in 1942 and he was in the Commandos then, and it wasn't at Andalsnes, but on a little island off the coast where the Commando boys pulled a fast raid."

"I see no need to be so hostile about it," Spencer said in an executive sort of voice. He was fooling with the yellow sheets in front of him now. I didn't know whether he was trying to stooge for me or was just sore. He picked up a slab of yellow script and weighed it on his hand.

"You going to buy that stuff by the pound?" I asked him.

743

He looked startled, then he smiled a small difficult smile.

"Eileen had a pretty tough time in London," he said. "Things get confused in one's memory."

I took a folded paper out of my pocket. "Sure," I said. "Like who you got married to. This is a certified copy of a marriage certificate. The original came from Caxton Hall Registry Office. The date of the marriage is August 1942. The parties named are Paul Edward Marston and Eileen Victoria Sampsell. In a sense Mrs. Wade is right. There was no such person as Paul Edward Marston. It was a fake name because in the army you have to get permission to get married. The man faked an identity. In the army he had another name. I have his whole army history. It's a wonder to me that people never seem to realize that all you have to do is ask."

Spencer was very quiet now. He leaned back and stared. But not at me. He stared at Eileen. She looked back at him with one of those faint half deprecatory, half seductive smiles women are so good at.

"But he was dead, Howard. Long before I met Roger. What could it possibly matter? Roger knew all about it. I never stopped using my unmarried name. In the circumstances I had to. It was on my passport. Then after he was killed in action —" She stopped and drew a slow breath and let her hand fall slowly and softly to her knee. "All finished, all done for, all lost."

"You're sure Roger knew?" he asked her slowly.

"He knew something," I said. "The name Paul Marston had a meaning for him. I asked him once and he got a funny look in his eyes. But he didn't tell me why."

She ignored that and spoke to Spencer.

"Why, of course Roger knew all about it." Now she was smiling at Spencer patiently as if he was being a little slow on the take. The tricks they have.

"Then why lie about the dates?" Spencer asked dryly. "Why say the man was lost in 1940 when he was lost in 1942?

Why wear a badge that he couldn't have given you and make a point of saying that he did give it to you?"

"Perhaps I was lost in a dream," she said softly. "Or a nightmare, more accurately. A lot of my friends were killed in the bombing. When you said goodnight in those days you tried not to make it sound like goodbye. But that's what it often was. And when you said goodbye to a soldier – it was worse. It's always the kind and gentle ones that get killed."

He didn't say anything. I didn't say anything. She looked down at the pendant lying on the table in front of her. She picked it up and fitted it to the chain around her neck again and leaned back composedly.

"I know I haven't any right to cross-examine you, Eileen," Spencer said slowly. "Let's forget it. Marlowe made a big thing out of the badge and the marriage certificate and so on. Just for a moment I guess he had me wondering."

"Mr. Marlowe," she told him quietly, "makes a big thing out of trifles. But when it comes to a really big thing – like saving a man's life – he is out by the lake watching a silly speedboat."

"And you never saw Paul Marston again," I said.

"How could I when he was dead?"

"You didn't know he was dead. There was no report of his death from the Red Cross. He might have been taken prisoner."

She shuddered suddenly. "In October 1942," she said slowly, "Hitler issued an order that all Commando prisoners were to be turned over to the Gestapo. I think we all know what that meant. Torture and a nameless death in some Gestapo dungeon." She shuddered again. Then she blazed at me: "You're a horrible man. You want me to live that over again, to punish me for a trivial lie. Suppose someone you loved had been caught by those people and you knew what had happened, what must have happened to him or her? Is it so strange that I tried to build another kind of memory – even a false one?"

745

"I need a drink," Spencer said. "I need a drink badly. May I have one?"

She clapped her hands and Candy drifted up from nowhere as he always did. He bowed to Spencer.

"What you like to drink, Señor Spencer?"

"Straight Scotch, and plenty of it," Spencer said.

Candy went over in the corner and pulled the bar out from the wall. He got a bottle up on it and poured a stiff jolt into a glass. He came back and set it down in front of Spencer. He started to leave again.

"Perhaps, Candy," Eileen said quietly, "Mr. Marlowe would like a drink too."

He stopped and looked at her, his face dark and stubborn.

"No, thanks," I said. "No drink for me."

Candy made a snorting sound and walked off. There was another silence. Spencer put down half of his drink. He lit a cigarette. He spoke to me without looking at me.

"I'm sure Mrs. Wade or Candy could drive me back to Beverly Hills. Or I can get a cab. I take it you've said your piece."

I refolded the certified copy of the marriage license. I put it back in my pocket.

"Sure that's the way you want it?" I asked him.

"That's the way everybody wants it."

"Good." I stood up. "I guess I was a fool to try to play it this way. Being a big time publisher and having the brains to go with it – if it takes any – you might have assumed I didn't come out here just to play the heavy. I didn't revive ancient history or spend my own money to get the facts just to twist them around somebody's neck. I didn't investigate Paul Marston because the Gestapo murdered him, because Mrs. Wade was wearing the wrong badge, because she got mixed up on her dates, because she married him in one of those quickie wartime marriages. When I started investigating him I didn't know any of those things. All I knew was his name. Now how do you suppose I knew that?"

"No doubt somebody told you," Spencer said curtly.

"Correct, Mr. Spencer. Somebody who knew him in New York after the war and later on saw him out here in Chasen's with his wife."

"Marston is a pretty common name," Spencer said, and sipped his whiskey. He turned his head sideways and his right eyelid drooped a fraction of an inch. So I sat down again. "Even Paul Marstons could hardly be unique. There are nineteen Howard Spencers in the Greater New York area telephone directories, for instance. And four of them are just plain Howard Spencer with no middle initial."

"Yeah. How many Paul Marstons would you say had had one side of their faces smashed by a delayed-action mortar shell and showed the scars and marks of the plastic surgery that repaired the damage?"

Spencer's mouth fell open. He made some kind of heavy breathing sound. He got out a handkerchief and tapped his temples with it.

"How many Paul Marstons would you say had saved the lives of a couple of tough gamblers named Mendy Menendez and Randy Starr on that same occasion? They're still around, they've got good memories. They can talk when it suits them. Why ham it up any more, Spencer? Paul Marston and Terry Lennox were the same man. It can be proved beyond any shadow of a doubt."

I didn't expect anyone to jump six feet into the air and scream and nobody did. But there is a kind of silence that is almost as loud as a shout. I had it. I had it all around me, thick and hard. In the kitchen I could hear water run. Outside on the road I could hear the dull thump of a folded newspaper hit the driveway, then the light inaccurate whistling of a boy wheeling away on his bicycle.

I felt a tiny sting on the back of my neck. I jerked away from it and swung around. Candy was standing there with his knife in his hand. His dark face was wooden but there was something in his eyes I hadn't seen before.

"You are tired, amigo," he said softly. "I fix you a drink, no?"

"Bourbon on the rocks, thanks," I said.

"De pronto, señor."

He snapped the knife shut, dropped it into the side pocket of his white jacket and went softly away.

Then at last I looked at Eileen. She sat leaning forward, her hands clasped tightly. The downward tilt of her face hid her expression if she had any. And when she spoke her voice had the lucid emptiness of that mechanical voice on the telephone that tells you the time and if you keep on listening, which people don't because they have no reason to, it will keep on telling you the passing seconds forever, without the slightest change of inflection.

"I saw him once, Howard. Just once. I didn't speak to him at all. Nor he to me. He was terribly changed. His hair was white and his face – it wasn't quite the same face. But of course I knew him, and of course he knew me. We looked at each other. That was all. Then he was gone out of the room and the next day he was gone from her house. It was at the Lorings' I saw him – and her. One afternoon late. You were there, Howard. And Roger was there. I suppose you saw him too."

"We were introduced," Spencer said. "I knew who he was married to."

"Linda Loring told me he just disappeared. He gave no reason. There was no quarrel. Then after a while that woman divorced him. And still later I heard she found him again. He was down and out. And they were married again. Heaven knows why. I suppose he had no money and it didn't matter to him any more. He knew that I was married to Roger. We were lost to each other."

"Why?" Spencer asked.

Candy put my drink in front of me without a word. He looked at Spencer and Spencer shook his head. Candy drifted away. Nobody paid any attention to him. He was like the prop man in a Chinese play, the fellow that moves things around on the stage and the actors and audience alike behave as if he wasn't there.

"Why?" she repeated. "Oh, you wouldn't understand. What we had was lost. It could never be recovered. The Gestapo didn't get him after all. There must have been *some* decent Nazis who didn't obey Hitler's order about the Commandos. So he survived, he came back. I used to pretend to myself that I would find him again, but as he had been, eager and young and unspoiled. But to find him married to that redheaded whore — that was disgusting. I already knew about her and Roger. I have no doubt Paul did too. So did Linda Loring, who is a bit of a tramp herself, but not completely so. They all are in that set. You ask me why I didn't leave Roger and go back to Paul. After he had been in her arms and Roger had been in those same willing arms? No thank you. I need a little more inspiration than that. Roger I could forgive. He drank, he didn't know what he was doing. He worried about his work and he hated himself because he was just a mercenary hack. He was a weak man, unreconciled, frustrated, but under-standable. He was just a husband. Paul was either much more or he was nothing. In the end he was nothing."

I took a swig of my drink. Spencer had finished his. He was scratching at the material of the davenport. He had forgotten the pile of paper in front of him, the unfinished novel of the very much finished popular author.

"I wouldn't say he was nothing," I said.

She lifted her eyes and looked at me vaguely and dropped them again.

"Less than nothing," she said, with a new note of sarcasm in her voice. "He knew what she was, he married her. Then because she was what he knew she was, he killed her. And then ran away and killed himself."

"He didn't kill her," I said, "and you know it."

She came upright with a smooth motion and stared at me blankly. Spencer let out a noise of some kind.

"Roger killed her," I said, "and you also know that."

"Did he tell you?" she asked quietly.

"He didn't have to. He did give me a couple of hints. He would have told me or someone in time. It was tearing him to pieces not to."

She shook her head slightly. "No, Mr. Marlowe. That was not why he was tearing himself to pieces. Roger didn't know he had killed her. He had blacked out completely. He knew something was wrong and he tried to bring it to the surface, but he couldn't. The shock had destroyed his memory of it. Perhaps it would have come back and perhaps in the last moments of his life it did come back. But not until then. Not until then."

Spencer said in a sort of growl: "That sort of thing just doesn't happen, Eileen."

"Oh yes, it does," I said. "I know of two well-established instances. One was a blackout drunk who killed a woman he picked up in a bar. He strangled her with a scarf she was wearing fastened with a fancy clasp. She went home with him and what went on then is not known except that she got dead and when the law caught up with him he was wearing the fancy clasp on his own tie and he didn't have the faintest idea where he got it."

"Never?" Spencer asked. "Or just at the time?"

"He never admitted it. And he's not around any more to be asked. They gassed him. The other case was a head wound. He was living with a rich pervert, the kind that collects first editions and does fancy cooking and has a very expensive secret library behind a panel in the wall. The two of them had a fight. They fought all over the house, from room to room, the place was a shambles and the rich guy eventually got the low score. The killer, when they caught him, had dozens of bruises on him and a broken finger. All he knew for sure was that he had a headache and he couldn't find his way back to Pasadena. He kept circling around and stopping to ask directions at the same service station. The guy at the service station decided he was nuts and called the cops. Next time around they were waiting for him."

"I don't believe that about Roger," Spencer said. "He was no more psycho than I am."

"He blacked out when he was drunk," I said.

"I was there. I *saw* him do it," Eileen said calmly.

I grinned at Spencer. It was some kind of grin, not the cheery kind probably, but I could feel my face doing its best.

"She's going to tell us about it," I told him. "Just listen. She's going to tell us. She can't help herself now."

"Yes, that is true," she said gravely. "There are things no one likes to tell about an enemy, much less about one's own husband. And if I have to tell them publicly on a witness stand, you are not going to enjoy it, Howard. Your fine, talented, ever so popular and lucrative author is going to look pretty cheap. Sexy as all get out, wasn't he? On paper, that is. And how the poor fool tried to live up to it! All that woman was to him was a trophy. I spied on them. I should be ashamed of that. One has to say these things. I am ashamed of nothing. I saw the whole nasty scene. The guest house she used for her amours happens to be a nice secluded affair with its own garage and entrance on a side street, a dead end, shaded by big trees. The time came, as it must to people like Roger, when he was no longer a satisfactory lover. Just a little too drunk. He tried to leave but she came out after him screaming and stark naked, waving some kind of small statuette. She used language of a depth of filth and depravity I couldn't attempt to describe. Then she tried to hit him with the statuette. You are both men and you must know that nothing shocks a man quite so much as to hear a supposedly refined woman use the language of the gutter and the public urinal. He was drunk, he had had sudden spells of violence, and he had one then. He tore the statuette out of her hand. You can guess the rest."

"There must have been a lot of blood," I said.

"Blood?" She laughed bitterly. "You should have seen him when he got home. When I ran for my car to get away he was just standing there looking down at her. Then he bent and picked her up in his arms and carried her into the guest house. I knew then that the shock had partially sobered him. He got home in about an hour. He was very quiet. It shook him when he saw me waiting. But he wasn't drunk then. He was dazed. There was blood on his face, on his hair, all over the front of his coat. I got him into the lavatory off the study and got him stripped and cleaned off enough to get him upstairs into the shower. I put him to bed. I got an old suitcase and went downstairs and gathered up the bloody clothes and put them in the suitcase. I cleaned the basin and the floor and then I took a wet towel out and made sure his car was clean. I put it away and got mine out. I drove to the Chatsworth Reservoir and you can guess what I did with the suitcase full of bloody clothes and towels."

She stopped. Spencer was scratching at the palm of his left hand. She gave him a quick glance and went on.

"While I was away he got up and drank a lot of whiskey. And the next morning he didn't remember a single thing. That is, he didn't say a word about it or behave as if he had anything on his mind but a hangover. And I said nothing."

"He must have missed the clothes," I said.

She nodded. "I think he did eventually – but he didn't say so. Everything seemed to happen at once about that time. The papers were full of it, then Paul was missing, and then he was dead in Mexico. How was I to know that would happen? Roger was my husband. He had done an awful thing, but she was an awful woman. And he hadn't known what he was doing. Then almost as suddenly as it began the papers dropped it. Linda's father must have had something to do with that. Roger read the papers, of course, and he made just the sort of comments one would expect from an innocent bystander who had just happened to know the people involved."

"Weren't you afraid?" Spencer asked her quietly.

"I was sick with fear, Howard. If he remembered, he would probably kill me. He was a good actor – most writers are – and perhaps he already knew and was just waiting for a chance. But I couldn't be sure. He might – just might – have forgotten the whole thing permanently. And Paul was dead."

"If he never mentioned the clothes that you had dumped in the reservoir, that proved he suspected something," I said. "And remember, in that stuff he left in the typewriter the other time – the time he shot the gun off upstairs and I found you trying to get it away from him – he said a good man had died for him."

"He said that?" Her eyes widened just the right amount.

"He wrote it – on the typewriter. I destroyed it, he asked me to. I supposed you had already seen it."

"I never read anything he wrote in his study."

"You read the note he left the time Verringer took him away. You even dug something out of the wastebasket."

"That was different," she said coolly. "I was looking for a clue to where he might have gone."

"Okay," I said, and leaned back. "Is there any more?"

She shook her head slowly, with a deep sadness. "I suppose not. At the very last, the afternoon he killed himself, he may have remembered. We'll never know. Do we want to know?"

Spencer cleared his throat. "What was Marlowe supposed to do in all this? It was your idea to get him here. You talked me into that, you know."

"I was terribly afraid. I was afraid of Roger and I was afraid *for* him. Mr. Marlowe was Paul's friend, almost the last person to see him who knew him. Paul might have told him something. I had to be sure. If he was dangerous, I wanted him on my side. If he found out the truth, there might still be some way to save Roger."

Suddenly and for no reason that I could see, Spencer got tough. He leaned forward and pushed his jaw out.

"Let me get this straight, Eileen. Here was a private detective who was already in bad with the police. They'd had him in jail. He was supposed to have helped Paul — I call him that because you do — jump the country to Mexico. That's a felony, if Paul was a murderer. So if he found out the truth and could clear himself, he would just sit on his hands and do nothing. Was that your idea?"

"I was afraid, Howard. Can't you understand that? I was living in the house with a murderer who might be a maniac. I was alone with him a large part of the time."

"I understand that," Spencer said, still tough. "But Marlowe didn't take it on, and you were still alone. Then Roger fired the gun off and for a week after that you were alone. Then Roger killed himself and very conveniently it was Marlowe who was alone that time."

"That is true," she said. "What of it? Could I help it?"

"All right," Spencer said. "Is it just possible you thought Marlowe might find the truth and with the background of the gun going off once already, just kind of hand it to Roger and say something like, 'Look, old man, you're a murderer and I know it and your wife knows it. She's a fine woman. She has suffered enough. Not to mention Sylvia Lennox's husband. Why not do the decent thing and pull the trigger and everybody will assume it was just a case of too much wild drinking? So I'll stroll down by the lake and smoke a cigarette, old man. Good luck and goodbye. Oh, here's the gun. It's loaded and it's all yours.'"

"You're getting horrible, Howard. I didn't think anything of the sort."

"You told the deputy Marlowe had killed Roger. What was that supposed to mean?"

She looked at me briefly, almost shyly. "I was very wrong to say that. I didn't know what I was saying."

"Maybe you thought Marlowe had shot him," Spencer suggested calmly.

Her eyes narrowed. "Oh no, Howard. Why? Why would he do that? That's an abominable suggestion."

"Why?" Spencer wanted to know. "What's abominable about it? The police had the same idea. And Candy gave them a motive. He said Marlowe was in your room for two hours the night Roger shot a hole in his ceiling – after Roger had been put to sleep with pills."

She flushed to the roots of her hair. She stared at him dumbly.

"And you didn't have any clothes on," Spencer said brutally. "That's what Candy told them."

"But at the inquest –" she began to say in a shattered kind of voice. Spencer cut her off.

"The police didn't believe Candy. So he didn't tell it at the inquest."

"Oh." It was a sigh of relief.

"Also," Spencer went on coldly, "the police suspected you. They still do. All they need is a motive. Looks to me like they might be able to put one together now."

She was on her feet. "I think you had both better leave my house," she said angrily. "The sooner the better."

"Well, did you or didn't you?" Spencer asked calmly, not moving except to reach for his glass and find it empty.

"Did I or didn't I what?"

"Shoot Roger?"

She was standing there staring at him. The flush had gone. Her face was white and tight and angry.

"I'm just giving you the sort of thing you'd get in court."

"I was out. I had forgotten my keys. I had to ring to get into the house. He was dead when I got home. All that is known. What has got into you, for God's sake?"

He took a handkerchief out and wiped his lips. "Eileen, I've stayed in this house twenty times. I've never known that front door to be locked during the daytime. I don't say you shot him. I just asked you. And don't tell me it was impossible. The way things worked out it was easy."

"I shot my own husband?" she asked slowly and wonderingly.

"Assuming," Spencer said in the same indifferent voice, "that he *was* your husband. You had another when you married him."

"Thank you, Howard. Thank you very much. Roger's last book, his swan song, is there in front of you. Take it and go. And I think you had better call the police and tell them what you think. It will be a charming ending to our friendship. Most charming. Goodbye, Howard. I am very tired and I have a headache. I'm going to my room and lie down. As for Mr. Marlowe – and I suppose he put you up to all this – I can only say to him that if he didn't kill Roger in a literal sense, he certainly drove him to his death."

She turned to walk away. I said sharply: "Mrs. Wade, just a moment. Let's finish the job. No sense in being bitter. We are all trying to do the right thing. That suitcase you threw into the Chatsworth Reservoir – was it heavy?"

She turned and stared at me. "It was an old one, I said. Yes, it was very heavy."

"How did you get it over the high wire fence around the reservoir?"

"What? The fence?" She made a helpless gesture. "I suppose in emergencies one has an abnormal strength to do what has to be done. Somehow or other I did it. That's all."

"There isn't any fence," I said.

"Isn't any fence?" She repeated it dully, as if it didn't mean anything.

"And there was no blood on Roger's clothes. And Sylvia Lennox wasn't killed outside the guest house, but inside it on the bed. And there was practically no blood, because she was already dead – shot dead with a gun – and when the statuette was used to beat her face to a pulp, it was beating a dead woman. And the dead, Mrs. Wade, bleed very little."

She curled her lip at me contemptuously. "I suppose you were there," she said scornfully.

756

Then she went away from us.

We watched her go. She went up the stairs slowly, moving with calm elegance. She disappeared into her room and the door closed softly but firmly behind her. Silence.

"What was that about the wire fence?" Spencer asked me vaguely. He was moving his head back and forth. He was flushed and sweating. He was taking it gamely but it wasn't easy for him to take.

"Just a gag," I said. "I've never been close enough to the Chatsworth Reservoir to know what it looks like. Maybe it has a fence around it, maybe not."

"I see," he said unhappily. "But the point is she didn't know either."

"Of course not. She killed both of them."

43

THEN SOMETHING MOVED softly and Candy was standing at the end of the couch looking at me. He had his switch knife in his hand. He pressed the button and the blade shot out. He pressed the button and the blade went back into the handle. There was a sleek glitter in his eye.

"Million de pardones, señor," he said. "I was wrong about you. She killed the boss. I think I –" He stopped and the blade shot out again.

"No." I stood up and held my hand out. "Give me the knife, Candy. You're just a nice Mexican houseboy. They'd hang it onto you and love it. Just the kind of smoke screen that would make them grin with delight. You don't know what I'm talking about. But I do. They fouled it up so bad that they couldn't straighten it out now if they wanted to. And they don't want to. They'd blast a confession out of you so quickly you wouldn't even have time to tell them your full name. And you'd be sitting on your fanny up in San Quentin with a life sentence three weeks from Tuesday."

"I tell you before I am not a Mexican. I am Chileno from Viña del Mar near Valparaíso."

"The knife, Candy. I know all that. You're free. You've got money saved. You've probably got eight brothers and sisters back home. Be smart and go back where you came from. This job here is dead."

"Lots of jobs," he said quietly. Then he reached out and dropped the knife into my hand. "For you I do this."

I dropped the knife into my pocket. He glanced up towards the balcony. "La señora – what do we do now?"

"Nothing. We do nothing at all. The señora is very tired. She has been living under a great strain. She doesn't want to be disturbed."

"We've got to call the police," Spencer said grittily.

"Why?"

"Oh my God, Marlowe – we have to."

"Tomorrow. Pick up your pile of unfinished novel and let's go."

"We've got to call the police. There is such a thing as law."

"We don't have to do anything of the sort. We haven't enough evidence to swat a fly with. Let the law enforcement people do their own dirty work. Let the lawyers work it out. They write the laws for other lawyers to dissect in front of other lawyers called judges so that other judges can say the first judges were wrong and the Supreme Court can say the second lot were wrong. Sure there's such a thing as law. We're up to our necks in it. About all it does is make business for lawyers. How long do you think the big-shot mobsters would last if the lawyers didn't show them how to operate?"

Spencer said angrily: "That has nothing to do with it. A man was killed in this house. He happened to be an author and a very successful and important one, but that has nothing to do with it either. He was a man and you and I know who killed him. There's such a thing as justice."

"Tomorrow."

"You're just as bad as she is if you let her get away with it. I'm beginning to wonder about you a little, Marlowe. You could have saved his life if you had been on your toes. In a sense you let her get away with it. And for all I know this whole performance this afternoon has been just that — a performance."

"That's right. A disguised love scene. You could see Eileen is crazy about me. When things quiet down we may get married. She ought to be pretty well fixed. I haven't made a buck out of the Wade family yet. I'm getting impatient."

He took his glasses off and polished them. He wiped perspiration from the hollows under his eyes, replaced the glasses and looked at the floor.

"I'm sorry," he said. "I've taken a pretty stiff punch this afternoon. It was bad enough to know Roger had killed himself. But this other version makes me feel degraded — just knowing about it." He looked up at me. "Can I trust you?"

"To do what?"

"The right thing — whatever it is." He reached down and picked up the pile of yellow script and tucked it under his arm. "No, forget it. I guess you know what you are doing. I'm a pretty good publisher but this is out of my line. I guess what I really am is just a goddam stuffed shirt."

He walked past me and Candy stepped out of his way, then went quickly to the front door and held it open. Spencer went out past him with a brief nod. I followed. I stopped beside Candy and looked into his dark shining eyes.

"No tricks, amigo," I said.

"The señora is very tired," he said quietly. "She has gone to her room. She will not be disturbed. I know nothing, señor. No me acuerdo de nada . . . A sus órdenes, señor."

I took the knife out of my pocket and held it out to him. He smiled.

"Nobody trusts me, but I trust you, Candy."

"Lo mismo, señor. Muchas gracias."

Spencer was already in the car. I got in and started it and backed down the driveway and drove him back to Beverly Hills. I let him out at the side entrance of the hotel.

"I've been thinking all the way back," he said as he got out. "She must be a little insane. I guess they'd never convict her."

"They won't even try," I said. "But she doesn't know that."

He struggled with the batch of yellow paper under his arm, got it straightened out, and nodded to me. I watched him heave open the door and go on in. I eased up on the brake and the Olds slid out from the white curb, and that was the last I saw of Howard Spencer.

★

I got home late and tired and depressed. It was one of those nights when the air is heavy and the night noises seem muffled and far away. There was a high misty indifferent moon. I walked the floor, played a few records, and hardly heard them. I seemed to hear a steady ticking somewhere, but there wasn't anything in the house to tick. The ticking was in my head. I was a one-man death watch.

I thought of the first time I had seen Eileen Wade and the second and the third and the fourth. But after that something in her got out of drawing. She no longer seemed quite real. A murderer is always unreal once you know he is a murderer. There are people who kill out of hate or fear or greed. There are the cunning killers who plan and expect to get away with it. There are the angry killers who do not think at all. And there are the killers who are in love with death, to whom murder is a remote kind of suicide. In a sense they are all insane, but not in the way Spencer meant it.

It was almost daylight when I finally went to bed.

The jangle of the telephone dragged me up out of a black well of sleep. I rolled over on the bed, fumbled for slippers, and realized that I hadn't been asleep for more than a couple of hours. I felt like a half-digested meal eaten in a greasy-spoon joint. My eyes were stuck together and my mouth was full of sand. I heaved up on the feet and lumbered into the living room and pulled the phone off the cradle and said into it: "Hold the line."

I put the phone down and went into the bathroom and hit myself in the face with some cold water. Outside the window something went snip, snip, snip. I looked out vaguely and saw a brown expressionless face. It was the once-a-week Jap gardener I called Hardhearted Harry. He was trimming the tecoma – the way a Japanese gardener trims your tecoma. You ask him four times and he says, "next week," and then he comes by at six o'clock in the morning and trims it outside your bedroom window.

I rubbed my face dry and went back to the telephone.

"Yeah?"

"This is Candy, señor."

"Good morning, Candy."

"La señora es muerta."

Dead. What a cold black noiseless word it is in any language. The lady is dead.

"Nothing you did, I hope."

"I think the medicine. It is called Demerol. I think forty, fifty in the bottle. Empty now. No dinner last night. This morning I climb up on the ladder and look in the window. Dressed just like yesterday afternoon. I break the screen open. La señora es muerta. Frio como agua de nieve."

Cold as icewater. "You call anybody?"

"Sí. El Doctor Loring. He call the cops. Not here yet."

"Dr. Loring, huh? Just the man to come too late."

"I don't show him the letter," Candy said.

"Letter to who?"

"Señor Spencer."

"Give it to the police, Candy. Don't let Dr. Loring have it. Just the police. And one more thing, Candy. Don't hide anything, don't tell them any lies. We were there. Tell the truth. This time the truth and all the truth."

There was a little pause. Then he said: "Sí. I catch. Hasta la vista, amigo." He hung up.

I dialed the Ritz-Beverly and asked for Howard Spencer.

"One moment, please. I'll give you the desk."

A man's voice said: "Desk speaking. May I help you?"

"I asked for Howard Spencer. I know it's early, but it's urgent."

"Mr. Spencer checked out last evening. He took the eight o'clock plane to New York."

"Oh, sorry. I didn't know."

I went out to the kitchen to make coffee – yards of coffee. Rich, strong, bitter, boiling hot, ruthless, depraved. The lifeblood of tired men.

It was a couple of hours later that Bernie Ohls called me.

"Okay, wise guy," he said. "Get down here and suffer."

44

IT WAS LIKE the other time except that it was day and we were in Captain Hernandez's office and the Sheriff was up in Santa Barbara opening Fiesta Week. Captain Hernandez was there and Bernie Ohls and a man from the coroner's office and Dr. Loring, who looked as if he had been caught performing an abortion, and a man named Lawford, a deputy from the D.A.'s office, a tall gaunt expressionless man whose brother was vaguely rumored to be a boss of the numbers racket in the Central Avenue district.

Hernandez had some handwritten sheets of note paper in front of him, flesh-pink paper, deckle-edged, and written on with green ink.

"This is informal," Hernandez said, when everybody was as comfortable as you can get in hard chairs. "No stenotype or recording equipment. Say what you like. Dr. Weiss represents the coroner who will decide whether an inquest is necessary. Dr. Weiss?"

He was fat, cheerful, and looked competent. "I think no inquest," he said. "There is every surface indication of narcotic poisoning. When the ambulance arrived the woman was still breathing very faintly and she was in a deep coma and all the reflexes were negative. At that stage you don't save one in a hundred. Her skin was cold and respiration would not be noticed without close examination. The houseboy thought she was dead. She died approximately an hour after that. I understand the lady was subject to occasional violent attacks of bronchial asthma. The Demerol was prescribed by Dr. Loring as an emergency measure."

"Any information or deduction about the amount of Demerol taken, Dr. Weiss?"

"A fatal dose," he said, smiling faintly. "There is no quick way of determining that without knowing the medical history, the acquired or natural tolerance. According to her confession she took twenty-three hundred milligrams, four or five times the minimal lethal dose for a non-addict." He looked questioningly at Dr. Loring.

"Mrs. Wade was not an addict," Dr. Loring said coldly. "The prescribed dose would be one or two fifty-milligram tablets. Three or four during a twenty-four-hour period would be the most I'd permit."

"But you gave her fifty at a whack," Captain Hernandez said. "A pretty dangerous drug to have around in that quantity, don't you think? How bad was this bronchial asthma, Doctor?"

Dr. Loring smiled contemptuously. "It was intermittent, like all asthma. It never amounted to what we term *status asthmaticus*, an attack so severe that the patient seems in danger of suffocating."

"Any comment, Dr. Weiss?"

"Well," Dr. Weiss said slowly, "assuming the note didn't exist and assuming we had no other evidence of how much

763

of the stuff she took, it could be an accidental overdose. The safety margin isn't very wide. We'll know for sure tomorrow. You don't want to suppress the note, Hernandez, for Pete's sake?"

Hernandez scowled down at his desk. "I was just wondering. I didn't know narcotics were standard treatment for asthma. Guy learns something every day."

Loring flushed. "An emergency measure, I said, Captain. A doctor can't be everywhere at once. The onset of an asthmatic flareup can be very sudden."

Hernandez gave him a brief glance and turned to Lawford. "What happens to your office, if I give this letter to the press?"

The D.A.'s deputy glanced at me emptily. "What's this guy doing here, Hernandez?"

"I invited him."

"How do I know he won't repeat everything said in here to some reporter?"

"Yeah, he's a great talker. You found that out. The time you had him pinched."

Lawford grinned, then cleared his throat. "I've read that purported confession," he said carefully. "And I don't believe a word of it. You've got a background of emotional exhaustion, bereavement, some use of drugs, the strain of wartime life in England under bombing, this clandestine marriage, the man coming back here, and so on. Undoubtedly she developed a feeling of guilt and tried to purge herself of it by a sort of transference."

He stopped and looked around, but all he saw was faces with no expression. "I can't speak for the D.A. but my own feeling is that your confession would be no grounds to seek an indictment even if the woman had lived."

"And having already believed one confession you wouldn't care to believe another that contradicted the first one," Hernandez said caustically.

"Take it easy, Hernandez. Any law enforcement agency has to consider public relations. If the papers printed that confession we'd be in trouble. That's for sure. We've got enough eager beaver reformer groups around just waiting for that kind of chance to stick a knife into us. We've got a grand jury that's already jittery about the working-over your vice squad lieutenant got last week."

Hernandez said: "Okay, it's your baby. Sign the receipt for me."

He shuffled the pink deckle-edged pages together and Lawford leaned down to sign a form. He picked up the pink pages, folded them, put them in his breast pocket and walked out.

Dr. Weiss stood up. He was tough, good-natured, unimpressed.

"We had the last inquest on the Wade family too quick," he said.

"I guess we won't bother to have this one at all."

He nodded to Ohls and Hernandez, shook hands formally with Loring, and went out. Loring stood up to go, then hesitated.

"I take it that I may inform a certain interested party that there will be no further investigation of this matter?" he said stiffly.

"Sorry to have kept you away from your patients so long, Doctor."

"You haven't answered my question," Loring said sharply. "I'd better warn you –"

"Get lost, Jack," Hernandez said.

Dr. Loring almost staggered with shock. Then he turned and fumbled his way rapidly out of the room. The door closed and it was a half minute before anybody said anything. Hernandez shook himself and lit a cigarette. Then he looked at me.

"Well?" he said.

"Well what?"

"What are you waiting for?"

"This is the end, then? Finished? Kaput?"

"Tell him, Bernie."

"Yeah, sure it's the end," Ohls said. "I was all set to pull her in for questioning. Wade didn't shoot himself. Too much alcohol in his brain. But like I told you, where was the motive? Her confession could be wrong in details, but it proves she spied on him. She knew the layout of the guest house in Encino. The Lennox frail had taken both her men from her. What happened in the guest house is just what you want to imagine. One question you forgot to ask Spencer. Did Wade own a Mauser P.P.K.? Yeah, he owned a small Mauser automatic. We talked to Spencer already today on the phone. Wade was a blackout drunk. The poor unfortunate bastard either thought he had killed Sylvia Lennox or he actually had killed her or else he had some reason to know his wife had. Either way he was going to lay it on the line eventually. Sure, he'd been hitting the hooch long before, but he was a guy married to a beautiful nothing. The Mex knows all about it. The little bastard knows damn near everything. That was a dream girl. Some of her was here and now, but a lot of her was there and then. If she ever got hot pants, it wasn't for her husband. Get what I'm talking about?"

I didn't answer him.

"Damn near made her yourself, didn't you?"

I gave him the same no answer.

Ohls and Hernandez both grinned sourly. "Us guys aren't exactly brainless," Ohls said. "We knew there was something in that story about her taking her clothes off. You outtalked him and he let you. He was hurt and confused and he liked Wade and he wanted to be sure. When he got sure he'd have used his knife. This was a personal matter with him. He never snitched on Wade. Wade's wife did, and she deliberately fouled up the issue just to confuse Wade. It all adds. In the end I guess she was scared of him. And Wade never threw her down any stairs. That was an accident. She tripped and the guy tried to catch her. Candy saw that too."

"None of it explains why she wanted me around."

"I could think of reasons. One of them is old stuff. Every cop has run into it a hundred times. You were the loose end, the guy that helped Lennox escape, his friend, and probably to some extent his confidant. What did he know and what did he tell you? He took the gun that had killed her and he knew it had been fired. She could have thought he did it for her. That made her think he knew she had used it. When he killed himself she was sure. But what about you? You were still the loose end. She wanted to milk you, and she had the charm to use, and a situation ready-made for an excuse to get next to you. And if she needed a fall guy, you were it. You might say she was collecting fall guys."

"You're imputing too much knowledge to her," I said.

Ohls broke a cigarette in half and started chewing on one half. The other half he stuck behind his ear.

"Another reason is she wanted a man, a big, strong guy that could crush her in his arms and make her dream again."

"She hated me," I said. "I don't buy that one."

"Of course," Hernandez put in dryly. "You turned her down. But she would have got over that. And then you blew the whole thing up in her face with Spencer listening in."

"You two characters been seeing any psychiatrists lately?"

"Jesus," Ohls said, "hadn't you heard? We got them in our hair all the time these days. We've got two of them on the staff. This ain't police business any more. It's getting to be a branch of the medical racket. They're in and out of jail, the courts, the interrogation rooms. They write reports fifteen pages long on why some punk of a juvenile held up a liquor store or raped a schoolgirl or peddled tea to the senior class. Ten years from now guys like Hernandez and me will be doing Rorschach tests and word associations instead of chin-ups and target practice. When we go out on a case we'll carry little black bags with portable lie detectors and bottles of truth serum. Too bad we didn't grab the four hard monkeys that poured it on Big Willie Magoon. We might have been able to unmaladjust them and make them love their mothers."

"Okay for me to blow?"

"What are you not convinced about?" Hernandez asked, snapping a rubber band.

"I'm convinced. The case is dead. She's dead, they're all dead. A nice smooth routine all around. Nothing to do but go home and forget it ever happened. So I'll do that."

Ohls reached the half cigarette from behind his ear, looked at it as if wondering how it got there, and tossed it over his shoulder.

"What are you crying about?" Hernandez said. "If she hadn't been fresh out of guns she might have made it a perfect score."

"Also," Ohls said grimly, "the telephone was working yesterday."

"Oh sure," I said. "You'd have come running and what you would have found would have been a mixed up story that admitted nothing but a few silly lies. This morning you have what I suppose is a full confession. You haven't let me read it, but you wouldn't have called in the D.A. if it was just a love note. If any real solid work had been done on the Lennox case at the time, somebody would have dug up his war record and where he got wounded and all the rest of it. Somewhere along the line a connection with the Wades would have turned up. Roger Wade knew who Paul Marston was. So did another P.I. I happened to get in touch with."

"It's possible," Hernandez admitted, "but that isn't how police investigations work. You don't fool around with an open-shut case, even if there's no heat on to get it finalized and forgotten. I've investigated hundreds of homicides. Some are all of a piece, neat, tidy, and according to the book. Most of them make sense here, don't make sense there. But when you get motive, means, opportunity, flight, a written confession, and a suicide immediately afterwards, you leave it lay. No police department in the world has the men or the time to question the obvious. The only thing against Lennox being a killer was that somebody thought he was a nice guy who wouldn't have done it and that there were others who could equally well have done it. But the others didn't take it on the lam, didn't confess, didn't blow their brains out. He did. And as for being a nice guy I figure sixty to seventy per cent of all the killers that end up in the gas chamber or the hot seat or on the end of a rope are people the neighbors thought were just as harmless as a Fuller Brush salesman. Just as harmless and quiet and well bred as Mrs. Roger Wade. You want to read what she wrote in that letter? Okay, read it. I've got to go down the hall."

He stood up and pulled a drawer open and put a folder on the top of the desk. "There are five photostats in here, Marlowe. Don't let me catch you looking at them."

He started for the door and then turned his head and said to Ohls: "You want to talk to Peshorek with me?"

Ohls nodded and followed him out. When I was alone in the office I lifted the cover of the file folder and looked at the white-on-black photostats. Then touching only the edges I counted them. There were six, each of several pages clipped together. I took one and rolled it up and slipped it into my pocket. Then I read over the next one in the pile. When I had finished I sat down and waited. In about ten minutes Hernandez came back alone. He sat down behind his desk again, tallied the photostats in the file folder, and put the file back in his desk.

He raised his eyes and looked at me without any expression. "Satisfied?"

"Lawford know you have those?"

"Not from me. Not from Bernie. Bernie made them himself. Why?"

"What would happen if one got loose?"

He smiled unpleasantly. "It won't. But if it did, it wouldn't be anybody in the Sheriff's office. The D.A. has photostat equipment too."

"You don't like District Attorney Springer too well, do you, Captain?"

He looked surprised. "Me? I like everybody, even you. Get the hell out of here. I've got work to do."

I stood up to go. He said suddenly: "You carry a gun these days?"

"Part of the time."

"Big Willie Magoon carried two. I wonder why he didn't use them."

"I guess he figured he had everybody scared."

"That could be it," Hernandez said casually. He picked up a rubber band and stretched it between his thumbs. He stretched it farther and farther. Finally with a snap it broke. He rubbed his thumb where the loose end had snapped back against it. "Anybody can be stretched too far," he said. "No matter how tough he looks. See you around."

I went out of the door and got out of the building fast. Once a patsy, always a patsy.

45

BACK IN MY dog house on the sixth floor of the Cahuenga Building I went through my regular double play with the morning mail. Mail slot to desk to wastebasket, Tinker to Evers to Chance. I blew a clear space on the top of the desk and unrolled the photostat on it. I had rolled it so as not to make creases.

I read it over again. It was detailed enough and reasonable enough to satisfy any open mind. Eileen Wade had killed Terry's wife in a fit of jealous fury and later when the opportunity was set up she had killed Roger because she was sure he

770

knew. The gun fired into the ceiling of his room that night had been part of the setup. The unanswered and forever unanswerable question was why Roger Wade had stood still and let her put it over. He must have known how it would end. So he had written himself off and didn't care. Words were his business, he had words for almost everything, but none for this.

"I have forty-six Demerol tablets left from my last prescription," she wrote. "I now intend to take them all and lie down on the bed. The door is locked. In a very short time I shall be beyond saving. This, Howard, is to be understood. What I write is in the presence of death. Every word is true. I have no regrets – except possibly that I could not have found them together and killed them together. I have no regrets for Paul whom you have heard called Terry Lennox. He was the empty shell of the man I loved and married. He meant nothing to me. When I saw him that afternoon for the only time after he came back from the war – at first I didn't know him. Then I did and he knew me at once. He should have died young in the snow of Norway, my lover that I gave to death. He came back a friend of gamblers, the husband of a rich whore, a spoiled and ruined man, and probably some kind of crook in his past life. Time makes everything mean and shabby and wrinkled. The tragedy of life, Howard, is not that the beautiful things die young, but that they grow old and mean. It will not happen to me. Goodbye, Howard."

I put the photostat in the desk and locked it up. It was time for lunch but I wasn't in the mood. I got the office bottle out of the deep drawer and poured a slug and then got the phone book off the hook at the desk and looked up the number of the *Journal*. I dialed it and asked the girl for Lonnie Morgan.

"Mr. Morgan doesn't come in until around four o'clock. You might try the press room at the City Hall."

I called that. And I got him. He remembered me well enough. "You've been a pretty busy guy, I heard."

"I've got something for you, if you want it. I don't think you want it."

"Yeah? Such as?"

"A photostat of a confession to two murders."

"Where are you?"

I told him. He wanted more information. I wouldn't give him any over the phone. He said he wasn't on a crime beat. I said he was still a newspaperman and on the only independent paper in the city. He still wanted to argue.

"Where did you get this whatever it is? How do I know it's worth my time?"

"The D.A.'s office has the original. They won't release it. It breaks open a couple of things they hid behind the icebox."

"I'll call you. I have to check with the brass."

We hung up. I went to the drugstore and ate a chicken salad sandwich and drank some coffee. The coffee was overstrained and the sandwich was as full of rich flavor as a piece torn off an old shirt. Americans will eat anything if it is toasted and held together with a couple of toothpicks and has lettuce sticking out of the sides, preferably a little wilted.

At three-thirty or so Lonnie Morgan came in to see me. He was the same long thin wiry piece of tired and expressionless humanity as he had been the night he drove me home from the jailhouse. He shook hands listlessly and rooted in a crumpled pack of cigarettes.

"Mr. Sherman – that's the M.E. – said I could look you up and see what you have."

"It's off the record unless you agree to my terms." I unlocked the desk and handed him the photostat. He read the four pages rapidly and then again more slowly. He looked very excited – about as excited as a mortician at a cheap funeral.

"Gimme the phone."

I pushed it across the desk. He dialed, waited, and said: "This is Morgan. Let me talk to Mr. Sherman." He waited and got some other female and then got his party and asked him to ring back on another line.

He hung up and sat holding the telephone in his lap with the forefinger pressing the button down. It rang again and he lifted the receiver to his ear.

"Here it is, Mr. Sherman."

He read slowly and distinctly. At the end there was a pause. Then, "One moment, sir." He lowered the phone and glanced across the desk. "He wants to know how you got hold of this."

I reached across the desk and took the photostat away from him. "Tell him it's none of his goddam business how I got hold of it. Where is something else. The stamp on the back of the pages shows that."

"Mr. Sherman, it's apparently an official document of the Los Angeles Sheriff's office. I guess we could check its authenticity easy enough. Also there's a price."

He listened some more and then said: "Yes, sir. Right here." He pushed the phone across the desk. "Wants to talk to you."

It was a brusque authoritative voice. "Mr. Marlowe, what are your terms? And remember the *Journal* is the only paper in Los Angeles which would even consider touching this matter."

"You didn't do much on the Lennox case, Mr. Sherman."

"I realize that. But at that time it was purely a question of scandal for scandal's sake. There was no question of who was guilty. What we have now, if your document is genuine, is something quite different. What are your terms?"

"You print the confession in full in the form of a photographic reproduction. Or you don't print it at all."

"It will be verified. You understand that?"

"I don't see how, Mr. Sherman. If you ask the D.A. he will either deny it or give it to every paper in town. He'd have to. If you ask the Sheriff's office they will put it up to the D.A."

"Don't worry about that, Mr. Marlowe. We have ways. How about your terms?"

"I just told you."

773

"Oh. You don't expect to be paid?"

"Not with money."

"Well, you know your own business, I suppose. May I have Morgan again?"

I gave the phone back to Lonnie Morgan.

He spoke briefly and hung up. "He agrees," he said. "I take that photostat and he checks it. He'll do what you say. Reduced to half size it will take about half of page 1A."

I gave him back the photostat. He held it and pulled at the tip of his long nose. "Mind my saying I think you're a damn fool?"

"I agree with you."

"You can still change your mind."

"Nope. Remember that night you drove me home from the City Bastille? You said I had a friend to say goodbye to. I've never really said goodbye to him. If you publish this photostat, that will be it. It's been a long time − a long, long time."

"Okay, chum." He grinned crookedly. "But I still think you're a damn fool. Do I have to tell you why?"

"Tell me anyway."

"I know more about you than you think. That's the frustrating part of newspaper work. You always know so many things you can't use. You get cynical. If this confession is printed in the *Journal*, a lot of people will be sore. The D.A., the coroner, the Sheriff's crowd, an influential and powerful private citizen named Potter, and a couple of toughies called Menendez and Starr. You'll probably end up in the hospital or in jail again."

"I don't think so."

"Think what you like, pal. I'm telling you what *I* think. The D.A. will be sore because he dropped a blanket on the Lennox case. Even if the suicide and confession of Lennox made him look justified, a lot of people will want to know how Lennox, an innocent man, came to make a confession, how he got dead, did he really commit suicide or was he helped, why was there no investigation into the circumstances, and how come the whole thing died so fast. Also, if he

774

has the original of this photostat he will think he has been double-crossed by the Sheriff's people."

"You don't have to print the identifying stamp on the back."

"We won't. We're pals with the Sheriff. We think he's a straight guy. We don't blame him because he can't stop guys like Menendez. Nobody can stop gambling as long as it's legal in all forms in some places and legal in some forms in all places. You stole this from the Sheriff's office. I don't know how you got away with it. Want to tell me?"

"No."

"Okay. The coroner will be sore because he buggered up the Wade suicide. The D.A. helped him with that too. Harlan Potter will be sore because something is reopened that he used a lot of power to close up. Menendez and Starr will be sore for reasons I'm not sure of, but I know you got warned off. And when those boys get sore at somebody he gets hurt. You're apt to get the treatment Big Willie Magoon got."

"Magoon was probably getting too heavy for his job."

"Why?" Morgan drawled. "Because those boys have to make it stick. If they take the trouble to tell you to lay off, you lay off. If you don't and they let you get away with it they look weak. The hard boys that run the business, the big wheels, the board of directors, don't have any use for weak people. They're dangerous. And then there's Chris Mady."

"He just about runs Nevada, I heard."

"You heard right, chum. Mady is a nice guy but he knows what's right for Nevada. The rich hoodlums that operate in Reno and Vegas are very careful not to annoy Mr. Mady. If they did, their taxes would go up fast and their police co-operation would go down the same way. Then the top guys back East would decide some changes were necessary. An operator who can't get along with Chris Mady ain't operating correctly. Get him the hell out of there and put somebody else in. Getting him out of there means only one thing to them. Out in a wooden box."

"They never heard of me," I said.

Morgan frowned and whipped an arm up and down in a meaningless gesture. "They don't have to. Mady's estate on the Nevada side of Tahoe is right next to Harlan Potter's estate. Could be they say hello once in a while. Could be some character that is on Mady's payroll hears from another guy on Potter's payroll that a punk named Marlowe is buzzing too loud about things that are not any of his business. Could be that this passing remark gets passed on down to where the phone rings in some apartment in L.A. and a guy with large muscles gets a hint to go out and exercise himself and two or three of his friends. If somebody wants you knocked off or smashed, the muscle men don't have to have it explained why. It's mere routine to them. No hard feelings at all. Just sit still while we break your arm. You want this back?"

He held out the photostat.

"You know what I want," I said.

Morgan stood up slowly and put the photostat in his inside pocket. "I could be wrong," he said. "You may know more about it than I do. I wouldn't know how a man like Harlan Potter looks at things."

"With a scowl," I said. "I've met him. But he wouldn't operate with a goon squad. He couldn't reconcile it with his opinion of how he wants to live."

"For my money," Morgan said sharply, "stopping a murder investigation with a phone call and stopping it by knocking off the witness is just a question of method. See you around – I hope."

He drifted out of the office like something blown by the wind.

46

I DROVE OUT to Victor's with the idea of drinking a gimlet and sitting around until the evening edition of the morning papers was on the street. But the bar was crowded and it wasn't any fun. When the barkeep I knew got around to me he called me by name.

"You like a dash of bitters in it, don't you?"

"Not usually. Just for tonight two dashes of bitters."

"I haven't seen your friend lately. The one with the green ice."

"Neither have I."

He went away and came back with the drink. I pecked at it to make it last, because I didn't feel like getting a glow on. Either I would get really stiff or stay sober. After a while I had another of the same. It was just past six when the kid with the papers came into the bar. One of the barkeeps yelled at him to beat it, but he managed one quick round of the customers before a waiter got hold of him and threw him out. I was one of the customers. I opened up the *Journal* and glanced at page 1A. They had made it. It was all there. They had reversed the photostat by making it black on white and by reducing it in size they had fitted it into the top half of the page. There was a short brusque editorial on another page. There was a half column by Lonnie Morgan with a by-line, on still another page.

I finished my drink and left and went to another place to eat dinner and then drove home.

Lonnie Morgan's piece was a straightforward factual recapitulation of the facts and happenings involved in the Lennox case and the "suicide" of Roger Wade – the facts as they had been published. It added nothing, deduced nothing, imputed nothing. It was clear concise businesslike reporting. The editorial was something else. It asked questions – the kind a newspaper asks of public officials when they are caught with jam on their faces.

About nine-thirty the telephone rang and Bernie Ohls said he would drop by on his way home.

"Seen the *Journal*?" he asked coyly, and hung up without waiting for an answer.

When he got there he grunted about the steps and said he would drink a cup of coffee if I had one. I said I would make some. While I made it he wandered around the house and made himself very much at home.

"You live pretty lonely for a guy that could get himself disliked," he said. "What's over the hill in back?"

"Another street. Why?"

"Just asking. Your shrubbery needs pruning."

I carried some coffee into the living room and he parked himself and sipped it. He lit one of my cigarettes and puffed at it for a minute or two, then put it out. "Getting so I don't care for the stuff," he said. "Maybe it's the TV commercials. They make you hate everything they try to sell. God, they must think the public is a halfwit. Every time some jerk in a white coat with a stethoscope hanging around his neck holds up some toothpaste or a pack of cigarettes or a bottle of beer or a mouthwash or a jar of shampoo or a little box of something that makes a fat wrestler smell like mountain lilac I always make a note never to buy any. Hell, I wouldn't buy the product even if I liked it. You read the *Journal*, huh?"

"A friend of mine tipped me off. A reporter."

"You got friends?" he asked wonderingly. "Didn't tell you how they got hold of the material, did he?"

"No. And in this state he doesn't have to tell you."

"Springer is hopping mad. Lawford, the deputy D.A. that got the letter this morning, claims he took it straight to his boss, but it makes a guy wonder. What the *Journal* printed looks like a straight reproduction from the original."

I sipped coffee and said nothing.

"Serves him right," Ohls went on. "Springer ought to have handled it himself. Personally I don't figure it was Lawford that leaked. He's a politician too." He stared at me woodenly.

"What are you here for, Bernie? You don't like me. We used to be friends – as much as anybody can be friends with a tough cop. But it soured a little."

He leaned forward and smiled – a little wolfishly. "No cop likes it when a private citizen does police work behind his back. If you had connected up Wade and the Lennox frail for me the time Wade got dead I'd have made out. If you had connected up Mrs. Wade and this Terry Lennox I'd have had her in the palm of my hand – alive. If you had come clean from the start Wade might be still alive. Not to mention Lennox. You figure you're a pretty smart monkey, don't you?"

"What would you like me to say?"

"Nothing. It's too late. I told you a wise guy never fools anybody but himself. I told you straight and clear. So it didn't take. Right now it might be smart for you to leave town. Nobody likes you and a couple of guys that don't like people do something about it. I had the word from a stoolie."

"I'm not that important, Bernie. Let's stop snarling at each other. Until Wade was dead you didn't even enter the case. After that it didn't seem to matter to you and to the coroner or to the D.A. or to anybody. Maybe I did some things wrong. But the truth came out. You could have had her yesterday afternoon – with what?"

"With what you had to tell us about her."

"Me? With the police work I did behind your back?"

He stood up abruptly. His face was red. "Okay, wise guy. She'd have been alive. We could have booked her on suspicion. You *wanted* her dead, you punk, and you know it."

"I wanted her to take a good long quiet look at herself. What she did about it was her business. I wanted to clear an innocent man. I didn't give a good goddam how I did it and I don't now. I'll be around when you feel like doing something about me."

"The hard boys will take care of you, buster. I won't have to bother. You think you're not important enough to bother them. As a P.I. named Marlowe, check. You're not. As a guy who was told where to get off and blew a raspberry in their faces publicly in a newspaper, that's different. That hurts their pride."

"That's pitiful," I said. "Just thinking about it makes me bleed internally, to use your own expression."

He went across to the door and opened it. He stood looking down the redwood steps and at the trees on the hill across the way and up the slope at the end of the street.

"Nice and quiet here," he said. "Just quiet enough."

He went on down the steps and got into his car and left. Cops never say goodbye. They're always hoping to see you again in the line-up.

47

FOR A SHORT time the next day things looked like getting lively. District Attorney Springer called an early press conference and delivered a statement. He was the big florid black-browed prematurely gray-haired type that always does so well in politics.

"*I have read the document which purports to be a confession by the unfortunate and unhappy woman who recently took her life, a document which may or may not be genuine, but which, if genuine, is obviously the product of a disordered mind. I am willing to assume that the* Journal *published this document in good faith, in spite of its many absurdities and inconsistencies, and these I shall not bore you with enumerating. If Eileen Wade wrote these words, and my office in conjunction with the staff of my respected coadjutor, Sheriff Petersen, will soon determine whether or not she did, then I say to you that she did not write them with a clear head, nor with a steady hand. It is only a matter of weeks since the unfortunate lady found her husband wallowing in his own blood, spilled by his own hand. Imagine the shock, the despair, the utter loneliness which must have followed so sharp a disaster! And now she has joined him in the bitterness of death. Is anything to be gained by disturbing the ashes of the dead?*

Anything, my friends, beyond the sale of a few copies of a newspaper which is badly in need of circulation? Nothing, my friends, nothing. Let us leave it at that. Like Ophelia in that great dramatic masterpiece called Hamlet, *by the immortal William Shakespeare, Eileen Wade wore her rue with a difference. My political enemies would like to make much of that difference, but my friends and fellow voters will not be deceived. They know that this office has long stood for wise and mature law enforcement, for justice tempered with mercy, for solid, stable, and conservative government. The* Journal *stands for I know not what, and for what it stands I do not much or greatly care. Let the enlightened public judge for itself. "*

The Journal printed this guff in its early edition (it was a round-the-clock newspaper) and Henry Sherman, the Managing Editor, came right back at Springer with a signed document.

Mr. District Attorney Springer was in good form this morning. He is a fine figure of a man and he speaks with a rich baritone voice that is a pleasure to listen to. He did not bore us with any facts. Any time Mr. Springer cares to have the authenticity of the document in question proved to him, the *Journal* will be most happy to oblige. We do not expect Mr. Springer to take any action to reopen cases which had been officially closed with his sanction or under his direction, just as we do not expect Mr. Springer to stand on his head on the tower of the City Hall. As Mr. Springer so aptly phrases it, is anything to be gained by disturbing the ashes of the dead? Or, as the *Journal* would prefer to phrase it less elegantly, is anything to be gained by finding out who committed a murder when the murderee is already dead? Nothing, of course, but justice and truth.

On behalf of the late William Shakespeare, the *Journal* wishes to thank Mr. Springer for his favorable mention of *Hamlet*, and for his substantially, although not exactly, correct allusion to Ophelia. 'You must wear your rue with a difference' was not said of Ophelia but by her, and just what she meant has never been very clear to our less erudite minds. But let that pass. It sounds well and helps to confuse the issue. Perhaps we may be permitted to quote, also from that officially approved dramatic production known as *Hamlet*, a good thing that happened to be said by a bad man: "And where the offence is let the great axe fall."

Lonnie Morgan called me up about noon and asked me how I liked it. I told him I didn't think it would do Springer any harm.

"Only with the eggheads," Lonnie Morgan said, "and they already had his number. I meant what about you?"

"Nothing about me. I'm just sitting here waiting for a soft buck to rub itself against my cheek."

"That wasn't exactly what I meant."

"I'm still healthy. Quit trying to scare me. I got what I wanted. If Lennox was still alive he could walk right up to Springer and spit in his eye."

"You did it for him. And by this time Springer knows that. They got a hundred ways to frame a guy they don't like. I don't figure what made it worth your time. Lennox wasn't that much man."

"What's that got to do with it?"

He was silent for a moment. Then he said: "Sorry, Marlowe. Shut my big mouth. Good luck."

We hung up after the usual goodbyes.

★

About two in the afternoon Linda Loring called me. "No names, please," she said. "I've just flown in from that big lake up north. Somebody up there is boiling over something that was in the *Journal* last night. My almost ex-husband got it right between the eyes. The poor man was weeping when I left. He flew up to report."

"What do you mean, almost ex-husband?"

"Don't be stupid. For once Father approves. Paris is an excellent place to get a quiet divorce. So I shall soon be leaving to go there. And if you have any sense left you could do worse than spend a little of that fancy engraving you showed me going a long way off yourself."

"What's it got to do with me?"

"That's the second stupid question you've asked. You're not fooling anyone but yourself, Marlowe. Do you know how they shoot tigers?"

"How would I?"

"They tie a goat to a stake and then hide out in a blind. It's apt to be rough on the goat. I like you. I'm sure I don't know why, but I do. I hate the idea of your being the goat. You tried so hard to do the right thing – as you saw it."

"Nice of you," I said. "If I stick my neck out and it gets chopped, it's still my neck."

"Don't be a hero, you fool," she said sharply. "Just because someone we knew chose to be a fall guy, you don't have to imitate him."

"I'll buy you a drink if you're going to be around long enough."

"Buy me one in Paris. Paris is lovely in the fall."

"I'd like to do that too. I hear it was even better in the spring. Never having been there I wouldn't know."

"The way you're going you never will."

"Goodbye, Linda. I hope you find what you want."

"Goodbye," she said coldly. "I always find what I want. But when I find it, I don't want it any more."

She hung up. The rest of the day was a blank. I ate dinner and left the Olds at an all-night garage to have the brake linings checked. I took a cab home. The street was as empty as usual. In the wooden mailbox was a free soap coupon. I went up the steps slowly. It was a soft night with a little haze in the air. The trees on the hill hardly moved. No breeze. I unlocked the door and pushed it part way open and then stopped. The door was about ten inches open from the frame. It was dark inside, there was no sound. But I had the feeling that the room beyond was not empty. Perhaps a spring squeaked faintly or I caught the gleam of a white jacket across the room. Perhaps on a warm still night like this one the room beyond the door was not warm enough, not still enough. Perhaps there was a drifting smell of man on the air. And perhaps I was just on edge.

I stepped sideways off the porch on to the ground and leaned down against the shrubbery. Nothing happened. No light went on inside, there was no movement anywhere that I heard. I had a gun in a belt holster on the left side, butt forward, a short-barreled Police .38. I jerked it out and it got me nowhere. The silence continued. I decided I was a damn fool. I straightened up and lifted a foot to go back to the front door, and then a car turned the corner and came fast up the hill and stopped almost without sound at the foot of my steps. It was a big black sedan with the lines of a Cadillac. It could have been Linda Loring's car, except for two things. Nobody opened a door and the windows on my side were all shut tight. I waited and listened, crouched against the bush, and there was nothing to listen to and nothing to wait for. Just a dark car motionless at the foot of my redwood steps, with the windows closed. If its motor was still running I couldn't hear it. Then a big red spotlight clicked on and the beam struck twenty feet beyond the corner of the house. And then very slowly the big car backed until the spotlight could swing across the front of the house, across the hood and up.

Policemen don't drive Cadillacs. Cadillacs with red spotlights belong to the big boys, mayors and police commissioners, perhaps District Attorneys. Perhaps hoodlums.

The spotlight traversed. I went down flat, but it found me just the same. It held on me. Nothing else. Still the car door didn't open, still the house was silent and without light.

Then a siren growled in low pitch just for a second or two and stopped. And then at last the house was full of lights and a man in a white dinner jacket came out to the head of the steps and looked sideways along the wall and the shrubbery.

"Come on in, cheapie," Menendez said with a chuckle. "You've got company."

I could have shot him with no trouble at all. Then he stepped back and it was too late – even if I could have done it. Then a window went down at the back of the car and I could hear the thud as it opened. Then a machine pistol went off and fired a short burst into the slope of the bank thirty feet away from me.

"Come on in, cheapie," Menendez said again from the doorway. "There just ain't anywhere else to go."

So I straightened up and went and the spotlight followed me accurately. I put the gun back in the holster on my belt. I stepped up onto the small redwood landing and went in through the door and stopped just inside. A man was sitting across the room with his legs crossed and a gun resting sideways on his thigh. He looked rangy and tough and his skin had that dried-out look of people who live in sun-bleached climates. He was wearing a dark brown gabardine-type windbreaker and the zipper was open almost to his waist. He was looking at me and neither his eyes nor the gun moved. He was as calm as an adobe wall in the moon-light.

48

I LOOKED AT him too long. There was a brief half-seen move at my side and a numbing pain in the point of my shoulder. My whole arm went dead to the fingertips. I turned and looked at a big mean-looking Mexican. He wasn't grinning, he was just watching me. The .45 in his brown hand dropped to his side. He had a mustache and his head bulged with oily black hair brushed up and back and over and down. There was a dirty sombrero on the back of his head and the leather chin strap hung loose in two strands down the front of a stitched shirt that smelled of sweat. There is nothing tougher than a tough Mexican, just as there is nothing gentler than a gentle Mexican, nothing more honest than an honest Mexican, and above all nothing sadder than a sad Mexican. This guy was one of the hard boys. They don't come any harder anywhere.

I rubbed my arm. It tingled a little but the ache was still there and the numbness. If I had tried to pull a gun I should probably have dropped it.

Menendez held his hand out towards the slugger. Without seeming to look he tossed the gun and Menendez caught it. He stood in front of me now and his face glistened. "Where would you like it, cheapie?" His black eyes danced.

I just looked at him. There is no answer to a question like that.

"I asked you a question, cheapie."

I wet my lips and asked one back. "What happened to Agostino? I thought he was your gun handler."

"Chick went soft," he said gently.

"He was always soft – like his boss."

The man in the chair flicked his eyes. He almost but not quite smiled. The tough boy who had paralyzed my arm neither moved nor spoke. I knew he was breathing. I could smell that.

"Somebody bump into your arm, cheapie?"

"I tripped over an enchilada."

Negligently, not quite looking at me even, he slashed me across the face with the gun barrel.

"Don't get gay with me, cheapie. You're out of time for all that. You got told and you got told nice. When I take the trouble to call around personally and tell a character to lay off — he lays off. Or else he lays down and don't get up."

I could feel a trickle of blood down my cheek. I could feel the full numbing ache of the blow in my cheekbone. It spread until my whole head ached. It hadn't been a hard blow, but the thing he used was hard. I could still talk and nobody tried to stop me.

"How come you do your own slugging, Mendy? I thought that was coolie labor for the sort of boys that beat up Big Willie Magoon."

"It's the personal touch," he said softly, "on account of I had personal reasons for telling you. The Magoon job was strictly business. He got to thinking he could push me around — me that bought his clothes and his cars and stocked his safe deposit box and paid off the trust deed on his house. These vice squad babies are all the same. I even paid school bills for his kid. You'd think the bastard would have some gratitude. So what does he do? He walks into my private office and slaps me around in front of the help."

"On account of why?" I asked him, in the vague hope of getting him mad at somebody else.

"On account of some lacquered chippie said we used loaded dice. Seems like the bim was one of his sleepy-time gals. I had her put out of the club — with every dime she brought in with her."

"Seems understandable," I said. "Magoon ought to know no professional gambler plays crooked games. He doesn't have to. But what have I done to you?"

He hit me again, thoughtfully. "You made me look bad. In my racket you don't tell a guy twice. Not even a hard number. He goes out and does it, or you ain't got control. You ain't got control, you ain't in business."

"I've got a hunch that there's a little more to it than that," I said. "Excuse me if I reach for a handkerchief."

The gun watched me while I got one out and touched the blood on my face.

"A two-bit peeper," Menendez said slowly, "figures he can make a monkey out of Mendy Menendez. He can get me laughed at. He can get me the big razzoo – me, Menendez. I ought to use a knife on you, cheapie. I ought to cut you into slices of raw meat."

"Lennox was your pal," I said, and watched his eyes. "He got dead. He got buried like a dog without even a name over the dirt where they put his body. And I had a little something to do with proving him innocent. So that makes you look bad, huh? He saved your life and he lost his, and that didn't mean a thing to you. All that means anything to you is playing the big shot. You didn't give a hoot in hell for anybody but yourself. You're not big, you're just loud."

His face froze and he swung his arm back to slug me a third time and this time with the power behind it. His arm was still going back when I took a half step forward and kicked him in the pit of the stomach.

I didn't think, I didn't plan, I didn't figure my chances or whether I had any. I just got enough of his yap and I ached and bled and maybe I was just a little punch drunk by this time.

He jackknifed, gasping, and the gun fell out of his hand. He groped for it wildly making strained sounds deep in his throat. I put a knee into his face. He screeched.

The man in the chair laughed. That staggered me. Then he stood up and the gun in his hand came up with him.

"Don't kill him," he said mildly. "We want to use him for live bait."

Then there was movement in the shadows of the hall and Ohls came through the door, blank-eyed, expressionless and utterly calm. He looked down at Menendez. Menendez was kneeling with his head on the floor.

"Soft," Ohls said. "Soft as mush."

"He's not soft," I said. "He's hurt. Any man can be hurt. Was Big Willie Magoon soft?"

Ohls looked at me. The other man looked at me. The tough Mex at the door hadn't made a sound.

"Take that goddam cigarette out of your face," I snarled at Ohls. "Either smoke it or leave it alone. I'm sick of watching you. I'm sick of you, period. I'm sick of cops."

He looked surprised. Then he grinned.

"That was a plant, kiddo," he said cheerfully. "You hurt bad? Did the nasty mans hit your facey-wacey? Well for my money you had it coming and it was damn useful that you had." He looked down at Mendy. Mendy had his knees under him. He was climbing out of a well, a few inches at a time. He breathed gaspingly.

"What a talkative lad he is," Ohls said, "when he doesn't have three shysters with him to button his lip."

He jerked Menendez to his feet. Mendy's nose was bleeding. He fumbled the handkerchief out of his white dinner jacket and held it to his nose. He said no word.

"You got crossed up, sweetheart," Ohls told him carefully. "I ain't grieving a whole lot over Magoon. He had it coming. But he was a cop and punks like you lay off cops – always and forever."

Menendez lowered the handkerchief and looked at Ohls. He looked at me. He looked at the man who had been sitting in the chair. He turned slowly and looked at the tough Mex by the door. They all looked at him. There was nothing in their faces. Then a knife shot into view from nowhere and Mendy lunged for Ohls. Ohls side-stepped and took him by the throat with one hand and chopped the knife out of his hand with ease, almost indifferently. Ohls spread his feet and straightened his back and bent his legs slightly and lifted Menendez clear off the floor with one hand holding his neck. He walked him across the floor and pinned him against the wall. He let him down, but didn't let go of his throat.

789

"Touch me with one finger and I'll kill you," Ohls said. "One finger." Then he dropped his hands.

Mendy smiled at him scornfully, looked at his handkerchief, and refolded it to hide the blood. He held it to his nose again. He looked down at the gun he had used to hit me. The man from the chair said loosely: "Not loaded, even if you could grab it."

"A cross," Mendy said to Ohls. "I heard you the first time."

"You ordered three muscles," Ohls said. "What you got was three deputies from Nevada. Somebody in Vegas don't like the way you forget to clear with them. The somebody wants to talk to you. You can go along with the deputies or you can go downtown with me and get hung on the back of the door by a pair of handcuffs. There's a couple of boys down there would like to see you close up."

"God help Nevada," Mendy said quietly, looking around again at the tough Mex by the door. Then he crossed himself quickly and walked out of the front door. The tough Mex followed him. Then the other one, the dried out desert type, picked up the gun and the knife and went out too. He shut the door. Ohls waited motionless. There was a sound of doors banging shut, then a car went off into the night.

"You sure those mugs were deputies?" I asked Ohls.

He turned as if surprised to see me there. "They had stars," he said shortly.

"Nice work, Bernie. Very nice. Think he'll get to Vegas alive, you coldhearted son of a bitch?"

I went to the bathroom and ran cold water and held a soaked towel against my throbbing cheek. I looked at myself in the glass. The cheek was puffed out of shape and bluish and there were jagged wounds on it from the force of the gun barrel hitting against the cheekbone. There was a discoloration under my left eye too. I wasn't going to be beautiful for a few days.

Then Ohls' reflection showed behind me in the mirror. He was rolling his damn unlighted cigarette along his lips, like a cat teasing a half-dead mouse, trying to get it to run away just once more.

"Next time don't try to outguess the cops," he said gruffly. "You think we let you steal that photostat just for laughs? We had a hunch Mendy would come gunning for you. We put it up to Starr cold. We told him we couldn't stop gambling in the county, but we could make it tough enough to cut way into the take. No mobster beats up a cop, not even a bad cop, and gets away with it in our territory. Starr convinced us he had nothing to do with it, that the outfit was sore about it and Menendez was going to get told. So when Mendy called for a squad of out-of-town hard boys to come and give you the treatment, Starr sent him three guys he knew, in one of his own cars, at his own expense. Starr is a police commissioner in Vegas."

I turned around and looked at Ohls. "The coyotes out in the desert will get fed tonight. Congratulations. Cop business is wonderful uplifting idealistic work, Bernie. The only thing wrong with cop business is the cops that are in it."

"Too bad for you, hero," he said with a sudden cold savagery. "I could hardly help laughing when you walked into your own parlor to take your beating. I got a rise out of that, kiddo. It was a dirty job and it had to be done dirty. To make these characters talk you got to give them a sense of power. You ain't hurt bad, but we had to let them hurt you some."

"So sorry," I said. "So very sorry you had to suffer like that."

He shoved his taut face at me. "I hate gamblers," he said in a rough voice. "I hate them the way I hate dope pushers. They pander to a disease that is every bit as corrupting as dope. You think those palaces in Reno and Vegas are just for harmless fun? Nuts, they're there for the little guy, the something-for-nothing sucker, the lad that stops off with his pay envelope in his pocket and loses the week-end grocery money. The rich gambler loses forty grand and laughs it off and comes back for more. But the rich gambler don't make the big racket, pal. The big steal is in dimes and quarters and half dollars and once in a while a buck or even a five-spot. The big racket money comes in like water from the pipe in your bathroom, a steady stream that never stops flowing. Any time anybody wants to knock off a professional gambler, that's for me. I like it. And any time a state government takes money from gambling and calls it taxes, that government is helping to keep the mobs in business. The barber or the beauty parlor girl puts two bucks on the nose. That's for the Syndicate, that's what really makes the profits. The people want an honest police force, do they? What for? To protect the guys with courtesy cards? We got legal horse tracks in this state, we got them all year round. They operate honest and the state gets its cut, and for every dollar laid at the track there's fifty laid with the bookies. There's eight or nine races on a card and in half of them, the little ones nobody notices, the fix can be in any time somebody says so. There's only one way a jock can win a race, but there's twenty ways he can lose one, with a steward at every eighth pole watching, and not able to do a damn thing about it if the jock knows his stuff. That's legal gambling, pal, clean honest business, state approved. So it's right, is it? Not by my book, it ain't. Because it's gambling and it breeds gamblers and when you add it up there's one kind of gambling – the wrong kind."

"Feel better?" I asked him, putting some white iodine on my wounds.

"I'm an old tired beat-up cop. All I feel is sore."

I turned around and stared at him. "You're a damn good cop, Bernie, but just the same you're all wet. In one way cops are all the same. They all blame the wrong things. If a guy loses his pay check at a crap table, stop gambling. If he gets drunk, stop liquor. If he kills somebody in a car crash, stop making automobiles. If he gets pinched with a girl in a hotel room, stop sexual intercourse. If he falls downstairs, stop building houses."

"Aw shut up!"

"Sure, shut me up. I'm just a private citizen. Get off it, Bernie. We don't have mobs and crime syndicates and goon squads because we have crooked politicians and their stooges in the City Hall and the legislatures. Crime isn't a disease, it's a symptom. Cops are like a doctor that gives you aspirin for a brain tumor, except that the cop would rather cure it with a blackjack. We're a big rough rich wild people and crime is the price we pay for it, and organized crime is the price we pay for organization. We'll have it with us a long time. Organized crime is just the dirty side of the sharp dollar."

"What's the clean side?"

"I never saw it. Maybe Harlan Potter could tell you. Let's have a drink."

"You looked pretty good walking in that door," Ohls said.

"You looked better when Mendy pulled the knife on you."

"Shake," he said, and put his hand out.

We had the drink and he left by the back door, which he had jimmied to get in, having dropped by the night before for scouting purposes. Back doors are a soft touch if they open out and are old enough for the wood to have dried and shrunk. You knock the pins out of the hinges and the rest is easy. Ohls showed me a dent in the frame when he left to go back over the hill to where he had left his car on the next street. He could have opened the front door almost as easily but that would have broken the lock. It would have showed up too much.

I watched him climb through the trees with the beam of a torch in front of him and disappear over the rise. I locked the door and mixed another mild drink and went back to the living room and sat down. I looked at my watch. It was still early. It only seemed a long time since I had come home.

I went to the phone and dialed the operator and gave her the Lorings' phone number. The butler asked who was calling, then went to see if Mrs. Loring was in. She was.

"I was the goat all right," I said, "but they caught the tiger alive. I'm bruised up a little."

"You must tell me about it sometime." She sounded about as far away as if she had got to Paris already.

"I could tell you over a drink – if you had time."

"Tonight? Oh, I'm packing my things to move out. I'm afraid that would be impossible."

"Yes, I can see that. Well, I just thought you might like to know. It was kind of you to warn me. It had nothing at all to do with your old man."

"Are you sure?"

"Positive."

"Oh. Just a minute." She was gone for a time, then she came back and sounded warmer. "Perhaps I could fit a drink in. Where?"

"Anywhere you say. I haven't a car tonight, but I can get a cab."

"Nonsense, I'll pick you up, but it will be an hour or longer. What is the address there?"

I told her and she hung up and I put the porch light on and then stood in the open door inhaling the night. It had got much cooler.

I went back in and tried to phone Lonnie Morgan but couldn't reach him. Then just for the hell of it I put a call in to the Terrapin Club at Las Vegas, Mr. Randy Starr. He probably wouldn't take it. But he did. He had a quiet, competent, man-of-affairs voice.

"Nice to hear from you, Marlowe. Any friend of Terry's is a friend of mine. What can I do for you?"

"Mendy is on his way."

"On his way where?"

"To Vegas, with the three goons you sent after him in a big black Caddy with a red spotlight and siren. Yours, I presume?"

He laughed. "In Vegas, as some newspaper guy said, we use Cadillacs for trailers. What's this all about?"

"Mendy staked out here in my house with a couple of hard boys. His idea was to beat me up – putting it low – for a piece in the paper he seemed to think was my fault."

"Was it your fault?"

"I don't own any newspapers, Mr. Starr."

"I don't own any hard boys in Cadillacs, Mr. Marlowe."

"They were deputies maybe."

"I couldn't say. Anything else?"

"He pistol-whipped me. I kicked him in the stomach and used my knee on his nose. He seemed dissatisfied. All the same I hope he gets to Vegas alive."

"I'm sure he will, if he started this way. I'm afraid I'll have to cut this conversation short now."

"Just a second, Starr. Were you in on that caper at Otatoclán – or did Mendy work it alone?"

"Come again?"

"Don't kid, Starr. Mendy wasn't sore at me for why he said – not to the point of staking out in my house and giving me the treatment he gave Big Willie Magoon. Not enough motive. He warned me to keep my nose clean and not to dig into the Lennox case. But I did, because it just happened to work out that way. So he did what I've just told you. So there was a better reason."

"I see," he said slowly and still mildly and quietly. "You think there was something not quite kosher about how Terry got dead? That he didn't shoot himself, for instance, but someone else did?"

"I think the details would help. He wrote a confession which was false. He wrote a letter to me which got mailed. A waiter or hop in the hotel was going to sneak it out and mail it for him. He was holed up in the hotel and couldn't get out. There was a big bill in the letter and the letter was finished just as a knock came at his door. I'd like to know who came into the room."

"Why?"

"If it had been a bellhop or a waiter Terry would have added a line to the letter and said so. If it was a cop, the letter wouldn't have been mailed. So who was it – and why did Terry write that confession?"

"No idea, Marlowe. No idea at all."

"Sorry I bothered you, Mr. Starr."

"No bother, glad to hear from you. I'll ask Mendy if he has any ideas."

"Yeah — if you ever see him again — alive. If you don't — find out anyway. Or somebody else will."

"You?" His voice hardened now, but it was still quiet.

"No, Mr. Starr. Not me. Somebody that could blow you out of Vegas without taking a long breath. Believe me, Mr. Starr. Just believe me. This is strictly on the level."

"I'll see Mendy alive. Don't worry about that, Marlowe."

"I figured you knew all about that. Goodnight, Mr. Starr."

49

WHEN THE CAR stopped out front and the door opened I went out and stood at the top of the steps to call down. But the middle-aged colored driver was holding the door for her to get out. Then he followed her up the steps carrying a small overnight case. So I just waited.

She reached the top and turned to the driver: "Mr. Marlowe will drive me to my hotel, Amos. Thank you for everything. I'll call you in the morning."

"Yes, Mrs. Loring. May I ask Mr. Marlowe a question?"

"Certainly, Amos."

He put the overnight case down inside the door and she went in past me and left us.

" 'I grow old . . . I grow old . . . I shall wear the bottoms of my trousers rolled.' What does that mean, Mr. Marlowe?"

"Not a bloody thing. It just sounds good."

He smiled. "That is from the 'Love Song of J. Alfred Prufrock.' Here's another one. 'In the room the women come and go/Talking of Michael Angelo.' Does that suggest anything to you, sir?"

"Yeah – it suggests to me that the guy didn't know very much about women."

"My sentiments exactly, sir. Nonetheless I admire T. S. Eliot very much."

"Did you say 'nonetheless'?"

"Why, yes I did, Mr. Marlowe. Is that incorrect?"

"No, but don't say it in front of a millionaire. He might think you were giving him the hotfoot."

He smiled sadly. "I shouldn't dream of it. Have you had an accident, sir?"

"Nope. It was planned that way. Goodnight, Amos."

"Goodnight, sir."

He went back down the steps and I went back into the house. Linda Loring was standing in the middle of the living room looking around her.

"Amos is a graduate of Howard University," she said. "You don't live in a very safe place – for such an unsafe man, do you?"

"There aren't any safe places."

"Your poor face. Who did that to you?"

"Mendy Menendez."

"What did you do to him?"

"Nothing much. Kicked him a time or two. He walked into a trap. He's on his way to Nevada in the company of three or four tough Nevada deputies. Forget him."

She sat down on the davenport.

"What would you like to drink?" I asked. I got a cigarette box and held it out to her. She said she didn't want to smoke. She said anything would do to drink.

"I thought of champagne," I said. "I haven't any ice bucket, but it's cold. I've been saving it for years. Two bottles. Cordon Rouge. I guess it's good. I'm no judge."

"Saving it for what?" she asked.

"For you."

She smiled, but she was still staring at my face. "You're all cut." She reached her fingers up and touched my cheek lightly.

797

"Saving it for me? That's not very likely. It's only a couple of months since we met."

"Then I was saving it until we met. I'll go get it." I picked up her overnight bag and started across the room with it.

"Just where are you going with that?" she asked sharply.

"It's an overnight bag, isn't it?"

"Put it down and come back here."

I did that. Her eyes were bright and at the same time they were sleepy.

"This is something new," she said slowly. "Something quite new."

"In what way?"

"You've never laid a finger on me. No passes, no suggestive remarks, no pawing, no nothing. I thought you were tough, sarcastic, mean, and cold."

"I guess I am – at times."

"Now I'm here and I suppose without preamble, after we have had a reasonable quantity of champagne you plan to grab me and throw me on the bed. Is that it?"

"Frankly," I said, "some such idea did stir at the back of my mind."

"I'm flattered, but suppose I don't want it that way? I like you. I like you very much. But it doesn't follow that I want to go to bed with you. Aren't you rather jumping at conclusions – just because I happen to bring an overnight bag with me?"

"Could be I made an error," I said. I went and got her overnight bag and put it back by the front door. "I'll get the champagne."

"I didn't mean to hurt your feelings. Perhaps you would rather save the champagne for some more auspicious occasion."

"It's only two bottles," I said. "A really auspicious occasion would call for a dozen."

"Oh, I see," she said, suddenly angry. "I'm just to be a fill-in until someone more beautiful and attractive comes along.

Thank you so very much. Now you've hurt my feelings, but I suppose it's something to know that I'm safe here. If you think a bottle of champagne will make a loose woman out of me, I can assure you that you are very much mistaken."

"I admitted the mistake already."

"The fact that I told you I was going to divorce my husband and that I had Amos drop me by here with an overnight bag doesn't make me as easy as all that," she said, still angry.

"Damn the overnight bag!" I growled. "The hell with the overnight bag! Mention it again and I'll throw the damn thing down the front steps. I asked you to have a drink. I'm going out to the kitchen to get the drink. That's all. I hadn't the least idea of getting you drunk. You don't want to go to bed with me. I understand perfectly. No reason why you should. But we can still have a glass or two of champagne, can't we? This doesn't have to be a wrangle about who is going to get seduced and when and where and on how much champagne."

"You don't have to lose your temper," she said, flushing.

"That's just another gambit," I snarled. "I know fifty of them and I hate them all. They're all phony and they all have a sort of leer at the edges."

She got up and came over close to me and ran the tips of her fingers gently over the cuts and swollen places on my face. "I'm sorry. I'm a tired and disappointed woman. Please be kind to me. I'm no bargain to anyone."

"You're not tired and you're no more disappointed than most people are. By all the rules you ought to be the same sort of shallow spoiled promiscuous brat your sister was. By some miracle you're not. You've got all the honesty and a large part of the guts in your family. You don't need anyone to be kind to you."

I turned and walked out of the room down the hall to the kitchen and got one of the bottles of champagne out of the icebox and popped the cork and filled a couple of shallow goblets quickly and drank one down. The sting of it brought tears to my eyes, but I emptied the glass. I filled it again. Then I put the whole works on a tray and carted it into the living room.

She wasn't there. The overnight bag wasn't there. I put the tray down and opened the front door. I hadn't heard any sound of its opening and she had no car. I hadn't heard any sound at all.

Then she spoke from behind me. "Idiot, did you think I was going to run away?"

I shut the door and turned. She had loosened her hair and she had tufted slippers on her bare feet and a silk robe the color of a sunset in a Japanese print. She came towards me slowly with a sort of unexpectedly shy smile. I held a glass out to her. She took it, took a couple of sips of the champagne, and handed it back.

"It's very nice," she said. Then very quietly and without a trace of acting or affectation she came into my arms and pressed her mouth against mine and opened her lips and her teeth. The tip of her tongue touched mine. After a long time she pulled her head back but kept her arms around my neck. She was starry-eyed.

"I meant to all the time," she said. "I just had to be difficult. I don't know why. Just nerves perhaps. I'm not really a loose woman at all. Is that a pity?"

"If I had thought you were I'd have made a pass at you the first time I met you in the bar at Victor's."

She shook her head slowly and smiled. "I don't think so. That's why I am here."

"Perhaps not that night," I said. "That night belonged to something else."

"Perhaps you don't ever make passes at women in bars."

"Not often. The light's too dim."

"But a lot of women go to bars just to have passes made at them."

THE LONG GOODBYE

"A lot of women get up in the morning with the same idea."

"But liquor is an aphrodisiac — up to a point."

"Doctors recommend it."

"Who said anything about doctors? I want my champagne."

I kissed her some more. It was light, pleasant work.

"I want to kiss your poor cheek," she said, and did. "It's burning hot," she said.

"The rest of me is freezing."

"It is not. I want my champagne."

"Why?"

"It'll get flat if we don't drink it. Besides I like the taste of it."

"All right."

"Do you love me very much? Or will you if I go to bed with you?"

"Possibly."

"You don't have to go to bed with me, you know. I don't absolutely insist on it."

"Thank you."

"I want my champagne."

"How much money have you got?"

"Altogether? How would I know? About eight million dollars."

"I've decided to go to bed with you."

"Mercenary," she said.

"I paid for the champagne."

"The hell with the champagne," she said.

50

AN HOUR LATER she stretched out a bare arm and tickled my ear and said: "Would you consider marrying me?"

"It wouldn't last six months."

"Well, for God's sake," she said, "suppose it didn't. Wouldn't it be worth it? What do you expect from life – full coverage against all possible risks?"

"I'm forty-two years old. I'm spoiled by independence. You're spoiled a little – not too much – by money."

"I'm thirty-six. It's no disgrace to have money and no disgrace to marry it. Most of those who have it don't deserve it and don't know how to behave with it. But it won't be long. We'll have another war and at the end of that nobody will have any money – except the crooks and the chiselers. We'll all be taxed to nothing, the rest of us."

I stroked her hair and wound some of it around my finger. "You may be right."

"We could fly to Paris and have a wonderful time." She raised herself on an elbow and looked down at me. I could see the shine of her eyes but I couldn't read her expression. "Do you have something against marriage?"

"For two people in a hundred it's wonderful. The rest just work at it. After twenty years all the guy has left is a work bench in the garage. American girls are terrific. American wives take in too damn much territory. Besides –"

"I want some champagne."

"Besides," I said, "it would be just an incident to you. The first divorce is the only tough one. After that it's merely a problem in economics. No problem to you. Ten years from now you might pass me on the street and wonder where the hell you had seen me before. If you noticed me at all."

"You self-sufficient, self-satisfied, self-confident, untouchable bastard. I want some champagne."

"This way you will remember me."

"Conceited too. A mass of conceit. Slightly bruised at the moment. You think I'll remember you? No matter how many men I marry or sleep with, you think I'll remember you? Why should I?"

"Sorry. I overstated my case. I'll get you some champagne."

"Aren't we sweet and reasonable?" she said sarcastically. "I'm a rich woman, darling, and I shall be infinitely richer. I could buy you the world if it were worth buying. What have you now? An empty house to come home to, with not even a dog or cat, a small stuffy office to sit in and wait. Even if I divorced you I'd never let you go back to that."

"How would you stop me? I'm no Terry Lennox."

"Please. Don't let's talk about him. Nor about that golden icicle, the Wade woman. Nor about her poor drunken sunken husband. Do you want to be the only man who turned me down? What kind of pride is that? I've paid you the greatest compliment I know how to pay. I've asked you to marry me."

"You paid me a greater compliment."

She began to cry. "You fool, you utter fool!" Her cheeks were wet. I could feel the tears on them. "Suppose it lasted six months or a year or two years. What would you have lost except the dust on your office desk and the dirt on your venetian blinds and the loneliness of a pretty empty kind of life?"

"You still want some champagne?"

"All right."

I pulled her close and she cried against my shoulder. She wasn't in love with me and we both knew it. She wasn't crying over me. It was just time for her to shed a few tears.

Then she pulled away and I got out of bed and she went into the bathroom to fix her face. I got the champagne. When she came back she was smiling.

"I'm sorry I blubbered," she said. "In six months from now I won't even remember your name. Bring it into the living room. I want to see lights."

I did what she said. She sat on the davenport as before. I put the champagne in front of her. She looked at the glass but didn't touch it.

"I'll introduce myself," I said. "We'll have a drink together."

"Like tonight?"

"It won't ever be like tonight again."

She raised her glass of champagne, drank a little of it slowly, turned her body on the davenport, and threw the rest in my face. Then she began to cry again. I got a handkerchief out and wiped my face off and wiped hers for her.

"I don't know why I did that," she said. "But for God's sake don't say I'm a woman and a woman never knows why she does anything."

I poured some more champagne into her glass and laughed at her. She drank it slowly and then turned the other way and fell across my knees.

"I'm tired," she said. "You'll have to carry me this time."

After a while she went to sleep.

In the morning she was still asleep when I got up and made coffee. I showered and shaved and dressed. She woke up then. We had breakfast together. I called a cab and carried her overnight case down the steps.

We said goodbye. I watched the cab out of sight. I went back up the steps and into the bedroom and pulled the bed to pieces and remade it. There was a long dark hair on one of the pillows. There was a lump of lead at the pit of my stomach.

The French have a phrase for it. The bastards have a phrase for everything and they are always right.

To say goodbye is to die a little.

51

SEWELL ENDICOTT SAID he was working late and I could drop around in the evening about seven-thirty.

He had a corner office with a blue carpet, a red mahogany desk with carved corners, very old and obviously very valuable, the usual glass-front bookshelves of mustard-yellow legal books, the usual cartoons by Spy of famous English judges, and a large portrait of Justice Oliver Wendell Holmes on the south wall, alone. Endicott's chair was quilted in black leather.

Near him was an open rolltop desk jammed with papers. It was an office no decorator had had a chance to pansy up.

He was in his shirtsleeves and he looked tired, but he had that kind of face. He was smoking one of his tasteless cigarettes. Ashes from it had fallen on his loosened tie. His limp black hair was all over the place.

He stared at me silently after I sat down. Then he said: "You're a stubborn son of a bitch, if ever I met one. Don't tell me you're still digging into that mess."

"Something worries me a little. Would it be all right now if I assumed you were representing Mr. Harlan Potter when you came to see me in the birdcage?"

He nodded. I touched the side of my face gently with my fingertips. It was all healed up and the swelling was gone, but one of the blows must have damaged a nerve. Part of the cheek was still numb. I couldn't let it alone. It would get all right in time.

"And that when you went to Otatoclán you were temporarily deputized as a member of the D.A.'s staff?"

"Yes, but don't rub it in, Marlowe. It was a valuable connection. Perhaps I gave it too much weight."

"Still is, I hope."

He shook his head. "No. That's finished. Mr. Potter does his legal business through San Francisco, New York, and Washington firms."

"I guess he hates my guts – if he thinks about it."

Endicott smiled. "Curiously enough, he put all the blame on his son-in-law, Dr. Loring. A man like Harlan Potter has to blame somebody. He couldn't possibly be wrong himself. He felt that if Loring hadn't been feeding the woman dangerous drugs none of it would have happened."

"He's wrong. You saw Terry Lennox's body in Otatoclán, didn't you?"

"I did indeed. In the back of a cabinet maker's shop. They have no proper mortuary there. He was making the coffin too.

The body was ice-cold. I saw the wound in the temple. There's no question of identity, if you had any ideas along those lines."

"No, Mr. Endicott, I didn't, because in his case it could hardly be possible. He was disguised a little though, wasn't he?"

"Face and hands darkened, hair dyed black. But the scars were still obvious. And the fingerprints, of course, were easily checked from things he had handled at home."

"What kind of police force do they have down there?"

"Primitive. The jefe could just about read and write. But he knew about fingerprints. It was hot weather, you know. Quite hot." He frowned and took his cigarette out of his mouth and dropped it negligently into an enormous black basalt sort of receptacle. "They had to get ice from the hotel," he added. "Plenty of ice." He looked at me again. "No embalming there. Things have to move fast."

"You speak Spanish, Mr. Endicott?"

"Only a few words. The hotel manager interpreted." He smiled. "A well-dressed smoothie, that fellow. Looked tough, but he was very polite and helpful. It was all over in no time."

"I had a letter from Terry. I guess Mr. Potter would know about it. I told his daughter, Mrs. Loring. I showed it to her. There was a portrait of Madison in it."

"A what?"

"Five-thousand-dollar bill."

He raised his eyebrows. "Really. Well, he could certainly afford it. His wife gave him a cool quarter of a million the second time they were married. I've an idea he meant to go to Mexico to live anyhow – quite apart from what happened. I don't know what happened to the money. I wasn't in on that."

"Here's the letter, Mr. Endicott, if you care to read it."

I took it out and gave it to him. He read it carefully, the way lawyers read everything. He put it down on the desk and leaned back and stared at nothing.

"A little literary, isn't it?" he said quietly. "I wonder why he did it."

"Killed himself, confessed, or wrote me the letter?"

"Confessed and killed himself, of course," Endicott said sharply. "The letter is understandable. At least you got a reasonable recompense for what you did for him – and since."

"The mailbox bothers me," I said. "Where he says there was a mailbox on the street under his window and the hotel waiter was going to hold his letter up before he mailed it, so Terry could see that it was mailed."

Something in Endicott's eyes went to sleep. "Why?" he asked indifferently. He picked another of his filtered cigarettes out of a square box. I held my lighter across the desk for him.

"They wouldn't have one in a place like Otatoclán," I said.

"Go on."

"I didn't get it at first. Then I looked the place up. It's a mere village. Population say ten or twelve thousand. One street partly paved. The jefe has a Model A Ford as an official car. The post office is in the corner of a store, the chanceria, the butcher shop. One hotel, a couple of cantinas, no good roads, a small airfield. There's hunting around there in the mountains – lots of it. Hence the airfield. Only decent way to get there."

"Go on. I know about the hunting."

"So there's a mailbox on the street. Like there's a race course and a dog track and a golf course and a jai alai frontón and park with a colored fountain and a bandstand."

"Then he made a mistake," Endicott said coldly. "Perhaps it was something that looked like a mailbox to him – say a trash receptacle."

I stood up. I reached for the letter and refolded it and put it back in my pocket.

"A trash receptacle," I said. "Sure, that's it. Painted with the Mexican colors, green, white, red, and a sign on it stenciled in large clear print: KEEP OUR CITY CLEAN. In Spanish, of course. And lying around it seven mangy dogs."

807

"Don't get cute, Marlowe."

"Sorry if I let my brains show. Another small point I have already raised with Randy Starr. How come the letter got mailed at all? According to the letter the method was pre-arranged. So somebody told him about the mailbox. So somebody lied. So somebody mailed the letter with five grand in it just the same. Intriguing, don't you agree?"

He puffed smoke and watched it float away.

"What's your conclusion – and why ring Starr in on it?"

"Starr and a heel named Menendez, now removed from our midst, were pals of Terry's in the British Army. They are wrong gees in a way – I should say in almost every way – but they still have room for personal pride and so on. There was a cover-up here engineered for obvious reasons. There was another sort of cover-up in Otatoclán, for entirely different reasons."

"What's your conclusion?" he asked me again and much more sharply.

"What's yours?"

He didn't answer me. So I thanked him for his time and left.

He was frowning as I opened the door, but I thought it was an honest frown of puzzlement. Or maybe he was trying to remember how it looked outside the hotel and whether there was a mailbox there.

It was another wheel to start turning – no more. It turned for a solid month before anything came up.

Then on a certain Friday morning I found a stranger waiting for me in my office. He was a well-dressed Mexican or Suramericano of some sort. He sat by the open window smoking a brown cigarette that smelled strong. He was tall and very slender and very elegant, with a neat dark mustache and dark hair, rather longer than we wear it, and a fawn-colored suit of some loosely woven material. He wore those green sunglasses. He stood up politely.

"Señor Marlowe?"

"What can I do for you?"

He handed me a folded paper. "Un aviso de parte del Señor Starr en Las Vegas, señor. Habla Usted Español?"

"Yeah, but not fast. English would be better."

"English then," he said. "It is all the same to me."

I took the paper and read it. "This introduces Cisco Maioranos, a friend of mine. I think he can fix you up. S."

"Let's go inside, Señor Maioranos," I said.

I held the door open for him. He smelled of perfume as he went by. His eyebrows were awfully damned dainty too. But he probably wasn't as dainty as he looked because there were knife scars on both sides of his face.

52

HE SAT DOWN in the customer's chair and crossed his knees. "You wish certain information about Señor Lennox, I am told."

"The last scene only."

"I was there at the time, señor. I had a position in the hotel." He shrugged. "Unimportant and of course temporary. I was the day clerk." He spoke perfect English but with a Spanish rhythm. Spanish – American Spanish that is – has a definite rise and fall which to an American ear seems to have nothing to do with the meaning. It's like the swell of the ocean.

"You don't look the type," I said.

"One has difficulties."

"Who mailed the letter to me?" He held out a box of cigarettes. "Try one of these."

I shook my head. "Too strong for me. Colombian cigarettes I like. Cuban cigarettes are murder."

He smiled faintly, lit another pill himself, and blew smoke. The guy was so goddam elegant he was beginning to annoy me.

"I know about the letter, señor. The mozo was afraid to go up to the room of this Señor Lennox after the guarda was posted. The cop or dick, as you say. So I myself took the letter to the correo. After the shooting, you understand."

"You ought to have looked inside. It had a large piece of money in it."

"The letter was sealed," he said coldly. "El honor no se mueve de lado como los congrejos. That is, honor does not move sidewise like a crab, señor."

"My apologies. Please continue."

"Señor Lennox had a hundred-peso note in his left hand when I went into the room and shut the door in the face of the guarda. In his right hand was a pistol. On the table before him was the letter. Also another paper which I did not read. I refused the note."

"Too much money," I said, but he didn't react to the sarcasm.

"He insisted. So I took the note finally and gave it to the mozo later. I took the letter out under the napkin on the tray from the previous service of coffee. The dick looked hard at me. But he said nothing. I was halfway down the stairs when I heard the shot. Very quickly I hid the letter and ran back upstairs. The dick was trying to kick the door open. I used my key. Señor Lennox was dead."

He moved his fingertips gently along the edge of the desk and sighed. "The rest no doubt you know."

"Was the hotel full?"

"Not full, no. There were half a dozen guests."

"Americans?"

"Two Americanos del Norte. Hunters."

"Real Gringos or just transplanted Mexicans?"

He drew a fingertip slowly along the fawn-colored cloth above his knee. "I think one of them could well have been of Spanish origin. He spoke border Spanish. Very inelegant."

"They go near Lennox's room at all?"

He lifted his head sharply but the green cheaters didn't do a thing for me. "Why should they, señor?"

I nodded. "Well, it was damn nice of you to come in here and tell me about it, Señor Maioranos. Tell Randy I'm ever so grateful, will you?"

"No hay de que, señor. It is nothing."

"And later on, if he has time, he could send me somebody who knows what he is talking about."

"Señor?" His voice was soft, but icy. "You doubt my word?"

"You guys are always talking about honor. Honor is the cloak of thieves – sometimes. Don't get mad. Sit quiet and let me tell it another way."

He leaned back superciliously.

"I'm only guessing, mind. I could be wrong. But I could be right too. These two Americanos were there for a purpose. They came in on a plane. They pretended to be hunters. One of them was named Menendez, a gambler. He registered under some other name or not. I wouldn't know. Lennox knew they were there. He knew why. He wrote me that letter because he had a guilty conscience. He had played me for a sucker and he was too nice a guy for that to rest easy on him. He put the bill – five thousand dollars it was – in the letter because he had a lot of money and he knew I hadn't. He also put in a little off-beat hint which might or might not register. He was the kind of guy who always wants to do the right thing but somehow winds up doing something else. You say you took the letter to the correo. Why didn't you mail it in the box in front of the hotel?"

"The box señor?"

"The mailbox. The cajón cartero, you call it, I think."

He smiled. "Otatoclán is not Mexico City, señor. It is a very primitive place. A street mailbox in Otatoclán? No one there would understand what it was for. No one would collect letters from it."

I said: "Oh. Well, skip it. You did not take any coffee on any tray up to Señor Lennox's room, Señor Maioranos. You did not go into the room past the dick. But the two Americanos did go in. The dick was fixed, of course. So were several other people. One of the Americanos slugged Lennox from behind.

Then he took the Mauser pistol and opened up one of the cartridges and took out the bullet and put the cartridge back in the breech. Then he put this gun to Lennox's temple and pulled the trigger. It made a nasty-looking wound, but it did not kill him. Then he was carried out on a stretcher covered up and well hidden. Then when the American lawyer arrived, Lennox was doped and packed in ice and kept in a dark corner of the carpintería where the man was making a coffin. The American lawyer saw Lennox there, he was ice-cold, in a deep stupor, and there was a bloody blackened wound in his temple. He looked plenty dead. The next day the coffin was buried with stones in it. The American lawyer went home with the fingerprints and some kind of document which was a piece of cheese. How do you like that, Señor Maioranos?"

He shrugged. "It would be possible, señor. It would require money and influence. It would be possible, perhaps, if this Señor Menendez was closely related to important people in Otatoclán, the alcalde, the hotel proprietor and so on."

"Well, that's possible too. It's a good idea. It would explain why they picked a remote little place like Otatoclán."

He smiled quickly. "Then Señor Lennox may still be alive, no?"

"Sure. The suicide had to be some kind of fake to back up the confession. It had to be good enough to fool a lawyer who had been a District Attorney, but it would make a very sick monkey out of the current D.A. if it backfired. This Menendez is not as tough as he thinks he is, but he was tough enough to pistol-whip me for not keeping my nose clean. So he had to have reasons. If the fake got exposed, Menendez would be right in the middle of an international stink. The Mexicans don't like crooked police work any more than we do."

"All that is possible, señor, as I very well know. But you accused me of lying. You said I did not go into the room where Señor Lennox was and get his letter."

"You were already in there, chum – writing the letter."

He reached up and took the dark glasses off. Nobody can change the color of a man's eyes.

"I suppose it's a bit too early for a gimlet," he said.

53

THEY HAD DONE a wonderful job on him in Mexico City, but why not? Their doctors, technicians, hospitals, painters, architects are as good as ours. Sometimes a little better. A Mexican cop invented the paraffin test for powder nitrates. They couldn't make Terry's face perfect, but they had done plenty. They had even changed his nose, taken out some bone and made it look flatter, less Nordic. They couldn't eliminate every trace of a scar, so they had put a couple on the other side of his face too. Knife scars are not uncommon in Latin countries.

"They even did a nerve graft up here," he said, and touched what had been the bad side of his face.

"How close did I come?"

"Close enough. A few details wrong, but they are not important. It was a quick deal and some of it was improvised and I didn't know myself just what was going to happen. I was told to do certain things and to leave a clear trail. Mendy didn't like my writing to you, but I held out for that. He undersold you a little. He never noticed the bit about the mailbox."

"You know who killed Sylvia?"

He didn't answer me directly. "It's pretty tough to turn a woman in for murder – even if she never meant much to you."

"It's a tough world. Was Harlan Potter in on all this?"

He smiled again. "Would he be likely to let anyone know that? My guess is not. My guess is he thinks I am dead. Who would tell him otherwise – unless you did?"

"What I'd tell him you could fold into a blade of grass. How's Mendy these days – or is he?"

"He's doing all right. In Acapulco. He slipped by because of Randy. But the boys don't go for rough work on cops. Mendy's not as bad as you think. He has a heart."

"So has a snake."

"Well, what about that gimlet?"

I got up without answering him and went to the safe. I spun the knob and got out the envelope with the portrait of Madison on it and the five C notes that smelled of coffee. I dumped the lot out on the desk and then picked up the five C notes.

"These I keep. I spent almost all of it on expenses and research. The portrait of Madison I enjoyed playing with. It's all yours now."

I spread it on the edge of the desk in front of him. He looked at it but didn't touch it.

"It's yours to keep," he said. "I've got plenty. You could have let things lie."

"I know. After she killed her husband and got away with it she might have gone on to better things. He was of no real importance, of course. Just a human being with blood and a brain and emotions. He knew what happened too and he tried pretty hard to live with it. He wrote books. You may have heard of him."

"Look, I couldn't very well help what I did," he said slowly. "I didn't want anyone to get hurt. I wouldn't have had a dog's chance up here. A man can't figure every angle that quick. I was scared and I ran. What should I have done?"

"I don't know."

"She had a mad streak. She might have killed him anyway."

"Yeah, she might."

"Well, thaw out a little. Let's go have a drink somewhere where it's cool and quiet."

"No time right now, Señor Maioranos."

"We were pretty good friends once," he said unhappily.

"Were we? I forget. That was two other fellows, seems to me. You permanently in Mexico?"

"Oh yes. I'm not here legally even. I never was. I told you I was born in Salt Lake City. I was born in Montreal. I'll be a Mexican national pretty soon now. All it takes is a good lawyer. I've always liked Mexico. It wouldn't be much risk going to Victor's for that gimlet."

"Pick up your money, Señor Maioranos. It has too much blood on it."

"You're a poor man."

"How would you know?"

He picked the bill up and stretched it between his thin fingers and slipped it casually into an inside pocket. He bit his lip with the very white teeth you can have when you have a brown skin.

"I couldn't tell you any more than I did that morning you drove me to Tijuana. I gave you a chance to call the police and turn me in."

"I'm not sore at you. You're just that kind of guy. For a long time I couldn't figure you at all. You had nice ways and nice qualities, but there was something wrong. You had standards and you lived up to them, but they were personal. They had no relation to any kind of ethics or scruples. You were a nice guy because you had a nice nature. But you were just as happy with mugs or hoodlums as with honest men. Provided the hoodlums spoke fairly good English and had fairly acceptable table manners. You're a moral defeatist. I think maybe the war did it and again I think maybe you were born that way."

"I don't get it," he said. "I really don't. I'm trying to pay you back and you won't let me. I couldn't have told you any more than I did. You wouldn't have stood for it."

"That's as nice a thing as was ever said to me."

"I'm glad you like something about me. I got in a bad jam. I happened to know the sort of people who know how to deal with bad jams. They owed me for an incident that happened long ago in the war. Probably the only time in my life I ever did the right thing quick like a mouse. And when I needed them, they delivered. And for free. You're not the only guy in the world that has no price tag, Marlowe."

He leaned across the desk and snapped at one of my cigarettes. There was an uneven flush on his face under the deep tan. The scars showed up against it. I watched him spring a fancy gas cartridge lighter loose from a pocket and light the cigarette. I got a whiff of perfume from him.

"You bought a lot of me, Terry. For a smile and a nod and a wave of the hand and a few quiet drinks in a quiet bar here and there. It was nice while it lasted. So long, amigo. I won't say goodbye. I said it to you when it meant something. I said it when it was sad and lonely and final."

"I came back too late," he said. "These plastic jobs take time."

"You wouldn't have come at all if I hadn't smoked you out."

There was suddenly a glint of tears in his eyes. He put his dark glasses back on quickly.

"I wasn't sure about it," he said. "I hadn't made up my mind. They didn't want me to tell you anything. I just hadn't made up my mind."

"Don't worry about it, Terry. There's always somebody around to do it for you."

"I was in the Commandos, bud. They don't take you if you're just a piece of fluff. I got badly hurt and it wasn't any fun with those Nazi doctors. It did something to me."

"I know all that, Terry. You're a very sweet guy in a lot of ways. I'm not judging you. I never did. It's just that you're not here any more. You're long gone. You've got nice clothes and perfume and you're as elegant as a fifty-dollar whore."

"That's just an act," he said almost desperately.

"You get a kick out of it, don't you?"

His mouth dropped in a sour smile. He shrugged an expressive energetic Latin shrug.

"Of course. An act is all there is. There isn't anything else. In here —" he tapped his chest with the lighter — "there isn't anything. I've had it, Marlowe. I had it long ago. Well — I guess that winds things up."

He stood up. I stood up. He put out a lean hand. I shook it.

"So long, Señor Maioranos. Nice to have known you — however briefly."

"Goodbye."

He turned and walked across the floor and out. I watched the door close. I listened to his steps going away down the imitation marble corridor. After a while they got faint, then they got silent. I kept on listening anyway. What for? Did I want him to stop suddenly and turn and come back and talk me out of the way I felt? Well, he didn't. That was the last I saw of him.

I never saw any of them again — except the cops. No way has yet been invented to say goodbye to them.

PLAYBACK

To Jean and Helga

1

THE VOICE ON the telephone seemed to be sharp and peremptory, but I didn't hear too well what it said – partly because I was only half awake and partly because I was holding the receiver upside down. I fumbled it around and grunted.

"Did you hear me? I said I was Clyde Umney, the lawyer."

"Clyde Umney, the lawyer. I thought we had several of them."

"You're Marlowe, aren't you?"

"Yeah. I guess so." I looked at my wrist watch. It was 6:30 A.M., not my best hour.

"Don't get fresh with me, young man."

"Sorry, Mr. Umney. But I'm not a young man. I'm old, tired and full of no coffee. What can I do for you, sir?"

"I want you to meet the Super Chief at eight o'clock, identify a girl among the passengers, follow her until she checks in somewhere, and then report to me. Is that clear?"

"No."

"Why not?" he snapped.

"I don't know enough to be sure I could accept the case."

"I'm Clyde Um –"

"Don't," I interrupted. "I might get hysterical. Just tell me the basic facts. Perhaps another investigator would suit you better. I never was an FBI man."

"Oh. My secretary, Miss Vermilyea, will be at your office in half an hour. She will have the necessary information for you. She is very efficient. I hope you are."

"I'm more efficient when I've had breakfast. Have her come here, would you?"

"Where is here?"

I gave him the address of my place on Yucca Avenue, and told him how she would find it.

"Very well," he said grudgingly, "but I want one thing very clear. The girl is not to know she is being followed. This is very important. I am acting for a very influential firm of Washington attorneys. Miss Vermilyea will advance you some expense money and pay you a retainer of two hundred and fifty dollars. I expect a high degree of efficiency. And let's not waste time talking."

"I'll do the best I can, Mr. Umney."

He hung up. I struggled out of bed, showered, shaved and was nuzzling my third cup of coffee when the door bell rang.

"I'm Miss Vermilyea, Mr. Umney's secretary," she said in a rather chintzy voice.

"Please come in."

She was quite a doll. She wore a white belted raincoat, no hat, a well-cherished head of platinum hair, booties to match the raincoat, a folding plastic umbrella, a pair of blue-gray eyes that looked at me as if I had said a dirty word. I helped her off with her raincoat. She smelled very nice. She had a pair of legs – so far as I could determine – that were not painful to look at. She wore night sheer stockings. I stared at them rather intently, especially when she crossed her legs and held out a cigarette to be lighted.

"Christian Dior," she said, reading my rather open mind. "I never wear anything else. A light, please."

"You're wearing a lot more today," I said snapping a lighter for her.

"I don't greatly care for passes this early in the morning."

"What time would suit you, Miss Vermilyea?"

She smiled rather acidly, inventoried her handbag and tossed me a manila envelope. "I think you'll find everything you need in this."

"Well – not quite everything."

"Get on with it, you goof. I've heard all about you. Why do you think Mr. Umney chose you? He didn't. I did. And stop looking at my legs."

I opened the envelope. It contained another sealed envelope and two checks made out to me. One, for $250, was marked "Retainer, as an advance against fees for professional services." The other was for $200 and was marked "Advance to Philip Marlowe for necessary expenses."

"You will account for the expenses to me, in exact detail," Miss Vermilyea said. "And buy your own drinks."

The other envelope I didn't open – not yet. "What makes Umney think I'll take a case I know nothing about?"

"You'll take it. You're not asked to do anything wrong. You have my word for that."

"What else do I have?"

"Oh, we might discuss that over a drink some rainy evening, when I'm not too busy."

"You've sold me."

I opened the other envelope. It contained a photograph of a girl. The pose suggested a natural ease, or a lot of experience in being photographed. It showed darkish hair which might possibly have been red, a wide clear forehead, serious eyes, high cheekbones, nervous nostrils and a mouth which was not giving anything away. It was a fine-drawn, almost a taut face, and not a happy one.

"Turn it over," Miss Vermilyea said.

On the back there was clearly typed material.

"Name: Eleanor King: Height five feet four inches. Age about 29. Hair dark reddish brown, thick, with a natural wave. Erect carriage, low distinct voice, well dressed but not over-dressed. Conservative make-up. No visible scars. Characteristic mannerisms: habit of moving her eyes without moving her head when entering a room. Scratches palm of right hand when tense. Left-handed but adept in concealing it. Plays fast tennis, swims and dives beautifully, holds her liquor. No convictions, but prints on file."

"Been in the coop," I said, looking up at Miss Vermilyea.

"I have no information beyond what is there. Just follow your instructions."

"No name, Miss Vermilyea. At twenty-nine a dish like this would almost certainly have been married. There's no mention of a wedding ring or any other jewels. That makes me wonder."

She glanced at her watch. "Better do your wondering at the Union Station. You haven't much time." She stood up. I helped her on with her white raincoat and opened the door.

"You came in your own car?"

"Yes." She went halfway out and turned. "There's one thing I like about you. You don't paw. And you have nice manners – in a way."

"It's a rotten technique – to paw."

"And there's one thing I don't like about you. Guess what it is."

"Sorry. No idea – except that some people hate me for being alive."

"I didn't mean that."

I followed her down the steps and opened her car door for her. It was a cheap job, a Fleetwood Cadillac. She nodded briefly and slid down the hill.

I went back up and loaded a few things into an overnight bag, just in case.

2

THERE WAS NOTHING to it. The Super Chief was on time, as it almost always is, and the subject was as easy to spot as a kangaroo in a dinner jacket. She wasn't carrying anything but a paperback which she dumped in the first trash can she came to. She sat down and looked at the floor. An unhappy girl, if ever I saw one. After a while she got up and went to the book rack. She left it without picking anything out, glanced at the big clock on the wall and shut herself in a telephone booth. She talked to someone after putting a handful of silver into the slot. Her expression didn't change at all. She hung up and went to the magazine rack, picked up a *New Yorker*, looked at her watch again, and sat down to read.

She was wearing a midnight blue tailor-made suit with a white blouse showing at the neck and a big sapphire blue lapel pin which would probably have matched her earrings, if I could see her ears. Her hair was a dusky red. She looked like her photograph, but a little taller than I expected. Her dark blue ribbon hat had a short veil hanging from it. She was wearing gloves.

After a while she moved across the arches outside of which the taxis wait. She looked left at the coffee shop, turned and went into the main waiting room, glanced at the drugstore and newsstand, the information booth, and the people sitting on the clean wooden benches. Some of the ticket windows were open, some not. She wasn't interested in them. She sat down again and looked up at the big clock. She pulled off her right glove and set her wrist watch, a small plain platinum toy without jewels. Mentally I put Miss Vermilyea beside her. She didn't look soft or prissy or prudish, but she made the Vermilyea look like a pick-up.

She didn't stay long sitting down this time, either. She got up and strolled. She went out into the patio and came back and went into the drugstore and stayed some time at the paperbook rack. Two things were obvious. If anyone was going to meet her, the date hadn't been for train time. She looked like a girl waiting between trains. She went into the coffee shop. She sat down at one of the plastic top tables, read the menu, and then started to read her magazine. A waitress came with the inevitable glass of ice water, and the menu. The subject gave an order. The waitress went away, the subject went on reading her magazine. It was about nine-fifteen.

I went out through the arches to where a redcap was waiting by the taxi starter. "You work the Super Chief?" I asked him.

"Yeah. Part of it." He glanced without too deep interest at the buck I was teasing with my fingers.

"I was expecting someone on the Washington–San Diego through car. Anybody get off?"

"You mean get off permanent, baggage and all?"

I nodded.

He thought about it, studying me with intelligent chestnut eyes. "One passenger got off," he said at last. "What your friend look like?"

I described a man. Someone who looked something like Edward Arnold. The redcap shook his head.

"Can't help you, mister. What got off don't look like that at all. Your friend probably still on the train. They don't have to get off the through car. She gets hitched on to Seventy-Four. Leaves here eleven-thirty. The train ain't made up yet."

"Thanks," I said, and gave him the dollar. The subject's baggage was still on the train, which was all I wanted to know.

I went back to the coffee shop and looked in through the glass wall.

Subject was reading her magazine and toying with coffee and a snail. I moved over to a phone booth and called a garage I knew well and asked them to send somebody for my car if I didn't call again by noon. They'd done this often enough to have a spare key on hand. I went out to the car and got my overnight bag out of it and into a two-bit locker. In the enormous waiting room, I bought a round trip to San Diego and trotted back to the coffee shop once again.

Subject was in place, but no longer alone. A guy was across the table from her smiling and talking, and one look was enough to show that she knew him and regretted it. He was California from the tips of his port wine loafers to the buttoned and tieless brown and yellow checked shirt inside his rough cream sports jacket. He was about six feet one, slender, with a thin conceited face and too many teeth. He was twisting a piece of paper in his hand.

The yellow handkerchief in his outside breast pocket sprayed out like a small bunch of daffodils. And one thing was as clear as distilled water. The girl didn't want him there.

He went on talking and twitching the paper. Finally he shrugged and got up from his chair. He reached over and ran a fingertip down her cheek. She jerked back. Then he opened the twisted paper and laid it carefully down in front of her. He waited, smiling.

Her eyes went down to it very, very slowly. Her eyes held on it. Her hand moved to take it, but his was quicker. He put it away in his pocket, still smiling. Then he took out one of those pocket notebooks with perforated pages, and wrote something with a clip pen and tore the sheet out and put that down in front of her. That she could have. She took it, read it, put it in her purse. At last she looked at him. And at last she smiled at him. My guess was that it took quite an effort. He reached across to pat her hand, then walked away from the table and out.

He shut himself in a phone booth, dialed, and talked for quite a while. He came out, found himself a redcap and went with the redcap to a locker. Out came a light oyster-white suitcase and a matching overnight case. The redcap carried them through the doors to the parking lot and followed him to a sleek two-toned Buick Roadmaster, the solid top convertible type that isn't convertible. The redcap put the stuff in behind the tipped seat, took his money, went away. The guy in the sports coat and yellow handkerchief got in and backed his car out and then stopped long enough to put on dark glasses and light a cigarette. After that he was gone. I wrote down the license number and went back into the station.

The next hour was three hours long. The girl left the coffee shop and read her magazine in the waiting room. Her mind wasn't on it. She kept turning back to see what she had read. Part of the time she didn't read at all, just held the magazine and looked at nothing. I had an early morning edition of the evening paper and behind it I watched her and added up what I had in my head. None of it was solid fact. It just helped to pass the time.

The guy who had sat at the table with her had come off the train, since he had baggage. It could have been her train and he could have been the passenger that got off her car. Her attitude made it pretty clear that she didn't want him around, and his that that was too bad but if she would glance at his piece of paper she would change her mind. And apparently she did. Since this happened after they got off the train when it could have happened more quietly before, then it followed that he didn't have his piece of paper on the train.

At this point the girl got up abruptly and went to the news-stand and came back with a pack of cigarettes. She tore it open and lit one. She smoked awkwardly as if she wasn't used to it, and while she smoked her attitude seemed to change, to become more flashy and hard, as if she was deliberately vulgarizing herself for some purpose. I looked at the wall clock: 10:47. I went on with my thinking.

The twist of paper had looked like a newspaper clipping. She had tried to grab it, he hadn't let her. Then he had written some words on a piece of blank paper and given them to her and she had looked at him and smiled. Conclusion: the dreamboat had something on her and she had to pretend to like it.

Next point was that earlier on he had left the station and gone somewhere, perhaps to get his car, perhaps to get the clipping, perhaps anything you like. That meant he wasn't afraid that she would run out on him, and that reinforced the idea that he hadn't at that time disclosed everything he was holding up his sleeve but had disclosed some of it. Could be he wasn't sure himself. Had to check. But now having shown her his hole card he had gone off in a Buick with his baggage. Therefore he was no longer afraid of losing her. Whatever held them together was strong enough to keep on holding them.

At 11:05 I tossed all this out of the window and started with a fresh premise. I got nowhere. At 11:10 the public address system said Number Seventy-Four on Track Eleven was now ready to receive passengers for Santa Ana, Oceanside, Del Mar and San Diego. A bunch of people left the waiting room, including the girl. Another bunch was already going through the gate. I watched her through and went back to the phone booths. I dropped my dime and dialed the number of Clyde Umney's office.

Miss Vermilyea answered by giving the phone number only.

"This is Marlowe. Mr. Umney in?"

Her voice was formal saying: "I'm sorry, Mr. Umney is in court. May I take a message?"

"Am in contact and leaving by train for San Diego, or some intermediate stop. Can't tell which yet."

"Thank you. Anything else?"

"Yeah, the sun's shining and our friend is no more on the lam than you are. She ate breakfast in the coffee shop which has a glass wall towards the concourse. She sat in the waiting room with a hundred and fifty other people. And she could have stayed on the train out of sight."

"I have all that, thank you. I'll get it to Mr. Umney as soon as possible. You have no firm opinion then?"

"I have one firm opinion. That you're holding out on me."

Her voice changed abruptly. Somebody must have left the office. "Listen, chum, you were hired to do a job. Better do it and do it right. Clyde Umney draws a lot of water in this town."

"Who wants water, beautiful? I take mine straight with a beer chaser. I might make sweeter music if I was encouraged."

"You'll get paid, shamus — if you do a job. Not otherwise. Is that clear?"

"That's the nicest thing you ever said to me, sweetheart. Goodbye now."

"Listen, Marlowe," she said with sudden urgency. "I didn't mean to be rough with you. This is very important to Clyde Umney. If he doesn't come through, he might lose a very valuable connection. I was just sounding off."

"I liked it, Vermilyea. It did things to my subconscious. I'll call in when I can."

I hung up, went through the gate, down the ramp, walked about from here to Ventura to get to Track Eleven and climbed aboard a coach that was already full of the drifting cigarette smoke that is so kind to your throat and nearly always leaves you with one good lung. I filled and lit a pipe and added to the general frowst.

The train pulled out, dawdled interminably through the yards and the back stretches of East L.A., picked up a little speed and made its first stop at Santa Ana. Subject did not get off. At Oceanside and Del Mar the same. At San Diego I hopped off quickly, chartered a cab, and then waited eight minutes outside the old Spanish station for the redcaps to come out with the baggage. Then the girl came out too.

She didn't take a cab. She crossed the street and rounded the corner to a U-Drive outfit and after a longish interval came out again looking disappointed. No driver's license, no U-drive. You'd think she would have known that.

She took a cab this time and it did a U turn and started north. Mine did the same. I had a little difficulty with my driver about the tail job.

"That's something you read about in books, mister. We don't do it in Dago."

I passed him a fin and the $4 \times 2\frac{1}{2}$ photostat of license. He looked them over, both of them. He looked off up the block.

"Okay, but I report it," he said. "The dispatcher may report it to the Police Business Office. That's the way it is here, chum."

"Sounds like the kind of city I ought to live in," I said. "And you've lost the tail. He turned left two blocks ahead."

The driver handed me back my wallet. "Lost my left eye," he said tersely. "What you think a two-way radiophone is for?" He picked it up and talked into it.

He turned left at Ash Street to Highway 101 and we merged with the traffic and kept going at a peaceable forty. I stared at the back of his head.

"You don't have a worry in the world," the driver told me over his shoulder. "This five is on top of the fare, huh?"

"Right. And why don't I have a worry in the world?"

"The passenger's going to Esmeralda. That's twelve miles north of here on the ocean front. Destination, unless changed en route – and if it is I'll get told – a hotel joint called the Rancho Descansado. That's Spanish for relax, take it easy."

"Hell, I didn't need a cab at all," I said.

"You got to pay for the service, mister. We ain't buying groceries giving it away."

"You Mexican?"

"We don't call ourselves that, mister. We call ourselves Spanish-Americans. Born and raised in the USA. Some of us don't hardly speak Spanish any more."

"*Es gran lástima,*" I said. "*Una lengua muchísima hermosa.*"

He turned his head and grinned. "*Tiene Vd. razón, amigo. Estoy muy bien de acuerdo.*"

We went on to Torrance Beach, through there and swung out towards the point. From time to time the hackie talked into his radiophone. He turned his head enough to speak to me again.

"You want to keep out of sight?"

"What about the other driver? Will he tell his passenger she's being tailed?"

"He ain't been told hisself. That's why I asked you."

"Pass him and get there ahead, if you can. That's five more on the top."

"A cinch. He won't even see me. I can rib him later on over a bottle of Tecate."

We went through a small shopping center, then the road widened and the houses on one side looked expensive and not new, while the houses on the other side looked very new and still not cheap. The road narrowed again and we were in a 25 mile zone. My driver cut to the right, wound through some narrow streets, jumped a stop sign, and before I had had time to size up where we were going, we were sliding down into a canyon with the Pacific glinting off to the left beyond a wide shallow beach with two lifeguard stations on open metal towers. At the bottom of the canyon the driver started to turn in through the gates, but I stopped him. A large sign, gold script on a green background, said: *El Rancho Descansado*.

"Get out of sight," I said. "I want to make sure."

He swung back on the highway, drove fast down beyond the end of the stucco wall, then cut into a narrow winding road on the far side and stopped. A gnarled eucalyptus with a divided trunk hung over us. I got out of the cab, put dark glasses on, strolled down to the highway and leaned against a bright red jeep with the name of a service station painted on it. A cab came down the hill and turned into the Rancho Descansado. Three minutes passed. The cab came out empty and turned back up the hill. I went back to my driver.

"Cab No. 423," I said. "That check?"

"That's your pigeon. What now?"

"We wait. What's the layout over there?"

"Bungalows with car ports. Some single, some double. Office in a small one down front. Rates pretty steep in season. This is slack time around here. Half price probably and plenty of room."

"We wait five minutes. Then I check in, drop my suitcase, and look for a car to rent."

He said that was easy. In Esmeralda there were three places that rented cars, time and mileage, any make you wanted.

We waited the five minutes. It was now just past three o'clock. I was empty enough to steal the dog's dinner.

I paid my driver off, watched him leave, and went across the highway and into the office.

3

I LEANED A polite elbow on the counter and looked across at the happy-faced young guy in the polka-dotted bow tie. I looked from him to the girl at the small PBX against the side wall. She was an outdoorsy type with shiny make-up and a horse tail of medium blond hair sticking out at the back of her noodle. But she had nice large soft eyes and when they looked at the clerk they glistened. I looked back at him and choked back a snarl. The girl at the PBX swung her horse tail in an arc and put the eye on me also.

"I'd be glad to show you what we have vacant, Mr. Marlowe," the young guy said politely. "You can register later, if you decide to stay here. About how long would you be likely to want accommodations?"

"Only as long as she does," I said. "The girl in the blue suit. She just registered. Using what name I wouldn't know."

He and the PBX girl stared at me. Both their faces had the same expression of distrust mixed with curiosity. There are a hundred ways of playing this scene. But this was a new one for me. In no city hotel in the world would it work. It might work here. Mostly because I didn't give a damn.

"You don't like that, do you?" I said.

He shook his head slightly. "At least you're frank about it."

"I'm tired of being cagey. I'm worn out with it. Did you notice her ring finger?"

"Why no, I didn't." He looked at the PBX girl. She shook her head and kept her eyes on my face.

"No wedding ring," I said. "Not any more. All gone. All broken up. All the years – ah, the hell with it. I've followed her all the way from – well, never mind where. She won't even speak to me. What am I doing here? Making a damn fool of myself." I turned away quickly and blew my nose. I had their attention. "I'd better go somewhere else," I said, turning back.

"You want to make it up and she won't," the PBX girl said quietly.

"Yes."

"I'm sympathetic," the young guy said. "But you know how it is, Mr. Marlowe. A hotel has to be very careful. These situations can lead to anything – even shootings."

"Shootings?" I looked at him with wonder. "Good God, what sort of people do that?"

He leaned both arms on the desk. "Just what would you like to do, Mr. Marlowe?"

"I'd like to be near her – in case she needs me. I wouldn't speak to her. I wouldn't even knock at her door. But she would know I was there and she'd know why. I'd be waiting. I'll always be waiting."

The girl loved it now. I was up to my neck in the soft corn. I took a deep slow breath and shot for the grand prize. "And I don't somehow like the look of the guy who brought her here," I said.

"Nobody brought her here – except a cabdriver," the clerk said. But he knew what I meant all right.

The PBX girl half smiled. "He doesn't mean that, Jack. He means the reservation."

Jack said, "I kind of gathered as much, Lucille. I'm not so dumb." Suddenly he brought a card out from the desk and put it down in front of me. A registration card. Across the corner diagonally was written the name Larry Mitchell. In a very different writing in the proper places: (Miss) Betty Mayfield, West Chatham, New York. Then in the top left-hand corner

834

in the same writing as Larry Mitchell a date, a time, a price, a number.

"You're very kind," I said. "So she's gone back to her maiden name. It's legal, of course."

"Any name is legal, if there's no intent to defraud. You would like to be next door to her?"

I widened my eyes. Maybe they glistened a little. Nobody ever tried harder to make them glisten.

"Look," I said, "it's damn nice of you. But you can't do it. I'm not going to make any trouble, but you can't be sure. It's your job if I pulled anything."

"Okay," he said. "I've got to learn some day. You look all right to me. Just don't tell anybody." He took the pen from its cup and held it out. I signed my name with an address on East Sixty-first Street, New York City.

Jack looked at it. "That's near Central Park, isn't it?" he asked idly.

"Three blocks and a bit," I said. "Between Lexington and Third Avenue."

He nodded. He knew where it was. I was in. He reached for a key.

"I'd like to leave my suitcase here," I said, "and go get something to eat and maybe rent a car, if I can. You could have it put in the room for me?"

Sure. He could do that for me easy. He took me outside and pointed up through a grove of saplings. The cottages were allover shingled, white with green roofs. They had porches with railings. He showed me mine through the trees. I thanked him. He started back in and I said, "Look, there's one thing. She may check out when she knows."

He smiled. "Of course. Nothing we can do about that, Mr. Marlowe. Lots of guests only stay a night or two — except in summer. We don't expect to be filled up this time of year."

He went on into the office cottage and I heard the girl say to him: "He's kind of cute, Jack — but you shouldn't have done it."

I heard his answer too. "I hate that guy Mitchell – even if he is a pal of the owner."

4

THE ROOM WAS bearable. It had the usual concrete couch, chairs without cushions, a small desk against the front wall, a walk-in closet with a built-in chest, a bathroom with a Hollywood bath and neon shaving lights beside the mirror over the basin, a small kitchenette with a refrigerator and a white stove, a three-burner electric. In a wall cupboard over the sink enough dishes and stuff. I got some ice cubes and made myself a drink with the bottle from my suitcase, sipped it and sat in a chair listening, leaving the windows shut and the venetian blinds dark. I heard nothing next door, then I heard the toilet flush. Subject was in residence. I finished the drink, killed a cigarette and studied the wall heater on the party wall. It consisted of two long frosted bulbs in a metal box. It didn't look as if it would throw out much heat, but in the closet there was a plug-in fan heater with a thermostat and a three-way plug, which made it 220 volts. I slipped off the chromium grill guard of the wall heater and twisted out the frosted bulbs. I got a doctor's stethoscope out of my suitcase and held it against the metal backing and listened. If there was another similar heater back against it in the next room, and there almost certainly would be, all I had between the two rooms was a metal panel and some insulation, probably a bare minimum of that.

I heard nothing for a few minutes, then I heard a telephone being dialed. The reception was perfect. A woman's voice said: "Esmeralda 4-1499, please."

It was a cool contained voice, medium pitch, very little expression in it except that it sounded tired. It was the first time I had heard her voice in all the hours I had been following her.

There was a longish pause, then she said: "Mr. Larry Mitchell, please."

Another pause, but shorter. Then: "This is Betty Mayfield, at the Rancho Descansado." She pronounced the "a" in Descansado wrong. Then: "Betty Mayfield, I said. Please don't be stupid. Do you want me to spell it for you?"

The other end had things to say. She listened. After a while she said: "Apartment 12C. You ought to know. You made the reservation . . . Oh. I see . . . Well, all right. I'll be here."

She hung up. Silence. Complete silence. Then the voice in there said slowly and emptily: "Betty Mayfield, Betty Mayfield, Betty Mayfield. Poor Betty. You were a nice girl once – long ago."

I was sitting on the floor on one of the striped cushions with my back to the wall. I got up carefully, laid the stethoscope down on the cushion and went to lie on the day bed. After a while he would arrive. She was in there waiting for him, because she had to. She'd had to come there for the same reason. I wanted to know what it was.

He must have been wearing crepe soles because I didn't hear anything until the buzzer sounded next door. Also, he hadn't driven his car up to the cottage. I got down on the floor and went to work with the stethoscope.

She opened the door, he came in and I could imagine the smile on his face as he said: "Hello, Betty. Betty Mayfield is the name, I believe. I like it."

"It was my name originally." She closed the door.

He chuckled. "I suppose you were wise to change it. But how about the initials on your luggage?"

I didn't like his voice any better than his smile. It was high and cheerful, almost bubbly with sly good humor. There was not quite a sneer in it, but close enough. It made me clamp my teeth.

"I suppose," she said dryly, "that was the first thing you noticed."

837

"No, baby. *You* were the first thing I noticed. The mark of a wedding ring but no wedding ring was the second. The initials were only the third."

"Don't call me 'baby,' you cheap blackmailer," she said with a sudden muted fury.

It didn't faze him in the least. "I may be a blackmailer, honey, but" – another conceited chuckle – "I'm certainly not cheap."

She walked, probably away from him. "Do you want a drink? I see you have a bottle with you."

"It might make me lascivious."

"There's only one thing about you I'm afraid of, Mr. Mitchell," the girl said coolly. "Your big loose mouth. You talk too much and you like yourself too well. We'd better understand each other. I like Esmeralda. I've been here before and I always wanted to come back. It's nothing but sheer bad luck that you live here and that you were on the train that was taking me here. It was the worst kind of luck that you should have recognized me. But that's all it is – bad luck."

"Good luck for me, honey," he drawled.

"Perhaps," she said, "if you don't put too much pressure on it. If you do, it's liable to blow up in your face."

There was a brief silence. I could see them in my imagination, staring at each other. His smile might be getting a little nervous, but not much.

"All I've got to do," he said quietly, "is pick up the phone and call the San Diego papers. You want publicity? I can arrange it for you."

"I came here to get rid of it," she said bitterly.

He laughed. "Sure, by an old coot of a judge falling to pieces with senile decay, and in the only state in the Union – and I've checked on that – where it could happen after the jury said otherwise. You've changed your name twice. If your story got printed out here – and it's a pretty good story, honey – I guess you'd have to change your name again – and start traveling a little more. Gets kind of tiresome, doesn't it?"

"That's why I'm here," she said. "That's why you're here. How much do you want? I realize it will only be a down payment."

"Have I said anything about money?"

"You will," she said. "And keep your voice down."

"The cottage is all yours, honey. I walked around it before I came in. Doors closed, windows shut, blinds drawn, car ports empty. I can check with the office, if you're nervous. I've got friends around here – people you need to know, people who can make life pleasant for you. Socially this is a tough town to break into. And it's a damn dull town if you're on the outside looking in."

"How did *you* get in, Mr. Mitchell?"

"My old man is a big shot in Toronto. We don't get on and he won't have me around home. But he's still my old man and he's still the real thing, even if he does pay me to stay away."

She didn't answer him. Her steps went away. I heard her in the kitchen making the usual sounds connected with getting ice out of a tray of cubes. The water ran, the steps came back.

"I'd like one myself," she said. "Perhaps I've been rude to you. I'm tired."

"Sure," he said equably. "You're tired." A pause. "Well, here's to when you're not tired. Say about seven-thirty this evening at The Glass Room. I'll pick you up. Nice place for dinner. Dancing. Quiet. Exclusive, if that means anything any more. Belongs to the Beach Club. They don't have a table unless they know you. I'm among friends there."

"Expensive?" she asked.

"A little. Oh yes – and that reminds me. Until my monthly check comes in, you could let me have a couple of dollars." He laughed. "I'm surprised at myself. I did mention money after all."

"A couple of dollars?"

"A couple of hundred would be better."

"Sixty dollars is all I have – until I can open an account or cash some traveler's checks."

"You can do that at the office, baby."

"So I can. Here's fifty. I don't want to spoil you, Mr. Mitchell."

"Call me Larry. Be human."

"Should I?" Her voice had changed. There was a hint of invitation in it. I could imagine the slow smile of pleasure on his face. Then I guess from the silence that he had grabbed her and she had let him. Finally her voice was a little muffled, saying: "That's enough, Larry. Be nice now and run along. I'll be ready at seven-thirty."

"One more for the road."

In a moment the door opened and he said something I didn't catch. I got up and went to the window and took a careful look through the slats of the blind. A floodlight was turned on in one of the tall trees. Under it I saw him stroll off up the slope and disappear. I went back to the heater panel and for a while I heard nothing and wasn't sure what I was listening for. But I knew soon enough.

There was quick movement back and forth, the sound of drawers being pulled open, the snap of a lock, the bump of a lifted lid against something.

She was packing up to leave.

I screwed the long frosted bulbs back into the heater and replaced the grille and put the stethoscope back in my suitcase. The evening was getting chilly. I slipped my jacket on and stood in the middle of the floor. It was getting dark and no light on. I just stood there and thought it over. I could go to the phone and make a report and by that time she could be on her way in another cab to another train or plane to another destination. She could go anywhere she liked, but there would always be a dick to meet the train if it meant enough to the big important people back in Washington. There would always be a Larry Mitchell or a reporter with a good memory. There would always be the little oddness to be noticed and there would always be somebody to notice it. You can't run away from yourself.

840

I was doing a cheap sneaky job for people I didn't like, but – that's what you hire out for, chum. They pay the bills, you dig the dirt. Only this time I could taste it. She didn't look like a tramp and she didn't look like a crook. Which meant only that she could be both with more success than if she had.

5

I OPENED THE door and went along to the next and pushed the little buzzer. Nothing moved inside. There was no sound of steps. Then came the click of a chain set in the groove and the door opened a couple of inches on light and emptiness. The voice said from behind the door: "Who is it?"

"Could I borrow a cup of sugar?"

"I haven't any sugar."

"Well how about a couple of dollars until my check comes in?"

More silence. Then the door opened to the limit of the chain and her face edged into the opening and shadowed eyes stared out at me. They were just pools in the dark. The floodlight set high in the tree glinted on them obliquely.

"Who are you?"

"I'm your next door neighbor. I was having a nap and voices woke me. The voices spoke words. I was intrigued."

"Go somewhere else and be intrigued."

"I could do that, Mrs. King – pardon me, Miss Mayfield – but I'm not sure you'd want me to."

She didn't move and her eyes didn't waver. I shook a cigarette out of a pack and tried to push up the top of my Zippo with my thumb and rotate the wheel. You should be able to do it one-handed. You can too, but it's an awkward process. I made it at last and got the cigarette going, yawned, and blew smoke out through my nose.

"What do you do for an encore?" she asked.

841

"To be strictly kosher I should call L.A. and tell the party who sent me. Maybe I could be talked out of it."

"God," she said fervently, "two of them in one afternoon. How lucky can a girl get?"

"I don't know," I said. "I don't know anything. I think I've been played for a sucker, but I'm not sure."

"Wait a minute." She shut the door in my face. She wasn't gone long. The chain came out of the groove inside and the door came open.

I went in slowly and she stepped back and away from me. "How much did you hear? And shut the door, please."

I shut it with my shoulder and leaned against it.

"The tag end of a rather nasty conversation. The walls here are as thin as a hoofer's wallet."

"You in show business?"

"Just the opposite of show business. I'm in the hide-and-seek business. My name is Philip Marlowe. You've seen me before."

"Have I?" She walked away from me in little cautious steps and went over by her open suitcase. She leaned against the arm of a chair. "Where?"

"Union Station in L.A. We waited between trains, you and I. I was interested in you. I was interested in what went on between you and Mr. Mitchell − that's his name, isn't it? I didn't hear anything and I didn't see much because I was out-side the coffee shop."

"So what interested you, you great big lovable something or other?"

"I've just told you part of it. The other thing that inter-ested me was how you changed after your talk with him. I watched you work at it. It was very deliberate. You made yourself over into just another flip hard-boiled modern cutie. Why?"

"What was I before?"

"A nice quiet well-bred girl."

"That was the act," she said. "The other was my natural personality. Which goes with something else." She brought a small automatic up from her side.

I looked at it. "Oh guns," I said. "Don't scare me with guns. I've lived with them all my life. I teethed on an old Derringer, single-shot, the kind the riverboat gamblers used to carry. As I got older I graduated to a lightweight sporting rifle, then a .303 target rifle and so on. I once made a bull at nine hundred yards with open sights. In case you don't know, the whole target looks the size of a postage stamp at nine hundred yards."

"A fascinating career," she said.

"Guns never settle anything," I said. "They are just a fast curtain to a bad second act."

She smiled faintly and transferred the gun to her left hand. With her right she grabbed the edge of her blouse at the collar line and with a quick decisive motion tore it to the waist.

"Next," she said, "but there's no hurry about it, I turn the gun in my hand like this" – she put it back in her right hand, but held it by the barrel – "I slam myself on the cheekbone with the butt. I do a beautiful bruise."

"And after that," I said, "you get the gun into its proper position and release the safety catch and pull the trigger, just about the time I get through the lead column in the Sports Section."

"You wouldn't get halfway across the room."

I crossed my legs and leaned back and lifted the green glass ashtray from the table beside the chair and balanced it on my knee and held the cigarette I was smoking between the first and second fingers of my right hand.

"I wouldn't get any of the way across the room. I'd be sitting here like this, quite comfortable and relaxed."

"But slightly dead," she said. "I'm a good shot and it isn't nine hundred yards."

"Then you try to sell the cops your account of how I tried to attack you and you defended yourself."

She tossed the gun into her suitcase and laughed. It sounded like a genuine laugh with real amusement in it. "Sorry," she said. "You sitting there with your legs crossed and a hole in your head and me trying to explain how I shot you to defend my honor – the picture makes me a little lightheaded."

She dropped into a chair and leaned forward with her chin cupped in a hand, the elbow propped on her knee, her face taut and drained, her dark red hair framing it too luxuriantly, so that her face looked smaller than it should have.

"Just what are you doing to me, Mr. Marlowe? Or is it the other way around – what I can do for you in return for you not doing anything at all?"

"Who is Eleanor King? What was she in Washington, D.C.? Why did she change her name somewhere along the way and have the initials taken off her bag? Odds and ends like that are what you could tell me. You probably won't."

"Oh, I don't know. The porter took the initials off my things. I told him I had had a very unhappy marriage and was divorced and had been given the right to resume my unmarried name. Which is Elizabeth or Betty Mayfield. That could all be true, couldn't it?"

"Yeah. But it doesn't explain Mitchell."

She leaned back and relaxed. Her eyes stayed watchful. "Just an acquaintance I made along the way. He was on the train."

I nodded. "But he came down here in his own car. He made the reservation here for you. He's not liked by the people here, but apparently he is a friend of someone with a lot of influence."

"An acquaintance on a train or a ship sometimes develops very quickly," she said.

"So it seems. He even touched you for a loan. Very fast work. And I got the impression you didn't care for him too well."

"Well," she said, "so what? But as a matter of fact I'm crazy about him." She turned her hand over and looked down at it. "Who hired you, Mr. Marlowe, and for what?"

"A Los Angeles lawyer, acting on instructions from back east. I was to follow you and check you in somewhere. Which I did. But now you're getting ready to move out. I'm going to have to start over again."

"But with me knowing you're there," she said shrewdly. "So you'll have a much harder job of it. You're a private detective of some sort, I gather."

I said I was. I had killed my cigarette some time back. I put the ashtray back on the table and stood up.

"Harder for me, but there are lots of others, Miss Mayfield."

"Oh, I'm sure there are, and all such nice little men. Some of them are even fairly clean."

"The cops are not looking for you. They'd have had you easily. It was known about your train. I even got a photo of you and a description. But Mitchell can make you do just what he wants. Money isn't all he'll want."

I thought she flushed a little, but the light didn't strike her face directly. "Perhaps so," she said. "And perhaps I don't mind."

"You mind."

She stood up suddenly and came near me. "You're in a business that doesn't pay fortunes, aren't you?"

I nodded. We were very close now.

"Then what would it be worth to you to walk out of here and forget you ever saw me?"

"I'd walk out of here for free. As for the rest, I have to make a report."

"How much?" She said it as if she meant it. "I can afford a substantial retainer. That's what you call it, I've heard. A much nicer word than blackmail."

"It doesn't mean the same thing."

"It could. Believe me, it can mean just that – even with some lawyers and doctors. I happen to know."

"Tough break, huh?"

"Far from it, shamus. I'm the luckiest girl in the world. I'm alive."

845

"I'm on the other side. Don't give it away."

"Well, what do you know," she drawled. "A dick with scruples. Tell it to the seagulls, buster. On me it's just confetti. Run along now, Mr. P. I. Marlowe, and make that little old phone call you're so anxious about. I'm not restraining you."

She started for the door, but I caught her by the wrist and spun her around. The torn blouse didn't reveal any startling nakedness, merely some skin and part of a brassière. You'd see more on the beach, far more, but you wouldn't see it through a torn blouse.

I must have been leering a little, because she suddenly curled her fingers and tried to claw me.

"I'm no bitch in heat," she said between tight teeth. "Take your paws off me."

I got the other wrist and started to pull her closer. She tried to knee me in the groin, but she was already too close. Then she went limp and pulled her head back and closed her eyes. Her lips opened with a sardonic twist to them. It was a cool evening, maybe even cold down by the water. But it wasn't cold where I was.

After a while she said with a sighing voice that she had to dress for dinner.

I said, "Uh-huh."

After another pause she said it was a long time since a man had unhooked her brassière. We did a slow turn in the direction of one of the twin day beds. They had pink and silver covers on them. The little odd things you notice.

Her eyes were open and quizzical. I studied them one at a time because I was too close to see them together. They seemed well matched.

"Honey," she said softly, "you're awful sweet, but I just don't have the time."

I closed her mouth for her. It seems that a key slid into the door from the outside, but I wasn't paying too close attention.

The lock clicked, the door opened, and Mr. Larry Mitchell walked in.

We broke apart. I turned and he looked at me droopy-eyed, six feet one and tough and wiry.

"I thought to check at the office," he said, almost absently. "Twelve B was rented this afternoon, very soon after this was occupied. I got faintly curious, because there are a lot of vacancies here at the moment. So I borrowed the other key. And who is this hunk of beef, baby?"

"She told you not to call her 'baby,' remember?"

If that meant anything to him, he didn't show it. He swung a knotted fist gently at his side.

The girl said: "He's a private eye named Marlowe. Somebody hired him to follow me."

"Did he have to follow you as close as all that? I seem to be intruding on a beautiful friendship."

She jerked away from me and grabbed the gun out of her suitcase. "What we've been talking is money," she told him.

"Always a mistake," Mitchell said. His color was high and his eyes too bright. "Especially in that position. You won't need the gun, honey."

He poked at me with a straight right, very fast and well sprung. I stepped inside it, fast, cool and clever. But the right wasn't his meal ticket. He was a lefty too. I ought to have noticed that at the Union Station in L.A. Trained observer, never miss a detail. I missed him with a right hook and he didn't miss with his left.

It snapped my head back. I went off balance just long enough for him to lunge sideways and lift the gun out of the girl's hand. It seemed to dance through the air and nestle in his left hand.

"Just relax," he said. "I know it sounds corny, but I could drill you and get away with it. I really could."

"Okay," I said thickly. "For fifty bucks a day I don't get shot. That costs seventy-five."

"Please turn around. It would amuse me to look at your wallet."

I lunged for him, gun and all. Only panic could have made him shoot and he was on his home field and nothing to panic about. But it may be that the girl wasn't so sure. Dimly at the extreme edge of vision I saw her reach for the whiskey bottle on the table.

I caught Mitchell on the side of the neck. His mouth yapped. He hit me somewhere, but it wasn't important. Mine was the better punch, but it didn't win the wrist watch, because at that moment an army mule kicked me square on the back of my brain. I went zooming out over a dark sea and exploded in a sheet of flame.

6

THE FIRST SENSATION was that if anybody spoke harshly to me I should burst out crying. The second, that the room was too small for my head. The front of the head was a long way from the back, the sides were an enormous distance apart, in spite of which a dull throbbing beat from temple to temple. Distance means nothing nowadays.

The third sensation was that somewhere not far off an insistent whining noise went on. The fourth and last was that ice water was running down my back. The cover of a day bed proved that I had been lying on my face, if I still had one. I rolled over gently and sat up and a rattling noise ended in a thump. What rattled and thumped was a knotted towel full of melting ice cubes. Somebody who loved me very much had put them on the back of my head. Somebody who loved me less had bashed in the back of my skull. It could have been the same person. People have moods.

I got up on my feet and lunged for my hip. The wallet was there in the left pocket, but the flap was unbuttoned. I went through it. Nothing was gone. It had yielded its information, but that was no secret any more. My suitcase stood open on the stand at the foot of the day bed. So I was home in my own quarters.

I reached a mirror and looked at the face. It seemed familiar. I went to the door and opened it. The whining noise was louder. Right in front of me was a fattish man leaning against the railing. He was a middle-sized fat man and the fat didn't look flabby. He wore glasses and large ears under a dull gray felt hat. The collar of his topcoat was turned up. His hands were in the pockets of his coat. The hair that showed at the sides of his head was battleship gray. He looked durable. Most fat men do. The light from the open door behind me bounced back from his glasses. He had a small pipe in his mouth, the kind they call a toy bulldog. I was still foggy but something about him bothered me.

"Nice evening," he said.

"You want something?"

"Looking for a man. You're not him."

"I'm alone in here."

"Right," he said. "Thanks." He turned his back on me and leaned his stomach against the railing of the porch.

I went along the porch to the whining noise. The door of 12C was wide open and the lights were on and the noise was a vacuum cleaner being operated by a woman in a green uniform.

I went in and looked the place over. The woman switched off the vacuum and stared at me. "Something you wanted?"

"Where's Miss Mayfield?"

She shook her head.

"The lady who had this apartment," I said.

"Oh, that one. She checked out. Half an hour ago." She switched the vacuum on again. "Better ask at the office," she yelled through the noise. "This apartment is on change."

I reached back and shut the door. I followed the black snake of the vacuum cord over to the wall and yanked the plug out. The woman in the green uniform stared at me angrily. I went over and handed her a dollar bill. She looked less angry.

"Just want to phone," I said.

"Ain't you got a phone in your room?"

"Stop thinking," I said. "A dollar's worth."

I went to the phone and lifted it. A girl's voice said: "Office. Your order, please."

"This is Marlowe. I'm very unhappy."

"What? . . . Oh yes, Mr. Marlowe. What can we do for you?"

"She's gone. I never even got to talk to her."

"Oh, I'm sorry, Mr. Marlowe." She sounded as if she meant it. "Yes, she left. We couldn't very well —"

"She say where to?"

"She just paid up and left, sir. Quite suddenly. No forwarding address at all."

"With Mitchell?"

"I'm sorry, sir. I didn't see anyone with her."

"You must have seen something. How did she leave?"

"In a taxi. I'm afraid —"

"All right. Thank you." I went back to my apartment.

The middle-sized fat man was sitting comfortably in a chair with his knees crossed.

"Nice of you to drop in," I said. "Anything in particular I could do for you?"

"You could tell me where Larry Mitchell is."

"Larry Mitchell?" I thought it over carefully. "Do I know him?"

He opened a wallet and extracted a card. He struggled to his feet and handed it to me. The card read: Goble and Green, Investigators, 310 Prudence Building, Kansas City, Missouri.

"Must be interesting work, Mr. Goble."

"Don't get funny with me, buster. I get annoyed rather easy."

"Fine. Let's watch you get annoyed. What do you do – bite your mustache?"

"I ain't got no mustache, stupid."

"You could grow one. I can wait."

He got up on his feet much more rapidly this time. He looked down at his fist. Suddenly a gun appeared in his hand. "You ever get pistol-whipped, stupid?"

"Breeze off. You bore me. Mudheads always bore me."

His hand shook and his face turned red. Then he put the gun back in the shoulder holster and wobbled towards the door. "You ain't through with me," he snarled over his shoulder.

I let him have that one. It wasn't worth topping.

7

AFTER A WHILE I went down to the office.

"Well, it didn't work," I said. "Does either one of you happen to have noticed the cabdriver who took her away?"

"Joe Harms," the girl said promptly. "You ought to maybe find him at the stand halfway up Grand. Or you could call the office. A pretty nice guy. He made a pass at me once."

"And missed by from here to Paso Robles," the clerk sneered.

"Oh, I don't know. You didn't seem to be there."

"Yeah," he sighed. "You work twenty hours a day trying to put enough together to buy a home. And by the time you have, fifteen other guys have been smooching your girl."

"Not this one," I said. "She's just teasing you. She glows every time she looks at you."

I went out and left them smiling at each other.

Like most small towns, Esmeralda had one main street from which in both directions its commercial establishments flowed gently for a short block or so and then with hardly a change of mood became streets with houses where people lived. But unlike most small California towns it had no false fronts, no cheesy billboards, no drive-in hamburger joints, no cigar counters or pool-rooms, and no street corner toughs to hang around in front of them. The stores on Grand Street were either old and narrow but not tawdry or else well modernized with plate glass and stainless steel fronts and neon lighting in clear crisp colors. Not everybody in Esmeralda was prosperous, not everybody was happy, not everybody drove a Cadillac, a Jaguar or a Riley, but the percentage of obviously prosperous living was very high, and the stores that sold luxury goods were as neat and expensive-looking as those in Beverly Hills and far less flashy. There was another small difference too. In Esmeralda what was old was also clean and sometimes quaint. In other small towns what is old is just shabby.

I parked midway of the block and the telephone office was right in front of me. It was closed of course, but the entrance was set back and in the alcove which deliberately sacrificed money space to style were two dark green phone booths, like sentry boxes. Across the way was a pale buff taxi, parked diagonally to the curb in slots painted red. A gray-haired man sat in it reading the paper. I crossed to him.

"You Joe Harms?"

He shook his head. "He'll be back after a while. You want a cab?"

"No, thanks."

I walked away from him and looked in at a store window. There was a checked brown and beige sport shirt in the window which reminded me of Larry Mitchell. Walnut brogues, imported tweeds, ties, two or three, and matching shirts for them set out with plenty of room to breathe. Over the store the name of a man who was once a famous athlete. The name was in script, carved and painted in relief against a redwood background.

A telephone jangled and the cabdriver got out of the taxi and went across the sidewalk to answer it. He talked, hung up, got in his cab and backed out of the slot. When he was gone, the street was utterly empty for a minute. Then a couple of cars went by, then a good-looking well dressed colored boy and his prettied up cutie came strolling the block looking in at the windows and chattering. A Mexican in a green bell-hop's uniform drove up in somebody's Chrysler New Yorker – it could be his for all I knew – went into the drugstore and came out with a carton of cigarettes. He drove back towards the hotel.

Another beige cab with the name Esmeralda Cab Company tooled around the corner and drifted into the red slot. A big bruiser with thick glasses got out and checked on the wall phone, then got back into his cab and pulled a maga-zine out from behind his rear-view mirror.

I strolled over to him and he was it. He was coatless and had his sleeves rolled up past the elbows, although this was no Bikini suit weather.

"Yeah. I'm Joe Harms." He stuck a pill in his kisser and lit it with a Ronson.

"Lucille down at the Rancho Descansado thought maybe you'd give me a little information." I leaned against his cab and gave him my big warm smile. I might as well have kicked the curbing.

"Information about what?"

"You picked up a fare this evening from one of their cot-tages. Number 12C. A tallish girl with reddish hair and a nice shape. Her name's Betty Mayfield but she probably didn't tell you that."

"Mostly they just tell me where they want to go. Quaint, isn't it?" He blew a lungful of smoke at his windshield and watched it flatten out and float around in the cab. "What's the pitch?"

"Girl friend walked out on me. We had a little argument. All my fault. I'd like to tell her I'm sorry."

"Girl friend got a home somewhere?"

"A long way from here."

He knocked ash from his cigarette by flicking his little finger at it still in his mouth.

"Could be she planned it that way. Could be she don't want you to know where she went. Could be you were lucky at that. They can drop the arm on you for shacking up in a hotel in this town. I'll admit it has to be pretty flagrant."

"Could be I'm a liar," I said, and got a business card out of my wallet. He read it and handed it back.

"Better," he said. "Some better. But it's against the company rules. I'm not driving this hack just to build muscle."

"A five interest you? Or is that against the rules too?"

"My old man owns the company. He'd be pretty sore if I was on the chisel. Not that I don't like money."

The phone on the wall jangled. He slid out of the cab and went over to it in about three long strides. I just stood planted, gnawing my lip. He talked and came back and stepped into the cab and was sitting behind the wheel all in one motion.

"Have to blow," he said. "Sorry. I'm kind of behind schedule. Just got back from Del Mar, the seven forty-seven to L.A. makes a flag stop there. Most people from here go that way."

He started his motor and leaned out of the cab to drop his cigarette in the street.

I said, "Thanks."

"For what?" He backed out and was gone.

I looked at my watch again. Time and distance checked. It was all of twelve miles to Del Mar. It would take almost an hour to ferry someone to Del Mar and drop him or her off at the railroad station and turn around and come back. He had told me in his own way. There was no point in telling me at all unless it meant something.

I watched him out of sight and then crossed the street to the booths outside the telephone company's office. I left the booth door open and dropped my dime and dialed the big O.

"I'd like to make a collect call to West Los Angeles, please."
I gave her a Bradshaw number. "Person to person, Mr. Clyde
Umney. My name is Marlowe and I'm calling from Esmeralda
4-2673, a pay phone."

She got him a lot quicker than it took me to tell her all
that. He came on sharp and quick.

"Marlowe? It's about time you reported in. Well – let's
have it."

"I'm in San Diego. I've lost her. She slipped away while
I was taking a nap."

"I just knew I'd picked a smart cookie," he said unpleasantly.

"It's not as bad as it sounds, Mr. Umney. I have a rough idea
where she went."

"Rough ideas are not good enough for me. When I hire a
man I expect him to deliver exactly what I order. And just
what do you mean by a rough idea?"

"Would it be possible for you to give me some notion
of what this is all about, Mr. Umney? I grabbed it off kind of
quick on account of meeting the train. Your secretary gave
me a lot of personality but very little information. You want
me to be happy in my work, don't you, Mr. Umney?"

"I gathered that Miss Vermilyea told you all there is to
know," he grumbled. "I am acting at the request of an important law firm in Washington. Their client desires to remain
anonymous for the present. All you have to do is trace this
party to a stopping place, and by stopping place I do not mean
a rest room or a hamburger stand. I mean a hotel, apartment
house, or perhaps the home of someone she knows. That's all.
How much simpler do you want it?"

"I'm not asking for simplicity, Mr. Umney. I'm asking for
background material. Who the girl is, where she came from,
what she's supposed to have done to make this job necessary."

"Necessary?" he yapped at me. "Who the hell are you to
decide what is necessary? Find that girl, pin her down, and

855

phone me her address. And if you expect to be paid, you better do it damn quick. I'll give you until ten o'clock tomorrow morning. After that I'll make other arrangements."

"Okay, Mr. Umney."

"Where are you exactly and what is your telephone number?"

"I'm just kind of wandering around. I got hit on the head with a whiskey bottle."

"Well, that's too bad," he said acidly. "I presume you had already emptied the bottle."

"Oh it might have been worse, Mr. Umney. It might have been *your* head. I'll call you around ten A.M. at your office. Don't worry about anybody losing anybody. There's two other guys working the same side of the street. One's a local boy named Mitchell and the other is a Kansas City shamus name of Goble. He carries a gun. Well, good night, Mr. Umney."

"Hold it!" he roared. "Wait a minute! What does that mean — two other operatives?"

"You asking me what it means? I'm the guy that asked you. Looks like you only got a piece of the job."

"Hold it! Hold it right there!" There was a silence. Then in a steady voice that didn't bluster any more: "I'll call Washington the first thing in the morning, Marlowe. Excuse me if I sounded off. It begins to look as though I am entitled to a little more information about this project."

"Yeah."

"If you make contact again, call me here. At any hour. Any hour at all."

"Yeah."

"Good night, then." He hung up.

I put the phone back on the hook and took a deep breath. My head still ached but the dizziness was gone. I breathed in the cool night air laced with sea fog. I pushed out of the booth and looked across the street. The old guy who had been in the taxi slot when I arrived was back again. I strolled across and asked him how to get to The Glass Room, which was where Mitchell had promised to take Miss Betty Mayfield to dinner – whether she liked it or not. He told me, I thanked him, recrossed the empty street and climbed into my rented car, and started back the way I had come.

It was still possible that Miss Mayfield had grabbed the 7:47 for Los Angeles or some way station. It was a lot more likely that she had not. A cabdriver taking a fare to the station doesn't stick around to watch the fare get on the train. Larry Mitchell wouldn't be that easy to shake. If he had enough on her to make her come to Esmeralda, he had enough on her to keep her there. He knew who I was and what I was doing. He didn't know why, because I didn't know myself. If he had half a brain, and I gave him credit for a good deal more, he would have to assume I could trace her movements as far as a taxi took her. The first guess I was working on was that he would have driven to Del Mar, parked his big Buick somewhere in the shadows, and waited for her taxi to drive up and unload. When it turned around and started back, he would pick her up and drive her back to Esmeralda. The second guess I was working on was that she wouldn't tell him anything he didn't already know. I was a Los Angeles private eye, unknown parties had hired me to follow her, I had done so and then made the mistake of trying to get too close. That would bother him because it suggested he didn't have the field to himself. But if his information, whatever it was, came from a press clipping, he could hardly expect to have it to himself forever. Anybody with enough interest and enough patience could turn it up in time. Anybody with enough reason to hire a private dick probably knew it already. And that in turn meant that whatever kind of bite he planned to put on Betty Mayfield, financial or amatory or both, would have to be put on fast.

A third of a mile down the canyon a small illuminated sign with an arrow pointing seaward said in script *The Glass Room.*

The road wound down between cliffside houses with warm lights in the windows, manicured gardens, stucco walls and one or two of fieldstone or brick inset with tiles in the Mexican tradition.

I drove down the last curve of the last hill and the smell of raw seaweed filled my nostrils and the fog-veiled lights of The Glass Room swelled to amber brightness and the sound of dance music drifted across the paved parking lot. I parked with the sea growling out of sight almost at my feet. There was no attendant. You just locked your car and went in.

A couple of dozen cars, no more. I looked them over. One hunch at least had paid off. The Buick Roadmaster solid top bore a license number I had in my pocket. It was parked almost at the entrance and next to it in the very last space near the entrance was a pale green and ivory Cadillac convertible with oyster-white leather seats, a plaid traveling rug thrown over the front seat to keep it dry, and all the gadgets a dealer could think of, including two enormous spotlights with mirrors on them, a radio aerial almost long enough for a tuna boat, a folding chromium luggage rack to help out the boot if you wanted to travel far and in style, a sun visor, a prism reflector to pick up traffic lights obscured by the visor, a radio with enough knobs on it for a control panel, a cigarette lighter into which you dropped your cigarette and it smoked it for you, and various other trifles which made me wonder how long it would be before they installed radar, sound-recording equipment, a bar, and an anti-aircraft battery.

All this I saw by the light of a clip-on flash. I moved it to the license holder and the name was Clark Brandon, Hotel Casa del Poniente, Esmeralda, California.

8

THE ENTRANCE LOBBY was on a balcony which looked down over the bar and a dining room on two levels. A curving carpeted staircase led down to the bar. Nobody was upstairs but the hat-check girl and an elderly party in a phone booth whose expression suggested that nobody better fool with him.

I went down the stairs to the bar and tucked myself in a small curved space that commanded a view of the dance floor. One side of the building was an enormous glass window. Outside of it was nothing but fog, but on a clear night with a moon low over the water it would have been sensational. A three-piece Mexican band was making the kind of music a Mexican band always makes. Whatever they play, it all sounds the same. They always sing the same song, and it always has nice open vowels and a drawn out sugary lilt, and the guy who sings it always strums on a guitar and has a lot to say about *amor, mi corazón*, a lady who is "linda" but very hard to convince, and he always has too long and too oily hair and when he isn't making with the love stuff he looks as if his knife work in an alley would be efficient and economical.

On the dance floor half a dozen couples were throwing themselves around with the reckless abandon of a night watchman with arthritis. Most of them were dancing cheek to cheek, if dancing is the word. The men wore white tuxedos and the girls wore bright eyes, ruby lips, and tennis or golf muscles. One couple was not dancing cheek to cheek. The guy was too drunk to keep time and the girl was too busy not getting her pumps walked on to think of anything else. I needn't have worried about losing Miss Betty Mayfield. She was there and with Mitchell, but far from happy. Mitchell's mouth was open, he was grinning, his face was red and shiny, and his eyes had that glazed look. Betty was holding her head as far as she could get away from him without breaking her neck. It was very obvious that she had had about all of Mr. Larry Mitchell that she could take.

A Mexican waiter in a short green jacket and white pants with a green stripe down the side came up and I ordered a double Gibson and asked if I could have a club sandwich where I was. He said, "*Muy bien, señor,*" smiled brightly, and disappeared.

The music stopped, there was desultory clapping. The orchestra was deeply moved, and played another number. A dark-haired headwaiter who looked like a road company Herbert Marshall circulated among the tables offering his intimate smile and stopping here and there to polish an apple. Then he pulled out a chair and sat down opposite a big hand-some Irish type character with gray in his hair and just enough of it. He seemed to be alone. He wore a dark dinner jacket with a maroon carnation in the lapel. He looked like a nice guy if you didn't crowd him. At that distance and in that light I couldn't tell much more, except that if you did crowd him, you had better be big, fast, tough and in top condition.

The headwaiter leaned forward and said something and they both looked towards Mitchell and the Mayfield girl. The captain seemed concerned, the big guy didn't seem to care much one way or another. The headwaiter got up and left. The big guy fitted a cigarette into a holder and a waiter popped a lighter at him as if he had been waiting all evening for the opportunity. The big guy thanked him without look-ing up.

My drink came and I grabbed it and drank. The music stopped and stayed stopped. The couples divided and strolled back to their tables. Larry Mitchell still had hold of Betty. He was still grinning. Then he began to pull her close. He put his hand behind her head. She tried to shake him off. He pulled harder and pushed his flushed face down on hers. She strug-gled but he was too strong for her. He chewed her face some more. She kicked him. He jerked his head up, annoyed.

"Let go of me, you drunken slob," she said breathlessly but very distinctly.

His face got a nasty look. He grabbed her arms hard enough to bruise her and slowly using his strength he pulled her tight against his body and held her there. People looked hard, but nobody moved.

"Whassa matta, baby, you no love poppa no more?" he inquired loudly and thickly.

I didn't see what she did to him with her knee but I could guess and it hurt him. He pushed her away and his face went savage. Then he hauled off and slapped her across the mouth forehand and backhand. The red showed on her skin at once.

She stood quite still. Then in a voice the whole joint could hear she said clearly and slowly: "Next time you do that, Mr. Mitchell – be sure to wear a bullet-proof vest."

She turned and walked away. He just stood there. His face had gone glistening white – whether from pain or rage I couldn't tell. The headwaiter walked softly up to him and murmured something with an inquiring lift of the eyebrow.

Mitchell brought his eyes down and looked at the man. Then without a word he walked right through him and the headwaiter had to stagger out of his way. Mitchell followed Betty, and on the way he bumped a man in a chair and didn't stop to apologize. Betty was sitting down now at a table against the glass wall right next to the big dark guy in the dinner jacket. He looked at her. He looked at Mitchell. He took his cigarette holder out of his mouth and looked at that. His face was quite expressionless.

Mitchell reached the table. "You hurt me, sweetness," he said thickly but loudly. "I'm a bad man to hurt. Catch on? Very bad. Want to apologize?"

She stood up, jerked a wrap off the back of the chair and faced him.

"Shall I pay the check, Mr. Mitchell – or will you pay it with what you borrowed from me?"

His hand went back for another swing at her face. She didn't move. The guy at the next table did. He came up on his feet in one smooth movement and grabbed Mitchell's wrist.

"Take it easy, Larry. You've got a skinful." His voice was cool, almost amused.

Mitchell jerked his wrist loose and spun around. "Stay out of this, Brandon."

"Delighted, old man. I'm not in it. But you'd better not slug the lady again. They don't often throw people out of here – but it could happen."

Mitchell laughed angrily. "Why don't you go spit in your hat, mister?"

The big man said softly, "Take it easy, Larry, I said. I won't say it again."

Mitchell glared at him. "Okay, see you later," he said in a sulky voice. He started off and stopped. "Much later," he added, half turning. Then he went out – unsteadily but quickly, looking at nothing.

Brandon just stood there. The girl just stood there. She looked uncertain about what to do next.

She looked at him. He looked at her. He smiled, just polite and easygoing, no come-on. She didn't smile back.

"Anything I could do?" he asked. "Drop you anywhere?" Then he half turned his head. "Oh, Carl."

The headwaiter came up to him quickly.

"No check," Brandon said. "You know, in the circum-stances –"

"Please," the girl said sharply. "I don't want other people paying my bills."

He shook his head slowly. "Custom of the house," he said. "Nothing to do with me personally. But may I send you a drink?"

She looked at him some more. He had what it took all right. "Send?" she asked.

He smiled politely. "Well, bring then – if you care to sit down."

And this time he pulled out the chair at his own table. And she sat down. And at that moment, nor a second before, the headwaiter signaled the orchestra and they began to play another number.

Mr. Clark Brandon seemed to be the sort of man who got what he wanted without raising his voice.

After a while my club sandwich came. It was nothing to brag about, but eatable. I ate it. I stuck around for half an hour. Brandon and the girl seemed to be doing all right. They were both quiet. After a while they danced. Then I left and sat in the car outside and smoked. She could have seen me although she didn't show it. I knew Mitchell hadn't. He had turned too quickly up the stairs, he had been too mad to see anything.

About ten-thirty, Brandon came out with her and they got into the Cadillac convertible with the top down. I followed it away without trying to hide because the way they went would be the way anybody would go back to the downtown part of Esmeralda. Where they went was to the Casa del Poniente, and Brandon drove down the ramp to the garage.

There was only one thing more to find out. I parked in the side lot and went through the lobby to the house phones.

"Miss Mayfield, please. Betty Mayfield."

"One moment, please" – slight pause – "Oh yes, she just checked in. I'm ringing the room, sir."

Another and much longer pause.

"I'm sorry, Miss Mayfield's room does not answer."

I thanked her and hung up. I beat it out of there fast in case she and Brandon should get off at the lobby.

I went back to my rented chariot, and poked my way along the canyon through the fog to the Rancho Descansado. The cottage where the office was seemed to be locked up and empty. A single hazy light outside showed the position of a night bell. I groped my way up to 12C, tucked the car in the car port, and yawned my way into my room. It was cold and damp and miserable. Someone had been in and taken the striped cover off the day bed and removed the matching pillowcases.

I undressed and put my curly head on the pillow and went to sleep.

9

A TAPPING SOUND awoke me. It was very light but it was also persistent. I had the feeling that it had been going on a long time and that it had very gradually penetrated my sleep. I rolled over and listened. Somebody tried the door and then the tapping started again. I glanced at my wrist watch. The faint phosphorescence showed it was past three o'clock. I got up on my feet and moved over to my suitcase and reached down into it for the gun. I went over to the door and opened it a crack.

A dark figure in slacks stood there. Some kind of windbreaker also. And a dark scarf knotted around the head. It was a woman.

"What do you want?"

"Let me in – quickly. Don't put any light on."

So it was Betty Mayfield. I pulled the door back and she slid in like a wisp of the fog. I shut the door. I reached for my bathrobe and pulled it on.

"Anybody else outside?" I asked. "There's nobody next door."

"No. I'm alone." She leaned against the wall and breathed quickly. I fumbled my pen flash out of my coat and poked a small beam around and found the heater switch. I shone the little light on her face. She blinked away from it and raised a hand. I put the light down on the floor and trailed it over to the windows and shut them both and lowered and turned the blinds. Then I went back and switched on the lamp.

She let out a gasp, then said nothing. She was still leaning against the wall. She looked as if she needed a drink. I went out to the kitchenette and poured some whiskey into a glass and carried it to her. She waved it away, then changed her mind and grabbed the glass and emptied it.

I sat down and lit a cigarette, the always mechanical reaction that gets so boring when someone else does it. Then I just sat there and looked at her and waited.

Our eyes met across great gulfs of nothing. After a while she reached slowly into the slanted pocket of the windbreaker and pulled out the gun.

"Oh no," I said. "Not that again."

She looked down at the gun. Her lip twitched. She wasn't pointing it anywhere. She pushed herself away from the wall and crossed to lay the gun down at my elbow.

"I've seen it," I said. "We're old friends. Last time I saw it Mitchell had it. So?"

"That's why I knocked you out. I was afraid he would shoot you."

"That would have fouled up all his plans — whatever his plans were."

"Well, I couldn't be sure. I'm sorry. Sorry I hit you."

"Thanks for the ice cubes," I said.

"Aren't you going to look at the gun?"

"I have looked at it."

"I walked all the way over here from the Casa. I'm staying there now. I — moved in this afternoon."

"I know. You took a taxi to the Del Mar station to catch an evening train and then Mitchell picked you up there and drove you back. You had dinner together and danced and there was a little ill-feeling. A man named Clark Brandon took you back to the hotel in his convertible."

She stared. "I didn't see you there," she said finally, in a voice that was thinking of other things.

"I was in the bar. While you were with Mitchell you were too busy getting your face slapped and telling him to wear a bullet-proof vest next time he came around. Then at Brandon's table you sat with your back to me. I left before you did and waited outside."

"I'm beginning to think you *are* a detective," she said quietly. Her eyes went to the gun again. "He never gave it back to me," she said. "Of course I couldn't prove that."

"That means you'd like to be able to."

"It might help a little. It probably wouldn't help quite enough. Not when they found out about me. I guess you know what I'm talking about."

"Sit down and stop grinding your teeth."

She moved slowly to a chair and sat down on the edge and leaned forward. She stared at the floor.

"I know there's something to find out," I said. "Because Mitchell found it out. So I could find it out too — if I tried. Anyone could who knows there is something to find. I don't know at this moment. All I was hired to do was to keep in touch and report back."

She looked up briefly. "And you've done that?"

"I reported in," I said after a pause. "I'd lost contact at the time. I mentioned San Diego. He'd get that from the operator anyway."

"You'd lost contact," she repeated dryly. "He must think a lot of you, whoever he is." Then she bit her lip. "I'm sorry. I didn't mean to say that. I'm trying to make up my mind about something."

"Take your time," I said. "It's only twenty past three A.M."

"Now *you're* sneering."

I looked towards the wall heater. It didn't show a thing, but there seemed to be a lessening of the chill if no more. I decided I needed a drink. I went out to the kitchen and got it. I put it down, poured some more and came back.

She had a small imitation leather folder in her hand now. She showed it to me.

"I have five thousand dollars in American Express checks in this — one hundred dollar size. How far would you go for five grand, Marlowe?"

I took a sip of whiskey. I thought about it with a judicial expression. "Assuming a normal rate of expenses, that would buy me full time for several months. That is, if I happened to be for sale."

She tapped on the chair arm with the folder. I could see that her other hand was almost pulling her kneecap off.

"You're for sale all right," she said. "And this would be merely a down payment. I can buy big. I've got more money than you ever dreamed of. My last husband was so rich that it was pitiful. I got a cool half million dollars out of him."

She put a hardboiled sneer on her face and gave me plenty of time to get used to it.

"I take it I wouldn't have to murder anybody?"

"You wouldn't have to murder anybody."

"I don't like the way you say that."

I looked sideways at the gun that I hadn't so far laid a finger on. She had walked over from the Casa in the middle of the night to bring it to me. I didn't have to touch it. I stared at it. I bent over and sniffed it. I still didn't have to touch it, but I knew I was going to.

"Who's wearing the bullet?" I asked her. The cold in the room had got into my blood. It ran ice water.

"Just one bullet? How did you know?"

I picked up the gun then. I slipped the magazine out, looked at it, slipped it back. It snapped home in the butt.

"Well, it could have been two," I said. "There are six in the magazine. This gun holds seven. You could jack one into the chamber and then add another to the magazine. Of course you could fire the whole supply and then put six in the magazine."

"We're just talking, aren't we?" she said slowly. "We don't quite want to say it in plain words."

"All right. Where is he?"

"Lying across a chaise on the balcony of my room. All the rooms on that side have balconies. They have concrete walls across them, and the end walls – between the rooms or suites, that is – are slanted outward. I guess a steeplejack or a mountain climber might get around one of the end walls, but not carrying a weight. I'm on the twelfth floor. There's nothing any higher but the penthouse floor." She stopped and frowned, then made a sort of helpless gesture with the hand

867

that had been squeezing her kneecap. "This is going to sound a little corny," she went on. "He could only have got there through my room. And I didn't let him through my room."

"But you're sure he's dead?"

"Quite sure. Quite dead. Stone cold dead. I don't know when it happened. I didn't hear a sound. Something woke me all right. But it wasn't any sound like a shot. Anyhow he was already cold. So I don't know what woke me. And I didn't get up right away. I just lay there, thinking. I didn't go back to sleep, so after a while I put the light on and got up and walked around and smoked. Then I noticed the fog was gone and it was moonlight. Not down on the ground, but up there on my floor. I could still see fog down below when I went out on the balcony. It was damned cold. The stars seemed enormous. I stood there near the wall for quite a while before I even saw him. I guess that sounds pretty corny too – or pretty unlikely. I can't imagine the police taking it very seriously – even at first. And afterwards – well, just take it this way. I haven't a chance in a million – unless I get help."

I stood up, tossed down what whiskey was left in the glass and walked over to her.

"Let me tell you two or three things. First off, you're not taking this with normal reactions. You're not icy cool, but you're too cool. No panic, no hysteria, no nothing. You're fatalistic. Next, I heard the entire conversation between you and Mitchell this afternoon. I took those bulbs out" – I pointed to the wall heater – "and used a stethoscope against the partition at the back. What Mitchell had on you was a knowledge of who you were, and that knowledge was something that if published could drive you into another switch of names and another dodge to some other town somewhere. You said you were the luckiest girl in the world because you were alive. Now a man is dead on your balcony, shot with your gun, and the man of course is Mitchell. Right?"

She nodded. "Yes, it's Larry."

"And you didn't kill him, you say. And the cops would hardly believe that even at first, you say. And later on not at all. My guess is that you've been there before."

She was still looking up at me. She came slowly to her feet. Our faces were close, we stared hard into each other's eyes. It didn't mean a thing.

"Half a million dollars is a lot of money, Marlowe. You're not too hard to take. There are places in the world where you and I could have a beautiful life. In one of those tall apartment houses along the ocean front in Rio. I don't know how long it would last, but things can always be arranged, don't you think?"

I said: "What a lot of different girls you are. Now you're making like a moll. When I first saw you, you were a quiet well-bred little lady. You didn't like dreamboats like Mitchell making a pitch at you. Then you bought yourself a pack of cigarettes and smoked one as if you hated it. Then you let him cuddle you – after you got down here. Then you tore your blouse at me ha, ha, ha, cynical as a Park Avenue pet after her butter and egg man goes home. Then you let me cuddle you. Then you cracked me on the head with a whiskey bottle. Now you're talking about a beautiful life in Rio. Which one of you would have her head on the next pillow when I woke up in the morning?"

"Five thousand dollars down. And a lot more to come. The police wouldn't give you five toothpicks. If you think different, you have a telephone."

"What do I do for the five grand?"

She let her breath out slowly as if a crisis was past. "The hotel is built almost on the edge of the cliff. At the foot of the wall there's only a narrow walk, very narrow. Below the cliffs are rocks and the sea. It's almost high tide. My balcony hangs right over all that."

I nodded. "Are there fire stairs?"

"From the garage. They start just beside the basement elevator landing, which is up two or three steps from the garage floor. But it's a long hard climb."

"For five grand I'd climb it in a diver's suit. Did you come out through the lobby?"

"Fire stairs. There's an all night man in the garage but he was asleep in one of the cars."

"You said Mitchell is lying on a chaise. Is there a lot of blood?"

She winced. "I – I didn't notice. I suppose there must be."

"You didn't notice? You went near enough to find out he was stone cold dead. Where was he shot?"

"Nowhere that I saw. It must have been under him."

"Where was the gun?"

"It was lying on the floor of the porch – beside his hand."

"Which hand?"

She widened her eyes slightly. "Does it matter? I don't know which hand. He's sort of lying across the chaise with his head hanging on one side and his legs on the other. Do we have to keep on talking about it?"

"All right," I said. "I don't know a damn thing about the tides and currents around here. He might wash up on the beach tomorrow and he might not show up for two weeks. Assuming, of course, we bring it off. If it's a long time they may not even find out he was shot. Then I guess there's some possibility that he won't be found at all. Not much, but some. There are barracuda in these waters, and other things."

"You certainly do a thorough job of making it revolting," she said.

"Well, I had a running start. Also I was thinking if there was any chance of suicide. Then we'd have to put the gun back. He was left-handed, you know. That's why I wanted to know which hand."

"Oh. Yes, he was left-handed. You're right. But not suicide. Not that smirking, self-satisfied gentleman."

"Sometimes a man kills the dearest thing he loves, they say. Couldn't it be himself ?"

"Not this character," she said briefly and finally. "If we are very lucky, they will probably think he fell off the balcony. God knows he was drunk enough. And by that time I'll be in South America. My passport is still valid."

"In what name is your passport?"

She reached out and drew her fingertips down my cheek. "You'll know all about me soon enough. Don't be impatient. You'll know all the intimate things about me. Can't you wait a little?"

"Yeah. Start getting intimate with those American Express checks. We have another hour or two of darkness and more than that of fog. You play with the checks while I get dressed."

I reached into my jacket and gave her a fountain pen. She sat down near the light and began to sign them with the second signature. Her tongue peeped out between her teeth. She wrote slowly and carefully. The name she wrote was Elizabeth Mayfield.

So the switch of names had been planned before she left Washington.

While I dressed I wondered if she was really foolish enough to think I'd help her dispose of a body.

I carried the glasses out to the kitchenette and scooped the gun up on the way. I let the swing door close and slipped the gun and the magazine into the tray under the broiler of the stove. I rinsed out the glasses and wiped them off. I went back into the living room and threw my clothes on. She didn't even look at me.

She went on signing the checks. When she had finished, I took the folder of checks and flipped them over one by one, checking the signatures. The big money meant nothing to me. I shoved the folder into my pocket, put the lamp out and moved to the door. I opened it and she was beside me. She was close beside me.

"Sneak out," I said. "I'll pick you up on the highway just above where the fence ends."

871

She faced me and leaned a little towards me. "Can I trust you?" she asked softly.

"Up to a point."

"You're honest at least. What happens if we don't get away with it? If somebody reported a shot, if he has been found, if we walk in on that and the place is full of policemen?"

I just stood there with my eyes on her face and didn't answer her.

"Just let me guess," she said very softly and slowly. "You'll sell me out fast. And you won't have any five thousand dollars. Those checks will be old newspaper. You won't dare cash a single one of them."

I still didn't say anything.

"You son of a bitch." She didn't raise her voice even a semitone. "Why did I ever come to you?"

I took her face between my hands and kissed her on the lips. She pulled away.

"Not for that," she said. "Certainly not for that. And one more small point. It's terribly small and unimportant, I know. I've had to learn that. From expert teachers. Long hard painful lessons and a lot of them. It just happens that I really didn't kill him."

"Maybe I believe you."

"Don't bother to try," she said. "Nobody else will."

She turned and slid along the porch and down the steps. She flitted off through the trees. In thirty feet the fog hid her.

I locked up and got into the rent car and drove it down the silent driveway past the closed office with the light over the night bell. The whole place was hard asleep, but trucks were rumbling up through the canyon with building materials and oil and the big closed up jobs with and without trailers, full of anything and everything that a town needs to live on. The fog lights were on and the trucks were slow and heavy up the hill.

Fifty yards beyond the gate she stepped out of the shadows at the end of the fence and climbed in. I switched on my headlights. Somewhere out on the water a foghorn was moaning. Upstairs in the clear reaches of the sky a formation of jets from North Island went over with a whine and a whoosh and a bang of the shock wave and were gone in less time than it took me to pull the lighter out of the dash and light a cigarette.

The girl sat motionless beside me, looking straight ahead and not speaking. She wasn't seeing the fog or the back of a truck we were coming up behind. She wasn't seeing anything. She was just sitting there frozen in one position, stony with despair, like somebody on the way to be hanged.

Either that or she was the best little scene stealer I had come across in a long long time.

10

THE CASA DEL Poniente was set on the edge of the cliffs in about seven acres of lawn and flower beds, with a central patio on the sheltered side, tables set out behind a glass screen, and a trellised walk leading through the middle of it to an entrance. There was a bar on one side, a coffee shop on the other, and at each end of the building blacktop parking lots partly hidden behind six-foot hedges of flowering shrubs. The parking lots had cars in them. Not everyone bothered to use the basement garage, although the damp salt air down there is hard on chromium.

I parked in a slot near the garage ramp and the sound of the ocean was very close and you could feel the drifting spray and smell it and taste it. We got out and moved over to the garage entrance. A narrow raised walk edged the ramp. A sign hung midway of the entrance said: Descend in Low Gear. Sound Horn. The girl grabbed me by the arm and stopped me.

"I'm going in by the lobby. I'm too tired to climb the stairs."

"Okay. No law against it. What's the room number?"

"Twelve twenty-four. What do we get if we're caught?"

"Caught doing what?"

"You know what. Putting – putting it over the balcony wall. Or somewhere."

"I'd get staked out on an anthill. I don't know about you. Depends what else they have on you."

"How can you talk like that before breakfast?"

She turned and walked away quickly. I started down the ramp. It curved as they all do and then I could see a glassed-in cubbyhole of an office with a hanging light in it. A little farther down and I could see that it was empty. I listened for sounds of somebody doing a little work on a car, water in a washrack, steps, whistling, any little noise to indicate where the night man was and what he was doing. In a basement garage you can hear a very small noise indeed. I heard nothing.

I went on down and was almost level with the upper end of the office. Now by stooping I could see the shallow steps up into the basement elevator lobby. There was a door marked: To Elevator. It had glass panels and I could see light beyond it, but little else.

I took three more steps and froze. The night man was looking right at me. He was in a big Packard sedan in the back seat. The light shone on his face and he wore glasses and the light shone hard on the glasses. He was leaning back comfortably in the corner of the car. I stood there and waited for him to move. He didn't move. His head was against the car cushions. His mouth was open. I had to know why he didn't move. He might be just pretending to be asleep until I got out of sight. When that happened he would beat it across to the phone and call the office.

Then I thought that was silly. He wouldn't have come on the job until evening and he couldn't know all the guests by sight. The sidewalk that bordered the ramp was there to walk on. It was almost 4 A.M. In an hour or so it would begin to get light. No hotel prowler would come around that late.

I walked straight over to the Packard and looked in on him. The car was shut up tight, all windows. The man didn't move. I reached for the door handle and tried to open the door without noise. He still didn't move. He looked like a very light colored man. He also looked asleep and I could hear him snoring even before I got the door open. Then I got it full in the face — the honeyed reek of well-cured marihuana. The guy was out of circulation, he was in the valley of peace, where time is slowed to a standstill, where the world is all colors and music. And in a couple of hours from now he wouldn't have a job, even if the cops didn't grab him and toss him into the deep freeze.

I shut the car door again and crossed to the glass-paneled door. I went through into a small bare elevator lobby with a concrete floor and two blank elevator doors and beside them, opening on a heavy door closer, the fire stairs. I pulled that open and started up. I went slowly. Twelve stories and a basement take a lot of stairs. I counted the fire doors as I passed them because they were not numbered. They were heavy and solid and gray like the concrete of the steps. I was sweating and out of breath when I pulled open the door to the twelfth-floor corridor. I prowled along to Room 1224 and tried the knob. It was locked, but almost at once the door was opened, as if she had been waiting just behind it. I went in past her and flopped into a chair and waited to get some breath back. It was a big airy room with french windows opening on a balcony. The double bed had been slept in or arranged to look that way. Odds and ends of clothing on chairs, toilet articles on the dresser, luggage. It looked about twenty bucks a day, single.

She turned the night latch in the door. "Have any trouble?"

"The night man was junked to the eyes. Harmless as a kitten." I heaved myself out of the chair and started across to the french doors.

"Wait!" she said sharply. I looked back at her. "It's no use," she said. "Nobody could do a thing like that."

I stood there and waited.

"I'd rather call the police," she said. "Whatever it means for me."

"That's a bright idea," I said. "Why ever didn't we think of it before?"

"You'd better leave," she said. "There's no need for you to be mixed up in it."

I didn't say anything. I watched her eyes. She could hardly keep them open. It was either delayed shock or some kind of dope. I didn't know which.

"I swallowed two sleeping pills," she said, reading my mind. "I just can't take any more trouble tonight. Go away from here. Please. When I wake I'll call room service. When the waiter comes I'll get him out on the balcony somehow and he'll find – whatever he'll find. And I won't know a damn thing about it." Her tongue was getting thick. She shook herself and rubbed hard against her temples. "I'm sorry about the money. You'll have to give it back to me, won't you?"

I went over close to her. "Because if I don't you'll tell them the whole story?"

"I'll have to," she said drowsily. "How can I help it? They'll get it out of me. I'm – I'm too tired to fight any more."

I took hold of her arm and shook her. Her head wobbled. "Quite sure you only took two capsules?"

She blinked her eyes open. "Yes. I never take more than two."

"Then listen. I'm going out there and have a look at him. Then I'm going back to the Rancho. I'm going to keep your money. Also I have your gun. Maybe it can't be traced to me but – Wake up! Listen to me!" Her head was rolling sideways again. She jerked straight and her eyes widened, but they looked dull and withdrawn. "Listen. If it can't be traced to you, it certainly can't be traced to me. I'm working for a lawyer and my assignment is you. The traveler's checks and the gun will go right where they belong. And your story to the cops won't be worth a wooden nickel. All it will do is help to hang you. Understand that?"

"Ye-es," she said. "And I don't g-give a damn."

"That's not you talking. It's the sleeping medicine."

She sagged forward and I caught her and steered her over to the bed. She flopped on it any old way. I pulled her shoes off and spread a blanket over her and tucked her in. She was asleep at once. She began to snore. I went into the bathroom and groped around and found a bottle of Nembutal on the shelf. It was almost full. It had a prescription number and a date on it. The date was a month old, the drugstore was in Baltimore. I dumped the yellow capsules out into my palm and counted them. There were forty-seven and they almost filled the bottle. When they take them to kill themselves, they take them all – except what they spill, and they nearly always spill some. I put the pills back in the bottle and put the bottle in my pocket.

I went back and looked at her again. The room was cold. I turned the radiator on, not too much. And finally at long last I opened the french doors and went out on the balcony. It was as cold as hell out there. The balcony was about twelve by fourteen feet, with a thirty-inch wall across the front and a low iron railing sprouting out of that. You could jump off easy enough, but you couldn't possibly fall off accidentally. There were two aluminum patio chaises with padded cushions, two armchairs of the same type. The dividing wall to the left stuck out the way she had told me. I didn't think even a steeplejack could get around the projection without climbing tackle. The wall at the other end rose sheer to the edge of what must be one of the penthouse terraces.

Nobody was dead on either of the chaises, nor on the floor of the balcony, nor anywhere at all. I examined them for traces of blood. No blood. No blood on the balcony. I went

877

along the safety wall. No blood. No signs of anything having been heaved over. I stood against the wall and held on to the metal railing and leaned out as far as I could lean. I looked straight down the face of the wall to the ground. Shrubs grew close to it, then a narrow strip of lawn, then a flagstone footpath, then another strip of lawn and then a heavy fence with more shrubs growing against that. I estimated the distance. At that height it wasn't easy, but it must have been at least thirty-five feet. Beyond the fence the sea creamed on some half-submerged rocks.

Larry Mitchell was about half an inch taller than I was but weighed about fifteen pounds less, at a rough guess. The man wasn't born who could heave a hundred and seventy-five pound body over that railing and far enough out to fall into the ocean. It was barely possible that a girl wouldn't realize that, just barely possible, about one tenth of one per cent possible.

I opened the french door and went through and shut it and crossed to stand beside the bed. She was still sound asleep. She was still snoring. I touched her cheek with the back of my hand. It was moist. She moved a little and mumbled. Then she sighed and settled her head into the pillow. No stertorous breathing, no deep stupor, no coma, and therefore no overdose.

She had told me the truth about one thing, and about damned little else.

I found her bag in the top drawer of the dresser. It had a zipper pocket at the back. I put her folder of traveler's checks in it and looked through it for information. There was some crisp folding money in the zipper pocket, a Santa Fe timetable, the folder her ticket had been in and the stub of the railroad ticket and the Pullman reservation. She had had Bedroom E on Car 19, Washington, D.C., to San Diego, California. No letters, nothing to identify her. That would be locked up in the luggage. In the main part of the bag was what a woman carries, a lipstick, a compact, a change purse, some silver, and a few keys on a ring with a tiny bronze tiger hanging from it. A pack of cigarettes that seemed just about full but had been opened. A matchbook with one match used. Three handkerchiefs with no initials, a packet of emery boards, a cuticle knife, and some kind of eyebrow stuff, a comb in a leather case, a little round jar of nail polish, a tiny address book. I pounced on that. Blank, not used at all. Also in the bag were a pair of sun glasses with spangled rims in a case, no name on the case; a fountain pen, a small gold pencil, and that was all. I put the bag back where I had found it. I went over to the desk for a piece of hotel stationery and an envelope.

I used the hotel pen to write: "Dear Betty: So sorry I couldn't stay dead. Will explain tomorrow. Larry."

I sealed the note in the envelope, wrote *Miss Betty Mayfield* on it, and dropped it where it might be if it had been pushed under the door.

I opened the door, went out, shut the door, and went back to the fire stairs, then said out loud: "The hell with it," and rang for the elevator. It didn't come. I rang again and kept on ringing. Finally it came up and a sleepy-eyed young Mexican opened the doors and yawned at me, then grinned apologetically. I grinned back and said nothing.

There was nobody at the desk, which faced the elevators. The Mexican parked himself in a chair and went back to sleep before I had taken six steps. Everybody was sleepy but Marlowe. He works around the clock, and doesn't even collect.

I drove back to the Rancho Descansado, saw nobody awake there, looked longingly at the bed, but packed my suitcase — with Betty's gun in the bottom of it — put twelve bucks in an envelope and on the way out put that through the slot in the office door, with my room key.

I drove to San Diego, turned the rent car in, and ate breakfast at a joint across from the station. At seven-fifteen I caught

879

the two-car diesel job that makes the run to L.A. nonstop and pulls in at exactly 10 A.M.

I rode home in a taxi and shaved and showered and ate a second breakfast and glanced through the morning paper. It was near on eleven o'clock when I called the office of Mr. Clyde Umney, the lawyer.

He answered himself. Maybe Miss Vermilyea hadn't got up yet.

"This is Marlowe. I'm home. Can I drop around?"

"Did you find her?"

"Yeah. Did you call Washington?"

"Where is she?"

"I'd like to tell you in person. Did you call Washington?"

"I'd like your information first. I have a very busy day ahead." His voice was brittle and lacked charm.

"I'll be there in half an hour." I hung up fast and called the place where my Olds was.

11

THERE ARE ALMOST too many offices like Clyde Umney's office. It was paneled in squares of combed plywood set at right angles one to the other to make a checkerboard effect. The lighting was indirect, the carpeting wall to wall, the furniture blond, the chairs comfortable, and the fees probably exorbitant. The metal window frames opened outward and there was a small but neat parking lot behind the building, and every slot in it had a name painted on a white board. For some reason Clyde Umney's stall was vacant, so I used it. Maybe he had a chauffeur drive him to his office. The building was four stories high, very new, and occupied entirely by doctors and lawyers.

When I entered, Miss Vermilyea was just fixing herself for a hard day's work by touching up her platinum blond coiffure. I thought she looked a little the worse for wear. She put away her hand mirror and fed herself a cigarette.

"Well, well. Mr. Hard Guy in person. To what may we attribute this honor?"

"Umney's expecting me."

"*Mister* Umney to you, buster."

"Boydie-boy to you, sister."

She got raging in an instant. "Don't call me 'sister,' you cheap gumshoe!"

"Then don't call me buster, you very expensive secretary. What are you doing tonight? And don't tell me you're going out with four sailors again."

The skin around her eyes turned whiter. Her hand crisped into a claw around a paperweight. She just didn't heave it at me. "You son of a bitch!" she said somewhat pointedly. Then she flipped a switch on her talk box and said to the voice: "Mr. Marlowe is here, Mr. Umney."

Then she leaned back and gave me the look. "I've got friends who could cut you down so small you'd need a stepladder to put your shoes on."

"Somebody did a lot of hard work on that one," I said. "But hard work's no substitute for talent."

Suddenly we both burst out laughing. The door opened and Umney stuck his face out. He gestured me in with his chin, but his eyes were on the platinum girl.

I went in and after a moment he closed the door and went behind his enormous semicircular desk, with a green leather top and just piles and piles of important documents on it. He was a dapper man, very carefully dressed, too short in the legs, too long in the nose, too sparse in the hair. He had limpid brown eyes which, for a lawyer, looked very trustful.

"You making a pass at my secretary?" he asked me in a voice that was anything but limpid.

"Nope. We were just exchanging pleasantries."

I sat down in the customer's chair and looked at him with something approaching politeness.

"She looked pretty mad to me." He squatted in his executive vice-president type chair and made his face tough.

"She's booked up for three weeks," I said. "I couldn't wait that long."

"Just watch your step, Marlowe. Lay off. She's private property. She wouldn't give you the time of day. Besides being a lovely piece of female humanity, she's as smart as a whip."

"You mean she can type and take dictation as well?"

"As well as what?" He reddened suddenly. "I've taken enough lip from you. Just watch your step. Very carefully. I have enough influence around this town to hang a red light on you. Now let me have your report and make it short and to the point."

"You talk to Washington yet?"

"Never mind what I did or didn't do. I want your report as of right now. The rest is my business. What's the present location of the King girl?" He reached for a nice sharp pencil and a nice clean pad. Then he dropped the pencil and poured himself a glass of water from a black and silver thermos jug.

"Let's trade," I said. "You tell me why you want her found and I'll tell you where she is."

"You're my employee," he snapped. "I don't have to give you any information whatsoever." He was still tough but beginning to shred a little around the edge.

"I'm your employee if I want to be, Mr. Umney. No check has been cashed, no agreement has been made."

"You accepted the assignment. You took an advance."

"Miss Vermilyea gave me a check for two hundred and fifty as an advance, and another check for two hundred for expenses. But I didn't bank them. Here they are." I took the two checks out of my pocketbook and laid them on the desk in front of him. "Better keep them until you make up your mind whether you want an investigator or a yes man, and until I make up my mind whether I was offered a job or was being suckered into a situation I knew nothing about."

He looked down at the checks. He wasn't happy. "You've already had expenses," he said slowly.

"That's all right, Mr. Umney. I had a few dollars saved up – and the expenses are deductible. Also I've had fun."

"You're pretty stubborn, Marlowe."

"I guess, but I have to be in my business. Otherwise I wouldn't be in business. I told you the girl was being blackmailed. Your Washington friends must know why. If she's a crook, fine. But I have to get told. And I have an offer you can't match."

"For more money you are willing to switch sides?" he asked angrily. "That would be unethical."

I laughed. "So I've got ethics now. Maybe we're getting somewhere."

He took a cigarette out of a box and lit it with a pot-bellied lighter that matched the thermos and the pen set.

"I still don't like your attitude," he growled. "Yesterday I didn't know any more than you did. I took it for granted that a reputable Washington law firm would not ask me to do anything against legal ethics. Since the girl could have been arrested without difficulty, I assumed it was some sort of domestic mix-up, a runaway wife or daughter, or an important but reluctant witness who was already outside the jurisdiction where she could be subpoenaed. That was just guessing. This morning things are a little different."

He got up and walked to the big window and turned the slats of the blinds enough to keep the sun off his desk. He stood there smoking, looking out, then came back to the desk and sat down again.

"This morning," he went on slowly and with a judicious frown, "I talked to my Washington associates and I am informed that the girl was confidential secretary to a rich and important man – I'm not told his name – and that she absconded with certain important and dangerous papers from his private files. Papers that might be damaging to him if

RAYMOND CHANDLER

made public. I'm not told in what way. Perhaps he has been fudging his tax returns. You never know these days."

"She took this stuff to blackmail him?"

Umney nodded. "That is the natural assumption. They had no value to her otherwise. The client, Mr. A we will call him, didn't realize that the girl had left until she was already in another state. He then checked his files and found that some of his material was gone. He was reluctant to go to the police. He expects the girl to go far enough away to feel safe and from that point to start negotiations with him for the return of the material at a heavy price. He wants to peg her down somewhere without her knowing it, walk in and catch her off balance and especially before she contacts some sharp lawyer, of whom I regret to say there are far too many, and with the sharp lawyer works out a scheme that would make her safe from prosecution. Now you tell me someone is blackmailing her. On what grounds?"

"If your story stood up, it could be because he is in a position to spoil her play," I said. "Maybe he knows something that could hang a pinch on her without opening up the other box of candy."

"You say if the story stood up," he snapped. "What do you mean by that?"

"It's as full of holes as a sink strainer. You're being fed a line, Mr. Umney. Where would a man keep material like the important papers you mention – if he had to keep them at all? Certainly not where a secretary could get them. And unless he missed the stuff before she left, how did he get her followed to the train? Next, although she took a ticket to California, she could have got off anywhere. Therefore she would have to be watched on the train, and if that was done, why did someone need me to pick her up here? Next, this, as you tell it, would be a job for a large agency with nation-wide connections. It would be idiotic to take a chance on one man. I lost her yesterday. I could lose her again. It takes a bare minimum of six operatives to do a standard tail job in any sizable place, and that's just what I mean – a bare minimum. In a really big city you'd need a dozen. An operative has to eat and sleep and change his shirt. If he's tailing by car he has to be able to drop a man while he finds a place to park. Department stores and hotels may have half a dozen entrances. But all this girl does is hang around Union Station here for three hours in full view of everybody. And all your friends in Washington do is mail you a picture, call you on the phone, and then go back to watching television."

"Very clear," he said. "Anything else?" His face was dead-pan now.

"A little. Why – if she didn't expect to be followed – would she change her name? Why if she did expect to be followed would she make it so easy? I told you two other guys were working the same side of the street. One is a Kansas City private detective named Goble. He was in Esmeralda yesterday. He knew just where to go. Who told him? I had to follow her and bribe a taxi driver to use his R/T outfit to find out where her cab was going so that I wouldn't lose her. So why was I hired?"

"We'll come to that," Umney said curtly. "Who was the other party you say was working the same side of the street?"

"A playboy named Mitchell. He lives down there. He met the girl on the train. He made a reservation for her in Esmeralda. They're just like that" – I held up two touching fingers – "except that she hates his guts. He's got something on her and she is afraid of him. What he has on her is a knowledge of who she is, where she came from, what happened to her there, and why she is trying to hide under another name. I overheard enough to know that, but not enough to give me exact information."

Umney said acidly: "Of course the girl was covered on the train. Do you think you are dealing with idiots? You were nothing more than a decoy – to determine whether she had any associates. On your reputation – such as it is – I relied on you to grandstand just enough to let her get wise to you. I guess you know what an open shadow is."

"Sure. One that deliberately lets the subject spot him, then shake him, so that another shadow can pick him up when he thinks he is safe."

"You were it." He grinned at me contemptuously. "But you still haven't told me where she is."

I didn't want to tell him, but I knew I'd have to. I had up to a point accepted the assignment, and giving him back his money was only a move to force some information out of him.

I reached across the desk and picked up the $250 check. "I'll take this as payment in full, expenses included. She is registered as Miss Betty Mayfield at the Casa del Poniente in Esmeralda. She is loaded with money. But of course your expert organization must know all this already."

I stood up. "Thanks for the ride, Mr. Umney."

I went out and shut his door. Miss Vermilyea looked up from a magazine. I heard a faint muffled click from somewhere in her desk.

"I'm sorry I was rude to you," I said. "I didn't get enough sleep last night."

"Forget it. It was a stand-off. With a little practice I might get to like you. You're kind of cute in a low down sort of way."

"Thanks," I said and moved to the door. I wouldn't say she looked exactly wistful, but neither did she look as hard to get as a controlling interest in General Motors.

I turned back and closed the door.

"I guess it's not raining tonight, is it? There was something we might have discussed over a drink, if it had been a rainy night. And if you had not been too busy."

She gave me a cool amused look. "Where?"

"That would be up to you."

"Should I drop by your place?"

886

"It would be damn nice of you. That Fleetwood might help my credit standing."

"I wasn't exactly thinking of that."

"Neither was I."

"About six-thirty perhaps. And I'll take good care of my nylons."

"I was hoping you would."

Our glances locked. I went out quickly.

12

AT HALF PAST six the Fleetwood purred to the front door and I had it open when she came up the steps. She was hatless. She wore a flesh-colored coat with the collar turned up against her platinum hair. She stood in the middle of the living room and looked around casually. Then she slipped the coat off with a lithe movement and threw it on the davenport and sat down.

"I didn't really think you'd come," I said.

"No. You're the shy type. You knew darned well I'd come. Scotch and soda, if you have it."

"I have it."

I brought the drinks and sat down beside her, but not close enough for it to mean anything. We touched glasses and drank.

"Would you care to go to Romanoff's for dinner?"

"And then what?"

"Where do you live?"

"West Los Angeles. A house on a quiet old street. It happens to belong to me. I asked you, and then what, remember?"

"That would be up to you, naturally."

"I thought you were a tough guy. You mean I don't have to pay for my dinner?"

"I ought to slap your face for that crack."

She laughed suddenly and stared at me over the edge of her glass.

"Consider it slapped. We had each other a bit wrong. Romanoff's could wait a while, couldn't it?"

"We could try West Los Angeles first."

"Why not here?"

"I guess this will make you walk out on me. I had a dream here once, a year and a half ago. There's still a shred of it left. I'd like it to stay in charge."

She stood up quickly and grabbed her coat. I managed to help her on with it.

"I'm sorry," I said. "I should have told you before."

She swung around with her face close to mine, but I didn't touch her.

"Sorry that you had a dream and kept it alive? I've had dreams too, but mine died. I didn't have the courage to keep them alive."

"It's not quite like that. There was a woman. She was rich. She thought she wanted to marry me. It wouldn't have worked. I'll probably never see her again. But I remember."

"Let's go," she said quietly. "And let's leave the memory in charge. I only wish I had one worth remembering."

On the way down to the Cadillac I didn't touch her either. She drove beautifully. When a woman is a really good driver she is just about perfect.

13

THE HOUSE WAS on a curving quiet street between San Vincente and Sunset Boulevard. It was set far back and had a long driveway and the entrance to the house was at the back with a small patio in front of it. She unlocked the door and switched on lights all over the house and then disappeared without a word. The living room had nicely mixed furniture and a feeling of comfort. I stood waiting until she came back with two tall glasses. She had taken her coat off.

"You've been married, of course," I said.

"It didn't take. I got this house and some money out of it, but I wasn't gunning for anything. He was a nice guy, but we were wrong for each other. He's dead now – plane crash – he was a jet pilot. Happens all the time. I know a place between here and San Diego that is full of girls who were married to jet pilots when they were alive."

I took a single sip of my drink and put it down.

I lifted her glass out of her hand and put it down too.

"Remember yesterday morning when you told me to stop looking at your legs?"

"I seem to remember."

"Try and stop me now."

I took hold of her and she came into my arms without a word. I picked her up and carried her and somehow found the bedroom. I put her down on the bed. I peeled her skirt up until I could see the white thighs above her long beautiful nylon-clad legs. Suddenly she reached up and pulled my head down against her breast.

"Beast! Could we have a little less light?"

I went to the door and switched the light off in the room. There was still a glow from the hall. When I turned she was standing by the bed as naked as Aphrodite, fresh from the Aegean. She stood there proudly and without either shame or enticement.

"Damn it," I said, "when I was young you could undress a girl slowly. Nowadays she's in the bed while you're struggling with your collar button."

"Well, struggle with your goddam collar button."

She pulled the bedcovers back and lay on the bed shamelessly nude. She was just a beautiful naked woman completely unashamed of being what she was.

"Satisfied with my legs?" she asked.

I didn't answer.

889

"Yesterday morning," she said, half dreamily, "I said there was something about you I liked – you didn't paw – and something I didn't like. Know what it was?"

"No."

"That you didn't make me do this then."

"Your manner hardly encouraged it."

"You're supposed to be a detective. Please put out all the lights now."

★

Then very soon in the dark she was saying, "Darling, darling, darling" in that very special tone of voice a woman uses only in those special moments. Then a slow gentle relaxing, a peace, a quietness.

"Still satisfied with my legs?" she asked dreamily.

"No man ever would be. They would haunt him, no matter how many times he made love to you."

"You bastard. You complete bastard. Come closer."

She put her head on my shoulder and we were very close now.

"I don't love you," she said.

"Why would you? But let's not be cynical about it. There are sublime moments – even if they are only moments."

I felt her tight and warm against me. Her body surged with vitality. Her beautiful arms held me tight.

★

And again in the darkness that muted cry, and then again the slow quiet peace.

"I hate you," she said with her mouth against mine. "Not for this, but because perfection never comes twice and with us it came too soon. And I'll never see you again and I don't want to. It would have to be forever or not at all."

890

"And you acted like a hardboiled pick-up who had seen too much of the wrong side of life."

"So did you. And we were both wrong. And it's useless. Kiss me harder."

Suddenly she was gone from the bed almost without sound or movement.

After a little while the light went on in the hallway and she stood in the door in a long wrapper.

"Goodbye," she said calmly. "I'm calling a taxi for you. Wait out in front for it. You won't see me again."

"What about Umney?"

"A poor frightened jerk. He needs someone to bolster his ego, to give him a feeling of power and conquest. I give it to him. A woman's body is not so sacred that it can't be used – especially when she has already failed at love."

She disappeared. I got up and put my clothes on and listened before I went out. I heard nothing. I called out, but there was no answer. When I reached the sidewalk in front of the house the taxi was just pulling up.

I looked back. The house seemed completely dark.

No one lived there. It was all a dream. Except that someone had called the taxi. I got into it and was driven home.

14

I LEFT LOS Angeles and hit the superhighway that now bypassed Oceanside. I had time to think.

From Los Angeles to Oceanside were eighteen miles of divided six-lane superhighway dotted at intervals with the carcasses of wrecked, stripped, and abandoned cars tossed against the high bank to rust until they were hauled away. So I started thinking about why I was going back to Esmeralda. The case was all backwards and it wasn't my case anyway. Usually a P. I. gets a client who, for too little money, wants too much information. You get it or you don't, depending on circumstances. The same with your fee. But once in a while you get the information and too much else, including a story about a body on a balcony which wasn't there when you went to look. Common sense says go home and forget it, no money coming in. Common sense always speaks too late. Common sense is the guy who tells you you ought to have had your brakes relined last week before you smashed a front end this week. Common sense is the Monday morning quarterback who could have won the ball game if he had been on the team. But he never is. He's high up in the stands with a flask on his hip. Common sense is the little man in a gray suit who never makes a mistake in addition. But it's always somebody else's money he's adding up.

At the turn-off I dipped down into the canyon and ended up at the Rancho Descansado. Jack and Lucille were in their usual positions. I dropped my suitcase and leaned on the desk.

"Did I leave the right change?"

"Yes, thanks," Jack said. "And now you want the room back, I suppose."

"If possible."

"Why didn't you tell us you were a detective?"

"Now, what a question." I grinned at him. "Does a detective ever tell anyone he's a detective? You watch TV, don't you?"

"When I get a chance. Not too often here."

"You can always tell a detective on TV. He never takes his hat off. What do you know about Larry Mitchell?"

"Nothing," Jack said stiffly. "He's a friend of Brandon's. Mr. Brandon owns this place."

Lucille said brightly: "Did you find Joe Harms all right?"

"Yes, thanks."

"And did you —?"

"Uh-huh."

"Button the lip, kid," Jack said tersely. He winked at me and pushed the key across the counter. "Lucille has a dull life,

Mr. Marlowe. She's stuck here with me and a PBX. And an itty-bitty diamond ring – so small I was ashamed to give it to her. But what can a man do? If he loves a girl, he'd like it to show on her finger."

Lucille held her left hand up and moved it around to get a flash from the little stone. "I hate it," she said. "I hate it like I hate the sunshine and the summer and the bright stars and the full moon. That's how I hate it."

I picked up the key and my suitcase and left them. A little more of that and I'd be falling in love with myself. I might even give myself a small unpretentious diamond ring.

15

THE HOUSE PHONE at the Casa del Poniente got no reply from Room 1224. I walked over to the desk. A stiff-looking clerk was sorting letters. They are always sorting letters.

"Miss Mayfield is registered here, isn't she?" I asked.

He put a letter in a box before he answered me. "Yes, sir. What name shall I say?"

"I know her room number. She doesn't answer. Have you seen her today?"

He gave me a little more of his attention, but I didn't really send him. "I don't think so." He glanced over his shoulder. "Her key is out. Would you care to leave a message?"

"I'm a little worried. She wasn't well last night. She could be up there sick, not able to answer the phone. I'm a friend of hers. Marlowe's the name."

He looked me over. His eyes were wise eyes. He went behind a screen in the direction of the cashier's office and spoke to somebody. He came back in a short time. He was smiling.

"I don't think Miss Mayfield is ill, Mr. Marlowe. She ordered quite a substantial breakfast in her room. And lunch. She has had several telephone calls."

893

"Thanks a lot," I said. "I'll leave a message. Just my name and that I'll call back later."

"She might be out in the grounds or down on the beach," he said. "We have a warm beach, well sheltered by a break-water." He glanced at the clock behind him. "If she is, she won't be there much longer. It's getting cool by now."

"Thanks. I'll be back."

The main part of the lobby was up three steps and through an arch. There were people in it just sitting, the dedicated hotel lounge sitters, usually elderly, usually rich, usually doing nothing but watching with hungry eyes. They spend their lives that way. Two old ladies with severe faces and purplish permanents were struggling with an enormous jigsaw puzzle set out on a specially built king-size card table. Farther along there was a canasta game going – two women, two men. One of the women had enough ice on her to cool the Mojave Desert and enough make-up to paint a steam yacht. Both women had cigarettes in long holders. The men with them looked gray and tired, probably from signing checks. Farther along, still sitting where they could look out through the glass, a young couple were holding hands. The girl had a diamond and emerald sparkler and a wedding ring which she kept touching with her fingertips. She looked a little dazed.

I went out through the bar and poked around in the gardens. I went along the path that threaded the cliff top and had no trouble picking out the spot I had looked down on the night before from Betty Mayfield's balcony. I could pick it out because of the sharp angle.

The bathing beach and small curved breakwater were a hundred yards along. Steps led down to it from the cliff. People were lying around on the sand. Some in swim suits or trunks, some just sitting there on rugs. Kids ran around screaming. Betty Mayfield was not on the beach.

I went back into the hotel and sat in the lounge.

I sat and smoked. I went to the newsstand and bought an evening paper and looked through it and threw it away. I strolled by the desk. My note was still in Box 1224. I went to the house phones and called Mr. Mitchell. No answer. I'm sorry. Mr. Mitchell does not answer his telephone.

A woman's voice spoke behind me. "The clerk said you wanted to see me. Mr. Marlowe —" she said. "Are you Mr. Marlowe?"

She looked as fresh as a morning rose. She was wearing dark green slacks and saddle shoes and a green windbreaker over a white shirt with a loose Paisley scarf around that. A bandeau on her hair made a nice wind-blown effect.

The bell captain was hanging out his ear six feet away. I said: "Miss Mayfield?"

"I'm Miss Mayfield."

"I have the car outside. Do you have time to look at the property?"

She looked at her wrist watch. "Ye-es, I guess so," she said. "I ought to change pretty soon, but – oh, all right."

"This way, Miss Mayfield."

She fell in beside me. We walked across the lobby. I was getting to feel quite at home there. Betty Mayfield glanced viciously at the two jigsaw puzzlers.

"I hate hotels," she said. "Come back here in fifteen years and you would find the same people sitting in the same chairs."

"Yes, Miss Mayfield. Do you know anybody named Clyde Umney?"

She shook her head. "Should I?"

"Helen Vermilyea? Ross Goble?"

She shook her head again.

"Want a drink?"

"Not now, thanks."

We came out of the bar and went along the walk and I held the door of the Olds for her. I backed out of the slot and pointed it straight up Grand Street towards the hills. She slipped dark glasses with spangled rims on her nose. "I found the traveler's checks," she said. "You're a queer sort of detective."

I reached in my pocket and held out her bottle of sleeping pills. "I was a little scared last night," I said. "I counted these but I didn't know how many had been there to start with. You said you took two. I couldn't be sure you wouldn't rouse up enough to gulp a handful."

She took the bottle and stuffed it into her windbreaker. "I had quite a few drinks. Alcohol and barbiturates make a bad combination. I sort of passed out. It was nothing else."

"I wasn't sure. It takes a minimum of thirty-five grains of that stuff to kill. Even then it takes several hours. I was in a tough spot. Your pulse and breathing seemed all right but maybe they wouldn't be later on. If I called a doctor, I might have to do a lot of talking. If you had taken an overdose, the homicide boys would be told, even if you snapped out of it. They investigate all suicide attempts. But if I guessed wrong, you wouldn't be riding with me today. And where would I be then?"

"It's a thought," she said. "I can't say I'm going to worry about it terribly. Who are these people you mentioned?"

"Clyde Umney's the lawyer who hired me to follow you – on instructions from a firm of attorneys in Washington, D.C. Helen Vermilyea is his secretary. Ross Goble is a Kansas City private eye who says he is trying to find Mitchell." I described him to her.

Her face turned stony. "Mitchell? Why should he be interested in Larry?"

I stopped at the corner of Fourth and Grand for an old coot in a motorized wheel chair to make a left turn at four miles an hour. Esmeralda is full of the damn things.

"Why should he be looking for Larry Mitchell?" she asked bitterly. "Can't anybody leave anybody else alone?"

"Don't tell me anything," I said. "Just keep on asking me questions to which I don't know the answers. It's good for my inferiority complex. I told you I had no more job. So why am I here? That's easy. I'm groping for that five grand in traveler's checks again."

"Turn left at the next corner," she said, "and we can go up into the hills. There's a wonderful view from up there. And a lot of very fancy homes."

"The hell with them," I said.

"It's also very quiet up there." She picked a cigarette out of the pack clipped to the dash and lit it.

"That's two in two days," I said. "You're hitting them hard. I counted your cigarettes last night too. And your matches. I went through your bag. I'm kind of snoopy when I get roped in on a phony like that one. Especially when the client passes out and leaves me holding the baby."

She turned her head to stare at me. "It must have been the dope and the liquor," she said. "I must have been a little off base."

"Over at the Rancho Descansado you were in great shape. You were hard as nails. We were going to take off for Rio and live in luxury. Apparently also in sin. All I had to do was get rid of the body. What a letdown! No body."

She was still staring at me, but I had to watch my driving. I made a boulevard stop and a left turn. I went along another dead-end street with old streetcar tracks still in the paving.

"Turn left up the hill at that sign. That's the high school down there."

"Who fired the gun and what at?"

She pressed her temples with the heels of her hands. "I guess I must have. *I* must have been crazy. Where is it?"

"The gun? It's safe. Just in case your dream came true, I might have to produce it."

We were climbing now. I set the pointer to hold the Olds in third. She watched that with interest. She looked around her at the pale leather seats and the gadgets.

"How can you afford an expensive car like this? You don't make a lot of money, do you?"

"They're all expensive nowadays, even the cheap ones. Fellow might as well have one that can travel. I read somewhere that a dick should always have a plain dark inconspicuous car that nobody would notice. The guy had never been to L.A. In L.A. to be conspicuous you would have to drive a flesh-pink Mercedes-Benz with a sun porch on the roof and three pretty girls sunbathing."

She giggled.

"Also," I labored the subject, "it's good advertising. Maybe I dreamed I was going to Rio. I could sell it there for more than it set me back new. On a freighter it wouldn't cost too much to ferry."

She sighed. "Oh, stop teasing me about that. I don't feel funny today."

"Seen your boy friend around?"

She sat very still. "Larry?"

"You got others?"

"Well – you might have meant Clark Brandon, although I hardly know him. Larry was pretty drunk last night. No – I haven't seen him. Perhaps he's sleeping it off."

"Doesn't answer his phone."

The road forked. One white line curved to the left. I kept straight on, for no particular reason. We passed some old Spanish houses built high on the slope and some very modern houses built downhill on the other side. The road passed these and made a wide turn to the right. The paving here looked new. The road ran out to a point of land and a turning circle. There were two big houses facing each other across the turning circle. They were loaded with glass brick and their seaward windows were green glass. The view was magnificent. I looked at it for all of three seconds. I stopped against the end curb and cut the motor and sat. We were about a thousand feet up and the whole town was spread out in front of us like a 45 degree air photo.

"He might be sick," I said. "He might have gone out. He might even be dead."

"I told you —" She began to shake. I took the stub of the cigarette away from her and put it in the ashtray. I ran the car windows up and put an arm around her shoulders and pulled her head down on my shoulder. She was limp, unresisting; but she still shook.

"You're a comfortable man," she said. "But don't rush me."

"There's a pint in the glove compartment. Want a snort?"

"Yes."

I got it out and managed to pull the metal strip loose with one hand and my teeth. I held the bottle between my knees and got the cap off. I held it to her lips. She sucked some in and shuddered. I recapped the pint and put it away.

"I hate drinking from the bottle," she said.

"Yeah. Unrefined. I'm not making love to you, Betty. I'm worried. Anything you want done?"

She was silent for a moment. Then her voice was steady, saying: "Such as what? You can have those checks back. They were yours. I gave them to you."

"Nobody gives anybody five grand like that. It makes no sense. That's why I came back down from L.A. I drove up there early this morning. Nobody goes all gooey over a character like me and talks about having half a million dollars and offers me a trip to Rio and a nice home complete with all the luxuries. Nobody drunk or sober does that because she dreamed a dead man was lying out on her balcony and would I please hurry around and throw him off into the ocean. Just what did you expect me to do when I got there — hold your hand while you dreamed?"

She pulled away and leaned in the far corner of the car. "All right, I'm a liar. I've always been a liar."

I glanced at the rear view mirror. Some kind of small dark car had turned into the road behind and stopped. I couldn't see who or what was in it. Then it swung hard right against the curbing and backed and made off the way it had come. Some fellow took the wrong road and saw it was a dead end.

"While I was on the way up those damn fire stairs," I went on, "you swallowed your pills and then faked being awfully terribly sleepy and then after a while you actually did go to sleep – I think. Okay. I went out on the balcony. No stiff. No blood. If there had been, I might have managed to get him over the top of the wall. Hard work, but not impossible, if you know how to lift. But six trained elephants couldn't have thrown him far enough to land in the ocean. It's thirty-five feet to the fence and you'd have to throw him so far out that he would clear the fence. I figure an object as heavy as a man's body would have to be thrown a good fifty feet outward to clear the fence."

"I told you I was a liar."

"But you didn't tell me why. Let's be serious. Suppose a man had been dead on your balcony. What would you expect me to do about it? Carry him down the fire stairs and get him into the car I had and drive off into the woods somewhere and bury him? You do have to take people into your confidence once in a while when bodies are lying around."

"You took my money," she said tonelessly. "You played up to me."

"That way I might find out who was crazy."

"You found out. You should be satisfied."

"I found out nothing – not even who you are."

She got angry. "I told you I was out of my mind," she said in a rushing voice. "Worry, fear, liquor, pills – why can't you leave me alone? I told you I'd give you back that money. What more do you want?"

"What do I do for it?"

"Just take it." She was snapping at me now. "That's all. Take it and go away. Far, far away."

"I think you need a good lawyer."

"That's a contradiction in terms," she sneered. "If he was good, he wouldn't be a lawyer."

"Yeah. So you've had some painful experience along those lines. I'll find out in time, either from you or some other way. But I'm still being serious. You're in trouble. Apart from what happened to Mitchell, if anything, you're in enough trouble to justify hiring yourself a lawyer. You changed your name. So you had reasons. Mitchell was putting the bite on you. So *he* had reasons. A firm of Washington attorneys is looking for you. So *they* have reasons. And their client has reasons to have them looking for you."

I stopped and looked at her as well as I could see her in the freshly darkening evening. Down below, the ocean was getting a lapis lazuli blue that somehow failed to remind me of Miss Vermilyea's eyes. A flock of gulls went south in a fairly compact mass but it wasn't the kind of tight formation North Island is used to. The evening plane from L.A. came down the coast with its port and starboard lights showing, and then the winking light below the fuselage went on and it swung out to sea for a long lazy turn into Lindbergh Field.

"So you're just a shill for a crooked lawyer," she said nastily, and grabbed for another of my cigarettes.

"I don't think he's very crooked. He just tries too hard. But that's not the point. You can lose a few bucks to him without screaming. The point is something called privilege. A licensed investigator doesn't have it. A lawyer does, provided his concern is with the interests of a client who has retained him. If the lawyer hires an investigator to work in those interests, then the investigator has privilege. That's the only way he can get it."

"You know what you can do with your privilege," she said. "Especially as it was a lawyer that hired you to spy on me."

I took the cigarette away from her and puffed on it a couple of times and handed it back.

"It's all right, Betty. I'm no use to you. Forget I tried to be."

"Nice words, but only because you think I'll pay you more to be of use to me. You're just another of them. I don't want your damn cigarette either." She threw it out of the window. "Take me back to the hotel."

I got out of the car and stamped on the cigarette. "You don't do that in the California hills," I told her. "Not even out of season." I got back into the car and turned the key and pushed the starter button. I backed away and made the turn and drove back up the curve to where the road divided. On the upper level where the solid white line curved away a small car was parked. The car was lightless. It could have been empty.

I swung the Olds hard the opposite way from the way I had come, and flicked my headlights on with the high beam. They swept the cars as I turned. A hat went down over a face, but not quick enough to hide the glasses, the fat broad face, the outjutting ears of Mr. Ross Goble of Kansas City.

The lights went on past and I drove down a long hill with lazy curves. I didn't know where it went except that all roads around there led to the ocean sooner or later. At the bottom there was a T-intersection. I swung to the right and after a few blocks of narrow street I hit the boulevard and made another right turn. I was now driving back towards the main part of Esmeralda.

She didn't speak again until I got to the hotel. She jumped out quickly when I stopped.

"If you'll wait here, I'll get the money."

"We were tailed," I said.

"What —?" She stopped dead, with her head half turned.

"Small car. You didn't notice him unless you saw my lights brush him as I made the turn at the top of the hill."

"Who was it?" Her voice was tense.

"How would I know? He must have picked us up here, therefore he'll come back here. Could he be a cop?"

She looked back at me, motionless, frozen. She took a slow step, and then she rushed at me as if she was going to claw my face. She grabbed me by the arms and tried to shake me. Her breath came whistling.

"Get me out of here. Get me out of here, for the love of Christ. Anywhere. Hide me. Get me a little peace. Somewhere where I can't be followed, hounded, threatened. He swore he would do it to me. He'd follow me to the ends of the earth, to the remotest island of the Pacific —"

"To the crest of the highest mountain, to the heart of the loneliest desert," I said. "Somebody's been reading a rather old-fashioned book."

She dropped her arms and let them hang limp at her sides.

"You've got as much sympathy as a loan shark."

"I'll take you nowhere," I said. "Whatever it is that's eating you, you're going to stay put and take it."

I turned and got into the car. When I looked back, she was already halfway to the bar entrance, walking with quick strides.

16

IF I HAD any sense, I would pick up my suitcase and go back home and forget all about her. By the time she made up her mind which part she was playing in which act of which play, it would probably be too late for me to do anything about it except maybe get pinched for loitering in the post office.

I waited and smoked a cigarette. Goble and his dirty little jalopy ought to show up and slip into a parking slot almost any moment. He couldn't have picked us up anywhere else, and since he knew that much he couldn't have followed us for any reason except to find out where we went.

He didn't show. I finished the cigarette, dropped it over-board, and backed out. As I turned out of the driveway towards the town, I saw his car on the other side of the street, parked left-hand to the curb. I kept going, turned right at the boulevard and took it easy so he wouldn't blow a gasket trying to keep up. There was a restaurant about a mile along called The Epicure. It had a low roof, and a red brick wall to shield it from the street and it had a bar. The entrance was at the side. I parked and went in. It wasn't doing any business yet. The barkeep was chatting with the captain and the captain didn't even wear a dinner jacket. He had one of those high desks where they keep the reservation book. The book was open and had a list of names in it for later in the evening. But it was early now. I could have a table.

The dining room was dim, candlelit, divided by a low wall into two halves. It would have looked crowded with thirty people in it. The captain shoved me in a corner and lit my candle for me. I said I would have a double Gibson. A waiter came up and started to remove the place setting on the far side of the table. I told him to leave it, a friend might join me. I studied the menu, which was almost as large as the dining room. I could have used a flashlight to read it, if I had been curious. This was about the dimmest joint I was ever in. You could be sitting at the next table from your mother and not recognize her.

The Gibson arrived. I could make out the shape of the glass and there seemed to be something in it. I tasted it and it wasn't too bad. At that moment Goble slid into the chair across from me. In so far as I could see him at all, he looked about the same as he had looked the day before. I went on peering at the menu. They ought to have printed it in braille.

Goble reached across for my glass of ice water and drank. "How you making out with the girl?" he asked casually.

"Not getting anywhere. Why?"

"Whatcha go up on the hill for?"

"I thought maybe we could neck. She wasn't in the mood. What's your interest? I thought you were looking for some guy named Mitchell."

"Very funny indeed. Some guy named Mitchell. Never heard of him, I believe you said."

"I've heard of him since. I've seen him. He was drunk. Very drunk. He damn near got himself thrown out of a place."

"Very funny," Goble said, sneering. "And how did you know his name?"

"On account of somebody called him by it. That would be *too* funny, wouldn't it?"

He sneered. "I told you to stay out of my way. I know who you are now. I looked you up."

I lit a cigarette and blew smoke in his face. "Go fry a stale egg."

"Tough, huh," he sneered. "I've pulled the arms and legs off bigger guys than you."

"Name two of them."

He leaned across the table, but the waiter came up.

"I'll have bourbon and plain water," Goble told him. "Bonded stuff. None of that bar whiskey for me. And don't try to fool me. I'll know. And bottled water. The city water here is terrible."

The waiter just looked at him.

"I'll have another of these," I said, pushing my glass.

"What's good tonight?" Goble wanted to know. "I never bother with these billboards." He flicked a disdainful finger at the menu.

"The *plat du jour* is meat loaf," the waiter said nastily.

"Hash with a starched collar," Goble said. "Make it meat loaf."

The waiter looked at me. I said the meat loaf was all right with me. The waiter went away. Goble leaned across the table again, after first taking a quick look behind him and on both sides.

"You're out of luck, friend," he said cheerfully. "You didn't get away with it."

"Too bad," I said. "Get away with what?"

"You're bad out of luck, friend. Very bad. The tide was wrong or something. Abalone fisher — one of those guys with frog feet and rubber masks — stuck under a rock."

"The abalone fisher stuck under a rock?" A cold prickly feeling crawled down my back. When the waiter came with the drinks, I had to fight myself not to grab for mine.

"Very funny, friend."

"Say that again and I'll smash your goddam glasses or you," I snarled.

He picked up his drink and sipped it, tasted it, thought about it, nodded his head.

"I came out here to make money," he mused. "I didn't nowise come out to make trouble. Man can't make money making trouble. Man can make money keeping his nose clean. Get me?"

"Probably a new experience for you," I said. "Both ways. What was that about an abalone fisher?" I kept my voice controlled, but it was an effort.

He leaned back. My eyes were getting used to the dimness now. I could see that his fat face was amused.

"Just kidding," he said. "I don't know any abalone fishers. Only last night I learned how to pronounce the word. Still don't know what the stuff is. But things are kind of funny at that. I can't find Mitchell."

"He lives at the hotel." I took some more of my drink, not too much. This was no time to dive into it.

"I know he lives at the hotel, friend. What I don't know is where he is at right now. He ain't in his room. The hotel people ain't seen him around: I thought maybe you and the girl had some ideas about it."

"The girl is screwy," I said. "Leave her out of it. And in Esmeralda they don't say 'ain't seen.' That Kansas City dialect is an offense against public morals here."

"Shove it, Mac. When I want to get told how to talk English I won't go to no beat-up California peeper." He turned his head and yelled: "Waiter!"

Several faces looked at him with distaste. The waiter showed up after a while and stood there with the same expression as the customers.

"Hit me again," Goble said, and snapped a finger at his glass.

"It is not necessary to yell at me," the waiter said. He took the glass away.

"When I want service," Goble yelped at his back, "service is what I want."

"I hope you like the taste of wood alcohol," I told Goble.

"Me and you could get along," Goble said indifferently, "if you had any brains."

"And if you had any manners and were six inches taller and had a different face and another name and didn't act as if you thought you could lick your weight in frog spawn."

"Cut the doodads and get back to Mitchell," he said briskly. "And to the dish you was trying to fumble up the hill."

"Mitchell is a man she met on a train. He had the same effect on her that you have on me. He created in her a burning desire to travel in the opposite direction."

It was a waste of time. The guy was as invulnerable as my great-great-grandfather.

"So," he sneered, "Mitchell to her is just a guy she met on a train and didn't like when she got to know him. So she ditched him for you? Convenient you happened to be around."

The waiter came with the food. He set it out with a flourish. Vegetables, salad, hot rolls in a napkin.

"Coffee?"

I said I'd rather have mine later. Goble said yes and wanted to know where his drink was. The waiter said it was on the way – by slow freight, his tone suggested. Goble tasted his meat loaf and looked surprised. "Hell, it's good," he said. "What with so few customers I thought the place was a bust."

"Look at your watch," I said. "Things don't get moving until much later. It's that kind of town. Also, it's out of season."

"Much later is right," he said, munching. "An awful lot later. Two, three in the A.M. sometimes. People go calling on their friends. You back at the Rancho, friend?"

907

I looked at him without saying anything.

"Do I have to draw you a picture, friend? I work long hours when I'm on a job."

I didn't say anything.

He wiped his mouth. "You kind of stiffened up when I said that about the guy stuck under a rock. Or could I be wrong?"

I didn't answer him.

"Okay, clam up," Goble sneered. "I thought maybe we could do a little business together. You got the physique and you take a good punch. But you don't know nothing about nothing. You don't have what it takes in my business. Where I come from you got to have brains to get by. Out here you just got to get sunburned and forget to button your collar."

"Make me a proposition," I said between my teeth.

He was a rapid eater even when he talked too much. He pushed his plate away from him, drank some of his coffee and got a toothpick out of his vest.

"This is a rich town, friend," he said slowly. "I've studied it. I've boned up on it. I've talked to guys about it. They tell me it's one of the few spots left in our fair green country where the dough ain't quite enough. In Esmeralda you got to belong, or you're nothing. If you want to belong and get asked around and get friendly with the right people you got to have class. There's a guy here made five million fish in the rackets back in Kansas City. He bought up property, subdivided, built houses, built some of the best properties in town. But he didn't belong to the Beach Club because he didn't get asked. So he bought it. They know who he is, they touch him big when they got a fund-raising drive, he gets service, he pays his bills, he's a good solid citizen. He throws big parties but the guests come from out of town unless they're moochers, no-goods, the usual trash you always find hopping about where there's money. But the class people of the town? He's just a nigger to them."

It was a long speech and while he made it he glanced at me casually from time to time, glanced around the room, leaned back comfortably in his chair and picked his teeth.

"He must be breaking his heart," I said. "How did they find out where his dough came from?"

Goble leaned across the small table. "A big shot from the Treasury Department comes here for a vacation every spring. Happened to see Mr. Money and know all about him. He spread the word. You think it's not breaking his heart? You don't know these hoods that have made theirs and gone respectable. He's bleeding to death inside, friend. He's found something he can't buy with folding money and it's eating him to a shell."

"How did you find out all this?"

"I'm smart. I get around. I find things out."

"All except one," I said.

"Just what's that?"

"You wouldn't know if I told you."

The waiter came up with Goble's delayed drink and took dishes away. He offered the menu.

"I never eat dessert," Goble said. "Scram."

The waiter looked at the toothpick. He reached over and deftly flicked it out from between Goble's fingers. "There's a Men's Room here, chum," he said. He dropped the toothpick into the ashtray and removed the ashtray.

"See what I mean?" Goble said to me. "Class."

I told the waiter I would have a chocolate sundae and some coffee. "And give this gentleman the check," I added.

"A pleasure," the waiter said. Goble looked disgusted. The waiter drifted. I leaned across the table and spoke softly.

"You're the biggest liar I've met in two days. And I've met a few beauties. I don't think you have any interest in Mitchell. I don't think you ever saw or heard of him until yesterday when you got the idea of using him as a cover story. You were sent here to watch a girl and I know who sent you – not who hired you, but who had it done. I know why she is being watched and I know how to fix it so that she won't be watched. If you've got any high cards, you'd better play them right away quick. Tomorrow could be too late."

He pushed his chair back and stood up. He dropped a folded and crimped bill on the table. He looked me over coolly.

"Big mouth, small brain," he said. "Save it for Thursday when they set the trash cans out. You don't know from nothing, friend. My guess is you never will."

He walked off with his head thrust forward belligerently.

I reached across for the folded and crimped bill Goble had dropped on the table. As I expected it was only a dollar. Any guy who would drive a jalopy that might be able to do forty-five miles an hour downhill would eat in joints where the eighty-five cent dinner was something for a wild Saturday night.

The waiter slid over and dumped the check on me. I paid up and left Goble's dollar in his plate.

"Thanks," the waiter said. "That guy's a real close friend of yours, huh?"

"The operative word is close," I said.

"The guy might be poor," the waiter said tolerantly. "One of the choice things about this town is that the people who work here can't afford to live here."

There were all of twenty people in the place when I left, and the voices were beginning to bounce down off the low ceiling.

17

THE RAMP DOWN to the garage looked just the same as it had looked at four o'clock in the morning, but there was a swishing of water audible as I rounded the curve. The glassed-in cubicle office was empty. Somewhere somebody was washing a car, but it wouldn't be the attendant. I crossed to the door leading into the elevator lobby and held it open. The buzzer sounded behind me in the office. I let the door close and stood outside it waiting and a lean man in a long white coat came around the corner. He wore glasses, had skin the color of cold oatmeal and hollow tired eyes. There was something Mongolian about his face, something south-of-the-border, something Indian, and something darker than that. His black hair was flat on a narrow skull.

"Your car, sir? What name, please?"

"Mr. Mitchell's car in? The two-tone Buick hardtop?"

He didn't answer right away. His eyes went to sleep. He had been asked that question before.

"Mr. Mitchell took his car out early this morning."

"How early?"

He reached for a pencil that was clipped to his pocket over the stitched-on scarlet script with the hotel name. He took the pencil out and looked at it.

"Just before seven o'clock. I went off at seven."

"You work a twelve-hour shift? It's only a little past seven now."

He put the pencil back in his pocket. "I work an eight-hour shift but we rotate."

"Oh. Last night you worked eleven to seven."

"That's right." He was looking past my shoulder at something far away. "I'm due off now."

I got out a pack of cigarettes and offered him one.

He shook his head.

"I'm only allowed to smoke in the office."

"Or in the back of a Packard sedan."

His right hand curled, as if around the haft of a knife.

"How's your supply? Needing anything?"

He stared.

"You should have said 'Supply of what?'" I told him.

He didn't answer.

"And I would have said I wasn't talking about tobacco," I went on cheerfully. "About something cured with honey."

Our eyes met and locked. Finally he said softly: "You a pusher?"

"You snapped out of it real nice, if you were in business at seven A.M. this morning. Looked to me as if you would be out of circulation for hours. You must have a clock in your head – like Eddie Arcaro."

"Eddie Arcaro," he repeated. "Oh yes, the jockey. Has a clock in his head, has he?"

"So they say."

"We might do business," he said remotely. "What's your price?"

The buzzer sounded in the office. I had heard the elevator in the shaft subconsciously. The door opened and the couple I had seen holding hands in the lobby came through. The girl had on an evening dress and the boy wore a tux. They stood side by side, looking like two kids who had been caught kissing. The attendant glanced at them and went off and a car started and came back. A nice new Chrysler convertible. The guy handed the girl in carefully, as if she was already pregnant. The attendant stood holding the door. The guy came around the car and thanked him and got in.

"Is it very far to The Glass Room?" he asked diffidently.

"No, sir." The attendant told them how to get there.

The guy smiled and thanked him and reached in his pocket and gave the attendant a dollar bill.

"You could have your car brought around to the entrance, Mr. Preston. All you have to do is call down."

"Oh thanks, but this is fine," the guy said hurriedly. He started carefully up the ramp. The Chrysler purred out of sight and was gone.

"Honeymooners," I said. "They're sweet. They just don't want to be stared at."

The attendant was standing in front of me again with the same flat look in his eyes.

"But there's nothing sweet about us," I added.

"If you're a cop, let's see the buzzer."

"You think I'm a cop?"

"You're some kind of nosy bastard." Nothing he said changed the tone of his voice at all. It was frozen in B Flat. Johnny One-Note.

"I'm all of that," I agreed. "I'm a private star. I followed somebody down here last night. You were in a Packard right over there" – I pointed – "and I went over and opened the door and sniffed the weed. I could have driven four Cadillacs out of here and you wouldn't have turned over in bed. But that's your business."

"The price today," he said. "I'm not arguing about last night."

"Mitchell left by himself ?"

He nodded.

"No baggage?"

"Nine pieces. I helped him load it. He checked out. Satisfied?"

"You checked with the office?"

"He had his bill. All paid up and receipted."

"Sure. And with that amount of baggage a hop came with him naturally."

"The elevator kid. No hops on until seven-thirty. This was about one A.M."

"Which elevator kid?"

"A Mex kid we call Chico."

"You're not Mex?"

"I'm part Chinese, part Hawaiian, part Filipino, and part nigger. You'd hate to be me."

"Just one more question. How in hell do you get away with it? The muggles, I mean."

He looked around. "I only smoke when I feel extra special low. What the hell's it to you? What the hell's it to anybody?

Maybe I get caught and lose a crummy job. Maybe I get tossed in a cell. Maybe I've been in one all my life, carry it round with me. Satisfied?" He was talking too much. People with unstable nerves are like that. One moment monosyllables, next moment a flood. The low tired monotone of his voice went on.

"I'm not sore at anybody. I live. I eat. Sometimes I sleep. Come around and see me some time. I live in a flea bag in an old frame cottage on Polton's Lane, which is really an alley. I live right behind the Esmeralda Hardware Company. The toilet's in a shed. I wash in the kitchen, at a tin sink. I sleep on a couch with broken springs. Everything there is twenty years old. This is a rich man's town. Come and see me. I live on a rich man's property."

"There's a piece missing from your story about Mitchell," I said.

"Which one?"

"The truth."

"I'll look under the couch for it. It might be a little dusty."

There was the rough noise of a car entering the ramp from above. He turned away and I went through the door and rang for the elevator. He was a queer duck, the attendant, very queer. Kind of interesting, though. And kind of sad, too. One of the sad, one of the lost.

The elevator was a long time coming and before it came I had company waiting for it. Six feet three inches of handsome, healthy male named Clark Brandon. He was wearing a leather windbreaker and a heavy roll-collar blue sweater under it, a pair of beat-up Bedford cord breeches, and the kind of high laced boots that field engineers and surveyors wear in rough country. He looked like the boss of a drilling crew. In an hour from now, I had no doubt he would be at The Glass Room in a dinner suit and he would look like the boss of that too, and perhaps he was. Plenty of money, plenty of health and plenty of time to get the best out of both, and wherever he went he would be the owner.

He glanced at me and waited for me to get into the elevator when it came. The elevator kid saluted him respectfully. He nodded. We both got off at the lobby. Brandon crossed to the desk and got a big smile from the clerk — a new one I hadn't seen before — and the clerk handed him a fistful of letters. Brandon leaned against the end of the counter and tore the envelopes open one by one and dropped them into a wastebasket beside where he was standing. Most of the letters went the same way. There was a rack of travel folders there. I picked one off and lit a cigarette and studied the folder.

Brandon had one letter that interested him. He read it several times. I could see that it was short and handwritten on the hotel stationery, but without looking over his shoulder that was all I could see. He stood holding the letter. Then he reached down into the basket and came up with the envelope. He studied that. He put the letter in his pocket and moved along the desk. He handed the clerk the envelope.

"This was handed in. Did you happen to see who left it? I don't seem to know the party."

The clerk looked at the envelope and nodded. "Yes, Mr. Brandon, a man left it just after I came on. He was a middle-aged fat man with glasses. Gray suit and topcoat and gray felt hat. Not a local type. A little shabby. A nobody."

"Did he ask for me?"

"No, sir. Just asked me to put the note in your box. Anything wrong, Mr. Brandon?"

"Look like a goof ?"

The clerk shook his head. "He just looked what I said. Like a nobody."

Brandon chuckled. "He wants to make me a Mormon bishop for fifty dollars. Some kind of nut, obviously." He picked the envelope up off the counter and put it in his pocket. He started to turn away, then said: "Seen Larry Mitchell around?"

"Not since I've been on, Mr. Brandon. But that's only a couple of hours."

"Thanks."

Brandon walked across to the elevator and got in. It was a different elevator. The operator grinned all over his face and said something to Brandon. Brandon didn't answer him or look at him. The kid looked hurt as he whooshed the doors shut. Brandon was scowling. He was less handsome when he scowled.

I put the travel folder back in the rack and moved over to the desk. The clerk looked at me without interest. His glance said I was not registered there. "Yes, sir?"

He was a gray-haired man who carried himself well.

"I was just going to ask for Mr. Mitchell, but I heard what you said."

"The house phones are over there." He pointed with his chin. "The operator will connect you."

"I doubt it."

"Meaning what?"

I pulled my jacket open to get at my letter case. I could see the clerk's eyes freeze on the rounded butt of the gun under my arm. I got the letter case out and pulled a card.

"Would it be convenient for me to see your house man? If you have one."

He took the card and read it. He looked up. "Have a seat in the main lobby, Mr. Marlowe."

"Thank you."

He was on the phone before I had done a complete turn away from the desk. I went through the arch and sat against the wall where I could see the desk. I didn't have very long to wait.

The man had a hard straight back and a hard straight face, with the kind of skin that never tans but only reddens and pales out again. His hair was almost a pompadour and mostly reddish blond. He stood in the archway and let his eyes take in the lobby slowly. He didn't look at me any longer than at anybody else. Then he came over and sat down in the next chair to me. He wore a brown suit and a brown and yellow bow tie. His clothes fitted him nicely. There were fine blond hairs on his cheeks high up. There was a grace note of gray in his hair.

"My name's Javonen," he said without looking at me. "I know yours. Got your card in my pocket. What's your trouble?"

"Man named Mitchell. I'm looking for him. Larry Mitchell."

"You're looking for him why?"

"Business. Any reason why I shouldn't look for him?"

"No reason at all. He's out of town. Left early this morning."

"So I heard. It puzzled me some. He only got home yesterday. On the Super Chief. In L.A. he picked up his car and drove down. Also, he was broke. Had to make a touch for dinner money. He ate dinner at The Glass Room with a girl. He was pretty drunk – or pretended to be. It got him out of paying the check."

"He can sign his checks here," Javonen said indifferently. His eyes kept flicking around the lobby as if he expected to see one of the canasta players yank a gun and shoot his partner or one of the old ladies at the big jigsaw puzzle start pulling hair. He had two expressions – hard and harder. "Mr. Mitchell is well known in Esmeralda."

"Well, but not favorably," I said.

He turned his head and gave me a bleak stare. "I'm an assistant manager here, Mr. Marlowe. I double as security officer. I can't discuss the reputation of a guest of the hotel with you."

"You don't have to. I know it. From various sources. I've observed him in action. Last night he put the bite on somebody and got enough to blow town. Taking his baggage with him, is my information."

"Who gave this information to you?" He looked tough asking that.

I tried to look tough not answering it. "On top of that I'll give you three guesses," I said. "One, his bed wasn't slept in last night. Two, it was reported to the office sometime today that his room had been cleaned out. Three, somebody on your night staff won't show for work tonight. Mitchell couldn't get all his stuff out without help."

Javonen looked at me, then prowled the lobby again with his eyes. "Got something that proves you are what the card reads? Anyone can have a card printed."

I got my wallet out and slipped a small photostat of my license from it and passed it over. He glanced at it and handed it back. I put it away.

"We have our own organization to take care of skipouts," he said. "They happen — in any hotel. We don't need your help. And we don't like guns in the lobby. The clerk saw yours. Somebody else could see it. We had a stickup attempted here nine months ago. One of the heist guys got dead. I shot him."

"I read about it in the paper," I said. "It scared me for days and days."

"You read some of it. We lost four or five thousand dollars' worth of business the week following. People checked out by the dozen. You get my point?"

"I let the clerk see my gunbutt on purpose. I've been asking for Mitchell all day and all I got was the runaround. If the man checked out, why not say so? Nobody had to tell me he had jumped his bill."

"Nobody said he jumped his bill. His bill, Mr. Marlowe, was paid in full. So where does that leave you?"

"Wondering why it was a secret he had checked out."

He looked contemptuous. "Nobody said that either. You don't listen good. I said he was out of town on a trip. I said his bill was paid in full. I didn't say how much baggage he took. I didn't say he had given up his room. I didn't say that what he took was all he had . . . Just what are you trying to make out of all this?"

"Who paid his bill?"

His face got a little red. "Look, buster, I told you *he* paid it. In person, last night, in full and a week in advance as well. I've been pretty patient with you. Now you tell me something. What's your angle?"

"I don't have one. You've talked me out of it. I wonder why he paid a week in advance."

Javonen smiled – very slightly. Call it a down payment on a smile. "Look, Marlowe, I put in five years in Military Intelligence. I can size up a man – like for instance the guy we're talking about. He pays in advance because we feel happier that way. It has a stabilizing influence."

"He ever pay in advance before?"

"God damn it . . . !"

"Watch yourself," I cut in. "The elderly gent with the walking stick is interested in your reactions."

He looked halfway across the lobby to where a thin, old, bloodless man sat in a very low round-backed padded chair with his chin on gloved hands and the gloved hands on the crook of a stick. He stared unblinkingly in our direction.

"Oh, him," Javonen said. "He can't even see this far. He's eighty years old."

He stood up and faced me. "Okay, you're clammed," he said quietly. "You're a private op, you've got a client and instructions. I'm only interested in protecting the hotel. Leave the gun home next time. If you have questions, come to me. Don't question the help. It gets told around and we don't like it. You wouldn't find the local cops friendly if I suggested you were being troublesome."

"Can I buy a drink in the bar before I go?"

"Keep your jacket buttoned."

"Five years in Military Intelligence is a lot of experience," I said looking up at him admiringly.

"It ought to be enough." He nodded briefly and strolled away through the arch, back straight, shoulders back, chin in, a hard lean well set-up piece of man. A smooth operator. He had milked me dry – of everything that was printed on my business card.

Then I noticed that the old party in the low chair had lifted a gloved hand off the crook of his stick and was curving a finger at me. I pointed a finger at my chest and looked the question. He nodded, so over I went.

He was old, all right, but a long way from feeble and a long way from dim. His white hair was neatly parted, his nose was long and sharp and veined, his faded-out blue eyes were still keen, but the lids drooped wearily over them. One ear held the plastic button of a hearing aid, grayish pink like his ear. The suede gloves on his hands had the cuffs turned back. He wore gray spats over polished black shoes.

"Pull up a chair, young man." His voice was thin and dry and rustled like bamboo leaves.

I sat down beside him. He peered at me and his mouth smiled. "Our excellent Mr. Javonen spent five years in Military Intelligence, as no doubt he told you."

"Yes, sir. CIC, a branch of it."

"Military Intelligence is an expression which contains an interior fallacy. So you are curious about how Mr. Mitchell paid his bill?"

I stared at him. I looked at the hearing aid. He tapped his breast pocket. "I was deaf long before they invented these things. As the result of a hunter balking at a fence. It was my own fault. I lifted him too soon. I was still a young man. I couldn't see myself using an ear trumpet, so I learned to lip-read. It takes a certain amount of practice."

"What about Mitchell, sir?"

"We'll come to him. Don't be in a hurry." He looked up and nodded.

A voice said, "Good evening, Mr. Clarendon." A bellhop went

by on his way to the bar. Clarendon followed him with his eyes.

"Don't bother with that one," he said. "He's a pimp. I have spent many many years in lobbies, in lounges and bars, on porches, terraces and ornate gardens in hotels all over the world. I have outlived everyone in my family. I shall go on being useless and inquisitive until the day comes when the stretcher carries me off to some nice airy corner room in a hospital. The starched white dragons will minister to me. The bed will be wound up, wound down. Trays will come with that awful loveless hospital food. My pulse and temperature will be taken at frequent intervals and invariably when I am dropping off to sleep. I shall lie there and hear the rustle of the starched skirts, the slurring sound of the rubber shoe soles on the aseptic floor, and see the silent horror of the doctor's smile. After a while they will put the oxygen tent over me and draw the screens around the little white bed and I shall, without even knowing it, do the one thing in the world no man ever has to do twice."

He turned his head slowly and looked at me. "Obviously, I talk too much. Your name, sir?"

"Philip Marlowe."

"I am Henry Clarendon IV. I belong to what used to be called the upper classes. Groton, Harvard, Heidelberg, the Sorbonne. I even spent a year at Uppsala. I cannot clearly remember why. To fit me for a life of leisure, no doubt. So you are a private detective. I do eventually get around to speaking of something other than myself, you see."

"Yes, sir."

"You should have come to me for information. But of course you couldn't know that."

I shook my head. I lit a cigarette, first offering one to Mr. Henry Clarendon IV. He refused it with a vague nod.

"However, Mr. Marlowe, it is something you should have certainly learned. In every luxury hotel in the world there will be half a dozen elderly idlers of both sexes who sit around and stare like owls. They watch, they listen, they compare notes, they learn everything about everyone. They have nothing else to do, because hotel life is the most deadly of all forms of boredom. And no doubt I'm boring you equally."

"I'd rather hear about Mitchell, sir. Tonight at least, Mr. Clarendon."

"Of course. I'm egocentric, and absurd, and I prattle like a schoolgirl. You observe that handsome dark-haired woman over there playing canasta? The one with too much jewelry and the heavy gold trim on her glasses?"

He didn't point or even look. But I picked her out. She had an overblown style and she looked just a little hardboiled. She was the one with the ice, the paint.

"Her name is Margo West. She is seven times a divorcee. She has stacks of money and reasonably good looks, but she can't hold a man. She tries too hard. Yet she's not a fool. She would have an affair with a man like Mitchell, she would give him money and pay his bills, but she would never marry him. They had a fight last night. Nevertheless I believe she may have paid his bill. She often has before."

"I thought he got a check from his father in Toronto every month. Not enough to last him, huh?"

Henry Clarendon IV gave me a sardonic smile. "My dear fellow, Mitchell has no father in Toronto. He gets no monthly check. He lives on women. That is why he lives in a hotel like this. There is always some rich and lonely female in a luxury hotel. She may not be beautiful or very young, but she has other charms. In the dull season in Esmeralda, which is from the end of the race meet at Del Mar until about the middle of January, the pickings are very lean. Then Mitchell is apt to travel – Majorca or Switzerland if he can make it, to Florida or one of the Caribbean islands if he is not in rich funds. This year he had poor luck. I understand he only got as far as Washington."

He brushed a glance at me. I stayed deadpan polite, just a

nice youngish guy (by his standards) being polite to an old gentleman who liked to talk.

"Okay," I said. "She paid his hotel bill, maybe. But why a week in advance?"

He moved one gloved hand over the other. He tilted his stick and followed it with his body. He stared at the pattern in the carpet. Finally he clicked his teeth. He had solved the problem. He straightened up again.

"That would be severance pay," he said dryly. "The final and irrevocable end of the romance. Mrs. West, as the English say, had had it. Also, there was a new arrival in Mitchell's company yesterday, a girl with dark red hair. Chestnut red, not fire red or strawberry red. What I saw of their relationship seemed to me a little peculiar. They were both under some sort of strain."

"Would Mitchell blackmail a woman?"

He chuckled. "He would blackmail an infant in a cradle. A man who lives on women always blackmails them, although the word may not be used. He also steals from them when he can get his hands on any of their money. Mitchell forged two checks with Margo West's name. That ended the affair. No doubt she has the checks. But she won't do anything about it except keep them."

"Mr. Clarendon, with all due respect, how in hell would you know all these things?"

"She told me. She cried on my shoulder." He looked toward the handsome dark-haired woman. "She does not at the moment look as if I could be telling the truth. Nevertheless I am."

"And why are you telling it to me?"

His face moved into a rather ghastly grin. "I have no delicacy. I should like to marry Margo West myself. It would reverse the pattern. Very small things amuse a man of my age. A hummingbird, the extraordinary way a strellitzia bloom opens. Why at a certain point in its growth does the bud turn

923

at right angles? Why does the bud split so gradually and why do the flowers emerge always in a certain exact order, so that the sharp unopened end of the bud looks like a bird's beak and the blue and orange petals make a bird of paradise? What strange deity made such a complicated world when presumably he could have made a simple one? Is he omnipotent? How could he be? There's so much suffering and almost always by the innocent. Why will a mother rabbit trapped in a burrow by a ferret put her babies behind her and allow her throat to be torn out? Why? In two weeks more she would not even recognize them. Do you believe in God, young man?"

It was a long way around, but it seemed I had to travel it. "If you mean an omniscient and omnipotent God who intended everything exactly the way it is, no."

"But you should, Mr. Marlowe. It is a great comfort. We all come to it in the end because we have to die and become dust. Perhaps for the individual that is all, perhaps not. There are grave difficulties about the afterlife. I don't think I should really enjoy a heaven in which I shared lodgings with a Congo pygmy or a Chinese coolie or a Levantine rug peddler or even a Hollywood producer. I'm a snob, I suppose, and the remark is in bad taste. Nor can I imagine a heaven presided over by a benevolent character in a long white beard locally known as God. These are foolish conceptions of very immature minds. But you may not question a man's religious beliefs however idiotic they may be. Of course I have no right to assume that I shall go to heaven. Sounds rather dull, as a matter of fact. On the other hand how can I imagine a hell in which a baby that died before baptism occupies the same degraded position as a hired killer or a Nazi death-camp commandant or a member of the Politburo? How strange it is that man's finest aspirations, dirty little animal that he is, his finest actions also, his great and unselfish heroism, his constant daily courage in a harsh world – how strange that these things should be so much finer than his fate on this earth. That has to be somehow made reasonable. Don't tell me that honor is merely a chemical reaction or that a man who deliberately gives his life for another is merely following a behavior pattern. Is God happy with the poisoned cat dying alone in convulsions behind the billboard? Is God happy that life is cruel and that only the fittest survive? The fittest for what? Oh no, far from it. If God were omnipotent and omniscient in any literal sense, he wouldn't have bothered to make the universe at all. There is no success where there is no possibility of failure, no art without the resistance of the medium. Is it blasphemy to suggest that God has his bad days when nothing goes right, and that God's days are very, very long?"

"You're a wise man, Mr. Clarendon. You said something about reversing the pattern."

He smiled faintly. "You thought I had lost the place in the overlong book of my words. No sir, I had not. A woman like Mrs. West almost always ends up marrying a series of pseudo-elegant fortune hunters, tango dancers with handsome sideburns, skiing instructors with beautiful blond muscles, faded French and Italian aristocrats, shoddy princelings from the Middle East, each worse than the one before. She might even in her extremity marry a man like Mitchell. If she married me, she would marry an old bore, but at least she would marry a gentleman."

"Yeah."

He chuckled. "The monosyllable indicates a surfeit of Henry Clarendon IV. I don't blame you. Very well, Mr. Marlowe, why are you interested in Mitchell? But I suppose you can't tell me."

"No sir, I can't. I'm interested in knowing why he left so soon after coming back, who paid his bill for him and why, if Mrs. West or, say, some well-heeled friend like Clark Brandon paid for him, it was necessary to pay a week in advance as well."

His thin worn eyebrows curved upwards. "Brandon could easily guarantee Mitchell's account by lifting the telephone.

Mrs. West might prefer to give him the money and have him pay the bill himself. But a week in advance? Why would our Javonen tell you that? What does it suggest to you?"

"That there's something about Mitchell the hotel doesn't want known. Something that might cause the sort of publicity they hate."

"Such as?"

"Suicide and murder are the sort of things I mean. That's just by way of example. You've noticed how the name of a big hotel is hardly ever mentioned when one of the guests jumps out of a window? It's always a midtown or a downtown hotel or a well-known exclusive hotel – something like that. And if it's rather a high class place, you never see any cops in the lobby, no matter what happened upstairs."

His eyes went sideways and mine followed his. The canasta table was breaking up. The dolled-up and well-iced woman called Margo West strolled off towards the bar with one of the men, her cigarette holder sticking out like a bowsprit.

"So?"

"Well," I said, and I was working hard, "if Mitchell keeps his room on the records, whatever room he had –"

"Four-eighteen," Clarendon put in calmly. "On the ocean side. Fourteen dollars a day out of season, eighteen in season."

"Not exactly cheap for a guy on his uppers. But he still has it, let's say. So whatever happened, he's just away for a few days. Took his car out, put his luggage in around seven A.M. this morning. A damn funny time to leave when he was as drunk as a skunk late last night."

Clarendon leaned back and let his gloved hands hang limp. I could see that he was getting tired. "If it happened that way, wouldn't the hotel prefer to have you think he had left for good? Then you'd have to search for him somewhere else. That is, if you really are searching for him."

I met his pale stare. He grinned.

"You're not making very good sense to me, Mr. Marlowe. I talk and talk, but not merely to hear the sound of my voice. I don't hear it naturally in any case. Talking gives me an opportunity to study people without seeming altogether rude. I have studied you. My intuition, if such be the correct word, tells me that your interest in Mitchell is rather tangential. Otherwise you would not be so open about it."

"Uh-huh. Could be," I said. It was a spot for a paragraph of lucid prose. Henry Clarendon IV would have obliged. I didn't have a damn thing more to say.

"Run along now," he said. "I'm tired. I'm going up to my room and lie down a little. A pleasure to have met you, Mr. Marlowe." He got slowly to his feet and steadied himself with the stick. It was an effort. I stood up beside him.

"I never shake hands," he said. "My hands are ugly and painful. I wear gloves for that reason. Good evening. If I don't see you again, good luck."

He went off, walking slowly and keeping his head erect. I could see that walking wasn't any fun for him.

The two steps up from the main lobby to the arch were made one at a time, with a pause in between. His right foot always moved first. The cane bore down hard beside his left. He went out through the arch and I watched him move towards an elevator. I decided Mr. Henry Clarendon IV was a pretty smooth article.

I strolled along to the bar. Mrs. Margo West was sitting in the amber shadows with one of the canasta players. The waiter was just setting drinks before them. I didn't pay too much attention because farther along in a little booth against the wall was someone I knew better. And alone.

She had the same clothes on except that she had taken the bandeau off her hair and it hung loose around her face.

I sat down. The waiter came over and I ordered. He went away. The music from the invisible record player was low and ingratiating.

She smiled a little. "I'm sorry I lost my temper," she said. "I was very rude."

"Forget it. I had it coming."

"Were you looking for me in here?"

"Not especially."

"Were you – oh, I forgot." She reached for her bag and put it in her lap. She fumbled in it and then passed something rather small across the table, something not small enough for her hand to hide that it was a folder of traveler's checks. "I promised you these."

"No."

"Take them, you fool! I don't want the waiter to see."

I took the folder and slipped it into my pocket. I reached into my inside pocket and got out a small receipt book. I entered the counterfoil and then the body of the receipt. "Received from Miss Betty Mayfield, Hotel Casa del Poniente, Esmeralda, California, the sum of $5000 in American Express Company traveler's checks of $100 denomination, countersigned by the owner, and remaining her property subject to her demand at any time until a fee is arranged with, and an employment accepted by me, the undersigned."

I signed this rigmarole and held the book for her to see it.

"Read it and sign your name in the lower left-hand corner."

She took it and held it close to the light.

"You make me tired," she said. "Whatever are you trying to spring?"

"That I'm on the level and you think so."

She took the pen I held out and signed and gave the stuff back to me. I tore out the original and handed it to her. I put the book away.

The waiter came and put my drink down. He didn't wait to be paid. Betty shook her head at him. He went away.

"Why don't you ask me if I have found Larry?"

"All right. Have you found Larry, Mr. Marlowe?"

928

"No. He has skipped the hotel. He had a room on the fourth floor on the same side as your room. Must be fairly nearly under it. He took nine pieces of luggage and beat it in his Buick. The house peeper, whose name is Javonen – he calls himself an assistant manager and security officer – is satisfied that Mitchell paid his bill and even a week in advance for his room. He has no worries. He doesn't like me, of course."

"Does somebody?"

"You do – five thousand dollars' worth."

"Oh, you *are* an idiot. Do you think Mitchell will come back?"

"I told you he paid a week in advance."

She sipped her drink quietly. "So you did. But that could mean something else."

"Sure. Just spitballing, for example, I might say it could mean that he didn't pay his bill, but someone else did. And that the someone else wanted time to do something – such as getting rid of that body on your balcony last night. That is, if there was a body."

"Oh, stop it!"

She finished her drink, killed her cigarette, stood up and left me with the check. I paid it and went back through the lobby, for no reason that I could think of. Perhaps by pure instinct. And I saw Goble getting into the elevator. He seemed to have a rather strained expression. As he turned he caught my eye, or seemed to, but he gave no sign of knowing me. The elevator went up.

I went out to my car and drove back to the Rancho Descansado. I lay down on the couch and went to sleep. It had been a lot of day. Perhaps if I had a rest and my brain cleared, I might have some faint idea of what I was doing.

18

AN HOUR LATER I was parked in front of the hardware store. It wasn't the only hardware store in Esmeralda, but it was the only one that backed on the alley called Polton's Lane. I walked east and counted the stores. There were seven of them to the corner, all shining with plate glass and chromium trim. On the corner was a dress shop with mannequins in the windows, scarves and gloves and costume jewelry laid out under the lights. No prices showing. I rounded the corner and went south. Heavy eucalyptus trees grew out of the sidewalk. They branched low down and the trunks looked hard and heavy, quite unlike the tall brittle stuff that grows around Los Angeles. At the far corner of Polton's Lane there was an automobile agency. I followed its high blank wall, looking at broken crates, piles of cartons, trash drums, dusty parking spaces, the back yard of elegance. I counted the buildings. It was easy. No questions to ask. A light burned in the small window of a tiny frame cottage that had long ago been somebody's simple home. The cottage had a wooden porch with a broken railing. It had been painted once, but that was in the remote past before the shops swallowed it up. Once it may even have had a garden. The shingles of the roof were warped. The front door was a dirty mustard yellow. The window was shut tight and needed hosing off. Behind part of it hung what remained of an old roller blind. There were two steps up to the porch, but only one had a tread. Behind the cottage and halfway to the loading platform of the hardware store there was what had presumably been a privy. But I could see where a water pipe cut through the sagging side. A rich man's improvements on a rich man's property. A one-unit slum.

I stepped over the hollow place where a step would have been and knocked on the door. There was no bell push. Nobody answered. I tried the knob. Nobody had locked the door. I pushed it open and went in. I had that feeling. I was going to find something nasty inside.

A bulb burned in a frayed lamp crooked on its base, the paper shade split. There was a couch with a dirty blanket on it. There was an old cane chair, a Boston rocker, a table covered with a smeared oilcloth. On the table spread out beside a coffee cup was a copy of *El Diario*, a Spanish language newspaper, also a saucer with cigarette stubs, a dirty plate, a tiny radio which emitted music. The music stopped and a man began to rattle off a commercial in Spanish. I turned it off. The silence fell like a bag of feathers. Then the clicking of an alarm clock from beyond a half open door. Then the clank of a small chain, a fluttering sound and a cracked voice said rapidly: "*Quién es? Quién es? Quién es?*" This was followed by the angry chattering of monkeys. Then silence again.

From a big cage over in the corner the round angry eye of a parrot looked at me. He sidled along the perch as far as he could go.

"*Amigo*," I said.

The parrot let out a screech of insane laughter.

"Watch your language, brother," I said.

The parrot crabwalked to the other end of the perch and pecked into a white cup and shook oatmeal from his beak contemptuously. In another cup there was water. It was messy with oatmeal.

"I bet you're not even housebroken," I said.

The parrot stared at me and shuffled. He turned his head and stared at me with his other eye. Then he leaned forward and fluttered his tail feathers and proved me right.

"*Necio!*" he screamed. "*Fuera!*"

Somewhere water dripped from a leaky faucet. The clock ticked. The parrot imitated the ticking amplified.

I said: "Pretty Polly."

"*Hijo de la chingada*," the parrot said.

I sneered at him and pushed the half-open door into what there was of a kitchen. The linoleum on the floor was worn through to the boards in front of the sink. There was a rusty three-burner gas stove, an open shelf with some dishes and the alarm clock, a riveted hot water tank on a support in the corner, the antique kind that blows up because it has no safety valve. There was a narrow rear door, closed, with a key in the lock, and a single window, locked. There was a light bulb hanging from the ceiling. The ceiling above it was cracked and stained from roof leaks. Behind me the parrot shuffled aimlessly on his perch and once in a while let out a bored croak.

On the zinc drainboard lay a short length of black rubber tubing, and beside that a glass hypodermic syringe with the plunger pushed home. In the sink were three long thin empty tubes of glass with tiny corks near them. I had seen such tubes before.

I opened the back door, stepped to the ground and walked to the converted privy. It had a sloping roof, about eight feet high in front, less than six at the back. It opened outward, being too small to open any other way. It was locked but the lock was old. It did not resist me much.

The man's scuffed toes almost touched the floor. His head was up in the darkness inches from the two by four that held up the roof. He was hanging by a black wire, probably a piece of electric light wire. The toes of his feet were pointed down as if they reached to stand on tiptoe. The worn cuffs of his khaki denim pants hung below his heels. I touched him enough to know that he was cold enough so that there was no point in cutting him down.

He had made very sure of that. He had stood by the sink in his kitchen and knotted the rubber tube around his arm, then clenched his fist to make the vein stand out, then shot a syringeful of morphine sulphate into his blood stream. Since all three of the tubes were empty, it was a fair guess that one of them had been full. He could not have taken in less than enough. Then he had laid the syringe down and released the knotted tube. It wouldn't be long, not a shot directly into the blood stream. Then he had gone out to his privy and stood on the seat and knotted the wire around his throat. By that time he would be dizzy. He could stand there and wait until his knees went slack and the weight of his body took care of the rest. He would know nothing. He would already be asleep.

I closed the door on him. I didn't go back into the house. As I went along the side towards Polton's Lane, that handsome residential street, the parrot inside the shack heard me and screeched: "*Quién es? Quién es? Quién es?*"

Who is it? Nobody, friend. Just a footfall in the night.

I walked softly, going away.

19

I WALKED SOFTLY, in no particular direction, but I knew where I would end up. I always did. At the Casa del Poniente. I climbed back into my car on Grand and circled a few blocks aimlessly, and then I was parked as usual in a slot near the bar entrance. As I got out I looked at the car beside mine. It was Goble's shabby dark little jalopy. He was as adhesive as a band-aid.

At another time I would have been racking my brains for some idea of what he was up to, but now I had a worse problem. I had to go to the police and report the hanging man. But I had no notion what to tell them. Why did I go to his house? Because, if he was telling the truth, he had seen Mitchell leave early in the morning. Why was that of significance? Because I was looking for Mitchell myself. I wanted to have a heart to heart talk with him. About what? And from there on I had no answers that would not lead to Betty Mayfield, who she was, where she came from, why she changed her name, what had happened back in Washington, or Virginia or wherever it was, that made her run away.

I had $5000 of her money in traveler's checks in my pocket, and she wasn't even formally my client. I was stuck, but good.

I walked over to the edge of the cliff and listened to the sound of the surf. I couldn't see anything but the occasional gleam of a wave breaking out beyond the cove. In the cove the waves don't break, they slide in politely, like floorwalkers. There would be a bright moon later, but it hadn't checked in yet.

Someone was standing not far away, doing what I was doing. A woman. I waited for her to move. When she moved I would know whether I knew her. No two people move in just the same way, just as no two sets of fingerprints match exactly.

I lit a cigarette and let the lighter flare in my face, and she was beside me.

"Isn't it about time you stopped following me around?"

"You're my client. I'm trying to protect you. Maybe on my seventieth birthday someone will tell me why."

"I didn't ask you to protect me. I'm not your client. Why don't you go home – if you have a home – and stop annoying people?"

"You're my client – five thousand dollars' worth. I have to do something for it – even if it's no more than growing a mustache."

"You're impossible. I gave you the money to let me alone. You're impossible. You're the most impossible man I ever met. And I've met some dillies."

"What happened to that tall exclusive apartment house in Rio? Where I was going to lounge in silk pajamas and play with your long lascivious hair, while the butler set out the Wedgwood and the Georgian silver with that faint dishonest smile and those delicate gestures, like a pansy hair stylist fluttering around a screen star?"

"Oh, shut up!"

"Wasn't a firm offer, huh? Just a passing fancy, or not even that. Just a trick to make me slaughter my sleeping hours and trot around looking for bodies that weren't there."

"Did anybody ever give you a swift poke in the nose?"

"Frequently, but sometimes I make them miss."

I grabbed hold of her. She tried to fight me off, but no fingernails. I kissed the top of her head. Suddenly she clung to me and turned her face up.

"All right. Kiss me, if it's any satisfaction to you. I suppose you would rather have this happen where there was a bed."

"I'm human."

"Don't kid yourself. You're a dirty low-down detective. Kiss me."

I kissed her. With my mouth close to hers I said: "He hanged himself tonight."

She jerked away from me violently. "Who?" she asked in a voice that could hardly speak.

"The night garage attendant here. You may never have seen him. He was on mesca, tea, marihuana. But tonight he shot himself full of morphine and hanged himself in the privy behind his shack in Polton's Lane. That's an alley behind Grand Street."

She was shaking now. She was hanging on to me as if to keep from falling down. She tried to say something, but her voice was just a croak.

"He was the guy that said he saw Mitchell leave with his nine suitcases early this morning. I wasn't sure I believed him. He told me where he lived and I went over this evening to talk to him some more. And now I have to go to the cops and tell them. And what do I tell them without telling them about Mitchell and from then on about you?"

"Please – please – *please* leave me out of it," she whispered. "I'll give you more money. I'll give you all the money you want."

"For Pete's sake. You've already given me more than I'd keep. It isn't money I want. It's some sort of understanding of what the hell I'm doing and why. You must have heard of professional ethics. Some shreds of them still stick to me. Are you my client?"

"Yes. I give up. They all give up to you in the end, don't they?"

"Far from it. I get pushed around plenty."

I got the folder of traveler's checks out of my pocket and put a pencil flash on them and tore out five. I refolded it and handed it to her. "I've kept five hundred dollars. That makes it legal. Now tell me what it's all about."

"No. You don't have to tell anybody about that man."

"Yes, I do. I have to go to the cop house just about now. I have to. And I have no story to tell them that they won't bust open in three minutes. Here, take your goddam checks – and if you ever push them at me again, I'll smack your bare bottom."

She grabbed the folder and tore off into the darkness to the hotel. I just stood there and felt like a damn fool. I don't know how long I stood there, but finally I stuffed the five checks into my pocket and went wearily back to my car and started off to the place where I knew I had to go.

20

A MAN NAMED Fred Pope who ran a small motel had once told me his views on Esmeralda. He was elderly, talkative, and it always pays to listen. The most unlikely people sometimes drop a fact or two that means a lot in my business.

"I been here thirty years," he said. "When I come here I had dry asthma. Now I got wet asthma. I recall when this town was so quiet dogs slept in the middle of the boulevard and you had to stop your car, if you had a car, and get out and push them out of the way. The bastards just sneered at you. Sundays it was like you was already buried. Everything shut up as tight as a bank vault. You could walk down Grand Street and have as much fun as a stiff in the morgue. You couldn't even buy a pack of cigarettes. It was so quiet you could of heard a mouse combin' his whiskers. Me and my old woman – she's been dead fifteen years now – used to play cribbage in a little place we had down on the street that goes along the cliff, and we'd listen in case something exciting would happen – like an old geezer taking a walk and tapping with a cane. I don't know if the Hellwigs wanted it that way or whether old man Hellwig done it out of spite. In them years he didn't live here. He was a big shot in the farm equipment business."

"More likely," I said, "he was smart enough to know that a place like Esmeralda would become a valuable investment in time."

"Maybe," Fred Pope said. "Anyhow, he just about created the town. And after a while he came to live here – up on the hill in one of them great big stucco houses with tile roofs. Pretty fancy. He had gardens with terraces and big green lawns and flowering shrubs, and wrought iron gates – imported from Italy, I heard, and Arizona fieldstone walks, and not just one garden, half a dozen. And enough land to keep the neighbors out of his hair. He drank a couple bottles of hooch a day and I heard he was a pretty rough customer. He had one daughter, Miss Patricia Hellwig. She was the real cream and still is.

"By that time Esmeralda had begun to fill up. At first it was a lot of old women and their husbands, and I'm tellin' you the mortician business was real good with tired old men that died and got planted by their loving widows. The goddam women last too long. Mine didn't."

He stopped and turned his head away for a moment, before he went on.

"There was a streetcar from San Diego by then, but the town was still quiet – too quiet. Not hardly anybody got born here. Child-bearing was thought kind of too sexy. But the war changed all that. Now we got guys that sweat, and tough school kids in Levis and dirty shirts, and artists and country club drunks and them little gifte shoppes that sell you a two-bit highball glass for eight-fifty. We got restaurants and liquor stores, but we still don't have no billboards or pool-rooms or drive-ins. Last year they tried to put in a dime-in-the-slot telescope in the park. You ought to of heard the town council scream. They killed it for sure, but the place ain't no bird refuge any more. We got as smart stores as Beverly Hills. And Miss Patricia, she spent her whole life working like a beaver to give things to the town. Hellwig died five years ago. The doctors told him he would have to cut down on the booze or he wouldn't live a year. He cussed them out and said if he couldn't take a drink when he wanted to, morning, noon or night, he'd be damned if he'd take one at all. He quit – and he was dead in a year.

"The docs had a name for it – they always have – and I guess Miss Hellwig had a name for them. Anyway, they got bumped off the staff of the hospital and that knocked them loose from Esmeralda. It didn't matter a whole lot. We still got about sixty doctors here. The town's full of Hellwigs, some with other names, but all of the family one way or another. Some are rich and some work. I guess Miss Hellwig works harder than most. She's eighty-six now, but tough as a mule. She don't chew tobacco, drink, smoke, swear or use no make-up. She give the town the hospital, a private school, a library, an art center, public tennis courts, and God knows what else. And she still gets driven in a thirty-year-old Rolls-Royce that's about as noisy as a Swiss watch. The mayor here is two jumps from a Hellwig, both downhill. I guess she built the municipal center too, and sold it to the city for a dollar. She's some woman. Of course we got Jews here now, but let me tell you something. A Jew is supposed to give you a sharp deal and steal your nose, if you ain't careful. That's all bunk. A Jew enjoys trading; he likes business, but he's only tough on the surface. Underneath a Jewish businessman is usually real nice to deal with. He's human. If you want cold-blooded skinning, we got a bunch of people in this town now that will cut you down to the bone and add a service charge. They'll take your last dollar from you between your teeth and look at you like you stole it from them."

21

THE COP HOUSE was part of a long modernistic building at the corner of Hellwig and Orcutt. I parked and went into it, still wondering how to tell my story, and still knowing I had to tell it.

The business office was small but very clean, and the duty officer on the desk had two sharp creases in his shirt, and his uniform looked as if it had been pressed ten minutes before. A battery of six speakers on the wall was bringing in police and sheriff's reports from all over the county. A tilted plaque on the desk said the duty officer's name was Griddell. He looked at me the way they all look, waiting.

"What can we do for you, sir?" He had a cool pleasant voice, and that look of discipline you find in the best ones.

"I have to report a death. In a shack behind the hardware store on Grand, in an alley called Polton's Lane, there's a man hanging in a sort of privy. He's dead. No chance to save him."

"Your name, please?" He was already pressing buttons.

"Philip Marlowe. I'm a Los Angeles private detective."

"Did you notice the number of this place?"

"It didn't have one that I could see. But it's right smack behind the Esmeralda Hardware Company."

"Ambulance call, urgent," he said into his mike. "Possible suicide in a small house behind the Esmeralda Hardware Store. Man hanging in a privy behind the house."

He looked up at me. "Do you know his name?"

I shook my head. "But he was the night garage man at the Casa del Poniente."

He flicked some sheets of a book. "We know him. Has a record for marihuana. Can't figure how he held the job, but he may be off it now, and his sort of labor is pretty scarce here."

A tall sergeant with a granite face came into the office, gave me a quick glance and went out. A car started.

The duty officer flicked a key on a small PBX. "Captain, this is Griddell on the desk. A Mr. Philip Marlowe has reported a death in Polton's Lane. Ambulance moving. Sergeant Green is on his way. I have two patrol cars in the vicinity."

He listened for a moment, then looked at me. "Captain Alessandro would like to speak to you, Mr. Marlowe. Down the hall, last door on the right, please."

He was on the mike again before I was through the swinging door.

The last door on the right had two names on it. Captain Alessandro in a plaque fastened to the wood, and Sergeant Green on a removable panel. The door was half open, so I knocked and went in.

The man at the desk was as immaculate as the desk officer. He was studying a card through a magnifying glass, and a tape recorder beside him was telling some dreary story in a crumpled, unhappy voice. The captain was about six feet three inches tall and had thick dark hair and a clear olive skin. His uniform cap was on the desk near him. He looked up, cut off the tape recorder and put down the magnifying glass and the card.

"Have a seat, Mr. Marlowe."

I sat down. He looked at me for a moment without speaking. He had rather soft brown eyes, but his mouth was not soft.

"I understand you know Major Javonen at the Casa."

"I've met him, Captain. We are not close friends."

He smiled faintly. "That's hardly to be expected. He wouldn't enjoy private detectives asking questions in the hotel. He used to be in the CIC. We still call him Major. This is the politest goddam town I was ever in. We are a goddam smooth bunch around here, but we're police just the same. Now about this Ceferino Chang?"

"So that's his name. I didn't know."

"Yes. We know him. May I ask what you are doing in Esmeralda?"

"I was hired by a Los Angeles attorney named Clyde Umney to meet the Super Chief and follow a certain party until that party came to a stop somewhere. I wasn't told why, but Mr. Umney said he was acting for a firm of Washington attorneys and he didn't know why himself. I took the job because there is nothing illegal in following a person, if you don't interfere with that person. The party ended up in Esmeralda. I went back to Los Angeles and tried to find out what it was all about. I couldn't, so I took what I thought was a reasonable fee, two hundred and fifty, and absorbed my own expenses. Mr. Umney was not very pleased with me."

The captain nodded. "That doesn't explain why you are here or what you have to do with Ceferino Chang. And since you are not now working for Mr. Umney, unless you are working for another attorney you have no privilege."

"Give me a break, if you can, Captain. I found out that the party I was following was being blackmailed, or there was an attempt at blackmail, by a man named Larry Mitchell. He lives or lived at the Casa. I have been trying to get in touch with him, but the only information I have is from Javonen and this Ceferino Chang. Javonen said he checked out, paid his bill, and a week in advance for his room. Chang told me he left at seven A.M. this morning with nine suitcases. There was something a bit peculiar about Chang's manner, so I wanted to have another talk with him."

"How did you know where he lived?"

"He told me. He was a bitter man. He said he lived on a rich man's property, and he seemed angry that it wasn't kept up."

"Not good enough, Marlowe."

"Okay, I didn't think it was myself. He was on the weed. I pretended to be a pusher. Once in a while in my business a man has to do a good deal of faking."

"Better. But there's something missing. The name of your client – if you have one."

"Could it be in confidence?"

"Depends. We never disclose the names of blackmail victims, unless they come out in court. But if this party has committed or been indicted for a crime, or has crossed a state line to escape prosecution, then it would be my duty as an officer of the law to report her present whereabouts and the name she is using."

"Her? So you know already. Why ask me? I don't know why she ran away. She won't tell me. All I know is she is in trouble and in fear, and that somehow Mitchell knew enough to make her say uncle."

He made a smooth gesture with his hand and fished a cigarette out of a drawer. He stuck it in his mouth but didn't light it.

He gave me another steady look.

"Okay, Marlowe. For now I'll let it lay. But if you dig anything up, here is where you bring it."

I stood up. He stood up too and held his hand out.

"We're not tough. We just have a job to do. Don't get too hostile with Javonen. The guy who owns that hotel draws a lot of water around here."

"Thanks, Captain. I'll try to be a nice little boy – even to Javonen."

I went back along the hall. The same officer was on the desk. He nodded to me and I went out into the evening and got into my car. I sat with my hands tight on the steering wheel. I wasn't too used to cops who treated me as if I had a right to be alive. I was sitting there when the desk officer poked his head out of the door and called that Captain Alessandro wanted to see me again.

When I got back to Captain Alessandro's office, he was on the telephone. He nodded me to the customer's chair and went on listening and making quick notes in what looked like the sort of condensed writing that many reporters use. After a while he said: "Thanks very much. We'll be in touch."

942

He leaned back and tapped on his desk and frowned.

"That was a report from the sheriff's substation at Escondido. Mitchell's car has been found — apparently abandoned. I thought you might like to know."

"Thanks, Captain. Where was this?"

"About twenty miles from here, on a country road that leads to Highway 395, but is not the road a man would naturally take to get to 395. It's a place called Los Peñasquitos Canyon. Nothing there but outcrop and barren land and a dry river bed. I know the place. This morning a rancher named Gates went by there with a small truck, looking for fieldstone to build a wall. He passed a two-tone Buick hardtop parked off the side of the road. He didn't pay much attention to the Buick, except to notice that it hadn't been in a wreck, so somebody just parked it there.

"Later on in the day, around four, Gates went back to pick up another load of fieldstone. The Buick was still there. This time he stopped and looked it over. No keys in the lock, but the car wasn't locked up. No sign of any damage. Just the same, Gates wrote down the license number and the name and address on the registration certificate. When he got back to his ranch he called the substation at Escondido. Of course the deputies knew Los Peñasquitos Canyon. One of them went over and looked at the car. Clean as a whistle. The deputy managed to trick the trunk open. Empty except for a spare tire and a few tools. So he went back to Escondido and called in here. I've just been talking to him."

I lit a cigarette and offered one to Captain Alessandro. He shook his head.

"Got any ideas, Marlowe?"

"No more than you have."

"Let's hear them anyway."

"If Mitchell had some good reason to get lost and had a friend who would pick him up — a friend nobody here knew

943

anything about – he would have stored his car in some garage. That wouldn't have made anyone curious. There wouldn't be anything to make the garage curious. They would just be storing a car. Mitchell's suitcases would already have been in his friend's car."

"So?"

"So there wasn't any friend. So Mitchell disappeared into thin air – with his nine suitcases – on a very lonely road that was hardly ever used."

"Go on from there." His voice was hard now. It had an edge to it. I stood up.

"Don't bully me, Captain Alessandro. I haven't done anything wrong. You've been very human so far. Please don't get the idea that I had anything to do with Mitchell's disappearance. I didn't – and still don't – know what he had on my client. I just know that she is a lonely and frightened and unhappy girl. When I know why, if I do manage to find out, I'll let you know or I won't. If I don't, you'll just have to throw the book at me. It wouldn't be the first time it's happened to me. I don't sell out – even to good police officers."

"Let's hope it doesn't turn out that way, Marlowe. Let's hope."

"I'm hoping with you, Captain. And thanks for treating me the way you have."

I walked back down the corridor, nodded to the duty officer on the desk and climbed back into my car again. I felt twenty years older.

I knew – and I was pretty damn sure Captain Alessandro knew too – that Mitchell wasn't alive, that he hadn't driven his car to Los Peñasquitos Canyon, but somebody had driven him there, with Mitchell lying dead on the floor of the back seat.

There was no other possible way to look at it. There are things that are facts, in a statistical sense, on paper, on a tape recorder, in evidence. And there are things that are facts because they have to be facts, because nothing makes any sense otherwise.

22

IT IS LIKE a sudden scream in the night, but there is no sound. Almost always at night, because the dark hours are the hours of danger. But it has happened to me also in broad daylight – that strange, clarified moment when I suddenly know something I have no reason for knowing. Unless out of the long years and the long tensions, and in the present case, the abrupt certainty that what bullfighters call "the moment of truth" is here.

There was no other reason, no sensible reason at all. But I parked across from the entrance to the Rancho Descansado, and cut my lights and ignition, and then drifted about fifty yards downhill and pulled the brake back hard.

I walked up to the office. There was the small glow of light over the night bell, but the office was closed. It was only ten-thirty. I walked around to the back and drifted through the trees. I came on two parked cars. One was a Hertz rent car, as anonymous as a nickel in a parking meter, but by bending down I could read the license number. The car next to it was Goble's little dark jalopy. It didn't seem very long since it was parked by the Casa del Poniente. Now it was here.

I went on through the trees until I was below my room. It was dark, soundless. I went up the few steps very slowly and put my ear to the door. For a little while I heard nothing. Then I heard a strangled sob – a man's sob, not a woman's. Then a thin, low cackling laugh. Then what seemed to be a hard blow. Then silence.

I went back down the steps and through the trees to my car. I unlocked the trunk and got out a tire iron. I went back to my room as carefully as before – even more carefully. I listened again. Silence. Nothing. The quiet of the night. I reached out my pocket flash and flicked it once at the window, then slid away from the door. For several minutes nothing happened. Then the door opened a crack.

I hit it hard with my shoulder and smashed it wide open. The man stumbled back and then laughed. I saw the glint of his gun in the faint light. I smashed his wrist with the tire iron. He screamed. I smashed his other wrist. I heard the gun hit the floor.

I reached back and switched the lights on. I kicked the door shut.

He was a pale-faced redhead with dead eyes. His face was twisted with pain, but his eyes were still dead. Hurt as he was, he was still tough.

"You ain't going to live long, boy," he said.

"You're not going to live at all. Get out of my way."

He managed to laugh.

"You've still got legs," I said. "Bend them at the knees and lie down – face down – that is, if you want a face."

He tried to spit at me, but his throat choked. He slid down to his knees, holding his arms out. He was groaning now. Suddenly he crumpled. They're so goddam tough when they hold the stacked deck. And they never know any other kind of deck.

Goble was lying on the bed. His face was a mass of bruises and cuts. His nose was broken. He was unconscious and breathing as if half strangled.

The redhead was still out, and his gun lay on the floor near him. I wrestled his belt off and strapped his ankles together. Then I turned him over and went through his pockets. He had a wallet with $670 in it, a driver's license in the name of Richard Harvest, and the address of a small hotel in San Diego. His pocketbook contained numbered checks on about twenty banks, a set of credit cards, but no gun permit.

I left him lying there and went down to the office. I pushed the button of the night bell, and kept on pushing it. After a while a figure came down through the dark. It was Jack in a bathrobe and pajamas. I still had the tire iron in my hand.

He looked startled. "Something the matter, Mr. Marlowe?"

"Oh, no. Just a hoodlum in my room waiting to kill me. Just another man beaten to pieces on my bed. Nothing the matter at all. Quite normal around here, perhaps."

"I'll call the police."

"That would be awfully damn nice of you, Jack. As you see, I am still alive. You know what you ought to do with this place? Turn it into a pet hospital."

He unlocked the door and went into the office. When I heard him talking to the police I went back to my room. The redhead had guts. He had managed to get into a sitting position against the wall. His eyes were still dead and his mouth was twisted into a grin.

I went over to the bed. Goble's eyes were open.

"I didn't make it," he whispered. "Wasn't as good as I thought I was. Got out of my league."

"The cops are on their way. How did it happen?"

"I walked into it. No complaints. This guy's a lifetaker. I'm lucky. I'm still breathing. Made me drive over here. He cooled me, tied me up, then he was gone for a while."

"Somebody must have picked him up, Goble. There's a rent car beside yours. If he had that over at the Casa, how did he get back there for it?"

Goble turned his head slowly and looked at me. "I thought I was a smart cookie. I learned different. All I want is back to Kansas City. The little guys can't beat the big guys – not ever. I guess you saved my life."

Then the police were there.

First two prowl car boys, nice cool-looking serious men in the always immaculate uniforms and the always deadpan faces. Then a big tough sergeant who said his name was Sergeant

947

Holzminder, and that he was the cruising sergeant on the shift. He looked at the redhead and went over to the bed.

"Call the hospital," he said briefly, over his shoulder.

One of the cops went out to the car. The sergeant bent down over Goble. "Want to tell me?"

"The redhead beat me up. He took my money. Stuck a gun into me at the Casa. Made me drive him here. Then he beat me up."

"Why?"

Goble made a sighing sound and his head went lax on the pillow. Either he passed out again or faked it. The sergeant straightened up and turned to me. "What's your story?"

"I haven't any, Sergeant. The man on the bed had dinner with me tonight. We'd met a couple of times. He said he was a Kansas City P.I. I never knew what he was doing here."

"And this?" The sergeant made a loose motion towards the redhead, who was still grinning a sort of unnatural epileptic grin.

"I never saw him before. I don't know anything about him, except that he was waiting for me with a gun."

"That your tire iron?"

"Yes, Sergeant."

The other cop came back into the room and nodded to the sergeant. "On the way."

"So you had a tire iron," the sergeant said coldly. "So why?"

"Let's say I just had a hunch someone was waiting for me here."

"Let's try it that you didn't have a hunch, that you already knew. And knew a lot more."

"Let's try it that you don't call me a liar until you know what you're talking about. And let's try it that you don't get so goddam tough just because you have three stripes. And let's try something more. This guy may be a hood, but he still has two broken wrists, and you know what that means, Sergeant? He'll never be able to handle a gun again."

"So we book you for mayhem."

"If you say so, Sergeant."

Then the ambulance came. They carried Goble out first and then the intern put temporary splints on the two wrists of the redhead. They unstrapped his ankles. He looked at me and laughed.

"Next time, pal, I'll think of something original – but you did all right. You really did."

He went out. The ambulance doors clanged shut and the growling sound of it died. The sergeant was sitting down now, with his cap off. He was wiping his forehead.

"Let's try again," he said evenly. "From the beginning. Like as if we didn't hate each other and were just trying to understand. Could we?"

"Yes, Sergeant. We could. Thanks for giving me the chance."

23

EVENTUALLY I LANDED back at the cop house. Captain Alessandro had gone. I had to sign a statement for Sergeant Holzminder.

"A tire iron, huh?" he said musingly. "Mister, you took an awful chance. He could have shot you four times while you were swinging on him."

"I don't think so, Sergeant. I bumped him pretty hard with the door. And I didn't take a full swing. Also, maybe he wasn't supposed to shoot me. I don't figure he was in business for himself."

A little more of that, and they let me go. It was too late to do anything but go to bed, too late to talk to anyone. Just the same I went to the telephone company office and shut myself in one of the two neat outdoor booths and dialed the Casa del Poniente.

"Miss Mayfield, please. Miss Betty Mayfield. Room 1224."

"I can't ring a guest at this hour."

"Why? You got a broken wrist?" I was a real tough boy tonight. "Do you think I'd call if it wasn't an emergency?"

He rang and she answered in a sleepy voice.

"This is Marlowe. Bad trouble. Do I come there or do you come to my place?"

"What? What kind of trouble?"

"Just take it from me for just this once. Should I pick you up in the parking lot?"

"I'll get dressed. Give me a little time."

I went out to my car and drove to the Casa. I was smoking my third cigarette and wishing I had a drink when she came quickly and noiselessly up to the car and got in.

"I don't know what this is all about," she began, but I interrupted her.

"You're the only one that does. And tonight you're going to tell me. And don't bother getting indignant. It won't work again."

I jerked the car into motion and drove fast through silent streets and then down the hill and into the Rancho Descansado and parked under the trees. She got out without a word and I unlocked my door and put the lights on.

"Drink?"

"All right."

"Are you doped?"

"Not tonight, if you mean sleeping pills. I was out with Clark and drank quite a lot of champagne. That always makes me sleepy."

I made a couple of drinks and gave her one. I sat down and leaned my head back.

"Excuse me," I said. "I'm a little tired. Once in every two or three days I have to sit down. It's a weakness I've tried to get over, but I'm not as young as I was. Mitchell's dead."

Her breath caught in her throat and her hand shook. She may have turned pale. I couldn't tell.

"Dead?" she whispered. "Dead?"

"Oh, come off it. As Lincoln said, you can fool all of the detectives some of the time, and some of the detectives all the time, but you can't –"

"Shut up! Shut up right now! Who the hell do you think you are?"

"Just a guy who has tried very hard to get where he could do you some good. A guy with enough experience and enough understanding to know that you were in some kind of jam. And wanted to help you out of it, with no help from you."

"Mitchell's dead," she said in a low breathless voice. "I didn't mean to be nasty. Where?"

"His car has been found abandoned in a place you wouldn't know. It's about twenty miles inland, on a road that's hardly used. A place called Los Peñasquitos Canyon. A place of dead land. Nothing in his car, no suitcases. Just an empty car parked at the side of a road hardly anybody ever uses."

She looked down at her drink and took a big gulp. "You said he was dead."

"It seems like weeks, but it's only hours ago that you came over here and offered me the top half of Rio to get rid of his body."

"But there wasn't – I mean, I must just have dreamed –"

"Lady, you came over here at three o'clock in the morning in a state of near-shock. You described just where he was and how he was lying on the chaise on your little porch. So I went back with you and climbed the fire stairs, using the infinite caution for which my profession is famous. And no Mitchell, and then you asleep in your little bed with your little sleeping pill cuddled up to you."

"Get on with your act," she snapped at me. "I know how you love it. Why didn't *you* cuddle up to me? I wouldn't have needed a sleeping pill – perhaps?"

"One thing at a time, if you don't mind. And the first thing is that you were telling the truth when you came here.

Mitchell *was* dead on your porch. But someone got his body out of there while you were over here making a sucker out of me. And somebody got him down to his car and then packed his suitcases and got them down. All this took time. It took more than time. It took a great big reason. Now who would do a thing like that – just to save you the mild embarrassment of reporting a dead man on your porch?"

"Oh, shut up!" She finished her drink and put the glass aside. "I'm tired. Do you mind if I lie down on your bed?"

"Not if you take your clothes off."

"All right – I'll take my clothes off. That's what you've been working up to, isn't it?"

"You might not like that bed. Goble was beaten up on it tonight – by a hired gun named Richard Harvest. He was really brutalized. You remember Goble, don't you? The fat sort of man in the little dark car that followed us up the hill the other night."

"I don't know anybody named Goble. And I don't know anybody named Richard Harvest. How do you know all this? Why were they here – in your room?"

"The hired gun was waiting for me. After I heard about Mitchell's car I had a hunch. Even generals and other important people have hunches. Why not me? The trick is to know when to act on one. I was lucky tonight – or last night. I acted on a hunch. He had a gun, but I had a tire iron."

"What a big strong unbeatable man you are," she said bitterly. "I don't mind the bed. Do I take my clothes off now?"

I went over and jerked her to her feet and shook her. "Stop your nonsense, Betty. When I want your beautiful white body, it won't be while you're my client. I want to know what you are afraid of. How the hell can I do anything about it if I don't know? Only you can tell me."

She began to sob in my arms.

Women have so few defenses, but they certainly perform wonders with those they have.

I held her tight against me. "You can cry and cry and sob and sob, Betty. Go ahead, I'm patient. If I wasn't that – well, hell, if I wasn't that –"

That was as far as I got. She was pressed tight to me trembling. She lifted her face and dragged my head down until I was kissing her.

"Is there some other woman?" she asked softly, between my teeth.

"There have been."

"But someone very special?"

"There was once, for a brief moment. But that's a long time ago now."

"Take me. I'm yours – all of me is yours. Take me."

24

A BANGING ON the door woke me. I opened my eyes stupidly. She was clinging to me so tightly that I could hardly move. I moved her arms gently until I was free. She was still sound asleep.

I got out of bed and pulled a bathrobe on and went to the door; I didn't open it.

"What's the matter? I was asleep."

"Captain Alessandro wants you at the office right away. Open the door."

"Sorry, can't be done. I have to shave and shower and so on."

"Open the door. This is Sergeant Green."

"I'm sorry, Sergeant. I just can't. But I'll be along just as soon as I can make it."

"You got a dame in there?"

"Sergeant, questions like that are out of line. I'll be there."

I heard his steps go down off the porch. I heard someone laugh. I heard a voice say, "This guy is really rich. I wonder what he does on his day off."

I heard the police car going away. I went into the bathroom and showered and shaved and dressed. Betty was still glued to the pillow. I scribbled a note and put it on my pillow. "The cops want me. I have to go. You know where my car is. Here are the keys."

I went out softly and locked the door and found the Hertz car. I knew the keys would be in it. Operators like Richard Harvest don't bother about keys. They carry sets of them for all sorts of cars.

Captain Alessandro looked exactly as he had the day before. He would always look like that. There was a man with him, an elderly stony-faced man with nasty eyes.

Captain Alessandro nodded me to the usual chair. A cop in uniform came in and put a cup of coffee in front of me. He gave me a sly grin as he went out.

"This is Mr. Henry Cumberland of Westfield, Carolina, Marlowe. North Carolina. I don't know how he found his way out here, but he did. He says Betty Mayfield murdered his son."

I didn't say anything. There was nothing for me to say. I sipped the coffee which was too hot, but good otherwise.

"Like to fill us in a little, Mr. Cumberland?"

"Who's this?" He had a voice as sharp as his face.

"A private detective named Philip Marlowe. He operates out of Los Angeles. He is here because Betty Mayfield is his client. It seems that you have rather more drastic ideas about Miss Mayfield than he has."

"I don't have any ideas about her, Captain," I said. "I just like to squeeze her once in a while. It soothes me."

"You like being soothed by a murderess?" Cumberland barked at me.

"Well, I didn't know she was a murderess, Mr. Cumberland. It's all news to me. Would you care to explain?"

"The girl who calls herself Betty Mayfield – and that was her maiden name – was the wife of my son, Lee Cumberland. I never approved of the marriage. It was one of those wartime idiocies. My son received a broken neck in the war and had to wear a brace to protect his spinal column. One night she got it away from him and taunted him until he rushed at her. Unfortunately, he had been drinking rather heavily since he came home, and there had been quarrels. He tripped and fell across the bed. I came into the room and found her trying to put the brace back on his neck. He was already dead."

I looked at Captain Alessandro. "Is this being recorded, Captain?"

He nodded. "Every word."

"All right, Mr. Cumberland. There's more, I take it."

"Naturally. I have a great deal of influence in Westfield. I own the bank, the leading newspaper, most of the industry. The people of Westfield are my friends. My daughter-in-law was arrested and tried for murder and the jury brought in a verdict of guilty."

"The jury were all Westfield people, Mr. Cumberland?"

"They were. Why shouldn't they be?"

"I don't know, sir. But it sounds like a one-man town."

"Don't get impudent with me, young man."

"Sorry, sir. Would you finish?"

"We have a peculiar law in our state, and I believe in a few other jurisdictions. Ordinarily the defense attorney makes an automatic motion for a directed verdict of not guilty and it is just as automatically denied. In my state the judge may reserve his ruling until after the verdict. The judge was senile. He reserved his ruling. When the jury brought in a verdict of guilty, he declared in a long speech that the jury had failed to consider the possibility that my son had in a drunken rage removed the brace from his neck in order to terrify his wife. He said that where there was so much bitterness anything was possible, and that the jury had failed to consider the possibility that my daughter-in-law might have been doing exactly what she said she was doing – trying to put the brace back on my son's neck. He voided the verdict and discharged the defendant.

"I told her that she had murdered my son and that I would see to it that she had no place of refuge anywhere on this earth. That is why I am here."

I looked at the captain. He looked at nothing. I said: "Mr. Cumberland, whatever your private convictions, Mrs. Lee Cumberland, whom I know as Betty Mayfield, has been tried and acquitted. You have called her a murderess. That's a slander. We'll settle for a million dollars."

He laughed almost grotesquely. "You small-town nobody," he almost screamed. "Where I come from you would be thrown into jail as a vagrant."

"Make it a million and a quarter," I said. "I'm not so valuable as your ex-daughter-in-law."

Cumberland turned on Captain Alessandro. "What goes on here?" he barked. "Are you all a bunch of crooks?"

"You're talking to a police officer, Mr. Cumberland."

"I don't give a good goddam what you are," Cumberland said furiously. "There are plenty of crooked police."

"It's a good idea to be sure – before you call them crooked," Alessandro said, almost with amusement. Then he lit a cigarette and blew smoke and smiled through it.

"Take it easy, Mr. Cumberland. You're a cardiac case. Prognosis unfavorable. Excitement is very bad for you. I studied medicine once. But somehow I became a cop. The war cut me off, I guess."

Cumberland stood up. Spittle showed on his chin. He made a strangled sound in his throat. "You haven't heard the last of this," he snarled.

Alessandro nodded. "One of the interesting things about police work is that you never hear the last of anything. There are always too many loose ends. Just what would you like me to do? Arrest someone who has been tried and acquitted, just because you are a big shot in Westfield, Carolina?"

"I told her I'd never give her any peace," Cumberland said furiously. "I'd follow her to the end of the earth. I'd make sure everyone knew just what she was!"

"And what is she, Mr. Cumberland?"

"A murderess that killed my son and was let off by an idiot of a judge – that's what she is!"

Captain Alessandro stood up, all six feet three inches of him. "Take off, buster," he said coldly. "You annoy me. I've met all kinds of punks in my time. Most of them have been poor stupid backward kids. This is the first time I've come across a great big important man who was just as stupid and vicious as a fifteen-year-old delinquent. Maybe you own Westfield, North Carolina, or think you do. You don't own a cigar butt in my town. Get out before I put the arm on you for interfering with an officer in the performance of his duties."

Cumberland almost staggered to the door and groped for the knob, although the door was wide open. Alessandro looked after him. He sat down slowly.

"You were pretty rough, Captain."

"It's breaking my heart. If anything I said makes him take another look at himself – oh well, hell!"

"Not his kind. Am I free to go?"

"Yes. Goble won't make charges. He'll be on his way back to Kansas City today. We'll dig up something on this Richard Harvest, but what's the use? We put him away for a while, and a hundred just like him are available for the same work."

"What do I do about Betty Mayfield?"

"I have a vague idea that you've already done it," he said, deadpan.

"Not until I know what happened to Mitchell." I was just as deadpan as he was.

"All I know is that he's gone. That doesn't make him police business."

I stood up. We gave each other those looks. I went out.

25

SHE WAS STILL asleep. My coming in didn't wake her. She slept like a little girl, soundlessly, her face at peace. I watched her for a moment, then lit a cigarette and went out to the kitchen. When I had put coffee on to percolate in the

handsome paper-thin dime store aluminum percolator provided by the management, I went back and sat on the bed.
The note I had left was still on the pillow with my car keys.

I shook her gently and her eyes opened and blinked.

"What time is it?" she asked, stretching her bare arms as far
as she could. "God, I slept like a log."

"It's time for you to get dressed. I have some coffee
brewing. I've been down to the police station – by request.
Your father-in-law is in town, Mrs. Cumberland."

She shot upright and stared at me without breathing.

"He got the brush, but good, from Captain Alessandro. He
can't hurt you. Was that what all the fear was about?"

"Did he say – say what happened back in Westfield?"

"That's what he came here to say. He's mad enough to
jump down his own throat. And what of it? You didn't, did
you? Do what they said?"

"I did not." Her eyes blazed at me.

"Wouldn't matter if you had – now. But it wouldn't
make me very happy about last night. How did Mitchell get
wise?"

"He just happened to be there or somewhere nearby.
Good heavens, the papers were full of it for weeks. It wasn't
hard for him to recognize me. Didn't they have it in the
papers here?"

"They ought to have covered it, if only because of the
unusual legal angle. If they did, I missed it. The coffee ought
to be ready now. How do you take it?"

"Black, please. No sugar."

"Fine. I don't have any cream or sugar. Why did you call
yourself Eleanor King? No, don't answer that. I'm stupid. Old
man Cumberland would know your unmarried name."

I went out to the kitchen and removed the top of the percolator, and poured us both a cup. I carried hers to her. I sat
down in a chair with mine. Our eyes met and were strangers
again.

She put her cup aside. "That was good. Would you mind looking the other way while I gather myself together?"

"Sure." I picked a paperback off the table and made a pretense of reading it. It was about some private eye whose idea of a hot scene was a dead naked woman hanging from the shower rail with the marks of torture on her. By that time Betty was in the bathroom. I threw the paperback into the wastebasket, not having a garbage can handy at the moment. Then I got to thinking there are two kinds of women you can make love to. Those who give themselves so completely and with such utter abandonment that they don't even think about their bodies. And there are those who are self-conscious and always want to cover up a little. I remembered a girl in a story by Anatole France who insisted on taking her stockings off. Keeping them on made her feel like a whore. She was right.

When Betty came out of the bathroom she looked like a fresh-opened rose, her make-up perfect, her eyes shining, every hair exactly in place.

"Will you take me back to the hotel? I want to speak to Clark."

"You in love with him?"

"I thought I was in love with you."

"It was a cry in the night," I said. "Let's not try to make it more than it was. There's more coffee out in the kitchen."

"No, thanks. Not until breakfast. Haven't you ever been in love? I mean enough to want to be with a woman every day, every month, every year?"

"Let's go."

"How can such a hard man be so gentle?" she asked wonderingly.

"If I wasn't hard, I wouldn't be alive. If I couldn't ever be gentle, I wouldn't deserve to be alive."

I held her coat for her and we went out to my car. On the way back to the hotel she didn't speak at all. When we got

959

there and I slid into the now familiar parking slot, I took the five folded traveler's checks out of my pocket and held them out to her.

"Let's hope it's the last time we pass these back and forth," I said. "They're wearing out."

She looked at them, but didn't take them. "I thought they were your fee," she said rather sharply.

"Don't argue, Betty. You know very well that I couldn't take money from you."

"After last night?"

"After nothing. I just couldn't take it. That's all. I haven't done anything for you. What are you going to do? Where are you going? You're safe now."

"I've no idea. I'll think of something."

"Are you in love with Brandon?"

"I might be."

"He's an ex-racketeer. He hired a gunman to scare Goble off. The gunman was ready to kill me. Could you really love a man like that?"

"A woman loves a man. Not what he is. And he may not have meant it."

"Goodbye, Betty. I gave it what I had, but it wasn't enough."

She reached her hand out slowly and took the checks. "I think you're crazy. I think you're the craziest man I ever met." She got out of the car and walked away quickly, as she always did.

26

I GAVE HER time to clear the lobby and go up to her room, and then I went into the lobby myself and asked for Mr. Clark Brandon on a house phone. Javonen came by and gave me a hard look, but he didn't say anything.

A man's voice answered. It was his all right.

"Mr. Brandon, you don't know me, although we shared an elevator the other morning. My name is Philip Marlowe. I'm a private detective from Los Angeles, and I'm a friend of Miss Mayfield. I'd like to talk to you a little, if you'll give me the time."

"I seem to have heard something about you, Marlowe. But I'm all set to go out. How about a drink around six this evening?"

"I'd like to get back to Los Angeles, Mr. Brandon. I won't keep you long."

"All right," he said grudgingly. "Come on up."

He opened the door, a big, tall, very muscular man in top condition, neither hard nor soft. He didn't offer to shake hands. He stood aside, and I went in.

"You alone here, Mr. Brandon?"

"Sure. Why?"

"I wouldn't want anyone else to hear what I have to say."

"Well say it and get done."

He sat in a chair and put his feet up on an ottoman. He flicked a gold lighter at a gold-tipped cigarette. Big deal.

"I first came down here on the instructions of a Los Angeles lawyer to follow Miss Mayfield and find out where she went, and then report back. I didn't know why and the lawyer said he didn't either, but that he was acting for a reputable firm of attorneys in Washington. Washington, D.C."

"So you followed her. So what?"

"So she made contact with Larry Mitchell, or he with her, and he had a hook of some sort into her."

"Into a lot of women from time to time," Brandon said coldly. "He specialized in it."

"He doesn't any more, does he?"

He stared at me with cool blank eyes. "What's that mean?"

"He doesn't do anything any more. He doesn't exist any more."

"I heard he left the hotel and went off in his car. What's it to do with me?"

"You didn't ask me how I know he doesn't exist any more."

"Look, Marlowe." He flicked ash from his cigarette with a contemptuous gesture. "It could be that I don't give a damn. Get to what concerns me, or get out."

"I also got involved down here, if involved is the word, with a man named Goble who said he was a private eye from Kansas City, and had a card which may or may not have proved it. Goble annoyed me a good deal. He kept following me around. He kept talking about Mitchell. I couldn't figure what he was after. Then one day at the desk you got an anonymous letter. I watched you read it over and over. You asked the clerk who left it. The clerk didn't know. You even picked the empty envelope out of the wastebasket. And when you went up in the elevator you didn't look happy."

Brandon was beginning to look a little less relaxed. His voice had a sharper edge.

"You could get too nosy, Mr. P. I. Ever think of that?"

"That's a silly question. How else would I make a living?"

"Better get out of here while you can still walk."

I laughed at him, and that really burned him. He shot to his feet and came striding over to where I was sitting.

"Listen, boy friend. I'm a pretty big man in this town. I don't get pushed around much by small-time operators like you. Out!"

"You don't want to hear the rest?"

"I said, out!"

I stood up. "Sorry. I was prepared to settle this with you privately. And don't get the idea that I'm trying to put a bite on you — like Goble. I just don't do those things. But if you toss me out — without hearing me out — I'll have to go to Captain Alessandro. He'll listen."

He stood glowering for a long moment. Then a curious sort of grin appeared on his face.

"So he'll listen to you. So what? I could get him transferred with one phone call."

"Oh, no. Not Captain Alessandro. He's not brittle. He got tough with Henry Cumberland this morning. And Henry Cumberland isn't a man that's used to having anyone get tough with him, any place, any time. He just about broke Cumberland in half with a few contemptuous words. You think you could get that guy to lay off? You should live so long."

"Jesus," he said, still grinning, "I used to know guys like you once. I've lived here so long now I must have forgotten they still make them. Okay. I'll listen."

He went back to the chair and picked another gold-tipped cigarette from a case and lit it. "Care for one?"

"No thanks. This bog Richard Harvest – I think he was a mistake. Not good enough for the job."

"Not nearly good enough, Marlowe. Not nearly. Just a cheap sadist. That's what comes of getting out of touch. You lose your judgment. He could have scared Goble silly without laying a finger on him. And then taking him over to your place – what a laugh! What an amateur! And look at him now. No good for anything any more. He'll be selling pencils. Would you care for a drink?"

"I'm not on that kind of terms with you, Brandon. Let me finish. In the middle of the night – the night I made contact with Betty Mayfield, and the night you chased Mitchell out of The Glass Room – and did it very nicely, I might add – Betty came over to my room at the Rancho Descansado. One of your properties, I believe. She said Mitchell was dead on a chaise on her porch. She offered me large things to do something about it. I came back over here and there was no man dead on her porch. The next morning the night garage man told me Mitchell had left in his car with nine suitcases. He'd paid his bill and a week in advance to hold his room. The same day his car was found abandoned in Los Peñasquitos Canyon. No suitcases, no Mitchell."

Brandon stared hard at me, but said nothing.

"Why was Betty Mayfield afraid to tell me what she was afraid of? Because she had been convicted of murder in Westfield, North Carolina, and then the verdict was reversed by the judge, who has that power in that state, and used it. But Henry Cumberland, the father of the husband she was accused of murdering, told her he would follow her anywhere she went and see that she had no peace. Now she finds a dead man on her porch. And the cops investigate and her whole story comes out. She's frightened and confused. She thinks she couldn't be lucky twice. After all, a jury did convict her."

Brandon said softly: "His neck was broken. He fell over the end of my terrace. She couldn't have broken his neck. Come out here. I'll show you."

We went out on the wide sunny terrace. Brandon marched to the end wall and I looked down over it and I was looking straight down on a chaise on Betty Mayfield's porch.

"This wall isn't very high," I said. "Not high enough to be safe."

"I agree," Brandon said calmly. "Now suppose he was standing like this" – he stood with his back against the wall, and the top of it didn't come very much above the middle of his thighs. And Mitchell had been a tall man too – "and he goads Betty into coming over near enough so that he can grab her, and she pushes him off hard, and over he goes. And he just happens to fall in such a way – by pure chance – that his neck snaps. And that's exactly how her husband died. Do you blame the girl for getting in a panic?"

"I'm not sure I blame anybody, Brandon. Not even you."

He stepped away from the wall and looked out to sea and was silent for a moment. Then he turned.

"For nothing," I said, "except that you managed to get rid of Mitchell's body."

"Now, how in hell could I do that?"

"You're a fisherman, among other things. I'll bet that right here in this apartment you have a long strong cord. You're a powerful man. You could get down to Betty's porch, you could put that cord under Mitchell's arms, and you have the strength to lower him to the ground behind the shrubbery. Then, already having his key out of his pocket, you could go to his room and pack up all his stuff, and carry it down to the garage, either in the elevator, or down the fire stairs. That would take three trips. Not too much for you. Then you could drive his car out of the garage. You probably knew the night man was a doper and that he wouldn't talk, if he knew you knew. This was in the small hours of the night. Of course the garage man lied about the time. Then you could drive the car as near as possible to where Mitchell's body was, and dump him into it, and drive off to Los Peñasquitos Canyon."

Brandon laughed bitterly. "So I am in Los Peñasquitos Canyon with a car and a dead man and nine suitcases. How do I get out of there?"

"Helicopter."

"Who's going to fly it?"

"You. They don't check much on helicopters yet, but they soon will, because they are getting more and more numerous. You could have one brought to you in Los Peñasquitos Canyon, having arranged in advance, and you could have had someone come along to pick up the pilot. A man in your position can do almost anything, Brandon."

"And then what?"

"You loaded Mitchell's body and his suitcases into the helicopter and flew out to sea and set the helicopter hovering close to the water, and then you could dump the body and the suitcases, and drift on back to wherever the helicopter came from. A nice clean well-organized job."

Brandon laughed raucously – too raucously. The laugh had a forced sound.

"You think I'd actually be idiot enough to do all this for a girl I had only just met?"

"Uh–uh. Think again, Brandon. You did it for you. You forget Goble. Goble came from Kansas City. Didn't *you*?"

"What if I did?"

"Nothing. End of the line. But Goble didn't come out here for the ride. And he wasn't looking for Mitchell, unless he already knew him, and between them, they figured they had a gold mine. You were the gold mine. But Mitchell got dead and Goble tried to go it alone, and he was a mouse fighting with a tiger. But would you want to explain how Mitchell fell off your terrace? Would you want an investigation of your background? What so obvious as for the police to think you had thrown Mitchell over the wall? And even if they couldn't prove it, where would you be in Esmeralda from then on?"

He walked slowly to the far end of the terrace and back. He stood in front of me, his expression completely blank.

"I could have you killed, Marlowe. But in some strange way in the years I have lived here, I don't seem to be that kind of guy any more. So you have me licked. I don't have any defense, except to have you killed. Mitchell was the lowest kind of man, a blackmailer of women. You could be right all along the line, but I wouldn't regret it. And it's just possible, believe me, just possible that I too went out on a limb for Betty Mayfield. I don't expect you to believe it, but it *is* possible. Now, let's deal. How much?"

"How much for what?"

"For not going to the cops."

"I already told you how much. Nothing. I just wanted to know what happened. Was I approximately right?"

"Dead right, Marlowe. Right on the nose. They may get me for it yet."

"Maybe. Well, I'll take myself out of your hair now. Like I said – I want to get back to Los Angeles. Somebody might offer me a cheap job. I have to live, or do I?"

"Would you shake hands with me?"

"No. You hired a gun. That puts you out of the class of people I shake hands with. I might be dead today, if I hadn't had a hunch."

"I didn't mean him to kill anyone."

"You hired him. Goodbye."

27

I GOT OUT of the elevator and Javonen seemed to be waiting for me. "Come into the bar," he said. "I want to talk to you."

We went into the bar, which was very quiet at that hour. We sat at a corner table. Javonen said quietly: "You think I'm a bastard, don't you?"

"No. You have a job. I have a job. Mine annoyed you. You didn't trust me. That doesn't make you a bastard."

"I try to protect the hotel. Who do you try to protect?"

"I never know. Often, when I do know, I don't know how. I just fumble around and make a nuisance of myself. Often I'm pretty inadequate."

"So I heard – from Captain Alessandro. If it's not too personal, how much do you make on a job like this?"

"Well, this was a little out of the usual line, Major. As a matter of fact, I didn't make anything."

"The hotel will pay you five thousand dollars – for protecting its interests."

"The hotel, meaning Mr. Clark Brandon."

"I suppose. He's the boss."

"It has a sweet sound – five thousand dollars. A very sweet sound. I'll listen to it on my way back to Los Angeles." I stood up.

"Where do I send the check, Marlowe?"

"The Police Relief Fund could be glad to have it. Cops don't make much money. When they get in trouble they have to borrow from the Fund. Yes, I think the Police Relief Fund would be very grateful to you."

"But not you?"

"You were a major in the CIC. You must have had a lot of chances to graft. But you're still working. I guess I'll be on my way."

"Listen, Marlowe. You're being a damn fool. I want to tell you —"

"Tell yourself, Javonen. You have a captive audience. And good luck."

I walked out of the bar and got into my car. I drove to the Descansado and picked up my stuff and stopped at the office to pay my bill. Jack and Lucille were in their usual positions. Lucille smiled at me.

Jack said: "No bill, Mr. Marlowe. I've been instructed. And we offer you our apologies for last night. But they're not worth much, are they?"

"How much would the bill be?"

"Not much. Twelve-fifty maybe."

I put the money on the counter. Jack looked at it and frowned. "I said there was no bill, Mr. Marlowe."

"Why not? I occupied the room."

"Mr. Brandon —"

"Some people never learn, do they? Nice to have known you both. I'd like a receipt for this. It's deductible."

28

I DIDN'T DO more than ninety back to Los Angeles. Well, perhaps I hit a hundred for a few seconds now and then. Back on Yucca Avenue I stuck the Olds in the garage and poked at the mailbox. Nothing, as usual. I climbed the long flight of redwood steps and unlocked my door. Everything was the same. The room was stuffy and dull and impersonal as it always was. I opened a couple of windows and mixed a drink in the kitchen.

I sat down on the couch and stared at the wall. Wherever I went, whatever I did, this was what I would come back to. A blank wall in a meaningless room in a meaningless house.

I put the drink down on a side table without touching it. Alcohol was no cure for this. Nothing was any cure but the hard inner heart that asked for nothing from anyone.

The telephone started to ring. I picked it up and said emptily: "Marlowe speaking."

"Is this Mr. Philip Marlowe?"

"Yes."

"Paris has been trying to reach you Mr. Marlowe. I'll call you back in a little while."

I put the phone down slowly and I think my hand shook a little. Driving too fast, or not enough sleep.

The call came through in fifteen minutes: "The party calling you from Paris is on the line, sir. If you have any difficulty, please flash your operator."

"This is Linda. Linda Loring. You remember me, don't you, darling?"

"How could I forget?"

"How are you?"

"Tired – as usual. Just came off a very trying sort of case. How are you?"

"Lonely. Lonely for you. I've tried to forget you. I haven't been able to. We made beautiful love together."

"That was a year and a half ago. And for one night. What am I supposed to say?"

"I've been faithful to you. I don't know why. The world is full of men. But I've been faithful to you."

"I haven't been faithful to you, Linda. I didn't think I'd ever see you again. I didn't know you expected me to be faithful."

"I didn't. I don't. I'm just trying to say that I love you. I'm asking you to marry me. You said it wouldn't last six months. But why not give it a chance? Who knows – it might last forever. I'm begging you. What does a woman have to do to get the man she wants?"

"I don't know. I don't even know how she knows she wants him. We live in different worlds. You're a rich woman, used to being pampered. I'm a tired hack with a doubtful future. Your father would probably see to it that I didn't even have that."

"You're not afraid of my father. You're not afraid of anyone. You're just afraid of marriage. My father knows a man when he sees one. Please, please, please. I'm at the Ritz. I'll send you a plane ticket at once."

I laughed. "You'll send *me* a plane ticket? What sort of guy do you think I am? I'll send *you* a plane ticket. And that will give you time to change your mind."

"But, darling, I don't need you to send me a plane ticket. I have —"

"Sure. You have the money for five hundred plane tickets. But this one will be *my* plane ticket. Take it, or don't come."

"I'll come, darling. I'll come. Hold me in your arms. Hold me close in your arms. I don't want to own you. Nobody ever will. I just want to love you."

"I'll be here. I always am."

"Hold me in your arms."

The phone clicked, there was a buzzing sound, and then the line went dead.

I reached for my drink. I looked around the empty room — which was no longer empty. There was a voice in it, and a tall slim lovely woman. There was a dark hair on the pillow in the bedroom. There was that soft gentle perfume of a woman who presses herself tight against you, whose lips are soft and yielding, whose eyes are half blind.

The telephone rang again. I said: "Yes?"

"This is Clyde Umney, the lawyer. I don't seem to have had any sort of satisfactory report from you. I'm not paying you to amuse yourself. I want an accurate and complete account of your activities at once. I demand to know in full detail exactly what you have been doing since you returned to Esmeralda."

"Having a little quiet fun — at my own expense."

His voice rose to a sharp cackle. "I demand a full report from you at once. Otherwise I'll see that you get bounced off your license."

"I have a suggestion for you, Mr. Umney. Why don't you go kiss a duck?"

There were sounds of strangled fury as I hung up on him. Almost immediately the telephone started to ring again.

I hardly heard it. The air was full of music.

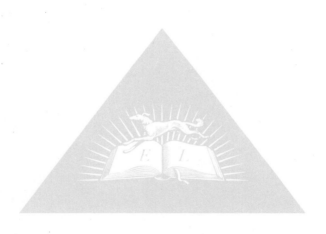